To Rule the Night

"and He made two great lights, one to rule the day and the other to rule the night"

Genesis 1: 10

"well-behaved women have seldom made history"

Unknown

"He brings the purple testament: bleeding war…"

Richard III Shakespeare

"On desperate ground, maneuver

On deadly ground, fight"

Sun Tzu the art of War

"In war everything is simple, but even simple things are difficult"

Von Clausewitz on War

"War is nothing less than a temporary repeal of the principles of virtue. It is a system out of which almost all the virtues are excluded, and in which nearly all the vices are included."

Robert Hall


"So this is the little lady who started the Great War?"

Abraham Lincoln on being introduced to Harriet Beecher Stowe ( Author of "Uncle Toms Cabin")


"Wisdom hath builded her house, she hath hewn out her seven pillars."

(Proverbs 9:1).


"The Archmetia is the Devil's highway"

Galax of Vale


People sleep peaceably in their beds at night only because rough men stand ready to do violence on their behalf.

George Orwell


"As it was feared from the beginning by its architects:  when the UFO cover-up perished, so would peace"

James Bergman

"On the willows by the river we hung up our harps and there our captors required of us mirth, saying, sing us one of the songs of Zion"

Psalm 137


"They have us surrounded. The poor bastards!"

*101st Airborne Trooper at Bastogne, Belgium 1944.*

## Prologue: To Rule the Night

Cassandra stepped out of the mouth of the furnace that the tower had now become, she clutched Hamster to herself tightly, and she could feel her clinging to her arm with her delicate hands. The tower ledge was white stone, the wind was harsh and cold, yet the baby did not cry but was still, as if full of stoic bravery. Cassandra looked down the hundred-story gulf beneath her feet, there were no rescuers, no helicopters poised to take them away from their perch, there was only bare cold concrete a mile below in the chaos. There was only the cold blue empty sky above here stretching off into blue galaxies in the blackness like snowflakes in a snowstorm spanning forever, merging into endless deep blue. She came to a decision, she held up the child to the endless blue galaxies of the sky, to her satisfaction the sky took the baby, bearing her off on the cold wind into the endless blue sky so she could no longer see her. *Now you are safe if I can keep silence. No one can know until it is time.* Cassandra then looked back to precarious ledge she stood on, and the gleaming white concrete below. There was no comfort between the searing heat and cold shear concrete cliffs in the cold wind. Jennifer, beside her on the ledge, leaped into the cold wind. Thousands of men in grey camouflage fatigues and space suits followed her over the edge with fierce war cries. Now Cassandra stood alone and took one last look at the crystal blue sky and the deep blue ocean beyond. She saluted the sky, the sea, and the Earth. She then plunged off the ledge as the flames sought her. She was going down, going faster and faster, the wind screaming past her as she saw the street full of fire trucks draw closer and then suddenly there was a feeling of impact and a crack of thunder.

Cassandra convulsed and tore at her hospital bed covers, her eyes flew open to see the hospital room bathed in blinding electric blue light. An earsplitting crack of thunder shook the hospital and rattled the plastic windows, a stream of bright yellow tracer shells flew up into the sky, followed by another blinding blue glare as an antiaircraft rocket burst from its launching tube a block from the hospital and shot skyward. Now a rising chorus of air raid sirens began to wail in the night, now with a sky full of deafening explosions and streams of antiaircraft tracers as batteries of 25 and 40-millimeter automatic cannons blazed from the heights around Arlington and cross the Potomac in Washington. Pamela had woken up and was screaming from her bed, Cassandra flew from her own bed to Pamela's and held her as she screamed in terror. The magnetometer in Pamela's bed was beeping and it red light flashing above the crashing noise and glare.

"MY GUN! GIVE ME MY GUN!" Pamela was screaming and Cassandra held her. A blinding flash and earsplitting explosion came out of the sky, and Cassandra felt Pamela's body convulse in terror as the sound washed over them. Cassandra felt desperately for the teddy bear in Pamela's bed and then tossed it aside to grab the 9 mm Berretta pistol Pamela kept beneath it. She passed the heavy firm gun into Pamela's hand while the tracers flew outside and the last explosion echoed. Pamela clutched the gun desperately. "THEY WON'T TAKE ALIVE! "Pamela screamed.

"No Baby you're safe! You're safe here!" cried Cassandra with tears flowing down her face, as she climbed into the bed beside her and wrapped her arms around her. The emergency power in the hospital came on, lighting a small light over the open doorway. There was the sound of running booted feet in the hallway, and other patients had awakened screaming and crying above the air raid sirens and crash of gunfire outside. A bereted head stuck itself into the room; it was one of their guards.

"You guys OK?" came a deep voice.

"Yes, yes were fine I think," gasped Cassandra, just then a series of sonic booms sounded, and several jet fighters roared over as Cassandra felt Pamela cringe. "Yes, we'll be OK" Finally, the crashing din ebbed and moved off to the distance. After what seemed like an eternity, an all-clear siren sounded Cassandra lay beside Pamela and fell into a dreamless sleep.

****

Deputy secretary of Defense James Bergman stepped out of the Black-Hawk helicopter into the leaf-strewn forest floor, followed by Major Jameson, his aide, a tall red headed paratrooper. He held his warm coat tight against the cold morning breeze. *Fight or flight reaction,* he thought. *Flight is impossible, so we fight...*Colonel Clifford and a dozen Army troops in camouflage bearing M-16 rifles and some heavily armed Virginia State Police stood by the wreckage of a saucer some thirty yards across lying smoking in the oak and hickory trees. It was silver, crumpled metal, with lots of ragged holes. He could see the metal was very thin and looked inside the craft in the open hatch. The walls were covered with delicately machined patterns, like a fine mosaic. But everywhere there were holes and on the floor, Bergman recognized a battered pre-sectioned prism of gleaming alloy steel, about an inch on a side. It was part of the storm of shrapnel over Washington DC the night before that had brought the craft down.

"You'd think by now they would have figured out how to make their ships bulletproof!"

said Bergman in amazement. "But I am grateful to God for even small favors."

"The last intel brief I heard, said they their ships can either fly or stop bullets but not both simultaneously, Sir. I guess they chose to fly over DC and take their chances." said Jameson, surveying the same scene grimly.

"Well looks like luck ran out for these guys," said Bergman with satisfaction.

They were twenty miles from Washington DC, in the Shenandoah Valley. The rumpled saucer was covered with autumn leaves. It was a casualty of the previous night's air raid over Arlington. Colonel Clifford, commander of the 34th antiaircraft battalion in Arlington, looked at Bergman with dismay. Bergman smiled back broadly. The troops looked cowed and fearful. Several small alien bodies lay on the ground dead. Bergman stood over them; they were childlike, pale, and delicate in their finely made silver coveralls, torn by the same chunks of raw steel that had brought down their ship. The contrast between their fine and delicate features and the gaping wounds and spewing entrails and brains from their ruptured heads was shocking. It gave the same impression as seeing fine china smashed by a crude sledgehammer. A gleaming steel prism projected partially from one alien's ruptured head.

7

"Well we brought one down again, probably by accident," said the Colonel. "It's got a lot of shrapnel hits or bullet holes."

"Well, then it wasn't an accident was it?" said Bergman smiling fiercely. "I want every antiaircraft crew in Arlington to get a medal for this." He reached out his hand and shook the Colonel's hand firmly.

"This is the tenth raid over Arlington, and the second saucer we've brought down over there, we should get those two women out of that hospital and someplace else. They are bringing too much heat there."

"Why would we want to do that Colonel? Your people seem to be getting better at this, "said Bergman looking at the wreck with satisfaction. *Two 5 billion dollar space ships lost, just to cause a little terror...*

"With all due respect Mr. Secretary, the greys can enter airspace over the Capitol at will, and sooner or later their just going to quit messing around and  bring a hydrogen bomb and drop it on the hospital."   At this, Bergman whirled to face him in anger.

"Perhaps you don't have the stomach for an interstellar war, Colonel?"

Bergman reached down and pulled the projecting piece of gleaming shrapnel from the dead alien's head. He wiped it off with his handkerchief as the Colonel flinched.

"With all due respect sir, these bodies may have an unexploded ordinance in them!"

Bergman handed it to Maj. Jameson wrapped in the handkerchief.

"I want this lucky piece of metal mounted on my office wall, Major," said Bergman. Bergman turned and stared at the Colonel with contempt.

The Colonel lowered his eyes. Bergman looked back at the crashed saucer. "Like any war Colonel, the most important battleground is up here!" Bergman pointed sharply towards his own silver-haired head.  A flight of F-51 Griffin's flew over with a roar as he spoke this.  "Now you secure this site and get this piece of shit up to Dayton!  But I want lots of pictures showing bullet holes for the news blogs!" Bergman paused.  "I see there's

8

four dead here, but you have a prisoner?" the Colonel nodded. "I want to see him." An armored recovery vehicle, moving on tank tracks through the forest, had arrived to drag the wreck to the highway. *I have to demonstrate that I am not intimidated by these people,* thought Bergman. *We need more mindless audacity around here!*

The Colonel turned and motioned to the soldiers, who brought forward a grey alien with a bandage on his head. He had been stripped naked and looked cold and confused. Bergman noted the complete lack of genitalia. For a moment, Bergman felt sorry for it. *A little fish,* Bergman thought in disappointment.

Bergman avoided the grey's large dark eyes, *watch for mind tricks,* he thought. *I shouldn't even be doing this, but I need to speak to him.*

"Do you speak English?" Bergman demanded. The creature nodded, looking dazed.

"Well, Welcome to planet Earth, but it appears your people have fucked with the wrong damn planet!" said Bergman with a smile. *He probably has no idea what I talking about.*

The dazed looking alien seemed to smile and bowed his head slightly.

"Thank you," said the alien with raspy low voice. "My name is Gintusk'ootan Wah" Bergman smiled awkwardly and nodded. He then motioned to the troops to take the alien away. *I shouldn't say anything else to him...Telepathy* thought Bergman.

"Sir, you should not be talking to this person," said Major Jameson. Only highly trained intelligence officers were normally allowed to interact with Greys, because of their telepathic abilities.

"Alright," said Bergman turning to the Colonel. "Now get him and the bodies out of here! And I want lots of pictures for the webs!" he added angrily. *I also need a new Colonel in charge of 34th Battalion, somebody who likes to fight. We need berserkers for this war,* thought Bergman as he re-boarded his helicopter. *This is going to be a long, bitter, war...*

Gintusk the alien was led away to a Humvee and given a warm coat and a candy bar to eat. He found himself quite happy as they drove him away. No one spoke further to him, they had been ordered not to. Gintusk had expected to be killed, so he was pleasantly surprised by all of these happenings.

An important personage had spoken to him, even spoken words of welcome to him, a great honor in his society, even if the personage was human dung-eater. He meditated on the sayings of Sootah, a renowned philosopher among his people. *Be content with fate; do not struggle against it...*

*But what of the great personage's words? Fate has led these words to be spoken by him to me. Instead of death, I received words. The human spoke crudely of the great coition with Erra, then said 'wrong damn planet' this is some sort of idiom, I must think about what he meant...It is part of my fate.*

Gintusk was indeed a thinker. Like many of his people, he had volunteered to come to Erra to gain pardon for past crimes on his home world. His crimes had been thought-crimes. He had been high caste but had been demoted and suffered the disgrace of having his genitalia taken from him. So he had come to the Erran front seeking a new chance at life, but he had seen only death and cruelty there. *I came to Erra hoping to recover my caste position, but look what has happened now.* Now he struggled to remain calm.

*Fate has dealt me a hard rock to tunnel through...*he thought as they drove on the highway.

\*\*\*\*

A policewoman with brown hair and silver sunglasses was beating her on the back with a nightstick ... She was writhing to protect her back.

Cassandra awoke wearily, she disentangled herself from Pamela in the bed, and pulled the pistol from Pamela's hand, placing it a safe distance away on the sheets. Dawn of a clear autumn day streamed in the windows. She found herself groggily worrying about Pamela's habit of sleep walking, this time with a loaded gun, but then realized that Pamela's legs were still paralyzed,

*Therefore, this is not a problem.* Cassandra thought sadly.

*But it will be Pammy! Because you're going to get well, I swear it!* she thought. *It's my fault you got wounded...This is all somehow my fault...* She felt herself sink into sadness and despair, tears welled in her eyes. *All my fault...* Cassandra gazed at Pamela's lithe form strewn across the bed, now sleeping soundly, her mop of long blonde hair spread over the sheets. *No, that is not true,* Cassandra thought again fiercely, fighting back against the despair. She wiped her eyes fiercely. *No, this is not all your fault. The Greys came here! They raped Pamela when she was fifteen! It's the fault of the Cosmos! Shit happens! This is our ration! The cost of existence! The cost of life!* Energized, she rose away from the bed by sheer force of will. Clad only in her hospital gown Cassandra cringed as her bare feet hit the cold hospital floor. She walked over to the bathroom they shared, dashed cold water on her face. Her back hurt, she felt the stitched up wounds on her back, slowly healing, and she was stuck with wonderment at this. *What happened to me?* But shook her head to chase the fearful doubts away. *Time to make an assessment,* she thought, in the mental habit she had adopted to periodically reassessing her situation and efforts to achieve her goals. It had gotten her to the peak of the news business and CNS. *Yes, to the peak on Earth, before all this trouble started. Before this train wreck...*

She gazed at herself in the mirror, smoothing her long raven hair so it parted in the middle, as she liked it, standing tall despite the pain in her back. *Empress of China,* she thought, noticing she had lost weight, *too much, perhaps, but the shape is still good. Almost ready for prime time,* she thought. *Pale, too pale, need more Sun. Despite all this, she found herself admiring herself. Beauty is power,* she thought, feeling a fleeting happy thought for the first time in a long time, *I will wield this power to get my revenge. I will get out of here. But, I look pale.* She noticed she had bandages on her fingertips, decided not to think about them. She turned and went out of the bathroom to the window. She and Pamela were in second story room in a new hospital facility formerly called The Golden Terraces that had formerly been an old people's home beside Arlington

Hospital. The Terraces looked out on a park, green, but with first leaves of autumn everywhere as the dawn gathered strength. Cassandra looked out the of second story window. She noticed with interest that parties of police and soldiers with dogs were moving through the park. Then she looked down to the grass below and near the window, something pale lay there, amid the leaves. It was a severed human arm lying in the grass. It was a woman's arm. Cassandra felt a wave of revulsion followed by fierce rage wash through her.

"No, you can't scare me... I have seen far worse..." Cassandra said to herself with a smirk, "and so will you Mr. Grey, before this is done. So will you see some real horror." But then another strange thought came, *No! No! It is not time yet, she is not safe yet... you must wait!*

Confused, Cassandra turned away from the window. Pamela was stirring and would need her help to get to the bathroom soon. Cassandra surveyed the notebooks full of delicate writing and the e-tablet on a table beside Pamela's bed. Pamela was taking calculus and other courses on-line from the Naval Academy at Annapolis; she was on track to get, in Pam's own words, "four-year paper", a Bachelor's degree, in a few months. *I am glad I was not forced to approve this academic plan at the Dean's office in Annapolis,* thought Cassandra humorously; *I would sleep even less well than I do now.* The study plan, which consisted of Pam getting college credit for her previous associates degree, work as a journalist, weather girl and "armchair cosmic war strategist" , as Pamela had put it laughingly, plus assortment of advanced on-line courses from the Naval Academy, had Pamela working diligently all day and into the night, in between air-raids.

"I never dreamed your Lieutenant Michael Donnelly, USN, had so much pull in the Navy..." said Cassandra to herself, looking a Pamela sleeping peacefully. "But you deserve every break you can get right now, Pamela sweety..." said Cassandra to herself she focused on Pamela's angelic face sleeping in the bed, and then looking down at Pam's inert legs. *Because if you weren't here in this room with me... I would die...* thought Cassandra to herself suddenly trembling, and leaned down and kissed Pamela on the cheek. Cassandra felt dizzy for a moment, and sat down, carefully keeping her back away from the back of the chair.  Her back felt strange and tingly. *I hope the nurse gets here soon with our magic beans.*

Pamela had enthusiastically tried to explain calculus to her on several occasions, saying it was a perfect woman's mathematics because it was 'about curves' rather than straight lines.

Cassandra had reacted to this by wailing in mock distress, 'what have you done with my friend Pammy?' *At least I am getting my sense of humor back*, thought Cassandra, and Pam had helped with this.

Pamela had a "theory" about her legs being paralyzed, that this was all "just a temporary setback , to get me to sit still and take courses from the Navy on-line, and get my four-year-paper finally." *You go, girl,* thought Cassandra, *I could never even balance my checkbook..."*

A nurse entered, took her and Pamela's temperature with an infrared ear thermometer, gave Cassandra pills: valium, *Yes! Good Shit!* Oxy-8s - a powerful painkiller, *Oh, Fabulous!* Aspirin, for inflammation, *Sure whatever...* Soon Cassandra felt a rosy glow filling her, as she looked out the window at the park, now apparently calm and peaceful.

*What beautiful day in the park,* Cassandra thought, *it would be so nice to go out there someday...*

So began another day in the Terraces.

****

The beautiful woman danced in the blue light, wearing only a loincloth of sparkling gems, she was beautiful in face and body, as she moved sensually. The jewels in her light brown hair sparkled in the intense blue light. Only the cruel brand of Batelgeen, an hourglass, on her upper right bicep, spoiled her otherwise perfect flesh.  Hontal of Alnilam sat at the banquet enraptured by her as she danced. He was ignoring his food now and drank only wine from his gold goblet.  All throughout the great hall the banquet continued, other dancing girls, many also from the Pleiades, it seemed,  danced in pools of intense light on the stage between the low banquet tables.

"You like her, I see. She is Pleiadian. We captured her and many other like her in our raid on the regions near Merope," laughed Bekar of Batelgeen and stroked his full beard, and ate beside Hontal. "She is yours for the night, as fits an honored guest. It is war-custom." Bekar waved his hand, festooned with many rings, at her. Hontal stroked his well-trimmed beard, now fully regrown and smiled at her with some awkwardness. His wife lay pregnant many light years away, but Hontal, wise to the protocols of Arnokal, the Capitol, knew he could not refuse the dancing girl honorably. It was war-custom, the sharing of the spoils of war with an honored guest that was part of Samaran traditions. Besides, Hontal was eager to show that he had recovered from his wounds and was now again a fully capable knight of the empire. He hoped to show his virtue had returned, for nothing mattered more among the Samarans than virtue.

Virtue meant skill at war, strength, toughness, endurance, cunning, and courage; it was the foundation of Samaran society, and its far-flung Empire. Hontal was shining example of Samaran virtue, a tall, rugged and handsome knight of the realm.

"I see you are finished with your food; come Hontal, let us walk in the garden," said Bekar rising. "He was short and swarthy and had a large scar on his right cheek. I have much to say to you about your new mission."

"My mission?" asked Hontal rising. He caught himself displaying too much curiosity, tempered it. "Yes, "you *must always listen much more than speak, especially in Arnokal,* he thought, remembering his father's words. *By Alkmar, the God of War, I sense a trap here...*

"Yes, you will be sent on a mission from the High Palace tomorrow, and it of this of which we must speak," said Bekar rising. Past the laughing guests, both lords, and ladies, they walked, past bearded guards in armor, to the cool of the evening in the garden outside. The garden held pillars of rose-colored stone, holding up cross beams of fragrant wood from which flowering vines hung. The mansion of Bekar was set in the hills above the great river, Oneen, that flowed peacefully to the ocean below them. All about them, away from the ocean shore, the light of the great city spread about them like a carpet of light-studded with brilliant towers, and in the night sky spacecraft and aircraft rushed back and forth with

14

gleaming and flashing lights to the five spaceports that served the vast city. The spacecraft bore news, and goods, and slaves, from the far corners of the Samaran empire, 'that expanded eternally' and held 400 billion souls, of whom three-quarters were of Samaran blood, and it was 800 light years across. The harbor, its water lit by the lights on shore, was full of ships, for the Samaran were traditionally a seafaring people, before they had been taught to sail the stars, before the bearers of war-magic had come. This whole broad vista was Arnokal, the capital of the Samaran Empire. On the cliffs on the opposite side of the great river stood the vast Grand palace of the Emperor, shining with light. Hontal knew that he was to be there the next morning. He had been badly wounded in battle against the Tlax, at Umax, on the battle front three hundred light years away, but had managed to recover after many months, and had been honored for heroic deeds in that same battle. Thus, his appointment at the Palace the next morning was the achievement of many years of, toil, ambition, and pain, within the empire's service. He was a knight of the Empire like his father and brothers, now gone, dead in the service of the Empire. They had died in the same battle.

"You are to be sent into the Quzrada to gather knowledge and report back to the High Palace what you see there, "said Bekar as he walked. He walked with a slight limp, for he was the scarred veteran of many battles.

"I see "nodded Hontal. *How does he know such things?*

"You must know young Hontal, that this mission is a great honor, and that you will go, with the authority of the Emperor, and also with the full permission of Batelgeen."

"I see" nodded Hontal warily. *Permission, yet I am being sent by the Palace?* he thought. He remembered his father's words before he had been killed in battle, *'beware the house of Batelgeen, they are the fathers and grandfathers of treachery.'* For the Batelgeen, were a powerful House of the Empire and had once, long ago, been the ruling House of the Samar.

"Do you really see this thing fully, Hontal?" asked Bekar carefully, pausing and motioning with his strong hand. "They say you are a wise man,

15

Hontal, capable, and a fine teller of tales. But, by the crimson light of Batelgeen, I warn you, to be sure that the tales you tell of the Quzrada are pleasing ones."

"Pleasing to whom?" asked Hontal as he stiffened. His hand grasped the hilt of his sword.

*Where is my retainer, Gamal? I was foolish not to bring him here,* thought Hontal. Gamal, a red-headed, older, but mighty warrior had served Hontal's family as a bodyguard for decades.

"I serve the Emperor," replied Hontal carefully. "I must give a true report of what I find." Bekar stopped and stared at him intently.

"Pleasing to the House of Batelgeen," said Bekar continuing to stare at him, "for the Quzrada and its affairs is our provenance. Verily, the Quzrada is our lake. You should consider this as your star rises, young Hontal."

"They are the provenance of the Empire as a whole, are they not?" Hontal deliberately phrased his reply as a question.

"But of course," said Bekar slyly, he seemed to retreat; Hontal could see calculation in Bekar's eyes. "However, the Quzrada is our outer border." Bekar paused, smiled slyly, "Besides, know you not of the prophecy?"

"What prophecy?" asked Hontal impatiently. He was looking around him now for eavesdroppers.

"Through the seed of the Quzrada, returns the Son of the Batelgeen to the throne," Bekar said with a laugh.

"I have not heard this prophecy."

"Then hear it now, Hontal of Alnilam" laughed Bekar," and lay your wagers accordingly!" There had been a gathering blue glow in the West, and now the star Rigel, the *Ruler of the Night*, rose brilliant and shimmering above the horizon, its intense blue light impossible to look at directly. Already its light was casting a shadow. Mighty Rigel lay only twenty light years from Telsamar, the golden home star of the Samaran

16

people. The light of Rigel was so brilliant that it could be seen clearly at noonday and, in the season of its appearance at night, it lit the night with a fierce blue light as bright as ten full Moons of Earth.

"Ah the light of Rigel, the second Sun, I could bask in it for hours, but you, yourself should rest Hontal, and enjoy our hospitality. You will have a busy day tomorrow," said Bekar with a broad smile. Hontal nodded thoughtfully, turned, and went back through the festive banquet, to his room. The Samar were the Lord of the Archmetia in the outer galaxy, the Archmetia being that swath of peoples across the galaxy who were not only extremely humanoid but genetically related, having been seeded apparently by some interstellar agency of unimaginable power and skill, and for purposes that were equally unimaginable.

****

Cassandra Chen walked down the hall of the hospital, pulling her IV stand on wheels behind her and sucking on a lollipop she had looted from a nurse's station. Her fingers had fresh bandages on their fingertips, she had been afraid to look when they were changed, so she hadn't looked. From the chrome IV stand hung a bottle of antibiotics for her back wounds and a tube from it fed a needle in her arm. She had come to get her daily dose of Oxy-8s and Valium. Because of what were described as "difficulties" at the hospital, those who could move now were required to come and receive Oxy-8 and other painkilling drugs from a central location with armed security guards in attendance. The war was not beginning well.

Cassandra was wearing light-blue slacks and a loose tee shirt with a long-sleeved, light blue blouse on top of this because she felt cold all the time. Her long black hair was combed, but her permanent was fading so her hair was losing its wave. She joined the line for Oxy-8s. She noted a man in a wheelchair beside her with a nurse helping him. He was missing his right leg and right arm and seemed to have other injuries. Despite this, he sat erect and alert in his wheelchair. The hospital was full of people like him and so this did not attract her attention. However, she noted with happiness that she recognized him from months before. She took her lollipop out of her mouth and put it carefully into her shirt pocket.

"Doctor Petrosian," she called out gently. He turned and looked at her, smiled warmly. The warm smile from one so terribly injured made her want to cry, but she did not. "It is Cassandra Chen, remember me? You

17

helped my friend Pamela when she had a breakdown." She noticed the nurse beside him began to weep gently.

"Oh yes, I heard she was wounded. How is she?" he asked, turning his wheelchair with his one good arm to face her with surprising agility.

"Oh, she is getting better, thank God," said Cassandra with a trembling voice. "I was wondering if maybe you could help me?"

"I can try," he said, smiling.

"You see, doctor, people have come to talk to me and I am afraid they think I am insane and they want to put me away in a cell someplace in some fortress or else put me on trial for treason," she said, starting to shake. She was waving her bandaged fingertips. "You see they want to know what happened to Cassandra Chen between the battle here and the battle at Morningstar and quite honestly I have learned Cassandra was taken prisoner by the secret government and they did awful things to her and she won't tell me what happened," she rambled fearfully. "I think they think I also cooperated with the secret government somehow. They think Cassandra made some sort of broadcast for the secret government and they want to try me for treason for it, but I know she would never do that, that she would rather die than do that. So if that happened she must be dead. Now, that's pretty common for people who are captured by people who do horrible things to people, that they don't want to talk about it. So if she won't tell me the things that happened how can I tell other people?" she asked plaintively. "Maybe if Cassandra could talk to you, they would stop trying to declare me insane and let me go home to my apartment and go back to work... Can you help?" she looked at him pleadingly. Tears rolled down her cheeks.

"Sure I can," he said, smiling.

"If you put me in between two mirrors, I think the seventh reflection will show me naked," she said firmly. "Then, you can see what they did to me, and if you record what I say in my sleep in Chinese and play it back backwards then you will understand what happened to me," she said, tearfully. "I mean... I have seen so many terrible things..." He lifted up his remaining hand and took hers and held it as they waited for their dose of Oxy-8. Her hand was trembling in his and she wiped her face with her other hand and composed herself.

"Thank you, doctor," said Cassandra. "I don't trust the people they send to talk to me. I am afraid of them. But I am not afraid of you because I know you were such a sweetie to my friend Pammy," she wept.

"What happened to you, Doctor?" she asked, gently.

"I can't remember, exactly," he said smiling. "The last thing I do remember was being at a National Guard Armory with women crying, and being given an M-16 rifle, with two ammo clips and one hundred rounds of loose ammunition. But thanks to you, I can now remember my name. I am Doctor George Petrosian, Chief of Psychiatry here. Isn't that right, nurse," he said, confidently, looking at the nurse.

"Yes doctor!" the nurse said, smiling with tears running down her cheeks.

"I am a psychiatrist, and a damn good one, so I will get through this. And I will help you get through this too," he said, grasping her hand tightly.


Cassandra then abruptly left the line and walked down the hall.

*Who was I just talking to? What was I talking just about? I must keep silent about all this! For Hamster! I can't even talk to myself! ...Am I going insane, or am I already insane?* She found herself trembling with fear and despite the pain in her back, went back to her room without her painkillers.

**** 

Colonel Robert Schwartzman walked painfully but determinedly in his hospital gown to his exercise area pulling his wheeled stainless steel IV "tree" beside him. His calves and ankles still had burn dressings on them but felt better. He had a small bandage on his face, on his left cheek, on a small wound that had gone septic and was healing slowly. Beside him, a buxom and attractive older black woman named Florence Rivers, the chief nurse, walked with a skeptical expression. Florence, dressed in blue surgical scrubs, was the chief nurse in the special section at Arlington Hospital for 'Extraterrestrially Exposed' patients. 'Chief Nurse Flo' wore her hair in red tinted brown ringlets at neck length and walked with an alert but world-weary expression. She carried an e-tablet and watched Schwartzman studying each patient's room on the hall as they walked by.

19

"Where's Cassandra Chen?" he asked dully. "I thought she was up here too."

"Oh they moved miss VIP's golden ass out of here last month," said Flo with a smirk. "They got her in the neurological section now. The Terraces"

*She has abandoned me,* thought Schwartzman in sudden desperation.

"Doctor Stephenson, said she had 'recovered sufficiently', meaning she was starting to become conscious," said Flo with some amusement. "I say, I thought we were supposed to keep all the ET exposed patients up here on this floor?  But the doctor just said 'out she goes to neurological.' I guess that's the new code word for 'deranged Big Wheel" Flo said with a laugh. The other patients in the rooms they passed all seemed to be horribly injured. Mostly captured facility guards or wounded servicemen from the storming of Devil's mesa at Morningstar. They passed by the last room.  A man sat on his bed in his hospital gown, bent over with a scowling look. He looked up as Schwartzman and Flo walked by, with staring wild eyes.

"That's Major Crawford, "said Flo. "He's Air Force,  or was. We heard they dug him out of some hole in the ground at Harshman Air Force Base." Schwartzman looked on him with pity. *That could  be me in there, one of the lost boys of Neverland... Who saved me from that?* he wondered.

"He looks pretty crazy, why doesn't he get a ticket out of here?"

"Yeah, he crazy, but he just a little wheel, apparently," said Flo.  She then turned to Schwartzman and studied him with her lovely hazel eyes. "Not a big hero like you... I've been meaning to ask you Colonel, what on Earth did you do to get in such big trouble? I swear you've had all the brass in the Pentagon come to see you, and the FBI too. They told us you got to be in the room by the nurse's station, so we can watch you all the time...

"I'm not supposed to talk about it." He said with a frown. "But here is the three sentence explanation" She stopped and listened attentively.

"Basically, Flo, I was part of a Pitch Black program that went berserk. So I mustered me and my men, and we busted out. Then we put the berserk program out of business, in royal fashion." He said with a big grin. Flo looked concerned and bit her lovely lower lip nervously.

"So you were working with outer space aliens...abducting people?"

Judging her reaction, he felt a deep abyss of despair open up in him. *I am abandoned. It's true, I'll never be able to join the human race ever again,* he thought hopelessly. *I can't explain the unspeakable...bones, millions of bones.* He shook it off. *Stay on mission, soldier.* He calmed. He decided to embellish his story more positively. "In addition, I was pirate Captain for a while," he added with a laugh. "Off the Coast of Africa. I kidnaped rich daughters of African businessmen. But, I am especially not supposed to talk about that part." Flo smiled at this. "Also," He said with a sly grin, "I rescued a bunch of nurses and other damsels in distress, out of that Morningstar place, without filling out the necessary paperwork. Which is why I may be the only man in this man's Army to get both a medal and Court Martial on the same day! And that's God's truth!"

"Oh, well that sounds a lot better, then!" said Flo looking happy and relieved.

"It had its compensations," he added. Flo laughed merrily at this, clutching her e-pad to her bosom. They stopped at the dead end of the hall.

"But just so you know girl," He said admiring the weights and treadmill he saw there. "They got furnaces all over this town that they are stoking day and night with documents and computer memorys , because of what went down in the UFO cover-up."

"I thought the cover-up was over," she said turned to him.

"Oh God no, girl," it's merely moved on to a new phase called CYA, that's 'Cover Your Ass'" said Schwartzman grinning, "and unless I show myself useful, I am going into one of those furnaces too."

"You shouldn't talk like that, Colonel," said Flo looking deeply into his eyes. "You're in my hotel; nobody messes with you here but me! And you got to get well so I can check you out and make your ass useful. That

21

means you have to have a good attitude." She paused. "So get well, that's an order Colonel. I want to see attitude!"

"Yes Flo" he nodded with a smile. "You're right, of course."

"Of course, I'm right. "She snapped, and then spoke again. "Alright Colonel Badass", said Flo, waving her arm at the end of the hall, "here is your exercise room. Courtesy of Chief Nurse Flo"

They had stopped at a small space at the end of the hall. A treadmill and a set of shiny free weights were set up there. "There you go Colonel, just like you requested. Big nurse Flo, she got some pull around here, you know what I'm saying? This hotel I am running has all the perks." She laughed.

"Oh, Babe! Thank you!" said Schwartzman happily. He limped quickly over to the weights, picked them up, and began doing curls. Soon he felt a good surge of endorphins as if his body was rejoicing. But he suddenly felt dizzy also. He shrugged it off. Flo watched dutifully with a slight smile, as his powerful muscles began to bulge with blood. He then stepped over to the treadmill and began walking as it glided along. He began to adjust its speed to move faster.

"Slow down Colonel," Flo said suddenly. Schwartzman kept walking swiftly.

"You mind me now, Colonel or all this stuff goes back," She said with an edge in her voice. Flo reached over suddenly and flicked a switch, and it slowed to a stop. She looked him with concern. He looked at her in protest. He was suddenly sweating profusely. His eyes were dilated.

"Colonel, you should slow down," she said. "You're my freaking responsibility, you know. My job is to get you well, and you don't look well all of a sudden." She reached over and checked his pulse. He looked at her warm brown face now full of concern. He squinted, her face was now blurry.

"Flo?" he said. "Flo, help me..." he gasped as he collapsed.

**** 

22

Cassandra was running through the dark forest, her long black hair flying, carrying the precious one in her arms, the one she had named Hamster. The sky was overcast and dark and the trees and brambles that tore at her were dark and dead in the cold of winter. But she had escaped the dark tower of the witch and carried Hamster with her to safety. They were coming after her, the witch's guards in black, but she was wearing dark tough armor and had a sword, she laughed to herself at her and Hamster's great escape.

How she had escaped was a blur, she only knew to run, ran as fast as she could through the forest that surrounded the dark tower. But she laughed "I am alive I am alive!"

"Don't worry Hamster, we will escape...My love for you will never end," she told little Hamster, as she held her and ran. She felt the warmth of the child's body as they clung to each other. Cassandra felt the child, drink in the love she was pouring into her as she held her. *This love I give you beloved will sustain you, my child*...thought Cassandra to the child and child looked up at her with love filled brown eyes.

Cassandra had been the prisoner of the witch in the dungeon of the dark tower, naked and in chains. The witch had kept her and tortured her there, and done unspeakable things to her in the darkness there so that she had died, but she had escaped none the less, and escaped armed and in armor and had carried away Hamster. She remembered great explosions and fire, and then she was free and running, she had fought the witch's guards and overcome them, she felt filled with pride as she ran. But she heard now the cry of the witch in the sky, the witch was flying after her on her broomstick from her dark tower, directing her troops to follow her. She turned and saw the great dark tower of the witch, she had run, far, but its shadow was long and was now casting on her. The witch flew after here in her dark sky. Despair now tore at Cassandra's heart.

"Don't look back, don't look at the dark sky" she told herself as she tore her eyes away and clutched Hamster tightly, who clung to her now, and she felt love flow between her and the child, as she ran again through the forest, and it made her feel warm and happy again. She ran, hearing the witch call to her, but ignoring her. She then came to the river.

A river dark and flowing cold and swift through the forest she was on the beach of round hard stones at its bank, searching for a way across. It was the river of Death. It was as broad and dark as the sky and flowing with ice and bodies floated in it, Lauren Davis floated by.

"How deep is the water?" asked Cassandra as Lauren floated by.

"It's cold here but you get used to it," Lauren called out to Cassandra, but Lauren smiled and revealed long fangs. Then Lauren rose from the dark water on a dark tower, she was naked, with dark hair, and Cassandra tried to pull out her sword but it would not come out of its scabbard. Then Lauren kissed her and the dark tower from the river enclosed them. Then she was a naked slave in chains back in the dungeon again. It was warm there and the dungeon walls caressed her flesh. Cassandra then remembered her beloved.

"Hamster! I must save her!" she cried out and awoke as if from a trance. She suddenly tore herself loose from the darkness, and once again, she was on the bank of the river in her armor. It had all been an evil spell of the witch who now circled above, the witch with her black robes and long dark hair flowing as she flew above her laughing.

But the witch now had Hamster with her. Cassandra cried out in anguish as she saw the witch fly away with Hamster back to her dark tower.

"Die! Die now! I have a hostage!" The witch screamed and as Cassandra looked, she saw herself naked riding on the front of the broomstick with her arms tied behind her and her hair flying. She rode helpless in front of the witch as the witch held Hamster, and Cassandra wept with despair as she saw the witch carry Hamster away and herself bound back to the dark tower, leaving Cassandra to die crying on the cold riverbank. The witch's guards were coming now to finish her off, Hamster was lost, she was lost, and with this, all was lost and she turned and looked at the dark river.

"God, help me God, help me!" she was wailing.

Then she suddenly had a thought. She remembered that Lauren had bitten her on the neck in the dungeon, making Cassandra a vampire princess, so that when she died Cassandra had become undead. "The witch had made a crucial error!" laughed Cassandra to herself. This filled Cassandra with sudden strength and encouragement. She turned and drew her sword. It made such a lovely sound of fine steel as it came out of its scabbard. She now gripped it with both hands, and with her dark armor flashing, she faced the horde of the witch's guards that had come from the tower, now pouring out of the forest onto the bare riverbank, a legion of dark goblins and monsters with huge black eyes and crab legs. Under the dark sky, they raced towards her on the bank of the river.

"My name is Jian! That means fighter! She yelled, and showed them all her fangs and then charged them on the stony, cold beach. "I will not die! I will live! I will save Hamster!" She was hewing them to pieces and stabbing them, but no matter that their dead lay in heaps finally they were pushing her back into the river, and her feet were then in the cold river, rushing by in a dark torrent. She was still hewing and slashing them to pieces. "Help me save Hamster!" she was pleading as she swung her sword with desperate strength at the dark horde, pressing her deeper into the cold river.

**** 

In the impromptu breakfast cafe on the ready line at Dutch Harbor Alaska , "Tiger " Douglass Forrester quickly smeared a thick layer of peanut butter on a slice of warm whole wheat bread with a butter knife following it with a layer of rich red strawberry jam. He then wolfed it down greedily, savoring its rich taste and washed it down with a deep drink of rich Hawaiian Kona coffee. He looked up briefly at his fellow fighter pilots doing the same in their pressure suits. They wore full space suits, their silver Mercury style metal astronaut helmets sat beside them on the tables. He glanced out at the window at the F-51 Griffin fighter planes of his squadron being hastily prepared for combat under a grey overcast sky. Airmen in green coveralls ran frantically amid the planes ripping red tagged safety pins off the missiles on the wings and still others loaded belts of 20-millimeter armor-piercing cartridges into the ammunition bays in the fuselages. Beyond them, the wintergreen forest of Sitka spruce

25

blew gently in the winds. The green of the evergreen trees seemed luminous in the dull light. There were cracks of thunder, telling of the gathering storm. Jet fighters were racing at supersonic speed in the overcast above them. Soon they would join them. He was mesmerized by the endless sea of trees for an instant but then found himself looking at the icy face of "Samurai " Nakajima, his wingman, as he walked past his line of sight and out the door to the flight-line carrying his helmet and personal air conditioning unit. Tiger swallowed his last gulp of coffee and followed him, and was in turn followed by the rest of the squadron to their planes, whose engines were now being started for them. The rest of his squadron was a wall of silver-suited men in astronaut helmets in front of him, reflecting the cold clouds. Tiger followed his wingman, into the cold wet wind. Behind him, pistol shots erupted. He grabbed his own Berretta 9 mm pistol from is holster on his hip and raised it, the gun feeling warm and comforting to his strong gloved hand, and fired three quick shots into the air towards the bay beyond the flight-line, as gunfire thundered. The flame of the muzzle blast was bright orange under the grey overcast. The airmen stood by watching this ritual , as he replaced his pistol in its holster, it was all against orders, but none of the sergeants protested , none of the ground crew said anything or even flinched , they just looked on with stoic calmness as the pilots marched past to their waiting planes and the engines roared to life. Tiger mounted the ladder to his open cockpit, looked on Samurai mounting his own plane next to his, and disconnecting his air-conditioning unit, and handed it to the sergeant. Samurai paused at the edge of his fighter's cockpit to survey the squadron preparing their planes around them. He then turned for an instant to look at Tiger, as if he sensed being watched. Despair covered Nakajima's normally stoic face. He locked eyes with Tiger for just an instant then averted his eyes, put on his helmet wordlessly, and got into his cockpit, and then lowered the canopy.

Tiger looked away from this sight and focused completely on the cockpit instruments as he put on his own helmet and locked it into place and then lowered his cockpit canopy. Half the squadron had been killed in the last battle, that day had begun as today was now beginning. He plugged in his pressure suit to the aircraft system and buckled on his parachute harness. He was listening now to the thunder of the twin engines of his fighter as they warmed up; they sounded good and comforting to him, as he scanned the instruments and activated the laser gyros and GPS systems. .A yellow flare flew up from the side of runaway telling them all to hurry.

On the runway on Dutch Harbor in Alaska, Tiger Forrester watched with ice-cold eyes as in the frozen landscape the engines of the Griffin fighters in front of him erupted into vortices of white-hot flame. A red flare rose into the dark overcast. The lead fighters began to roll swiftly down the runaway into the frigid distance. He snapped down his helmet visor into place and threw forward the twin throttles of his own plane's engines and began rolling swiftly after them. The planes ahead of him went to full afterburner, twin daggers of blue flame shooting from their twin engines, brilliant in the arctic overcast. The planes were suddenly airborne, their wings covered with missiles, and he was now slammed back into his seat as he likewise threw on the afterburners, and leapt skyward into the grey heavens.

****

Semjase of Pleione awoke suddenly and rolled out her bunk on the cramped spaceship, she wore the same simple coverall that was also her garment during the day. She had dreamed of someone crying for help from Erra, it troubled her. Tam still slept in his bunk. Sanjeed sat at the controls; his face looked weary but alert. . The viewscreens above the controls showed the unblinking stars of deep space. They were in the asteroid belt, hiding. Ships of the Samar had flown near looking for them. Ships under command of Nor of Rigel, who had sworn a blood oath to make a Semjase the honored guest at a Samaran feast of revenge. Ships of the Unash, the allies of the Samar, known to humans as "Greys" also had swept past in the days previous. But Semjase's ship orbited in free fall with a swarm of asteroids, her ships systems ran at minimum power to minimize any gravo-electromagnetic emissions. No one had detected them, so far.

"Have we received any response to our transmissions?" she queried. Sanjeed turned around in his chair looking startled. He was a handsome lug of a man, bearded, tall and strong, the Pleiadians were a handsome people. She had grown fonder of him as the weeks of confinement on their ship had worn on. But she dismissed the thought of any intimacy with him.

*"I have no time for such distractions,* "she thought. *Besides, it would be a breach of my command discipline.*

"Yes, an hour ago, the computer is decoding it now." he said pointing a strong finger at the control console. "It is from the Unull."

"I will wash then," she said with satisfaction. He turned his back obediently, as she unfastened her garment, stepped out of it naked, and dropped the garment into a cleaning device. On the cramped ship, not meant for women passengers, privacy was scarce and discretion the only thing that preserved dignity.

Semjase stepped gracefully over to the center of a tight metal ring in the center of the floor, pulled It up to attach to the ceiling. As it came up from the floor, a transparent plastic membrane stretched from it to the floor. She pushed it with both hands held over her head to attach to the ceiling and as it locked into place, jets of warm water came from the ceiling. It refreshed her as she pulled a soap gun on the end of a tube from the ceiling and sprayed white foam all over herself and her long brown hair. She kept far from her mind that the water she bathed in had been recycled at least a hundred times on the ship already and had probably passed through her and fellow crewmen's bodies at least half that many times.

Sanjeed, watched the computer screen indicate the decoding process progress, but he had kept the screen brightness low deliberately so he could watch the reflected light of Semjase's lovely nude body writhe sensuously in the shower. He dismissed thoughts that these actions were improper.

*I gallantly volunteered to accompany this unpredictable young wench to Erra, the least I can do is get some morsel of enjoyment out of it?* he thought.

\*\*\*\*

28

The Pleiadian dancing girl arrived at his door clad only in a cloak, accompanied by two guards. The Pleiadian appeared to know only two phrases of Samaran: "yes", and "My Lord" Her stay was pleasant but perfunctory, her eyes expressionless. After this she left with the cloak wrapped around her naked body again, Hontal found himself unable to sleep, he arose naked and paced the floor like a caged lion, his body now healed, and rippling with muscle again. He paced in his room until dawn.

****

Tiger and the rest of his squadron were flying over the grey sea of the Gulf of Alaska, under a grey low overcast. Below him, the frigid grey sea would kill an unprotected human in three minutes. The flames of the afterburners of the Griffin engines were brilliant around him as he flew. They were nearing the fleet anchored off Adak; already they saw smaller warships and supply ships, all painted grey like the sea, flying past them on the ocean's surface. Then the planes in front of him pitched up their noses and rocketed upwards into the grey overcast and Samurai followed them, and Tiger followed his wingman. With his g-compensation, equipment on Tiger felt the change in acceleration only dully. In an instant, he was flying upwards through the dense grey cloud, with only the faint light of the afterburner flames of the neighboring planes dimly visible. Suddenly they tore through the cloud layer into a clear layer below an even higher grey overcast. The squadron looked like shooting stars in the vast dark gulf flying upwards towards the higher layer. The afterburner flames were blue and brilliant and studded with white shock diamonds. In a moment, they had entered the second cloud layer.

****

Feeling clean and refreshed, and clothed in fresh coveralls, her long hair carefully combed with its usual part in the middle. Semjase stared at the decoded message narrowly. She turned to Sanjeed.

"The Unull cannot help us, they say that the Samar are about in force, at least four battlecruisers patrol the system now, and the Unull have been forced to pull back to the far outer system. They advise we continue to hide until the Samar forces must leave."

29

Sanjeed nodded. Tam, a more slender and boyish looking man, was up and also stood by and agreed. "However, I think we should return to Erra, "said Semjase. Tam and Sanjeed expressions turned to dismay.

"Why?" sputtered Sanjeed.

"Because I have sensed a cry of help from Erra."

"There is a little mystery in that! Erra is under a death sentence! Everyone on the planet with any brains cries out for help." said Sanjeed. "That doomed place is the last place we should go near!"

"No, we will be safer there than here, "she insisted.

"No! We are much safer here! They must search vast regions of space full of rocks here. For what reason do you say that Erra is safer?" asked Tam angrily. "You know what will happen if you are captured alive by the Samar."

"That will not happen," she said flatly. "Besides, Erra is safer because the Samar will not expect it, they will expect us to go outwards from Sol," she said with a flip of her elegant head and a sly smile. "Instead, we will return inwards."

"I disagree," said Sanjeed flatly.

"I am in command here!" said Semjase sharply. Both Sanjeed and Tam lowered their eyes. The Pleiadians were a people of iron discipline.

"Yes, Captain" muttered both Sanjeed and Tam in unison, as they all began to get their armored spacesuits on.

****

Tiger burst through the second cloud layer into a radiant blue sky. The planes of his squadron were rising almost vertically now. The Griffin had the highest rate of climb of any plane in the Air Force. They were rising like rockets into the dark blue sky above him.

They were now rising in a cold blue sky above a sea of white cloud, with the sun low on the horizon, white contrails filled the sky above them all converging in one place. Tiger was leaning on his throttles straining to keep his wingman Nakajima ahead of him, his fighter plane like a blazing comet above him. Soon they were rising through layers of other fighters with inferior climb rates to the Griffin. Tiger saw American, Canadian, and Japanese. Mostly they were F-15s and F-18s but he saw F-22s also and cringed mentally, for already in this war, only a few months old, the F-22 had acquired the nickname of "flying coffin" because its complex electronic systems were so susceptible to jamming, rendering it unflyable. They were flying up and through the other fighters like they were sitting still. Above him, another group of contrails was coming from the East, they were Russian MIG 31s Super Foxbats. Now they had the clear sky to themselves, except for one lonely silver speck above them, at this sight, a chill swept through him, and Cowboy, their squadron commander, was yelling.

"Bogy! Bogy! at 1:00 O 'clock, arm Firefox 1, Firefox 2, close with bogey and engage! Close and engage! "Cowboy was yelling. Tiger adjusted his protective visor to protect his eyes from possibly melting. Then pressed his throttles to go even faster as the silver speck began to swell into a grey orb above him in the sky. Suddenly off to his right a sharp flash occurred, orange fire and black smoke as one of the Russian Super Foxbats vanished into wreckage.

"Ghost riders! Break Formation! Break, Break! Bre…" The lead plane in his squadron exploded in a cloud of burning aluminum, titanium, and jet fuel. The grey orb was now huge, smooth, and eyeless; it looked as large as an aircraft carrier. Tiger had one moment of awe mixed with terror before he joined the rest of the squadron in releasing every long-range missile on their wings. The sky ahead of him exploded into orange fire and burning wreckage and black smoke, his plane was buffeted by shock waves, but he was mesmerized now following only the twin daggers of flame from Nakajima's fighter ahead of him. Nakajima's plane flashed brilliantly with rocket exhaust as he ripple-fired his long-range missiles then flew on, now lighter and faster, closer to their vast featureless enemy. It now filled Tiger's windscreen as he followed Nakajima closer, the twin daggers of his wingman's jet exhaust brilliant against the dull silver of the great orb.

31

The Super Foxbats were now flying past him heavy armor piercing rockets blazing off their wings like flares of light. They looked like darts of brilliant flame, but he knew, invisible amid the glare, were tungsten carbide tipped spikes of titanium alloy. Tiger now was firing his own unguided hyper-velocity rockets, as Nakajima did the same. Tiger was now firing his cannon, it was impossible to miss the thing, or aim at any feature on it, there were none, then there was a tremendous flash and feeling of unbearable heat on his face.

****

On the far side of the Moon at the great Unash base in Mare Moscovienes, Tatiana Semonov, walked swiftly down an endless corridor, she wore a dark silver grey form fitting coverall, with a wide black belt. It was open slightly at the neck. She was a blonde, with shoulder length hair, and very attractive but expressionless face. She walked with Nora Goldberg, shorter a brunette, younger woman, who was similarly attired and who wore an equally stoic facial expression. Between them perched on top of a silver cylinder of roughly waist height, rode the shaved head of Murray Rosen. They approached an iris doorway to the ship that that was to take Nora and what was left of Murray to the home worlds of the Unash, the race called by the humans "Greys". Two Unash waited at the doorway. One was an Unash middle-caste technician, with their usual blank expression, the other was a high caste Unash, Doctor Ukla, looked on them with visible relief and agitation.

"Were you stopped by security? "he asked Tatiana frantically, his eyes squinting in the Unash expression of fear.

"No, I simply showed them your pass and they waved us by," said Tatiana impassively.

"Good! Let us go! We must hurry!" said Ukla turning to the technician. The iris diaphragm opened into the ship. "You must listen to number seven in my absence, he can be trusted, and I have his oath he will protect you as best he can! These two must come with me! It is my only hope to save them and stop this war! "Both Nora and Murray hesitated at the doorway and turned to look at Tatiana; she raised her hand and waved it without expression. Murray burst into tears, and tears filled Nora's eyes.

32

Ukla looked pained at this. "We must hurry!" He looked at Tatia and then covered his eyes in the Unash expression of unbearable grief, and they all moved through the hatchway and it closed with a bang. Tatiana looked after it, glanced up at the surveillance cameras looking down at her, and turned and walked back down the corridor. She felt dully the waves of gravity fluctuation as the ship took off and lifted into the sky. She felt an avalanche of relief inwardly. It had been an emotionally enormous strain to accompany them to the embarkation zone. She had nearly lost control of her facial expression for a moment. She walked back into the main chamber of the embarkation area. It was in near chaos; Toman Daz warriors were arriving from newly docked ships to reinforce the garrison, and in the future to form the occupying army of Erra. Supplies for the war were being unloaded by blue lower caste aliens with medicast officers barking orders and raining blows on them. Scores of upper caste officials were being evacuated with their staffs. Tatiana simply walked through the confusion expressionless. She waved her pass at a harried looking medicast who waved her past, as two Toman Daz warriors beside him glared at her in hatred. She avoided their eyes. That was all you could do. Prolonged eye contact with them, for a human, was dangerous before, and was now often fatal, now that war had begun. She moved down the hall. She passed a group of human men, heads shaven, a work detail for the airlocks, and all carrying bags of tools. They were lower caste captives. They were similarly attired as her, and like her, they had no expression. "Novocain face" the human captives of the Unash called it. Her blue eyes avoided them as did their eyes avoid her's. She walked on back to the medical section where she normally performed her duties. She passed another procession of Toman Daz warriors, then some Hadden Daz military marched by, who all glared at her fiercely, she simply stared straight ahead. She finally stepped with relief through the doorway of the medical laboratory where she worked as a supervisor of other human captives, mostly women. However, her relief was instantly replaced by barely hidden terror.

Oyka, a particularly sadistic Unash medicast security guard was in the laboratory. He turned from staring at Katherine, a red-headed newly arrived captive, who was sitting paralyzed with fear on a laboratory stool. Oyka turned and glared at Tatiana with his huge black eyes full of rage. Normally, Oyka was kept out of the labs by doctor Ukla, but he had somehow figured out that Ukla was gone now. Tatiana looked at him impassively.

"Yes Donu," Donu was a Unash expression of respect, roughly translated as 'Sire'

"Look at these test vessels!" yelled Oyka. "They are filthy!" he swiftly walked over to Tatiana and held the small glass cylinder up in her face. She tried not to flinch.

"What do you see?" he screamed.

"I see mineralization Donu "she said levelly, looking at water spots on the clear glass-like ceramic.

"It is oomani filth!" he spat. He pulled out his pain wand and struck her in the throat with it. Tatia gasped in agony and fell to the floor. He bent over her hitting her again on the bare skin of her neck. It felt like the slash of meat cleaver. The pain wand induced agony on bare skin by nerve induction, it did not do direct damage to tissue, though many captives had died because of it, screaming their lives away naked in the punishment chambers on the lower levels. Tatiana blacked out from the pain for an instant.

"Officer Oyka!" came a harsh voice, "Why are you not at your post?" It was number seven; Tatiana fought the blackness and regained consciousness. She looked up desperately from the black smooth floor. Number seven was standing at the door in a rage. Oyka looked petrified and bowing his head, walked out of the laboratory past number seven. Number seven, looked at her gasping on the floor for a moment, then turned and left shutting the door.

Tatiana rose, now shaking with rage and staggered over to Katherine Davenport, who sat still looking petrified. Kathy's face dissolved into tears. Tatiana stepped over and spat blood from her mouth into a sink. Despite her attempt to prepare for the pain wand; she had bitten the edge of her tongue when the wand had hit her.

"NO TEARS!" yelled Tatiana through bloody teeth as she turned to Kathy again. "I told YOU NO TEARS ON THE MOON!" Tatiana slapped her hard across the face and then slapped her hard again as Kathy's face melted into tears. Kathy fell from her lab stool and Tatiana was pounding her with her fists on her back as she curled into a fetal position on the floor. Finally, Tatiana stood over her, panting from the exertion.

"Listen to me Katya; I am done covering for your mistakes. You must decide whether to live or die here. Many die here, few live long." She took a deep breath. "I looked after you because of Murray Rosen, but he is gone now. Now you must decide whether you will live or die here. LIFE OR DEATH! YOUR CHOICE! DO YOU UNDERSTAND?"

Kathy nodded tearfully from the floor. She rose; the corner of her mouth was bleeding.

"NOW CLEAN THIS GLASSWARE AGAIN! No food! No food until they are spotless!"

"Where have they gone," stammered Kathy tearfully, "Nora and Murray?"

"They are gone… Hopefully, they will enjoy a quick death back in the Unash home worlds. Do not look to ever see them again. "said Tatiana with a shrug, scanning the rest of the lab glassware, her blue eyes squinting. "A trip to the Unash world is always a one-way train ticket. None has ever returned."

"How can you be so different than your sister…?" sobbed Kathy. "Your sister Pam is so kind." Tatiana whirled on Kathy in anger at these words. Kathy cringed in terror anew.

"My sister is under a death sentence from the Prime One," said Tatiana icily, "I count her dead already, so do not mention her again to me…" hissed Tatiana. "Do not remind anyone here she is my sister, or they might just decide to use me in a dress rehearsal for her execution. Tatiana's eyes grew cold as ice. "If you do mention her again, I promise I WILL GET A PAIN WAND AND KILL YOU MYSELF WITH IT! " Kathy froze at this warning. Tatiana leaned close to her as Kathy trembled. "DO YOU UNDERSTAND?" Kathy nodded in terror. Amber, Tatiana's deputy, came in the door,

35

looked at Kathy on the floor and then Tatiana with the same blank expression she always wore. Amber, like Tatiana and Kathy, was attractive and slim, with shoulder length dark reddish-brunette hair. 'They only bring the pretty ones to the Moon,' was the saying. Tatiana looked at Amber.

"There is no problem here," said Tatiana to Amber, who turned and left.

Tatiana then turned and they left Kathy crying alone in the laboratory. "

****

Edgebright the messenger rode in the antigravity craft with his mind deliberately focused on the clouds around him. It was stormy day and the craft was periodically buffeted as it rode swiftly. His bodyguards sitting near him in the cabin, all hardened warriors, kept their blonde and red-bearded faces motionless as they rode. He knew the message he carried in his heavy leather pouch was of high importance, even if he remained ignorant of its contents. He was the chosen courier for messages of great importance. As they flew over the vast bright city of Vela below them, he noted ruefully the silver spires of the Samaran embassy, rising above every building in the city except the palace itself. The palace sprawled ahead of them on the side of Mount Vela, it was the center of government of the Vikhelm people, on their planet of genesis, Vale.

"Such impudence," he muttered to himself, as he regarded the Samaran spires. But who else but the Samar would challenge the Vikhelm in their own capital. For it was said, that 'there was no man known, who was born a slave but who died a king, except he was a Samaran.'

He felt the inquiring minds from the Samaran embassy and elsewhere in the city probing him, looking for some hint as to what his message pouch contained. But his long training made him immune to such psychic probes; they were confronted with only his visage wearing a faint smile. Soon they landed at the palace and escorted by the guards who had accompanied him he walked swiftly down the palace halls to quarters of the Lord Protector. He passed more guards of the palace in body armor, their faces often bearing scars from the battles that had earned them this honored duty, armed with swords and ray guns, and then at every other station, a fully armed war robot.

He paused at the outer guard station while his identification was checked by stern sergeants of the guard and sensors scanned every cell of his body. His guards from the ship remained there as he passed through the inner security ring. Only after passing two more portals of security was he brought with his message pouch to the council chamber of the Lord Protector there was granted entrance.

The room was small and circular with a large round table of fine wood in its center, and a domed ceiling, Edgebright knew they were deep inside the Vela Mountain. The walls and ceiling were of polished white stone. As he was escorted into the room, all eyes of the Lord Protector's council were on him. Quantal of Valekone, The Lord protector, a tall strong man, who kept his face shaved like the Archmetans, and whose dark brown hair was long but whose head was bald on top, rose from his great chair and looked at Edgebright sternly. The Marshall, Swarus of Vanon, a dark bearded grim-looking man with a patch on his left eye, and who, it could be seen, wore armor beneath his fur-lined coat, who stood always at the right hand of the Lord Protector, stepped forward and took the pouch from Edgebright's hand as Edgebright bowed and withdrew to leave the room. Swarus opened the pouch and handed the piece of paper it contained to the Lord Protector who looked around the room at the assembly of grey-bearded faces. It was folded to conceal its contents and sealed in blue wax with the seal of Jagal, master of the Vikhelm star fleets. The Lord Protector held it up to all, before breaking the seal and reading it.

"There is war in the Quzrada," said the Lord Protector grimly, "At Erra...the Errans fight the Unash" the last words fell like heavy stones in the room. His eyes rose and probed the room; most of the men lowered their eyes. One man with a rich white beard, Ragnar the Bold, a leader of war of great renown in times past, and who still wore a sword always, met his gaze without flinching.

"It is as I foretold my Lord," spoke Ragnar, "the Unash have provoked this war, for are not the Errans also the seed of the Archmetans! Therefore, they are people of virtue! The Unash have only had the courage to do this thing because they have been egged on by the Samarans!" The Lord Protector waved his hand and Ragnar fell silent, looking down at the table

37

in the center of the room. The table bore a simple map of their sector of the galaxy, looked at from above its disk. The Quzrada lay outwards from them from the galactic core. The Quzrada was shaded in a greyish blue. The Eshalon, the zone of peace, with the stars of Vikhelm and their allies were separated from the Quzrada region by the pale blue stars of the Araras, but also the stars of the Vikhelm, near the red giant Antares, marked in blue and white and their allies shown in green, , butting up against them, two hundred light years from the star Velakone, which Vale orbited, lay the deep red stars of the Xix.

"Alnas Al Nach, (Alas, there is nothing to be done.) We can do nothing my Lord, Alas. We cannot risk another great war in the Quzrada," came an old thin voice. It was Norden the Wise, who had spoken up. "We must keep all our strength turned against the Xix, for already our allies waver."

The last great interstellar war of the Quzrada that had raged for a thousand years, wiped out three civilizations, and left countless fertile worlds desolate, had begun at Erra. Therefore, the Quzrada had been declared a neutral zone by the powers that survived the war, the Samar, The Pleiadians, Vikhelm, Anak, and Arras. Alas, the Unash were a newly emerged power and had not signed the treaty. The war of the Quzrada, it was said had thrown back civilization in the galaxy for 3 thousand years and wiped out several generations of the young. It had been called the 'dagger thrust to the heart' of the Archimedean peoples, who had dominated the galaxy before this.

The Lord Protector stepped to the table, took pen and paper, and wrote firmly, and spoke as he wrote

**To Krayus of Rigel, Lord Ambassador of the Samarans to Vale:**

*What doest thou in the Quzrada?*

*Come; let us look one another in the eye*

**Signed, Quantal of Velakone, the Lord Protector of the Vikhelm**

He then folded it and sealed it with hot blue wax. The Lord Protector looked around the room. All cast their eyes downwards in agreement.

38

Unspoken was the understanding that the Samaran move must be challenged. 'Show anything to a Samaran but weakness' went the saying. Edgebright was ushered in and the Marshall bore the paper to him, it was placed in his pouch and he was dispatched to Samaran embassy.

"The Errans fight the Unash, as true seed of the Archmetans." Began the Lord Protector gravely, "So does the brave ram turn  to face the wolf pack in the snow of winter, but alas, it is for nothing." He looked down deep in thought.

"Alas, Alnach" he muttered, "we can do nothing." He looked around the room, eyes, sad and grim, nodded assent to his words.

Suddenly, voices cried out and the door to the chamber burst open.

Setyya the Poetress , her long dark hair streaked with grey, blue lines on her ancient face marking her as part Arrasian, strode in dressed in a black cloak. She carried a long wooden staff. Around her neck, she wore a jeweled dagger with a bare blade. The guards followed her in with bowed and fearful heads.  Only Quantal the Lord Protector, fastened his eyes on her, she walked past him oblivious, to the north wall of the room. In one graceful motion, she punctured the side of her right index finger and wrote in rich red blood on the white wall it large letters: **Avert not your eyes**

 She then turned as glared at the Lord Protector, and swept a contemptuous glance around the room. Only Norden the wise and Ragnar the Bold met her dark-eyed gaze. Setyya then spoke loudly.

"From the Throne of the Gods comes this message to you Quantal of Velakone, Lord Protector of the Vikhelm. It concerns the Errans, Hear it or perish…" she motioned to the now blood stained wall, then she turned and left the room, holding her thumb tightly against her wounded finger. The Lord Protector shook with rage.

"Impudent witch!" he said, "I want her seized before she can leave the palace!" his voice trembling in anger.

"My Lord," please calm yourself" came the voice of Norden the Wise. His voice was imploring. The Lord Protector glared back at him.

"It will magnify the trouble if you try to detain her. It is best to humor her in this."

The Lord Protector now stared at the bloody message on the wall, then looked down at the Quzrada on the star map on the table and became lost in troubled thought.

****

Tiger awoke falling and strangling in a cloud. Mental confusion overwhelmed him. The front of his helmet visor had a jagged hole in it, and he desperately tried to clamp his hands over it to allow pressure to build up inside so he could breathe. One arm, his left, did not work, he used his right hand. It seemed to work, and he could breathe again and his thought stream began to form a recognizable form. He had to press his hand against the visor with all his strength to contain the oxygen pressure inside the visor so he could breathe. His face was burning and freezing at the same time. His parachute had either not opened or was damaged and was only slowing his fall. He realized he was at least 70,000 ft. and falling at 400 mph in the thin frigid air. He heard thunder, saw flashes of light below him, and realized that he had somehow ejected from his doomed fighter. Suddenly he fell clear of the upper overcast straight into a battle raging furiously below him. Hundreds of fighter jets were swarming around the formerly featureless orb. Missile trails from antiaircraft were also striking it. The orb looked smaller now. It was obviously chaos below, as he saw one anti-aircraft missile strike a fighter. The orb was now heavily marked and had gaping holes in it, some of which spewed flames; Tiger's satisfaction at this was deep. He wanted to move his hands off the hole in his visor to get a better look, but he dared not.

"GOT YOU MOTHERFUCKER! If it bleeds, it can be killed! Ha, Ha!" he yelled in triumph, but his satisfaction was momentary and was replaced choking panic. He was plummeting to the cold grey Gulf of Alaska at a terminal velocity he knew would probably be fatal even if the cold water did not kill him soon after. He looked up at his deflated parachute streaming above him, his left arm seemed paralyzed or broken. He fell through the thin

40

arctic air. The flashes of the battle raging below him lighted the parachute and clouds above him. He took a deep breath, took his hand off the hole in his visor and felt for his reserve parachute on his chest. It was still there and seemed undamaged, his face was now freezing, and he slammed his gloved hand back over the hole in his visor, let the oxygen level build up and then breathed again. His arm was now incredibly tired from pressing his hand over the hole in his visor and holding in the oxygen pressure. But the sensed the air getting denser around him, as he fell, the thickening air which was now his staff of life.

"Thank God my reserve is still there, "he thought. Can't release my reserve chute now, it will tangle around the main chute lines...Got to cut away the main parachute lines so I can use my reserve chute, he thought with a calmness that surprised him. But I have to wait until I am below 10,000 feet so I can breathe and still use my good arm to cut the cords from the main chute free. He marveled that he was now working out a plan to survive while falling to the sea surface at 400 mph. A sudden flash startled him. He was falling straight into the battle. Oh shit, he thought.

Suddenly he felt shock waves strike him and blinding flashes light his helmet, as he went into a tumble and tried to pull up himself into a ball to protect himself as he breathed deeply, each breath perhaps his last. Then after what seemed like an eternity of being buffeted by turbulent air, concussions, and flashes, he fell through the battle zone into another layer of overcast and the flashes dimmed and concussion dulled to thunder. He felt something smack into his left leg below the knee and felt it go numb. He then heard a tremendous impact on his helmet as a high-speed fragment of debris hit it. He sensed the air getting ever thicker around him. He waited in the fog blasting past him, pulled his hand off his visor, and breathed the thin rushing air, he coughed but his lungs began to work with the thin air, he could breathe again. His weary right arm rejoiced as he let it rest and breathed deeply the cold moist air. My left arm must have broken in the eject, but at least it's numb. He could smell the sea beneath him, and mixed with the smell of the sea was the smell of burning oil, cordite, and ozone. He heard thunder and saw flashes from below. He reached down with his good right arm and found his field knife on his belt, he carefully freed it. His right leg was beginning to hurt; he suppressed his awareness of it. I don't need my leg right now. He reached

41

up and by feel found a taut main parachute line and cut it easily. As it gave way, he sensed this rate of fall increasing as his chute lost some of what little inflation it had. He could not look up well because of his helmet, so he felt for another cord and cut it. He felt an explosive concussion from above him and saw a flash and now felt a deep vibration throughout his body. Reflexively he desperately felt for another cord and cut it, this time, the cord gave way easily, the shock of its release was so sudden and intense he lost his grip on his knife. As he sensed it fly away he felt a despair fill him as deep and cold as the waters gulf of Alaska that now rushed up to embrace him. Now he was plummeting at a terrible speed, his useless parachute now trailing behind him on a single line but still hanging on to him by the death grip. He knew his reserve chute could not deploy fully with the main chute still trailing above him. His reserve chute was small even when deployed fully. He was falling very fast now. He found himself doing a grim mental calculation, of rates of fall, impact energies, time in the cold water. *I guess I am not going to survive this battle after all.* He found himself thinking of his mother and father, his brothers, his sister, *our Father who art in heaven hallowed be thy name...*he was praying reflexively. Suddenly his mother appeared to him screaming at him, *"Don't give up! Don't give up!"*

There was a bright flash and a concussion that shook his whole frame. The cloud vanished away as he fell out of the lower overcast and revealed the dark grey sea beneath him studded with fire, smoke, and lightning. Ships were burning; the sea was covered with burning oil. He could see an aircraft carrier burning like a furnace in the distance.

Other ships were firing streams of tracers of brilliant colors , blue and red and yellow salvos of rockets with bright blue exhaust like welding arcs were flying all over his head. He could now see the flames on a vast oil slick studded with debris beneath him rushing up to meet him. The merging of the shocks and thunder was a continual deafening roar. A burning jet fighter fell past him; it looked Canadian. Rockets were now flying straight at him but flashed above him as he fell at increasing speed. He dully wondered where the orb was that they were shooting at. He suddenly felt a vibration and reflexively looked above him as he fell. He heard a piece of shrapnel smash into his helmet again. Above the flash-lit failed white parachute, that was now his banner, the orb was directly

42

above him, in flames with tracers and missile after missile hammering it. It was coming down right on top of him. He instinctively reached for his pistol with his good arm and filled with rage, emptied the pistol at the orb above him. Its muzzle flame brilliant in the dark sky as he fired past his useless parachute.

"GOT YOU MOTHERFUCKER!" he yelled, suddenly feeling energized.

Suddenly the remaining line on his main parachute broke and he was now falling end over end as tracers and missiles flew past him, the pistol flying out of his hand. He frantically struggled to stop spinning as he became dizzy and sensed he was near to blacking out. Miraculously, he resumed his fall feet first.

He was closing with burning dark sea rapidly, the air now screaming past the hole in his visor. His hand found the reserve chute handle and pulled it. His chute opened with a massive jolt. Then he slammed into the cold sea. Cold seawater hit his face and he went under before he could inflate his life vest. For a moment, he felt cold and darkness enclose him. He bobbed to the surface with his helmet full of numbing cold seawater, he managed to frantically struggle with his helmet with his one good arm and pull it off before he drowned from water inside it, and bobbed in the icy stormy sea, topped nearby with red flame and oily black smoke. Without his helmet, his ears were bombarded with the merged crashing of hundreds of tons of high explosive detonating. He managed to inflate his life vest. Tracers and rocket trails were filling the dark sky above him as grey waves washed over him, paralyzing cold water was now pouring down into his pressure suit he sensed its weight now fighting with the floating vest to try to pull him under. He began to look around desperately for a piece of debris to cling to with his good arm and to try to move to keep his head above water. Shrapnel was hitting the water around him. He looked up, the orb was now coming down flaming above him.

He saw it veer away from him and slow itself, all the time being hammered relentlessly, then impact the sea in flames, a vast wreck , and then begin to sink, then rise again above the waves with white streams water pouring out of the holes in its surface and begin to fly slowly away. He heard the scream of high-speed turbines, and thunder of heavy automatic cannon  and looked up to see a  British Navy Frigate slicing through the waves,  its smokestacks flaring black smoke and flame as it rammed through the sea at full military power , obviously burning out its engines  in pursuit of the wounded orb. Its missile racks now empty it was now obviously emptying its magazine of gun ammunition and tracers and bright flashes of muzzle flame leaped from it decks as it raced straight towards him and he floated numb and mesmerized. Suddenly and the prow began to loom above him and he could see sailors in helmets and life jackets frantically feeding deck guns. Then it suddenly heeled over and turned, its deck nearly awash as it rode past him. He sat dull and now numb and exhausted in the water waiting for the next wave to take him under as the strange apparition of the fast warship, its gas turbines screaming like banshees, at full emergency power shot past him. The grey water was coming over its deck, as it heeled  near him so close he could see the white teeth of the helmeted sailors clenched as they held on to their 40-millimeter automatic deck cannon, now silent because the Orb was out of their field of fire. Tiger saw the ships name written in bold white letters on its bow **HMS Thunderchild,** as it rammed past him, the Union Jack of the Royal Navy snapping defiantly. The waves of its passage now rose like a wall and overwhelmed him, pulling under into icy darkness. He held his breath as until his lungs were bursting then opened his mouth and choked on the cold water. He duly was aware of being able to breathe between coughs; a tall grey wave had lifted him. He was shivering spastically now, his teeth chattering even as he coughed up water and gasped for breath. A grey US Navy helicopter firing rocket after rocket crashed past him just over his head, startling him even in his benumbed state, he saw the door gunner's face looking straight at him for an instant, saw the American flag symbol on the doorframe as it shot over. The helmeted door gunner had a surprised look as their eyes met; he had a mustache and needed a shave. The helicopter flashed past leaving thunder and the smell of kerosene. Then from his vantage point on the high wave, he looked with dazed eyes and saw the awful spectacle of the HMS Thunderchild, its forward and deck guns blazing brilliantly in the dim light, and launching torpedoes,   close the final 100 yards with the orb. The frigate rammed the battered orb at full speed even as the orb seemed to try to rise again in flames from the sea. The two vessels, the orb twice as large as the frigate, clung tightly in a death embrace and then both

44

rapidly began to sink between the dark waves, now lit from beneath by the fires burning below the surface. The frigate's stern with propellers visible as its prow was pulled under the water with the sinking orb. Sailors were jumping from her into the sea. Then, it too went under with the orb. All this Tiger beheld even the wave he rode now carried him down. He felt the wave take him under the icy darkness even as the sea and sky lit up with a tremendous flash and he felt a concussion crush out what little breath remained in him. Then all was icy blackness.

****

In armored spacesuits, Semjase and her crew clung to their chairs as their cramped spacecraft give one sharp impulse and began a new trajectory back to Erra. She tried to look absolutely calm, in the next hours they would find out if their strategy had worked. If the impulse had been detected they would all be dead soon. If it succeeded they would reach Erra in a week.

*"I am coming,"* she thought fiercely to Erra. *"I am coming to help."*

****

On the back on the dark river, Cassandra had battled her way out of the dark water. Her back was wounded and was in agony, but the slain of the witch's guards were in piles, she was swinging her sword on those who remained. They were turning and running...

"I must keep fighting! Help is coming!" she shouted to encourage herself.

Cassandra awoke tearing at the covers.

*****

In the inner chamber of the Kormain, the great palace of the government of the Anakan people, the First Minister, in a golden robe, stood waiting in apprehension. The chief councilor stood beside him with his staff, looking grim, his once green scales now grey with age. Boltaan, the supreme commander of the Anakian military forces, stood nearby in an armored spacesuit and did his subordinates, for the coded message had been sent under red coding- a Warning of War, so he had placed all his forces on

45

alert. Other ministers of the great council stood also in robes of green and silver. Some bared their fangs in nervousness as they waited. The plight of the Anakin people, who had lost a recent war with the Samar, was desperate, and any news was regarded with dread. Suddenly the doors of the chamber burst open and three officers of the guard in armored space suits entered with grim faces. Their chief officer held high the message in a red envelope, as the doors were shut and made fast. Many of the ministers gasped and muttered prayers at the sight of the code red message. It was borne to the First Minister who stretched forth his hand and took it grimly and tore open the envelope and read the message in red letters.

"It is from Talkin of Trakken:

"He reports that that there is now war at Erra in the Quzrada, and the Errans fight against the Unash there." the First Minister read further.

Gasps of fear filled the room from the lesser ministers. Boltaan however, looked at the First Minister sternly and in anger at this news.

"He also reports that Taon of Trakken ordered the evacuation of our mission in the Solerra system , due to attacks and increased forces, of the Unash," continued the First Minister.

"Death to the Unash!" cried out one of the officers in armor besides Boltaan, who looked on with a face of iron. The First minister suddenly wept and covered his face.

"Talkin reports that Taon of Trakken has been killed in battle. He reports that he died valiantly, in fighting at Erra with the Unash, in order to cover the withdrawal of our Mission. "

"War! War!" shouted Boltaan. "We must have war! The Quzrada is our eastern border! The Unash are the slaves of the Samarkin! If they take the Quzrada, then we are crushed by the Samarkin from two sides!"

"No! No! We can do nothing!" shouted the Great Councilor. "We cannot oppose the Samarkin; they are too strong for us! Better Erra perishes alone than we perish with them!" He then burst into tears. "Taon is dead! How has our great light perished?" He then collapsed.

"It was I who ordered him sent there.....all things perish now..." the Great Councilor gasped as the other ministers tried to carry him from the chamber, but they were too late and he died before doctors could arrive to help.

****

Hontal, after an hour of having his identification gems checked at several gates, was finally ushered into the inner palace, leaving Gamal, his bodyguard, behind, and Hontal was told to wait in an outer office, before his audience with Dakon, who was the Emperor's Marshall. Hontal had dressed in the plain everyday garb of a knight of Empire, of brown leather armor, studded with glittering alloy at vulnerable points. His sword was at his side, as signified and befitted his station in Samaran life where all able-bodied men were first men of war. For a sword or dagger was a Samaran mark of manhood as surely as his beard.  He paced slowly in the office, whose walls were of smooth white marble, inlaid with gold, observed by a line of bearded guards at the walls in glittering armor, bearing both swords and laser pistols.  He had come far and fast from his home star near Alnilam, and the low status of his father's house. His father, dead now, in battle, as was usual for older men, but his two older brothers had perished also, in battle with the Tlax the outer galactic arm.  This had left Hontal as the family patriarch. Yet he had distinguished himself in the same battle, also, and been badly wounded, but had recovered.   Now he had been chosen for a high mission from the palace.  A white-haired minister appeared, his beard grey and wearing the long blue cloak of the royal court, and bid him follow through a gold edged doorway where guards stood at either side.

In a large office filled with shelves holding scrolls and one whose wall showed a luminescent map of the galaxy stood Dakon of Rigel likewise clad in the plain leather armor of a knight. Dakon was an impressive man, tall and of legendary strength. His beard was grey but his manner was a vigorous young man.  Hontal was ushered in and the minister, whose

47

name was Janek of Saiph, sat with seeming weariness in a chair near where Dakon stood.

Hontal bowed himself as Dakon acknowledged him with usual Samaran salute of the clenched fist struck over his heart.

"Welcome Hontal of Alnilam," said Dakon with a smile. " I regret we cannot talk long, We must move quickly this morning to send you on your journey"

"Yes My Lord"

"First, you must swear the oath of secrecy for what you are about to hear, for you are to receive high secrets of the palace and to gather such knowledge and from reports which will also become high secrets of the palace. You may refuse this responsibility and honor at this time, for the penalty of betrayal of such secrets is the death of salt. Do you understand this?"

"Yes My Lord," said Hontal reflexively, though inwardly he shook. The death of salt was a gruesome form of execution among the Samar, normally reserved for spies, traitors, and cowards in battle. It was a high death for the highest of crimes.

Dakon smiled and raised his right hand. Hontal did likewise.

"I swear by the light of Rigel and the High Palace that I will faithfully carry out the trust I am about to be given, and if I fail I shall suffer the death of salt." said Dakon looking at Hontal intently in the eyes as Hontal repeated the words after him. Dakon nodded and smiled, as he clapped his hand on Hontal's strong shoulder.

"You are the true son of your father, Hontal" said Dakon, turning to Janek, who handed Dakon a sealed envelope and a blue jewel, the Imperial signet, set in gold on a heavy gold necklace chain.

"I send you on mission of the highest importance to the Emperor," he handed Hontal the envelope sealed with the Imperial seal, and hung the signet on its chain around Hontal's neck, "You must go to the Quzrada, into its very heart, and observe what transpires there, in particular with our military mission at Erra. Your vessel will be the battle cruiser, Tlakmar. "Tlakmar was a renowned warship of the main fleet.

Hontal betrayed an expression of confusion. "The Imperial signet is your protection and sign that you are on a mission of the High Palace; wear it all times." added Janek gravely. "Beware, for the heart-spaces of the Quzrada you travel into, are the realms of death."

"You were not aware that we had a military mission there?" asked Dakon to Hontal pointedly.

"My Lord, it was my understanding that the Quzrada was a neutral zone..."

"That is correct, so our involvement there is a High Secret of the Palace, do you understand this?"

"Yes My Lord"

"You have a reputation as a reliable man, with keen eyes, a good military sense, and a teller of fine tales. For this reason, you have been chosen. You father's house is honored, but not great, therefore your mission will be less conspicuous."

"Yes my Lord"

"Janek here will explain the situation that faces the Empire in the Quzrada," said Dakon and motioned to Janek. Janek rose and pointed to the large Map on the wall. The map depicted the galaxy viewed from above its disk. The blue stars of the Samarans were a wide swath in the center of the map extending outward to the outer galaxy; a lighter circle was the Quzrada, which formed the border of the Samaran star swath in its portion nearest the galactic core. Going clockwise around the white region from the Samaran-Quzrada border was the Golden stars of the Pleiadians, then a turn to a small green area which were stars of the Unash and a purple star area which were another lesser species, the Unul, then was the region of red stars opposite the Samarans across the Quzrada called the Arras, and finally a large group of silver stars which was the Anak. However, Hontal's eyes were drawn to the region inward

49

toward the galactic core, where a large mass of orange stars lay. These stars belonged to the fearsome people known as the Vikhelm.

"The Quzrada is also known as the neutral zone and it forms the inner border of the Empire with the galaxy toward the core of the galaxy. The four powers of the treaty that emplaced it are the Anak to the east, the Pleiadians in the west and the Vikhelm in the inner galaxy. Together with the Samar, they guard the neutrality of the Quzrada. The entrance of any significant forces into the Quzrada will lead to the dissolution of the armistice and interstellar war. "

Hontal felt a stunning sense of foreboding at this statement. For the Samar existence was war, they knew no peace with their neighbors, only lulls in violence when 'trifles could be exchanged' in trade. To hear a minister of the palace speak of interstellar war with trepidation was astonishing. Hontal, like every Samaran was taught that the power of the empire was limitless, and its war fleets invincible. He grasped suddenly that even the Samaran Empire, did not have unlimited resources, and might be taxed too severely by a war in the inner galaxy when all their efforts were being spent on the Tlaxian war in the galaxy's outer regions. He also realized it was the prospect of war with the Vikhelm that was obviously the main fear, for they were renowned for their skill in war and ferocity.

"We have tasked the Unash to manage things in the Quzrada, at Erra, and we have paid them. They are not bound by the treaty," Janek paused "technically," he added. The Unash are to neutralize the Errans and prevent them from becoming a complication within the Quzrada. The Errans are, of course, an Archmetan people, and thus could cause troubles if they rise up in power. "

"Neutralize? The Unash are to guard them and keep them bound to Erra. "

"They are to prevent the Errans from becoming a power in the Quzrada..." said Janek firmly "by whatever means are necessary. We can have no Archmedean power in the Quzrada. But, none the less, we want this done quietly and efficiently. No one can see the hand of the Samar in this."

"Do you know how much we paid the Unash people 60 years ago for this service to the Samaran Empire?" continued Dakon.

"No my Lord," replied Hontal.

"We paid them one-thousand great-stone's weight of fine gold..." said Dakon slowly, emphasizing each word. He stared at Hontal intently. "That and we granted them possession of fertile Erra forever." Dakon added. Even the idea of that much wealth made Hontal feel dizzy.

"But my Lord, good planets have been bought and sold for less..." gasped Hontal.

"Yes," nodded Dakon with a look of seething anger. "But this planet is in the heart of the Quzrada. Its value is beyond measure."

Dakon was shaking with rage now, so Hontal became nervous. Hacking apart of subordinates occasionally happened in the Samaran military, sometimes just so leaders could publically register displeasure at unwelcome reports. 'Hard duty is to be the bearer of bad tidings,' was the old saying that Hontal's father had instructed him several times. "So, for this treasure of gold, and the everlasting title to fair Erra," continued Dakon. "The Unash were to snuff out the Errans like a man licks his fingers and snuffs out a candle flame. Thus it was to be done, quickly and quietly."

Hontal nodded in awe.

"But, we have received poor service from the Unash for this treasure, so we hear..." said Dakon

Hontal nodded, "We have also our people there to observe?" he asked.

"Yes, a small mission, a hundred men, to monitor the Unash.

"What do they report?"

"Their reports are not sufficient, they are trash. These men are mostly of the Batelgeen tribe, close to the Unash. We want a different set of eyes to survey the matter first hand," said Dakon gruffly

51

"They keep reporting that everything is going well, yet we also have monitored Unash communications recently indicating serious problems," said Janek. "The light of Erra still burns, it has not been snuffed out!"

"We suspect the Monchkini have made a mess of this situation," interjected Dakon sharply, using the Samaran derogatory term for the Unash. Monchkini meant 'monkey-bug' or 'monkey lizard.' "We want you to find out how bad this mess is and be able to recommend solutions."

"As you know, Bekar of Batelgeen had me to his mansion for a banquet last night." said Hontal.

"Yes, we know this. Did he attempt to bribe you, to give a good report? "

"Only a dancing girl of Merope, my Lord, for the night," said Hontal with slight embarrassment, "I received her only as war-custom, since I was a guest there." Dakon nodded with a slight smile at this.

"It is custom," said Dakon nodding, "but did Bekar say anything of import to you?"

"Bekar did speak of this mission my Lord, and asked me to give a good report, however, and he spoke of Quzrada as their provenance"

Janek and Dakon looked at each other in shared anger.

"Did he say anything else of consequence? "

"No my Lord, except for one strange thing, he spoke me of a prophecy concerning Erra and the throne."

"What did he say, exactly?" asked Dakon intently.

"He said that through a son of Erra the Batelgeen would achieve the throne of the Samar again."

"This borders on treason," muttered Janek

"Bah!" said Dakon. "This so-called prophecy he told you is but is but a song of drunkards, wrapped in an intrigue. That is not even the prophecy!"

52

"But they perhaps seek advantage from this rumor." said Janek turning to Dakon, "to twist it to their own ends."

The tribe of Batelgeen had once held the throne of Rigel, many generations before, but lost it due to crimes of Taggon the Unwise, and the war of succession that followed. It was known among the Samar that the house of Batelgeen schemed endlessly to replace the house of Mylex, and become the Royal house of Rigel once again.  Hontal nodded in shared concern at these words.

"No matter what a snake hisses, he is still a snake," said Dakon with a shrug. "Beware the Batelgeen, Hontal of Alnilam, especially Bekar. And see to it that when return from Erra in the Quzrada with your report, you bring your report directly here to the High Palace. "And also, "Dakon paused and smiled, "No more dancing girls of Merope, at least not until you have delivered your report here at the Palace to me. Is that understood?"

"Yes, my Lord"

"You might also know that the dancing girl you bedded last night cost Batelgeen dearly," said Janek with a smirk. "When they raided the Merope sector, the Pleiadians struck them as they withdrew and the Batelgeen lost 3-star cruisers and two slave ships, full of captives, many other ships were damaged. Hence, our forces in the outer galaxy were later found deficient at Umax. You may have wondered why that battle at Umax was so ill-fortuned, as you lay in your hospital bed. Now you know why. I suppose it fitting you received the Meropean as war-custom now."

"I knew there was a raid near Merope, but I heard no mention of losses," said Hontal in astonishment. "I did not know the Pleiadians fought anymore so fiercely."

"No, you did not hear of these losses, or of the return of manly firmness to the Pleiadians. That is a high Secret of the Palace. You should also know the Pleiadians spared not their own, but counted those held captive on board those slave ships, as already dead, when they destroyed them." Dakon nodded in admiration at this contempt for life.  "We have decided that it is not auspicious to trifle with the Pleiadians further at this time.

That raid also had no sanction from the Palace here, either, but was taken 'on a venture' as they say. "

"What reckless fool ordered this raid then that ended so disastrously? We could have used those ships at Umax! " exploded Hontal, the pain he had endured returned to his memory like fire, the long days hovering at death's door, the fear of being left crippled, and the death cries of his shipmates. *My father and brothers.*

"The fool who ordered this, "said Dakon darkly, "was none other than Bekar of Batelgeen, your host last night. But that is all a secret of the Palace. But now you must fly Hontal of Alnilam, fly swiftly as a black hawk, and have eyes as keen as an eagle, to Erra in the heart of Quzrada." Dakon placed his heavy strong hand on Hontal's shoulder, "and get us true knowledge, true-facts, be our sharp eyes there, and then report back as swiftly as you went there, here to me and Janek, of the real situation there, as best you can estimate it. We will want also your recommendations for any actions that appear required. We can have no Archmetan power rise in the Quzrada. "

"Yes my Lord"

"May Elon, the King of the Gods guard your path, Hontal. May Alkmar, the god of war profit your efforts," said Janek rising as Hontal saluted by placing his clenched fist over his heart, then, grasping his envelope of orders and bearing the signet of palace around his neck he turned and strode swiftly out of the room into broad corridors of the palace, a detachment of four guards escorted him. His family retainer, Gamal, joined him there. Gamal, sturdy and strong yet old, and bearing the scars of many battles, with greying red hair, unusual among the Samar, fell into lock step behind Hontal, carrying their bags. They were warriors of the Samaran Empire and traveled light. The palace guards walked them both to the spaceport of the Palace where the cruiser Tlakmar awaited him.

Back in the conference room, Dakon stood deep in thought. He turned to Janeck.

"Janek, the master of secrets, behold, I have sent a bold knight to the heart of Quzrada, to discover its truths. I now send you on a similar mission here in Alkmar "

"Yes my lord, "said Janeck leaning close to listen.

"You and your most trusted men, go, find out what brave Hontal was talking about, about that devilry Bekar spoke of. That matter of a prophecy... about a son of Erra and the throne"

Janeck nodded gravely.

"It is probably some tale out of a Batelgeen ale bottle, "said Dakon looking troubled at the wall map. But it also could be a venomous serpent, coiled near the throne of Rigel."

"You find out which it is for me," he said turning back to Janek's now stony face.

"And, brave Janeck... "Dakon added, "Stop at nothing...".

Janeck looking grim, saluted and left the room, as Dakon stood pondering the map of the galaxy, his eyes fixed on the center of the Quzrada, on Erra.

****

On planet Janus, there was a loud cry in the night and with it, Karlac of Janus awoke on the floor of his simple room. He arose trembling, and wrapped his simple white cloak, which was also his bed cloth, and spoke the word 'luma' to turn on the lights. A scream echoed in his head, a woman's scream. He listened carefully, so see if he had actually heard it, or if was a dream. The house and neighborhood slept peacefully, it seemed. He heard urgent knocking on the door to his bedchamber.

"My lord, my Lord! How is it with you?" came the voice of his older housekeeper, Mistress Hena.

"I am well...I had a frightful dream. That is all, Mistress, peace be unto you..." he responded. *So I dreamed. But a dream of what?*

55

"I will make you a vegetable broth then…so you can sleep." she said through the door.

"Very good…" he responded reluctantly and heard her depart. In the distance, he heard thunder. He glanced at the window; saw the flicker of far way lightning. *What was the dream?* He trembled again as he tried to remember. All he could remember was darkness and terror, pain… He glanced at himself in the mirror near his bed; he was Archimedean, like all the inhabitants of Janus, tucked near the Vikhelm worlds. His hair was white and short, as was his well-trimmed beard. He shook his head in disbelief at his appearance; he looked completely disheveled and horrified. *The dream has left its mark on me…*

He immediately fell to his knees and prayed to the Creator for guidance. "The dream, someone calls me My Lord, someone who needs help… Who is it? Please help me remember!" he gasped desperately. Karlac of Janus had made a name for himself as a mediator of disputes and as a voice for the helpless in the regions of Eshalon. He sensed within himself, that the dream was of vast importance, but he could remember only the woman's scream. Suddenly he rose, grasping paper and pen from a small wooden table, sat, and began to write quickly. *The scream was not just a scream, it was a word…* Terror, terrain, Terran, Terra, error … he scribbled. Suddenly he wrote *Erra.* He dropped his pen trembling; the word filled him with fear. Fear was an emotion he had not felt for many years. Now he felt it, deep within himself.

*No, you cannot mean Erra that is so very far from here…* Karlac of Janus, the Great Sayer of Peace, and also known as the Father of Conciliation, fell back upon his knees and prayed anew. *No, it is too far from the stars of the Eshalon…You cannot ask me to go there …*

## Chapter 1: Not in Kansas Anymore

Hontal of Alnilam, a high knight of the realm strode down the dark grey corridor to the bridge of the battle cruiser starship Tlakmar in his armored spacesuit, carrying his space helmet. A gold chain with a large blue sapphire set in gold hung around the neck ring of his spacesuit, marking his as a special emissary of the Samaran Empire. His sword in its scabbard on his spacesuit belt showed his status as a knight, and his dark jeweled dagger was on his sash, the badge of manhood for every Samaran male. He passed young officers with smooth shaven faces, also in armored spacesuits, and more senior officers with mustaches and beards. All their faces told the same story of grueling wariness and alarm. They had journeyed now three days into the forbidden zone of the Quzrada, into its outer zones. Hontal had been awakened by alarms as the Tlakmar had fallen out of hyperspace and as he had hurried dressed in his quarters, he had heard the straining of the normal space engines. His mission, as an emissary of the palace, was to journey to the very heart of the Quzrada, to Erra, to observe and return with a report on the progress in the Quzrada of the allies, the Samar and the Unash. He now wondered, in his warrior's heart, if he would make it even halfway there.

He strode through the hatchway, its guardian in armored spacesuit and space helmet, the Zoldarm, one of the able fighting men of the Samar, saluted by bringing his fist across his chest to be over his heart. On the bridge of the starship, the officers sat tensely at their consoles in armored spacesuits, with space helmets at the ready. The ship was on high alert, higher even than the levels of alert that had been maintained since entering the Quzrada, which was obviously now a zone of war. Twice before, they had had to drop out of hyperspace because sensors indicated Unull warships following them. He entered the bridge of the warship and quickly, with practiced eyes, scanned the view screens and data panels being studied by the ship's captain. To Hontal's amazement, he saw they were now in an asteroid belt, around a dull red star. The other officers and crew of the bridge stood at their posts with that calm look assumed by the Samar when extreme danger was present.

The Captain of the Tlakmar, a balding strong man, named Quinton of Rigel, stood in his armored spacesuit stroking his short well-trimmed beard. He was standing by his command chair staring at the main viewscreen in the front of the bridge. The Captain, his bearded face etched with wary calmness, turned and saluted Hontal quickly, before turning back to gaze at the view screen.

"We have detected a large Unull fleet, "he said in a hushed tone, "three heavy cruisers of their type 2 class, at least, perhaps four destroyers, class 1." Hontal felt dread and amazement at this. *Too much for even the Tlakmar to handle alone. How dare the Unull bring such a force this near to Samar space?*

"Have they detected us? "

Captain Quinton shook his head slowly, still studying the view-screens.

"I think not, they have bigger quarry to seek," the Captain said grimly and turned to the Communications officer. "Put the com channel through the large speaker, "he said in a low voice. From a speaker above their heads now poured forth a rushing noise of sub-space background hum mixed with faint voice communications and then punctuated with sharp blasts of static. To Hontal, after his years of service on the Tlaxian war-front, the blasts of static and their tones were unmistakable: a space battle was in progress, several light years in the distance. He looked up at the speaker and strained to discern the voices and if possible the types of weapons being used. He heard the guttural voices of the Unash, one crying out in alarm, then after a loud blast of static with a shrill keening noise, more Unash, then harsh clicking voices. Hontal recognized these clicking voices as Unullain battle-speech.

"Did you here that last burst of static, with the screeching? That was a large ship going up; the Unash main drives make that sound when they disintegrate. The Unull are attacking an Unash convoy if I do not miss my guess...." Suddenly what sounded like a woman's voice, yelling in Samaran was heard, followed by more static. Hontal glanced at the Captain in surprise, who also looked at him in amazement. More bursts of static flowed with more Unash and Unullain voices, then there was the male voice of a Samaran speaking in the precise code of battle, honed over ages of warfare to transmit clear information in the chaos of combat.

Hontal felt a sense of pride rise in him. *Ah! The swords of the Samar are unsheathed! The Sword of Orion! Always victorious! May their realm expand eternally!* His mind chanted ritually. Rapidly the noise and voices of the battle ebbed and became more indistinct. The combat was moving away from where they sat.

"Why wait we here? We should join this battle!" urged Hontal "Are not our brave Samarkin engaged here?" The Captain looked deep in thought at this.

"No, "the Captain said gravely, after a long silence, "My orders from the Palace are clear, to take you to Erra and bring you back with your report." The Captain then smiled slightly. "Don't worry, young buck, there will be no shortage of battle-glory in your life," he said and clapped Hontal on the shoulder. Hontal looked and saw the small, silver, four pointed star insignias, filling the chest of the Captain's armored space suit, marking him as a veteran of hundreds of battles. Hontal carried only five such stars. For a Samaran male, to live was to serve the Empire, and to die in battle in its service was the highest death. For this reason, the death of a relative in battle was never mourned publically.

"Yes, Captain," Hontal said, lowering his eyes.

****

The group, known as the "A team" arrived in several Air Force vans near dusk. Travel problems, common in that time, and security clearance delays at the main gate offices had made the first day of Project Prometheus run hours behind schedule. But the students were eager to for the tour to start and agreed to have dinner brought to them in Building 34 so they could begin.

Doctor Hans Bergenholm, resplendent in a suit and tie and with his beard now greying stood beside Colonel Headman of the US Air Force as he checked the tablet for the list of names, as the students filed in the doorway. He was reading their ID badges as they walked by Trevor Adamson, Tobias Levinson, Quami Housa, Indira Patel, Fredrick Wilhelm, Susan Yang, Takashi Omira, Theodore Lodge, Jessica Hanson, Mohamed Ansari, Joshua Resnick, James Byrnes... the best and brightest students in engineering , physics, and biology, drawn from MIT , Georgia Tech, Cal Tech, and Texas A&M. All of them that could be cleared to the above Top Secret Level, that is, together with several of their professors. They had arrived at Site 51, in the middle of a war, to view a gallery of captured alien specimens and technology.  They were all smartly dressed, the men in suits and ties, the women in dresses and pantsuits. The Sun was setting; its russet light shining through the front doors of the hall, which was obviously a converted airplane hangar.  The students walked immediately into the hall followed by several white-haired professors.   Hans Bergenholm followed them.   He noted that all paused before several Unash alien bodies, preserved in formaldehyde.  The women particularly lingered, some approaching closely, eyes wide with wonder, or in one case grief, to examine the details of their inert skin and eyes.  The young men had pushed on to examine a small captured saucer whose skin had been cut away to reveal in cross section its intricate inner mechanisms.  One could walk inside its roughly forty foot circumference, to view the complex inductor array on its bottom portion and the crew cockpit with its strange instruments on top.

One young woman asked him a question as he passed the preserved alien bodies.

"They use hemocyanin   as a blood pigment?  But how can that work? Copper has less oxygen affinity than iron; it must be much less efficient than hemoglobin." she asked in amazement.

"Oh, apparently it is much more advanced than hemocyanin found on Earth," said Bergenholm as he walked by, "but you are right, they run a little oxygen lean all the time.  Bad choice, iron is much more common in the universe for one thing, and it made trying to hybridize with humans a real biochemical mess.  But I am merely a physicist," he said waving his hands and smiling as he walked past the women.  "You should ask Dr. Clifford, our biologist about this during the briefing."

"It looks like a child..." said one young woman wiping her wide eyes, yet standing near the specimens in fascination.

A cluster of young men and women and several older professors were standing mesmerized near the cut-away saucer. The look on their faces

60

was a mixture of wonder and intense concentration. They spoke in low tones, but most expressed awed silence. One student wearing a yamaka was tracing some circuit element with his finger from the lower inductor assembly, up through the innards of the saucer, up to the control console in the cockpit, as several other students stood watching in amazement.

"What is this metal? Was it easy to cut open like this?" asked a young black man with a large afro, as Bergenholm walked up. A young man, with heavy framed glasses, was looking carefully at the cross-cut metal at the saucer's edge.

"They use a family of magnesium aluminum alloys, often with some chrome and other metals. The alloy is very hard and strong, apparently with multi-ply directional crystals, but we can cut it with diamond or Borazon saws, and it won't stop 50 caliber bullets, which is fortunate."

"You are?"

"Hans Bergenholm and you?"

"Quami Housa, from MIT, I work for Doctor Levine over there." He motioned to a grey-haired professor examining the cockpit.

"Have you noticed it has patterned layers? Could it be the skin is part of the field control system and not just structure?" asked Quami pointing down at the cross section of the metal skin.

"Yes, good observation, Quami, but save your questions for the briefing," said Hans smiling. "This was just an intellectual appetizer, and we are behind schedule."

The students were moving further down the gallery of exhibits, of human-Unash hybrids, of machinery recovered from Morningstar and other overrun bases. One exhibit showed examples of alien spacesuits and life support packages. Another exhibit showed alien death ray weapons, which fired spin-polarized proton beams or laser beams modulated to disrupt human DNA and hemoglobin.

"These inductors, they obviously support a rotating tesla type EM field! Do they use one frequency or do they add harmonics?" asked one student aggressively.

"They mix in harmonics and use them to control the field distributions using interference patterns, "said Bergenholm smiling. Standing there in the middle of the students, he felt bathed in a bubble of sheer intelligence and curiosity, "But they also vary the electric to magnetic field mix. We need your help on understanding this, we see evidence they use fluid-space time duality dynamics to control the gravity around the saucer. But let's get back to the main table for the briefings..." Bergenholm pointed at a large table and computer projector and screen near the entrance of the hall. He stood aside and let the students troop by, back to the table.

"So far so good, "said Colonel Headman smiling, as Bergenholm walked up to the table. "Nobody ran out of the hall screaming," he added. A group of physicists, biologists, metallurgists, electro-gravitic engineers and an anthropologist stood by wearing ID badges, ready to deliver briefings to the assembling students and professors.

"Yeah, they are eager, you can sense it," said Bergenholm watching the students take their seats. One young woman was still crying. He noted the name on her ID badge, Jessica Hansen. *This is a bad sign,* he thought, *she may not last in this program*. But he encouraged himself as he saw the solemnly determined looks on the faces of many others.

"I pray to God these people can work some miracles here, "said Colonel Headman losing his smile, "we just lost our four thousandth fighter pilot last night. We can't train them fast enough now; we are now drawing on airline pilots and calling men out of retirement."

Bergenholm nodded soberly and stepped up to the podium.

"Thank you all for being here," he said loudly to the students. " I know you've all had a long journey here, and we are behind schedule, so let's get started. We are going to give you all a collection of briefings representing the basic sets of knowledge we now have concerning Unash alien technology, physiology, and social psychology. I myself work on EM–Gravity unification theory, trying to understand the physics they use to drive their spacecraft. I will tell you now that, you represent the very best this country has and we are counting on your insights and ideas to help us master the technologies you have just looked at so we can drive the Unash out of the Solar system .

"Once again, we are counting on your help. We have, for a half century of contact with the Unash, been studying intercepted communications, bodies , crashed spacecraft , even studying of captives, yet despite this prolonged effort, much of their science , technology and motivations remain mysterious to us. So we are counting on your help and fresh insights in this effort…" He was scanning each young determined face now in the audience, even Jessica was now staring at him soberly and composed, and he was filled with hope. He put his first viewgraph up on screen: "Introduction to Electromagnetic Spacetime Geometrodynamics - Antigravity 101 or *'how to build a flying saucer'*"

*Operation Prometheus is now rolling,* he thought with determination as he saw the students and professors lean closer.

****

Douglas Forester awoke in a hospital room to the roar of jet engines in the distance. He felt dull pain throughout his body and his every breath was painful. His arm was in a cast. In the window, the sky was a heavy grey overcast. He managed to reach a nurse call button and pressed it until someone showed up. A sweet-faced young nurse in a white pantsuit came bursting through the door and looked at him.

"Nurse, where am I? What day is it? "Doug demanded.

"You're in Elmendorf Hospital, and its Friday, flyboy." said the nurse.

"Friday the what? How long have I been out?" Doug said angrily.

"You shouldn't talk so much, you have three fractured ribs." The nurse cautioned. She stuck an infrared thermometer in his ear and read its dial, seemed pleased. "You were brought in last night from the battle at Adak, you're lucky you just woke up, you have a visitor."

Samurai Nakajima stuck his head in the door. He was wearing flight overalls and looked tired and haggard. Despite this, his face lit up in a smile at the sight of Doug awake.

"Samurai! Come on into my luxury suite!" said Doug happily, and then felt pain from his ribs straining against his lungs.

"Don't let him talk too much or too loudly, he has broken ribs, a broken arm, and a concussion." said the nurse to Samurai. Samurai nodded and sat down wearily in a chair at the foot of the bed.

"Well, we kicked their ass, didn't we? The last thing I saw from the water was the Brit Frigate ramming the thing and it blowing up!" said Doug smiling.

"Yeah we brought it down," said Samurai with a weary smile. "We chased off two smaller escorts too, and brought down a third, seagull class, I think. It went in the drink a few klicks from the big one." He pulled out a sigma, which was an electronic cigarette favored by the military and primed it. Samurai had lines on his face Doug had never seen before. Samurai then starred out the window at the grey sky, blowing the cigarette vapor out of his mouth slowly. He looked half dead.

"Well at least I get a few days' vacation here," said Doug, "that nurse isn't bad either. Did they say when I can come back to the squadron?"

"No, you rest up buddy, they're redeploying us anyway back to the lower forty-eight. They say we're done here, they're sending in another griffin squadron. "

"That's too bad; I was just getting to like this place."

"Yeah Tiger, me too," said Samurai smiling weakly.

"They are transferring me to a Scorpion squadron Tiger, so you'll have to get a new wingman," said Samurai looking at the floor. Doug reacted slowly to this.

"That's good buddy, what's a Scorpion?" said Doug trying to mask his disappointment. Samurai had been his wingman for a year now, through all the battles of what was being called the ET war.

"It's the new fighter upgrade of the SR-71 , fresh off the assembly line, buddy, F-71 , it's Mach 5 plus; they're using it for high altitude combat air patrol over the lower forty-eight states now." Samurai brightened slightly in discussing the new fighter. "The dumb ass Greys keep abducting people, and then they chop 'em up and drop them on the suburbs. My new squadron's job is to stop them. I am being based out of Vandenberg."

"Sounds good buddy, where's the rest of the squadron going?" asked Doug. Samurai looked down at the floor.

"We're it Tiger, you and me..." Nakajima's voice became tough and harsh. "Everybody else in the squadron bought it yesterday." Doug looked at him in disbelief. Samurai looked up at him grimly, dragged on his e-cig. "Yeah, it's true. You're the only one who went down who could even eject."

"I had to sit up all last night," Samurai continued, now staring out the window at the grey sky. "After I got back from graves registration, I had to write letters home to their families. The hell of it is, two of our planes got hit by Navy Standard missiles, and I didn't know what to write. I sat there for maybe three hours paralyzed.  So finally I lied and said they went down due to enemy fire." He paused, blinked. "That way I could use the same basic letter twenty times," he laughed slightly, and then looked back at Doug blankly. Doug looked down at the floor beside the bed.  He held his face immobile.

**\*\*\*\***

The view screen was centered on a dazzling blue-white point of light. Hontal paused, mesmerized by the beauty of the star.

"Prime Officer, when do we assume orbit?" demanded the Captain.

"Five periods my Captain, by our present course." answered the officer, after checking his console.

"What is that star ahead of us, I thought we were in the Solerra system?" asked Hontal.   Solerra, he knew, was golden, like the star of Samar, Telsmar.

"That is Erra.  It is a bright planet. The area crawls with Unull interceptor ships, and we have the view-sensors sensitivity turned up, to watch for them." said the Captain turning to look at Hontal, grimly before turning back.  "This is the fifth time I have voyaged here, to the heart of the Quzrada, and every time Erra looks more beautiful and dreadful."

Hontal felt the dread of the place also, for it was here, at Erra that the Great War had begun 7 thousand years before.

"If the dead of this place could speak, they would deafen us." said the Captain.   "To evade detection by the Errans we will approach in the planet's shadow then make a short transit to the shadow of Una, the moon of Erra."

"We fear detection by the Errans?" asked Hontal incredulously.

"The last time we were here they tracked us with radar, despite our countermeasures. Now the Errans are at war with the Unash, and have warned all ships to stay away."

"Why should we fear if they see us?" asked Hontal with a laugh.

"They have nuclear weapons, and missiles to deliver them at a considerable distance into space."

"If they launch a warhead at us, what is that to us?" asked Hontal, with a slight smirk. The report he had read as he had traveled, had described the Errans as brave primitives.

Missiles, at least those that traveled at sub-light speed, were considered primitive and obsolete weapons by the Samar, who, like the other regional powers, fought exclusively with long-range directed energy weapons.

"They will not launch one at us, they will launch five hundred," said the Captain grimly.

"Trust me, we do not want a battle here." added the Captain. "My orders are to deliver you to Una, and return you with your report." Hontal, tried to hide his consternation at hearing this information, nothing of this had been mentioned in his report book, not the heavy presence of the Unull, no the situation of war at Erra, not their dangerous, if primitive, weapons. *I have obviously been sent here to find out everything here for myself,* thought Hontal, with anger.

Hours crawled by, they neared Erra and slipped into its shadow. Erra appeared then as a red ring, like the evil eye of Ental, the Samaran god of evil. After some period in Erra's shadow, they made a brief dash into the shadow of Una as they approached it.

****

On Earth, as the full moon neared an eclipse Duncan Lowery, the amateur astronomer stood on a bare mountain in the Mojave Desert watching the stardust filled the sky as the cold wind blew. He was a portly man with a scraggly beard and a ponytail. He wore a black beret. Before the stars had been a comfort to him, but now, since the beginning of the war, the stars filled him with fear. He and his friends with him all carried an assortment of guns that night and wore magnetometers. They were on a "truth seeking expedition" into the desert at night, given the times; it was not something done lightly.

"My God look!" he exclaimed as he beheld a spark of light near the Moon's disk. "Do you see it?" he cried out to his friends who were watching a laptop viewscreen that showed what he saw through the eyepiece. His friends, six other men, stared mesmerized at the viewscreen.

"Yes I see it!" exclaimed one pointing at the screen. "Even if that is just a glint, the thing must be enormous, as big as an aircraft carrier!" Duncan Lowery, watched as the spark moved and went out near the Moon.

"It's entered the Moon's shadow, I can't see it anymore." Lowery gasped. His heart sank.

"It's all true, somebody is on the Moon, and there obviously being reinforced." He said as he turned to his friends, who all looked at him in shock.

"It's true..." he said.

"I still say the government is lying to us!" said one of them, a short wiry fellow named Linus Quisling, who wore a bandana around his head. "They have invented this threat from aliens to stifle dissent. This war is their fire in the Reichstag! This whole war is their invention!"

"You saw the ship moving to the Moon!"

"The government is the one with bases there, not the aliens!" insisted Quisling.

"Linus, you are the one always telling us the government never went the Moon, that the Apollo program was a hoax!" yelled Lowery.

The man named Linus looked down at the ground in the dim light of the laptop viewscreen. He folded his arms defiantly.

"LINUS! NOTHING EVER HAPPENS ON THIS PLANET EXCEPT IT'S AN U.S. GOVERNMENT CONSPIRACY! THE REST OF THE COSMOS DOESN'T EXIST TO YOU!" yelled Duncan at him. THAT BELIEF IS YOUR SECURITY BLANKET! " he screamed. "THE TRUTH IS WE ARE AT WAR WITH ALIENS FROM OUTER SPACE! AND THEY'RE ON THE MOON! AND THAT'S FAR MORE FRIGHTENING THAN ANY GOVERNMENT CONSPIRACY, ISN'T IT!

"And that's why I refuse to give into that belief," said Linus quietly, looking up. "Because it is intended to frighten me." he turned and walked to his car, got in it and drove away down the desert road, back towards the glow of Palm Springs in the distance.

Lowery looked around at the sad and worried faces of those remaining. He was embarrassed at his outburst, but no one looked at him as if they disagreed.

"Help me take this stuff down, we have to get out of here," Lowery said grimly. He felt his heart failing him, and his fingers were trembling as he began to quickly disassemble the telescope and pack it into its case. This observation was the culmination of weeks of effort by him and his friends, to try to find out the "real truth" of their situation. *Nothing is so terrifying as when someone who you know has lied to you continually, suddenly starts telling you the truth,* he thought.

****

Number 7 sat silently as usual in the high council chamber. He had been warned not to speak at the meetings, since he was only an Idelkite and technically a slave species.

"Doctor Acra, at my request, has developed a potent plague germ to spread terror and death among the Errans. It is a genetically modified version of a disease endemic to Erra in the area of our former base in the mountains. He will provide a report on its effectiveness and use.

Dr. Acra, a scientist from the Daedalus crater fortress, who was experimenting on Errans extensively, rose and spoke to the assembled commanders.

"The Dung-eaters on Erra are subject to many communicable diseases, things that have been unknown in our civilization for centuries, due to its strict cleanliness and genetic conditioning. We have, therefore, at Number 1's suggestion, developed a weapon from one of the diseases we have studied on Earth. This disease is called the "Red Plague" because it causes Errans to suffer red hemorrhages. In order to serve the primary purpose of creating death and terror among the Errans we have modified it to be extremely lethal, contagious, and aggressive, causing death in mere hours after exposure. To assist its spread we have made it cause mental confusion and extreme fear by having it attack certain nerve centers in the brain. The view screen showed several horrific images of naked dead humans whose bodies were covered with red blotches and bleeding wounds. We, of course, have also ensured that it will not infect Unash or any of our slave species. "

"How about the mutation aspect?" asked Sadok Sar, seeming pleased. I want it also to mutate rapidly so that the dung-eaters on Erra will not be

69

able to make an effective vaccine against it. This will make its ability to inspire terror complete."

"Yes my Lord, that will also be done"

"It is essential!" said Sadok Sar sharply. "Otherwise, the dung eaters will make vaccines against it as all this work will have been for nothing! I know things are difficult, our people must load this plague into ships and take to Earth and disperse it low in the atmosphere , all while suffering danger of attack from their aircraft.  So this difficult task must have maximum effectiveness!  The terror aspect is most important and that requires it to mutate rapidly!"  Sadok Sar continued.  "I have studied the dung-eaters on Erra for many years and they have made vaccines against many diseases. This must not happen with this Red Plague.  It must be a perfect terror weapon!"

"Yes my Lord," said Doctor Acra. Number 7 noted that Acra looked extremely uncomfortable, but Number 7 simply looked away.

"You have proposed a test of this red plague on a large group of dung-eaters here, have you not?" prompted Sadok Sar.

"Yes, my Lord. We have selected the medical staff here, of dung-eaters, since they are female and are much more compliant, than the males."

"Number 7!" said Sadok Sar sharply "You will assist doctor Acra in selecting a group of the female dung-eaters in the medical department which you are in charge of, for this test of the Red Plague."

Number 7 was seized with fear at this order and an overwhelming feeling of death.

"Yes my Lord!" he answered robotically.

****

"Karlac of Janus, I tell you again, do not go into the Quzrada, you have no conception of what lies there, "said Ragnar of Vale emphatically.

70

"I think I do," replied Karlac calmly, his pale forehead now covered with perspiration, as he sat in the palace of Vale at a table across from Ragnar of Vale. "I have heard a voice crying out to me for help, and I cannot ignore it. To do so, would be to deny what I have become; a messenger for peace."

"What voice have you heard?"

"It was in a dream, it was a woman with long dark hair, she was very fair but unusual looking. She cried out for me to help Erra." Karlac shivered as he remembered it.

Ragnar looked at him incredulously.

"I have heard of such exotic women on Erra, but if it is an exotic woman you seek, we can provide you with one." He said quietly.

"I do not go there seeking a woman's company! As you know, I have forsworn the company of women, and all riches in order to best serve the cause of peace! I am here because I must go to Erra, and I am told I cannot go without your clearance. No one will tell me why."

"By the Gods, you could use a wife now! She would then warn you against this folly. But, that you may have heard a soul cry for help from Erra is no great thing, several others have reported it. But, nothing can be done, it is fate, most noble Karlac."

"This affair of Erra and Quzrada, is not a dispute over nectar wine within the stars of the Echelon," continued Ragnar, or the proper duties of Quetan chamber maids," reiterated Ragnar, referring to previous disputes the Karlac had helped resolve. "What I will tell you now noble Karlac, must be between us, you must not speak outside this palace of Vale." Karlac became less indignant and leaned forward intently to hear what Ragnar had to say. *Finally, the truth...* thought Karlac.

"I will now enlighten you, concerning the doings in the Quzrada," said Ragnar, stroking his rich beard. "And you will see how they do not relate to you at all. However, if these things spread beyond the palace it would

71

disturb the peace of the Echelon. Do I have your word? "Ragnar now stared at him intently.

"I give you my word," said Karlac. "Just explain to me why I cannot go there, alone, in my one small ship. I know if I do, I can help this situation."

"You have mediated many disputes in the Echelons, and we are all grateful." said Ragnar looking grim." The Alliance against the Xix has thus been strengthened. But that was within this civilized stellar region, dealing with people who have tears for things. If you go to the Quzrada and try to speak peace, they will cut your tongue out. You will pour out your blood on the desert sands of Issus, and it will swallow every drop as if they had never been. Then, what happens if another trade dispute erupts? Who will we ask to convene a council of mediation? I have seen the Echelon Alliance tremble over nectar wine and other trifles, and with it, our whole way of life."

Seeing Karlac resisting his line of logic, Ragnar switched to a different tact.

"Have you ever dealt with the Unash people?"

"No, but I have been studying them recently. I have prepared for this journey in ways besides the provisioning of my ship. I know they are a minor people, insectoid, from regions near the outer Archmetia."

"They are a ruined people!" said Ragnar in anger. "They are a self-made abomination, who destroyed their own genome under the rule of terrible tyrant hundreds of years ago. He tried to alter the Unash genome to improve it. He was determined to refashion his people into something better, stronger, wiser, and greater in the Cosmos, but he failed. In the process, he destroyed the last traces of their natural genetic makeup. Their children are born in hatcheries now, unnaturally, and more than half of them are deformed at birth so they abandon them, feeding them back into biodigesters alive in some cases." Karlac sat in horror at hearing these words. He had not heard of such things before.

"The Unash used to be a fair and wise race, now they are but a race of slaves and slave masters. They are an atrocity on the natural order of things, and so are now famous for their atrocities upon others. Now they

72

roam the stars seeking fresh genomes to hybridize with, to try to repair their own irreparably damaged genome, but you cannot bind up that which has become utterly corrupt. That is why they are at Erra, to try to become part Archmetan." Hearing this Karlac felt again the deep trembling he felt the night of the dream. *No, this is too horrible to imagine. The genomes are so different. How could they even attempt this?*

"But if the Errans are then Archmetan, are they, not our kindred? Should we not help them?" he asked suddenly.

"Help is only possible when there is something to be done, and there is no help possible there. It would be like trying to help a fly already caught in a spider's web. Erra is in the heart of Quzrada, the neutral zone. The Unash should not be there, but they did not sign the Neutral Zone treaty. The Unash, we know also, are only the bloody glove on the mailed fist of the Samar. They are their hired dagger men. But we cannot chase the Unash out of there without violating the Neutral Zone treaty, and risking war with the Samar."

"But are not the Samar Archmetan also? I could reason with them..."

"Have you ever dealt with the Samar? Do you know anything about them?
"

"I dealt with some Samaran merchants once, they seemed to be reasonable men "

"They were Hotten then, they wore black clothing and you probably noticed the conditions of their hands," said Ragnar emphatically, leaning over the table.

"Yes, I remember they all had no thumbs..." said Karlac. A creeping feeling of horror swept over him as he remembered the encounter. The men had all worn black clothing and had crude prosthetic thumbs.

"That is because they were born into the merchant class, Hotten-Samar, considered almost the bottom of Samar society, and they chop off the thumbs of their male children at two weeks, so they cannot become men of war later. Those who are born into a warrior house, however, are trained for war almost from birth." Ragnar smiled derisively at Karlac's ignorance, and Karlac lowered his eyes. *I obviously don't know anything about this dispute,* Karlac thought with regret. *It was folly of me to come here without preparation.*

"Tell me, do you own a sword, Peacesayer?"

"No, I am of Janus; you know we Jain have foresworn war and its implements."

"Yes! But the Vikhelm have not! How convenient that we Vikhelm stand between Janus and the Xix!" said Ragnar angrily. He then regretted immediately what he had said. Karlac looked at him vacantly.

"I am sorry most noble Karlac," said Ragnar regretfully, " this whole matter has the entire palace here at Vale on a sword's edge. Truly, it is very good that one people of the Eshalon have embraced peace and studies it... otherwise, we should be at each other's throats constantly. But I tell you, if you do not wear a sword, the Samar will not even bother to speak with you, and if you try to talk to them they may just draw their sword and take your head off with it, for trying to speak to them without permission. In their eyes, a man without a sword or dagger is not a man. So you may be informed, noble Karlac, if you speak to the high Samar, they will rattle their swords in their scabbards if they become angry before they draw their swords. It is customary, this will mean they actually respect you and are warning you to be quiet. I myself have heard this sound. By coincidence, some say the only thing like this sound is the sound of the venomous rattle-serpent that lives on Erra. It has rattles on its tail and warns those who are wise enough to know what it means - that it will strike. Many a stranger on Erra has died because of this serpent's fanged bite. Usually, they die because they heard the rattling noise and wondered what it meant. So you may take heed in the future, know this, that once a Samar draws his sword, he will not sheath it un-blooded."

"You Vikhelm have a similar custom. I have heard," said Karlac somberly.

"Yes, but we can sheath the sword un-blooded without loss of honor if proper appeals by third parties are made, which is a custom among us," said Ragnar in mild embarrassment. *It is a foolish custom, but useful.*

Besides, only officers carry swords here, and daggers are forbidden unless one carries also a sword. So we are much more enlightened in this." said Ragnar emphatically. Karlac nodded skeptically.

"But you see most noble Peacesayer that you know nothing of this matter or the peoples involved. This dispute, this little fire, must burn itself out in the deep forest, without meddling by you or anyone else from the Eshalon worlds," continued Ragnar.

"But if there is a war at Erra, in the heart of Quzrada, is this not truly like a fire in the forest that will spread to the surrounding regions?"

"Some fires must simply burn themselves out, Sayer of Peace, as this one will surely do in a short while. Do not meddle there; let it go its way. Also, I hold you to your word, do not repeat what you have heard here today, there is nothing to be done about this thing at Erra, so speaking of it will only disrupt the peace, nothing more. We of the Eshalon cannot do anything about this, it is fate."

"We at the palace here have thought deeply on this." continued Ragnar, looking weary. "If the Unash swallow Erra alive, it really matters little to us. The Unash are a minor power. But as for the Samar, things are difficult enough for them, even with them far away from our affairs, across the Quzrada. But if the Samar are drawn into this, into the Quzrada, then the Eshalon has the Xix in front of us and the Samar at our outer gate. So, let no one give occasion for trouble between us. Preserve this peace on our outer gate. It is a sad thing, passing sad, but you must turn away from it and go about your business."

"But, this is my business...peace must be brought to that place..." said Karlac. But his eyes were downcast. *I truly knew nothing about this. Indeed, how could I know, the conflict at Erra is being kept a secret matter...*

"No, not that place, it is not yours, nor even our business, to meddle with. This thing belongs to the endless stars, Karlac, it is fate...Therefore, you may not cross the Eshalon frontier into the Quzrada and you may certainly not go to Erra. That is the decision of the high Council of the Eshalon

Alliance, and I have told you why because we value your work." said Ragnar with finality and rose from the table.

Karlac rose, they both bowed, Ragnar turned and left the room. Karlac turned also and left out the other door full of sorrow. *How could I have been so foolish to meddle in this matter? Alas, it is a deep ocean, and I am seemly just a wader in puddles.*

****

"So, no one will tell me what happened to me..." said Cassandra, looking out the window from her chair at the blue sky. "Not even Pamela, she said you told her not to." She trembled and was very pale. "I vaguely remember knowing something when I came here, things that made me afraid. Now even when I try to think about what happened to me, how I got here, my mind, it simply goes blank."

"It will pass," said Petrosian "The mind does this sometimes, to give itself time to heal."

"But I feel like my mind is shrinking to a point!" responded Cassandra. "As if in a while, I won't even remember my own name or recognize my own face in a mirror! So I am afraid now...And I don't even know what I am afraid of," she said trembling. She was sitting in an overstuffed chair in Doctor Petrosian's office; he sat in his wheelchair facing her. She remained staring out the window.

She turned and looked at Doctor Petrosian in his wheelchair. His own face looked conflicted. *Should I tell her?* He thought, *No, not yet, too traumatic.*

"Your own mind knows what happened, Cassandra," said Petrosian, "and when it decides to let you know, it will. Let's say your mind has put a bandage on this experience, and it's not ready to come off yet. It needs to heal and process it. You must respect this about yourself." He paused, looked sad, and then forced a smile. "I see this a lot in the Post-Traumatic Stress patients that I normally treat. So, don't feel bad, I myself can't even remember how I lost my arm and leg, the night of the coup." He looked down at his missing right leg, frowned. He looked up found her staring at

76

him with those ghostly mesmerizing eyes. *Still beautiful after all this.* He thought in wonder. *But she looks very pale and thin this morning, more than last week*, he noted with sudden concern. *Her progressive amnesia, is it purely psychological or organic at this point? I must proceed carefully...*

"This is just our first therapeutic session Cassandra. Therapy exists because the slings and arrows of outrageous fortune sometimes stay imbedded in us, a therapist's job is to find these arrows and then to help remove them so healing can occur." Cassandra nodded, looking transfixed. "So let's start like I start with all my patients, with you telling me about your childhood, " said Petrosian. Cassandra stared at him blankly.

"I'll make you a deal doctor," she said with a sudden faint smile. "You answer me one question, and I'll tell you all about my favorite goldfish growing up."

He reacted in shock to her change in demeanor. *One minute a helpless victim, the next a scheming countess,* he thought in awe. *What happened? She seems driven by a desire to find information...*

"That depends on the question," Petrosian said with a faint smile. *The sudden change, was this to throw me off guard? The duel begins, this patient is clever...too clever. I must be careful.*

"Oh it's a cosmological question," she smiled sweetly as she spoke, "not about my condition, more a question like whether the Earth moves around the Sun, or vice versa,"

"Cosmology? But all cosmic models have the self as their centers don't they?" he replied warily. *What has happened to her, right in front of me?*

"We are at war with the Greys, now," she said suddenly, looking at him intently. "Aren't we?" she added quickly. His eyes answered. She saw his pupils contract to points, and he blinked. *So we are at war,* she thought suddenly. She felt suddenly weak and frail. But she smiled.

77

"Your childhood? In San Diego, how was it?" he asked intently. *This is not going well. She is reverting to being an investigative journalist from being a victim! A hardened professional!* He thought. *She's too smart for her own good. She is also getting paler as we speak.*

"So the UFO cover-up ended! Pammy and I succeeded! She said beaming. She sat up erect in her chair. "Then it was just as she predicted might happen, we are at war now! Aren't we?"

He merely looked back at her, patiently. Perspiration suddenly covered her face, and she felt suddenly cold. "What happened to their big base at Morningstar Colorado?" she asked.

"I think we should stop now Cassandra, for one thing, you don't look well," he replied worriedly. "I mean, you just got off of your IV antibiotics yesterday." He began to roll back slightly in his wheelchair, using his remaining arm.

"I had this goldfish when I was a child, back in San Diego," she started talking quickly. "Actually, I had hundreds, in this big aquarium, then I dreamed one night I was swimming in the tank with them..." she began to stammer. She was turning pale white in front of him. Tears ran down her cheeks. He looked at her in growing alarm. He pressed the pager button by his side for the nurse.

"Then the aquarium became the aquarium of the great Tyrant in the city of the night on Tau Ceti 4! "she was now speaking frantically "and I was a prisoner there, in the dungeon, in this aquarium naked and the Dictator!" her voice was a wail now. She rose out of her chair, "THE DICTATOR WAS HURTING ME, HE HURT ME SO BAD... SO I DIED!" Two nurses entered looking apprehensive. She felt dizzy, she wrapped her thin arms around herself. "They hurt me so I died..." she wailed. She sank to the floor weeping, her back was in agony, she felt arms grab her, and all was blackness.

\*\*\*\*

Semjase and Sanjeed walked quickly in the cool early evening darkness. Several jet fighters flew over thunderously, wings covered with missiles, as

78

Semjase and Samjeed closed in on a shed on the back of the mansion in Arcturus, on the Potomac River south of Washington DC. A helicopter flew swiftly over them, following the river. There was thunder in the distance and flashes in the clouds, either from lightning or from battles in the sky; she sensed both.

"I sense the voice coming from here, in this place in front of us," she whispered worriedly. The place looked deserted. She felt raw pain suddenly; it was wrapped around the mental voice calling for help. All Semjase's concern that it was a trap laid by the Samar evaporated from her mind. She found herself rushing into the darkness of the shed. There was a door, unlocked as it turned out, and she plunged through it into the darkness beyond. She triggered a light on her uniform and saw a compact, saucer-shaped spacecraft parked in the darkness. It was Vikhelmian,

"Vikor!" she gasped "he is inside and badly injured!"

She leaped up to the doorway on it and worked the controls, mercifully the door opened. It had not been locked or even coded. A sense of complete despair and desperation filled her from the mental voice calling for help. However, she was afraid to send a thought in return. Too many ears were listening at Erra for it to be safe.

A horrible stench of bodily waste and decay greeted them; she and Sanjeed plunged into the small ship oblivious. There lying in a puddle of his own filth lay Vikor, he was barely conscious and delirious. She understood from his mind that he had been savagely beaten and was suffering from several infections and internal injuries.

"Vikor, It is me Semjase, we have come to help you" she wept, as Sanjeed helped her to pull him out of the pool of filth and pulled off his fouled pants.

"He is near death," said Sanjeed grimly, as they stripped off his clothing. We need fresh water to wash his wounds. "Semjase nodded and ran out of the ship to find some water and basin to carry it in, as Sanjeed opened his medical kit and went to work on the worst of Vikor's injuries.

****

79

Cassandra opened her eyes; tears fell from them as she stared at the ceiling of the hospital room. She felt light and glowing. A figure in space helmet appeared in her vision and she recoiled in fear. Florence, the nurse bent over Cassandra smiled as best as she could through the bio-isolation suit.

"Its OK honey, we had to move you back to the ET ward. You're going to be OK."

"What wrong with me?" she gasped. Florence looked at her silently. Even through the helmet visor, Cassandra could see fear and doubt in the nurse's eyes.

"Doctor Stephanson says that you have an infection, it may be an X-ray infection, that's what we call an infection from outer space. That's why we're wearing these space suits, but we have it isolated, and we can cure it. He wanted me to tell you that.

"You're lying..." gasped Cassandra in despair. "I am dying and you can't do anything about it, can you ..." *Good, I will die now,* she thought, *it's better this way...*

"Now Ms. Chen don't be talking like that, "said Florence. "Now you rest, don't think about anything." Cassandra turned her face away with great effort, closed her eyes. Florence turned away from Cassandra's bed in resignation. She checked the box on Cassandra's chart, that she had checked her vital signs, and walked out of her room into the hall. Workers in bio-suits were laying plastic film in layers on the floor. She walked into the next patient's room where Doctor Stephanson, stood in a transparent bio-suit, a solid middle-aged man with glasses and a full head of brown hair. He was turning from the bed of a patient. It was a horribly injured guard from the base at Morningstar. The Doctor looked at Flo grimly through his helmet visor.

"Flo, This one is dead now too, it's X-ray. Get your people to roll him out of here STAT in a bio-bag. His body is loaded with X-ray bacteria so tag it for immediate incineration." Flo nodded fearfully.

"We can't have anybody up here without an X-ray clearance until we stabilize this outbreak," the doctor added. Florence turned and walked out into the hall, motioned to two orderlies in bio-suits, and handed one of them a red biohazard tag with a skull and crossbones on it from the pocket in her suit, she motioned silently to the room she had just been in as Doctor Stephanson stepped out of it somberly. The orderlies went into the room to bag and remove the body.

"We have one thing working in our favor Flo," said Stephanson. This X-ray bug has a long incubation period, so it's not that vigorous, and Schwartzman over there in room 1 was one of the first to get it, and he is still alive. So we know a strong patient can fight it." He then turned and went back to nurse's station.

Florence went into the next room. Robert Schwartzman was lying on the bed in a coma. An IV was draining medicine into him. They were giving him a cocktail of antibiotics hoping one would be effective against the extraterrestrial bacteria now coursing through his blood. Flo bent over him, looked at the display showing his heartbeat pulse and brain waves, they continued to beat on.

"Colonel Schwartzman, Ms. Chen is up here and tells you to get well. She's sick with X-ray too, so if you get well, we'll pull her through too. You got that? So you get well, that's an order." She looked up hopefully to see if his signs had reacted. "No way is you checking out of Flo's Hotel till I say so!" she added, looking at the vital signs display. Seeing no change, she sadly left and turned out the light.

In the darkness, a long moment passed. Then, suddenly the heartbeat began to beat more vigorously and the brain activity increased on the displays.

****

Alicia Sepulveda Steel, dressed in a black pantsuit, stood at the hospital room window and watched as a Super-Patriot missile burst from its launcher tube a mile away with a blinding blue-white flame and plunged into the clear night sky, as the air raid sirens wailed. Her rich brown eyes squinted against the glare as her lovely bronze face grimaced in preparation for the torrent of sound she knew raced towards her. In the distance, she saw the lights illuminating the Capitol fail, and the rest of Washington, DC, plunge into darkness as another missile exploded from its launcher tube with a blue-white light like a welding arc and tear up into the sky after the previous one. From around the city, dozens of missiles were rising into the dark night sky. The delayed scream of the rocket engine hit and then deepened into a thundering howl that rattled the windows and the whole building. A third missile launched as this happened. It was the new fuel she knew in the rockets, it used magnesium to burn hotter and push harder.

"Yes!" called out Pamela's voice behind her in the room as the thunder shook the building. "YES!" she cried, as the thunder of the second launch arrived. Alicia watched as the three missiles raced at an incredible speed up into the sky, turning murderously to chase some unseen target, and then detonating in three brilliant electric blue flashes high in the sky amid the cold stars. Other missiles were detonating amid the stars. "Oh yes!" cooed Pamela, before breaking into laughter, as the third batch of thunder arrived from the launches. Pamela's magnetic alarm beeped from beneath her pillow. "I know if I am thinking more about pulling one of my hunky young doctors into bed with me, than about anything else, that means I am getting better," Pamela laughed. "That's how I know Cassie will be getting better soon, Alicia, and will be back here with me because I am better." Pamela said more seriously, "She and I will die in the same hour, I know, and I am getting better. So, she must be getting better too."

The hospital room lights dimmed then brightened again as an emergency diesel generator cut in to maintain power. Alicia turned with a weak smile to look at Pamela sitting up in her hospital bed, smiling, with her arms folded behind her head, her blonde hair spilled over her pillows. The air raid sirens continued to wail in the distance. The alarm beeped on. The sound of jet fighters flying overhead rattled the windows anew.

"How do you sleep with all that going on every night?" asked Alicia. "You'd think they wouldn't put that missile site so close to the hospital here!"

"I sleep a lot better with it close by, actually," laughed Pamela. "It's Cassie and my own private missile battery. Besides, the missiles go supersonic about a thousand yards up and we are in the sonic shadow of the Mach cone. It's people farther away who really get knocked out of bed at night." Three claps of thunder from the warheads going off at high altitude shook the building. Pamela's face broke into a beautiful smile.

"That's half a ton of HMX in each warhead, with 50,000, 1-gram, pre-sectioned steel prisms for fragmentation," said Pamela.

"What's HMX?" asked Alicia, in slight embarrassment. "Is that like TNT? I should know this stuff now. "

"HMX stands for Her Majesty's explosive because it was invented by some Brit scientist who was having a torrid affair with Queen Elizabeth II and he thought she was explosive in bed."

"You're making that up!" laughed Alicia in annoyance. "Doesn't HMX stand for hexanitro something?"

"Actually, its formula is Cyclo-tetra methylene tetra-nitramine. I learned that in my defense systems course I took online from Annapolis last month," said Pamela, looking angelic and slightly mischievous. "Maybe the affair with the queen part is, as Cassie calls it, a slight embellishment, but it was noisy."

"What, the sex?"

"That too, but I meant the explosives," laughed Pamela. "See, I know this all means I am getting better."

"I am sure someone complains about the noise of the missiles too," said Alicia, ruefully, returning to her chair beside Pamela's bed. Pamela looked beautiful despite her hospital gown. Her light blonde hair cascaded in waves over her shoulders. Her large, light-blue eyes were heavily made up and she wore silver angel-wing earrings. Stuffed animals sat around her in the bed. Despite the fact that Alicia was a very attractive woman, the contrast between them was stark. Alicia wore her thick black hair, now slightly streaked with grey, in a no-nonsense, mid-neck hairstyle; her black pants suit was professional looking despite her slim but curvaceous figure. Her earrings were simple turquoise set in silver.

"Yes, some do complain about the noise," said Pamela, her smile fading. "We are in a dark place on this collective human journey, I must admit.

When that occurs, there will always be some idiot who asks, 'is this trip really necessary? We are now crossing the dark plains of Mars, and two stars rule the night above that place, named fear and terror. It is little wonder some hearts have failed already."

"To triumph then, those moons must first be conquered, yes?" said Alicia, staring off into space, her bronze features pensive. More thunder arrived from the sky.

"Oh, but you know how that is done Alicia!" said Pamela smiling. "To conquer fear requires courage, to conquer terror, requires preparation. God and those two things are our companions on this journey. I recognize my own role in starting the human race on this road." Pamela looked more thoughtful. "But you yourself know that fate compels us to go on some journeys we did not anticipate, or choose, but these journeys must be finished just the same. You know that probably better than anyone else on Earth." The air raid sirens wail ended in the distance. The all clear sounded. The beeping alarm also fell silent under her pillow.

"Your husband is a very good professor at the Academy, by the way. I am taking his Space Systems course online. I watch his lectures every day," said Pamela, happily.

"Good. He wants to go back up into space again, but I will tell his superiors your comments so they will keep him on Earth," said Alicia, with a worried smile.

"You look beautiful, Alicia. You have this radiant glow. Have you picked out any names for the baby yet?" asked Pamela.

"Who says I am pregnant?" retorted Alicia, with a laugh. Pamela smiled angelically.

"Yes, we are having another baby," said Alicia, with a sudden smile. "It was an accident, but we are both happy. Nobody is supposed to know that yet, comprendo?"

Pamela beamed at this, and then she was looking off in the distance. Pamela was suddenly looking over at the empty hospital bed nearby. A toy stuffed Tiger sat on it. Pamela's smile had faded.

"They are coming for you Alicia," said Pamela turning back to Alicia. Pamela grabbed a large teddy bear from beside her on her bed, kissed it, and handed it to Alicia with a look of deep worry. Underneath, where the teddy bear had lain was a Berretta 9 mm pistol. A spare clip of ammunition was next to it.

"As I told you earlier, I know she will be back here again, in this room with me," said Pamela, looking at Alicia with determination. "And she will be, I know it. But you give her this for me."

Alicia took the teddy bear and nodded, her own eyes began to brim with tears.

Pamela tried to smile and blinked back tears. "Tell Cassie that if she doesn't get well soon she's fired!" she said with a weak laugh. "On second thought, don't tell her that." Pamela lost her smile and then stared deeply into the distance for a moment, then smiled again. She turned to Alicia, she looked determined.

"Give Cassie my love, and tell her the Dark Carnival has saddled up and prepares to ride for us, and that her child awaits." Tears filled Pamela's eyes, yet she smiled. "Yes, tell her that."

Suddenly a nurse appeared at the door to the room. Her face was devoid of expression.

"Doctor Sepulveda, you must come now, we haven't much time," said the nurse.

Alicia rose and embraced Pamela. Pamela smiled bravely, tears rolling down her cheeks, as Alicia dutifully carrying the teddy bear, followed the nurse out of the room. She stepped past two armed guards in the hallway outside Pamela's room.

Alicia and the nurse walked down a long corridor, to a nurse's station. A military policeman stood nearby wearing a pistol. An older nurse simply took the teddy bear away from Alicia wordlessly and gave her a plastic badge. Alicia then followed the nurse grimly down the hall to the isolation—intensive care ward. Large red signs saying "Biohazard" "Isolation Zone," and the triple crescent symbols in red were everywhere. They passed troops in helmets and combat fatigues with MP-5 submachine guns standing guard. The nurse and Alicia both showed the badges to the guards who waved them through. Down the hall, they passed through sealed doors past more armed guards, this time in white plastic isolation suits and respirators. Alicia was given an isolation suit and respirator that was in the form of a helmet with a wide clear faceplate. She pulled them on, and after being checked by a medical technician likewise garbed, she passed through an airlock into the isolation zone, kept at below atmospheric pressure to prevent biohazard escape, then down the hall to the intensive care ward.

In Room 5, she was led in to see Cassandra lying on her bed on her stomach. Cassandra looked up as Alicia entered. Alicia wept to see her. Cassandra was very thin and pale, wearing only a hospital gown open in the back to show her infected back. Alicia's gloved hand clasped Cassandra's and she sat down by Cassandra's bed in a simple plastic chair. Cassandra's eyes were dilated; they were large black dots.

"I am sure they have told you... what happened to me," rasped Cassandra, hoarsely, her voice nearly a whisper, her eyes burning with intensity. "It's an X-ray infection. It got into the wounds on my back. Bob's got it too; he's in the next room... He's worse off than me, in a coma now ...." Tears rolled down her cheeks. "I wanted to see you... to say thank you for helping us." Cassandra's voice seemed to fail, every word seemed like it took a supreme effort. "The bacterium is slow, it waited till the other normal infections were gone, then it blossomed, so it's weak... but they tell me it's killing us. Gram negative...blood infection now...They can't do anything for us, none of the antibiotics work on it..."

Alicia, her tears visible even through the faceplate of her respirator, clasped Cassandra's hand between hers. She could feel the burning heat of Cassandra's hand even through her plastic gloves—could feel the fever raging in her.

"Cold, I feel so cold..." said Cassandra. She paused and seemed to gather her strength. "But tell me now, certainly with everything that has happened... you can tell me now..." rasped Cassandra. Despite her state, Cassandra's voice was a voice of command.

"Tell you what, Cassie?" gasped Alicia. *Donna Cassandra,* she thought, *you always want to know what I cannot tell.*

86

"Tell me about the Sepulveda Asteroid... We all... defeated it... You, Pam, and I. ..." her voice failed her. "Tell me how we did it... tell me all the hidden things... before it's too late... I want to hear it...how did the journey begin for you?"

Alicia wept and looked at Cassandra for a long time.

Cassandra, even in her near delirium was still beautiful, her dark eyes large, full of a ghostly light as she stared at Alicia. "I feel like I am slowly falling now, falling... my world... my world ..." she gasped out. Her eyes implored Alicia. Her burning hand gripped Alicia's tightly.

Alicia could not bear it, looking into those eyes, but she could not look away either. *Donna Cassandra, I always end up telling you what you want to know,* thought Alicia in resignation.

"Tell me..." Cassandra gasped.

"The journey began with a dream; I dreamed of the King's Highway," began Alicia slowly, looking straight into Cassandra dark eyes. "A dream on a night that many things happened which I only found out about later.... But for me that night, it began with this vivid dream of a highway of stars..." As Cassandra heard these words, the room, and Alicia's face, seemed to spin slowly and fall away and she was falling into a sea of stars... *It ends now, my whole dark dream...*

"She's slipped into a coma, Ms. Sepulveda, you'll have to go now," said the nurse, in a bio-isolation suit. She was looking at brain activity display beside Cassandra's bed.

Alicia felt tears cover her face, as another nurse in a bio-isolation suit, pulled on her arm. She let go of Cassandra's now limp hand, looked at her peaceful, still face. Alicia rose from her chair. "What will you do for her now?" gasped Alicia, to the nurse beside her.

The nurse simply shook her head.

Just then, a woman doctor burst in through the doors of the room in a bio-suit. She looked at Cassandra.

"She's gone into a coma like the others did," reported the nurse who stood beside Cassandra to the doctor.

"Move her bed to the side! We're going to try an emergency real-time electrophoresis! Move her bed to the wall!" The doctor whirled to look at Alicia. "Get her out of here!"

Alicia and the nurse beside her retreated to the hallway. Bio-suited workers were rolling a large piece of apparatus swiftly down the hallway, their faces stern with concentration.

"What are they doing? Are they trying to save her?" gasped Alicia.

"I don't know! The electrophoresis procedure is new and requires a live blood donor for anti-toxin …"

The apparatus disappeared into Cassandra's room just as around the corner came rolling swiftly a gurney surrounded by doctors and nurses in bio-suits. One of the doctors was arguing with a pale and emaciated figure on the gurney. At the sight, Alicia's heart leaped for joy. It was Colonel Robert Schwartzman; he was alive, awake, and apparently in a bad mood.

"But, you're our only survivor, Colonel! Three others are dead! You just came out of a coma! You need time to recover!" one doctor was protesting, as he walked along beside the swiftly rolling gurney.

Schwartzman was merely offering his still muscular arm to another doctor to disconnect an IV and plug it into another tube. "Doctor, with all due respect, get the fuck out of the way, and let me get hooked up!" grasped Schwartzman, his grey eyes blazing with intensity. They then also disappeared into Cassandra's room. The nurse, overcome with emotion beside her, silently led Alicia out of the X-ray isolation ward.

****

Cassandra awoke; it was a beautiful morning. She saw Pamela sleeping peacefully in the other hospital bed near her. She rose from her bed. She was connected to an IV drip from a bottle on a slender silver stand with small wheels. She moved carefully to keep it close to her. She tearfully leaned down and kissed Pamela on the forehead as she slept. Outside the birds were chirping. The tall birch trees outside her window had beautiful golden leaves against a powder blue sky. The Washington, DC, Capitol lay in the distance, beautiful and shining across the deep blue Potomac River. She rose from the hospital bed and walked in wonder to the door leading to the beautiful terrace balcony that formed the patio of their room. She opened the window a crack and breathed the fresh cool breeze. It was fall now, she realized to her confusion. All the leaves were turning a riot of colors. She breathed the air, and all the fall fragrances filled her with hope.

"It's a beautiful morning, isn't it Cassie," came Pamela's voice, behind her.

"Yes, but I'm confused. How long have I been unconscious," asked Cassandra?

"Long enough to get well apparently," said Pamela, smiling. She was sitting up in bed. "They said you made a miraculous recovery, and a lot of other people died of what you had."

"You're getting better! Your legs!" exclaimed Cassandra rushing, with her IV stand in tow, to Pam's bedside.

"Yeah, look at this," said Pamela, "I can wiggle my toes again." She presented her toes and carefully moved one at a time. "They're better every day."

"Oh! That is so wonderful!" wept Cassandra.

"Soon, I am going to walk out of here and across Key Bridge," said Pamela, "in heels."

"Did the Doctor tell you that?" asked Cassandra, happily.

"No, but I am in charge here," insisted Pamela. "They have to follow my orders."

"Pammy, how did I get here? I can't remember anything, since... "

"Never mind, Cassie," said Pamela, "just concentrate on this beautiful morning, and being alive. The past is the old world; it has ended. But the world is renewed every morning, as if it emerges from the valley of the shadow of death, changed from what it was, to a new brighter world. We are renewed with it also."

****

Arizona and Mongoose, resplendent in their combat fatigues and green berets, stood watching Col Robert Schwartzman's tall, muscular frame pacing back and forth in his hospital room clad only in his hospital gown. He was strong again, his muscular arm hauling along his IV tree on rollers as he as he listened with a furrowed brow to Arizona's report of the fighting on Adak.

"So we, out of the blue, get this radio transmission in the clear, and it says 'we want a truce of four days to bury our glorious dead, and we ascertained it comes from their stronghold in Mount Bering. So, Admiral Thomas put us on a B-1 bomber down here pronto to talk to you and get your advice. He's worried they're expecting another attempt at resupply and they want to get it through under this truce.

"Nah!" Schwartzman said abruptly, shaking his head.    If they were expecting another resupply attempt, they wouldn't give us a heads up. Tell Admiral Thomas I definitely think this is legit. He should grant them a truce. These guys apparently look like us," Schwartzman said waving at a folder of photos of the dead Samar that Badge had brought down. "And they fight like us, so my first guess is that they have similar customs. The Samar are obviously a warrior society. The old intel suggested this and that guy's body confirms it." Schwartzman stared at both Mongoose and Arizona with a look of deep thought. His face was lean and hard, his hair slightly greyer but neatly combed. "I mean why else would the guy Badge dropped be carrying a sword? That's Samurai tradition, right?"

"Yeah that's what Goose thinks too."

"I told Admiral Thomas, don't think Samar, Admiral, think Samurai!" said Mongoose emphatically. "We should be studying Bushido, the way of the warrior if we want to understand these people!"

"That would fit" nodded Schwartzman. "You also tell Admiral Thomas, what he really needs is me! He needs me up on the line in the Aleutians, fighting this war! Not sitting around here getting a thermometer shoved up my ass every three hours to see if I'm still alive!" He glanced at the clock. He lowered his voice, "speaking of which...I got to meet with the girls of my own intel network here." he said with a grin. "At least all the nurses here are good looking. They seem to be some handpicked group." Schwartzman suddenly raised his hand with fingers together and thumb straight out. At this signal, both Arizona and Goose became more attentive. "Especially the girl out there at the nurse's station with the long hair tied back. I think she's Cajun."

90

"Why is that boss?" said Arizona with a smile.

"Her eye makeup is always perfect," said Schwartzman with a smile, "sure sign of a girl from Louisiana."

"Goose," he turned to Mongoose, "Next time you're here Goose could you get me a jukebox or something so I can listen to some music? A little mineral water would be good too. This hospital tap water is not satisfactory. If you guys could do that for me, it would be real good. Also..." Schwartzman paused deep in thought.

"There's another thing bothering me. I have had a parade of brass in here from the Pentagon for weeks pumping me for every piece of intel, and I can tell they don't have a clue as to how we are going to win this war. It shows on their faces. So as near as I can estimate, nobody in this town has conceptualized a master war strategy to win this war. That's fatal guys, you know that anyone who studies military history knows that: 'no strategy, no victory.' The Pentagon has no strategy to win this war. They are just making it up as they go along, and I can see it clear as day even from this hospital room. So Goose, remember when we had the CNS HQ wired for sound months ago, and Blondie gave that big speech on a master war strategy to their staff? It was what convinced her bosses they could bring down the Cover-up."

Mongoose nodded thoughtfully.

"Yeah, I remember it; that was mesmerizing. I remember we all stopped and listened to it, then played it back and listened again. I remember everybody thinking we had fighting chance if the situation with the Greys went south after that. Suddenly, we could see daylight. I remember she compared it to the Colonists starting the Revolutionary war with Britain knowing it would be hard, but knowing they could win, because the colonies had a large population compared to Britain, that British supply lines across the Atlantic were precarious, and that because the previous French and Indian wars had become World Wars involving the other European rivals of Britain. So the colonists wagered they could bite and hang on, chew away, inflict major defeats on the British, and that if the war dragged on long enough and the other powers saw the British getting in trouble, they would wade into the war on the American side. Which is

91

exactly what happened? The French joined the war against Britain, so did the Spanish and even the Dutch!"

"RIGHT!" exclaimed Schwartzman. "So I want you to get that tape, and write up the strategy just like she laid it out, that day! Try to footnote it or something. I remember she even used something called Chatelier's principle! Find out whatever the hell that is, and put that in there too! It sounds technical! She brought the Pleiades in there too. They're in the Bible for God's sake! Put everything in there! Then I want you to get it down to the Pentagon somehow. Call it an official report from the Carney Cosmic Strategy Unit! Maybe then the brass down their will get their shit in one sock and figure out how to fight this war to win it!"

"But suppose they find out the author of this strategy is just a blonde weather girl from Cleveland?" asked Mongoose.

"We are still the Carney! The brass at the Pentagon still thinks we have knowledge of all cosmic mysteries! Use it! Goose, use your imagination! Call it the Carney Strategy! Just write it up and get it down to the Joint Chiefs! I'll be damned if we are going to lose this war while I stuck in this hospital room with a thermometer up my ass because nobody can figure out what a blonde abductee weather girl from Cleveland has figured out!"

"Alright chief," said Mongoose. Schwartzman, Mongoose, and Arizona saluted. "We got to get back up to Adak!" said Arizona scooping up the file of images.

"You tell Badge to quit letting those nurses coddle him at Bethesda! I want his ass back up on the line pronto!" said Schwartzman forcefully as Arizona and Mongoose trooped out of the door of his hospital room, and he clapped them both on the shoulder.

"And get that Carney Strategy report written up and to the Joint Chiefs somehow! I want that done yesterday!" said Schwartzman as Mongoose and Arizona marched out the door. "Now get that shit done!" he yelled after them.

Florence, the Chief Nurse on the floor, walked in followed by a younger white woman, named Jennifer, with brown hair, they were both in light blue nurse's pant-uniforms.

"Colonel, what the hell are you doing out of bed?" asked Flo indignantly.

"This beds a lonely place, Flo, why don't you slide in there with me? "said Schwartzman with a sly grin. Florence laughed as the white woman shut the door.

"Aren't we feeling better, though? said Flo with a smile.

Schwartzman sat down on the bed with a smile and offered his arm for a blood sample as Florence found a vein and slipped the needle into it.

"So, how are the two girls, Jade and Blondie, I was asking about?" asked Schwartzman. "Did you give Jade that note?" Florence turned with a grim look to the other nurse. Jennifer had leaned against the wall cradling her computer notebook.

"So, what are Pamela Monroe and Cassandra Chen's conditions? How are they doing?" he asked in a concerned voice.

"They have them over in the neurological ward in the Terraces. That's our new long-term care section. We took it over to house casualties; it used to be a nursing home."

"So, what's the story? How are they? Did you give Cassandra the note?"

Jennifer's face fell, and with it his heart.

"Monroe is improving slowly, but the doctors don't think she'll ever walk again."

Schwartzman looked at the floor as he absorbed this. His eyes then rose to Jennifer again. He stared at her intently.

"What about the other one?" Jennifer's face grew sad.

"How is Cassandra Chen?" he said her name painfully.

93

"She's pretty messed up I heard, post-traumatic stress, like the others they got out of the Morningstar base. She seemed to shrug everything off initially after her back healed up. But apparently, she started falling apart a few days ago. Most of them do, they say."

"What's her prognosis?" asked Schwartzman quickly.

"I don't know, I'm not a doctor Colonel," said the nurse sadly.

"What about the note?"

He continued to look at her until she again spoke in low tones.

"I gave it to her Colonel, but she looked at it and tore it up..." Schwartzman looked at her with a stoic face.

"I'm sorry Colonel," continued the nurse. "I've worked psych and neurological wards for over two years. I've known a lot of people who go through things like she went through, they aren't ever the same after that," said Jennifer sadly. "A lot of them never reconnect with people they knew before. I heard her parents even came to see her, but she refused to meet with them. Several of the others from Morningstar have cracked up completely, even while on heavy meds." She lowered her eyes and looked away. Schwartzman sat silently on the bed staring at the wall expressionless. He sat immobile like that as the blood samples taken, Florence stuck an infrared thermometer in his ear and took his temperature.

"Excellent temperature Colonel," said Florence with a smile, then turned and went to the door. He silently sat here as the two women left. However, he noticed another nurse out at the nurse's station looking at him intently as the two nurses exited. The door shut. Schwartzman had memorized her face. He stared at the door intently, frowned.

*Is she gone...?*

He glanced up at the television camera with a microphone in the upper corner of the room, looking down on him, listening to his every word. He raised his hand with his middle finger extended, then grinned.

94

*I am sitting duck here, and if I don't miss my guess that chick with the perfect eye shadow is French intelligence, who is now my biggest fan club.* He thought deeply, controlled his breathing to keep from panicking. *But the guys will get me out of here, I will be up on the line soon again, out of this glorified prison, guarded by pretty amazons...*

\*\*\*\*

Alicia Sepulveda, let her body go limp with relief and pulled the oxygen mask off her face. The two-seat version of the sleek F-51 Griffin jet fighter she was riding in was descending rapidly to the runway at Andrews Air Force base outside of Washington DC. It was late afternoon and she had flown across the country from St. Louis, Missouri. The jet fighter touched down with great skill and soon rolled to a stop at a hanger. She then spit out a glass capsule of cyanide she had kept in her mouth during the trip. The two escort fighters, both also Griffins, had also touched down and rolled to a stop beside them. The cockpit raised, she thanked the pilot and climbed out of the cockpit, taking off her helmet and handing it to an airman on the ground crew. As the youngest and healthiest person on the War Defense Science Board, she had volunteered to act as a liaison between St. Louis, where much of the actually industrial planning and production for the war was occurring, near the center of the country, and Washington DC from where the war was being directed. Since she carried in her mind so many wartime secrets, and the ability of the Greys to snatch planes right of the air was well known, she always carried a cyanide capsule on a plastic tether when she made the flights. After ten flights with only one close call, she no longer thought about the capsule. A Humvee containing several military officers appeared and whisked her away to the officer's quarters and a welcome bath, however, all she could think of was seeing her son and Blue, her husband.

\*\*\*\*

Nurse Florence carefully dialed the phone. It rang several times before Pamela picked it up in her and Cassie's room.

"Hello honey, this is nurse Florence from the ET ward, is Cassandra awake? I have Colonel Robert Schwartzman here and he is hoping to talk

95

to her. Florence handed the phone to Schwartzman, who was standing by the nurse's station grinning in his hospital gown.

"Let me see if she is awake, "said Pamela turning to were Cassandra stood looking out the window at the trees of the park, as she always did. Cassandra turned to Pamela with a look of alarm. Pamela covered the phone mouthpiece and spoke to her.

"Cassie, it's Colonel Robert Schwartzman, he wants to talk to you."

"No," said Cassandra shaking her head fearfully. Tears suddenly ran down her cheeks.

Pamela stared at her sadly then put the phone back to her head.

"I'm sorry she is asleep now," said Pamela quietly.

"NO! TELL HIM TO GO AWAY!" Cassandra screamed hysterically. Tears now streamed down her face. She then rushed over to her own bed and fell on it, face down, weeping.

Schwartzman heard her scream over the phone, then heard her sobs afterward. Pamela looked sadly at Cassandra crying on the bed. Pamela was temporarily paralyzed.

Florence watched Schwartzman's smile evaporate he listened on the phone. *Alone, I am utterly alone here now. No one knows what I have seen anymore, except me.* He thought in sudden despair.

"She can't talk to you right now, Colonel…" said Pamela quietly.

"I see that Ms. Monroe, thank you… "said Schwartzman sadly. He then handed the phone back to Florence and walked back to his room.

*I have to get out of here before I go insane too.*

****

Number 7 called the group of forty women together. They all stood at attention with their hands at their sides in blue silky coveralls in a room with grey metal walls. They all lined up in rows. Tatiana noted the look in

96

Number 7's eyes and by reflex stood nearest to him and had Amber stand one row down. After reflection Tatiana had someone stand in between her and Kathy.

"Count off by twos," said Tatiana without emotion as they all stood at attention. The woman counted off by twos, Tatiana, Amber, and Kathy were in the group of ones.

"Those who were in the group of twos follow me," said Number 7.

The group of women followed him down the hall to a small room with a metal ceiling and walls, full of chairs and he ordered them all to sit.

"You must wait here for more instructions on new medical techniques," said Number 7 and then he left the room and the hatchway was sealed. After several minutes, a puff of vapor was released from the ceiling. Some of the women noticed this fearfully but did nothing. It did not profit anyone to become afraid on the Moon since fear had no rewards in terms of survival. Number 7 left Dr. Acra in a control room watching the women and went to a meeting with the Unash space officers to request more spacesuits for his crews to wear on combat missions to Erra.

This was causing difficulty because normally space suits were worn only by officers on ships. This had caused many deaths when the hulls on the ships were punctured and cabin pressure was lost. However, to get spacesuits issued for all crew, Erra would have to be officially declared a war zone. However, Sadok Sar had forbidden Erra to be termed a war zone, because this would complicate the reports they were sending back to Nashan, which Sadok Sar insisted must only emphasize progress on the coition at Erra.

"If we request more space suits, in our supply shipments, people on Nashan will ask 'why?' And what will we tell them?" replied an Unash officer to his request.

So Number 7 returned from his fruitless meeting with the Unash space commanders with no more space suits.

Number 7 returned to find Doctor Acra laughing with delight as he saw the scene in the sealed room was now bloody chaos with the women running wildly about screaming with their faces covered with blood. This sight horrified Number 7, but he could not show this. Finally, mercifully, all the women collapsed and died after another hour of terror.

"You must disinfect the room with composition 6 and incinerate all of the bodies, "said Dr. Acra.

"Yes my Lord, "said Number 7.

****

## Chapter 2: Hard X-rays

Hontal and his retainer Gamal, walked into the transporter room on the Tlakmar as the mighty ship sat at the L2 Lagrange point above the far side of the Moon from the Earth. Hontal stared at the shimmering light around him as he de-materialized and then materialized in a transported facility in the massive Unash base in Mare Moscoviens known as Rabmag. He turned to check that Gamal had materialized also with him. Two Samaran officers and an Unash official stood nearby facing him. He raised his fist to his chest above his heart and the Samaran's did likewise. The Unash stood motionless.

"Welcome to Una my Lord." said the most senior looking Samaran, a tall strong man in armor with blonde curly hair and a beard. "I am second officer Zomal of Alnik."

"Where is Koton of Betalgeen? I need to speak with him!" demanded Hontal. "I am here under the full authority of the Palace to take his sworn report."

"He now drinks wine in the great hall of Alkmar, My Lord" responded Zomal without emotion.

Hontal starred at him in shock. This signified Koton had died in battle. A deep feeling of unease filled Hontal. *The reports didn't mention all this trouble in the Quzrada because the palace does not know it is happening!* The realization swept through him like a shock. He gripped the hilt of sword, looked around warily. *I am now the only official witness to the situation here.* This thought filled him with caution.

"Where did he fall, on what battlefield?" demanded Hontal.

"On Erra my Lord. He died in battle with the Errans." said Zomal looking uncomfortable. Hontal looked at Zomal in astonishment.

"How is that possible?" asked Hontal, "The palace reports mentioned no battles at Erra involving our people. I thought we were not supposed to be fighting anywhere in the Quzrada, much less at Erra?"

"Come, my Lord, enjoy our quarters." said Zomal with some weariness. "I will report to you the things that have happened here of late."

****

"The Greys came over to Washington DC again last night," the Army officer began. He was a Colonel in combat fatigues, motioning with a laser pointer at a projector screen with pictures from last night's action. The President, sat looking weary, on his right sat the Defense Secretary Senator Clayborne, on his left sat James Bergman, the National Security Advisor and Deputy Defense secretary. The Colonel, a stocky blonde man with close-cropped hair, continued. "We estimate four ships of seagull class. Two came down to low altitude near Arlington Hospital where they were driven off by antiaircraft and missile fire. One ship crashed in the Shenandoah later, and we believe it was one of the ships that came over here. It was full of shrapnel; we are analyzing some of the shrapnel to see if it came from the antiaircraft batteries here. "They were in a deep, electromagnetically shielded bunker near the Whitehouse and this was the President's daily military briefing.

"I notice many of the attacks seem to focus on the Arlington Hospital area. What do we have there?" asked Alicia Sepulveda. She was dressed in a tight black pantsuit, her shapely form, well-toned, her black hair now streaked with grey. Yet her dark eyes darted around the room constantly assessing everyone's face. Her lovely bronze face kept a look of severe intelligence. She was now the president's Science Advisor for War.

"It may be what we don't have there; the core of the DC area has heavier defenses. They may be going where defenses are weaker," said the Colonel.

"Yes but why there?" asked Alicia rhetorically, "Why not Bethesda Naval Hospital? She said looking at James Bergman, who looked deep in thought. "I suggest its Jade and Blondie who in the hospital there." said Alicia. I can't think of anybody else there who would interest them. We have files from the Magi suggesting the Greys regarded Pamela Monroe as a high value target. "

100

"Why would they risk ships night after night to try and kill or abduct one person?" asked the Secretary of Defense.

"I don't know," said Alicia, "I merely suggest it as a pattern." *This whole situation is a mystery.* She thought.

"I tend to agree with Dr. Sepulveda," said Bergman. "We should put more defenses in Arlington near the hospital, we can attrite them there," he said levelly. There were nods around the table.

The Colonel clicked a controller and map of the Alaska area appeared.

"In the Aleutians, the lull in activity since the aliens last tried unsuccessfully to resupply the fortress there continues. We have now lost 4,253 men, the aircraft carrier Essex, two destroyers, 1 frigate, and 221 aircraft, but we have the Samaran garrison, which we believe consists of a force of twenty to thirty individuals, now cornered in a mountainside fortification on Mount Bering. The Samar have requested a truce to mourn their dead, which Admiral Thomas has decided to grant, under advice from the Carney. We feel this reveals not only have they experienced casualties, but also reveals something about their culture, which appears to be very warlike. "

*No shit,* thought Alicia.

"Also the fast attack submarine USS. Monterey is now missing." continued the Colonel, "All contact was lost yesterday after investigating the Bering Abyss area of the ocean, where sightings of grey spacecraft entering and leaving the water surface have been made. COM NORPAC in Hawaii is now readying contingency plans for a major operation there should we find an alien base on the ocean floor there.

Alicia looked around the room. The faces of everyone showed dismay at this news. Finding additional alien bases on Earth and destroying them was the major focus of the war effort, but the sheer number of them found, even though many were abandoned, was taxing allied military and mental resources. *We are being overwhelmed,* she thought, then shook herself mentally, steeled herself. *No, we have destroyed five bases, found 3 others abandoned, we just need to keep this effort up! We have them off balance, we need to keep pushing them so they can't catch their breath. The next place this war will move is space, if we can push them completely off the Earth's surface.* Then a terrible thought hit her. *Blue, he's an astronaut and wants to go fight in space...*

"Doctor Sepulveda, what can you report on the sharp increase in solar and auroral activity recently? I can't ever remember seeing Northern lights here in Washington before. "asked the President, jolting her out of her thoughts. She rose, clicked a controller and a graph of solar activity over the past decades appeared on the screen. It showed a rising trend going back two years, before the war started.

"Yes Mister President, I can report right now that this pattern of increased solar activity, while unusual in its severity, actually started before the crisis and is normal, at least in its timing." she adopted her most academic demeanor. "We also note that the solar outbursts, while a nuisance to us, appear to have significantly impeded grey space activities, as we notice drop in sightings and other activities when the outbursts reach their peak."

"You mean they abduct less people and dismember them to dump over our cities?" asked the President.

"Yes Sir, the increased levels of proton radiation appear to hinder their ability to fly as many sorties from the Moon, when they reach their highest intensity." she said nodding for emphasis. *Not even the Aztecs would imagine such a nightmare as this,* she thought, but the thought of the Aztec and Spanish blood flowing in her veins, both peoples known for their toughness and bravery in the face of every horror imaginable, suddenly made her feel suddenly strong. *Sharp as Obsidian, tough as steel. Bravado, Machismo. I am Mexican.*

"Well, I am grateful for small favors then." The President said smiling. The rest of the officials laughed slightly. "I think that concludes the briefing then, keep up the good work, I see we have them off balance and on the run, let's keep up the pressure on them."

****

Hontal and Gamal his retainer sat at a banquet table and raised their glasses, full of Betalgeen ale, as Zomal, the acting commander, raised a toast. His second in command also sat at the table.

"To the Samarian Empire, may it expand endlessly! May its stars burn forever!" said Hontal loudly.

"Araah! The Sword of Orion!" said the men in unison.

"I do apologize for the poor state of our rations here! The Monchkini supply them and our cook does the best he can with them." said Zomal.

"They are very savory, Zomal, and this ale is superb!"

"Yes, it from the stars of Batelgeen province, we save it for very special occasions! As we save other things!" said Zomal smiling, who then drained his glass and then banged it on the table to be refilled by a retainer. Retainers then cleared away the dishes and poured more ale for the four men at the table.

"Now I will show you the whole purpose of our operations here Hontal, brave knight of the realm," said Zomal rising and turning his chair around so it faced away from the table. Hontal noticed that several men bearing musical instruments had entered the room and took seats on cushions on the floor in a corner. "And when you report back this thing we will now show you to the Palace, concerning Erra, they will understand the entire reason for our being here!" Hontal and Gamal both turned their chairs around. Zomal clapped his hands and looked to the darkened doorway. Hontal followed his eyes. The musician began to play.

Through the door came three beautiful Erran women, wearing only jeweled loincloths and bracelets that flashed in the lights as they moved. *War custom,* thought Hontal in satisfaction. After a month in space his eyes drank in the sight of the women dancing sensuously like it was strong sweet wine. One woman had black hair and bronze skin, one had brown hair and lighter skin and one had hair like light gold and pale white skin. They were slightly slender for Samaran taste, but Hontal did not even think of that and he watched hypnotized, as the blonde woman smiled at him with big blue eyes. *Part Vikhelmkin,* he thought in awe.

103

"You see here the fair jewels of Erra! Not in all the stars of the Archmetia, will you find women so fair and of such various hues as those found at Erra. "said Zomal rising and gesturing to the women as they danced.

"If it was up to me," said Zomal laughing " I would bring a mighty space fleet here, slay all the men of Erra and take all these women of Erra back to the stars of Rigel as slaves and turn to a ball of glass this accursed planet!" said Zomal drinking more ale. "And whatever happens in the Quzrada after that, our comely prizes warming our beds in Rigel would make it all be more than worth the trouble!" He turned and looked at Hontal. The other Samaran officer in attendance rose smiling, excused himself and left the room.

"The golden haired one, she is your's for the night as war custom, brave knight of the realm. So you will see that we have managed to get a few things right here in the Quzrada. "Call her Tatiana, they all wear translator earplugs, so she will do anything you require of her..." continued Zomal smiling. He rose and took the hand of the black haired dancing girl. The golden haired one danced closer to Hontal and smiled sweetly as these words were said.

****

Suddenly Cassandra was awake, she held up her hands, saw them pale and strong, but unwounded; no chains were on her wrists. Not like in the dream, when the palms of both hands had been bleeding. She had been naked in a dark prison and in chains. But she saw her fingertips had bandages on them, she realized she had not noticed them before. She rose from her bed in wonder. Saw Pamela sitting up in bed smoking an electronic cigarette. Pamela looked at her with slight amusement.

"Where did you get those?" asked Cassandra, feeling bewildered. Pamela looked around warily.

"The male nurse named Gibson, he traded me this pack for an Oxy-8, and apparently those are the new currency around here." she said mischievously. Oxy-8s were a powerful painkiller dispensed in the hospital.

104

Cassandra rose. Went into the bathroom and closed the door, urinated then rose and brushed her teeth and brushed her hair and showered. As she stepped out of the shower, she suddenly looked at her back. Her ribs were all visible; she had lost a lot of weight. But across her back, on her pale skin, crisscrossed, were eight long purple scars, looking as if she had been cut apart and crudely welded back together. She looked at them in astonishment, and ran her fingers over their rough surface. Cassandra began shaking. She had taken showers every day, how had the scars gotten there? She bolted out the door naked, standing still dripping wet in front of Pamela who looked up at her from her bed in surprise, her e-cigarette dangling from her mouth. Pamela's hand grabbed for the nurses call button, found it on the bed and she pressed it with all her strength.

"How did I get these scars on my back?" asked Cassandra with a trembling voice. Pamela stared at her wordlessly, and then took a long drag on her cigarette. Cassandra looked at her hands then at the bandages on her fingers; she frantically pulled off the bandages, saw that her fingernails were gone, and were only slowly beginning to grow back.

"What happened to me?" asked Cassandra. "WHAT HAPPENED TO MY FINGERS!" she shrieked. She remembered the dream, the dark tower rising from the forest, and being held prisoner there. Tears flowed down her cheeks.

"They took me to Morningstar!" Cassandra stammered "They took me to Devil's Mesa didn't they? DIDN'T THEY!???!" screamed Cassandra.

"Yes, you were captured, and then Swartz and the Carney rescued you," said Pamela levelly, her eyes were now wide and red rimmed. Tears began streamed down Pamela's cheeks.

Then Cassandra began to scream, she saw rat-crabs climbing on her and was trying to bat them off her arms. Two nurses burst thought the doorway into the room, grabbed her, and gave her a shot of sedative in the arm; blackness enclosed her as she struggled screaming against them on the floor.

**** 

105

Hontal, after enjoying the Erran woman, lay back on his bed. The wonderful fragrance of her body filled him with comfort. The Erran woman known as Tatiana now smothered him with soft kisses. He had enjoyed the delights of war custom several times, but never with a woman who supplied it with such enthusiasm. After all he endured in the past year, he felt whole again. *These Erran women are full of ardor for love. Just as the legends said. She acts as if she has not been with man in ages,* he thought, *or enjoyed a good meal either,* he thought looking at her slender frame. If she were my housemaid, *I would fatten her up just a little.* He felt overwhelmed with desire and concern for her.

But she was apparently not done in making him happy. She slid on top of him straddling his stomach and smiled at him in the dim light of his room.

"Oh no! my precious," he said smiling. "No, we can have none of that, it is against custom. "He gently pushed her over to be beside him again. She looked slightly confused and afraid.

"It is nothing Tatia, but among the Samar customs is that man always rules in the bed. The man must be on top." he said reassuringly. *She has not been trained that thoroughly,* he thought, *these Erran women are wild in bed!* She smiled fearfully, and began to rub her hands gently on the scar on his shoulder.

"Yes I got that in battle, far from this place," he said. "You see, among my people the men are supposed to be very strong and brave and rule everything in their houses. Our women are taught to obey everything we say, all the time." *Hah,* he thought, *such fables I tell!*

"Tell me of your home world, brave Hontal." said Tatiana smiling, as she cuddled close to him naked.

"Yes," said Hontal. *I had better be careful,* he thought, *I could easily tell her everything I know...* "My family owns a great estate on a world similar to yours, very green. We have wide fields, and many cattle, many servants work our lands for us. "*That's enough* he thought, *soon I will be bragging about our space fleets.* "I will tell you a funny story which shows some of the customs of my people." *Yes tell an amusing story,* he thought. *If she learns anything important, the Monchkini may tear it out of her when I am gone.* He thought sadly. "This is a story about manhood and duty."

"A story?" she said softly.

"Yes, there was once a man who had a son who was a simpleton, and the man thought, I must teach my son to do a man's work. So he set him a simple task to educate him. He said, son, our cow needs to be serviced by a bull; here is money to go hire a bull ox at the market place in town. See to this business, that calves may be born of this cow and our herd will increase! Now the man watched with satisfaction as the son prepared a pen, complete with a trough by the fence where good hay was laid, so the cow and bull would be happy together and the servicing would occur, then the son went off to town with the bag of fine gold, and sought a bull to hire.

But the son encountered a shyster in the market place, and from him hired a great horned bull that was old and tired, and cared only for hay! So the bull was brought back from the town and let into the pen and the cow was also let in. But instead of the bull servicing the cow, he trotted over to the feed trough and began to eagerly eat the good hay. So eager was his eating, that great bundles of hay soon adorned his horns. Then the cow, seeing this, followed the bull, but the bull would not let her near the feed trough, but greedily kept it to himself. So at length the hungry cow, feeling neglected, climbed on the bull's back from behind and began to eat the bundles of straw caught in his horns! Now the father returned to see how his son's task was being accomplished, and was displeased at this.

He said to his son" Behold my son, I wanted the bull to service the cow, but instead the cow has mounted the bull!"

"Tatiana laughed at this vision and cuddled close to him.

"So the son responded, 'my father, this is a mystery!'"

"So among my people whenever a situation gets completely confused and mismanaged, we say the "The Cow has mounted the Bull!"

107

With that he rolled over on top of her, kissed her warmly, and further enjoyed her warmth.

*Oh Erra, thy jewels are fairer than a thousand worlds,* he thought. *No wonder a terrible war began over this place.*

****

"So how was Washington?" asked Goldberg, as Alicia Sepulveda walked through the door. Goldberg was sitting behind a steel desk covered with briefing papers. He was not looking at her, but staring intently at a projection screen on the wall where a computer projector was running a movie file. The lights in the office were dim. Alicia's eyes immediately were attracted to the green images on the view screen.

"It was very noisy in DC, the saucers are coming almost every night," she said starring at the green images in mounting wonder. "And between the rockets and antiaircraft fire and the air raid sirens I couldn't get any sleep there-what is this?"

"Shut the door, I want you to see this. It's some combat footage they got me today," said Goldberg, looking fit and trim. He suddenly grinned ear to ear. "I have been watching this thing for an hour, over and over. It green because it's taken through a night vision scope."

She starred at the film sequence, could see it was a night combat sequence through a night vision scope. She had also lost weight and was looking careworn. She was wearing a black tight sweater and a dark grey business suit. She watched the sequence transfixed. It was a saucer, in the sky, so brilliant it was visible just as lens shaped glowing blob, the stars were brilliant, the saucer was dodging streams of tracer bullets, dancing back and forth, almost as if to taunt the people shooting at it. Once in a while, a rocket would fly by saucer uselessly, as it deftly dodged it. It looked almost like an early computer game with poor monochrome graphics. But Alicia's keen dark eyes noticed something. She noticed the stars would get noticeably brighter in the greenish night sky of the night vision scope whenever the saucer darted one way or another. Finally, the saucer, seemly bored, darted upward out of sight and the camera and tracers tilted upward in a hopeless attempt to find it in the green stardust.

108

"Did you see that?" asked Goldberg "the way the night vision gain changed whenever the saucer darted around. They took this footage last night at Umatilla Army Depot. "

"Yes! Why would that happen?" asked Alicia looking a Goldberg. He was stroking his mustache as the film looped to repeat again.

"Big Magnetic field, that's got to be it" said Goldberg in wonderment. "I just called up the specs on the night-vision scope they were using at Umatilla. It uses a micro-channel plate, electrons stream down the channels in the plate, when a magnetic field pulse hits, the electrons in the micro-channels must hit the wall more often, and it creates a momentary diminishing of the gain, followed by a flash of higher gain when the pulse changes."

"That would make sense," said Alicia nodding, her trim bronze face intent with thought.

"Absolutely it would!" exploded Goldberg, "I am amazed we didn't think of this before! And if we put magneto-sensors in the tracers they will explode near the saucer every time it tries to dodge them! We can trigger their explosives off the magnetic pulses!" said Goldberg exultantly. "Cranston get in here!" yelled Goldberg into an intercom "And bring Brubaker with you! I got an idea!" Alicia turned to face the door with a smile appearing on her face.

"Yes, the saucer drives are electromagnetic, that should work!" she said to herself. *Hope*, she thought suddenly, realizing she was happy for the first time in weeks. Two men came bursting through the door, one an Air Force officer, and another a civilian in a sports-shirt. Both looked unkempt and exhausted. They both stopped in front of Goldberg's desk and stared at him intently. Goldberg rose unsteadily; his leg had never fully healed from the shrapnel he took in the truck bombing at JPL during the Sepulveda asteroid encounter.

"OK you guys, I want miniature magnetic sensor fuse chips put in every size shell 50 caliber and above and every missile warhead we have, we want the chip to trigger explosive fragmentation of the shell whenever they sense a big change in the local magnetic field. That way the shells will blow up whenever the saucer tries to dodge them! Make the magnetic sensor chips so they have some logic and can be programed just before they are fired to trigger on strong magnetic pulses! Got that? I want to see a plan for them made for test deployment in two days! The officer was writing on a clipboard furiously, the civilian was pulling out a coded cell phone and calling someone.

"OK, now go make it happen guys!" yelled Goldberg sternly. The two men turned and rushed out of the office, shutting the door behind them. Goldberg turned and smiled at Alicia and then sat down wearily.

"So they keep coming over Washington DC at night," said Goldberg. A sudden roar sounded outside the building. It was a group of jet fighters taking off. They were in St. Louis, Missouri, near an aircraft plant churning out Griffin jet fighters at a rate of four a day. They were being flown out fully armed with veteran fighter pilots at the controls. In a nearby area of Saint Louis, they were building F-71 scorpions, a fighter version of the SR-71 Mach 5 aircraft at a rate of two a day.

"Why? If they were smart they would come here and blow up our jet fighter production lines, but they don't, instead we keep building up our air-strength and they keep buzzing Washington and other cities trying to scare people. Every night they lose, one or sometimes two saucers, we lose fighter planes pilots, but we can replace them, all this so they can abduct people and chop them up and drop them in parking lots..." said Goldberg, his voice trailing off.

"I think they are after Jade and Blondie," said Alicia abruptly.

"What?" asked Goldberg in astonishment. "That wouldn't make any sense! They must be trying to make the President suffer sleep deprivation"

"No he sleeps fine, so he tells me" said Alicia leaning back in her chair. "He sleeps in a bunker near the White house with electromagnetic shielding and good sound proofing." She looked around the office, it was cluttered with charts and graphs on the walls- fighter production, night intercepts flown, saucers downed, fighters lost.

110

"But that would mean they are not just waging psychological warfare, "said Goldberg in wonder. "They are after some sort of propaganda coup. It's as if they believe they can break our will if they can abduct Jade and Blondie from their hospital beds," He paused and shot Alicia a look. "They are being well guarded of course, so that can't happen, right?"

"I told the President that their guard should be tripled, he agreed. They already have three missile batteries around the hospital and automatic antiaircraft guns too. It's the only thing this government seems to have done right in past two months, everything else seems completely confused."

"That's really crazy though, it doesn't make sense. Those two women have no military value, and everyone has pretty much forgotten them, now that the war has started"

"Well I haven't forgotten them," said Alicia with a hint of anger.

"No of course and I haven't either, but they haven't exactly been on the news every night. When they show up back on the news, that will be something."

"I went and saw them when I was there," said Alicia. "Cassandra contracted an infection by some extraterrestrial strain of bacteria, apparently in the wounds on her back. But they pulled her though with blood serum from the only known infection survivor, none other than Colonel Schwartzman himself. He pulled through and they used his blood to make anti-serum for her. "Despite herself, Alicia's voice trembled as she reported this. Goldberg's face fell and he nodded.

"So he survived too." Goldberg shook his head in wonder. "He is one tough bastard; I'll say that for him..."

"So Cassandra is now recovering," said Alicia, "but can't remember what happened to her at Morningstar apparently, which is not surprising since she was tortured while captive there. But she was doing better when I left. Pamela can now wiggle her toes too, so the doctors are becoming more hopeful that her spinal concussion is getting better." Alicia added with a slight smile. Pamela told me she is going to walk out of the hospital in heels."

"Yeah, I remember them both from the asteroid thing; that's good to hear." said Goldberg. He sat down. Looked at Alicia intently then looked away.

"So the goals of the Grey war effort are almost completely psychological, at this stage," said Goldberg in wonder, starring off into space. "That is the cheapest sort of war possible, but the Greys seem convinced Jade and Blondie are vital to our war effort?"

"Yes, it's like Hitler becoming obsessed with taking Stalingrad, because of its name," said Alicia.

"So that hospital in Arlington with two women in it is Stalingrad?" said Goldberg in wonder.

"Apparently, I also noticed we are having a lot of aurora activity. The Greys can't be causing that can they?" asked Alicia with a hint of fear in her voice.

"Yeah that's weird, the Sun has gotten really active lately, but that's normal for this time in the Sunspot cycle. At least we should expect increased activity now. General Standish thinks it's causing problems for the greys, so he says he's happy, I think he may be right but it means we have to call off space fighter missions sometimes because of radiation, so it's causing us some problems, and it's causing them some problems too, I know. So right now, it's just pretty lights; it hinders both sides equally.

"It's as if the Sun is expressing outrage at what is happening here at Earth." said Alicia.

****

"You got to get Colonel Schwartzman out of there!" said Mongoose to Major Prescott who sat behind his desk. The Carney Cosmic War Strategy Report sat in the middle of Prescott's desk where they had left it. They were deep in the Pentagon. "The French may have infiltrated the nursing staff in the isolation section where they have him!"

Prescott, his face haggard, shook his head. Arizona sat in his Special Forces uniform and nodded grimly. Both he and Mongoose were now thoroughly jet lagged from flying to Alaska and back, and cranking out a Cosmic War Strategy the previous night.

"Down here, we think it's safer for him there, for now," said Prescott sharply. "We don't even know if he is stabilized medically," Prescott paused. "You guys got to look at the big picture here. We have a hundred emergencies we are dealing with now, and the fate of one Colonel is nowhere near the top of that list. Colonel Schwartzman is just going to have to sit tight until he has a medical release and we can figure out what to do with him. The World Court Indictment and order for his arrest took everyone by surprise here. We know the French are after him, but we haven't seen any credible Intel they are coming here to get him or that they even know where he is."

"Well he thinks they know where he is!" said Mongoose. "It's not hard to figure out!"

"You got any evidence for that? Or is that just his opinion?" Prescott looked at his watch. "Look you guys, I got to I meet with General Burnham in twenty minutes, and all he wants to know is how many jet fighters and pilots we lost last night, versus how many of their ships we brought down. Besides that he wants to know where are all the fucking magnetometers our troops are supposed to have. We ordered ten million units to be built and shipped a month ago and no units have gotten them yet! Colonels and ship Captains are buying them off the internet from UFO websites because the GI version hasn't arrived yet!" Prescott yelled "Units are making them from kits from Radio Shack for God's sake!"

Major Prescott's face lost its anger.

"Look, the Big Guy knows Schwartz is in a jam, and he hasn't forgotten him, but until we get evidence Colonel Schwartzman's location is actually compromised he is staying put there. It's simply an "if it ain't broke, don't fix it" situation with a hundred other situations in the war theatre where things are busted to hell or completely non-existent. You get that?"

"Well, when it breaks, Colonel, the French will be up there at the Hospital for him!" yelled Mongoose. "Don't fix it till it breaks Major, them is famous last words I've heard many a man say in this business, just before he bought it!" Prescott absorbed this.

"Alright I'll do what I can! But I need evidence the French know where he is!" said Prescott. "Evidence, gentlemen! When you find it, I'll get it in front of General Burnham immediately. So get me some Intel, and don't come back here without it. Do I make myself clear gentlemen?" Prescott then rose and saluted them as Mongoose and Arizona rose and saluted smartly, put on their berets and left the office.

"Can you get him a Juke unit for the surveillance he's under Goose? It's the least I can do for him?" Mongoose nodded.

"Yeah, I'll get it to him tomorrow. Arizona, you better get back up North to deliver the boss's advice to the Admiral; that will help him get back on the line quicker too, it will make him seem important, and they'll spring him faster."

****

Goose sat in Schwartzman's hospital room with a CD player and a bottle of mineral water. "So chief, on the bright side, the boys up North are happy with your advice, and we got your Big Picture report from the Weather Girl, delivered to the appropriate desk." But the news, that no help from the Pentagon was forthcoming for him personally, had sunk in hard to Schwartzman.

"But until your uncle hears some funny noises out of your truck, he won't fix it, and until he hears some noises, he thinks his truck is running fine down here," said Mongoose solemnly. He saw what he thought was despair forming on Schwartzman's face.

"Well, tell my uncle I would rather run the truck off a cliff, than have it break down some day in the neighborhood. With my compliments"

"Sorry boss."

"Yeah, only I'll be the one who's really sorry when I am riding in the truck when it breaks down." said Schwartzman looking at the floor. Schwartzman rose. He felt ill and weak. *I know they are coming for me here. Please God don't let them take me here,* he thought desperately. *Help me get out of here.* "You better get back up North, Goose. Thanks for stopping by with the stuff and the update.

Mongoose left. Schwartzman poured some of the mineral water into a plastic hospital cup and drank it down. It was Stolinoika vodka as he had requested. It burned his throat. He calmed himself, forced himself to think deeply.

He opened the battery bay on the CD player, fished out the thin black tubular "juke box" unit with its coaxial TV connectors on both ends and its small square control unit. Conscious that people could be watching the TV images from the room he made the fussing with the CD player look like he was having trouble playing the music. He put in a disk of Wagner's ride of the Valkyrie, and listened to it play. He looked at his watch; the nurse was not due for another half hour. Inspired by the music and the sip of vodka, he suddenly sprung up on the bed, out of what he estimated was the camera's field of view. The room had thin windows up near the ceiling to let in light. He stood on the bed and looked out the window at Washington DC, seeing was late afternoon. He then quickly installed the coax cable from the TV camera, connected the jukebox unit on the cable, and then connected the other end of the juke unit to the camera. To the undiscerning eye, it looked like the cable to the TV was simply a few inches longer. *Let's hope this works,* he thought. The sense of danger gave him a massive erection. *Fortune favors the brave* he thought fiercely, to reassure himself. He calmed himself as he looked out the window and the city under a clear blue sky with autumn colors spreading everywhere. "Down boy" he said to his erect member. "Time for that later when you get out of here." Suddenly he heard the door open.

"Colonel, you get down from there or I am going to have to take your temperature Old School," said Florence in an irate voice. He turned around and grinned, aware his hospital gown was open in the back.

115

"We'll Flo, that would be fine by me," he said slyly, "as long as I could take yours the same way. "

He nimbly stepped down off the bed. He had a sudden inspiration. *Time to take my intel network in this hospital to a new level of performance,* he thought. *He who dares, wins.* He looked out the door, his heart leaped. No one was at the nurse's station watching the monitors. Florence shut the door to the room smiling. She moved gracefully, like a dancer. He noticed her nurse's uniform was not buttoned up completely at the top that day, exposing some of her generous cleavage.

"That would be hard to do Colonel since I have control of the thermometer. Now let's get this done shall we, before the next shift arrives," she said coming over to him. He clicked the jukebox control unit. The camera would now report simply an endless loop of the last few minutes to the monitors, basically Florence standing inside the closed door talking to him in artificially muffled tones.

He sat dutifully down on the bed and sat down beside him; he smelled her rose perfume. She sat smiling at him warmly then her face suddenly looked surprised. He had put his upturned hand flat under her well-shaped behind.

"I can see somebody is feeling better. Now Colonel will you kindly move your hand? We got no time for such nonsense today." He pulled his strong hand gently out from under her bottom. He then circled it around her waist, and pulled her close. She looked down with irritation and stuck the thermometer in his ear and read it carefully with a smile.

"How long have I been your honored guest here, Flo, and not once have you fluffed up my pillow for me? Did I ever tell you that the first girl I ever went to bed with was a cute black girl like you? It was down is Shreveport, Louisiana, the night I ran away from home in Texas and joined the Army."

He moved his hand up to touch the bottom of her full breasts, pulled her even closer. Her face changed to amusement and she laughed.

"There she was in the hallway of the hotel the Army put me in, looking so beautiful, "continued Schwartzman. "She was trying to get a coke out of the machine to mix with her bottle of Rum. So I gave the machine a thump for her, and out it came. And she was so grateful that she invited me back to her room and dipped me in chocolate..." He kissed her fully on the lips. "So I ran away from home, joined the Army and became a man, all in one day and night." he said with a smile. "I've had a taste for brown sugar and rum ever since."

"Colonel, you best not squeeze me so tight, "she said with big dreamy eyes.

"I do have a rectal thermometer, "he said smiling slyly. It's long and fat and takes forever to read a temperature. In fact, it causes a fever. "

"Yeah but we are being recorded on TV" she said looking up at the corner of the room.

"Not for another hour we're not" he said holding up the juke box control unit. *I am 'all in now,'* he thought. She looked astonished at seeing it then looked at him again in puzzlement. He then kissed her deeply on her rich chocolate lips. She broke the kiss with a smile then looked amazed at him.

"Colonel, it's true what they said, that you are a notorious man" she gasped. "They say you were working with outer space aliens and then fighting them and rescuing people..."

"Mostly lies, girl, I was actually a buccaneer of off Africa. I kidnapped Nubian princesses for ransom in bright gold." He kissed her deeply felt her melt in his arms, she was dropping the thermometer on the bed. "They called me Captain Doggy style then." he whispered to her as she sank on the bed he was kissing her and undoing the button on her uniform in record time with his quick strong fingers. Soon he was kissing her swelling brown nipples and then her stomach as she writhed on the bed, she was winding her slender arms around the pillow as he kissed her trim , soft stomach above and then below her navel and pulled off her pants and panties, and began kissing her slender strong thighs. He then sucked her large and swollen clitoris as she arched her back and convulsed with an orgasm, then another. He then rolled her over and pulled her up on her knees and plunged his large aching member into her from behind as he held her swollen breasts with one arm and squeezed her clitoris with the

117

other, she had her head turned and was kissing him desperately and holding him with her arms above her own head as he felt her have another orgasm while he smothered her cries with kisses and gently lowered her back down on her stomach and lay on top of her caressing her as she moaned with pleasure. They lay there, a pile of throbbing pleasure for what seemed like forever. She suddenly raised her head and looked around at him in alarmed and annoyed look.

"I declare, Colonel Schwartz, you be a wanted man for a good reason." she said irately. She then looked serious and rose and gracefully and pulled on her underwear and light blue uniform, he sat up and returned his hospital gown to its proper position of covering the front of his body. He reached down and picked up one of her slip-on tennis shoes, which she took warily from him. She was redoing her buttons, all the way to her neck, and she stood up and picked up her thermometer. She rolled her eyes up to the ceiling then looked down at him in annoyance. He stood up and kissed her again, she started to melt again but then pulled herself away smiling.

"No Colonel, we better let this be as it is," she said then kissed him again. "But Colonel, I now understand why you have managed be at the center of so much trouble..."

She picked up her clipboard and started for the door. Can I ask you one favor Flo?" he said from the bed with boyish grin.

"Sure Captain Bad," she smiled and paused in front of the door.

"He rose and stood close to her, his still grey eyes were hypnotic to her.

"I think that nurse, Rene, who sits out there a lot, is a French spy. You know they're after my ass to pack me off to Devil's Island, right?"

"Yeah, your face is in the papers Colonel" she said, her eyes narrowed as if deep in thought.

He pressed an email address on a piece of paper into her still-warm hand.

"I need you to get her personal file scanned and sent to this email address," he paused, "unless you want to see the French cart my ass off to

Timbuktu." He paused, "In which case I will no longer be a honored guest at this five star hotel of yours…"

She looked concerned and nodded, then kissed him again, and then motioned for him to go back to the bed. She then turned and opened the door, looked around and left, shutting the door behind her. Schwartzman lay down on the hospital bed. The orange sunset was now shining through the thin windows of his prison.

"I am going to get out of here," he thought with determination, "and if I got to break a few rules to do it, so be it." He then flicked off the jukebox and let the camera resume its surveillance of his room.

****

The meeting about the defense of the skies over Washington DC dissolved. Alicia rose and sought out the Army Colonel who had just given the briefing. He smiled at her approach from around the table.

"Colonel, what sort of fusing and guidance are you using on the Patriot missiles you are deploying over Washington DC?" He looked slightly awkward.

"The Greys deploy a lot of electronic jamming; it prevents our radar from tracking them well. So we fire salvos of four missiles, two where we try to home in on the interference sources themselves and two we try to optically guide with night vision scopes and have them detonate at best guess locations. Each warhead has a quarter million pre-sectioned steel prisms, so we try saturate the most likely location are of the seagull with shrapnel. "He shrugged. "We have brought down three this way in the last month." he added.

"You should have magnetic sensors in warhead fuses and big superconducting three-axis magnetometers on the ground. The Russians use them and report a good kill rate - one saucer a night over Moscow and Novosibirsk. They just briefed us yesterday." she blurted out. "Here I have a briefing on a thumb drive, I also have some US vendors for magnetometers…" She pulled out another thumb-drive from her bag. The Colonel's eyes lit up.

119

"We might be able to field modify some warheads in DC…" he was mentally calculating. She liked him. He reminded her of her husband that she hadn't seen in weeks. *Blue,* she thought.

****

In the late afternoon, Schwartzman, sweating and clad in a tee shirt, dog tags and athletic shorts, walked back to his room from his exercise area. He had just run the equivalent of 3 miles and worked out with weights. He felt like himself again. The ET ward was empty now except for him and Crawford, the head case from Harshman. The rest of the patients had died of the X-ray infection or injuries, or in one case, a badly injured man had been cured of the X-ray bug and been moved to a regular hospital wing. Accordingly, staff in the ward had been sharply reduced, and most had been moved elsewhere in the hospital where they were needed. Rene, the uber-surveillance nurse, still sat at her console at the nurse's station. She looked up at as he approached the nurse's station on his way back to his room to shower, her perfectly made up eyes examined him blankly. He was not only the most interesting person in the ward, he was the only person who left and entered his room under his own power.

"How are we doing today, Rene?"

"Fine Colonel," she said looking at him with faint smile he had not seen before. She was attractive in an intelligent sort of way. *Good choice for intelligence work,* he thought. He noticed a faint twinkle in her eyes, as he trudged by.

*Did I see what I think I saw?* Schwartzman thought gleefully. *Target fascination? The bane of all dive-bomber pilots! In war, morals go low, so morale can rise.*

****

"Bingo!" said Mongoose staring at the computer screen. "Nurse Rene is not who she says she is. The real Rene Howard died in a car accident in high school in Baton Rouge 10 years ago."

120

"Well let's get this to Major Prescott then!" said Arizona. "This means we have to spring the boss now!"

**\*\*\*\***

After dark, Schwartzman called Nurse Rene on the intercom.

"Nurse I am slightly dizzy, and I think I have a temperature," he told her.

She appeared in his room, finding him sitting on the bed in his hospital gown. She had the ear infrared thermometer in her hand. She sat down next to him; she was wearing lilac perfume. When she was done taking his temperature, finding it normal, he turned his head and kissed her on the lips. She suddenly embraced him with one arm and began tearing off her clothes with the other, and smothering him with more kisses. To his surprise, she then got on her knees beside the bed and began sucking his enormous erect penis. Soon she was in the bed and he was driving his large long member into her, and rolling his hips rhythmically as she cried in ecstasy. Finally, she lay beside him and drifted off to sleep cuddled up next to him. He freed his muscular arm out from under as she moaned. He spoke into her ear quietly as she slept next to him.

"L'amore, moi cheri, tres beautiful..." he muttered, as she responded by smiling sweetly in her sleep and moved closer to him.

He laughed mentally. *That's two sure things in this ward! , Why would I want to escape this place?* But then serious thoughts returned.

*Ok, I'm made, she's French Intelligence, and she's getting a little careless.* He then thought deeply. *Maybe this means were in the end game on this little cosplay?*

**\*\*\*\***

Alicia and Blue (Patrick) Steele lay cuddled up in bed, and down the hall their son lay sleeping sweetly. All was right with the world again. But as Alicia lay awake beside Blue her body aching with pleasure , she was troubled by thoughts that arose in her mind. She had noticed that he was extremely fit again, like before and occasionally, even now that they were seeing each other for the first times in weeks, she had seen a faraway look in his eyes.

*He wants to go to war, to go into space again...* she thought and tears welled up in her eyes.

****

Semjase walked into the Wendy's up on Wilson Boulevard in Arlington, near where the office buildings transitioned to small shops and suburban neighborhoods. She looked down the street out the wide windows and saw the Washington Capitol dome rising in the distance across the Potomac; it was beautiful clear fall day, like the many she had enjoyed on her home planet in the Pleiades star cluster. *Same blue sky, same trees.* She thought. She had been attracted to this particular place by strange thoughts she had felt emanating from the area, but also a desire to get out in some fresh air now that the battered Vikhelmian was recovering. He was doing well, though still not able to walk, or do more than sit up painfully in bed. But he was a powerful and determined man. He kept asking for "cheeseburger and fries, with a coke", much to Samjeed's puzzlement and annoyance. So Semjase, having spent enough time on Earth to understand this request, decided to go get him such a meal while on her usual intelligence gathering forays. She wanted to be able to make a complete report, back on her home world, a report on the Errans and their heroic and hopeless war against the Unash.

The people around her marching into the Wendy's at noon were numerous, which is what she wanted, and a nice mix of multihued office workers, mothers with children, high school kids, and an occasional soldier in combat fatigues. She was wary now of walking into any place alone, because she saw now that the Errans seemed to notice her exotic features in isolation, though not in a group situation. She was afraid that soon someone would report her if she were not careful. She wore her long light brown hair parted in the middle, a windbreaker, blue jeans, and boots. She was shorter than most humans were and slender in a healthy looking way. However, her face had beautiful hazel eyes that were catlike and attracted attention along with her high cheekbones. She worried that the repeated glances of men were not just due to their shared Archmetan

122

form and the natural inclinations that went with that. *They sense I am not from here, some of them. They do not recognize their own latent psychic abilities as fellow Archmetans. However, their authorities will start looking for humanoid aliens soon, once they get organized*, she thought. *I must be careful.*

The fact that the Errans seemed to make the war simply a day-to-day exercise in psychological survival, was something Semjase picked up easily from the people around her as she stood in line. Despite the slight gaiety of the crowd, she sensed an underlying depression, fatigue, and desperation below the surface. The Unash had staged another raid the previous night, and once again the sky had been lit up with tracers, missile trails, deafening cracks of thunder and sonic booms of jet fighters; and in the morning the recovery of human body parts scattered piecemeal over the metropolitan area along with two crashed fighters. *How long before the aliens simply came down and vaporized the place?* This was a thought she picked up more than once. Another thought was, *how long before I find my neighbor's severed head lying on my front lawn some morning?* Mothers seemed to keep their children close to them, and after the smile and greeting came to a sleep deprived and haunted look. *How long before we are crushed? Why are they toying with us?* One woman was thinking clearly in front of her while holding a young child.

She ordered a cheeseburger meal with a coke and to her surprise found herself ordering two meals to go, with a slightly mischievous curiosity. Pleiadians were a highly advanced people who had given up eating meat long ago as part of a reform of their culture. A "Model to all Peoples" was the Pleiadian saying for their ambitions. However, the Samar had savagely raided a star system on their shared border recently, she knew, and this had caused a great deal of doubt, about the 'way of the Pleiadians, and doubt about the Pleiadians themselves. Hence, her government had sent her again into the Quzrada, to its very heart, Erra, to find out what particular information, Semjase could only guess. *I don't even think the council knows what knowledge they are seeking here.* She thought in sudden anxiety. *Are we doomed like the Errans? Become too gentle and kind to survive?* She shook the terrible thought off as a bird shakes water of it feathers. She had been well trained. *Do I want onions on that burger?* she wondered instead.

She found herself sitting down and taking out the cheeseburger without onions she had ordered. The bag for the Vikhelm was next to hers. People were chatting happily, children fussing, and mothers were combing their daughter's hair as they ate French fries. She took the cheeseburger out of its aluminized wrapper. Smelled in skeptically, and then to her great surprise took a small bite.

"Oh!" she said to herself as her taste buds were suddenly overwhelmed with the unfamiliar taste of a cheeseburger. *Oh... that's not bad... not bad at all*, she thought in wonderment. *Moral implications aside, this is quite good actually.* She took a slightly larger bite, savored it. She washed it down with a sip of Coke. Suddenly felt a sense of strength and well-being fill her. But it fled instantly when she noticed a small crowd gather outside the window, watching something down a side street. Then she heard an approaching helicopter. Others in the Wendy's were noticing something amiss also. Teenagers and men were walking outside to see, mothers were suddenly looking fearful and pulling their children closer. She threw her cheeseburger back into the bag, scooped up the other bag and went outside without thinking. As she exited the door a police car roared by and then another. She looked up and saw a police helicopter descend and begin to hover a few hundred feet away over some houses in the nearby neighborhood, it was turning to face something. A chorus of sirens was now rising in the air. A chill coursed through her, as black SWAT team armored car flew past with combat-armed police hanging on its outside. She glimpsed several of their faces framed by helmets. *How brave they look.*

Then suddenly a thought hit her, a strange twisted utterly black thought with sharp, cold edges like hard black ice. *Vespectian,* she instantly sensed. *Many of them are here!* That was her last coherent thought before all hell broke loose.

A shot, then a deafening barrage of gunfire exploded followed by a chorus of screams from nearby on the side street. A policeman leaped from a car and was on the sidewalk yelling at everyone.

"GET DOWN! GET DOWN!" he yelled. Then the top of his head exploded into blood and brains. Semjase jerked her eyes away from the horrible sight, up to the blue sky where with her highly trained vision she watched the police helicopter hovering then dissolve into a brilliant ball of fire and a tremendous shock wave visible as a change in refraction in the clear air expanding out from it. The next thing she knew, she was lying inside the Wendy's on a floor strewn with broken glass, blood, and bodies of screaming wounded. Her hearing returned with the deafening cascade of automatic gunfire, wounded were screaming, children were shrieking in terror, mothers were crying and praying beside her, holding their shrieking children. Police Sirens wailed in a deafening chorus as they came screaming down Wilson boulevard to join the battle. She saw one policeman, his face covered with blood, sitting against a wall outside on the sidewalk calmly firing his pistol repeatedly down the street in the din, then ejecting a clip, reloading a new one, and resuming firing, this time with more care, amid the deafening gun battle. Another Black SWAT armored car rolled by with SWAT police running behind it firing M-16s. Above the noise, a mother was wailing.

"MARY! MOTHER MARY, HELP US!" she wailed as she covered her screaming child with her own body. A new thunder of a helicopter arrived, she saw it was a green Army Cobra gunship, it stopped in the sky and unleashed a stupefying staccato roar as it fired a Vulcan cannon, and then fired two hellfire missiles thunderously as a curtain of brass cartridges fell ringing into the street and two deafening explosions shook the whole building and blew what was left of the window glass out of the frames. Clouds of black smoke filled with fire rose from the nearby neighborhood.

"MOTHER MARY! MOTHER MARY!" the women was screaming , but now almost everyone was falling into terrified silence in the Wendy's, even the wounded, as they heard bullets fly through the air above their heads and crash and ricochet in the walls and street. Everyone put their heads down on the floor as low as possible. Now in addition to the endless chorus of sirens and gunfire was added a dull rumble shaking even the floor beneath them, and above it a roar of huge diesel engines. Suddenly two US Army armored personnel carriers roared past in the street covered with troops in full combat gear. The only impression Semjase could form was of young hard faces in helmets and utter determination. *So brave, so brave are the Errans ,* she thought, as a Sheridan Fighting Vehicle rolled past with troops

125

jumping off it and it opened fire in an ear-splitting staccato roar with its automatic cannon.

Semjase, suddenly by reflex, discovered she still held the bags of food and realized she had to deliver them, or perhaps it was from a sheer desire to escape, she rolled into a dark corner of the room strewn with wounded and terror-stricken people and teleported herself back to the Landau Mansion in Arcturus.

She rose from the patio, walked numbly to the boat house, and entered the spacecraft parked there. Sanjeed and Vikor both turned and looked at her in wonder. Vikor sat up painfully, his shirtless muscular frame looking fitter as he looked at her with concern, despite his own condition. In the distance, muffled thunder could be heard as the violent battle continued, upriver in Arlington, many miles away.

"Here is your cheeseburger with fries, and a coke," she stammered. She still clutched both sacks in nerveless hands and offered him a sack. He took it eagerly and began eating and drinking its contents with gusto. "Some of the coke has spilled in the sack, "he complained between bites. Sanjeed looked at her in growing concern.

"Your forehead is bleeding!" said Sanjeed crossly. Semjase put her hand up to her forehead and touched it, then looked with wonder at her hand covered with red blood, her own. Her legs grew weak and she sat down on the deck of the spaceship abruptly. Sanjeed wiped off her forehead and scanned it with a mediprobe. He then robotically withdrew a small shard of metal. He then looked at the wound carefully and put a bandage on it from his kit.

"What happened? You're lucky this fragment didn't go right through your pretty skull and out the other side!" said Sanjeed angrily, holding up the small fragment of metal, in front of her face.

"The Errans, they are so brave. So brave in battle..." she said to him with glassy eyes. "I saw a battle." she motioned with her head to the thunder in the distance. He looked at her carefully, then suddenly reached into his medical kit, got an injector, carefully chose a setting on its dial, and then quickly injected her in the neck with a sedative, as she protested absently.

126

Cushioned by his arm, she gently slumped to the deck and slept, the thunder continued in the distance.

"I am really hungry, can I have the stuff in the other sack she has there?" asked Vikor, as he ate the last of his coke-soaked French fries.

****

Major Prescott walked into the cold storage room, an impromptu morgue, at Ft. Myers. An Army Captain, still in sweat-stained combat gear, followed him. The scene was grim, the bullet and explosion shattered bodies of five strange looking men, plus parts of three others, lay on wooden forklift pallets.

"Who was in command of the rapid response combat teams?"

"I was sir; this all started with a call to the Arlington police about a strange character in someone's backyard. The police responded thinking this was some kids having a cosplay. It turns out it was a nest of Hard-X-ray Men in Black, eight of them. They were heavily armed every one of them fought to the death. We are talking hard X-ray MIBs. Not like some of the others who surrendered out West. We found evidence in the house wreckage that they had been camped out there for at least three months. It looked like they hadn't left the house, and they had all groceries delivered. The place was knee-deep in trash. The delivery people say that is consistent with their weekly grocery orders. They would charge them over the phone starting three months ago. We also found two dead women in the house and both have been missing for three months, since the balloon went up, actually.

"What were our other casualties?" asked Prescott.

"We lost 5 KIA with 10 wounded, 3 seriously. The Arlington police really got hit bad though, they lost fourteen officers, including half their SWAT team, they lost two EMS people and a fireman. We had ten civilians killed also. Hundreds were wounded; we had a knock-down drag out firefight in the middle of a suburban neighborhood. We told the police to hang back because we had a rifle company on the way, but they went in any way. I

127

told them, Major, to wait for the Army! I told them that SWAT team personnel are not combat troops. But they wouldn't listen. "

Prescott looked in amazement at the MIB bodies, all clad in black hats and black trench coats and dark glasses. Their skin was very pale and their faces resembled Laplanders.

Look at this Captain, these people have not changed their operating mode since the balloon went up! They are wearing the same uniforms and gear as during the Cover-up!

Prescott saw the mental image of a grey with his pants down around his ankles, trying to run.

"Is it possible Captain that these people have received no orders or resupply since the balloon went up and simply didn't know what to do? You know we barely have our shit together, but is it possible our enemy is so disorganized that they haven't even issued new orders to their ground intelligence units three months after the situation here has completely changed?

"It sure looks that way sir, in any case, though, their playbook hasn't changed, but they sure put up a fight once the shooting started. I thought we were going to need tank support for a while. We leveled a whole block of houses nailing them."

They looked numbly at a heavily damaged Black Cadillac with silver trim, tail fins, and no wheels. It apparently floated with antigravity and only projected the images of wheels to mask its real identity when moving around in daylight.

"A couple of them tried to make a run for it in this thing but ran into crossfire from 3rd platoon covering the street. It's got metal trim that's luminous, but the metal was no way bullet proof. This thing is a showboat for scaring people, not a combat vehicle. We call it the MIB "Pimp-wagon."

What weapons did they use?

"A variety of small arms, mostly Uzzie's bought in the 80's during the high cover-up. But they also had a semi-portable proton beam projector, the standard grey death ray. The techs say it threw a Megajoule each pop, with a billion volts beam energy. It looked mostly intact when new captured it so the science people took it for analysis. Fortunately, the MIBs only got off two shot with it before the Swat team knocked down the operators.

Prescott turned to the Army Captain and saluted.

"Good job by you and your men, Captain! I am now going to make a personal report to the Joint Chiefs about this action; expect your unit will receive a citation. Tell your people we want a written catalog with pictures and a paragraph on the recovered alien gear and its disposition. "Prescott then saluted and turned and walked outside. A heavy rain was now falling from a thunderstorm that had blown in from the west, but he could see smoke still rising from the resulting fires of the battle in the housing to the Southwest of Ft Myers.

****

In Arlington Hospital, the hall outside Cassandra and Pamela's room was now filled with screaming and crying wounded as the casualties of the battle in the Arlington suburb arrived and overwhelmed the emergency room. Outside sirens from ambulances and police cars wailed in a relentless chorus as they pressed in carrying wounded. It was raining now torrentially outside in a violent thunderstorm and the wounded were being carried or helped into the hospital to any available sheltered space. Cassandra was in the hall trying to help by holding blood bags. Finally, the hospital ran out of blood and both Cassandra and Pamela gave blood that was drained from their arms right into bags to help save the wounded lying outside in the hallway or in their room. They were giving blood out of one arm and drinking bottled juice with the other arm to make up for the fluid loss. Surgeons even had to amputate a young woman's leg in their room, with only Novocain as an anesthetic, while Cassie held her hand and tried to soothe her as the thunderclaps from the storm outside threw many of the wounded in the hall into hysterical screaming, thinking that the battle had started again.

Finally, by nightfall, the chaos was mostly over and the halls cleared of wounded as nearby hospitals absorbed the cases that could be moved. The blood on the floor in their room from the amputation performed there still remained; Cassandra simply covered it with towels. The MIBs had apparently used hollow point bullets in the fighting and this had resulted in massive wounds for anyone not wearing body armor. Cassandra's bed was covered with blood also. So she collapsed into Pamela's bed and wept beside her as they awaited the expected air raid. They lay beside each other with bandaged arms from emergency blood transfusions.

As she lay beside Pamela, both of them exhausted physically and emotionally, Cassandra spoke.

"Pam, don't ever imagine that I don't see all of this... don't ever imagine that I don't know how lucky I am to even be alive..." she gasped.

The first sonic boom of the night arrived before Pamela could think of something to say in response.

\*\*\*\*

In a bunker near the Pentagon, Major Prescott pushed past officers in dress uniforms and soldiers in combat gear to find General Burnham talking on the phone frantically with the Commander at Andrews Air Force Base. He was talking into an old fashioned telephone connected to a secure line while at the same time while signing a succession of documents being brought into him and laid down on the desk in front of him.

"OK, I want maximum air strength over the city tonight! I want you to pull in fighter strength from Philly, New York, and Boston and get them over DC! Tell your pilots, I want to make the Greys pay tonight for this! Yes, use every magneto warhead missile you have! Tell your pilots they are to ram the Greys and eject if they have too! This city is in near panic! It needs to see a maximum air effort tonight!" he put down the phone, it began ringing again as soon as he put it down. He looked up at Prescott, his face covered with sweat.

"What have you got Major? What happened in Arlington?" said Burnham
, signing several documents.

"The police stumbled on a pod of hard X-ray Men In Black in the Arlington
suburbs at a safe house, and Army arrived to back them up. They took it
down with heavy casualties both police and civilian. The MIBs all fought
to the death," Prescott paused. "Preliminary analysis is that the pod was
not a recent insert, but was stranded at a safe house without orders or
resupply when the war started and went to ground, then got careless
General." I interpret this as indications of extreme disorganization and
confusion on the enemy side General since the MIBs were just sitting
there rather than engaging us! We caught them with their pants down sir,
three months ago, and they still have their pants around their ankles! Also
General, this is consistent with what I have received in this document
from Major Garret of the Carney, it is an analysis and master war strategy
for winning this war, Sir. It basically says the alien supply lines are long
and vulnerable and that other interstellar powers such as the Pleiadians
will intervene if we can hold the Greys here long enough." Major
Prescott offered the stapled memo of five pages. "It's called the Monroe-
Monochencko doctrine General," said Prescott. "It is similar to the US
strategy during the Revolutionary war," General Burnham grabbed the
document, looked at it, then rolled it up and clutched it in his large right
hand. The phone continued to ring.

"How sure are we the Pleiadians will decide to join this war?" asked
General Burnham frowning.

"Major Garret says they're mentioned in the Bible, their aliens who look
like us. So they have been involved here a long time. We're probably
related. "

"Who is Monroe and who is Monochencko?"

"I don't know sir, probably people in the Carney"

Burnham suddenly smiled, "Well, I haven't heard any better ideas
recently. Good. The Carney know who they're dealing with, they've been
fighting ETs since they first arrived."

131

"OK Major, "Burnham continued, "I am inaugurating Operation Dragnet, and you are in command!" he said pointing the rolled up memo at Prescott. "You are hereby field promoted to Brigadier General, Major, and you are to take two battalions of armored infantry from Ft Myers, with two companies of military police and an attached Army air company of helicopter gunships and troop helicopters. You are to get Graceson's remaining Carney battalion out of White Sands with every X-ray K-9 unit they have and bring them out here to DC metro area. Operation Dragnet is to be an operation to find and destroy every X-ray safe house or pod existing in the DC metro area! Once located you are to attack such X-ray concentrations immediately with maximum firepower, concern for civilian casualties is to be secondary! Do I make myself clear General? You will find and destroy all alien safe houses, pods or recon units operating or dug in in this area using immediate and maximum force! Find them and Attack, Attack, Attack!" Burnham looked at the rolled up strategy document, paused. *Thank you, Jesus,* he thought desperately. *Please let this Monroe-Monochencko document be what we need! We are losing this war right here in the suburbs and skies over DC! They are winning the war every night here with sheer terror!*

"Colonel Bronson!" bellowed Burnham. Take Brevet General Prescott here and get Operation Dragnet fully staffed and requisitioned! It has maximum priority!" He then shot a salute to Gardener and then, still clutching the rolled up memo, picked up the ringing phone, as Prescott left the office.

"Yes Mister President, we have the situation contained," began Burnham. "Arlington police stumbled on a stranded, Men in Black, team at a safe house and wiped it out with Army support! We have indications from this that alien operations are extremely confused and disorganized in response to our present war plan. Consistent with this, I have also just received from our best people, the Carney unit, who are seasoned veterans at fighting the X-rays, an expanded war plan, and victory strategy. We are also preparing for a major air effort over DC tonight with reinforced air forces using the new magneto proximity fused cannon shells and missile warheads! Yes, sir! Yes, Mr. President! We have the situation completely contained Sir! All indications are sir that we caught them with pants down three months ago and they are still running around with their

132

pants down around the ankles and a turd stuck in their asses!" he said grinning.

*Help Us Jesus!* he thought desperately as he put down the phone and began signing more documents.

"Colonel Bronson! Bring General Prescott back in here! I have another job for him!"

****

Cassandra was staring out the window, sadly as usual. She didn't cry as much as she used to, but she had been in tears all that day, still in shock over the avalanche of wounded from the fighting the previous day.

Pamela was taking a break from her studies and was surfing the net. She suddenly clutched her breasts and smiled.

"Cassie! Our girls are saved!"

"What?"

"Our boobs, Cassie! They are safe! They have just discovered a "penicillin for cancer". It's called, Proviron, and it shuts off the ATP energy channel discovered to be shared by all cancer cells! The zombie cells fall over, are paralyzed, and the body attacks them because they are just trash! This is incredible! In the middle of this war and all this horror, some researchers just were patiently working on a cure for cancer and have found it! They have cured three women with breast cancer in one week! Cancer free after a week!"

"Pammy! That is really good news!" said Cassandra suddenly fondling her own breasts.

"It is based on some little-known research last year, which we didn't pay attention to because of the Star Gate story. " Pamela continued reading with large eyes. "They found out that almost all human cancers are actually an "evolved organism" a sort of metavirus hiding in the human genome. It's like a parasite that infects cells turning them into zombies. Everyone thought the zombies were mindless killers, but they noticed that

133

the zombies would check into the body like it was a hotel and then order room service. Not the run of mill expected zombie behavior- they even used company credit cards to pay! The cancer cells, supposedly mindless disordered cells, were actually issuing orders to the rest of the body to build blood vessels that deliver blood with oxygen and nutrients to the site of the tumors. So, not mindless zombies after all. They also discovered the cancers were issuing fake IDs to their cells so they could avoid attack by the body's immune system. So the researchers alerted the body to the presence of cancer in several patients, and Bingo, the supposedly mindless cancer cells suddenly issued orders to each other to switch to new fake IDs so the body's immune systems would still continue to think they were part of the body. So they found this was all being coordinated through a small group of genes found in all common cancer cells, and Bingo, they found the power switch for the cancer cells in the gene group and shut it off!" Pamela laughed at this. "Imagine the mindless zombie in a hotel room, suddenly ordering 50 pizzas, with everything on them, and a gallon of Coke from his room; and then using the hotel's own visa card to pay for it! It's sort of ridiculous now that we see it."

"Yes, how strange to have so much hope for the future suddenly, in the middle of despair," said Cassandra turning once again to look out the window.

****

Now Captain Douglas Forester stood in the conference room at Turner Air Force Base near Atlanta Georgia. The base Commander was introducing him to a room full of haggard and tired looking fighter pilots, who appeared to regard him and his arm, still in a cast, with skepticism. Night was falling. He knew the squadron had lost seven planes and pilots in the last seven nights. He had been flown, together with five new Griffin fighters to the air base that morning. He had surveyed the assortment of aging F-15 Eagles, F-16 Falcons and even a Phantom II fighter aircraft that they had pressed into service.

Captain Tiger Forester has flown to you straight from victories in the Aleutians where he personally helped shoot down a large alien craft *"I am*

134

*being awarded that kill because everyone else is dead except for Samurai and me,* he thought, "and coming off of two air kills on alien spacecraft over Washington DC." *One was a complete accident,* thought Tiger.

Suddenly, he was standing at the podium. He felt a strange elation come over him, suddenly his arm and still healing ribs felt better. He stood tall in his flight suit, jutted out his chin. The squadron of disheveled men also reacted, suddenly sitting up straight and gaining half smiles.

"All right you men! As your new squadron commander I hereby christen this squadron the 'Wolverines', instead of being just the 54th Air Force Fighter squadron!" began Tiger loudly. "As you know the wolverine sees at night as well as it does during the day! I am handing out red goggles and I want you all to start wearing them and eating carrots this afternoon to prepare for tonight! These are old night fighting techniques from the Second World War. With our new fighters that we have taken delivery of today, with more coming, and with the new magnetometers and magnetically fused cannon shells and missile warheads, we are going to start ruling the night over Georgia! Now I am going to tell you of my combat experiences against the Greys, dwelling on lessons learned over DC and the Aleutians. I am going to tell you how you can take advantage of the what we called in the "ghost riders" squadron , the 'golden second' when you have an alien craft in your sights and then push the fire control button on your control stick!" He noticed the men all looking more encouraged, and this encouraged him further. *We will rule the night,* he suddenly thought.

**** 

Karlac awoke bathed in sweat, in his ship, **Song of Peace;** the woman had appeared in his dream again crying, naked and in chains in some sort of horrifying prison. The ship was flying swiftly on automatic pilot back to Janus from Vale. He and ship were deep in tachyonic space, and outside the windows of the ship the strange spiral of faint rainbow lights were sweeping by as he appeared to travel down the large spiral tunnel. Scientists had conjectured that the lights were diffracted images of stars in ordinary space, but no one knew. He rose from his bed as sorrow tore at his heart. Two standard days before he had left Vale in sadness and in a feeling of deep humiliation, a feeling that the situation in the Quzrada was all hopeless and that his own efforts were naïve and pathetic. He had therefore resolved to forget the dream and forget Erra. *I can do nothing; I would be struggling futilely against fate.*

Now he arose from his bed, wrapped his simple cloak around him, and then advanced to the pilot's console of his ship. For one long moment, he paused in thought, and then he began re-programing the automatic pilot. His ship had been fully provisioned for the journey. Outside the spiral tunnel of dim rainbows suddenly dissolved into chaos then reformed in a different direction. He had reset the course for the Quzrada, on a course directly for the Soleran system, to Erra.

"I am coming, Oh maiden of Erra, Karlac of Janus comes to help with all the skills of peace that I possess," said Karlac to himself. "To the heart of the Quzrada, to Erra, I go. May the Creator help me." He suddenly felt at peace, for the first time in weeks, he then sat and watched the rainbows streaking around him, they seemed suddenly brighter and more numerous to him.

****

## Chapter 3: Nightmares

Tiger Forrester rammed forward the throttles of his dark blue F-51 Griffin fighter, christened again Vivacious Veronica, and it rocketed down the runway on full afterburner like two blowtorches and into the overcast night sky of Georgia. The rest of his squadron followed him, Griffin fighters first, F-15 Eagles and F-16 falcons afterward, as they scrambled the squadron to support two Griffin fighters on Night Combat Air Patrol or NiCAP, already in the sky and moving to engage a reported two alien craft.

"Come on you wolverines! We rule the Night!" he yelled. "Do you copy?"

"Roger Squadron leader! We copy came a chorus of voices, some enthusiastic, some thin with fear.

"I want standard wing dispersal, as we move to support Nighthawk flight! Look sharp and get kills!"

They soon were up above the overcast and under the dome of stars and Tiger slid back his goggles to use his own night vision; he scanned the cockpit, its lights turned low to keep his eyes acute. He felt safer up above the clouds. Civilians were now shooting at anything in the sky over Georgia at night and had already damaged two fighters. He had his wrist mounted US Army magnetometer on his arm cast, It was the best that could be gotten on short notice, and he glanced at its dial. He had had to dial down its sensitivity due to the electronic interference level from the Griffin's mechanisms. But the Griffin was designed to have low electronic emissions, so this did not hinder him greatly. However, in the older planes, it rendered the Army magnetometers almost useless.

"This is Nighthawk! Bogey! Bogey! Sector 8 bearing 5 niner!" came a yell over the radio. "Tiger instantly rolled his fighter to bring it on a course to intercept. He was arming his guns and missiles. His wingman, Captain Gerald 'Irish' O'Malley, an older but legendary pilot, pulled out of retirement, followed him closely.

Suddenly a brilliant electric blue flash, followed by the orange of burning jet fuel lit up the clouds below them.

"Nighthawk! Nighthawk! This is Tiger please advise!"

"They got Shark! Repeat, they got Shark!   Come quickly.." Another brilliant blue flash lit up the sky as Tiger and Irish went to full afterburner. Suddenly Tiger's magnetometer began to beep.

"Irish I got magneto alert. Start Thatch Weave!"   Tiger began to go zigzag across the sky followed by his wingman.  It was an old fighter technique from the Second World War in the Pacific, intended for American planes to fight the much more maneuverable Japanese Zero.  The magnetometer began flashing brightly. Suddenly Tiger noted a small dull shape in his peripheral vision, silhouetted against the starlit clouds, and with lighting reflexes, pulled his Griffin into a split-S and then rolled out to meet it.  He could feel the gravity adjustment gear powering up as he first dove then rolled out.  The alien was now right below and ahead of them, but Irish had ended up in front of him.   It was a Scarab A type with a manta ray shape, the type used for abductions and mutilations.  Suddenly Irish opened up ahead of him with two Aram missiles with magneto-proximity warheads and the craft darted out of their way, triggering the magneto warheads to explode in a two sharp orange explosions.  Tiger heard shrapnel pieces hitting his plane.  Irish was now opening up with his cannon, a stream of blue tracers cutting across the dark clouds. Then, by instinct Tiger did a snap roll to confuse any sensor-lock that was forming on his plane,  as the alien darted to the side to avoid the stream of tracers, and for one golden second, the alien was right in front of him. Tiger instantly pressed every fire control button on his stick and the cannon fired, and Sidewinders and AMRAMs tore off his wings with blinding light emitting twin streams of blue tracers and rocket exhaust.  Then the whole sky erupted into a brilliant blue flash followed by the flare of burning blue-white magnesium-aluminum as the hull of the alien craft ignited and it fell in a stream of blue fire into the clouds below, lighting them as it fell. Tiger looked away to try to preserve his night vision.  The flare of light disappeared into the clouds and was then followed by a brilliant white flash, lighting up the clouds from below.

"Bogey Down! Confirm Bogey Down!" yelled Tiger.  "Irish do you copy on that?" he then asked.  Silence followed as he realized his wingman had also fallen.  He wheeled his plane around and noted the black trail of smoke against the dull white clouds below him. He saw no parachute. Tiger sadly banked his plane to rejoin the rest of the squadron that was now swarming in from every direction. The magnetometer was now clear.

"Tower, confirm bogey down, but lost Irish," Tiger said tersely.

This is tower, we confirm, the other bogey has departed straight up.

"Continuing NiCAP.," said Tiger.

****

After a night of battle in the skies over Washington, the Sun rose in a beautiful dawn. Semjase rose and she and Sanjeed checked on Vikor's condition which continued to improve. The swelling on his face had gone down and he seemed to be regaining his strength. He wanted another cheeseburger and fries for breakfast but Sanjeed made him eat a medical porridge instead. Semjase, feeling restless at the resulting bickering between Sanjeed and Vikor, decided to go for a walk. The sky was beautiful but chilly, as she walked from behind the house to the front yard. She was suddenly aware that a police car had pulled up to the yard, and following this was an Army Humvee with military personnel in it that was now coming down the street towards the house. Two policemen got out of the car, one with an M-16, and were looking at her from a distance of about 100 yards. She froze in fear. The Humvee rolled up into the driveway after the police car and out sprung two men in fatigues and fatigue hats, followed by a German Shepherd dog. The German Shepard looked at her and began barking furiously. Semjase read its thoughts and realized to her astonishment that it was trained to recognize non-humans by scent and sound, and it had recognized her as an extraterrestrial. She turned and ran as fast as she could back to the shed where Sanjeed and Vikor were. The men were yelling at her but did not follow her. She had her Deathstar out in her hand and set it for stun as she ran, she could hear the dog barking furiously but they did not turn it loose. *It is too valuable to risk,* she realized. She heard sirens and sensed military units with armor racing to the scene. She mentally alerted Sanjeed to secure his patient and prepare to take off in the Vikhelm spacecraft. Vikor was still too weak to teleport, and besides their ship was on the other side of the planet in orbit.

She plunged through the hatchway of the craft and shut the hatch behind her, before jumping into the pilot's seat of the craft. She had been studying the controls in the long hours spent waiting for Vikor to get well. *Thank the Gods*, she thought. Sanjeed had given Vikor a sedative, had strapped him to the bed and now was strapping himself into the seat beside her. She waved her hands over the controls, the craft power plant activated and the magneto-plasma reactor whined to life and stabilized. She sensed that military armored vehicles with heavy automatic guns had arrived outside on the street and she jammed the gravity drive into full engagement. She grabbed the single control stick and pulled it back as far as it would go. The craft responded instantly, and rose swiftly, plowing right the roof and into the blue morning sky, pulling fragments of the roof behind it in its gravity wake. Suddenly the hull rang with the impact of bullets as she saw in the view screen, police and army troops opening fire on the craft as it darted up into the sky, now scattering broken pieces of wood and roof shingles everywhere. Tracers from quad mounted 50 caliber machine guns mounted in turrets on the two light armored vehicles in the streets flew around the ship as she now dived below the trees and flew as fast as she could over the surface of the Potomac river. An Apache helicopter appeared and began to pursue her ship, firing wildly as she zigged and zagged. Geysers of water churned up by the heavy slugs flew upwards all around the ship as it skimmed the river surface. Semjase was frantically darting the ship this way and that as she desperately tried to outguess the helicopter gunner. Finally, she made it put out on a burst of blinding speed by instinct and breathed a sigh of relief as the helicopter dropped far behind. *I must fly low along the river so their radar cannot gain a lock on us!*

"We have to fly away from the Capitol! They have all their defenses there!" shouted Sanjeed from the seat beside her.

"I am flying way from the city, but we have to stay low to avoid their sensors!" she yelled back.

She hoped against hope that she had chosen the right path on the river but then as she turned a bend in the river, he saw a sight that filled her with terror.

Three Griffin fighters were now swooping down out of the sky and flying down the river directly at her ship, and she now realized that in her confused evasion of the helicopter she was not going down the river toward the sea, as she had supposed, but flying straight up the river to the hornet's nest of air defenses around Washington DC. She instantly darted the ship to the side in time to evade a missile launched by one of the fighters. *Thank god this Vikhelm ship is built for speed and maneuver,* she heard herself exclaim mentally. She then pressed on in a burst of speed and flew right under the three fighter planes, which were diving at high speed. She saw them instantly pull Pugchacov Cobras maneuvers, stopping in mid-air, and thrust vectoring into flips and the resuming their pursuit of her ship. She debated trying to operate the weapons on the craft, but the idea filled her with unbearable sorrow so she abandoned it and diverted all power to flight systems.

More fighters were diving down on her, so she gave a burst of speed, as canon shells began to rain down on them, throwing up splashes of water all around them. She was now flying madly under the bridges over the Potomac as she flew the ship madly only a yard above the water. They were in deep gravity-ground-effect, hauling tons of river water along behind them in a wave as the power plant strained. She then yanked the stick back.

**\*\*\*\***

In the river entrance parking lot of the Pentagon, General Burnham was surrounded by staff and bodyguards as watched General Prescott who was showing him new pieces of equipment that were being deployed on operation Dragnet. Burnham was particularly pleased by the dummy 50 caliber cartridges he was being shown with the magneto-proximity fuses. The fuses were already proving to be effective in combat everywhere they were being issued. Prescott had also shown him a new quad-mounted 50 caliber turret on a Light Armored Vehicle or LAV. The standard quad mounts had been a manned turret on the Armored Personal Carrier or

141

APC; but since these vehicles were tracked, they tore up the roads and were slow. The manned turret had also been so tall the quad mount could not squeeze under some overpasses. The new LAV mounted one was lower in a sleek teardrop remote turret, a design derived from the WW II Black Widow, and the LAV had six wheels instead of tracks and was much faster on roads.

"We also have this new lightweight automatic 20 mm cannon we are just starting to deploy, General," said Prescott happily pointing to a slim automatic cannon on a table, with metal belts of dummy 20 mm cannon shells beside it. "It's called a Webber Machine-rifle, it's a new British design and uses gas dynamic rifling in the gun barrel, similar to an air bearing. The result is a dramatic loss in barrel friction and a vast increase in muzzle velocity. This means the gun is lighter..." Suddenly sirens were blaring and the air was filled with the thunder of automatic cannon fire. Both Burnham and Prescott, and everyone else, whirled their heads to see a flying saucer, pursued by three Griffin fighters on full afterburner, skimming the Potomac River. Women were screaming, men were cursing, everyone dove for the pavement and the quad 50's on the LAVs suddenly swung around to track the saucer, uselessly, it turned out since they were unloaded.

Prescott and Burnham watched in astonishment as the saucer emerged from under a bridge over the Potomac and flew straight up into the blue sky, pursued by the fighters. Burnham was grinning broadly. "THAT'S WHAT I LIKE TO SEE!" he yelled.

****

"Mother Mary help us!" Semjase cried out as they shot straight up into the blue sky and Griffin jet fighters turned rapidly, the g-forces on the pilots, neutralized by electronic anti-gravity in their cockpits. She found herself, flying straight up into the mass of them. Several of them opened fire, tracer bullets sprayed all around them, but miraculously the shells missed them and the fighters scattered in seeming confusion to avoid collisions and fratricide. She then leveled off at high altitude and put the craft into as much speed as possible to the west, and finally outran the fighter planes. She rose to high altitude out of gravity ground effect so

142

she could fly faster even faster to the West, not knowing what else to do. An alarm went off indicating that the gravitic inductors were overheating! She looked over at Sanjeed. He had fainted!

They flew on at top speed for an hour with high-speed fighters at high altitude giving chase, but she outran them still darting from side to side to break sensor locks. She flew this way and that, but the ships systems had overheated due to all the maneuvering and she did not dare push them harder to escape into space. Instead, she skimmed the top of the atmosphere trying to take maximum advantage of aerodynamics to keep the ship aloft and let the ship's gravitics return to normal temperatures. They fell in temperature, back to the normal range as she watched desperately. Finally, they neared the Pacific coast and she began to prepare to give another burst of power and fly into space. But the ship was suddenly shaken by a strong electromagnetic pulse, then another. Semjase looked in desperation as many of the ships systems began shutting down.

"OH GOD HELP US!" she cried out as the ship began a free fall into the dark Earth below. The ship was dark now and began to tumble. She was pressed against the straps of the seat as the ship fell "Help me Help me!" she screamed. She was working the control stick desperately and switched all power to flight.

Suddenly several lights on the ship came back on and the control panel regained life. The view screen came back on and showed the star-lit landscape below rising up to meet them. Desperately she grabbed the control stick and tried to regain control of the ship. Sluggishly the ship responded and she slowed its decent. Its landing gear would not deploy. She looked around fearfully and found a forested area on the slopes of a small mountain, she managed to guide the ship into the forest over a small brook and managed to bring the ship in without its landing gear down and plop in with a gentle thud, onto the ground under some trees. She then shut down the ship's drive systems, or what was left of them. She smelled overheated power systems and frantically made sure all the ship's power systems were turned off as well. She then wept with relief. Finally, she wiped her face with her hands and trembling she unstrapped herself and got out of her seat to check on Sanjeed. He was still unconscious, and Vikor was still obviously sedated and strapped to his bed. She then stumbled across the tilted floor of the craft to the hatch. She paused and carefully turned off all the lights in the ship before opening the hatch. The smell of forest greeted her and she drew strength from it. She could see the stars through the trees above them. She carefully stepped out and saw the lights of a small city many miles away. She walked carefully over to the small brook and felt the water with her hands, then wiped her face with her wet hands.

"Thank you," she said, realizing that by accident they had put down in an isolated area, yet close enough to civilization that they could get food and other supplies if they needed them. She took stock of their situation: Sanjeed had told her that they could not teleport Vikor out until he grew stronger, and she knew the longer she and Sanjeed stayed on Erra the more likely it was that the Samar or Unash would detect their Pleiadian thought patterns.

"Here we are then," she said aloud, "but we cannot stay"

**\*\*\*\***

The President, surrounded by secret service men in silver sunglasses, stood resplendent and confident, in the hospital room with Cassandra and Pamela. Cassandra stood looking solemn; Pamela sat likewise, but with a faint smile in her wheelchair. The visit had been arranged on only twenty minuet's notice. Cassandra and Pamela had barely time to comb their hair and put on makeup - but they had done it effectively. Cassandra recognized that this was being done to boost public morale, after the first fight in Arlington and the saucer escaping the fighters the other day. She understood it and was trying to help carry it off.

"It is my honor, to present you both, the Medal of Freedom, for your courageous roles in ending the UFO Cover-up and saving humanity from destruction, he leaned down and placed the bronze medal on a red, white and blue ribbon around Pamela's blonde head, with her now shortened hairstyle. She looked up tearfully and said thank you. The president then turned to Cassandra, who was trembling helplessly and screaming mentally, *NO, NO, I Can't!* and whose face was melting into tears. The President began to put the ribbon over her trembling head when suddenly a grim-faced man stepped through the doorway like a dark wraith, walked swiftly up to the President and whispered something in his ear. Cassandra, fighting the impulse to refuse the medal and run away down the hall screaming, was suddenly seized by an icy calmness as she watched the President's smile vanish as he absorbed the whispered message.

Cassandra watched the President's face in front of hers grow pale like a dead man's. He seemed to shrink in front of her eyes. Her eyes now saw, a foot away, instead of happy confidence and affection, of the previous moment, despair. Despair as deep and black as she had ever seen in a man's eyes. The President seemed paralyzed now, holding the ribbon above her head. He was trembling. His secret service men saw this and began to move towards him. Cassandra suddenly reached up and pulled his trembling hands bearing the ribbon down over her raven-haired head.

"Mister President, "she heard herself say, "it will be OK, thank-you. I am a little shaky now, but I am going to get well soon, and I am going to help you win this war." she heard herself say with a trembling voice gaining strength. "Pam's going to prance out of here in heels and cross Key Bridge, and I am going to be reading the news again and testifying before Congress." Her voice trembled despite her best efforts to keep it steady. She nodded tearfully and found herself smiling. The president looked dazed. "We will be reporting on our victories from the front lines!" *Yes! I can speak this into being!*

"We are going to help you win this war I started," she said firmly. "You just watch us," he smiled faintly in a confused way at this and nodded. Medal emplaced around her neck, he stepped back, and smiled weakly.

"I am sorry, but something has come up, and I have to cut this ceremony short, but we will do this right in the Rose Garden when you both check out of here!" he paused "Right?" said the President with sudden confidence again.

"Yes, Mister President!" Both Cassandra and Pamela said in eerie unison. The President stepped back, some pictures were taken with everyone managing brave smiles, and he looked at both Pam and Cassie and seemed to gain strength from them. With that, he turned, looking haunted and left wordlessly with his entourage following him. A crowd of nurses, guards, and doctors followed the President and his party down the hall, many pausing to look in at Cassandra and Pamela with their new shiny medals. Pamela beamed at them; Cassandra looked at them with as brave a face as she could muster.

*Yes, I started this war. Their eyes tell me I started it, thought Cassandra. I might as well own it!* But another voice said to her, *No not yet! It is not time yet!* And this caused her to be seized with doubt. One foot on the brake pedal, one foot on the brakes inside me! "Ahh!" she cried in mental anguish.

Finally, the hospital hall calmed, and Pamela shut the door. Cassandra resumed her normal station, staring out the window, forlornly.  She turned and helped Pamela, who was now looking exhausted, back into her bed from her wheelchair. Then Cassandra went and stood at the window again.

"The President just got some really bad news. Did you see that?" commented Pamela resuming her studies of calculus.

"Yes, the way he looked, we may have just lost the war..." said Cassandra. "What do think he was told?" Cassandra asked.

"The Greys may have sent a big space fleet... who knows. Ignorance is bliss for me right now..." said Pamela turning on her electronic tablet and donning her reading glasses. "When I need to know, I'll know..."

Cassandra turned stared out the window for a long time.

"Did I really start this war Pammy?"  asked Cassandra, as she stared out the window.

"I helped you, remember that? This is my war too," said Pamela, with a slight tone of irritation.

"Forget all the details, did I start this war?" asked Cassandra turning to Pamela.

"No, the Greys started it by coming here and they can end this war anytime they want. They can go back to their shithole of a home star system and leave us alone! So you didn't start the war. It simply comes under the category of "shit happens in the Cosmos. I didn't create the Sepulveda asteroid either, as some people at NBC have claimed."

"Oh," said Cassandra sounding dejected.

"Alright! If it will make you feel better, Cassie, you did start the war. You pulled the trigger on it!" said Pamela with sudden exasperation. "The gun was loaded and pointing in the right direction, the Mexican standoff was all there waiting for one shot, and you fired it! There, is that better?" said Pamela with amused annoyance.

Cassandra was silent but stood taller by the window looking out of it.

"You take your place in American history," continued Pamela, "right beside George Washington, who started the last French and Indian war, called historically the Seven Year's war, with skirmishes out in the wilderness near Pittsburg, this skirmish mushroomed into a world war with land and naval battles in every ocean and major landmass on Earth, and that saw Britain and Prussia defeat France. Austria, Spain, and Britain became the world's greatest empire. Except George Washington then defeated the British in the next big war, which we call the Revolutionary War."

"Do you think he ever felt guilty about starting the Seven Year's War?" asked Cassandra with her voice trembling, she saw tears streaming down her face in her reflection on the window. She kept her face hidden from Pamela. "So many people got killed." Cassie wiped her face.

"No, George Washington was a realist." He knew war on the frontier was inevitable." said Pamela sadly. "I don't have to be a historian to know this. It's obvious from his conduct afterward." Pamela paused. "You know, Cassie, the real 64,000 dollar question here is not about how the war with the Greys started, it's how to win it," added Pamela, after some thought.

"I learned in my online calculus course," she continued, "that when a number is a square root of a negative number, it's called imaginary. And when a number is partly real and partly imaginary, it's called a complex number. And that is all of life. Life is a complex number, Cassie, it's partly real, what we know, and partly imaginary, what we believe. So George's life was complex," said Pamela, "your's is too."

"George knew he had screwed up and provided the start of a world war," continued Pamela now staring at Cassandra's back intently. "But he also had this feeling of destiny, a feeling he was going to do some great thing in his life." Pamela held up her hands with her index finger raised on each. "So really, that is our situation, and imagination, that is our destiny..."

"Did George Washington lose any sleep over it?" asked Cassandra. "Being blamed for starting for Seven years war, I mean?  People must have blamed him," asked Cassandra, seemingly ignoring Pamela's last statements.

"No, Washington knew the French, Indians and British, and their Colonists were on a collision course. His role in starting it he seemed to consider it as just a learning experience in the school of war. He put on his big britches after that! He reportedly considered if he could start world war single-handed he must truly be a person of destiny!  He simply used the Seven Years War as a school of generalship for the revolution later. The only people who were mad at him were the British army, who considered him an incompetent fool.  As it turns out this was a particularly useful fiction for him to cultivate! It enabled him to win the revolution later!"

"So he owned up to it?" asked Cassandra turning around to face Pamela with a brave smile. "Did he put it on his business cards?"

"Yes! yelled Pamela.  "He used the hashtag '**I started this war!**' on all his tweets!  His attitude was: 'if the fool shits, wear it, remember that joke?" said Pamela with a laugh; that had been their private joke during the Sepulveda asteroid crisis. "It was either take on the world war Washington started as a project or commit suicide! He didn't commit suicide, no he instead committed himself to winning the war he started.  He then kicked the French and then later the British's asses."

"So he said, yes, I started this war! And I am going to damn well finish it!" said Cassandra with a flourish.

"Yes, he achieved a level of comfort with his role in history; history being all about gore and destruction," said Pamela.

Washington knew by the way, as the result of the French and Indian War, that the British Army could be defeated; he had seen the British Army routed at Braddock's Defeat. He and the other founding fathers also knew that the British supply line across the Atlantic, which was 3000 miles long, and very stormy, would prevent the British from effectively supplying their troops in America in the event of a war. And they learned something else from the French and Indian war; they learned the British had powerful enemies in Europe who would join any war that broke out in America and fight against the British, hence their real hope they could win the war. "Pamela got a faraway look in her eye as she said this.

"Yes," said Cassandra standing taller and then resuming her quiet stare out the window, taking up once again the endless vigil , looking for something she could only guess. "So Washington started the Seven Years War and he also learned from that that they could win the War of Independence from Britain?"

"Yes, and I have to write all this up for one of my professors named Henderson at Annapolis! Because we can win the war against the aliens the same way..." said Pamela pulling out her laptop.

"It's late august, and the leaves are turning colors. Isn't it early for that to be happening?" said Cassandra in puzzlement. *Cassandra Washington!* she thought, picturing herself in a white wig. *General of the Armies!*

****

"Congratulations General Prescott!" said General Burnham, rising from behind his desk clapping Prescott on the shoulder "You flushed out some aliens and gave everyone in DC an airshow to boot! Did you realize people got out of their cars and cheered our jets flying over! This was a big morale booster! Especially, since we knocked down two saucers last night!"

"They probably would have gotten this one but they used up all their magneto-proximity fused ammunition last night. They were flying with just straight tracer and explosives this morning," said Prescott

"But my people were just on their toes," said Prescott, "I will say that!" He was leaning back in his chair in Burnham's bunker office. "Space command says the ship was brought down in Southern Oregon and crashed in the woods. There trying to find the wreckage with ground teams now. So I can say Operation Dragnet has been a success in its first week, and we've had no casualties, civilian or military. "

"Ok, now I want you to hand off Dragnet to General Rawlings out of Fort Meade. You are obviously my Tiger team here, so I am re-tasking you to be my eyes and ears on Operation Royal Flush, "said Burnham returning to his chair.

"Yes General, but begging the General's pardon, what is Operation Royal Flush?" asked Prescott.

"The Air Force has been tasked to prepare for a Low Earth orbit surge, to seize control of near-Earth space, General Prescott. And I want you to ride General Arnold's and Standish's asses to see that it comes off on schedule and is successful. The operational kickoff is in two weeks."

"But General Sir, the Greys own space now, and we have not technically even gained air superiority," said Prescott.

"That's right General, and that means the Greys will have to fight the Air Force at two levels, in the atmosphere, and in low Earth Orbit, and we have now got a 10 to one advantage in the atmosphere."

"With respect General, I thought the plan was to gain air superiority first, then build into space from that?"

"Yes, but the plan has changed. Why the plan has changed will become apparent in a few months," said General Burnham looking suddenly grim. "Right now we have them running with their pants down around their ankles, and we are going to keep them running that way. I remember reading a report on past Unash behavior, and at one time the US was

150

zapping Unash ships with radar and making them crash, and it took the Greys two years to figure what we were doing and fix it so we couldn't do it anymore. So they are smart and methodical but appear to be slow on their feet. I just need a year of such behavior and we'll be on the Moon and end this thing."

**\*\*\*\***

They stood in the main meeting room of the Samar quarters. Zomal and his second in command sat at a conference table with Hontal. Several other officers also sat down in splendid dark uniforms. How much did the battle stars and armor gleam that day?

"So the Unash have not subjugated the Errans at all," began Zomal, "in all this time. The Errans have instead grown stronger. They have advanced in power, and even captured some of the technology of the Unash and learned how to use it. Basically, the recent crisis began with the Unash strategy to subjugate Erra by cultivating a group of traitors within the government of the first nation of Erra, called America. *Leave it to the Unash to try to affect by treachery what they should have done by brute force and power,* thought Hontal with contempt. *They could have taken Erra sixty years ago in one night!*

Zomal continued, "but this plot using the traitors, was discovered by two women, and then broken up by loyal military forces." Zomal flashed a picture of Cassandra Chen and Pamela Monroe up on the view screen." The women were both very brave! Many attempts were made on their lives! The golden haired one was sorely wounded in the battle leading a charge of young cadets!"

Hontal looked at the two women, both were beautiful and well dressed in the type of bright, form-fitting clothing the Erran women obviously favored. Pamela Monroe looked strikingly like the women Tatiana that he had been with the night before, but he kept his amazement hidden. *The planet must thrive with women who look like her,* he thought, *we should seize it, not destroy it!* The two women, posing in front of the US capitol smiling, baffled him. In Samaran culture, women wore dark colors, kept covered up in long dresses, were expected to stay at home, keep house and bear sons for the wars. Daughters were valued because they could

151

bear sons at a later date. Though occasionally women of the aristocracy could be seen in public and at banquettes, Samaran public life was very much a man's world.

Zomal flashed another image of Casandra Chen, looking serious and brave, upon the view screen. Her dark oriental eyes bewitched him. Such eyes were unusual in the Archmetia, and rarely seen among the Samar. He mentally shook himself, *Do not look on her with desire or admiration, this witch has caused us a near disaster here! But she looks like the warrior queen Xenoba!*

"So" Zomal continued, now with a smile on his face. "There was then A GREAT BATTLE!"

*Yes, the Battle!* thought Hontal, no great account by a Samar would be complete without a report of the battle. "In the very Capitol between the traitors supporting the Monchkini who attacked by treachery, and the true sons of Erra, who gathered themselves and fought against them. There was a truly great battle in the night and the next morning! We Samar watched this battle with brave hearts on the Erran broadcasts! We all began to shout when the brave Errans counterattacked against the traitors, again and again, with fire and sword! Each time the Errans were thrown back with great loss, but then pressing their attacks! They counted their lives as water! I must confess we poured ale, as we watched and toasted the brave Errans as they pressed their attacks over the bridges in the city. Despite ourselves, we toasted them, for they fought for their people, whereas the traitor slaves of the Monchkini fought for gold. But we all wondered, where are the Monchkini? Why do they not attack now to help their slaves on Erra? For the battle turned on a swords edge! So we Samar poured ale and drank as we watched the battle and shouted at each attack and counterattack! Many men drew their swords and struck the table with them! We all made wagers in gold on this table as we watched, and every man placed wagers for the Errans because our hearts were stirred by their brave attacks!" continued Zomal. But the wretched Monchkini were afraid! Instead of attacking the Errans that night they merely flew about over the Capitol above the clouds, one aircraft of the Errans came up and shot up one of their ships, and the Monchkini then fled disgracefully! They fled like beaten dogs crying with

152

their tails between their legs!" laughed Zomal bitterly. Hontal looked around the room as the other Samaran officers looked on in bitter merriment and nodded assent. "So, we brave Samar cursed the Monchkini for their cowardly retreat! We cursed them by the gods Alkmar and by Hontal! Many brave Samar then stood in this room that night and cried out 'Brave commander! Give us spaceships! Send us now to Erra and we will turn the tide of battle! We will fight the brave Errans sword to sword! But our brave commander Koton forbade it. "He said, NO! No Samaran blood shall be mixed this night with the cowardly piss of Monchkini! This is their defeat! Let this cowardly disgrace of the dickless Monchkini cling to them like the contents of their bladders! Let their piss-stained pants be their banner this night! He said this to all of us! In this very room, by the name of Alkmar, he said this before all of us!" Zomal turned and gestured to his other officers, who eagerly nodded their assent. Hontal was shocked at this description and was now in a rage at the cowardly conduct of the Monchkini. *We hired them for much gold! Instead of taking Erra at a rush of armed strength many years ago, they chose to take Erra by stealth and treachery! Then like hired dagger men they abandon their own slaves! Now I know why you chose to die in battle on Erra brave Koton, rather than give an account of this disgraceful episode! No wonder no report of this occurrence in the Quzrada has reached the Palace! Who could report it without fear? Disgrace and utter dishonor!* Hontal shook himself. *Much fine gold, wasted!*

Zomal returned eagerly to the account of the battle.

"The gold-haired woman, she fell sorely wounded in the battle at the Capitol, she fell leading a victorious attack of the brave Errans! So they bore her away to safety, though she was near death. *Oh no!* thought Hontal and clutched his sword's hilt. *She looks so much like Tatiana . Do not tell me she has died!*

"The leaders of traitors fled and left their troops leaderless; the loyal Errans put all of them to death! But the brave woman Cassandra was then captured by the traitors at the Capitol by treachery, those who were slaves to the Unash. They retreated and took her to their secret base!"

*"Oh no! She was dishonored by these slaves!"*

153

"They put her to torture there and forced her to make a broadcast from the secret base, which was no longer a secret by then, but surrounded by the Erran forces! "The Americans gave the Unash an ultimatum, but the traitors were hoping to buy time by this woman's speech in order for the Unash to rescue them with a great attack at the end of the deadline. The Unash did plan a large attack, but their plans were upset by this same woman! For she revealed their secret plans by the very speech they forced her to make!"

*"So she was unbroken though tortured! She defied them! Huzzah!"*

"Then there was another great battle at the fortress! Brave men of war then rescued the dark haired one from the fortress, even as the Errans, counting their lives as water, pressed the attack and overran the fortress. The Unash and the human traitors on their side fought very hard in the tunnels, but alas, the brave Erran men of war overwhelmed them. The Monchkini were much upset in their plans by the rapidity and boldness of the Erran attack! Though many of the Unash fought bravely that day, their plans were broken by the woman's speech, which they forced her to make, which revealed to the Errans that the attack was coming! So she got revenge on them for their cruelty to her! For the Unash and their slaves had bragged to her before her speech! They revealed everything to her because she bewitched them, though she was their captive, and then by secret code words in her speech, she then laid before all the Errans the plans of the Monchkini and their slaves! So the Monchkini and their slaves were undone by this woman in their own stratagem!"

*Huzzah!* Thought Hontal, *Such a tale of battle and bravery and beautiful women!*

"So there was a great battle at the formerly secret fortress in a mountain, when the Errans attacked suddenly, before the deadline they had been given, because they now saw clearly the treachery of the Unash. The Unash launched a great attack on their base here to try to rescue the fortress, but it was too little and too late and at half the strength it should have been. So many brave of the bravest Unash and their ships were wasted in the skies over the fortress and over the Capitol. For the Unash unwisely divided their forces! So it was all for naught. What the

Monchkini lost by their cowardice in the battle at the Capitol, they could not make up for by bravery at the mountain fortress. But those two women, were the real cause of their disaster, that and the bravery of the brave sons of Erra who followed them and counted their lives as drops of water! So it was by the lips of a beautiful dark haired woman who was as brave as Queen Xenoba, and by brave battles that the treachery of the Unash was undone and made a disgraceful disaster..."

"By the Gods, such a tale of war is this! Treason discovered by brave women, great attacks pressed bravely! Wiley stratagems of war undone by a brave woman! Bold rescues! Battles in earth and sky!" exclaimed Hontal. "A tale worthy of a great song were these people not our enemies!"

Zomal nodded with a slight smile.

"It is a sorry day when one admires one's enemies and despises one's allies," said Zomal. "But that is the day that we saw here." He continued. "To make matters worse, a squadron of the Anak lay in wait for the Unash and destroyed many more of them as they retreated into space after the battle at the fortress, to return to the Moon base. So the losses were very grievous, only one in three ships that had departed for Erra returned." Zomal continued. "Then said Koton, our brave and honorable commander, to me and my fellow officers here, after the battles had been finished and the losses counted. He said 'by the gods, a more perfect, disgraceful, disaster I have never seen, nor heard of in all our history, as if a crowd of fools had attempted to build a temple and had produced only a heap of flaming shit...'"

The other officers nodded in assent, some even chuckled.

"So the whole episode was a disaster brought about by these two women!" said Zomal laughing. His face then adopted a guarded look.

"This was, in fact, a disaster, and after this we had a visit from Bekar of Batelgeen so he could consult with Sadok Sar of the Unash, as to what was to be done, and he had with him some forces of the Belletrans, and they had Nor of Bellatrix with them, a high lady of that place. Koton, our commander, had some dispute with Bekar and this Beletran woman, and

155

was very displeased with them and he felt they had treated him with dishonor. It was some private matter." Zomal looked away uneasily after speaking about this.

"After Bekar and the Beletran  lady conferred with The Unash, they left the system. But Koton was angry.  He told me he wanted to die in battle to cleanse the stain on his honor, and of this whole episode on Erra, and so he did. For he said 'how can I report this thing to the Palace, should they ask me about it?' For this reason, Koton went to Erra to command the island base we had there. It was but a small base.  Sadok Sar told Koton we should evacuate the base. But Koton said it was shameful to retreat before the Errans and so said he would stay there with the garrison until it was relieved.  He made Sadok Sar swear an oath that the base would be sustained."

"Who is Nor of Belatrix?" asked Hontal. Remembering the woman's voice overheard shouting orders in subspace, during a battle.

"She is a fair high maiden of the house of Belatrix and allied with Bekar," said Zomal warily. "I know nothing of this business.  Nothing. She acts and dresses as a knight of the realm and commanded several ships here.  I know nothing else except she grievously insulted our commander.  You must ask Bekar for details of this shameful matter. "Zomal then changed the subject. He dismissed his men from the room.  When they had left, he lowered his voice and spoke carefully.

Also, your man Gamal of the red hair, he has spent two nights with the Erran women Amber. The Unash own these women and only provide them to us as a courtesy. One night's war custom is not considered a problem, but more than that and the chances are that the woman could be gotten with child." Zomal eyes narrowed and his voice became a hiss. "If this occurs the Unash take the woman away and then rip her child out of her, to study.   So Gamal must not see the woman again. We take this precaution for the women's sake. "Hontal felt sick at this statement. " The Monchkini seem to take pleasure in having this happen, "continued Zomal grimly, "We have said nothing about the woman remaining with him, out of courtesy to you. But she must be sent back, now, for her sake."

"I am sorry I gave him permission because he lost two sons at Umax. He is a brave man of war, veteran of many battles," said Hontal with embarrassment. "I thought to cheer his heart. But I will see to it that the woman is sent back."

"I must show you something else, that illustrates this situation here now since the crisis began three months ago, "said Zomal grimly. "He pulled a case from its place on the floor, pulled two cylindrical objects from the case. Both were cut away to expose their interiors.

"The Errans have sent us and the Unash these messages." continued Zomal. Hontal took one of the objects and examined it. Inside were several fine and intricate mechanisms and a hollow sphere of bronze-like metal.

"I see no message," said Hontal in puzzlement.

"Oh! the message is very clear," said Zomal. "The bronze metal is meant to represent plutonium and the plastic around it represents explosive." The humans have showered the place here with them using their rockets, thousands of them. The Unash spent much time and effort shooting at them but five or six got through anyway. Each represents an Erran nuclear weapon. "Hontal dropped the cylinder and was seized with amazement.

"Yes, the Errans can drop nuclear weapons on this place and anywhere else on this moon at any time. They do not because they fear the Unash will respond in like kind."

"But the Errans are supposed to be a primitive people without such weapons or capabilities!"

"You have obviously been given outdated reports my Lord. Did the reports the Palace provided you with mention that the Errans have landed on this moon six times in the past? Did they mention that they pounded an asteroid to pieces with very large nuclear weapons several years ago? These things I have just spoken of are kept secret among the Unash they send here, to prevent panic. But, one Unash commander I spoke with, who was wise and brave, told me: "The Errans have destroyed the asteroid, and we are next..."

157

****

Cassandra noticed some milling around in the park outside. In front of her amazed eyes suddenly a group of several hundred demonstrators lined up in the park below her window. Some of whom looked like freshly scrubbed preppies from Georgetown University  and others like they had not changed clothes or taken a bath since the Vietnam war, suddenly pulled signs out of backpacks and large shopping bags and began chanting. "STOP THE WAR! STOP THE MADNESS! CASSANDRA CHEN YOU CAN'T WIN! CASSANDRA CHEN YOU CAN'T WIN!"

*We are at war! They can't do that!* Cassandra thought in amazement.

Cassandra whirled in amazement to look at Pamela, now sitting in her wheelchair in preparation for her daily Physical therapy.  Pamela sat there in shock, her blue eyes wide as saucers.

"THOSE BASTARDS!"   yelled Cassandra and tore out of the room and down the hall. "That's against the rules!" she yelled as she marched swiftly down the hall to its end doors leading to the emergency room.

"STOP THE MADNESS! END THE WAR!" she heard the chorus of voices yelling just outside the door to the parking lot. Nurses and doctors were rushing around; security guards were hurrying down the hall after her. Behind them, Pamela was rolling along in her wheelchair. *My troops are coming*, thought Cassandra. She kicked open the door and stood face to face with twenty demonstrators and a man in a business suit with a megaphone. At her appearance, the demonstrators abruptly fell into stunned silence. She walked up to the man with the megaphone and grabbed it from his hands as he stood in astonishment, she recognized him. It was senator Tunney of Massachusetts, a noted critic of the war.

YOU WANT PEACE? she yelled out of the megaphone at the demonstrators I'LL SHOW WHAT PEACE WITH THE GREYS IS LIKE!! With that she threw down the megaphone behind her, shattering it, and frantically pulled off her white shirt and then as the crowd stood stunned. She quickly pulled off her tee shirt and bra and stood topless before them.

158

She then whirled and lifted her long black hair above her head with her now bare skinny arms still with bandages on her fingertips and showed them all her scarred back. Pamela, her face a mask of rage, came bursting out of the hospital door with security guards and MPs following her. Cassandra heard women scream in horror at her back. Cassandra whirled back to face the demonstrators, glaring at them in hatred. Many of them looked horrified, several women were crying and screaming and backing away, the Senator looked ashen and stunned.

"THAT'S WHAT PEACE WITH THE GREYS WILL MEAN!!!! YOU STUPID SHITS! She screamed, her voice becoming raw and tears pouring down her cheeks. LOOK AT ME AND PAMMY YOU IDIOTS! WE DID THIS TO SAVE YOUR WRETCHED, COWARDLY ASSES! A doctor ran up with a blanket and wrapped it around her, strong arms then wrapped around her and dragged her screaming and crying back into the hospital as police cars came into the parking lot with sirens wailing. An Armored Personnel Carrier with troops in combat gear riding on it suddenly came roaring around the hospital corner, followed by an APC carrying a full rack of sidewinder antiaircraft missiles, causing the demonstrators to break and run screaming.

"NO! NO! LET ME DEBATE THEM!" Cassandra was wailing as they took her back to her room, with Pamela was being pushed in her wheelchair by a security guard behind her, and was muttering obscenities all the way down the hall. Outside the riot police arrived in a chorus of sirens and flashing lights.

****

Pamela sat in her wheelchair in an office opposite a trim short doctor named Fitzgerald, with a trim greying beard, balding head, and glasses who sat behind a desk.

I am Doctor Fitzgerald, Ms. Monroe, as acting Chief of Psychiatry here I am doctor Petrosian's superior and ultimately in charge of Cassandra Chen's treatment here." He then paused and looked angrier. "Ms. Monroe, you broke the rules by which we have been allowing Ms. Chen to stay with you in the terraces, rather than in a room by herself with the other ET exposed patients. Doctor Petrosian recommended she be allowed to stay with

159

you, but I am strongly considering moving her back to the ET ward. We keep the TV off and have told the staff not to talk to her, but this does us no good if you tell her things! She found out somehow we are at war and you told her about her being held captive at Morningstar, and that makes me think she shouldn't stay with you anymore."

"There are air raids every night!" retorted Pamela. "It's obvious we are at war! We had peace demonstrators blaming her for the war! As for finding out about being captive, she suddenly stumbles out of the shower dripping wet with her scarred back and holds up her fingers with barely growing back fingernails at me! What am I supposed to tell her? That she got a tight manicure?"

"I think she should be put back in the ET ward. If we had the resources, I would want her in a room alone that was underground, "said Fitzgerald.

"Why?"

"So she could have a sense of safety and isolation, it helps some patients recover faster!"

"But that was the sort of place they rescued her from!" said Pamela in amazement.

"Well in any case she should go back to the ET exposed ward, such as it is."

"I would strongly advise you against that Doctor"

"You are not a psychiatrist Ms. Monroe. "

"Yes, I am not a psychiatrist!" said Pamela impatiently. "But I have been through similar things as Cassandra and I know that having a supportive human being around is really useful. Call me her therapy cat, if you want! I know that if she stays with me I can help her get better. She is suffering from traumatic amnesia, right? So did I. And when I was able to confront what happened to me, I got better. Besides, on the day she took the shower, she suddenly recognized that her fingernails were growing back after being ripped out and noticed the scars on her back for the first time, and that means her mind is ready to process what happened to her, in a

160

basic sense. So she suddenly recognized what she had been actually seeing for weeks, every time she had showered. That is actual progress. I don't need to be a psychiatrist to understand that, do I?"

"Alright then, but no more telling her information about the trauma she went through. As you obviously understand, she probably actually knows everything subconsciously it's just that her mind won't release the information to her consciousness. Dr. Petrosian and I think it best that she releases it to herself on her own timeframe, that she discovers these things herself." replied Fitzgerald. "Petrosian and I have dealt with a lot of political refugees in this town and many were victims of secret police prisons and torture, and many suffered from amnesia about their experiences. We have found that it very important to proceed slowly and carefully when recovering memories in these secret-police-type instances. Sometimes it's even better if the patients never remember fully what happened. These are the worst sort of cases, the secret-police cases, much worse than POW cases, in our experience. The memories themselves in such secret-police cases can induce a secondary trauma that is as bad as the actual experience, and even lead to a complete breakdown." Fitzgerald continued.

This sort of thing is not like your usual amnesia case caused by someone seeing their dog getting run over," continued Fitzgerald, where often we dose them up with sodium pentothal and let them relive and examine it to get well. No, cases of this type are of a completely different character and have to be handled differently. As I said, in some cases the patients never remember what happened and may be organically unable to do so, due to deep brain damage. I want you to understand Cassandra's case may be one of those.

"Why isn't Doctor Petrosian here? He is her doctor!" demanded Pamela.

"Because you are a former patient of his, and we thought it best that I delivered this warning. Doctor Petrosian is actually a trauma victim too, so this whole case is sort of ridiculous! I shouldn't even allow him to be treating her, but she refuses to talk to anyone else!" The doctor said with exasperation. So this is completely unorthodox and borders on the absurd!"

161

"She likes to run things," Dr. Fitzgerald. "To me, it shows she is getting better." The doctor looked at Pamela with a deep frown. *That's my Cassie! Running rings around everyone!* thought Pamela in sudden elation. *There is always a method in her absurdity!*

"Are we clear then? No information to Cassandra!" demanded Fitzgerald with finality.

"Sure, clear as crystal, doctor," said Pamela forcing herself to have a serious face. *Hah! You obviously have no idea about the people you are dealing with here! Not a clue...*Thought Pamela with a mental smirk. *You're dealing with Jade and Blondie!*

I want you to keep one thing in perspective, Ms. Monroe, and that is that your friend, while we consider her deeply traumatized, is a lot better off than most of our psychological cases. The fact that she can walk, talk and stare out a window all day, is actually much better than most of the other cases we see. This war, as a matter of fact, is producing psychological trauma causalities at a far higher rate than any previous wars this country has ever been involved in. We have people in this hospital whose bodies are crushed and whose minds are gone, and we have people whose bodies are mending nicely but whose minds may never recover. This is happening at far higher rate than even World War II, I or Vietnam.

"Why is that, do you think? Are people more fragile nowadays?"

"No, Ms. Monroe, the people are the same, it is the war that is different. The factor that makes this war different from any other war we fought, in my opinion, is despair: the absence of rational hope. Despair in the presence of mortal danger is what really gets people unhinged Ms. Monroe." He paused, seemed to be struggling with what to say next.

"I will confide in you something Ms. Monroe," he said quietly, "so will understand my motivation better in regard to your friend's treatment, and why I am letting Dr. Petrosian treat her, even though I consider it borderline unethical to let a trauma patient treat another trauma patient." He paused and looked out the window. "It's because, in the end, I don't think any of this really matters. I want you to know I consider this war a nightmare, and this is only its beginning. It's going to get much worse. Sometimes I question everything Ms. Monroe, even my own sanity sometimes." He turned to look at her with haunted eyes. "So, I wanted to give you that. It makes me less certain than normal, about what is correct and incorrect in a patient's treatment…"

"On the contrary, Dr. Fitzgerald, I think we will win this war in the end. I am extremely confident of that," said Pamela with a serene smile.

"That sounds almost delusional. Ms. Monroe," he said to her blankly and then glanced at the clock.

"Thank you doctor," she said and wheeled her chair expertly around to leave. *Am I the only person here who understands the grand cosmic strategy of this war?* thought Pamela. *We'll fix that!*

****

Cassandra had discovered that she could slip out of the room when Pamela was at physical therapy, and go to the cafeteria. She got herself some coffee, sat there and listened carefully, concentrating on every stray word. Soon three nurses came in in surgical scrubs came sat near her. Naturally, they noticed her and began talking about her. *Perfect,* she thought, carefully sipping her coffee with a blank expression. *I am such a good investigative journalist, I can even investigate myself…*

"Look it's Miss VIP.," said one, "the chick that started the war"

"That's the bitch?"

"Yeah, one broadcast out of that mountain in Colorado and the whole world gets turned upside down. Then my boyfriend and my brother and uncle get called up from the reserves and sent to Alaska. And we here in DC get free fireworks every night." *Infamy has its benefits…* thought Cassandra. *Who needs a private detective when other people tell me everything.* She had a feeling of mischievous glee.

"I thought it was some sort of parody at first when she came on television." began another voice. "I remember thinking, did the channel just flip to the comedy channel? I remember she wore a lot of weird eye makeup,"

163

"Oh, that's what did it, her eye makeup," chimed in another.

Cassandra suddenly got flashes of memory at his, of eye makeup like an Egyptian princess, of staring into a camera, with men in black combat fatigues and helmets with black cloth helmet covers, she suddenly felt ill and dizzy. She got up and began walking back to her room. Voices were calling her ... *Cassandra, Cassandra*, she was trembling. She saw a man in black fatigues and blue vest come straight up to her and point a gun right at her head. Then suddenly, she was in her room. She took up her normal place of sanctuary, standing by the window looking out into the park. Tears ran down her cheeks after a while like always. But today she wiped them away.

Cassandra was still there when Pamela returned looking tired. She wheeled into the room and a nurse helped her back into bed.

"Pammy?" asked Cassandra sweetly, when the nurse had left. She was still staring out the window. *Oh Cassie is up to something,* thought Pamela instantly as she analyzed Cassandra's tone of voice. *Go Cassie!*

"Yes, Cassie," Pamela said smiling sweetly.

"Did I, by chance, make a broadcast from Morningstar when I was being held captive there?"

"I was in a coma, when they took you to Morningstar, Cassie, the last thing I remember was storming Key Bridge with a bunch of cadets with me being armed with a microphone. The next thing I knew I woke up here and you were here too after they rescued you," said Pamela glancing up at the ceiling. *I hope to God she knows what she is doing...*

"That's certainly a really long way to say, 'I don't know...' but thank you." said Cassandra sweetly, and turned and looked at Pamela carefully. *Bingo! It's true, Pammy is telling me they are watching us and that she can't say anything! Good Pammy!* Cassandra smiled wickedly, Pamela felt a chill go through her at the sight of that smile.

"Are you OK baby?"

"Never better," said Cassandra turning back to the window.

164

Cassandra had resumed her forlorn observation out the window. Pamela pondered what to do and finally decided to simply watch Cassandra and judge her reaction to her discovery. To inform Petrosian was unthinkable. *She is investigating*, thought Pamela with sudden amusement. *She is investigating herself! And that's my Cassie! She is returning. She is zooming down the dark highway laughing, in her black information Cadillac...Like before...Please, God don't let her get in a wreck again...*

**** 

Cassandra was twisting the towel in her hands tighter and tighter and then releasing it. It dulled the pain from her back that was now becoming, after 36 hours of no pain medication, almost unbearable.

Crawford the male nurse, a swarthy fellow with a short reddish beard, arrived to change the bed sheets and towels in the room. Pamela was off at her physical therapy. Gibson was carrying a bag on the cart with his supply of sheets and towels. He smiled at her and she frowned at him.

"You're late" she hissed and handed him three Oxy-8 pain pills, which he took with a slight smile. He changed her bed sheets and Pamela's, put fresh towels in the bathroom, as Cassandra stood and stared out the window with pain gnawing at her. Finally, after she heard him connecting something to their useless TV, he left the room. She turned around and saw that Gibson had left, as they had agreed, a video disk player and several second-hand video disks bought at a thrift store. The video player was connected to the TV. Cassandra looked around, closed the door almost completely. *Can't close it completely, they'll get suspicious*, she thought. She rifled through the used video disks, opening each case and then closing it. Finally, after what seemed like an eternity, she found the last one on the bottom of the stack and opened it. It was a writable disk marked "broadcast." Cassandra, with a mischievous glee that made her forget all about her back, placed the disk with trembling hands in the machine.

*Try to keep the truth from me, you fools! Idiots!* she thought laughing mentally. "Idiots, I am running rings around you!" She then reached up and turned on the TV, keeping the volume low. She turned on the disk player. It worked! A picture appeared, she tensed. *Popcorn! I forgot to*

165

*order popcorn!* She thought gleefully. *Eyeshadow? How did I start the war with eye shadow?* She thought trying to remember precisely what the nurses had said.

It was an NBC news broadcast. *Why not CNS?* Cassandra thought indignantly. A commentator was speaking.

"Here, again, in its entirety, is Cassandra Chen's historic broadcast from the Devil's Mesa near Morningstar Colorado, which she just made a half hour ago which has caused a media firestorm around the world... She sat staring mesmerized. She suddenly found herself staring at herself on the screen.

*Oh my God, my eye makeup, I look like an outer space zombie drag queen! Why?*

"I speak on a matter of life and death for our people, life or death, now!" She heard herself say. She began to tremble, *"No, no....NO!"*

"Surrender, for resistance, is fertile," the image of her on the screen said.

"NOO!" she shrieked and burst into to tears shaking. She was running to the bathroom and opened the door, she looked at the mirror above the sink, saw her face in it and slammed her fist into it with all her might, shattering it. She frantically scooped up a shard of glass and turned on the sink and put a plug in the bottom and turned on both faucets. She filled it as she looked at herself with cold determination, in a fragment of the mirror remaining. She pushed the door shut and locked it.

"They have no patience with the human race..." she heard herself saying on the broadcast still coming from the television outside. The sink was now filled and overflowing. She gritted her teeth and pulled the shard of glass across one wrist, gasped in pain, then swapped hands and gritted her teeth again and slashed her other wrist, this time, her grip was bad so she tried again slashing it deeper frantically. Then plunged her wrists into water filled sink as her face flooded with tears. The water killed the pain in her wrists, felt almost comfortable. *So they broke me. I became a traitor...*

166

"I must say something! A note!" she gasped as she tried to lock her knees and lean into the sink to steady herself. She pulled up one bloody wrist and wrote crudely on the smooth white wall with the blood in as big of letters as could make.

"I AM SORRY, C CHEN "

The water was on the floor now and she had thrown herself off balance writing the big letters in blood on the wall. She plunged her hands into the lukewarm water in the sink again, felt the pain in her wrists diminish. Her feet slipped as she tried to lean again into the sink. She stared at her tear stained face in the fragment remaining of the mirror , gave a sad smile of determination as she  felt herself grow dizzy and dreamy.

"Yes, this is me, Cassandra Jian Chen, and I am fully recovered now…" she said to herself.

Then blackness engulfed her.

Pamela rolled through the door sensing trouble. She stopped in astonishment at the sight of Cassandra on the TV screen, in strangely hypnotic eye makeup.

"CASSIE!" she screamed. She heard water running, she whirled around in the chair and saw a bloody stream of water coming out from under the bathroom door.

"HELP ME SOMEBODY!" screamed Pamela.  Gibson the nurse came charging in, his face a mask of astonishment. He ran up to the bathroom and slipped into the bloody water. Another male nurse and female ran in. Gibson whipped out a key on a chain and frantically opened the bathroom door. Cassandra was slumped in a bloody heap on the floor underneath the sink. They frantically wrapped towels around her wrists to stop the bleeding. The female nurse was yelling.

CODE RED! CODE RED!

****

Cassandra was drifting in what felt like a warm sea, but she was thirsty. *Mustn't drink*, she thought, dully. *Sea water is bad. Thirsty.* She struggled to open her eyes. *Pain,* her hands hurt terribly, but she could not move them. *Thirsty.*

She heard voices talking. She recognized Pamela's voice. She suddenly felt happy.

*Pammy... thirsty.*

"I think you did quite enough on this case Dr. Fitzgerald, leave this to me and Dr. Petrosian from now on." came Pamela's voice.

"Dr. Petrosian, this woman is not a psychiatrist, she is not competent to give advice on this case" came an indignant voice Cassandra did not recognize.

"If I were you, Dr. Fitzgerald, I would not throw the word "competence" around just now!" came Pamela's angry reply

"That will be enough out of you, Ms. Monroe!" said the voice.

"You almost lost this patient! Bozo!" retorted Pamela.

"She's not supposed to find out this information this way! She was supposed to remember it!"

"Jesus! She is an investigative journalist! She brought down the fucking UFO cover-up! This is how she finds out things she wants to know!" retorted Pamela.

"OK, OK, Dr. Petrosian, you better handle this then; I leave this to your discretion. But this is highly irregular!" came Fitzgerald's voice.

"Irregular? Eat more bran then! It will help you think better!" shot back Pamela sarcastically.

"Pamela!" came Dr. Petrosian's voice scolding. "Knock it off!"

There was a long silence, she felt people drawing near. She heard the noise of two wheelchairs.

"She is waking up! Let me talk to her!" came Pamela's voice quietly.

"Ok try to wake her up gently..." came Petrosian's voice.

"Cassie... it's Pamela, Starbuck... wake up..." came Pamela's angelic voice.

Pammy ... I'm so thirsty, I need water," gasped Cassandra.

"Here sip this water through a straw..." Cassandra felt a straw brush against her lips. Slowly moved her lips over it and sipped cool fresh water. It felt heavenly. Cassandra opened her eyes. The room was very dim. She saw Pamela's lovely face looking down on her like an angel. Further away she saw Dr. Petrosian's face, he was smiling also. She felt safe and reassured.

"My hands hurt Pammy... I can't move my arms."

"Can we cut that tape, she is not going to try anything again, Doctor. I know her, this was some impulse she acted on...It won't happen again. I promise..."

"Are you sure?" asked Petrosian.

"If she really wanted to kill herself, she'd be dead!" said Pamela with annoyance. "Believe me, Doctor, she is normally very thorough."

"All right," said Petrosian in weary resignation. Cassandra felt the restraints on her arms loosen removed. She suddenly felt at ease, a faint smile crossed her face.

"See that's progress! Right there!" said Pamela.

"All right, talk to her, then let's get this show on the road."

"Cassie!" said Pamela.

"Yes?"

"Wake up!" said Pamela loudly. Cassandra awoke at this with a start. A thousand questions suddenly flew around in her mind like a flock of frightened birds. She was in a new hospital room; Pamela was sitting next to her bed in her wheelchair. Doctor Petrosian sat in his wheelchair, few feet away, smiling warily.

"I am sorry I made such mess... my plan to obtain the video disc part went perfectly... you must admit...I just didn't plan on my reaction to watching it very well.." gasped Cassandra with a faint smile. Tears welled in her dark eyes.

"Listen idiot! If you kill yourself you can't win the war you started, can you?" said Pamela with annoyance. "It would be a poor strategy! Right?" Cassandra stared ahead. Pamela heard Petrosian let out a low moan.

"Yes?" she heard herself say.

"Are you curious, about how exactly you started this war, especially the eye-makeup part?"

"Yes?" said Cassandra faintly.

"How much of the broadcast that you made did you actually watch?"

"Enough," said Cassandra as her face dissolved into tears. "I knew they had broken me ... I felt it. Then I saw the broadcast I did for them...it confirmed it. "

"Well, your wrong Cassie! You turned the whole thing around on them! You put a secret message in the broadcast that made the government pre-empt an alien attack! That's why everyone thinks you started the war! Actually, you just started it two hours earlier than the aliens planned! They forced you to do a broadcast and you used it to warn about an impending alien attack! I know this because I just watched your broadcast five times, while you were out. I had never seen it before. They wouldn't let me see for fear I would talk about it.   Dr. Petrosian watched it with me!" Pam gestured at Petrosian.

"Yes! It's all true Cassandra. "said Petrosian. " I have talked to people at the Pentagon who confirm everything Pam just said. They had given the aliens an ultimatum, a deadline, and you warned in the broadcast that the aliens were going to attack when it ran out. So the President ordered a preemptive attack. So you girl, are a hero, they didn't break you at all."

"How is that possible?" asked Cassandra, sitting up. "How could they let me put a warning in the broadcast? How could they be that stupid? "

"Watch it silly!" said Pamela laughing. "You obviously bedazzled them with your eyes, and they were so hypnotized, they didn't pay any attention to what you were saying. You were obviously very wily and read them like a book! "She then put her arm around Cassandra's shoulders and they adjusted the bed so she could sit up. "That's my Cassie!" Pamela held her tight. They then played the tape. Cassandra watched the entire bizarre broadcast with a mixture of astonishment and relief, all the while holding Pamela's hand. "Here's the real finale," said Pamela, when they came to the part where Cassandra flicked off the bandages on her fingertips, showing the world she had been tortured. "We found out that when the President saw that last part he decided to preempt because he had warned the people holding you at Devil's mesa that they were not to harm you." said Pamela more seriously.

"How did I do it?" she asked herself. "I don't understand it, this is astonishing"

They watched it again.

"I don't understand," gasped Cassandra, who despite herself laughed at several parts. She had mangled the words so thoroughly that unless one paid close attention, it appeared she was just having a series of nervous mental hiccups. She then buried her head into Pamela's shoulders and cried for several minutes. She cried with both sorrow and relief. Finally, at Petrosian's suggestion, a nurse came and injected Cassandra with a sedative. She drifted off, a comfortable cloud enveloped her, and she became in her last dream a Sphinx, with incredible eye shadow, speaking riddles while behind her a mountain burned with fire in the night.

Pamela conferred with Petrosian as they sat next to each other in their wheelchairs and Cassandra slept.

"George, I will stay here with her until tomorrow morning, you get some rest, she said. "I also want you to get every piece of information we have available on her condition when she was rescued and what the other survivors said about what happened to her. Can you do that?" Petrosian

171

nodded. "I also want her to be able to watch the news and anything else she wants. She just got over this hurdle, I know she can keep getting better the more she knows.

****

Now in a deep violet sky at 80,000 ft. and the shock wave around it slightly luminous, the F-71 Scorpion cruised at Mach 5, driven by its two massive engines. Its 50 yard black frame was festooned with a pair of blister turreted 20 mm guns behind the cockpit, and another flush turret with dual 20 mm guns on the bottom of its flat black fuselage, Samurai Nakajima, surveyed the world outside of the cockpit of his F-71 Scorpion jet fighter, named the Black Arrow, an updated fighter version of the legendary SR-71. His eyes scanned the curved Earth below, still sunlit, the band of blue sky above it on the horizon and above that a dark violet dome filled with stars. Through his space helmet visor, his roving eyes scanned inside the cockpit instrument dials by their hundreds, dancing over the important ones, engine temperature, oil pressure, altitude, speed, and he ignored those that were not important to his task of flying the plane. The roar of the F-71's massive engines was muted by his spacesuit, but he felt the hum of power from the craft around him and felt one with it. His eyes rested momentarily and reassuringly on his samurai sword in its scabbard, leaning against the knee of his silver spacesuit. He was utterly dedicated now to Bushido - the way of the warrior - and this comforted him. He felt utterly alone now, except for that warrior code, as he flew above most of the Earth's atmosphere.

*I am death mounted on my steed,* he thought. But he also knew that unless he was able to fire his six super-ARAM missiles with magneto warheads, carried internally in his enormous aircraft, at an alien ship, at long range, that despite his two forward firing cannons and remote control turret guns, his chances of survival in close combat with a saucer were actually low. His aircraft took a hundred miles to turn at Mach 5, and if he tried to dive too rapidly, at that speed, the titanium skin of his fighter might ignite like magnesium. But this did not bother him, he was now officially an ace with five kills now credited to him. *I am death...* He was closing on the Earth's shadow now and in the Eastern distance, a wall of blackness on the horizon. He soon passed into it, entering the world of

172

night.  During his daily patrols over the Continental US now, he saw multiple sunrises and sunsets.  He knew the plane could be flown by computer, but not in combat when the aliens could hack into any data link with the ground or sophisticated flight computer on board.  *So I am the essential part that makes this craft a deadly weapon against the Greys...* He thought as he now rode above the brightly lit cities below, along the Mississippi valley.

"Victor Tango Charlie, this is flight November Echo twelve, any bogey contacts? "

"Negative, November Echo twelve, no contacts so far." came back the Vandenberg Tower.

"Roger that Victor Tango Charlie, but what a shame it is..."replied Samurai with a laugh,  as he crossed the dark Mississippi far below.

****

"Can I climb into bed with you, like we used to sleep together?" asked Cassandra pleadingly as it grew dark outside.  Pamela smiled and nodded and Cassandra   climbed into bed with her.  It felt so good to be in bed together again.   *Human warmth, how precious...*Cassandra  thought snuggling up close to her. Cassandra had been surfing the net furiously for days after seeing the broadcast, analyzing the war's progress from every angle.  The last two nights had been ominously quiet.  Everyone expected a raid that night.

"So I did start the war, apparently, but just an hour and a half early.  If it was scheduled to begin in earnest, I apparently just helped it along.  I have always been a little impatient. "said Cassandra lying beside Pamela.

"Yes, I have always warned you about that Cassie!  Hastiness, always be on guard against hastiness! "

"How did I look in the broadcast?"

"You looked fabulous. I especially liked your eye makeup.  It was so 'look at me! I am the Queen of Outer Space."

173

"Yes, the eye makeup, I am especially proud of that aspect."

They drifted off to a deep sleep until the Greys showed up in four ships over DC later that night.

**** 

"Can I read you some of this?" asked Pamela the next morning. "For a shameless whitewash this Groveland Commission report on the UFO Cover-up has some surprisingly good writing," said Pamela from her bed.

"Sure," said Cassandra looking up from her laptop. She was now obsessed with the war, and eager to get out of the hospital and report on it. Pamela had printed out a copy of the Groveland Commission report on the UFO Cover-up that the government had produced, in record time, to try to explain to the public how they had come to be involved in an interstellar war.

"This is a good passage that pretty much summarizes this whole report," said Pamela adjusting her reading glasses and clearing her throat.

"The United States Government became aware of the alien presence on Earth in the late thirties because of a secret incident that occurred over Pearl Harbor naval base in Hawaii in June of 1938. In this heretofore secret incident, known as the Pearl Harbor incident in old War department files, an alien craft flew over Pearl Harbor and was pursued by navy biplane fighters, which it easily evaded. The Navy viewed this incident with great alarm and formed a secret special group of scientists and aviation specialists to study the incident. The working groups were simply code-named GM to appear inconspicuous. The chief fear of the Navy GM group was that the craft represented new Japanese technology, and this was made more extreme because Japan was already a military ally of Germany at the time and the Second World War was looming. However, the performance of the craft while pursued by Navy biplane F4Bs was so astonishing that many doubted that it was Japanese or German. Reports of the great airship on the late 1890's were therefore reexamined and it was considered that the craft may have had the same origin. A second watershed event for the US Government, however, was the infamous "War of the Worlds" Broadcast on Halloween in 1938. The

174

panic and hysteria created by the broadcast, apparently feeding off of fears of the coming in Europe, caused the US Government to seriously consider that the Pearl Harbor Incident may have involved an extraterrestrial craft, possibly from the planet Mars. The GM group, in particular, began to consider the Pearl Harbor incident in this way after the Halloween broadcast and some participants even began joking that "GM" stood for Grovers Mill, the supposed site of the Martian invasion in the broadcast.

These two incidents, The Pearl Harbor Incident, and the War of the Worlds broadcast panic, coming as they did with the looming threat of a world war, linked an alien presence with mortal threats to national security from the outset. This was reinforced by other alien craft sightings by the Navy and Army, and also reports from the British military. Finally, with the war in Europe already begun, the April 1941 Cape Giraedue, Missouri saucer crash occurred, confirming the extraterrestrial nature of the craft. From that point on the US government had to deal with not only the prospect of the war with the Axis powers but also a war with aliens from outer space. Its biggest fear was that the aliens might align themselves with the Axis.

This association of the confirmed arrival of extraterrestrials at Earth, the Greys, with fear of war with the Axis, colored the perception of the US government to view the grey aliens as a mortal threat. However, this was fortunate, as it turned out, for the later Roswell Incident after the Second World War confirmed the hostile intentions of the grey aliens when they were caught trying to disable our then-minuscule nuclear weapon stockpile. Despite frequent hostile encounters, the continuing presence of the aliens led to attempts to communicate with them, to gain more knowledge of their precise intentions and technology."

"So the government is saying that they knew the Greys were nasty people all along. No sir, they didn't have us fooled for a minute!" said Cassandra grinning.

"These attempts at communication began in the late 1950's." continued Pamela. "These efforts culminated in face to face meetings at Holloman Air Force Base in the early 1960's and despite strong distrust of the grey aliens by the military, a secret agreement to provide for scientific and diplomatic exchange was negotiated and signed by both agencies at Holloman on June 21, 1971."

"This agreement was originally managed by the CIA and Air Force, during the 70's and 80's under the code name MAJIC but persistent problems occurred." Pamela raised her eyebrows in mock surprise, then continued. "With the end of the Cold War in the 1980's, the program was reorganized under a new , and much smaller, civilian agency called NATEX and became known as MAGICIAN under the guidance of a panel of scientists and military officers known as the MAGI."

"Oh! here is where we come in babe!" said Cassandra gleefully.

"Yes the tone of this executive summary changes quite abruptly here!" laughed Pamela. "It goes into frantic Cover-Your-Ass mode in this next paragraph."

"Unfortunately, the extremely compartmentalized nature of MAGICIAN and the small size of NATEX, compared to the CIA, led quickly to extreme isolation of the MAGICIAN program, and a complete loss of oversight or information-sharing by other agencies." Pamela laughed as she read it. "So, the MAGI quit going out for drinks with the other agencies, and all sharing of gossip ended!"

"Oh my God! The program became so secret nobody knew what they were doing anymore!" exclaimed Cassandra.

Pamela read the next few lines and burst out laughing.

"Oh, these next few sentences are hilarious!" Pamela exclaimed. She then cleared her throat again and held up the report proudly, and resumed reading.

"The isolation and lack of oversight of MAGICIAN led to a confusion of goals and methods within the MAGI, as to their posture towards the grey aliens..."

"Oh, like confusion as to who is screwing who?" said Cassandra.

"This resulted in a breakdown in communications with other agencies, and dissension within the MAGI itself." Pamela then paused. "As a result of the distractions of the Sepulveda Asteroid Crisis, and this complete lack of transparency, the US government did not know that the MAGICIAN program had gone completely rogue until it was too late...." read Pamela.

"Oh, that is so lame! Pammy. We didn't stop the car going the wrong way on the freeway because the driver said he was on a secret government mission!" laughed Cassandra.

"Lame indeed Cassie," said Pamela. "There you have it, the complete confession of the US government. The great Mea Culpa," she said with sudden bitterness. "And it's as lame as I am now." She looked at her inert legs and suddenly began to cry. Cassandra rushed to her side and held her.

"Don't worry Pammy, everything is going to be OK," Cassandra said over and over as she held her.

*We are going to get out of here and make somebody pay for this...*thought Cassandra vehemently. *They are going to pay and pay and pay...*

**\*\*\*\***

## Chapter 4: Revelations

Pamela was devouring the Groveland Commission report with fascination.

"The Navy GM group was merged after the Cape Girardeau crash, which established a top-secret group called, in the then Department of War, the "Jamaica Group" originally started in Jamaica, New York; and they began meeting at Point Montauk on Long Island. British Intelleigence then informed the Americans that the Nazie elites were expecting a group of aliens called the 'Vril' to come and help them. This did not help matters, even though the Vril were considered imaginary by the British.

The Jamaica group, consisting of several prominent scientists, and Army and Navy officers was selected to study the remains from the Cape Girardeau crash, and given the outbreak of war in Europe, all participants entertained theories that the aliens were somehow associated with the forces of the Axis, i.e. Nazi Germany or Imperial Japan."

"Well, I guess it's sort of understandable, then" said Cassandra. "The US government had a really full radar screen. In fact, radar had only just been invented. So they saw threats everywhere." she said in wonder. "You must admit they had to be really tough-minded, considering how many unknowns they faced. Imagine facing war with Hitler, Imperial Japan, and even the Soviet Union, who was their ally initially, then people arrive from outer space."

"Coming as it did during the first year of War in Europe," continued Pamela. "The Cape Girardeau crash in April 1941 was viewed with great alarm and prompted President Roosevelt to declare an Unlimited State of National Emergency in the weeks following the crash. The Jamaica group, while initially a small study group, grew in numbers and importance after Pearl Harbor and then grew even more after the so-called 'Battle of Los Angeles' in late February 1942. The so-called Battle of Los Angeles reinforced the theory of a Space Alien-Axis connection, when following the surfacing of a Japanese submarine off the coast of Southern California and its bombardment of an oil refinery on the night of Feb 23rd the next night, saw a formation of alien craft fly right over Los Angeles and into a barrage of antiaircraft fire. The subsequent recovery of two crashed alien craft apparently brought down by antiaircraft fire, one recovered by the

Army on Feb 26 in the Los Angeles national forest and another on Catalina Island the same day by the US Navy, reinforced the feeling that the aliens had deliberately probed the antiaircraft defenses of Los Angeles and were acting in coordination with the Japanese Navy."

"They flew over Los Angeles right after Pearl Harbor and had two of their ships shot down! That is so stupid!" said Cassandra in amazement. "How did these people ever get here in the first place?"

"I know, let me finish..." said Pamela reading along.

"This theory, aliens-allied-with-the-Axis, was considered a worst case scenario by the government and was never completely discredited until the end of the war when interrogations of high ranking German and Japanese officials revealed that they had seen the aliens also and thought the aliens to be part of the Allied War effort. The Japanese submarine attack near Los Angles and the battle of Los Angeles the next night is now considered to have been a complete coincidence. During the war, The Luftwaffe had had on several occasions brought down alien craft and attempted with some success to duplicate its antigravity drives, though the lack of a portable nuclear power source doomed the project to merely producing a laboratory demonstration of the antigravity effect. "Pamela paused and wrote some notes in a notebook. Then Pamela continued.

"However, the coincidence of the arrival of the Unash with the outbreak of the Second World War in Europe, and especially following the 1938 'War of the Worlds" broadcast panic, permanently linked the Unash with the possibility of an existential threat to the human race, and made all studies of alien craft and alien intentions, to be the most carefully guarded secret of both the Second World War and the Cold War that followed it." Pamela continued.

"This attitude was so ingrained in the government people studying the problem, that when the Roswell incident happened, with the government shooting down two saucers spying on our total nuclear weapons stockpile, that they even recycled the code name for breaking the Japanese codes: MAGIC, from during the Second World War for the new program to gather intelligence on the aliens. Shortly after Roswell, they reorganized the entire defense and intelligence establishment." Pamela paused to digest these last words.

"So that's where they got the name? It was a cool name! Even I admit this!" said Cassandra laughing. She found this all delightful, for in contrast with the dark days of bringing down the UFO Cover-up, when people said she was crazy, now even the US Government was agreeing with her. She realized that her vindication was also the world's disaster, but did not dwell on it.

"The Russian interpretation of the alien presence on Earth was, for the most part, one of unremitting hostility and began in the late 30's," continued Pamela, "as did the American attitude, with the assumption that the alien craft were associated with Axis powers. During the Second World War, the Russians were unsuccessful in bringing down any alien craft and hence continued to regard them as a Nazi or Japanese secret weapon, since many were seen in the Soviet Far East. In the Cold war that followed the Russians interpreted any unidentified flying object flying over Soviet Territory as American Intelligence gathering aircraft, and they redoubled their efforts to bring them down. Finally aided by improved radar, missile and jet aircraft technologies, the Russians succeeded in bringing down various alien craft, only to discover, to great consternation in the Kremlin, that they were not American!" Pamela laughed at this last passage.

"Nyet Amerikinski!" chortled Cassandra. "I'll bet even Joe Stalin was puzzled by that one."

"However," continued Pamela, "by this time the KGB had detected signs of a possible US-Unash rapprochement and decided that even if the aliens were not American, then they were allied with them. The aliens apparently retaliated also, massacring a dozen wilderness hikers in one incident. Therefore, attack-on-sight remained the Soviet response to alien craft sightings. The Americans became aware of this attitude in the Kremlin, felt it would destabilize the Cold War and lead to a nuclear war by mistake, and so on several occasions the U.S. Government tried to assure the Soviets that any American-alien détente was purely defensive and "informational" in nature, with one American Air Force General, even telling his Soviet counterpart "the aliens, the Greys or Unash, are the common enemies of all mankind", these assurances were followed by a secret treaty of alliance between the NATO and the Warsaw pact against the Aliens, later amended secretly to include all nations on the UN security Council."

"That's really interesting, so the aliens were considered space Nazis from the beginning, but where does the shameless whitewash enter logically?" asked Cassandra.

"Oh," Pamela rolled her big blue eyes, "Their logic is actually pretty seamless." Pam continued. "They parlayed the 'we thought they were space Nazis' and 'the War of the World broadcast caused a panic' themes to say that the whole UFO cover-up was justified to 'protect public morale' and led to a situation where secret compartmentalization took over during the Cold War."

"In the name of morale, we committed gross immorality!" declared Cassandra smiling.

"So part of the government" continued Pamela "was actually telling the public and the rest of the government that UFOs were merely 'sightings of the planet Venus,' and another part was studying them in top secret compartments. If the government was a person, it would have required heavy medication. As could be predicted, at one point in the 1960's the UFO problem became so compartmentalized and secret among the rival Armed Services and the intelligence services, that quite literally, it says "all central control or supervision was lost for a period, and a situation of complete disorganization persisted for several years." So when they literally say later "the UFO program became so secret that oversight was impossible," they aren't really exaggerating. To paraphrase, on more than one occasions the UFO cover-up turned into a complete 'goat-fuck." said Pamela laughing. "So, yes, our work was so secret, we didn't even know what we were doing for a period!'

"They even say in the last chapter," continued Pamela, "in this little gem of government-speak: The MAGI working group, in the late 90's began abusing its authority in this realm, exceeding all its directives, and without informing anyone, undertook its own negotiations with the Unash, essentially becoming a rogue operation, allowing unspeakable crimes and treasonous activities to occur while keeping the rest of the government in complete ignorance of their activities!"

"Those dastardly MAGI, it was all their fault! OH! That is sooo bogus!" said Cassandra with irritation.

"Yes! World class bogosity! "said Pamela laughing. "To paraphrase, 'we didn't know that part of the government had gone from gathering intelligence on the aliens, to jumping into bed with them, because it was all supposed to be  a top secret government program! "  So that essentially is their big excuse, are you ready for this...impossibly implausible denial!" Both Pamela and Cassandra stared at each other and nodded gravely in agreement.

"But the report does have a lot of good stories in it," began Pamela again brightly, "and general information and they certainly make it clear why they kept the whole situation secret. They point out that in air combat between our jet fighters and their saucers; we lost jet fighters at a rate of 20 for every saucer brought down. That is unless we caught them by surprise. So the military assessments were that the human military stood no chance against a determined alien attack. So the government never could figure out what to say to the public.  There never was any good news to report. Hence, we kept the whole thing secret, and as for the aliens, we always threatened to start a nuclear war to destroy the Earth if the Greys ever invaded.  So that's how it stood for 50 years.  They also say that in addition to the Greys, the US government became aware of at least 20 other species visiting Earth, including some that look just like human beings..."

Cassandra got a deep chill when Pamela read this but shook it off.  Pamela continued.

"There's also a cool chapter on Hollywood, which explains why this whole scenario with the Greys sounds like the plot of a 1950's science fiction movie. That's because the whole scenario was leaked to Hollywood in the 50's and Hollywood wrote a bunch of movies around it."

"Mars needs women?" asked Cassandra arching her eyebrows.

"Yes, exactly!"

"Any other gems?" asked Cassandra.

"Oh some colossal screw-ups occurred," said Pamela. "These were predictable based on compartmentalization and intense rivalries between the services, the CIA and even the FBI, then there were some incidents where the aliens clearly fucked up. Like one embarrassing episode when an alien ship was obviously hot-dogging close to the ground for the benefit of some security guards at the gate of an ICBM base in Montana. One of the guards panicked and shot a single bullet into the saucer with his .38 revolver, which to the astonishment of the guards, and I am sure especially the astonishment of the alien crew, caused the whole ship to fall out of the air and crash!"

"My God that is embarrassing!" said Cassandra laughing. "That's almost as bad as flying right over a big city covered with antiaircraft guns, right after Pearl Harbor and losing two saucers."

"Then there was another incident where the US Army surprised and alien landing party underneath a hovering saucer in the woods near Fort Dix New Jersey," said Pamela reading intently. "The hovering saucer simply took off and left the ground party stranded, some of whom scattered into the woods and the rest who meekly surrendered to the Army. Then, two days later a little grey alien came wandering out of the woods, obviously lost and hungry, up to the gates at Fort Dix and was shot by a guard who obviously had not been told, because of compartmentalization, anything about aliens from outer space wandering in the woods.

"Oh that's sad," said Cassandra frowning. "But it also shows again that the Greys can screw up, and that's an important piece of information. No wonder the government found this whole situation so confusing."

"Then there's the time in the late 50's when the Navy set up a big radar station on a Pacific island to track missile tests and instead it turned into a giant bug-zapper for grey ships." read Pamela eagerly. "Two of the ships crashed on a nearby island after the Navy simply turned the radar on and they flew into its beam. So then the government learned a new trick from this and found out they could bring down grey ships by simply focusing

184

every available radar beam in the area on them when they showed up. In two years, the government brought down twelve grey ships without even firing a shot. They had so many grey bodies at one point they started just burning them at the crash sites rather than even shipping them to Wright-Patterson Air Force Base for study. The most amazing thing was that it took the Greys two years to fix the problem with their ships so the radar trick wouldn't work anymore. So this explains a little why the Greys haven't been able to take over this place. They were certainly militarily capable and advanced over us, but they are at the same time sort of incompetent.

"So in the late sixties under Johnson and Nixon," read Pamela. "The government actually established contact with the Greys and began negotiations with them. This culminated with a secret meeting at Holloman Air Force Base, in the early 70's, in the middle of the Cold War." Pamela paused and grinned impishly. "At the secret meeting, the Greys assured the Air Force General who was present, that they were not only friendly but 'staunch anti-communists.'" Pamela then exploded into laughter.

"Well then, we like you already!' says the General" laughed Cassandra.

"But the best one, you'll love this Cassie, is an exchange of emails between our old buddy the MAGI leader, Arthur Bremer and the alien commander at Morningstar. This is unintentionally hilarious." continued Pamela smiling. "Bremer to alien commander: 'Will you please stop mutilating the cattle around Morningstar, its attracting attention to the area where we have your top secret base, so please stop!" Pamela laughed, as did Cassandra.

"Your secret dog is pooping on everyone's lawn at night!" laughed Cassandra. "How can we keep your dog secret if it keeps making classified projects out of everyone's front lawn! You know we have a no pet's policy here!"

"Alien Commander to Bremer:" continued Pamela laughing, "we don't know what you are talking about. Your own government says these cattle are being mutilated by wild animals! Stop being silly! He says."

185

"Stop being Silly! Oh my God! That's rich! He knows enough English to misuse it! My secret dog never poops! It's your dog that doing the pooping!" laughed Cassandra.

"Whereupon Bremer responds: Quit lying! We know your people are involved. These mutilations are very counterproductive for our maintaining the security of your base. If you desire cattle parts, we can easily obtain and deliver them to you in any quantity you desire! says Bremer."

"We can hire a pooper scooper service! Just tell us when your dog needs to poop! They'll be right there with a baggy!"

"The Alien Commander responds:" recited Pamela gravely, "You know nothing! Why would we want parts of your dirty livestock? You know my people are vegetarians! You must apologize at once for calling me a liar and accusing my people of the barbarous practices which your primitive people do!"

"I repeat, my secret dog never needs to poop on your poopy lawn unless I order it too!" laughed Cassandra.

"So apparently the MAGI people and the aliens were thoroughly sick of dealing with each other by the time we started investigating," said Pamela.

"You must apologize for saying my dog pooped on your poopy lawn since my dog is secret and therefore does not exist, and certainly doesn't poop either!" laughed Cassandra. "Ah, vindication Pammy! It feels so good!" With Pamela's recital concluded, she resumed her studies of calculus and Cassandra resumed her endless meditation of staring out the window into the park, now littered with autumn leaves. She had a faint smile on her face.

****

"I agree you can't stay here any longer Colonel," said General Burnham pacing back and forth in Schwartzman's Hospital room in the ET exposed ward. The General's staff, including Major Prescott, stood at ease beside

186

Burnham, with bodyguards in green berets out in the main ward. Schwartzman stood at attention in his dress uniform by his bed. "But Major Prescott, here, my aid de camp, has figured out what to do. Unfortunately, we are in an alliance, and like all wartime alliances, it's like a bad marriage where a lot of give and take is required to get things done. Unfortunately, the French have declared you a wanted man because of your role in the cover-up and gotten the World Court at the Hague to issue a warrant, U.S. Presidential pardon or no,   and while the French don't carry much weight in the alliance, they talk the loudest, imagine that. Now, with the other major figures dead or in prison in the U.S., you are the biggest fish left in the pond, so to speak. You copy Colonel?"

"Roger, General, I copy," said Schwartzman without emotion. He had noticed that Rene, the uber-surveillance-nurse with the nice behind, had not shown up for work that morning. *Au Revoir moi Cheri!*

"Unfortunately, Schwartz," continued General Burnham, "this latest French move has derailed your Congressional Medal of Honor and your promotion to General officer, for the time being, both of which have to be approved by Congress. So you'll have to settle for my written commendation, which goes in your files. *Yes, French moves indeed!* Schwartzman thought hilariously, while trying to keep a straight face.

"Yes General, thank you," said Schwartzman blankly. *Yes, my highly classified files...What would I do without them!* he laughed a sad mental laugh. *Just get me out of here!*

"So we can offer you a choice of deep cover in the FBI witness protection program somewhere in-country, or else you will be transferred immediately to Special Operations Command and be assigned to combat operations there. If anybody asks where you are, we will simply say we have no knowledge of your whereabouts due to compartmentalization and would not be at liberty to divulge your whereabouts if we knew them. You will be working for SOCOM 100% and the missions profiles will be classified pitch-black, compartmentalized."

"General, send me to SOCOM.," said Schwartzman levelly.

"Good choice Schwartz," said General Burnham and pulled out an envelope with his new orders on it. We're *just like old times*, thought Schwartzman with resignation. He imagined living as a civilian in the FBI witness protection program, watching the war on the news, but his mind rebelled. *Living death,* he thought. *In hiding until death, like some rabbit in a hole! A guest of the damned Shoes! Never! Better to die in battle somewhere, much, much, better. One death with honor, rather than a million days of living death in hiding! Live like a lion!* He had decided instantly.

"General, I request assignment to SOCOM combat operations, for the duration," said Schwartzman. *The duration of my life. With any luck, I will not survive this war,* he thought, *God, I ask and hope for a good death on the battlefield! Grant me this I pray! Grant Me A Brave and Honorable Death!* He felt a sudden heavy burden lift off him. *Death with honor on a battlefield, not in a cage or some hidey-hole, with my heart going pitter patter! Let it be said of me, that 'Robert Schwartzman was Killed-in-Action!'*

"Excellent Colonel! I need every man up on the line now. We especially need men like you who are veterans of combat with the X-rays. This war has barely started and it's not going well." He handed Schwartzman an envelope. Schwartzman opened it.

General Burnham spoke as Schwartzman read the orders and confirmed them. "You are hereby ordered to report to General Ross, SOCOM-NorPac, at Fort Greely, Alaska, which is our rear staging area for the Aleutians campaign. Your Military Airlift Command flight will be out of Andrews tomorrow morning. A car will appear here at precisely 1000 hours to pick you up and transport you to Andrews Air Force Base. DIA personnel will secure you at this facility until you depart.

Schwartzman rose to full attention and saluted. General Burnham stood at attention also and saluted. He then reached out and shook Schwartzman's hand.

"Good luck Colonel, may God be with you." Burnham then turned and started for the door followed by Major Prescott. Schwartzman sighed and sat down on the bed; he began packing his things. General Burnham paused at the door, his face broke into a smile and he turned back to Schwartzman.

"I am curious Colonel. As you are probably aware, we just detained your nurse Rene Howard, real name Rene Schneider of French intelligence, this morning at her apartment. Things being as they are in the Alliance, we escorted her sweet French ass to Dulles airport in the company of the French Defense attaché', where they both received free tickets to Paris, France, courtesy of your Uncle Sam. My question to you, is how did you figure out she was French Intelligence?" asked General Burnham.

"She talks in her sleep," said Schwartzman, with a sly smile. At this, General Burnham exploded into rich laughter.

"Well done Colonel!" he said loudly, and departed out the door, laughing, with his staff and bodyguards following him. He was acting Chairman of the Joint Chiefs of Staff of the Armed Forces of the United States of America and acting Commander in Chief of all Allied Forces, United Nations of Earth.

"Major, such a multi-talented officer, has only one place! That is on the front line, in the thick of the action!" said Burnham to Prescott. They walked swiftly out of the ET exposed ward, before breaking again into laughter.

"Yes General," said Prescott checking his watch. "May I remind the General, that we are late for your 0900 meeting at the Pentagon."

"You may!" laughed Burnham feeling warm inside. *Colonel Schwartz will help me win this war! God helping us, we will win it!* Burnham thought as he laughed, *I see it! I see it! Victory,* as the nurses and staff all, stood aside at a civilian pose of attention. As he passed, a particularly attractive older black nurse with a name tag that said Florence, she beamed at him as he passed.

*Lord have mercy,* Burnham thought as he glanced at her, and laughed anew. *This is going to be a good day in this war.*

****

Arizona and Schwartzman walked down the hospital halls in full uniform, both wearing green berets. They walked tall, their polished black army boots shone, as did their campaign ribbons. Nurses and staff watched them in stunned silence and stood aside.

Suddenly, around the corner appeared Pamela in her wheelchair, wheeling herself down the hall to physical therapy. She stopped at the sight of Schwartzman and Arizona, a confused mix of emotions covered her face.

"Well if it isn't Pamela Monroe, amazon hero of the battle at Key bridge," said Schwartzman with a broad smile. "I heard about you leading the charge of the VMI cadets. Good Job." Pamela sat silently as they walked up to her.

"Good day to you Colonel" she finally said. "You hear lots of things don't you Colonel?"

"I have heard you're recovering nicely," said Schwartzman, still smiling.

"Yes I am," she said bravely. "I am going to walk out of this place in heels, Colonel"

"Is Cassandra in her room?" he asked. Pamela's face darkened, she stared at him with deep blue eyes squinting.

"Yes, but if I were you, Colonel, I would keep right on walking out of this hospital and leave her alone."

"Boss we got seven minutes, we got to go," said Arizona nervously.

"Why do you say that? I may not get to see here again for a long, long time." *Forever, in fact,* responded Schwartzman.

"Because she is not well Colonel, she is still traumatized. I think seeing you would not help her, it could even make her condition worse," said Pamela levelly. "I think if you really cared for her you would respect that and keep going." He huge blue eyes stared into his.

190

Schwartzman turned and walked on soberly in response. Arizona followed him dutifully. Pamela looked after them. Schwartzman turned to look back at her.

"Ms. Monroe, when you prance out of here in heels, you should start an advice column." He said flatly. She glared back at him, then turned and simply started down the empty hall in front of her.

"Arizona, if you got to amputate your own leg in a war zone, what's the best way to do it?" asked Schwartzman grimly, as they trudged on down the hall. *But I have to see her. I won't be able to live with myself if I don't see her one last time...*

"I don't know boss," replied Arizona fearfully. They had arrived outside Cassandra and Pamela's room.

"The best way to amputate your own leg ," said Schwartzman checking his watch and holding up three fingers, is to do it quickly," he said. "Wait here and give me a two minute warning sign," he said to Arizona and ducked into the room.

In the hospital room, Cassandra stared out of the window vacantly at the fall leaves and blue sky. Fall it seemed was coming early. She was wearing blue jeans and a deep green French tee shirt, and an open white shirt with long sleeves. Her long dark hair was in waves. The bandages on her wrists were still there. Schwartzman knocked on the side of the open door and entered, he took off his beret and stood before her.

"Cassandra, it's me, Bob Schwartzman," he said quietly.

Cassandra turned sadly to look at him. He looked at bandages on her wrists, winced inwardly. She saw him looking and pulled the cuffs of her shirt down to hide them. She then looked at him with a strange mixture of sadness, hope, and annoyance. Then her face changed.

She looked at him softly, then her beautiful face grew angry. Her dark eyes glistened. He was transfixed by her. *It wasn't a beautiful dream I had, in the middle of a landscape of nightmares,* he thought, *I was actually with her. It was real.*

"Cassandra I have to go now, I got orders. But I wanted to tell you I love you and I want to marry you," he said softly. She looked at him, a vision of loveliness, even in her emaciated state, and she began to shake.

"You've got a lot of goddamn gall coming here and telling me that!" she suddenly yelled at him.

She stepped closer to him. Her large dark eyes narrowed.

"You know what they did to me at Morningstar?" she gasped. "If you really loved me you would have left me to die there!!!" she yelled. "Go to Hell!" Then she turned her back to him again and folded her arms around herself as if to keep warm. Voices in her head were deafening, *Cassandra, Cassandra save us...*Schwartzman recovered from his shock and fumbled with his beret in resignation. He looked again sadly at the bandages on her wrists. Finally, his face grew hard again. *Nice ass*, he thought despite himself, looking at her backside. *Oh well, another crazy female exits my crazy soldier's life.* He saw out of the corner of his eye that Arizona was frantically waving two fingers at him.

"Well Princess, I will take that as a no." He paused drew himself up to his full height put on his beret and straightened it, "Now I got to go finish this little war we started." he said quietly, and if I was you I would get my shit in one sock and my sweet ass in gear, girl, because this is your war too." He then turned and left, his face hard as stone. Soon they were down the hall where the unmarked brown car had appeared for them. They both got in after flashing IDs at the two military men in the front seat and the car darted out of the parking lot. Schwartzman breathed a sigh of relief as they grew farther from the hospital. *The blue sky looks so sad*, he thought.

"Boss I got something to show you," said Arizona eagerly. Schwartzman could see he was trying to distract him and took the bait.

"Ok let's see it," he said quietly. Arizona pulled out a small rectangle of stainless steel and then a similar rectangle of bronze colored metal from his fatigue shirt pocket. Arizona dragged a corner of the bronze piece of metal across the stainless steel with his strong hands staining at the force he was applying. The steel was scoured deeply.

He tossed the piece of bronze metal to Schwartzman; it was warm from the friction.

"Wow, it's really light," said Schwartzman, now fascinated, "what is it?"

"It's a new alloy called Tallin, it's Titanium Aluminum Nickel Nitride, it's lighter than titanium and much stronger than steel. It was made by an experimental metallurgist named Tallant, whom I know, who also likes to make ancient swords and armor for collectors. I get my best dueling swords from this guy. So he shows me this stuff. I gave a piece to Mongoose, and he has gone crazy over it. He and I then came up with a plan to use it to pry the Samaran garrison out of the mountain on Adak. Goose has a brief for you to see on the Plane at Andrews.

"Good," said Schwartzman holding the bronze metal and examining it. He welcomed the chance to think about something else. But the color of the metal reminded him of Cassandra's bronze skin, so he looked away out the window.

Back at the hospital, Cassandra suddenly whirled around in a daze and looked incredulously at the empty room. She had been too distracted by the voices in her head to hear him leave. She bolted out of the room and began to run down the hall. She suddenly was face-to-face with Marcy Braxton and Madihira Kapoor, her two colleagues from CNS.

"Cassie! We heard you were well! We wanted to come see you and Pam!" blurted out Madihira as Cassie skidded to halt in front of them.

"Hurry I need you to drive me someplace!" she pleaded. Marcy and Madihira both looked at each other in confusion and then Cassandra rushed past them. "Hurry! He's getting away!" She turned and yelled at them frantically as they turned and ran after her. A nurse down the hall was pointing at her and talking to a doctor in the hall.

"Come on!" she yelled as they all charged out the hospital doors into the cool air of the parking lot. They ran to Marcy's car, a blue Mercedes, and Cassandra piled into the back seat, she saw a brown car with men in it in green uniforms rolling down the street away from the hospital.

"FOLLOW THAT CAR! HURRY!" she screamed as Madihira jumped in the car, and Marcy , acting by reflex, pulled the car out and tore out of the parking space after the brown car Cassie was pointed at frantically.

In the Army unmarked car, the two men in the front seat suddenly motioned to one another. The car sped up and was soon cruising swiftly down Wilson Blvd, the main street in Arlington toward the Capitol on the other side of the Potomac and the freeway on-ramp to Andrews AFB. The man riding in the front passenger seat pulled out a cell phone.

"Andrews gate this is FEDEX, and we have an Alpha Foxtrot condition." he said without emotion.

He then turned to Schwartzman and Arizona, handed them two Berretta pistols in holsters. He was holding an M-4 carbine.

Schwartzman and Arizona both took the pistols eagerly and checked the clips of ammunition. Schwartzman cradled it with satisfaction.

"Colonel some people are following us, but they can't catch us. So just sit tight and don't turn around. We always deliver our goods, where they're supposed to go." said the man with a blank look.

In the car following them, Cassandra watched tensely as the car got on the freeway headed in the direction of the Pentagon and Andrew's Air Force Base.

"Andrews! He's headed for Andrews!" Cassandra yelled, "follow him!" As Marcy followed as best she could. But police cars were everywhere, it seemed, and Marcy pointed at them helplessly as Cassandra keep yelling at her to hurry. Finally, Cassandra lapsed into mesmerized silence as she watched the car, now many cars ahead, pass the Pentagon and head for the Wilson bridge.

*Andrews, and plane out of here,* she thought helplessly. Marcy was managing to keep the car in sight. Cassandra was praying over and over, *Lord please let them hold him up at the Andrews's gate! Please, Lord! I wasn't finished with him yet!*

Schwartzman and Arizona were nearing Andrews and military traffic and checkpoints became more numerous. In an island in the freeway, a tank and several APCs sat with sober looking troops in camouflage standing beside them carrying M-16s. They were waved through the gates, and an APC then rolled in front of the gates after it closed. They were inside the main gates of the fortress that was now Andrews Air Force base.

Ten minutes later, the Mercedes bearing Cassandra, Marcy Braxton and Madihira Kapoor approached the gates of Andrews and was stopped at an outer checkpoint 100 feet from the main gate. Cassandra leaped out of the car as Madihira jumped out after her. Air police and Army soldiers raised their M-16 rifles and began pointing them at her as Air Police shouted at her to stop. Finally, Cassandra stopped and covered her mouth in speechless terror as the guards, many with guns drawn, began to move towards her warily.

"She's sick! Don't shoot!" Madihira was yelling, waving her arms, as she approached, she stopped running in fear, then resumed a slow walk to Cassandra. "My friend is crazy! Don't shoot her!" Madihira was yelling. Cassandra stood frozen, speechless, in between the outer checkpoint and the main gate. The APC in front of the main gate now had its 50 caliber machine gun trained on her.

"He didn't let me finish!" Cassandra cried out. "I, I wasn't finished talking to him!" she wailed and collapsed to the pavement as Madihira tried to put her arms around her. An Air Policeman in full combat gear approached and holstered his gun, looking a Cassandra in frightened amazement.

"Nobody lets me explain how I feel! NOBODY!" Cassandra wailed.

Just then, an enormous grey C-17 military cargo jet roared over thunderously headed North West. Cassandra stared up at, burst into tears.

"I hate you! I hate you! I HATE YOU! She screamed at the plane as Madihira, now joined by Marcy pulled her up from the ground. "WHY DIDN"T YOU JUST LEAVE ME TO DIE! WHY? WHY? she wept as Madihira, Marcy, and several guards carried her back to the car, and a car full of

195

MPs and medical personnel from Arlington hospital arrived to take her back.

Madihira rode back to the hospital holding her, as Cassandra murmured over and again.

"Why… why… why…"

****

On the plane, Schwartzman sat in the Spartan cargo bay of the C-17 with other members of the Carney, now christened the 42nd Ranger battalion. They were all in combat gear and cradled M-4 carbines. They were headed for Alaska and the front. He sat in his dress uniform still, beside Arizona, who had produced a bottle of rum from his pack. Schwartzman looked off into space. He took the bottle and took a deep drink before handing it back to Arizona.

"Too bad Badge ain't here," said Schwartzman, with a sudden smile.

"Yeah, but they'll get him patched up, Boss, and he'll join us later," said Arizona, he took a drink himself.

"Arizona, I'm damned lucky to have this war…" said Schwartzman smiling grimly. "It's shelter over my head, a meal ticket, and a warm bed to sleep in. It is purpose…" he said grimly. *And a good death.*

"Yeah Boss, for sure, we are some lucky sons of bitches!" said Arizona grinning, and taking another drink and handing it back to Schwartzman.

"This war, it is my one true love now…" said Schwartzman taking another deep drink and looking off into space, as the plane roared on through the sky to Alaska.

****

Cassandra was staring out the window forlornly at the park, and as usual, Pamela was doing calculus on-line when suddenly a scream and a flurry of shouts and curses sounded out from down the hallway.

196

"Motherfuckers! You can't take him out of here! Can't you see he's sick!" came a shrill voice.

Cassandra bolted for the doorway. A group of men in strange green uniforms and black berets and hard, shiny combat boots were marching a barefoot man, in a hospital gown, down the hall in handcuffs. His eyes were wide with terror and his mouth was taped shut. Behind this group were Nurse Flo and several other nurses following them. Flo was crying angrily.

"You got no right to do this!" she screamed. "He is MY PATIENT!" A grim-faced male doctor appeared and grabbed Flo's arms to hold her back, and the group of nurses stood with her as the procession continued down the hall.

The men walked on with their captive, oblivious to everyone's stares, and paused at Cassandra's door, a tall officer with a grim face and silver sunglasses stopped as the other men went past with their captive who was making muffled cries. Cassandra was filled with terror at this sight and began to shake, but steadied herself. Her dark eyes, like laser beams, bore into the silver sunglasses. The man studied her.

"Bonjour Mademoiselle Chen, "said the iron-faced man. "I am Colonel Duvalier of the French National Police, acting as an officer of the World Court at The Hague; we have an order for the arrest of your boyfriend, this man, Colonel Robert Schwartzman. He pulled out a sheet of paper and held in front of her astonished face. It held a picture of Schwartzman in his uniform and green beret and below it was writing in French, which she tried to decipher, "Colonel Schwartzman is wanted on charges of crimes against humanity and war crimes." He lowered the paper, stared at her. The procession of the men had stopped in the hall and everyone was looking at her now, including the captive barefoot man, whose eyes looked at her pleadingly. Down the hall, the group of nurses and doctors stared at her in stunned silence.

She rose to full height, glared at Duvalier. Suddenly she grabbed the paper out his hand with lightning speed and looked at it. He looked momentarily startled but then resumed his iron look. She read it in French quickly, and then rapidly tore it to pieces in front of his face. She then glared with her

197

huge dark eyes straight thought his silver glasses so that she saw him blink behind them.

"I remember you, Colonel Duvalier," she said slowly, "I never forget a face. You were at Lac Fortune in Quebec in the Canadian civil war, weren't you?" she hissed. He suddenly looked uncomfortable, and glanced away to other French soldiers, turned back to her, now iron faced again. "I also remember what you did to Chico Chicomague after you arrested him...You dumb motherfucker..." she hissed. She saw sweat appear on his upper lip.

"But you need to tell us where he is Mademoiselle!" Duvalier insisted, recovering himself. "He is a war Criminal! The world court will find you guilty of collusion also if you withhold information from us!"

"You're the only war criminal around here, Colonel," she sneered leaning close to him. "And I know it; you and your magic cattle prod!" yelled Cassandra at Duvalier. Pamela had somehow gotten into her wheelchair without Cassie's help. Pamela suddenly rolled up in her wheelchair beside her. Cassie was now trembling visibly.

"Hey! Leave my friend alone, Motherfucker!" Pam shouted at Duvalier. "Who the hell is this asshole, Cassie?" she asked.

"Just a creature from my dark past Pamela," said Cassandra through her teeth, boring her eyes into the Colonel's glasses. She could see him blink again. She began to curse him in French

"L'anal! Piece de Merde!" she yelled into his face.

He suddenly turned and walked away to the group of men who now proceeded down the hall again.

"Au Revoir Mademoiselle until we meet again," said Duvalier over his shoulder. He then pulled off his silver glasses and looked at them with obvious dissatisfaction and turned to another officer.

"Merde!" Duvalier said to the other officer, waving the glasses and laughing. They disappeared out the door down the hall.

198

Florence, the nurse, wrenched herself away from the doctor and ran up to Cassandra.

"Are you just going to stand there Miss High and Mighty? DO SOMETHING!" Flo screamed at her, then exploded into tears.

Cassandra turned away from Flo, trembling, her own face melted into tears, and she collapsed trembling on to the floor with Pamela grabbing her arms to break her fall. Flo was trying to help her also.

"THIS IS A NIGHTMARE! Oh God, Oh God, HELP ME!" Cassandra was screaming. She was seeing men in black combat fatigues and black masks hauling her away down an endless hall of white tiles, white tiles going on forever, then a black steel door... then blackness...

\*\*\*\*

At the tree-lined French Embassy the steel gate rolled back, and in the car was Duvalier, his men, and his "catch of the day", the unfortunate Major Crawford. They pulled swiftly through the gate. General La Farge of the French national Security Service rushed up in his uniform and looked at Duvalier's obviously deranged human cargo.

"Duvalier you fool! I send you to catch a shark and you bring back a minnow!" exclaimed La Farge waving his hand a Crawford in the back seat. "Who is this madman?"

"Mon General this man was an important Colonel in The U.S. Air Force at Harshman Air Force Base; he knows much of the American activities!" La Farge opened the door and recoiled from the smell in the back seat.

"He is mad! How can we present him to the Court at the Hague in this state? He will shit himself in the witness box!" said La Farge, walking away in disgust.

\*\*\*\*

199

So you didn't break, you weren't a traitor, you are a hero." said Petrosian. Petrosian was sitting in his wheelchair in his office at the hospital; Cassandra was sitting in a comfortable overstuffed chair. It was their bi-weekly regular therapy session.

"Yes, I see that. But I was certain that they had broken me. It was my worst fear when I woke up here and realized I had survived captivity there."

"Tell me, why did you think they had broken you."

"They can break anybody nowadays Dr. Petrosian. It is a terrible fact of modern life. I guess I just assumed it. But I know I felt it too. That's why I was so afraid to find out what I did and what happened to me."

"But the tape... that was the last thing that happened to you... as far as we know...."

"I still feel broken" she began to cry. "Despite the broadcast with the secret message..."

"But you made the broadcast and warned everyone. Someone who is broken doesn't do that. I have dealt with people who were broken by secret police; they don't act like you did."

"I don't care, I know what I feel, I know somehow they broke me."

"How? Can you remember?"

Her face changed became a mask of pain. Tears rolled down her cheeks

"They broke me... I know that deep inside."

"Can you describe it?"

"They broke me! They broke me!" she wailed. "I remember them breaking me!"

I was naked and they hurt me over and over again and I was screaming 'I'll do anything you want'," she sank to floor from the chair screaming and crying, I said I'll do anything you want, JUST PLEASE DON'T HURT ME

ANYMORE!" she screamed . "They broke me in a million pieces and skinned each piece alive... please don't hurt me anymore," her voice became a whimper as she lay with her face on the floor

**\*\*\*\***

"I don't care what Doctor Clausen says," said Pamela with trembling voice, as the morning light filled the room. "I am walking out of here in heels and I am going to walk across Key Bridge!" Pamela insisted. Cassandra nodded and helped her friend slide out of bed into her wheelchair. "Within the year!" Pamela added as Cassandra helped her lift her inert legs so she could put her feet on the steel footplates of the wheelchair. Pamela was due in Physical therapy soon. But her rapid progress she had made earlier had now 'hit a wall' in her words and no improvement was now seen in three weeks, and Clausen had advised Pam not to expect any more improvement. It was one thing to wiggle her toes, and another to walk. Pam had been devastated at first but was now defiant. Cassandra walked to the door with Pam as she wheeled her way out, kissing Pam on the top of the head as she departed and rolled determinedly down the hall.

Cassandra grew afraid in the room alone after Pamela left. The voices would come even during the day now. A chorus of voices she couldn't understand, the 'hubbub' she called it, and she was afraid to tell Doctor Petrosian about them. Alone also she might hallucinate that rat-crabs were crawling rapidly across the floor, and there would be no one there who could not see them and reassure Cassandra that they were just hallucinations. But the room was warm, so she took off her bathrobe and put on a white long sleeved shirt over her dark blue tee shirt and bra, and pulled on dark blue slacks and socks. She was worried her head would get cold, so she wrapped a red cotton scarf around her head like a gypsy with her long black hair hanging down.

*Like the pirate I am!* she thought, with sudden satisfaction, a faint smile crossed her face and made her feel better. She put on makeup and then put on mirrored sunglasses to avoid being recognized. Then she launched herself out into the hallways of the hospital. *My prison and my sanctuary,* she thought as she walked down the hall past chatting nurses and rooms filled with horribly wounded people. *And my insane asylum. Actually, I*

201

*should really advise Pamela to see a psychiatrist too, since she is so upset now about her legs.* Cassandra suddenly found herself laughing, *Oh déjà vu; such advice from me would reassure Pamela that things were returning to normal!* This made her feel stronger.

After wandering around, she found herself in the cafeteria sitting at a table enjoying a cup of coffee. The cafeteria was half-full of walking wounded, visitors, doctors, nurses and technicians, all talking at once. The mood seemed better. There had been a lull in night raids since the battle of last week and people seemed to be feeling a cautious optimism. She sat there and the hubbub came, but then emptied itself from her mind as the murmur of real voices chased the unreal voices away. *I can do it!* she thought, *I can defeat this and get well!* Then she heard a real pair of voices speaking that made her heart leap. It was Doctor Clausen speaking to someone about spinal cord treatment.

"I'm sorry Phil, almost all the military cases I get here are severe damage or severed cords. They send us the worst cases."

"Look, Fred, my study grant says I have to have military patients, but I need mild cases right now. I know you have a lot of severed cord cases but we need some mild spinal cord concussion cases to start this treatment out on. It's gotten excellent results up in Boston. Anyway, I thought I would ask while I was coming by here." Cassandra stood and walked over to the table where Clausen sat across from a tall bespectacled doctor. Clausen looked up with slight unease as she approached. She whipped off her glasses and smiled as sweetly as she could muster. Clausen smiled warily. Cassandra was acquiring a reputation, she knew, as being slightly unhinged.

"Doctor Clausen!" she beamed at him. "And this is?" she asked as she turned to the other doctor.

"Doctor Petrosky," said the doctor rising and shaking her offered hand. He at least smiled warmly. *I am skinny but I still got it. The power,* she thought with satisfaction.

"I am Cassandra Chen, the lady who started the war, "she said smiling. Clausen looked stunned at this introduction and looked away uncomfortably for a moment. "I just heard you say you have a new spinal treatment for mild spinal cord injuries. I may have just the patient for you..." she turned to Clausen. "We know who I mean, right doctor Clausen?"

"But Pamela is not military! She's a civilian!" said Clausen with slight indignation. He shot Petrosky a look that Cassandra decided to ignore. *This is for Pammy, so I don't care...*

"Au contraire Doctor, she's a naval cadet, technically." *Technically, technically ...*

"Is that true?" asked Petrosky, sounding excited, "that might work..." He looked at Clausen who shrugged.

"Well let's go meet her then, "said Cassandra suddenly grabbing his hand and pulling him along. To her delight, he followed dutifully as Clausen rose sputtering and followed them. "She would be delighted to meet you Doctor Petrosky, this is, by the way, the same lovely Pamela Monroe who helped me bring down the UFO Cover-up. They have been keeping her legs in good muscle tone with therapy and she can wiggle her toes. *"My muscle tone is excellent too if that's what it takes to get Pamela this new treatment,* thought Cassandra seriously, *I'll just wear a shirt to cover my back scars.* They boarded an elevator to the second floor where she knew Pamela was in physical therapy. Clausen now looked happy and 'onboard' with this scheme. *Pammy is too important for you to keep her as your own special patient,* thought Cassandra indignantly. But she now felt mounting joy and power. *Here I am leading the cavalry to rescue Pammy!*

"If she can wiggle her toes, that's a good sign for this treatment," said Petrosky.

"Will she be able to walk again?"

"If the treatment is successful. We have gotten remarkable results in cats," said Petrosky. Cassandra tried to smile at this but felt her heart sink momentarily. *Pammy is sort of catlike!* She thought desperately. "It's a stem cell treatment, we would take fat cells from her stomach and culture them and inject them at the injury site." said doctor Petrosky. Cassandra digested this, felt joyful again.

"Oh my friend will love that, walking again, and liposuction at the same time," said Cassandra nodding. The elevator door opened. Pamela was out in the hall looking forlorn. She had apparently just finished her therapy and was heading back to their room. Cassandra fairly yanked the man out of the elevator and led him up to Pamela. Clausen followed, now smiling. They all approached Pamela smiling. Who looked up at them with a wary grin.

"Pammy, I want you to meet Doctor Petrosky, "said Cassandra with trembling voice, and motioning to him with her hand. "Who is going to make you walk again, baby." With that Cassandra collapsed in tears on her knees beside Pamela's wheelchair.

****

"I keep having this odd dream, " said Cassandra, she was sitting in Petrosian's office, wearing slacks and a gold French tee shirt with a long sleeved white shirt thrown over it. " I dream I am parked in my sports car next to this big tree, like an oak tree. It the car I used to own before they blew it up, down in Adam's Morgan, before the coup. The big tree is very beautiful. And my car is chained to it, with this big chain around its trunk. Then this police woman comes by; she is wearing dark silver glasses. She has a tan uniform. But I think I recognize her. She is this woman named Lauren Hill; she worked at the White House before the Magi people killed her. She appears in my dreams a lot, but it's strange because I only met her once, and then she yelled at me. It was down at the white house."

"But anyway she is this policewoman," continued Cassandra. "And she brings this tow truck and they attach this big rusty chain to the rear of my car and then the tow truck starts to pull it with its winch. And I start pleading with her, because the car is chained to the tree, and they are tearing my car apart in front of me. I get down on my knees and I am begging her not to destroy my car, then she pulls out this big nightstick..." Casandra paused stared off into space.

"Then she forces it into my mouth... and I wake up"

204

Cassandra woke up; a beautiful golden light of morning filled the room. It was cold outside, but bright. She glanced over to Pamela's bed, saw she was gone, then glanced down reflexively and saw her wheelchair beside the bed. In a sudden panic, she launched herself out of bed and looked around wildly.

"Looking for me, Cassie?" said Pamela. Pamela was standing by the window in her white pajamas looking like an angel in the morning light. Cassandra spun around and stared at her in astonishment.

"You can walk again!" Cassandra exclaimed.

"Yes, I can. Watch this!" Pamela pushed herself away from the window and took several unsteady steps across the room to where Cassandra stood. With each step, she seemed to gain confidence and balance. Finally, she stood smiling radiantly in front of Cassandra, her blonde hair how spilling over her shoulders. They embraced.

"Oh! This is so wonderful!" cried Cassandra.

"I need some of my heels from the house Cassie!" said Pamela with determination . "So get Madihira or Marcy to get them! I am walking out of here soon, and then across Key Bridge!"

****

Cassandra put her boot in the stirrup and mounted the nightmare that was her steed, she wore a full suit of black gleaming armor, but no helmet, her black hair streaming as she rode. The black cavalry had come to help her, and with her leading, they rode up into the sky. They flew above the clouds until Casandra saw the Black Witch flying and her armies below on the plain, Cassandra then drew her sword and ordered her dream cavalry down, and watched the witch's armies scatter in panic. This filled her with joy. Casandra now pursued the Black Witch across the sky swinging her gleaming sword after her. The witch fled on her broomstick to her dark tower in the forest. Cassandra rode around and around the tower's crown screaming at the witch to come out and fight.

"You cannot kill me, for I am undead! Cassandra yelled.

But the Black Witch called back that "it was not time," and Cassandra saw her face, the face looked familiar, strong, smart and scared. Casandra drew satisfaction from this. Cassandra also saw the baby Hamster, held hostage in the tower, and her own self, naked and in chains crying, and Cassandra wept at this. She saw however that her forces had chased the witch's army back into the tower, and she landed to inspect the siege works. *It would take a long siege* she thought, *to break this place.* She pulled off her black steel gloves and saw written on the palm of her left hand, 'I love you', and on the palm of the other 'be strong;' then the words turned into red wounds in the palms of her hands.

****

It was October 17, at Key Bridge, stretching over the Potomac between Rosslyn in Virginia and Georgetown in DC. It was grey and overcast, the temperature was below freezing, but Pamela's blue eyes were on fire. She was dressed in a warm dark blue goose-down jacket, warm blue pants, dark blue gloves and despite Cassandra's protests, cowboy boots. A film crew was there from CNS, at Pam's insistence, as Cassandra hovered anxiously at Pamela's side dressed in a black ski outfit with a black goose down jacket, grey mukluk boots, and black gloves. They stood on the sidewalk at the Rosslyn side of the bridge as traffic poured by on a normal workday in DC. They were both out of the hospital "on leave" but had to come back by nightfall. This had been granted over the objections of nearly everyone at the hospital. *I got pull*, thought Cassandra with satisfaction. 344 people had died taking Key Bridge on the Morning after the attempted Coup, 97 of them VMI cadets, some barely 17 years old. VMI had now added Key Bridge to its battle standard as a victory. A make-shift memorial stood beside Pamela, it was of chiseled grey granite, sitting on the sidewalk like a massive gravestone. It was from New Hampshire and commemorated their deaths in an another universe it seemed, just six months previously.

"Ready?" said Pamela and began walking as the film crew recorded. She was walking slowly, grasping the railing once every few steps, her face a mask of concentration. Cassandra took her place behind the film crew on

206

the far side of the bridge, encouraging Pamela forward. Cassandra had wanted Pamela to get another week of practice and physical therapy, but Pamela had insisted, and Clausen and Petroski had given their grudging OK's. Pamela was eager to move ahead and wanted to cross Key bridge before it got any colder. Both Cassandra and Pamela had discussed the fact that the Fall was turning out to be much colder than normal, and Winter was to be even worse. Pamela was soon halfway across, but she was slowing and obviously becoming tired as she trudged ahead with measured steps. She no longer seemed to see Cassandra or the film crew but was instead focused on just the sidewalk in front of her and occasionally the shops and fashionable bars of M street at the end of the bridge in Georgetown. At three-quarters of the way across, she suddenly faltered and grabbed on to the bridge railing for support. Cassandra was praying for her and wanted to rush up and help her but Pamela suddenly stepped away from the railing and resumed her progress with steady but slow steps. Finally, with apparently tremendous effort, she reached the Georgetown end of the bridge and collapsed into Cassandra's ecstatic arms. Pamela, now beaming, leaned on the end of the bridge railing and rested for a few minutes.

"I did it! Now let's get a drink at Omar's!" Pamela yelled, pointing at the nearest bar on M street. "After that, let's go dancing, Cassie!" she yelled over the noise of traffic as they crossed the street joyfully, under the cold overcast sky.

****

At the short airstrip at Fort Riley Alaska, the C-130 Hercules screamed in, to slam its wheels down on the runway in the gloom of a cloudy afternoon. As it hurtled down the runway, its four massive turboprops crashed into reverse pitch and roared to maximum power to provide reverse thrust to slow the plane. Inside Schwartzman, Arizona and the other members of the 42nd Ranger Battalion braced themselves in their harnesses as the plane came to an abrupt halt on the runway. Schwartzman looked up as the back cargo bay doors opened and the loading ramp deployed with a crash out of the back of the plane. He was warily clutching his loaded Berretta 9 mm, his constant companion now.

The cold wind of Alaska blew through the cargo bay heavy with the smell of jet fuel as he arose unsnapping his safety harness.

"Let's go you Rangers!" he yelled as all through the hold men rose and donned backpacks and clutched M-4 carbines. Schwartzman strode strongly down the loading ramp to where two men in berets waited by a Humvee on the ground. It was major Garret or "Mongoose" and he snapped to attention as his black face broke into a bright smile. Schwartzman stopped and returned his salute with a wide grin.

"Good to see you Colonel!" yelled Mongoose above the wind and din of the busy airfield.

"Excellent to see you Major!" yelled Schwartzman. They shook hands as Arizona ambled up with Schwartzman's gear, threw it into the Humvee, and all got in after it. In an instant, the Humvee was racing down the flight line to the 42$^{nd}$ Battalion's quarters.

"What have you got going in operation Valhalla?"

"Oh, Boss you are gonna love this. I got three platoons, all volunteers, training for this fight, right now with steel armor and equipment, but we have the new Tallin gear arriving every day from Seattle. The men are sharp as razors! I have never seen a unit so itching for a brawl!"

"Good work Goose!" said Schwartzman as Mongoose handed him a report filled with pictures of the new equipment. "I sure am looking forward to this Op!"

****

Cassandra, clad in a loose-fitting French tee shirt and slacks, lay down on the padded medical table in Petrosian's office and offered her arm to the nurse, who inserted an IV. Pamela, standing beside her looking apprehensive, held her hand. Doctor Petrosian, looking grim, sat nearby in his wheelchair.

"Cassandra" began Dr. Petrosian, "I am going to ask you for the last time before we begin the Pentothal treatment if you are certain you want to do this? In cases such as yours involving imprisonment and torture, the recovered memories can sometimes lead to renewed trauma. Also, we have no need to do this now. We can easily wait for several weeks."

"No, Doctor, let us proceed," said Cassandra grimly. *I can't remember what happened and I can't get well until I do... I have to get well as soon as possible.* She was staring up at the ceiling gripping Pamela's hand. Petrosian nodded and took out a clipboard with notes. The nurse's face appeared above Cassandra and asked her to start counting backward from 100 as the sodium pentothal flowed into her veins. Cassandra began counting backward, 100, 99, 98, 97...

"Where are you now Cassandra?" asked Petrosian.

"I am in handcuffs, and Virgil Jackson is hustling me off the Learjet onto the landing strip near Devil's Mesa. There are troops in black fatigues and black helmet covers around us. Everyone is afraid. My arms are handcuffed behind me and I am afraid I will fall, but Virgil Jackson holds my arms and helps me and we run to an entrance at the base of the mesa. Inside the place is full of gunfire and smoke. There are dead bodies everywhere. It looks like chaos. These are horrible tarantula or crab-like things running around and eating the dead bodies. I see some of the police looking people in black shoot some of of the crab-things. It almost deafens me, because I can't cover my ears."

"Then they put me in a cell," continued Cassandra," and take off my handcuffs. Virgil Jackson says I will be safe there. He is being nice to me and he assigns guards with special blue traffic vests to guard me. There is more shooting and screams in the halls further away, and I am afraid. Then he goes with several other guards with blue vests. They send in women guards and tell me to take off my clothes because they say they need to wash my clothes and let me shower. Then they give me this clean white lab coat to wear and take me to a shower so I can wash all the sweat, dirt and blood off me from the past two days. I am afraid, but I do what they say. Then they take me back to the cell and I wait for them to bring me my clothes. This lady guard brings me my clothes, and they're all clean and pressed like magic. But I get angry with her and she slaps me. So I put on my clothes again and lay down on the bed in the jail cell and they lock the door. Then I fall asleep, and I dream about this policewoman with shiny dark glasses and then suddenly I am awake and somebody in the next cell is talking to me. I get angry with them too. Then Virgil Jackson comes back and says I have to go meet the big boss, and Virgil says I have to do what the big boss says. The big boss is the Wizard, the head of the UFO cover-up.

So, they handcuff me again with my arms behind my back, and Virgil and some other troops with blue vests take me to some sort of meeting room.

And everyone is happy to see me and cheers when I walk in, and then I see it's because they think I am going to make this broadcast for them, to save them. And that is what the guy in the wheelchair, the Wizard, who looks half dead, says to me. And I tell him, 'no, I won't do it'." Cassandra froze staring off into space.

"So then they take me away," Cassandra gasped. "And I see Virgil, he looks like he wants to help me but can't, so they march me down this endless corridor with white tiles to this black steel door. Then they take me inside.

"They, strip off my clothes," said Cassandra, "all except for my panties because the man in charge with a beard, they are all afraid of him, won't let them take them off. Some of the men, they want to rape me, but the man in charge, with a beard, he says they have to break me first. So they tie me down on my stomach on this table and they tell me I have to agree to give this broadcast or they're going to tear out my fingernails. I am afraid, I am afraid they are going to kill me.."

"They tear out my fingernails," stammered Cassandra, "one by one in front of me, with this pliers looking thing, and I am screaming and crying, but my fingertips are numb since they blew up my car a few weeks before, so it hurts but I can bear it. But I think they are destroying my body …

210

They get really angry now and they turn on some machine with high voltage.. and they hold this wire up in front of my face, and then beginning shocking me with the electricity. They are raising the voltage and I am screaming , they shock me all over my body, and I start to black out but then they hook the voltage up to this whip, and they hit on the back with it...and I scream some more.."

Cassandra paused and stared off into space

"It feels like they are cutting me in two with a razor, and they keep yelling at me to do the broadcast. But somehow I won't do it, and I think I will die now. And I won't do what they say... They hit my back some more times, and I feeling like am dying ... My back feels like a slab of rubber , numb."

"Then..."

"Then everything changes. I am floating, I am above my body looking down on it, and I can see my back is all bloody, but I floating free and I don't care anymore. Then I am floating upwards towards this bright light, and it is so beautiful, I want to join to it...

Then her face changed from a smile to disappointment, then twisted into grief.

"Then I am floating down away from the light..."

"No, No, I don't want to go back...Please don't make me go back..." she wept.

Then suddenly I am looking at Virgil Jackson, and he is talking to me. I can't understand what he is saying. Then there is all this noise. Then we are out of the dark torture room and into the light and Virgil has wrapped me in a blanket and is carrying me down the hall. I am hanging on to him."

"Then they take me to a safe place, and Virgil has a nurse come and give me Novocain for my back where they hit me, and she staples the gashes shut. Virgil pleads with me to do the broadcast so I can save the nurses and other guards in this place who are trying to get out. He says the government troops are outside the mesa with big guns and are going to destroy the place and everyone will be killed unless I can buy them some time to escape. He begs me to do this for the others."

"And I believe him. I want to help him save the people in this place who are trapped there, even if it dooms me. I don't care if I live anymore. I feel like I am dead already. Then they take me to this television studio and the guy, Bremer, the Wizard, in the wheelchair is there, and he is obviously on drugs. And he is bragging about how the aliens are going to attack at the end of the government deadline. I don't know what to do. I want to save the people who tried to help me, and the nurses and technicians who are trapped there, but I don't want to help Bremer and the aliens. So to buy time I ask him for his speech and it's mostly illegible, so I suddenly think, 'I can say what I want because his speech is gibberish and he won't know the difference. So I decide to mangle the speech and put in double meanings. So I decide to give the speech and I am doomed, and I know it...

"Then I give the speech, and Bremer applauds because he thinks the speech is so good." Cassandra's face turns into a contemptuous smile. "But then they figure out I tricked them, and I am afraid they are going to torture me again. But Virgil walks up and puts a gun to my head, and pulls the trigger," Cassandra looked astonished. "but then nothing happens... he forgot to reload his gun. So he uses this to have me taken away to be executed, but then some of his men try to rescue me..."

"And they have me in this chamber, to be executed, but then the Carny comes, with Bob, and they rescue me. They get me dressed in some dead guard's uniform, then we go down into the base's lower levels, and things get blurry. I am so tired I can hardly walk anymore, but I do..."

"And we are looking at all these bones, bones of millions of people..." gasped Cassandra staring wide-eyed. And Bob he wants to kill himself because he said he let this happen, but I tell him no, that I love him, it wasn't his fault, and that he has to rescue me and get me out of there." Cassandra paused. "So he believes me, and the Carny and I finally walk up this passage out of that hell. Then the Carny blows up the last door holding us in. And we go out, and the air is smoky but fresh, and the sky is dark now, and the mountain and the mesa are burning. I am so exhausted,

I think I might pass out after that…" Cassandra paused looked astonished. "Then I was here, at the hospital. "

*So I feel doomed, but I have saved people I loved, but I am doomed, but also alive then, and free…*

****

"Here you go, Colonel.   We had this made according to your specifications." Arizona laid the sword, of English late middle Ages design, down on the table. It was polished bronze-colored metal, Tallin alloy. It has long hilt of fine leather, suitable for two hands if required, and a solid bronze crosspiece to protect the hands.   The hilt ended with a bulb of bronze metal with large synthetic blue diamond set in it.   Schwartzman, now in camouflaged fatigues, took up the sword, mesmerized by it, and stood away from the table slowly moving it through the air, feeling its exquisite balance and heft.   He looked carefully and saw the words **Agincourt** etched into the hard metal.

*Yes,* thought Schwartzman, *I am where I belong.* As he looked down the gym and saw dozens of men in bluish steel armor, rehearsing with swords and heavy two-handed axes, with drill instructors balling out fierce directions.

****

**Chapter 5: Tallin**

At Fort Riley, Alaska, Robert Schwartzman had taken his seat in front of the desk of Brigadier General Festus Ross, commander of Special Forces for the Alaskan theater. In the small office, a large map showed the southwestern part of Alaska including the Aleutian island chain with the island of Adak circled in red. Ross was a greying but rugged man, a highly decorated veteran of Iraq and Afghanistan, Libya and Syria. Schwartz regarded him with both respect and awe. He wondered how his arrival on the front was going to be received, working with a regular army command, in an actual state of war, for the first time in a decade. Ross had his file in front of him and he was reading Schwartzman's orders.

"Colonel Schwartzman we have been waiting for your arrival with great anticipation. I understand your unit has cooked up a new tactic that might get us all out of this jam we're in here. As I see from your file, you have been involved in combat operations with hostile X-rays on many occasions, *and babysitting them too,* thought Schwartzman with chagrin, *depending on the weather.*

"Therefore, you're just the sort of man we need here now."

"I am here to get the job done general," said Schwartzman trying to muster a smile. "That's for sure."

"You have been in theater here for a week, what is your assessment of morale Colonel? "

"Permission to speak frankly sir?"

"Of course! Let's have it!" said the general, rising and pacing around like a caged lion.

"Morale does not look good General, down in the town where you got me quartered, in the Hilton, the troops are all drunk or passed out or in bed with some whore. The men are not looking sharp sir, I can see it, in their uniforms and their eyes, when they're not too bloodshot, that is."

"You might say you detect an atmosphere of depression, in the army units here."

215

"Yes Sir," said Schwartzman with some awkwardness.

"Well around here depression is considered a sign of intelligence, Colonel. Despite what all the news services say, we have gotten the shit kicked out of us in the past weeks. The Air Force lost almost its entire saucer buster squadron, and just barely stopped an alien resupply mission last month. Sure, they flew in another Griffin squadron, but General Peterson of the Air Task Force confided in me that one more victory like that and he is afraid pilots will start ejecting at the first sign of another alien vessel. Morale is at rock bottom. The same situation is holding in the naval units offshore. After that battle last month when they lost five ships, they say the ship's crews are scared shitless. True we have the Xrays bottled up in Mount Bering, but they holding off a force of two divisions with what we estimate is a force of no more than twenty combatants. The firepower they control is stupefying, tanks and APCs are death traps for their crews. So we are forced to advance by digging trenches, like in World War I. Even then are trenches are wiped out by their weapons, so we have not been able to advance to less than two kilometers of what we believe are the alien positions. We are simply blasting them night and day with bombing and artillery, but as soon as we try to advance, they come out and drive us back with heavy casualties. I happen to know that General Foster, the CINC in theater has asked for nuclear weapons to be released repeatedly, but has been denied. The X-rays here don't use proton beams like the Greys, they are using some sort of hypersonic kinetic energy weapons, from some kind of rail gun, and it goes through 100 feet of earth like it was paper... to say we are outgunned is an understatement of the first magnitude. Naturally, going up against such firepower day after day has had its cost in lives and confidence. The place where our lines are closest to the enemies is called the "butcher shop." The bravery displayed by the front line units is almost suicidal, but we cannot continue like this. People are literally starting to have mental breakdowns on the front lines at a much higher than expected rate. It's combat fatigue. To make matters worse, Weather is also deteriorating rapidly, we are having an early winter it looks like, and this will increase our difficulties."

Suddenly an officer stepped into the office and saluted someone outside in the outer office.

"Commanding General on site Sir!" Both General Ross and Schwartzman jumped to attention and saluted, as Lieutenant General Foster, the theater commander in chief, marched in with two staffers and saluted smartly. Foster was tall, and massively built, a giant of a man.

"At ease gentlemen," said General Foster, looking haggard and exhausted, eyed Schwartzman carefully, then smiled grimly and shook his hand.

"Colonel Schwartzman, I have heard from General Foster here, that your boys have cooked up something to break this bloody stalemate here? I want to hear about it. I am all ears!"

"Yes, sir, I was just about to lay it out for General Ross, so with your permission, I will do so now."

"Permission granted, let's see it. Schwartzman advanced to a map on the wall showing Adak Island with Mount Bering surrounded by siege lines and the eastern side marked with what was believed to be the alien's near-surface fortress. Schwartzman motioned with his strong hand between the 5th infantry divisions lines, the ones closest to the fortress, and the alien lines.

"The following operation plan, called Valhalla, was cooked up by my people in 42nd Battalion while I was reconnoitering in the hospital," he thought of his nocturnal encounters with nurse Flo and the French woman then grinned to himself.

"First, some background: Valhalla is based on our combat experience with various X-rays including the Samar, who are identified as the species on Adak, and our fragmentary knowledge of their culture. In brief, the Samar are an extremely humanoid, warrior race, similar in culture to the Spartans or Samurai. Out best guess is they were a Medieval sort of culture similar to Meiji Japan when some outside actor arrived and provided them with highly advanced weaponry and space technology, hence you have a society that fights with lasers and flies starships, but carries swords as a badge of manhood. We think we understand these people also because genetic studies have concluded that we are part Samar, due to their earlier visits to Earth in deep antiquity. We believe

217

this episode is mentioned in the Bible as the Nephilim or sons-of-God episode in genesis. It reads that they took earth women as wives and their offspring were legendary heroes."

"Is that really in the Bible Colonel?" asked General Foster, looking stunned.

"Yes, Sir. It in Genesis, just before the story of Noah's flood," said Schwartzman. "So in the case of the Samar we are dealing with our cousins, General. At least that is our best theory right now, based on that Biblical account and previous unit encounters." Schwartzman paused while General Foster digested this. *I would have thought everybody would know this by now...* thought Schwartzman in dismay. *This Op may be a harder to sell than I thought.*

"So we think we know these people to a degree because they are our cousins, and therefore we can develop an approximate predictive model of their behavior," continued Schwartzman. "Operation Valhalla is also based on the fact that they asked for a truce to cremate their dead, which I requested you grant. When the armistice went into effect, what we saw was them cremating several of the KIA in full view of our lines. They wanted to show us they had taken casualties also. This is called historically the 'brotherhood of the warrior' a mutual respect between foes who share an admiration for each other's fighting prowess and bravery, it often develops between opposing armies in war. So our heavy casualties were not for nothing General, they bought a few hundred meters of ground and those casualties also, in our view, brought respect. So we are going to use these things to pry them out of this mountain. To further this I have asked 5th Division to restore the bodies of the two Samar KIA we recovered to as pristine a state as possible, with all their armor and weapons and return these bodies to the Samar garrison so they can likewise be cremated according to the Samar customs.

"You're hoping to get these people to parley Colonel?" asked General Foster, intently. "Maybe agree to withdraw?"

Schwartzman grinned and shook his head.

218

"No sir, these people are not looking to surrender, withdraw, or even talk. In our estimation they are looking for only one thing now, which is what the Spartans called a "beautiful death": death in battle face-to-face, mano-a-mano, with their enemy, which is us. We intend to offer that to them in the most attractive way possible to them as Samurai-Spartans. We are helped in this by a new metal alloy called Tallin that roughly matches the strength and toughness of the sword and dagger blades the Samar KIA carried. They use some sort of Titanium Vanadium steel alloy, which we can't duplicate, but this Tallin alloy is just as strong and hard. So that's the background, here is Operation Valhalla."

I am equipping and intensively training two companies of my battalion, handpicked and augmented with volunteers from other units, by men who like hand to hand fighting. We are giving them Tallin body armor, and helmets and arming them with swords and axes, we also have several platoons of archers with arrows tipped with Tallin points just in case, and we are going to advance here," He motioned, between the American lines and the alien fortress at its shortest separation, "by tunneling in with high-speed tunneling equipment, breaking through into their fortress, and storming through the tunnel and fighting them in Medieval style combat."

General Foster smiled skeptically. "Won't they hear you tunneling in?"

"Oh we are going to tell them we are coming in, General," said Schwartzman with a slight swagger, "We will challenge them to meet us in personal combat with sword and axe."

"Suppose they don't want to play that way?"

"Well, we are wagering that, since they are surrounded and cut off from supplies, and either cannot or refuse to withdraw, that they will welcome this challenge, especially since we will have demonstrated respect for their dead. They don't want a ticket home General; they want a ticket to Valhalla, by dying sword-in-hand."

General Foster laughed uproariously at this. He looked relieved. He motioned to one of his staffers, who produced a box of fine Cuban cigars from a leather briefing case. Despite the no smoking signs in evidence on the wall, everyone, including Schwartzman took one. The staffer then went around with a lighter shooting out a huge flame, and lit everyone's cigar. The room filled with fragrant smoke. Schwartzman was reminded of the many conferences of the Carney, just before combat – spike operations against the X-rays.

"This is the craziest, asinine idea I have ever heard of Colonel!" said Foster blowing cigar smoke at the ceiling with a big grin. "You are basically challenging these people to a duel! And I like it! If it works, and your men are as sharp as I think they are, we can finish this campaign in an afternoon! I approve Operation Valhalla to proceed as soon as can be made practicable! Give them their ticket back to the stars." He then added thoughtfully. "However, I hope you are prepared to write a lot of letters home Colonel. "

"Oh yes, I even wrote my own, because I intend to be point man down in that tunnel when we break through!" said Schwartzman grinning past his cigar and squaring his shoulders as he faced his two superiors.

"Are you sure that a good idea Colonel?" asked General Ross.

"General, we are either going to chew their ass, or be incinerated in the first seconds when that tunneling machine breaks through! I wouldn't miss this battle for all the gold in Fort Knox!"

"All right! I like it!" said Foster turning to General Ross. "General Ross, make this thing happen! This is SOCOM's operation, just tell us anything the Colonel needs."

"Yes sir!" said both General Ross and Schwartzman standing at attention and saluting. Foster returned their salute as he rose to leave.

****

"Oooh! This is so outrageous!" yelled Cassandra indignantly. "Pictures of me confronting the peace-at-any-price demonstrators are all over the net and social media! Only they only show me from the front topless! They hardly show any pictures of my back!" she exploded in frustration at Pamela who was sitting in her bed working away furiously on her laptop.

220

Pamela paused and did a quick web search herself. Pamela quickly confirmed what had exasperated Cassandra so much and then gave her a look of amused sympathy. Pamela rose from the bed walked over to Cassandra and ceremoniously gave her a hug.

"Welcome to the new age of Journalism Cassie! At least most of them pixel out your nipples," said Pamela.

"But that's so unfair! It's ridiculous in fact! Most of them didn't even report me turning my back to them! Or even that I was arguing with a bunch of numb-skulled peaceniks"

"Yes! Unfair! Yes, voyeuristic! Yes, shocking, shallow!" laughed Pamela jumping back on her bed. " It is obvious that the fine intellectual point you were trying to make by going topless, itself  proved much too sophisticated  for the pooled intellects of the web to appreciate, " said Pamela with slight amusement. "It's a good thing that despite being a little thin, you still look hot!" she added with a grin.

"Do you really think so?"  asked Cassie studying the images. "I normally get upset when the camera adds ten pounds, but in this case, it did some good. It took me from being emaciated to just looking skinny." *What's done is done,* thought Cassandra, *someday I'll understand all this. At least I didn't look fat!*

"Oh definitely! I expect it will stimulate a new look!" said Pamela smiling. "I would consider the fact that no one comments on what you said, to be a sure sign of victory, congratulations! At least, now, no one thinks we are up here at Arlington Hospital, watching the war every night and munching popcorn."

"Just to change the subject, what are you working on so hard over there?" asked Cassandra shutting off her laptop.

"Cosmic war strategy.  Remember how I gave that big lecture to everyone at CNS when we started to unravel the Stargate scandal, and we all knew it could lead to war if the UFO cover-up was ended?" asked Pamela. "I used that analogy to the American Colonists in the Revolutionary War."

"Yes! It was magnificent Pammy! I was blown away, so was everybody else. I became convinced after that that we could win! That we could end the UFO cover-up and deal with whatever came afterward!" said Cassandra feeling ecstatic.

"So yes! So I am sending a write-up of it to one of my professors at Annapolis. I asked him to issue it under his own name if he thinks it makes sense." said Pamela. "People need to know that we have a way to win this thing. I don't care who gets credit, I just want to win."

"But it is your great idea!" said Cassandra.

"Yeah but I am just a blonde former weathergirl from Cleveland," said Pamela, looking a little dejected.

"Oh, you're so much more than that! For instance, where did you get this great idea?" said Cassandra walking over to Pamela looking concerned.

"Oh, that an interesting question. I have actually reconstructed it. I got the original inspiration from the Mr. Big alien I met when I was being abducted. When I said 'Mene Mene Tekle Uphraisin' at him, which is from the Bible, it turns out, though I didn't know at the time. And when I said that he became really afraid, and I picked up his thoughts. He was thinking the Pleiadians or some other interstellar power will come and intervene. In one instant, I knew he was thinking that and what had made him really afraid. So even though it was part of my suppressed memories as an abductee, I still was processing that information somehow, deep in my unconscious. Then when I found out what had happened to me, the whole analysis suddenly appeared in my mind also."

"Oh Pammy, that makes me feel so sad," said Cassandra suddenly bursting into tears. She then embraced Pamela and buried her face into Pamela's shoulder, and wept inconsolably.

**** 

The Navy Captain stood next to a projection screen showing the estimated depth and position of the fast attack submarine USS Monterey before all contact was lost.    Alicia sat with other Navy and scientific personnel as the Captain pointed with a laser pointer at the first point.

"Based on our reconstruction of the last five minutes of Monterey's mission from long range hydrophone data, we believe it started here at 151 W and 52 N at 0410 hours moving at 30 knots at a depth of 500 ft. The Monterey was equipped with downward looking sonar with a synthetic aperture and was conducting sea bottom surveys to try to locate possible alien bases.  Ocean depth at his location is 5,000 ft. plus.  Long range hydrophones, picked up what seems to be a side scattered sonar, at 0415 hrs. indicating a possible deep, large, rising object approaching the Monterey from below.   At 0418 propeller and rudder cavitation is heard indicating the Monterey went to flank speed  and applied  hard right rudder, indicating it was moving to engage a target rising from below.  At 0421 we have signatures that four Mark 48 torpedoes were launched from bow tubes.  A second rudder cavitation is heard  at 0425 indicating hard left rudder,   at 0427 three torpedo detonations in 10-second intervals begin.  At 0431, we have crash-back, which means the Monterey reversed propeller pitch to brake, followed by sounds of the USS Monterey blowing ballast. An unidentified sound follows at 0435 followed by sounds of a hull implosion, believed to be the Monterey descending below crush depth, sounds of major debris hitting the ocean floor follow approximately 25 minutes later. Based on this record and the recovery of some debris at the surface two days later, we now believe USS Monterey was lost in action with all 135 of its crew.

From this we also conclude that the Monterey engaged an alien submersible, probably rising up to protect a base in the area. Alicia felt a deep chill go through her at this report, she imagined the last moments of the crew, perishing in the cold, dark depths.

"Consistent with this Admiral Haynes has ordered the assembly of a large task force code named Typhoon  to locate and destroy the suspected alien base in  the approximate area where the Monterey  went down."

**\*\*\*\***

223

Schwartzman, covered in sweat from training in full armor with his sword, wandered into his battalion HQ office as the men took a break from endless physical and weapons training. Two men were looking at a computer terminal chuckling and both looked around by instinct as he entered the room and rose to attention.

"At ease, gentlemen," said Schwartzman wearily, waving a salute at them. Then his eyes fastened on the computer screen. It was Cassandra Chen in the video, she was topless and angry, and despite looking thin, presented a distracting image. Pamela was beside her in a wheelchair obviously also in a bad mood. Then he fastened his gaze on her face, it was twisted in anger, she then lifted her long black hair and whirled around to present her scarred back to the camera. The camera then turned to view troops in combat gear coming around the side of the building with an APC then also rolling around the building carrying a rack of ground-launched sidewinder missiles and troops in combat gear riding on the top. The camera work became very confused after this. It was obvious the local military commander wanted the cameraman and his fellow protestors to leave.

"Cassandra Chen," said one of the soldiers, "she came out of the hospital and confronted a bunch of nit-war protestors then showed them her back, apparently, the local commander at the hospital then sent everything available to break up the demonstration."

"Shit for brains protestors! Don't they know what happened at Morningstar?" yelled Schwartzman. "You can't negotiate peace with that!" He turned and walked away, back out to the gymnasium to where the men had resumed practice with swords and axes. The drillmaster, a master of swordsmanship, was yelling a drill sequence endlessly. In a moment, he was back into the rhythm of parrying and thrusting mindlessly. *She came out and did battle,* he thought, *the only way she knows how. It's a good thing I wasn't there,* he thought in a rage. *I might have lost control and killed some of the protestors. Better I am here, where I can kill and be killed and it's considered perfectly normal.* However, the image of Cassandra's scarred back haunted him, filling him with such a mixture of helpless rage and sorrow he could hardly bear it. Finally, as he resumed the exercises, he swung his sword in time with the shouted drillmaster's commands, every thought dissolved into one. *In a*

*few days, when I am first in the breakthrough tunnel, it won't matter*
*anymore what I think or feel.*

****

Hontal was ushered into a vast hall with gothic architecture. At the end of
the hall sat Sadok Sar the Unash commander on the Moon, on a stepped
stone platform. Two staffers sat near him on the platform. Hontal could
not help but feel he was in the presence of an evil so vast that it eclipsed
the stars. He gripped his royal star pendant, symbol of his authority from
the palace and walked forward down the long hall. The Toman Daz
security guards had tried to take his sword and dagger from him in the
outer chambers, but he had refused, citing Samaran customs. This had
resulted in a tense standoff, broken only when he was ushered in without
further comment. He sensed even now that several blaster weapons were
trained on him. But he was Samar, a knight of the realm, therefore used
to danger.

Hontal approached Sadok Sar and bowed his head and saluted. The
platform was taller than he and stepped so that that the Unash
commander could look down on the much taller Samaran. Sadok Sar
bowed his large head slightly as Hontal stopped in front of the platform.
Sadok Sar was dressed in an ornate robe of many colors and sat on a short
chair. His two staffers sat on the floor beside him. The light was dim in the
chamber and only a ray of sunlight from a large multicolored window
could be perceived in a far corner. The large chamber was bare grey stone
except for a carpet where Sadok Sar sat. Sadok Sar looked older and
greyer than most Unash Hontal had seen. His head was much larger,
relative to his body than a human, making his head appear much larger,
when in fact, his head and brain was nearly the same size as a human's,
and he had a pronounced brow ridge over his round eyes. He had only
two, round nostrils where a human would have had a nose and had a wide
slit-like mouth, with no visible lips.

"Greetings Hontal of Alnilam, I am wondering why you have been sent
here, so far from your home stars," said Sadok Sar in a thin voice. Hontal
stood and noticed no chair was available to sit in and was filled with

225

annoyance. However, mindful of the telepathic abilities of the Unash, he kept his emotions and thoughts under strict control.

"My Lord Sadok Sar, I am sent by the Palace of Rigel to collect information on your progress here. I am informed that your attempts to cultivate a group of partisans to your cause in the foremost nation on Erra has failed, and the partisan's forces have been defeated in battle, and many have been killed or arrested for treason. I am also informed that the nations of Erra have formed an alliance against the Unash forces here, and have declared war against you. "

"These things are minor matters. We are preparing operations against the Errans to restore the yoke of fear upon them, and bring about their complete surrender to our wishes. The wisest among them already know their situation is hopeless, so this will not take long."

"I note that you are mounting many operations against the Errans, but I also note you are losing many spacecraft in these operations. Please describe to me the operational goals of these operations, so I may include it in my report to the palace."

"These are part of my war plan, which has many components," said Sadok Sar. "Large reinforcements will shortly arrive to aid this war plan. However, the war plan is highly secret to this place and my government, I do not wish to discuss it, since the way back to Rigel is long, and the Quzrada, is, as you know, a dangerous place now. I will only assure your government that our operations here on their behalf are progressing, despite minor setbacks."

"I must also raise the question of our own Samaran garrison on a northern island on Erra. It is my understanding that repeated efforts to resupply them have failed and that they are under siege by Erran allied Forces. I must ask why a major operation has not been mounted to break this siege and evacuate them?" said Hontal. Sadok Sar tensed at this question and his large black eyes developed a slight squint. Beside him his two staffers became rigid. Sadok Sar sat silent for a long time, and Hontal sensed he was trembling with rage.

"The Samar garrison you speak was established against my recommendation, and was offered evacuation when the recent crisis on Erra developed, however, they refused," said Sadok Sar, in a thin, almost hissing, voice. "Your local commander, Koton, even made a point of journeying there to join the garrison, also against my recommendation. We have many personnel in many bases on Erra, and they follow my recommendations, and we supply them as best we can during these temporary difficulties. So the predicament of 23 of your personnel on the island is of concern, but I have thousands of personnel of on Erra, and I must also see to their support." Sadok Sar paused.

"If this garrison is of such importance, I recommend you deploy the starship Tlakmar to go to their rescue. We will support such an operation."

"I will discuss this with the Captain of the Tlakmar," answered Hontal. *This would be a great battle!*

"Good I will eagerly await further communications on this matter. I must also, at the behest of my government, raise the issue of payments for our services here. The situation here at Erra has become more complex as well as in the Quzrada region as a whole. This has greatly increased expenses and supply requirements for operations here. "Sadok Sar paused. "Therefore, we will need more money..."

"I can take no such request back to the palace, my mission here is purely to gather information," answered Hontal quickly. *I am glad for Dakon's orders. I have no wish to haggle with these people!*

"The increased complexity of the situation here, and its consequent increased expenses is important information to carry to Rigel," insisted Sadok Sar.

"I am not the right person to carry such a message. Your government must send a special emissary to discuss this grave, matter with the palace directly."

"Very well, Hontal of Alnilam, I believe this concludes our discussions for the day. I will await word from you concerning a joint operation between our forces and your starship the Tlakmar."

Hontal , now seething with rage, turned and walked out of the great hall.

Sadok Sar turned to one of his aides.

"I want that one killed, can this be arranged?" he hissed.

"Not here my Lord, it would cause great difficulties with the Samarans."

"Later then," said Sadok Sar, looking at the door where Hontal had departed. "But tell that dungeater Bekar of Batelgeen, that I want this impertinent one dead."

****

"We managed to bring down two saucers last night with the loss of no fighters, this was due to the apparent effectiveness of the magneto proximity fused cannon and missile warheads," said Alicia addressing the War Science Board. They were in the Pentagon in Washington. Abe Goldberg sat smiling supportively as she continued. He had come out by armored train from the Midwest, to chair the War Science Board. Most of the men looked heartened by this, but one, a white-haired thin fellow named Loomis, looked as dour as ever.

"Altogether, alien craft losses are up , and fighter losses are down. We brought down five total last night, nationwide, one over France and two over Russia, for a total of eight brought down with the loss of twenty aircraft. So this trend is good," said Alicia with satisfaction.

"One week does not constitute a trend," said Loomis. He was a professor of engineering from MIT with long grey hair and beard.

"The magneto proximity fused ammunition has barely gone into production, Dr. Loomis, and everywhere it has arrived and has been employed it has resulted in a better kill ratio," said Alicia. "I expect, that when widely employed, the magneto-proximity fuses will produce even greater alien losses."

"The aliens will counter measure them shortly, remember they are a thousand years ahead of us in technology, Dr. Sepulveda, " said Loomis.

228

"Well, following that logic Dr. Loomis, we should have been conquered in 1947 right after Roswell." retorted Alicia, becoming angry. "So your logic is bogus."

"Bill, you're up right after Alicia, why don't you reserve your comments on war strategy until after Dr. Sepulveda finishes here." Loomis sat seething in response to this. *Someone got up on the wrong side of the bed this morning,* she thought.

"What war strategy , Abe?" asked Loomis acidly.

"We have three new technologies that we are bringing online as fast as possible also," continued Alicia, ignoring Loomis and regaining her composure, "They should become factors in here over DC by next week and elsewhere following that." DC had now become the focus of the war in the skies at night. "First, we have a new fragmentation warhead design for missiles and perhaps even cannon shells, it is called CORTEX, which stands for Coordinated Tomography Explosive." She put up a power point slide showing a missile warhead with an array of detonators dispersed in the explosive, rather than one detonator. The usual array of pre-fragmented steel prisms for shrapnel stays around the explosive. "A simple computer using optical logic detects the probable direction of the alien ship based on magnetic field sensors or radar data and triggers the array of detonators to launch a focused shock wave and thus a jet of fragments, preferentially in the probable direction of the target. CORTEX basically converts a block of explosive into a directed energy weapon. Given that almost all the craft brought down over Moscow and Washington DC have been riddled with shrapnel, as well as several ships that have crashed outside of the metro areas, we believe this new technique will further increase our kill ratio."

"That is if the aliens don't hack the computers on the warheads like they hack everything else!" interjected Loomis.

"Bill, your twenty minutes is coming up right after she finishes," said Goldberg sharply.

"We also have a new Russian system ," continued Alicia. "The high power Carbon Monoxide laser, with 95% electric efficiency and low absorption in

229

the atmosphere. They can throw 1-second pulses of 5 megawatts, using after burning turbo-jet engines with MHD generators called Alexandrov generators. They even use phase conjugation to self-aim the laser off of reflected light pulse wave fronts, it's sort of like using a radar beam pulsed with a phased array to steer the next radar pulse wavefront. They are already being deployed around Moscow and Novosibirsk, so we should get data on their effectiveness soon.

Finally, our own people have now built a 2 Megawatt portable Copper Vapor laser firing 1-second pulses. It shoots green light. They will begin deploying that in two days here in Washington into the air defense ring.

"That should produce quite a light show," said one scientist, named Turner, enthusiastically. "We better make sure everyone has anti-laser goggles, in case they try to watch."

"Yes, good idea, even though we have warned everyone to stay indoors and watch it on TV. Finally, the Sun continues to make above normal numbers of Coronal mass ejections and solar flare events. The flares, in particular, seem to interfere with alien operations and so we are hoping for two nights of peace and quiet here later this week when a large flare pops. Northern lights should be visible the next few nights after that."

"Overall, the standard operation of this war appears to be small-scale alien attempts to defend established bases or else evacuate from them when they are discovered and attacked. The aliens have also resorted to terror attacks on major cities, by abducting people and then dismembering them, and attempts to cause power failures, however, they have avoided hard, heavily defended targets such as aircraft factories or launch sites.

Any Questions? Alicia looked around the room. Everyone looked as happy as they could during a war, on a day without big news. All except Loomis, who assumed the podium with an aura of barely suppressed rage. He plugged in a thumb drive and it began to open a video.

"Dr. Loomis of MIT is here to talk about radar." said Goldberg with a wary smile.

The video showed a mouse falling into a pool of water with a snapping turtle, the snapping turtle bit off the bottom half of the mouse, while its front half, head and front legs kept pathetically swimming. Alicia looked away from the horrid sight.

"Bill this is very funny, why are you showing us this?" said Goldberg rising with a more threatening smile. The snapping turtle finally swallowed the front half of the mouse in one bite, putting an end to the horrid spectacle.

"Because that mouse is us!" said Loomis looking straight at Goldberg. "I have just found out what the aliens are really up to in this war, these air raids are nothing but a distraction, and I have found out what you have been keeping from us, how the aliens are going to crush us in six months and why we can do nothing about it!" A new image had appeared on the view screen, it showed the Earth-Moon system and the Sun and the Earth-Sun L1 Lagrange point at a distance of four lunar orbits towards the Sun.

"Bill! This meeting is only cleared for Top Secret!" said Goldberg in obvious anger.

"The aliens have moved a large space platform to the L1 Solar Lagrange point! They are dumping Moondust into the Lagrange point region to cut off Sunlight from the Earth! And we can do nothing to stop them! NOTHING! This whole war effort is just a pathetic struggle against the inevitable..."

"This meeting is hereby adjourned for an hour!" yelled Goldberg. "As for the Lagrange point business, we have operations to deal with this!"

"We should be suing for peace! That is the only recommendation of conscience a scientist can make!" yelled Loomis. "SUE FOR PEACE! The aliens are just playing at this war with these dismemberments! They are going to cut off sunlight to the Earth and the..." The microphone was cut off and armed military police suddenly entered the room and Goldberg motioned to them to escort Loomis out of the room. He glared in anger at Abe Goldberg, as he was led out of the room. Alicia looked around the room, on the faces of the scientists remaining emotions ranged from despair to shock.

The door shut behind Loomis and the guards. Goldberg was standing tall at the podium now and reactivating the microphone. Goldberg calmed himself. Alicia looked at him, she could see from Goldberg's expression that what Loomis had said was true. An abyss of despair opened up within her, she struggled not to fall into it.

"Colleagues, the situation you have just heard referred to, draws on intelligence information that is compartmentalized and classified high above the level for which this room is cleared. This is a serious breach in security and you will all have to be debriefed."

"Abe , is what he said true? " asked another scientist.

"We have highly classified operations directed against the situation Loomis just spoke of, and I would risk not only the lives of the men involved in those operations if I spoke of them but also any chance of success they might have," said Goldberg calmly. "As I said , we are on top of this situation, and you will all be debriefed."

"The solar activity, the coronal mass ejections from it would blow any Moondust out of the Libration point halo orbits. Are we actually creating Solar flare activity somehow to prevent the aliens from accumulating any dust in the libration point?" asked a woman scientist.

"Like I said, this room is not cleared for these discussions," said Goldberg with a faint smile. "However, rest assured, that if we could stop the six mile long Sepulveda asteroid four years ago, then we can deal with this problem."

"Yes! " said Alicia, " We can deal with this!" She was rising and nodding. *We did stop the asteroid! I know they have a plan to deal with this, I know they do,* she thought fiercely. Then another thought came, that froze her soul. *They will do deep space operations, a long reach into space. They will need Blue to help them...* She watched the scientists in the room face's turn from gloom to calm optimism. She suddenly quit thinking about this.

"Do we actually have a strategy for winning this war?" asked another scientist named Cooper.

"Of course, you will be briefed on its Top Secret level details at our next meeting, it's called the Henderson plan."

"Who is Henderson ?" asked Cooper.

"He is a naval war strategist. Like I said, you will be briefed on the details later at our next meeting" said Goldberg with a broad smile.

"Alright, we have to adjourn for an hour," said Alicia rising. Everyone filed out of the room. Goldberg and Alicia stood calmly until the last person left.

"Thanks, Alicia, they are now convinced we somehow control Solar flare activity, and I want them to keep believing it. Also, I am reading you into the Archangel Program, follow me."

"What is Archangel?" she asked vacantly.

"Come with me, this room isn't cleared for it."

"What about Loomis?"

"He broke compartmentalization, in the middle of a war," said Goldberg angrily, "and I am going to supervise his debrief personally, and then if he wises up and tells us where he learned this libration point thing, it's a trip to Extended Stay America for the duration. A fate, which in my view, is too good for the smart ass! "

"Where is that?"

"It's where we send people who know too much to send to Fort Leavenworth Prison in Kansas: a little tropical paradise known as Kwajalein," said Goldberg grimly, as they filed out of the room to another corridor.

"I also need you to study a recent report by a guy named Henderson from Annapolis who works for the Navy and figure out if it makes any sense," said Goldberg as they proceeded down the hall through heavy steel doors, which shut behind them.

"My lord, we are losing too many ships to continue this operation!" said Number 4 to Sadok Sar. "Even if they are not lost outright, many ships are damaged during operations in the Erran atmosphere, with their hulls punctured, and cannot make the return trip back to the Moon! Their crews run out of air! Others that are slightly damaged are picked off by Unal raiders operating in stealthy ships between here and the Moon." Number 7 sat impassively as he watched the meeting progress. He was astounded at Number 4's bluntness.

*Why don't we simply have more spacesuits for the crews?* thought Number 7.

"We will soon receive reinforcement, our losses will be made up," said Sadok Sar calmly. "I cannot end this operation now, the Samar have sent observers, and they must see only normal operations. Therefore, operations will continue as they have. "

"But we are not only losing ships , we are losing their crews! These people are trained veterans of operations at Erra." protested Number 4.

"The crews will be replaced also," said Sadok Sar, looking calm. "Our war plan will see the Errans surrender in a few months' time." At this response, Number 4 fell into silence. The meeting ended with Sadok Sar leaving without further comment.

In the morning, with their son spending today at a sitter, Alicia was sitting in a bathrobe drinking Coffee when Blue, clad also in a bathrobe, came up and dropped a file of papers on the table in front of her. She looked at it fearfully. It was a navy flight surgeon's report. Blue had passed a physical for flight duty.

"No!" she screamed at him. "NO!" tears streaming down her cheeks. "What about our son? What about our next child?"

"You see this man?" he held up a portrait photo of himself in a spacesuit, as the astronaut he formerly was. "That is the man you married! Not a

234

college professor. I am a U.S. Marine Chiquita, and there is no way in hell I am sitting out this war!"

****

Alicia dreamed of the last great king of the Aztecs, Cuauhtémoc. He had gotten himself  bronze from Michoacán, and from his brother, the Great Inca in the far south. He used captured Spanish crossbows as a model and had equipped an army of Eagle and Jaguar warriors with bronze weapons and armor.  They had pushed the Spanish back to Veracruz on the coast. They had then constructed a great "Spirit Bow" to launch pots full of flaming pine oil and sulfur at the Spanish in their  fortifications . When the great Spirit Bow was drawn back and loaded with a great flaming arrow, a great drum would sound like thunder. With great bellows, they would blow a cloud of burning pine tar  and sulfur smoke at the Spanish, and let the great arrow fly up and over the walls that the Spanish  had constructed.  So the sound and smoke and damage were greater than even the cannons of the Spanish. All the warriors of the Aztecs would give a great shout when the Spirit Bow was fired. Then at a signal, a thousand war canoes with hawk warriors armed with flaming arrows  had swarmed out from thousand hidden bays at night and attacked the Spanish ships, offshore,  setting them all ablaze,  while the bronzed armored warriors took the city. So were the Spanish defeated.   She awoke trembling, and Blue was beside her.

"You are my brave eagle warrior," she said and embraced him as if he were about to die the next day.

"I need you to go into space and fight, and save us!" she wept.

****

"So this war strategy of  Henderson's, it's actually written by Pamela Monroe," said Alicia to Goldberg. They were sitting in his new office near the Pentagon. "He said she takes his class at Annapolis, she sent it to him, and said to publish it under his own name. I remember she talked about this when she and  Cassandra Chen were doing their Stargate exposé. She said if things went south when the UFO cover-up collapsed, and there was war,  she thought we could win."

235

"Did he change it at all ?" asked Goldberg, looking amazed.

"He basically just spell-checked it and added some references. He was big enough to tell me all of this and send me her original manuscript. He said it was the first thing he had ever read about the war that made sense. So he published it as a Center for Naval Analysis report. Which is what you gave me."

"What do you think?" asked Goldberg intently.

"I agree with Henderson, it makes sense, even if it's based on some big assumptions. We are apparently in some sort of neutral zone here, since many different species have been known to visit here, and she takes that fact and assumes that geopolitics occurs outside this neutral zone between the species. She would be in better position to know than anybody, since she was an abductee and reportedly met the local alien commander himself. "

"Her strategy is  basically the strategy of the American Colonies in the Revolutionary war, which was successful." continued Alicia. "The American colonists  knew the British had difficulty supplying their armies here from across the Atlantic, knew the British army could be defeated from Braddock' defeat in the French and Indian War, and they knew that if the colonists  made the war here go on long enough, Britain's enemies in Europe would join the war on their side.  Pamela proposes the same thing will happen here since the surrounding powers would want to preserve the status quo of a neutral zone not dominated by any one specie.  So she says we should fight and drag this out, in the hopes that other space powers, who are rivals of the Greys, will intervene on our side. It seems reasonable. I would say that, therefore, this strategy provides a basis for rational hope. In a war, hope is a weapon as surely as a high power laser."

"Good I want you to brief the war science board on this strategy at our next meeting. I want this spread around as far and wide as possible at the Top Secret Level."

"You've read it, what did you think?" asked Alicia.

"I think it sounds like a plan, and that's what we need right now, a plan…" he said with a smile.

****

Schwartzman sat in a trench behind the brow of a hill extending from the fog enshrouded Mount Bering volcano. The bare rock and grey volcanic ash of the landscape were broken only by patches of green moss or lichen, barely surviving an existence above the shallow timberline below them. The hill was known simply as hill 205, for its height in meters, and the slope beyond it up the mountain was known as the "Butcher Shop" for the number of men that had died there. Hill 205 was the point of closest American lines to the alien fortress up further on the side of the mountain. It was estimated that the alien fortress, sunk into the mountain side up above them, was 300 yards from the top of Hill 205. General Ross and several officers and soldiers, all in combat fatigues and helmets, sat or stood nervously in the trench beside Schwartzman. Schwartzman however, was clothed in bronze-colored chain mail and plate armor and wore a grizzly bear robe, requisitioned from a rug in a hotel lobby, draped over his head and hanging down over his shoulders. Schwartzman noticed that four tracked vehicles, with troops riding on them, of an unfamiliar shade of wintergreen were churning up the slope below the hill, protected from direct fire from the mountain. In a side trench stood a large but docile black horse named Gabriel. Schwartzman would have preferred a more spirited stallion, but Gabriel, older and more gentled, was all that was available for the operation on short notice. *Just like me*, thought Schwartzman.

"Well Colonel, we decided to add a new event to the dance card this morning," said General Ross beside him.

"I thought we were going to keep this operation simple this morning, " said Schwartzman with a frown.

"Oh, this should make your job, simpler, if it works," said Ross with a grin. "Think of you as the main course and this as an appetizer." Ross continued with a laugh. "Our faithful allies, the Russians, have arrived

237

with some new technology they want to test out here." Schwartzman frowned and turned to look at the foremost tracked vehicle now roaring loudly and belching black diesel smoke into the fog as it slowed and then churned past them with troops jumping off it to the ground. The troops were obviously Russian from their wintergreen camouflaged uniforms and helmet covers with AK-74 rifles over their shoulders. The tracked vehicle carried a large cylindrical clamshell, which Schwartzman guessed enclosed a large squat missile. The Russians were carrying satchels as they fanned out in the trench. One Russian officer was moving towards them with several satchels as the tracked vehicle, apparently now being driven remotely by a long control cable, churned up to just below the brow of the hill and in the direct line of fire from the alien fortress further up the mountain slope. The Russian officer had a mustache and a big grin on his face.

"Good Morning, I am Major Karpov!" he said as moved up beside Ross and Schwartzman. "Thank you for allowing us to test this new technology!" Schwartzman nodded grimly.

The Russians were putting on heavy goggles and handing them out to all the Americans. Schwartzman could see the Russians were hooking up what appeared to be a long optical control cable to the vehicle. On the vehicle , the whine of hydraulics started and the clamshells parted to reveal a long cylinder with a rounded front end that now itself opened and folded back. Suddenly a jet engine on the vehicle roared into life , with a plume of flame directed upwards.

"This is the auxiliary power unit for the laser! It turns big generator!" shouted Karpov above the roar of the jet engine. The smell of jet fuel filled the air above the mounting roar.

"Laser?" asked Schwartzman "What about the fog?" Karpov grinned a golden bridgework grin in response.

"The Fog means nothing! The is a Carbon Monoxide laser! It is 3 megawatts! 95% efficient! It will cut through fog in a nanosecond! This is Good Russian technology!" proclaimed Karpov above the roaring engines. He was looking around . He suddenly frowned and pointed at the horse in the nearby trench. "Cover horse's eyes with a towel! Scattered laser light

238

will blind Horse!" Karpov yelled. Ross motioned to some nearby troops who wrapped a heavy scarf around the horse's eyes while the horse sat there docilely as this happened. Karpov nodded and reacquired his grin. "Let us get going before our friends up there can figure out what we are doing!" Ross grinned and gave the thumbs up sign. A soldier nearby raised a flare pistol and fired a red flare. It arced brightly into the foggy, dark sky.

Schwartzman put on his goggles and watched with apprehensive fascination as the low silhouette tracked vehicle, with its cylindrical burden and now roaring jet engine spouting flame, rolled boldly up to the top of the hill. Suddenly the jet engine spun up giving a surge of power and its exhaust flame shot outward and turned to a brilliant yellow flame.

The air around them suddenly exploded with cracks of thunder as the Samar opened fire with kinetic energy weapons and the megawatt laser blasted the projectiles in midair causing them to explode into blossoms of blue-white hot burning fragments. Blue white hot fragments burned in the sky above them as the laser blasted away repeatedly. Schwartzman could smell jet fuel and hot burning metal as white chunks of ash fell down on them in the trenches. The flame of the vehicle's jet engine-driven generator reacted by shortening and developing shock diamonds every time the laser fired, making a sizzling sound in the air that was barely audible against the thunder and shock waves of the hypervelocity projectiles exploding in mid-air. Suddenly the battlefield grew comparatively silent except for the roar of the jet engine.

"Hah! Alien projectiles hyper velocity is big fast, but laser light is faster!" chortled Karpov. "We aim by conjugate wave fronts, Laser Self Aims! MHD generator of jet exhaust makes big power! Very Excellent Success!" Karpov waved his arm and the tracked vehicle suddenly backed off from the brow of the hill to the relative safety of the slope away from the mountain. A thin wisp of smoke was now rising from its now scorched looking jet exhausts. The realization that the Russian laser had now neutralized the alien's most feared weapon was sinking in and troops in the trenches as both Americans and Russians began to cheer and whistle. Several soldiers bellowing obscenities for the alien's benefit were also heard. Schwartzman looked down the slope behind the hill. Men everywhere were climbing off the other tracked vehicles and cheering and hugging each other.

Suddenly the air was full of cracks of thunder as the Samar, in oblivious frustration unleashed a barrage of hypervelocity projectiles at the empty hillside facing them and the air above it. The ground shook as projectile after projectile buried itself harmlessly in the ash and rock on the far side of the hill. Small Rock fragments fell around them into the trench. Several hyper-projectiles flew like meteors above them in the sky to burn up noisily, but harmlessly, miles away in the air beyond them.

"They're obviously thinking about what they just saw and aren't happy about it!" laughed Ross above the din. "Let's let them piss fire a little and then calm down for a while before you go out there, Colonel. "A bottle of vodka had appeared in Karpov's hand and he was drinking from it, apparently one of several bottles now being furnished by the Russians. Ross took a long drink from it. The ecstatic Karpov drank a big swallow and passed it on to Schwartzman, who also downed a big drink before passing it back down the line. The alien barrage ended abruptly, and an eerie quiet ensured. After a few minutes of further calm, General Ross spoke.

"I think if you ride out there now Colonel, them boys up there on that mountain will be all ears for what you have to say!" said Ross with a smile. Schwartzman, feeling the burn of the vodka, ran over to the horse and mounted it. His grizzly bear robe was arranged such that his face framed by the mouth and teeth of the bear with the bear's ears sticking up alertly above his head. Now mounted and with his robe and armor in order, Schwartzman spurred his horse up a dirt ramp out of the trench and up to the brow of the hill. *Here goes nothing,* he thought, as he mounted the crest of the hill in full sight and line of fire of the enemy. *It is a good day to die.*

At what he thought was the proper point, Schwartzman threw back his bearskin robe to expose his bare greying head to the cold. He then drew his great sword **Agincourt** from its sheath and raised it in a golden salute. He pulled out a one handed axe from his saddle with the other hand and held it aloft so its brutally functional shape was clearly visible.

"Brave warriors of the Samar! You have fought most valiantly." Schwartzman bellowed. "Now let us put away these childish toys and fight as true men of war! Let us meet in the tunnels below, with sword and axe! Let us look one another in the eye as true men, and let our blood mingle on the ground of battle! We vow as brothers in war, and by our common brave fathers, that your bodies will receive honorable treatment in accordance with your customs." Schwartzman paused, listened to the cold wind blowing. He then spoke again.

"To show our good faith we return to you the bodies of your brave fallen ones, with their bodies, armor, and weapons whole, and grant armistice so you may deal with their remains according to your glorious customs! "

A dozen soldiers in combat fatigues appeared bearing the two embalmed bodies on stretchers, the soldiers marched out slowly, left the stretchers bearing the bodies on the ashen ground 100 yards in front of Schwartzman and then marched back over the brow of the hill to safety.

Schwartzman then sheathed the sword and axe and turned his horse and galloped back over the hill.

Back at the trench, he gave Gabriel, the horse, a nice red delicious apple he had kept in a pouch for that moment.

****

Professor William Loomis sat in a conference room at the brig at Quantico normally reserved for meetings with lawyers and prisoners.

Goldberg entered flanked by two marines who stood just outside the door. Goldberg carried a notepad. Loomis looked up at him hopefully.

"Hey their Bill, thought it all over?" said Goldberg blankly.

"Sure Abe, I can tell you that I heard about the Lagrange point stuff from my nephew, Lt. William Farnsworth down at the Pentagon. You know, I was only trying to see if you had some strategy against this. I was just feeling that if we didn't have a strategy, then the humanitarian thing to do would be to sue for peace. I was just interested in saving lives, Abe." Goldberg wrote down the name of Lt. Farnsworth carefully on the notepad and then tore the paper from the pad in a quick motion. *It will probably mean a firing squad for the nephew, too bad.*

"Is this the right spelling?" Goldberg asked, as he showed the name to Loomis, who, looking ashamed, nodded.

"Now I have given you what you asked, and I apologize for breaking the rules. I would hope we could forget this whole episode happened Abe. Members of my family served on the MIT War Sciences Board in World War II, you know, " said Loomis.

"You know what my family did in World War II?" asked Goldberg, carefully placing the paper in his vest pocket.

"No," said Loomis smiling.

"My pop served in the combat infantry in the Battle of the Bulge, in Patton's army. We only found out about it when he died, because he would never talk about it. You know what my uncles and their wives and children did in World War II? "

"No, Abe"

"They were killed at Auschwitz," said Goldberg, matter-of-factly. "That fact kind of gives a certain outlook on this war were are fighting now."

"Sure Abe, I understand."

"Oh, I don't think you do understand it at all, Bill," said Abe, rising from the table. "I'll do what I can for you Bill." With that, he turned and left the room.

Lt. Farnsworth was arrested at the Pentagon in the next hour, he was executed for treason four days later. It was a war and things were done quickly.

242

****

"So if the Greys are waging psychological warfare, we wage it back!" said Alicia to the War Science Board at the Pentagon. "During the first Gulf war, Saddam Hussein started shooting Scuds at Israel. The Scud was a terror weapon, and it worked in that it caused terror. People in bomb shelters were dying of heart attacks in Israel, not from any real damage caused by the missiles. They were dying of terror. Then the U.S. brought in Patriot missile batteries, and boom everything changed. People would sit on their rooftops, watch the battle, and cheer rather than cowering in shelters. Analysis showed very few of the missile warheads were intercepted, but it didn't matter. It was a psychological weapon versus a terror weapon. People didn't feel helpless anymore, now it was a fight! A big battle in the sky! Once they started firing Patriots at the Scuds the heart attack deaths went away, people were happy, felt protected, even if in reality there was little danger in the first place; and the Patriots didn't really do that much! So my proposal is to hand out red infrared proof goggles to everyone in DC and tell them to take cover, knowing full well they will want to watch the show. We arrange flyovers by ten squadrons of jet fighters in the afternoon, Griffins, and Scorpions! We move lasers, antiaircraft guns, and missiles all around town all day like we are parading them! We will say we are deploying them according to a dynamic secret strategy. We roll in the Russian carbon monoxide lasers, but also the big copper vapor lasers that shoot green light. The Copper lasers are probably less effective than Carbon Monoxide, but people can see them shoot! This means the people can see the lasers shoot up the night! Not only will it let the people see we are putting up a fight, but they also will have to squint a lot to avoid getting dazzled by the green lasers, which operate near the peak of light sensitivity of the human eye. So they will be less likely to get their eyes burned by the 5-micron carbon monoxide lasers, which are more powerful but are invisible."

"The way I see it, we turn this attempt by the Greys to demonstrate the government's lack of control of the skies over DC into a killing zone! Like this place was a giant bug zapper!" said Professor Carter.

"Yes , and we will get kills here," said Alicia, "lots of them."

243

****

After two days of no activity, the heavy solar flares stopped and the Air defenses over DC prepared for another night of terror.    However, following Alicia's strategy,   the roads were crowded everywhere with military traffic moving high powered lasers, missiles and antiaircraft guns around the city all day.   Goggles, opaque to the carbon monoxide wavelength, and also blocking green light, were handed out en-mass with printed warnings to stay indoors and not use them.  A run of the stores to buy beer, popcorn and chips was reported, and numerous people ignored the warning. They set up lawn chairs on balconies and patios to watch the battle.   One commentator noted that DC had not turned out to witness such a military encounter since the Battle of Bull run in the Civil War.

Finally, in the afternoon, hundreds of jet fighters flew over the city with cheering crowds below.  Blue F-51 Griffins and then jet-black Mach 5-capable, F-71 Scorpions all with ammunition bays full of magneto –fused cannon shells and missiles.  The plan was actually for the fighters to move in a great vortex around the city over the suburbs with missiles, automatic cannon flak, and lasers covering the core of the city, a sort of fighter hurricane with an eye full of lasers.  Perched on the hills of Arlington was an anti-aircraft battery at Ft Myers overlooking Arlington cemetery and the Washington Capitol across the Potomac. At the anti-aircraft battery, Alicia and Abe  sat in combat fatigues, flak vests, and helmets, in a labyrinth of sandbagged trenches and bunkers, dug in what used to be a well-tended Army Golf Course.

"This reminds me of the good old days of your asteroid, Alicia," said Abe as they waited for night to fall. The weather was beautiful - a clear, cold, cloudless sky.  "Excellent for laser propagation," commented Alicia." The parade of hardware around the city and the fighter flyover was really impressive.  Now if we can just deliver a good kill ratio tonight, it will be perfect."

Night fell deeply with the absence of the Moon for most of the night. However, some aurora became visible, presenting an eerie spectacle to the North.  Alicia was scanning the city with binoculars and noted that parties were forming on rooftops around the city as if waiting for a fireworks show.

Then at just after 1000 hours came the word.

"Radar contact, magnetometer activity, here they come!" shouted an officer "Goggles! Goggles!" as air raid sirens began to wail and sonic booms thundered in the clear night sky. Suddenly a blue-white flare of light appeared in the South East.

"The fighters got one!" a soldier shouted. Then suddenly all hell broke loose as tracers missiles and blinding green laser beams suddenly lit up the sky. Another blue-white magnesium flare was seen, indicating the hull of a grey ship had ignited. Cheers rose up from thousands of throats above the thunder and staccato automatic cannon fire. In the distance, an orange ball of fire, probably a jet fighter, blossomed and fell to Earth in the far north. Then a surge in laser blasts and missile launches and tracers again, with the sky full of missile warhead explosions and flak bursts, whose shock waves rattled across the sky. This was followed by a lull in which only sonic booms were heard. Then the action surged again with clouds of tracers of red and yellow. Nearby to Alicia and Goldberg, several 40 mm automatic cannons opened up and sprayed red tracers across the sky with a deafening roar. This was followed by a firecracker string of flak bursts low over Georgetown. This time, two blue-white magnesium balls of fire blossomed in the night over Washington DC, one streaking like a meteor into the Potomac river near the 14th street bridge, the other disintegrating before it reached the ground in a shower of white ashes. These were greeted by raucous cheering and yelled obscenities from hundreds of nearby rooftops. The surge in action continued and another two magnesium flares blossomed , then two more!

"Oh my God we are slaughtering them!" cried out Abe Goldberg. "That's seven grey ships shot down! They must have thought our big buildup was a challenge!"

There was then a deep lull in activity, followed by a sudden upsurge in the firing of laser beams, and missiles flying and exploding in a staccato of thunder and dazzling lights. The whole sky seemed to become an inferno at times, and this time, three blossoms of blue-white fire appeared. Then

245

suddenly all the activity stopped, and even the sound of sonic booms diminished to simply a faraway thunder. There was a long wait with everyone scanning the skies, and new missile and ammo magazines being loaded. Finally, a stunned silence  settled over the battery and seemly over the whole city.

After what seemed like an eternity, dawn began in the East.  Alicia had fallen asleep in her helmet and fatigues somehow, and Abe Goldberg roused her from a tent. The long terrible night was over.  At the sight of dawn, cheers began to go up from every throat, and in the city below them, cars began honking their horns,  and people set off fireworks. Some Griffin jet fighters flew over doing big victory rolls to waves and cheering from people on rooftops and in the streets.

"Let's go to Denny's for breakfast," said Abe Goldberg to  Alicia as she looked around at the dawn in wonder. "I hear they have a special  this morning," he added.

****

"NO! NO! Absolutely not!" yelled  the Captain of the Tlakmar rising from his chair. Hontal sat with the Captain in his cabin at a table of fine wood. "I will not endanger this ship! If I try to bring the ship close to Erra to save the garrison, the Errans will fire salvos of nuclear weapons at us! Thousands of them. We can stop a hundred,  but only one needs to detonate close to us, and we will never get back to Rigel! Then I will have failed in my mission!"

"Can you not respond with the ray batteries on the launch sites?" asked Hontal.

"Listen, boy," said The Captain angrily. Hontal stood, and his  hand flew to his sword hilt at these words. The Captain and Hontal stared at each other in silence for a moment.  Both had their hands on their swords.

"Listen,  young brave knight of Rigel" resumed the Captain , causing Hontal to let go of his sword.  They both sat down. " I will explain to you the foundation of our operations here in the Quzrada and realities of this place.  We are a treaty power here if a Samar ship comes to Erra and turns

246

it to glass that could trigger another War of the Quzrada with the other treaty powers! Do you know what the Palace would do to me and you if that occurred?" The Captain let his words sink in. "My orders are clear, and so were the warnings given to me and all Captains who come here. If we start an interstellar war here among the major powers in the Quzrada again, the palace will not give us a banquet of honor for this, but a banquet of quite another variety..." Hontal looked down in resignation. "I, for one, do not wish to see someone munch on part of my roasted ass!" added the Captain.

"But the island garrison?" Hontal asked, "Can't we do anything for them?"

"You should have asked this question of that pimp of an Unash who runs this place. We have been watching his ships fly hundreds of sorties to Erra. If he concentrated his forces he could relieve the garrison."

"He insists he cannot do this. He says he must follow his war plan"

"Then the garrison dies and the fault is Sadok Sar's," said the Captain grimly.

"So the garrison dies?" asked Hontal incredulously.

"They are brave Samar!" exploded the Captain. "If they are trapped on Erra it is because they chose to stay rather than withdraw! Either that or they believed the Unash when they said they would rescue them! In that latter case, they were fools to believe the Monchkini and must die a brave death to cleanse themselves of their folly..."

Hontal rose and saluted the captain, who stood and bowed his head and saluted with a look of complete sorrow and anger.

"I return to Una to finish gathering information on the situation here," said Hontal. "Then we will leave this accursed place."

****

"Mr. President," began now-General Prescott, "I am here to present the war strategy developed by the Carney, the one military unit charged with both combat and surveillance on extraterrestrial species for the past several decades. They were also instrumental in bringing down the MAGI conspiracy. They call this strategy the Burnham-Monroe-Monachenko strategy. The strategy is basically as follows: they believe, based on fifty years of observation of ET activities here that the zone of space containing the solar system is a neutral zone not controlled by any one species of ET. They base this upon encounters with many different species of ET, most of whom were friendly and simply curious about Earth. This neutrality of the region of space we are in also implies that surrounding interstellar species will act to maintain this region's neutrality and combat any actors attempting to change that status quo by achieving dominance here. This is supported by many observations of combat between Greys and other species, especially over Russia during the period after the collapse of the Soviet Union. The effort to maintain the status quo of the neutral zone, we believe, will create great difficulties for the Greys in trying to bring major space forces here or to mount either the destruction or large-scale invasion of Earth. Other species will interfere with their efforts to reinforce and resupply, and may also intervene directly in response to any major military move in the neutral zone.

Our war strategy is thus to continue to take advantage of what we perceive to be shock and confusion of the enemy side caused by our aggressive moves against their bases on Earth, in order to force the Greys to try and undertake major efforts at resupply, which will be opposed. In other words, we think they will have supply line problems and we will exacerbate these problems by creating an even higher demand on their supply lines. We will take control of near-Earth space, the Moon, and Mars. We will drive the aliens into the outer solar system, taking and destroying any bases or prepositioned supplies, in the Solar System to deny them their use, thus placing, even more, stresses on their supply system. In the long term, we believe these moves will cause other space powers in the stellar neighborhood to intervene to prevent grey supply convoys from reaching here with supplies and reinforcements. Thus we believe that if we are aggressive enough and cause enough losses here the grey war effort here will starve due to poor supply lines and that any major intervention by the Greys will prove either impossible or be strongly opposed."

"The precedent for such a war strategy in American history," continued Prescott, "was the Revolutionary War, where the colonies counted on the difficulty of the British moving and resupplying their armies across the stormy Atlantic and the knowledge that if the war went on long enough and revealed British difficulties enough, the other European enemies of the British, France, Spain and the Netherlands, would intervene on the American side, which they did. Crucial in that effort was the destruction of the British Army at Saratoga and the battle of Germantown where Washington's army fought the British army to a standstill. Therefore, a war effort of strongly aggressive tactics is considered crucial, both to keep the Greys disorganized and to expose their weakness here to other interstellar powers. But we also to take advantage of what General Burnham believes to be the fact that we caught the aliens in an extremely 'forward deployed posture' with large forces and many bases in exposed positions that they cannot evacuate from. They basically deployed too much material and personnel into forward positions than they could actually support with their available airspace forces because they anticipated a short violent campaign of conquest after securing the US government as their vassal. However, they failed utterly, of course, and they must now supply their forces trapped here from the Moon." Prescott summarized.

"This strategy is based scientifically on the Principle of Mediocrity, a foundation of SETI research before the collapse of the cover-up , which assumes that human beings and their behavior are typical of intelligent species in the Cosmos, rather than being exotic. We are, quite frankly, projecting human

geopolitics on the surrounding universe. However, this principle has actually explained many of the behaviors of the Greys. So we regard it as reliable, and a good basis for this strategy. "

The President listened to this gravely, then smiled. Beside him, Defense Secretary Clayborne Thomas nodded and looked deep in thought. James Bergman, the Deputy Defense Secretary, and National Security Advisor, finally broke the silence.

249

"Well, it's not the sort of war strategy that the United States is used to, being based on so many unknowns, but if it was good enough for George Washington and Ben Franklin, I guess we should embrace it. When does General Burnham think we can achieve control of near-Earth space?"

"The General has ordered plans for a near-Earth Space surge, Mr. Secretary, in the next few months. He has told us on his staff that he does not want to wait for air supremacy before seeking space control. He has argued that if the aliens want to run around and abduct people in the atmosphere that leaves that many fewer craft they have in space to contest our near-Earth surge." said Prescott.

"That makes sense," said the President nodding and looking around. "Very well, tell General Burnham we like this strategy and his near-Earth surge, and we will support both," said the President. "Thank you for your briefing General Prescott." With that, General Prescott saluted, turned, and left the top secret briefing room.

With Prescott out of the room, a grim mood prevailed.

"Well it's good to hear that somebody has a plan for this war that at least makes sense on paper!" said the President shaking his head wearily. "It presumes a lot, I mean about how the neighboring interstellar powers will react, but that all makes sense too, I guess..." The President looked deep in thought , then continued. "The crucial factor then becomes the surge, do you think it will be in time? I mean this overall strategy sounds reasonable, but it is a long-term plan. It will do us no good unless this space surge succeeds. I can even tell temperatures are dropping and we can't count on these Solar storms to help us much longer."

"I believe it will be in time Mr. President." said Bergman "General Burnham has been completely briefed on what we are facing this winter. I believe this proposed space-surge is his response to our near-term crisis."

"Well, let us hope to God it succeeds," said the President.

****

"General Arnold! I want your's and Space Command's plans for the near-Earth surge by tomorrow morning! Is that clear?" said General Burnham. General Prescott was standing in front of General Burnham's desk, having just returned from the White House.

"Yes sir, but I do not see the great urgency in this operation General," said General Arnold, looking uncomfortable. He looked around at his staff at the table across from General Burnham's desk and facing his staff. "We are obviously still struggling to achieve air superiority in the atmosphere. Why not wait until we have that achieved before moving forces into space? Clear air superiority will support this space surge."

"Take my word for it, the urgency is there General, I want the Air Force and Space Command to focus every possible resource to gain space superiority as soon as possible in near-Earth-space. Is that clear?" Burnham paused, took off his glasses, looked around the room at both his own and the Air Force Staff." I want every captured saucer in Foxtrot squadron flying , and I want every transatmospheric fighter available and rolled out to gain a foothold in space and hold it on to it! Russian Space Command has said they will give us maximum launch support out of Plesetsk , Baikonur, and Vostok! So I want near-space control! ASAP! Is that clear?" He turned to General Standish of Space Command.

"Loud and clear General! My men are ready!" said Standish looking utterly determined.

"Now I want a supporting air superiority surge also. If the Greys are still trying to contest air superiority over our cities at night, then that leaves fewer ships to fight in space, correct? Every ship they lose in the atmosphere to one of our fighters is one more ship they can't use in space!" General Arnold, nodded in nervous response to this.

"Yes, General. Every enemy ship we can bring down in the atmosphere means one less for our people to face in space. I agree," said General Arnold, as if trying to convince himself. "But it means stretching my forces to the maximum."

"The Greys are already stretched thin General Arnold, if you press them, they will break!" said General Burnham. "I will see to it that Admiral

Haynes puts as much naval aviation in the air over the coasts as possible to support your people."

"Yes, General," said Arnold grimly.

"Good, then I want your briefing tomorrow at 0600 on the Space Surge!" said Burnham rising.

"I have heard we have an overall strategy General, how can we craft our strategy to support it?"

"Do the air-space Surge! Attack! Attack! Attack!" said General Burnham emphatically, "That is our strategy right now, General. We have apparently caught the aliens with their pants down around their ankles, and they are on the run, and the last thing we want them to do, is to give them a chance to catch their breath or pull up their pants. We have them on the run, your job General Arnold, the job of all my commanders, is to keep those bastards running! So the order is Attack, Attack, Attack! Understood?"

"Yes, General"

General Arnold saluted before turning to leave the meeting, followed by his staff.

****

Schwartzman moved forward through the double column of hard-faced men in the darkly lit tunnel. Like himself, every man was clad in a suit of arc-welded chain mail made of bronzed colored Tallin alloy. Like himself, everyone wore a dome-shaped Tallin helmet , a compromise between ancient Greek and Roman designs , with wide flip-up cheek guards, a visor above the face and a nose guard. They all wore Tallin breast plates. The men were armed with a murderous-looking variety of swords and axes. Schwartzman himself carried a large medieval sword with a Tallin blade. It was estimated they would break through the last few feet of basalt rock into the alien fortress in less than an hour. Schwartzman passed the final row of men, all chosen for their size, strength, and skill. A big strong soldier named Comacho who had shown himself an expert in

252

swordsmanship was the last in the row. Comacho wore a classic 1000 yard stare familiar to Schwartzman from his many years in combat zones. Beyond him was a sandy-haired powerfully built man named Lundquist, armed with a massive two-handed sword, who looked as if he was in a trance and about to turn into a werewolf. Beyond him was Tomaga, a Japanese American and an expert with a samurai sword with a Tallin blade. He also stared ahead, as if staring death itself in the face without flinching. Finally, Arizona, armed with a medieval sword and beyond him the massive forms of Van Buskirk and Washington, both armed with massive Tallin battle axes with wide crescent shaped blades sharpened to razor edges on thick shafts made of fire-hardened Hickory. Both Van Buskirk and Washington stared ahead wordlessly, with faces like chiseled steel. Schwartzman had chosen himself to be point. He took his place and unsheathed his own sword, admired the sound it made as it was unsheathed, and how the reflections of the lights on the tunnel roof played on the bronze metal. The sound of the tunneling machine cutting head grinding its way through the hard, black, volcanic, basalt overwhelmed everything. Schwartzman muttered a prayer to himself.

"Lord let me and my men do valiantly this day, and get victory!" Schwartzman gasped. The men were ready for whatever was coming. The whistle sounded as was agreed, two minutes or less until breakthrough. When the breakthrough came it would create a 2-yard diameter hole in the center of the 6-yard wide drill face and the tunneling machine centerpiece would then withdraw to leave a path into the fortress through the hot 2-yard diameter hole.

A siren sounded and Schwartzman tensed and leaned forward, crouching down to leap through the entrance when it opened up. There was a crashing noise of collapsing stone and then crying hydraulics as the tunneling head center withdrew and the door opened. The smell of hot rock and drill steel assailed him as he strained to see into the dusty doorway opening up. He saw dim golden light, a moving in the dusty light beyond, figures!

The air in the tunnel was suddenly filled with shrill screams as a dozen or so disheveled women, some completely naked, stampeded out through the tunnel, the still-hot rock burning their bare feet. Schwartzman starred at their terror-stricken faces in astonishment and pressed his body to the wall of the tunnel to let them run past him. *If they wanted to break our concentration, that was effective,* he thought in admiration of the Samar inside the fortress. He caught the same look of amazement on the faces of his men behind him, then turned to try and regain his fighting mind and posture, as he prepared to run through the now empty passageway lit by the dim golden light. *Well, back to business!* Suddenly a figure pushed him aside and leaped through the passage ahead of him. It was a naked figure with a sword, bellowing. Schwartzman lunged after him and heard shouted war cries and the crash of metal on metal. Behind Schwartzman followed the rest of the men in a bronze wave now all bellowing "HUZZA!"

Schwartzman leaped through the circular doorway his sword point gleaming. Screams, war cries and metal ringing off metal were now a chorus of noise. He was in a larger stone tunnel, blood was already on the floor, a bearded man in silver armor lay dying then another and beyond that a melee' of men with a naked man swinging his sword wildly and bellowing "VAHAALA!" Schwartzman plunged into the melee' and a bearded face with blue eyes turned to face him in rage, but Schwartzman struck with his sword in the bearded man's throat, as behind him he heard HUZZA's come from a chorus of throats as an armored wave of huge, superbly trained men poured into the tunnel and Schwartzman was carried ahead by their momentum. He was fighting another man sword to sword when the blow of Washington's axe hewed the man nearly in two and Schwartzman covered him, while he extricated his axe. Then Van Buskirk and Washington were in the front, swinging their huge axes in the melee', pressing the bearded men back. Then the bearded armored men seemed to rally and press forward screaming "SAMAR! RIGEL!" in a harsh chorus before Schwartzman and his men, now in much larger numbers in the tunnel, could counter-attack, and they pressed forward like cutting machines.

In a few minutes, the bloody carnage was over. The last Samar, who had reddish hair and green eyes, was wounded and cornered against a closed hatch. He screamed defiance at the circle of humans surrounding him. The Samaran's blood was deep red like a human's. Arizona, himself bleeding from a face wound, cast aside his shield and leaped forward and dueled the Samar sword to sword, finally wounding the already wounded

254

Samar in the stomach. The Samar stood unbowed and bled as Arizona stood and watched. Then the Samar suddenly smiled and fell upon his own bloody sword.

Schwartzman leaped forward and stood over the fallen Samar to prevent the men from venting their fury on his fallen corpse. He swept his gaze around the tunnel, its floor now covered in red human and Samar blood and bodies and fragments of bodies, its walls splattered everywhere with blood and fragments of flesh. A wall of fierce clean-shaven faces stared at him, many splattered with blood or themselves bleeding. He motioned them all back, and they retreated down the tunnel as he twisted the circular handle to try and open the closed hatch. To his pleasant surprise, it did not blow up in his face, and the hatch opened to reveal a smoke filled room, full of destroyed and burned equipment. In the middle of the floor, a red-haired woman's body lay face down. She was clad in a silk-like luminous emerald green gown. Her copper red hair was carefully braided and she wore a jeweled headband. She was completely still. Schwartzman stepped into the room through the hatch, followed by Arizona and a few officers, saw the tunnel ran deep into the mountain and that everywhere was destroyed or burned equipment. *Well, that was done honorably,* he thought, with grudging admiration. *They went out like men and have left us nothing useful in the fortress.* He approached the woman's body, leaned down and gently turned it over. The woman had a beautiful, tear-stained face, wearing makeup. Her green eyes were open and staring. Schwartzman closed them. The face now appeared calm and at peace. A Samaran dagger was buried in her heart, and her own right hand gripped it, in her other hand Schwartzman noticed a plastic card, it was her Alaskan state driver's license. He picked it up with mailed hand. He looked around again and saw a red luminous line appear on a large metal box next to the wall. The line was flashing and getting shorter as he watched.

"Retreat! Everybody retreat from the tunnel ! NOW!" Schwartzman yelled. "FIRE IN THE HOLE!" He turned and leaped back out of the hatchway into the bloody tunnel outside and then followed his men, now bearing wounded and their own dead, which were numerous, back through the breakthrough passage. Roughly twenty dead Samarans lay dead on the blood-soaked rock floor. As Schwartzman retreated,

255

stepping over the bodies , he was moved by the bravery of their dead foes, laying bearded and armored , on the floor like a band of brothers. Schwartzman paused at the breakthrough passage and stood tall, holding his still bloody sword straight up from his chest, the blade in front of his face as he touched the front of his helmet with it, in a salute. He now noticed his hands were bleeding from several wounds and so was his face, and that his body was exhausted, but he felt moved with strange pride as he looked over the carnage, and blood soaked floor, where Samaran and human blood had mingled freely, both rich and red, in the battle.

*We are now blood brothers with these people, and therein lies hope,* he thought, before turning and running for his life.

The tunneling machine was being withdrawn. Schwartzman and his men retreated behind it as it moved until they reached a side tunnel half covered with a huge steel door. Going into it, the able-bodied not bearing dead or wounded, pushed the massive door shut. Just in time, as the main tunnel was filled with searing blue-white heat. The Samaran fortress everywhere disintegrated into molten rock as if it was packed with thermite. It then slumped inward, forming a wide, steaming depression in the side of the mountain.

As they waited for medical help to arrive down in the tunnel, Schwartzman was talking to Washington, who had been badly wounded, and was laying on the cold stone of the tunnel as they pulled his blood-soaked armor off him. Van Buskirk was dead, Tomaga also. Lundquist had died of multiple wounds after storming into the Samaran naked except for his sword. Schwartzman looked at his hewn body with wonder, wondering whether to regard his bold charge as either madness or extreme bravery. Of the first four men into the Samaran fortress, only Schwartzman had survived. He regarded this fact with astonishment.

"You tell my mama, I died like a brave man, will you boss?" gasped Washington. "You tell her that..."

"Sure Vernon, but you ain't gonna die, you just keep talking and the medical people are going to come in here as soon as the out tunnel gets a little cooler..." But Washington was gone, his brown eyes wide open and dilated , his wide black face now holding a serene smile. The medic, who

256

had been holding up an IV draining blood into him, checked his pulse and shut his eyelids. Schwartzman rose and wandered down the tunnel, to the still hot door leading to the main tunnel. It was noticeably cooler now, soon crews would come and free them.

****

Hontal watched the transmission from the Adak fortress grimly. The last Samar, who had reddish hair, wounded and bleeding profusely, battled an Erran in bronze colored armor and a helmet with a nose guard. The Erran was bleeding from a face wound, his blood deep red like that of the Samar, but the Erran seemed oblivious to his wound as the Samaran was to his own wounds. To Hontal's astonishment, the Erran was incredibly skillful with the sword and obviously very strong. What was more impressive, was that the Erran was a least a head taller than the Samaran. Hontal watched grimly as the Samaran, obviously weakened from several wounds finally was badly wounded, and the Erran stood back while the Samaran threw himself honorably onto his own sword.

The other samaran beside him in their quarters on the Moon, stood and placed their clenched fists over their hearts in salute to the brave deaths of the Samaran garrison, that they had just watched. During the bloody melee' they had witnessed, Hontal had to resist the urge to draw his own sword and try to jump through the view screen to join the battle. He turned and saw everywhere grim looks of rage and sadness. Everywhere the Samar gripped the hilts of their own swords.

Zomal, the acting lunar garrison commander, spoke grimly and pointed at the now-blank view screen.

"That last man to fall was the brave Samus, he of the ruddy hair, he was well known to us here. He boldly volunteered to accompany our commander Koton to the island fortress. He is high-born, and we must inform the Palace of his honorable death," Zomal paused, then spoke again.

"My Lord Hontal! The vermin Monchkini, it is their fault! They made only feeble efforts to break the Erran's siege of the island fortress. They are too busy abducting people with their ships and disemboweling them over the Erran cities! For what?  You saw the Errans fight! Their blood was mingled in torrents with the blood of our brave Samar! Truly they are our children and sneer at the terror tactics of the Monchkini! The Monchkini spared only a few ships to bring our people supplies! What are they doing with the many pieces of gold the Throne  gives them? Tell the Palace the Monchkini  are robbing the Samarkin!"  Hontal, stood shaking with rage. He turned and strode out.

*How am I to report on all of this!* thought Hontal in astonishment . *Our enemy  the Errans fight like Samarkin and our allies act like goblins, stealing helpless people from their beds and killing them to try to terrorize others. It is contemptible.*  Then a new thought seized him. *The Palace does not know of the situation here! I must return to The Palace and report all of this.*  Then came another thought. He thought of Bekar of Batelgeen, and his warning: make sure your report is pleasing to the Batelgeans.  Hontal stood taller and gripped his sword tightly. *I must beware. I must get myself and Gamal my retainer out of here and back on the Tlakmar at once. I will write my report on the way back to the Palace.*

He went to his quarters and packed his things. He looked out in the hall and saw Gamal walking down the hall showering kisses on the now laughing  Erran woman called Amber and waved for him to pack also by holding up his full bag.     Gamal looked at him,  bowed slightly in abeyance, and then kissed the woman Amber a last time, motioning her down the hall and  swatting her on her round behind as she walked away smiling at him.   Around the corner came Tatiana, who smiled at him. Hontal's heart tore at him when he saw her.  He walked over and kissed her one last time. She looked surprised then her face lost its smile and her blue eyes suddenly regained the stone-like emptiness he had seen before when she had danced for him the first night. *Truly the Unash know what they are doing by providing these women to us, they have bewitched us!*

"I go, Tatiana, but I will return for you, to take you from this place!" he gasped . *How? How am I going to do that?* He then turned and joined Gamal his retainer, who now took his bag and trudged on dutifully and looked about warily.  Hontal could see that Gamal now understood the danger that surrounded them. They walked down the hall swiftly towards the transporter room. He then turned at last and saw Tatiana's face looking at him, her face was without emotion, but her eyes now looked at him with desperation. He tore his eyes away. *I have promised her the impossible!* In that instant, he felt his heart would break, but his warrior's instincts and training arose in him and made his heart as cold as ice. *Enough, we must go now and make our report!*

*At the transporter room the guards, both Unash and Samaran, looked startled and uneasy at Hontal's and Gamal's arrival and gripped their weapons. Finally, the garrison commander, Zomal, arrived, saluted Hontal, and bid him farewell. Zomal came close and looked Hontal in the eye gravely.*

*"Tell The Palace to get my men and I out of this accursed place," said Zomal in a low voice. Then Zomal stood away and watched impassively as Hontal and Gamal stood in the transporter and were teleported to the Tlakmar.*

*The captain of the Tlakmar met them as they emerged from the transporter room. His face looked grave.*

"It is good you are here." said the Captain gravely. "An Unash convoy is involved in a battle with Unull forces eleven light years from here. If they survive and come here , major Unullain forces may follow them and things could become difficult for us. As I said I was not sent here to gain more battle stars, but to convey you here and back to the palace to give your report. So, it is time to go."

*Hontal nodded.*

"I trust you have you gained sufficient knowledge to make a report?" said the Captain.

Hontal nodded gravely. The Captain nodded with sober satisfaction. He turned to his first officer.

"Prepare the ship to get underway within the hour!"

"On what course my Captain?" asked the first officer.

"To Rigel and the stars of home," said the Captain with a faint smile. The first officer nodded.

**** 

Cassandra arose in the middle of the night and found herself staring at the cold overcast sky out the window. The nightly air raids had ended.

"Even you, have your limit of pain, don't you?" she said to the sky. *What now? What do I do now?*

****

They were beginning their journey home to Rigel. Hontal stood beside the captain on the bridge of the Tlakmar in his armored spacesuit, helmet held ready under his this arm. The Captain stood beside likewise attired. On the main viewscreen, they saw the Moon's far side and beyond in the brilliant blue and white, Erra shining like a star. Hontal could see the Moon and Erra receding now as the ship picked up speed away from them.

Suddenly Erra appeared to explode into blue flame like water and expand and embrace the Moon rapidly submerging it in blue fire with the Unash main base of the far side now a shrinkling island of silver as the Moon sank in blue liquid flame, and out of the shrinking island, Hontal saw Tatia's face screaming in terror. He looked away shaken at this strange sight, he then looked back at the view screen, the apparition was gone and Erra was again but a blue-white star shrinking in the distance, and the Moon but a silver dot receding into blackness.

The Captain turned to him amazed.

"You saw it also, the blue flame, swallowing Una? " said the captain. Hontal looked at him speechless and slowly nodded.

"Every time I come here, we see such apparitions." continued the captain. "It is said that the God of Erra is the God of gods, and He guards this place. Indeed I tremble at what we Samaran may be trifling within this place." The captain's voice trembled slightly.

"But there are gods on every world," said Hontal with false bravado, shaking himself. *I am fatigued, it was a glint of blue light...*

"Fight a hundred battles like I have brave knight,  and journey to this haunted place five times, then instruct me on the ways of the gods!" retorted the captain angrily, "I see what I see!" He quickly pointed to his eyes. The captain then strode off to consult with his first officer. Hontal returned to his cabin shaking and began to compile his report. He now feared what he must write, and feared the reaction to his report at the palace. *Truly, I am the bearer of ill tidings.*

****

## Chapter 6: Pacifica

"I can't stay here anymore," said Cassandra to Pamela tearfully. "I am barely sane now and I think I will go completely insane if I stay here."

"I understand," said Pamela also weeping. They embraced by the doorway to their room and Cassandra packed up her things and simply walked out of the hospital with a group of visitors, caught a cab, and departed, much to the consternation of the hospital officials.

Later that evening Petrosian and Fitzgerald held a conference concerning their escaped charge.

"She apparently studied the procedures we were following at the exits and noted that nobody checked IDs for exiting visitors," said Fitzgerald morosely. "One last gesture of defiance... I'm worried, though, that, once again, she has proven too clever for her own good. She did call in, however, and arrange for an appointment with you tomorrow." Fitzgerald paused. "Do you think we should detain her here if she shows up?"

"No!" responded Petrosian. "She is getting better, stronger, more confident. Even this last move of simply walking out of the hospital I interpret as a sign she thinks she is well enough to function in society again. It was damn clever for one thing."

"Well, suppose she has miscalculated?" retorted Fitzgerald. "She attempted suicide once before..."

"She has taken risks before, getting the tape of her broadcast, going under pentothal, and she has emerged much stronger," said Petrosian in awe. "I have never had a patient cover so much nightmarish territory so quickly. Have you?" He looked at Fitzgerald, who shook his head.

"Many people would be permanently crippled emotionally by even a fraction of what she went through, but she has emerged as her former vivacious self, for the most part," said Petrosian.

"I will concede that," said Fitzgerald grudgingly. "But I think she still has major issues to deal with; I am just not sure what they are, however."

"Well, I'll see her and keep the conversation going. I think we are through the worst of this. She understands mostly what happened to her, and seems to understand that she actually emerged as a rather heroic figure, even in her own eyes."

"There is one thing that bothered me when I reviewed the pentothal tapes with you. And I must confess what she went through what would have broken most people, so she triumphed and is certainly the bravest person I have ever encountered in this business. I will say, I have gone from regarding her as simply a troublesome patient to admiring her, and I am used to having supposed heroes confess in my office that they simply got confused in a firefight and ran the wrong way straight into the enemy rather than away from them. So she has impressed me, I will admit. But there was one odd thing that I found myself puzzling over. That was the aspect of the dream she had while in the cell," said Fitzgerald.

"Yes, that was strange," responded Petrosian. "I confess I was focused on the most dramatic parts of her account and helping her get through the knowledge of her near death experience in the torture chamber, her rescue, and risking death again to make her infamous mangled syntax broadcast. The dream seemed a minor detail, but you are right, it actually represents something, something important." Petrosian said in awe, then laughed. "You must admit, she has run intellectual rings around us just like she did her captors, and from what I can gather from talking to them, she ran intellectual rings around her bosses at CNS even before she was captured by the cover-up people."

"But the dream she reported in the cell before anything else happened," said Fitzgerald. "It was similar to the dream she has reported to you several times. It is a dream of someone she recognizes as a dead person, robed in authority as a policewoman, beating her, then sometimes violating her orally with a nightstick. Then her car is torn apart by a tow truck. The car is easy to understand as representing herself, being threatened with dismemberment. Her car was blown up when they tried to kill her. But who does the masculine dead woman represent? Is it herself, forcing herself to go through this ordeal when she could have simply folded?"

"You know we all fall back on Freud's interpretations  in this business when we can't think of anything else," said Petrosian. "She told me the dead woman was Lauren Hill, a staffer at the White House who was murdered in a gruesome manner in the early parts of the Stargate cover-up story she was covering. Perhaps she views Lauren Hill as the standard she must measure herself against. That she had to be willing to risk such a gruesome death if she was to bring down the UFO cover-up."

"So Lauren Hill represented her determination to do her duty even in the face of horrific death?" asked Fitzgerald. "But Lauren Hill was just a victim, and she was reputed to be the President's mistress before she was found murdered.  So it seems odd that  Cassandra's  superego, the conscience that supposedly demands absolute service to  humanity even in the face of threats of horrific death, would make a presentation in that form. Where did she even get this fixation of saving humanity anyway? It makes no sense. It's a messiah complex..."

"However, she also did mention that Lauren Hill confronted her at the White House one day," responded Petrosian, "after Cassandra  gave the President a rough time at a press conference. She said this encounter with Lauren Hill made a real impression on her. Obviously, a mistress protecting her man, who just happens to be the President, but to Cassandra, she may represent a protective person and also someone who is also sexually involved with power. Which, seems to be something she also seems to find fascinating and admirable," Petrosian said, then laughed, shook his head, and smiled. "I have even watched a copy of the movie Barbarella recently, to try and figure out why she keeps talking about it," he laughed. "I admit it's the first I have ever watched a cheesy French sci-fi movie, and took careful notes,  to try to gain insight into a patient's condition. I couldn't see anything useful.  It shows also this patient's ability to both confide and confuse at the same time." Petrosian laughed.  "But it fits your model  Fitz. The Jane Fonda character is held captive in a dark city, but saves everyone, and the city is destroyed. The Fonda character is sort of a messiah figure of sorts."

"George, have you considered this is all some sort of smoke screen, some sort of dodge, by this woman?" responded Fitzgerald. "Look, she went through a terrible ordeal, granted, but she was actually sort of disturbed before she went into this. Doing what she did, attacking the UFO cover-up, is not normal behavior. Heroic yes, but it's like it was a death wish and messianic complex tied together. That's the real issue underlying this, in my opinion."

"So she was crazy before she got held captive by the secret police? Fitz, we are trying to analyze the workings of a remarkable female mind," he continued. Somebody who is obviously smarter than either of us and someone that does not think down ordinary channels." Petrosian reached into his drawer and pulled out a bottle of Jack Daniels and two shot glasses. He poured two glasses and then put the bottle back in the drawer. "Fitz, I concede temporary defeat."

"Yeah, you're right George, I do too," said Fitzgerald smiling with resignation while and taking the glass from Petrosian. "But, still, with her deep under pentothal, what do we end up confronting but a dream within a dream. Whatever it represents to her, even under pentothal, it is still presented in a highly symbolic form. I have never seen that before; it's fascinating."

"You notice something else, Fitz?" said Petrosian downing his drink in one gulp. "It's after dark and it's quiet. This may be the third night in a row with no air raid. Even the aliens may have reached their level of unacceptable pain after that battle last week."

"Now there would be an interesting study, the psychology of the aliens!" said Fitzgerald laughing. "What motivates someone to come 100 light years across interstellar space to try and terrorize a bunch of primitive savages like us? Who, being primitive, are used to terror, and therefore somewhat immune to it. And then, the poor saps try to continue to accomplish this terrorization and do so at enormous losses. It is as if they are still following orders written a year ago, even though everything has changed now…"

"Terror motivates them…" said Petrosian. "In my cases involving political refugees who had been captives of various secret police organizations, I even noted commonalities among the secret police themselves that my patients encountered. These commonalities of the secret police operatives crossed all national and cultural boundaries and boundaries of

266

right or left politics. These commonalities, I think, cross even light years and they are the commonalities of all personalities motivated by terror and the addiction to naked power. So I think I understand the aliens to that degree. They are behaving like classic minions of a dictatorship. And it's not pretty. That means this war is going to be long one my friend, and we're are going to have no shortage of patients."

****

Cassandra was riding the Washington metro endlessly, she had braided her hair and wore dark glasses and would sometimes spend all day riding the metro. She would ride north into Maryland and south into Virginia across the Potomac. She would watch the people, women with children, lonely looking old people, and soldiers, thousands of soldiers, riding the trains. Once after a large party of soldiers exited the train, she pulled out a picture of Bob Schwartzman, standing in his green beret and uniform, from her purse, and stared at it. She then wrote on it, I HATE YOU and stuffed it back into her purse.

****

At their observation post above Arlington Cemetery, Alicia, and Abe Goldberg, both in combat fatigues, helmets and anti-laser goggles, watched the sky warily.

"The solar flares have ebbed. There is no reason for the aliens not to show up, except one: these air defenses." said Goldberg, as midnight finally approached with no sign of the aliens.

"They are hitting New York and Philadelphia," said Alicia scanning the sky with light intensified binoculars.

"That means, then after losing 10 craft in one night a week ago, that we can mount enough air defense over one city to stop them. It means we can create unacceptable losses," said Goldberg. "Your plan of fighting terror weapons with psychological weapons has succeeded!"

"Of course, it did!" said Alicia laughing. "I am not an astrophysicist for nothing! Now we must extend this air defense over the other major

267

cities." After another half hour with the aliens a 'no-show', Alicia went back to a tent and went to sleep on an Army Cot. She slept well through the quiet night.

****

The saucer had its landing ramp down as the large Toman Daz hacked the naked Erran apart with an electric blade while his victim screamed. They were high over Moscow, at night, and the limbs of the Erran were dumped to the streets thousands of feet below, while rocket, laser and flak explosions in the sky lit the inside of the ramp as the Russian air defenses groped blindly to find them.

Number 4 was unhappy with the Toman Daz's work. "hurry up!" he snarled. "we must close the ramp and depart!" Number 4 turned to the pilot of the ship, a medicast as usual, and complained to him bitterly. "It is bad enough they were running so short of spacecraft that we have to risk my own ship to do this business! Now this Toman has become squeamish! "

The Toman Daz was working on cutting off the Erran's head when a Sukhoi 27 Jet fighter, flying at Mach 2, rammed the saucer and both plane and saucer disintegrated into a cloud of falling flaming debris. Number 4, commander of Unash space forces on the Moon, however, remained fully conscious as he fell screaming and flailing his arms and legs for the several thousand feet to the icy streets of Moscow.

****

Cassandra found herself back at her old apartment. She talked to the astonished apartment manager, who looked as if he was seeing a ghost, who gave her a new key and she entered her apartment. It seemed like an alien landscape to her, belonging to another universe. But, she noted with satisfaction that the water and other utilities were still on, the bills being paid by CNS apparently. She went to her equally astonished neighbors and was reunited with her black cat Jasmine, who meowed pathetically at her. *My hallucination insurance,* she thought, as she carried Jasmine, purring, back to her apartment. After some dusting and defrosting some food from the freezer, she found herself sitting in front of her large screen

268

TV that night, watching the Old movie channel, with Jasmine purring on her lap. She watched an old French movie called the 'The Roads to the South' about a man who dedicated himself to overthrowing Franco in Spain, and who becomes a lost man when Franco dies of natural causes.

*I wanted to save the world I knew, but that world is all gone now,* she thought as she drifted off to sleep.

****

Cassandra walked in the door at CNS the next morning dressed as well as she could muster. Everyone from the security guards at the entrance to Manny Berkowitz looked at her with astonishment. She wanted to read a piece of the news, about the victory in the Aleutians, but when she tried to read it in front of the cameras for later broadcast, she broke down and could not finish it. Manny sadly brought her back to his office.

"Cassie, you're trying to do everything on the first day out of the hospital." he said plaintively. "It's too much, too soon. I want you to start back here first by just acting as a contributor. Ok," she nodded tearfully.

She abruptly left and went to the Hospital for her appointment with doctor Petrosian. She expected a scolding from Petrosian about leaving the hospital without checking out, but to her relief, he said nothing about it.

"So how was your first day home?" asked Petrosian.

"Very strange. I feel like I am a ghost or something. Everything seems like it's from someone else's life."

"It will pass, that is normal when you have been through something like you've been through, and you get to go home for the first time in months."

"I feel like I am going to die soon, though like I am actually already dead, but somehow walking around for a while," she said. Petrosian looked at her with concern. "I feel like I have an arrow stuck in my soul, I can't live with it, and I can't pull out either."

"We can put you on medication, that is normal in post-traumatic stress. Think of it as a pain killer for the mind, while it heals."

" What kind of medication? What do you normally prescribe?"

"Prozac"

"One size fits all I suppose," said Cassandra with a smirk.

"Well you won't be alone, half this town is on Prozac now, and the other half is medicating themselves with more traditional palliatives"

"What's that"

"Alcohol mostly"

"I don't drink that much, it makes my face puffy. You know , for the cameras?" she said vacantly. She then continued.

"You realize I trying to do the impossible doctor. I am trying to find peace of mind in the middle of a war."

"Yeah, well at least the night raids have stopped for now. But you can't expect actual life to cooperate, you saved the world, but since the world was saved it goes right on living and creating problems for everyone."

"Yes, I suppose your right."

"By the way, when are you going to replace your car? You can only ride around in cabs or the Metro for so long."

"My car was my baby," she said sadly. "Men failed me, but my love affair with my car, it was successful, then that young girl with long black hair like me got into it one night and got blown up. She was only seventeen, you know, she could have been my daughter if I had stayed married when I was younger."

"Well, you say CNS, your employer, has kept you on the payroll all these months and your bills here are paid by the US government, so you think about getting yourself a new Maserati. Good, get one! Pamper yourself!"

"Now let's talk about what we learned in the past few months. We have learned that you are one tough cookie Ms. Chen and that you are a hero. You brought down the UFO cover-up, which was being used by some traitors to try to surrender the world to some evil aliens, and you got captured and managed to outwit your captors at great risk to yourself. You saved the world."

"A thankless task doctor," said Cassandra. "Some people think I created this whole situation rather than saving them from it."

"Well, you have just confronted the fact that the population as whole is neurotic and a significant portion of that neurotic population is very neurotic and blames everything on the most shiny visible object when anything goes wrong. I have patients who think this entire war is some sort of plot by a bunch of Wall Street bankers. I even have patients who still are convinced the 911 attack was planned by the government so we could invade Afghanistan and get all the oil there."

"There's no oil in Afghanistan, is there?" she asked incredulously.

"Exactly."

" So we have a segment of the population that is not really there completely." continued Petrosian. "Unfortunately, they often are the noisiest part of the population on the web! Think of yourself as the messenger that is being blamed for the bad news you have reported."

\*\*\*\*

"Well, how do you thinks she is doing?" asked Foster, "she certainly looks good."

"Yeah, I don't know how she does it," said Berkowitz. "Most people go through something like she went through and it destroys them, others like her , they just bounce back looking just as beautiful and somehow more noble. But mentally, she is still pretty shaky, we can't put her on camera yet."

"What is your prognosis, I mean do you think she'll recover emotionally," asked Foster.

271

"I think she'll need to get out of DC for a while. I am worried she will simply crack up if she hangs around here; too many people recognize her. I mean she attracts attention wherever she goes anyway, and somebody is bound to figure out who she is and make a scene. You know some people blame her for this whole fucking war."

"Well, she always liked attention before," said Foster. He was staring out the window at the Capitol.

"Yeah, but I have seen people lose their marbles before, and she shows all the signs. For one thing, I can tell she's looking at stuff that isn't there. She was in my office and I could see her eyes following something on the wall, so I sneaked a look, and there was nothing there, not even a shadow..."

"You've seen people do that before?" asked Foster turning to look at Berkowitz.

"Hey, I worked in Hollywood! Have I watched people lose their marbles? See things that weren't there? Sure! I had this one starlet who swore I had extra windows in my office with things flying by them, one day she saw Dumbo the elephant, out my extra nonexistent window."

"What happened to her?"

"Oh, she ended up selling real estate and made millions"

****

She was taking Zumba dance lessons and Prozac. The Zumba was nice but he Prozac made her feel like she was a toy doll 'stuffed with plastic'. She would troop into work every day, try to write copy, and end up simply staring out the window of her office. She kept her medal of freedom hung from a tack on the wall. Then she would call Pamela at the hospital and see how she was doing.

On Pamela's advice, she found herself at Madam Talleyrand's escort service and procured the company of Christopher, also on Pamela's recommendation.

Christopher waited in bed for her, naked, back in her apartment, and she after fortifying herself with several shots of brandy, climbed in after him , wearing only a long sleeved shirt open in the front.

"Please just hold me," was all she could muster, to his disappointment. This continued for several nights. Finally, she was invited to a consultation by Ms. Talleyrand, herself, an older attractive woman in a business suit with shoulder length sandy blond hair, in her office. She had several paintings of nudes posing provocatively and a whip and a leather masquerade mask hanging on the wall. Cassandra was told that Christopher was not available.

"But I like him!" said Cassandra. "What difference does it make whether we screw or not?"

"I am running a business here Ms. Chen, we traffic here in discreet physical company, not affection," said the madam while Cassandra sat fuming. "There are dating services for that." the madam added.

"All right! Then I want you to do something discreet for me, right here!" said Cassandra. "and here is a thousand dollars for your services!" Casandra pulled out her customary fee in 100 dollar bills and laid it on the woman's desk. The madam eyed it with a look of deep thought.

"Yes?" said the madam, leaning back in her chair with a bemused smile. "What do you want me to do for you?"

"I want you to whip me, right here in your office. Nine strokes should be sufficient. I am going to take off my top , that 's more than 100 dollars a stroke with the whip." said Cassandra quietly. "that whip or cat-of-nine-tails there will do nicely." said Cassandra pointing to the whip, which consisted of a leather handle and nine or so long leather strips hanging from the wall. The madam looked at Cassandra carefully. Cassandra rose and took off her tan jacket and then her dark blue blouse, and then undid her bra, she had gained some weight back, and with her Zumba dancing presented a picture of slightly voluptuous loveliness naked down to her navel. She laid her clothes on the chair she had been sitting in. She then pulled her long braided hair up on top of her head with both hands, turned , presenting her scarred back to the woman. The scars

273

were wide and reddish on her bronze skin and made her back look like it had welded together. Cassandra stood with her hands pulling her long hair on top of her head and holding it, staring at the woman, who looked at her now looking pale.

"How did you get those scars?" asked the woman.

"I got them as a guest of the secret government," said Cassandra bitterly. "you might say I displeased the powers of the heavens... Now can we proceed?"

"Ok, but I am not going to hit you hard," said the women rising and taking off her jacket. "That's for other places down the street here in Georgetown." The madam went to the wall and took the whip off the wall. Cassandra wordlessly got down on her knees in front of the woman's desk. She pulled up her long dark hair from off her back again, held it with both hands on top of her head. "do you want me to say anything to you when I hit you? " asked the woman.

"I want you to tell me you love me..." said Cassandra with her voice shaking.

"Ok," said the woman, after a pause. She stared at the long cruel scars on Cassandra's back. She then took off her tie, and unbuttoned her blouse several buttons, and drew back the whip, then flicked against Cassandra's bare back. "I love you," she said. Cassandra felt joy rising in her as the leather strips hit her back and the words rang in her ears.

"Harder please " gasped Cassandra closing her eyes. She absorbed another seven flicks of leather thongs, the woman saying "I love you" in a cadence with the whip.

"Ms. Chen , I think we are done here," said the woman suddenly.

"That was only seven... I paid for nine!"

"no charge... you can keep your money ..." said the woman in a shaking voice.

Cassandra rose dejectedly , *Am I going insane,* she thought, *what did I just do? Sometimes I am running on automatic, like a zombie, doing things I don't understand. It's like I am trying to tell myself something...* Cassandra put her bra and blouse back on. She picked up the money. The madam was sitting back in her chair, she was now smoking an e-cig. She looked blankly at Cassandra. Her eyes looked red.

"Ms. Chen , don't come back here..." said the woman looking sad now. " I think you need services of a different kind than we offer here." Cassandra buttoned up her blouse and put on her jacket. She left the building and went out into the cold street. It was starting to snow lightly. *Someday I'll understand,* she told herself. *I have to get these scars removed, if possible,* she thought. She thought of a Hollywood plastic surgeon she and Pamela had patronized for some small cuts and other things after the Sepulveda asteroid crisis. He had done a great job for both of them.

****

Cassandra one day rode the metro all day and into the night, then as if in a waking dream got off and wandered to a park. She wandered to the middle of the park without thinking and fell down on the cold grass, looking up at the bright blue stars. She then fell asleep and dreamed she was dancing amid the blue star holding a little child, loving it. *I love you hamster...*

She then awoke with a start, it was morning and she felt nearly frozen. *What am I doing here?* She thought in a panic. *I could have been killed here!*

"I have got to talk to Petrosian before I go insane..." she said to herself as she got up gathered her purse and ran to the metro. Soon she had gone home, showered and changed, and was riding the metro to Arlington Hospital to see Pamela and Petrosian.

****

"Cassie you look marvelous!" exclaimed Pamela as she rose from sitting on her bed studying and rushed to embrace Cassandra. "Whatever you're

275

doing for yourself, it's working!" However, Pamela looked with some dismay at the bright red streak in her braided hair, starting above her forehead.

Cassandra managed a brave smile. She was dressed to kill in a black dress and stylish boots.

"And those boots! Where did you get them?" exclaimed Pamela happily looking down.

"Oh a place in Georgetown, next to Madam Talleyrand's, she added with a smirk.

"How was Christopher?" asked Pamela eagerly.

"Oh he was fine, but I guess I am not ready for all that yet, all I could manage was have him hold me in his arms," said Cassandra walking idly around the room and looking out the window. Pamela looked sad at this, shrugged. "Basically, I used him as a big Teddy bear to help me sleep."

"Have you been back to work?" asked Pamela.

"Yeah, but Manny won't put me back on camera, the son of a bitch!" said Cassandra with her eyes flashing. She rubbed the red streak in her hair indignantly. "But, how are you doing, you're looking great too," asked Cassandra. "How is the physical therapy ..."

"Oh, they are going to discharge me next week! They have me running on the treadmill for miles. They say my legs are recovered completely." said Pamela excitedly. "And I am getting my four-year paper! You know, my Bachelor's degree, from Annapolis too. They gave me all this college credit because of my work as a Journalist and even as a weather girl! I aced my Calculus course too!"

"That's my girl," said Cassandra with a vacant smile. She turned and stared out into the Park like she used to. Sadness was filling her. "Listen, I have to go see Petrosian now. You keep studying and getting better Ok?" said Cassandra turning. Her smile had faded. Pamela looked at her sadly and nodded.

"Oh, I did hear one thing," Pamela said as she rose and walked with Cassandra towards the door. "My Navy buddies told me that one of the Carny people got wounded , fighting up in the Aleutians , and they have him I up in the Naval hospital at Bethesda. He's a former Navy Seal. I was wondering if you could do me a favor, and go visit him. It will show the Navy people I still have some pull in this town…"

"Sure, I'll go visit him. Do you know his name?"

"Yes , it's Captain John Badgio, he was your Colonel's right-hand man. They don't want the French to know he's there, so keep this quiet."

"Oh! He was one of the people who rescued me!" exclaimed Cassandra suddenly. "Of course I'll go see him!" she said emphatically. A thousand different emotions, ranging from sadness to fear, tore at her. She came back and hugged Pamela one more time, then turned and left.

Minutes later Cassandra was sitting in Petrosian's office like always.

"So, how are things on the outside Cassandra?" he asked, from his wheelchair. She looked beautiful and radiant but sad in the chair facing him. *She looks very well physically, and is obviously taking care of herself,* he thought. *So that's an accomplishment. But why the red streak in the hair?*

"Oh… Fine I guess, doctor." She said sadly. "I can function, I guess. Pammy has really gotten better too, so I feel like I helped her, and this makes me feel like I was supposed to survive, you know, to help her. That's the one thing that has stuck out in my mind recently, a reason for me being alive, that's because I survived that I could help her walk again. So that kind of blows my whole theory I had, about how strange and kind of inconvenient it all was, that I should survive and get rescued."

"Why do you think it's strange?" asked the doctor. *Now we are getting someplace.* He thought.

"Well, when I started this UFO cover-up thing, I actually thought I would probably die. I counted the costs, and that's what it looked like it would cost. So I accepted that. So my surviving, it's sort of strange and

277

unplanned. But Pammy needed me afterward, and I helped her. You know she is not only walking and running again, but they are going to award her a four-year degree from Annapolis!" Cassandra brightened. "A four-year degree, she did study a lot of stuff on-line. Calculus, Advanced Algebra, Physics, Space Technology! My God! She even tried to explain it all to me!" Cassandra laughed. "Me! I could never even balance my checkbook!"

*She laughed again. She is truly getting better! It is a miracle!* thought Petrosian trying to mask his happiness.

"Someone at Annapolis even managed to conflate Pammy's years as a weather girl in Cleveland into credit hours in meteorology or something! This is hilarious! And typical!" laughed Cassandra. "Seriously, I'm glad they're doing it for Pam, she earned it, but I am also glad I don't have that particular bit of creative scholastic bookkeeping on my conscience!" said Cassandra still smiling. But her smile soon faded.

"How are you sleeping?"

"Ooh, better than the officials at Annapolis I suppose..." said Cassandra with a weak laugh.

"Have you been working? I was hoping to see you back on the news..." asked Petrosian. *Not really* thought Petrosian. *She still isn't out of the woods on this. There is something else...*

"Ooh, I am still a little shaky in front of the camera I mean," she said looking at the floor. "And I keep having strange dreams. They bother me. I dreamed a woman was beating me again, with a whip, and I was shouting, 'I love you' every time she hit me." *That's it, I only dreamed it...* she thought feverishly.

"Then I dreamed I was dancing in the stars with this little baby again, I call her Hamster... That was a happy dream."

"What do you think these dreams mean? One good dream, one bad dream?"

"I think it means, one of those arrows, you spoke of doctor, one of those arrows that wounds us, that we have to remove to get well, it is still lodged in me..." she was now looking at him with a sad beauty. "This one is planted really deep, doctor, and I can't remember it, and I can't get past it either..." she said levelly.

Petrosian sat transfixed by her, felt overcome by sorrow, *she is so brave, so beautiful, what can I tell her?*

****

At Bethesda naval Hospital, James Bergman was shaking with anger, as he stared at the chief of the Psychiatric section. Bergman stood in his overcoat, because of the cold outside and one of his Marine bodyguards stood beside him.

"You mean you have been keeping this man in a drug induced stupor! For five years! Based on secret orders from the UFO cover up people?!" Bergman roared. " I could have you and all your staff court marshaled for this! Don't you know every order issued by the MAGI is rescinded now! The cover-up is over! Just when I think we are getting out of the woods on the human rights violations of that nightmare program doctor, I find this! Still running, like nothing ever happened!

The doctor, a dignified looking man in a naval dress uniform, now looking completely cowed, looked down at his desk.

"This is a military facility Dr. Bergman, and we have to follow orders, especially regarding patients who are labeled a national security risk." said the doctor quietly. " We only discovered this order was issued by the MAGI years back when we checked his file recently. The order had such high classification we had to bring somebody down from the White House with a high clearance to even read it. We had no idea whatsoever, that it was no longer operative."

"That's because we ordered his files, and everyone else's files reviewed," said Bergman. "This man used to be my right-hand man! Now you get him off that drug regime and back to his normal state! "

279

"We will, of course, wean him off the drugs. We can't just end them immediately, it may cause irreparable harm. And I cannot guarantee anything about his final mental state when we do this. You yourself must know he had to be admitted here after a mental breakdown."

"Good, you get Richard off those drugs, as close to sanity as you can, and inform me immediately when he is well enough for me to see him!" said Bergman angrily. He then turned and went back into the viewing room, where through a two-way mirror, he watched Richard Metternich, or what used to be Metternich, sitting in a stupor in a bare white room.

"Please, Jesus, let this man recover... I need him! The country, the whole human race needs his insights!" muttered Bergman, "May he be healed good as new!"

With horror tearing at him Bergman turned and left, it was getting colder outside, and Bergman glanced at the dull reddish Sun in the sky. Despair rose up in him, but he shook it off and got in the limousine with is body guards and shut the door. It was warm inside.

"Where to Doctor Bergman?" asked the marine who was his driver.

"Where else? The Pentagon!"

\*\*\*\*

Cassandra walked into the front door of the Bethesda Naval Hospital. The presence of numerous Marines and Shore Police in the lobby, with two police dogs, made her want to turn and run outside again. But she forced herself to keep walking up to the group of officers at the front desk. Everyone was looking at her, she took off her silver glasses and heard gasps of recognition from people out of her field of vision. But she pressed on. She was wearing a black pantsuit and long warm coat, it was freezing outside in October.

*I must see him* , she thought. *Human decency requires it, my own soul craves it. I must ask how I looked when they found me...*

280

"I am Cassandra Chen, and I am here to see one of your patients, Captain John Badgio, who was one of the men who rescued me from the alien base at Morningstar," she said to the group of amazed Naval and Marine officers behind a polished wooden counter.  A women officer in a white Navy dress uniform immediately  picked up a phone and called someone. She sat looking at the desk for a long time, then looked up at her.

"A doctor is coming Ms. Chen, please sit over there. He will be here shortly," she said with an amazed look.

After a few minutes,  an older doctor in a white coat appeared and walked up to her, then sat down next to her.

"I am doctor Mathews, Ms. Chen. I am not sure if the patient you want to see is really here."

"Oh I believe he is, and if you are worried about  the French Intelligence service following me in here, I can assure you they are nowhere near here."

The doctor looked at her in deep thought.

"There is another problem, the patient you want to see is still in a serious condition, I am not sure seeing you would  do him good right now."

"Sometimes seeing an old friend can do wonders for a patient's recovery, wouldn't  you say doctor?" said Cassandra. "After all,  isn't a  patient's mental state a key to recovery?" she said silkily.

The doctor looked deep in thought again.

"OK, follow me, but you can only see him for five minutes. That's five minutes exactly to the second. He is supposed to be sleeping now."

After an endless trip up and elevator and walking down long corridors filled with horribly wounded men struggling to get well, she suddenly found herself in the orthopedic ward of the hospital. A nurse ushered her into a room. There, with his legs raised off the bed and cruel bolts coming out of their flesh lay the emaciated form of John Badgio, USN. His black hair looked unkempt and his thick beard needed a shave.  His still brawny

281

arms were folded over his stomach.  He suddenly looked up.  His face lit up with a bright smile.  The smile coming from such a horribly wounded man made her almost begin to cry, but she forced herself to smile back.

"Cassie! What's shakin babe!" he gasped in a hoarse voice.  She immediately pulled up a chair near his bed and sat in it.

"Oh, I'm much better!  Captain!" she gasped. She tried not to look at his battered legs.

"Just call me Badge babe. Yeah, I got shot up pretty bad up there on Adak. But I nailed an alien right in front of me right after I got hit!"  he said with a beaming smile.

"What kind was he. I heard the aliens up at Adak are different; they're not Greys" she asked, burning with curiosity. *I am still a reporter, I should know what's going on.*

"Yeah,  this was a Samar, that what we call them anyway. He looked just like any human being, except for his surprised look.  He thought I was dead and instead I nailed him right in the gut with a shaped charge grenade round. Ruined his whole day,"  said Badge with a laugh.

At the mention of his human appearance, a deep chill went through Cassandra, but she shook it off and was determined to be as pleasant as possible.  *There I was feeling sorry for myself...*she thought, glancing at his legs.  *My sufferings are nothing...*

"How soon till you get better?  What are they telling you?"

"Oh," he looked deep in thought. She saw a hint of despair  in his dark eyes. "Yeah, my legs are held together with titanium alloy, so it's going to be a while, they say. I got enough metal in me to open a hardware store." He managed a weak laugh.   She looked sad. Tears formed in her eyes. He apparently saw them .

"But I'm gonna be fine soon!" he said with a big smile.   "Yeah, Cassie, couple months,  tops,  and I'll be marching out of here with my seabag on my shoulder again."

282

"Where too then Badge?   Hawaii ?" she asked smiling and wiping her eyes.

"To wherever the war is!" he laughed.   "My only worry is that Bob Schwartzman and the boys will win this war before I can get back into it!" Badgio laughed.  She laughed also. *This guy really likes to fight I guess...*

"Badge I have to ask you something.  I want to know what I looked like when you guys pulled me out of that plastic chamber at Morningstar," she asked leaning next to him. "I mean does anything stick out in your mind?"

"Well, you weren't wearing any clothes, I remember that part!  But aside from your back and fingernails, you actually looked pretty good.  Hell, You looked a lot better off than most of the other people in that place that day, that's for fucking sure!" he laughed.   He looked off in the distance and smiled. " You looked happy to see us too! As I remember!"

"I'm asking you because I am having a hard time remembering things from that day. I mean I am having a hard time getting over it." she wept.

"Oh Cassie, don't be like that OK. You got to be brave like you were back then.  I mean you really inspired us, you and that blonde friend of yours. You were our heroes.  You both were fearless!" he said quickly.  He smiled at her. Touched her cheek. She tried to smile again and wiped her eyes.

"You'll get over it, you need to get over it . Just like I'm gonna walk out of here with my seabag on my shoulder.   I mean a lot of guys here don't have any legs, so I figure I gotta get well for their sake, and get back into action..." he said. "You too, I order you to get well, and get back in this fight..."

Just then a nurse came in and looked at both of them.

"Sorry captain but visiting hours are over." said the Nurse.  "Sorry, the doctor is outside and insists."

"OK, I just want to say thank you for rescuing me. I'll get well and make it worth it that you all rescued me... I promise," she said tearfully.

Cassandra leaned over and kissed him on his stubbly cheek, then rose and waved goodbye sadly to him as the nurse escorted her out. Badge beamed at her fiercely as she left and waved at her with his powerful right hand.

*Hawaii,* she thought as she walked down the halls with the doctor. She wiped her eyes, walked tall. She felt energized. *I could get better quicker in Hawaii. I am going to get better and get back in this fight... I now have orders!*

****

"Your new unit deployment orders Colonel," said General Ross, handing Schwartzman an envelope. They were both sitting in Ross's office at Fort Riley. The stitches had come out of Schwartzman's two facial cuts, and they were healing nicely. The 42$^{nd}$ Ranger Battalion was now back up to full strength, with replacements integrated and funerals performed. The unit was rested and refitted after the fight at Adak. The orders were marked SOCOM.

****

She had been having groceries delivered, but finally decided, with the nightly air raids a thing of the past and semi-normal routine returning to the capitol, to go shopping herself. It was not a good decision, as it turned out.

She was stuck in a checkout line sipping a coke through a straw in a tall paper cup, behind someone having endless trouble with a credit card. She had a full shopping cart. She liked to shop. But she discovered to her horror the tabloids all had pictures of her topless, with some pixelizations on the front cover, with the comments 'Cassandra Chen goes berserk at hospital.' *At least I don't look fat,* she thought. She had nervously slipped on her dark glasses. Finally, the line was moving and she was being checked out.

A young man with long hair and a goatee was right behind her.

"Hey aren't you Cassandra Chen  the person who started this war?" he said to her.  She ignored him.  She had her credit card out to pay.

"Yeah, it's you! You started this fucking war! Didn't you?"  he said, his voice rising.  Rage filled her.  She whirled around and tore off her dark glasses, her dark eyes blazing.

"Hey shut the fuck up moron!" she yelled.  He was angry and pushed her cart, making it run over her foot.  The cashier, an older woman, started trying to help her.

"Leave her alone! She's just trying to buy some groceries!"

"You want a war fuckhead?  I'll give you a war!" yelled Cassandra as  she flipped her half full cup of coke and ice right into the young man's  face, blinding him temporarily, then slugged him in the face as hard as she could.  He collapsed in a heap on the floor.  She wanted to stomp on him with her high heels but a bagger held her back. She was screaming now.

"Let me go! Let me go!" she cried angrily, then her voice became a wail.  Please don't hurt me!"

**** 

Manny Berkowitz walked swiftly into the Alexandria police station.  He found Cassandra quietly crying in a chair being watched by several sympathetic policemen and women.

"I am her boss from work," said Berkowitz breathlessly. "This is Cassandra Chen, the newscaster."

The police sergeant looked  up from offering a box of Kleenex to Cassandra.  Cassandra took Kleenex from the  box and blew her nose noisily.

"Yeah, we know.  And we know what she's been through, so we didn't put her in a cell." said the sergeant.

"Are there going to be charges? You know she is still pretty traumatized by what happened to her."

285

"No, the jerk who started it was wanted for parole violations anyway, so back he goes to the state pen." said the police sergeant matter of factly. "Witness's said he started it anyway. But, uh, yeah if she has PTSD, which we understand, she should be on medication or something don't you think?"

"Yeah, I think she needs some help," said Berkowitz. He turned to Cassandra. She looked up at him mournfully, picked up her purse and followed him out of the building. He was driving her in his car.

"Manny, I think it would be good if I left town for a while," Cassandra said sadly. "I have to go to get treatments for the scars of my back in Los Angeles, and after that is done, maybe I should lay low for a while. I think this town is driving me crazy now. It's the center of the political universe. After today, I sense my mental state is maybe a little precarious."

" Yeah, well you just dodged a big bullet today Cassie. We want to report headlines, not make them, right? Now, you're going out to Los Angeles to go to Malvik's clinic for your back, right. So you book a room down in Chinatown and lie low in Los Angeles. I have to tell you now, we had the FBI in here yesterday saying there are people who want to kill you out there, so you have to be careful. So I am thinking about this. Then, I think I have this idea, I have a friend from way back in school, he is a Frenchman, sort of Jacque Cousteau wanna-be, but he is a good guy, and he is out on his research yacht in the Pacific near Hawaii studying whales. His name is Renoir, and you speak French, right? We at CNS could kick in some money to support his research, you could be a passenger on his ship. Do you think you could handle that for a few months? The most important question is would it help? You'd be out at sea near Hawaii for long periods, no news, no tabloids. Can you handle that? Studying whales in the middle of a war?"

*Hawaii*, she thought, and a smile appeared on her face.

**** 

Schwartzman watched with calm ruthlessness in the night as the figure in the nightgown floated in the blue light underneath a flying saucer in the suburbs of Baltimore. The woman was being abducted, and he and his

286

men and vehicles had now arrived and were deploying. He did a quick mental calculation as she rose towards the faintly glowing saucer in the blue beam. *We got them...*he thought.

"Open Fire!" he yelled into his radio. From around him and from several other locations nearby, streams of red tracer shells and several Stinger missiles, all with magneto-proximity warheads, flew upwards at the saucer and impacted it with deafening concussions. The hovering saucer exploded into brilliant blue fragments and fell burning into the nearby houses. He tempered his joy at getting another kill, with the sure knowledge that the woman being abducted was probably dead in the inferno that now engulfed the suburban row of houses. People in night clothes were now running from the houses, some carrying children.

"She was already dead, Chief. This way she died quickly..." said Arizona standing beside him, his face now lit with the light of the fires. Fire truck sirens were now beginning to sound. They would be arriving soon. *If you truly loved me you would have left me to die...*he thought, remembering Cassandra's last words to him.

"Yeah, and that's one Seagull that won't be flying on any abduction-mutilation missions again," said Schwartzman grimly. *A billion dollar spacecraft lost trying to create a little terror.*

"Xray recovery teams forward!" he ordered into the radio.

****

"Alright, so you're going away for a while, I recommend against it, but I understand. Promise me you'll keep taking your medication and that you'll come back to see me when you get back to Washington DC," said Petrosian soberly. "So let's summarize where we are now. You and Pamela successfully brought down the UFO cover-up and disrupted a plot by the aliens to take over the world by terror and treachery. In the process, Pamela was wounded, but you helped her recover. You were captured and tortured, but at no time did you betray your country or species, even though you were near death. In fact, you managed to warn

287

the government of an impending alien counterattack at great risk to yourself and then were rescued. You then got an extraterrestrial botulism-like infection and managed to survive it also. Would you agree with things I have just said?"

"Yes, I suppose so," said Cassandra sadly. "However, it doesn't make me feel better. You also neglected the minor detail that bringing down the cover-up started a war with a civilization vastly superior to us in technology. A few people are upset with me about this, also."

"Well, that's not your problem, that's everybody's problem now. I am going to cut the crap with you, Cassandra, and tell you what I really think for once, as one human being on planet Earth to another, instead of hiding behind being your psychiatrist," said Petrosian. OK? Are you going to pay attention for once?" Cassandra nodded and leaned forward in her chair.

"Look, you're talking to somebody who lost and arm and leg that night the cover-up ended," began Petrosian. "And I am not mad at you. No! I am grateful! I have never questioned the decisions I made that night. I lost my arm and leg fighting the secret government because I am Armenian and I know what genocide is, unlike most of the public, and I was determined to die fighting it. The fact that I only lost an arm and a leg, and my other vital plumbing was left intact, I consider a blessing and so does Mrs. Petrosian, by the way. Someday, in fact, I am told, they will be able to graft a new arm and leg on me. If there is anything this war is providing right now, it is an abundance of useful body parts. So, you saved the human race but started a war of survival in the process. This war was unavoidable, its only alternative was the quiet acceptance of extinction! Almost everyone with a brain on this planet knows this! The fact that some people don't accept that fact is part of the phenomenon we call denial and one reason being a psychiatrist is such a good career! However, you shouted fire in a crowded theater, and there was, in fact, a fire! The result wasn't pretty, but somebody had to say it! Tell me you didn't consider that a war might result if the aliens plan was disrupted."

"Yes, we knew that and we even warned people about that possibility..." she said vacantly. "But that was in the abstract, a sci-fi movie with happy ending. Now it's a reality, and it's horrible."

" Yes, so, this aftermath, what we are going through now,  is called Legitimate Suffering in my business, as opposed to the illegitimate suffering we were going through when the aliens were abducting and abusing people and no one would acknowledge or talk about what was happening. Legitimate Suffering is part of psychiatric therapy, no healing of any kind is possible without it. Why do you think good mental health is rare? It's rare because  people are constantly trying to avoid the legitimate suffering we all must go through to face the true problems of our lives and deal with them. I have to deal with pain every day. But I like it! It's a good pain! It is a good pain because it means I am still alive and capable of fighting!" said Petrosian with vehemence. He then relaxed, sat back in his wheelchair and looked at her for a moment in silence.

"There, I said it. Now I am going to go back to being a therapist," said Petrosian  with a smile. "Now tell me again, that this narrative I told you earlier about yourself is true or false."

"I guess it's true," said Cassandra.

"I would say these are things you should  feel proud of," said Petrosian.

"Yes, but  I don't feel very brave or strong right now. I feel broken and weak."

"Well just before your near death experience, you said yourself you were breaking, so that's probably the residual feeling from that.  Feelings are important, but the truth about feelings is they can just as much be out of synch with reality as any other mental process," said Petrosian.

"OK, I understand that. But I also feel bad that so many people got killed, and I survived.  Just at Devil's Mesa, I must have seen a thousand people die ..."

"Perhaps you survived for a reason..." said Petrosian.

"What reason would that be? I helped Pammy, but she is better than I am now. Why am I still alive now?" said Cassandra in wonder.

"That, Cassandra, you must find out for yourself."

**** 

Cassandra and Pamela tearfully embraced back in what had been their old room at the hospital. They were both standing by the window that Cassandra had spent so much time staring out of. Pamela was still undergoing physical therapy and had added Zumba lessons at the hospital. It had also been pointed out that she had an army battalion and several anti-aircraft batteries protecting her at the hospital, and that protection against abduction could not be guaranteed if she left the hospital.

"I am going out to get my back fixed as best they can in Los Angeles, at Doctor Malik's clinic," said Cassandra. Pamela nodded tearfully.

"Yes , he was good"

"Then I don't know where I am going, but I have to find someplace away from here, someplace quiet, to get well," said Cassandra wiping her eyes. "Pammy, I see things, I hear things, that aren't there, and I am afraid to even talk about it. They might lock me up if I tell anyone. I have to go someplace away from all this, to get well. To make the voices go away. I hope you understand." Pamela nodded tearfully.

"Promise me you'll come back," said Pamela

"I will," wept Cassandra. She suddenly smiled. "Oh, Doctor Petrosian, he seems sad I am leaving, so why don't you go talk to him. To cheer him up." Pamela nodded smiling. "Develop penis envy or some other neuroses like that, to give him something to do...," continued Cassandra, "To give him something to work on. He tells me I am his most interesting patient." laughed Cassandra wiping her eyes again.

"Oh I am sure I can come with something complex for him to work on," said Pamela nodding tearfully with a smile.

Number 7, the Idelkite, kept his face controlled, as the ship plunged from space through the dark night sky over the Northern Pacific and into the ocean. The gravity drives adjusted to moving the thick water past them rather than warping space as they drove deeper and deeper into the dark ocean. Number 7 turned to the team of four Toman Daz soldiers and a timid looking medicast called number 17 who had been sent with him on this mission. *Why do I get this cull of the hive as an assistant?* thought Number 7 ruefully *Because all the smart and brave ones are dead!* However, Number 7 knew he had only been promoted to commander of space forces as a temporary measure because Number 4, an Unash, had been killed and there was no-one that Sadok Sar trusted to replace him. Number 7 also knew that as an Idelkite, and thus a Hybrid, it was not certain that anyone in the undersea base, called Kadaul by the Unash, would listen to his orders unless an Unash was standing beside him seconding them. As the saucer dove deeper into the ocean, the hull began to creak and shudder and the Toman Daz warriors began to look about nervously. The medicast Unash simply sat stoically in the seat next to him. Number 7 shot a look to the commander of the saucer, who also looked nervous.

"This is normal, the hull bears some pressure not compensated for by the gravitic drives. It is nothing," said the saucer commander.

*Liar!* thought Number 7 fiercely. Many ships are lost in the Erran oceans! It means the hull is badly maintained! Number 7 had watched the losses of the space forces on the Moon mount as Sadok Sar, Number 1, had ordered a festival of terror on Erra after the Errans had overrun the base at Morningstar. Their ships, reinforced after the crisis had begun, had been roughly 300 then, but now due to the wear and tear of nightly trips from the Moon to Erra and back again, the effect of atmospheric buffeting and corrosive effects of oxygen from the Erran atmosphere on ships designed primarily for space flight in vacuum, the damage produced by high explosive shrapnel from Erran missile and cannon shells being fired at them constantly, plus the fact that Unull ships prowled constantly in near-Earth space to pick off damaged ships trying to make it back to the Moon, had resulted in steady losses. They now had only 185 ships left, that were fully armed and space capable.  He had mentioned, obliquely, the problem of high attrition rate that accompanied the terror campaign to Sadok Sar, but he had ignored it and merely said. "The festival must continue, and reinforcements will arrive soon to replace our losses."

*"How soon will we reach Kadaul?" demanded Number 7. "We must reach there as soon as possible!"*

"We must be careful, in the depths of Erra's oceans, some large creatures dwell here. If we attract attention  and one grabs our ship it could short out the gravitic fields and the hull will then implode" said the Commander watching his control view screen.

Finally, after what seemed an eternity, the ship set down on the circular landing pad on the oceans bottom, 2 miles down, in the cold blackness.  A split dome rose and cupped around them, then pumps forced all the water out and the hatch was opened.  The landing team composed of Number 7 ,number 17 and the four Toman Daz guards, all armed with death ray carbines,  marched through a tunnel into the main dome of the vast undersea base. Number 7 felt himself panting. *Low oxygen,* he thought in horror.

The base was a dark cold and damp place.  Number 7 looked above him and could see the dim outlines of the elaborately  ribbed geodesic structure of the dome far above them. Beneath the dome many white colored structures were built in a simple box and rectangular shapes.  On the way they walked between the structures, Number 7 could see a spire with a red beacon light ahead of them in the distance. This, he knew, was the base command center. The dome was crowded with Unash, many in stasis tubes hibernating to conserve life support capacity, with the stasis tubes lined up in long rows. Many other Unash rushed up to meet them in a mob in the near darkness.  There were not enough stasis tubes for all of them, nor, it was reported, enough food  either for them.  Even enough oxygen was barely being provided. Disease was now rampant in the dome, it had been reported. The crowd  then parted and stood in expectant rows alongside the route to the command center of the dome.  Number 7 looked nervously to the Toman Daz guards he had brought with him. He knew he came with bad tidings for those at the base.

Then a choir of greeting came forward, four Unash dressed in blue robes, and sang the song of greeting. The base commander, Scama, and his second and third in command then came walking towards them. The base commander wore a simple silver coverall like most of the other Unash.

"Number 7, how good of you to come here!" said the commander. "What undersea weapons and reinforcements have you brought us? We must clear the docking area to bring in the other ships with the supplies immediately! We have been the evacuation point for many bases , we need food and medicine here desperately!"

"My lord Scama, we have only brought one ship, and we bear no supplies. I bear orders from Number 1 to my Lord Scama, to return with us to the Moon. "

The Commander, Scama, stared at Number 7 for a long time in silence. He then squinted deeply.

"You have not brought the weapons and supplies  I requested or reinforcement?"

"No, my Lord , I only bring orders from my lord Sadok Sar, for you to return. He needs your presence on the Moon." Number 7 saw shock spreading on the faces of the other Unash in the dark dome. He was amazed that the base commander would speak so frankly in the presence of the crowd of onlookers. *Discipline is breaking down here! We must get out of here!* Thought Number 7 in near panic.

"I cannot abandon my post here! We have evacuated many lesser bases to this location!" said the commander angrily. "The Errans have discovered this place! If Number 1 will not send weapons for undersea fighting or reinforcements he must evacuate this place! This place is not defensible as it is, we have only three submersible aircraft for fighting and one cargo ship that is no longer space-capable! We need many spacecraft to evacuate these personnel! We need food and medicine until they are evacuated!"

Number 7 looked to Number 17, who meekly stated, "My Lord, Lord Sadok Sar needs your counsel on the Moon. You must obey his orders."

"He does not listen to my counsel! He is without honor and a fool!" said Scama. "Very well! But I must prepare myself to leave." He stepped into a nearby box-shaped enclosure. Number 17 followed him, then suddenly reappeared.

"He has made a death statement to me!" said Number 17 in horror. Number 7 went into the building, found Commander Scama lying inert on the floor. A vial of what appeared to be poison lay beside him. Number 7 turned and went outside. He pointed at the Number 2 in-command.

"If the commander will not come with us you must come." He said to the Number 2 officer. "I cannot return to the moon without somebody." To Number 7's relief, the number 2 Unash nodded and came along with them. The shock of the statements and the absence of the base commander from the group as they turned a walked back to the ship began to register with the crowd of Unash standing by the road, and they began to follow. Even the choir of greeting began to follow them.

"Officer! Maintain order here!" barked Number 7 to the Toman guard team. They reacted by raising their weapons. They were now in the tunnel, and the crowd of Unash was now looking like a desperate mob. Soon a cry went up, "They are abandoning us here!" The Toman guards fired their guns over the heads of the crowd, blinding some, but causing the rest to retreat in screaming panic. "Take us with you! Do not leave us!" they began to scream. Number 7 ordered the door to the tunnel sealed and then directed everyone on to the ship. "We cannot get out! WE CANNOT GET OUT!" the crowd outside the door was wailing in unison.

"Secure the ship, we must leave immediately!" said Number 7. The Number 2 commander of the base, sat down looking highly relieved as the dome filled with water and they launched back into the dark depths. After what seemed like hours they emerged from the ocean surface and flew swiftly up into the star filled the sky. Soon they were in space returning to the Moon.

"What shall we report to Lord Sadok Sar? " asked Number 17.

"We shall report that Base Commander Scama, was unable to travel due to poor health, and therefore his acting commander has been brought back to the Moon instead," said Number 7.  *Yes,  and Sadok Sar will simply believe this account because he does not like adverse reports. Therefore, all the reports that reach his ears are of progress and good developments.*

\*\*\*\*

Cassandra sat in a Starbucks coffee shop in Pacifica, a pleasant suburb of San Francisco,  and nursed her coffee.   It had been hard to get to San Francisco, and Pamela had had to exert her influence with the Navy to get her an uncomfortable seat in a Navy transport jet full of sailors and marines to get her there. She had arranged  for her flight to Hawaii, two weeks from then. It was now considered a perilous trip only accomplished by day and with fighter escort.  In a city so full of Asians, no one seemed to notice her.  She was dreaming of her own planet lost in the stars, that she named Pacifica, the planet of peace.

Soon she would drive down to Los Angeles, and have her back treated.

\*\*\*\*

Cassandra sat topless in Doctor Malvik's  examining room looking in the mirror ahead of her, it, in turn,  faced another mirror, and she could see endless reflections of her back going away to infinity.

"Well we have done the very best we could, Cassandra, but the scars are pretty bad. "Cassandra looked, and her heart sank. The scars were much less ugly and ragged but were still there. She rubbed her fingers across her back. The scars did not protrude as much but were still like raised welts.

"Thank you,  doctor. I see they are much improved." Tears ran down her cheeks. *I guess some things can't really heal as good as new.*

"Perhaps after the treatments we've done have a chance to fully heal, we can try some new treatments." said the Doctor.  However, Cassandra could read his eyes, and had to accept that the scars would never go away.

"Of course, I can come back in six months or so," she said with her voice trembling.

"Yes, that time frame would be good."

**\*\*\*\***

Cassandra looked over Pearl Harbor through her dark glasses. It was full of grey navy ships.

Later in the day, she was at the statue of King Kamehameha the Great, in Honolulu. King Kamehameha the great king, had united the Hawaiian islands under one rule. His name meant "lonely warrior." In him Cassandra saw Robert Schwartzman, but turned away from the thought, it was too painful. She looked back and saw also herself. *Lonely are the brave,* she thought. But then she encouraged herself. *My name is Jian, which means 'fighter ',* she thought. *I am recovering.*

**\*\*\*\***

In the harbor at Maui, Cassandra boarded the Research Yacht La Mirage de Mare, carrying a small bag of belongings, and was introduced to the captain and chief scientist, Dr. Charles Renoir, a noted ocean biologist, and his wife, Genevieve. They were a handsome greying couple, whose appearance bespoke many years at sea. She was shown to her quarters by their handsome, mid-20's son, Mathew, who had sandy hair and deep blue eyes.

Her 'nom de voyage' was Jian, it had been agreed. The crew had been told not to talk to her.

They then departed out to sea, soon after she was aboard. It was a beautiful day, and the ocean was smooth as glass. Cassandra lay for a long time in her bunk. And then arose to walk the decks after dark. She wore a black scarf with a skull and crossbones on it over her head, tied like she was a gypsy or pirate. It made her feel better. The ship was headed south to try to locate schools of Humpback whales, coming to Hawaiian waters to calve. The research plan was explained to Cassandra by Genevieve as observation of the migration calving with precision sonar and broad spectrum hydrophone recordings. Then they would follow the further migration north to Alaska by the Humpbacks and their young to feast on fish and shrimp in the bio-rich northern waters.

So she walked the deck silently at night. No one spoke to her, which was her wish. She found herself staring at the blackness of the  sea  to the south, where the southern cross, and nearby a brilliant golden star, Alpha Centauri, shown above the waters . She found herself staring at it for hours, letting her mind empty of all the voices that filled it, before returning to her  small cabin and falling into a dreamless sleep.

****

In the warm sea off of Maui, Cassandra was swimming furiously in her snorkeling outfit, to keep up with Liani, Cassandra's  name for the pregnant Humpback whale. The team on the Mirage was studying the whale, soon to be a mommy, and several others like her, but Cassandra had bonded with this one, much to the irritation of Dr. Renoir. Dolphins were occasionally flitting by and making noises at her, as the sun danced in the deep blue water. "I love you Liani!" Cassandra gurgled as she hung on to the whale's side fin as it gracefully moved through the water.

****

Cassandra, crowned with a wreath of red flowers, joined in the ritual chant of permission with the other women at the hula school. She began to sway with the music with the other women, almost all of them Asian like her with long black hair. She had shown the school officials  her scarred back, and the people at the school had allowed her to wear a black silk blouse instead of a bikini top to dance. If anyone recognized her, no one said anything, they were all there to dance and forget the war as Navy ships and planes moved across the sea and sky constantly. Cassandra and the Mirage were ashore in Maui, waiting for the main group of humpback whales to arrive for calving season.

Their dancing, Cassandra, and the other students were told if done with concentration, intensity,  and the proper frame of mind, would create Pono, or righteousness,  and this would prolong the life of the land forever. So Cassandra threw herself into the hula and danced.

297

****

Pamela was sitting in Petrosian's office. Petrosian was looking at her smiling, which was not hard. She looked stunning, and had her hair done short, as per Navy cadet regulations. She was dressed in a Navy blue cadet uniform with a skirt, which set off her big blue eyes. She kept shifting herself in the chair, crossing and uncrossing, and shifting her gorgeous legs. The Zumba dance classes had been added to her repertoire of physical therapy now that her legs had recovered.

"Yes, the uniform!" said Pamela cheerfully. " Well, I get to go to my graduation today at Annapolis, and pick up my four year degree! I also get an official reserve commission of ensign in the U.S. Navy, thanks to Cassandra's fast-talking so I could get my spinal cord treated. My network is even sending me up there by limousine . So I am in a good mood!"

"So why do you think you need to see me?" asked Petrosian with a smile. "What would you like to talk about?"

Well, doctor, Cassandra suggested I should see you because you helped her so much with her PTSD. I believe I suffer from it to a degree, though I must admit catching bullet in the middle of battle and waking up in hospital was much less traumatic than what she went through." said Pamela smiling. "And of course you know I had plenty of reason to be screwed up emotionally because of what happened to me even before."

"Hmm, let us discuss your childhood again..." said Petrosian shifting in his wheelchair.

"But of course doctor!" said Pamela nodding, with a slight grin. "And I keep having this dream of being in bed with this gorgeous guy, only he's asleep..."

****

"Well today I check out of the hospital..." said Pamela to the 800 assembled troops on the lawn at Arlington Hospital. She was dressed to kill in a clingy short electric blue dress, she also wore a red scarf to ward

298

off the cold wind that blew that day. Manny stood beside her, as did Bernard Foster, and the whole thing was being carried live by CNS. "And I just wanted to thank you all for protecting me and Cassandra while we were here. I am informed the 112th Anti-aircraft Battalion has received a unit citation for your service here, and is credited with 3 Unash spacecraft shot down." Cheers arose from the crowd of family and onlookers.

"And as you all may have noticed, the Unash ships do not come around DC anymore! We have won the Battle of Washington DC!" wild cheering arose. She waited for it to die down.

"Now you all know that we warned you that a war might result if we tried to stop the Unash, who are only one of several ET peoples that have come here, from their intention to conquer the Earth and destroy Humanity. Now war is never good, and the Unash know they can stop this war anytime they want by simply going back home. However, I tell you now that having met the Unash personally and seen their handiwork, we have no choice but to prosecute war against them until they leave the Solar System, and WE WILL!" More thunderous cheering followed. "The immediate strategy of this war is to produce homesickness among the Unash," laughed Pamela . "Which you of the 112th Battalion have done, through inflicting unacceptable losses on them to force them to withdraw from here!" More applause followed. "However, the long-term goal is to establish the human place in the Cosmos, with friendly relations with all our neighbors in the stars, many of whom are very friendly and we believe will be helping us to end this war. To understand this you must realize that space is not a vacuum. It is a cloud of stars, and the stars have intelligent peoples who live around them. The Unash, who are causing us all this trouble, are only one of the many peoples out there in the stars, most of whom have only good intentions towards us, and just like on the Earth, the war of any two nations affects the whole family of nations on the Earth. So the war here is affecting all peoples in this galactic neighborhood. I know that this war is being watched by many others, and the more successful we are in resisting the Unash, the longer this goes on, the more pressure from other species will build up on the Unash to cease their war of aggression here. So continue your good service, and as Cassandra wanted me to pass on to you all , THANKS FOR ALL THE GREAT FIREWORKS!" With this last remark the crowd broke into wild cheering and even the ranks of the assembled soldiers in dress uniform dissolved into a wave moving up to the podium with hundreds of hands being offered for Pamela to shake.

Later in the limousine heading back to CNS headquarters, Pamela looked at Berkowitz beside her with a sad expression. "I kept thinking, how good it would have been if Cassie could have been there. Have you heard anything from her?"

"No and you know better than to ask me Pam," said Manny. "Like I told you, I arranged it so I wouldn't even know where she is, but no news is good news. So just assume she is someplace where she is getting the rest she needs and getting better."

Pamela looked at him with her big blue eyes, then they squinted.

"That's so unfair! Why would you make an arrangement like that?" asked Pamela sharply.

"So no one could wheedle her location out of me," said Berkowitz smiling broadly. Pamela frowned and looked at Bernard Foster, who smiled and looked away as the limousine sped past the Pentagon in the afternoon sun. Suddenly, Foster turned back to her, looking serious, almost sad.

"Pam, we received an email today saying the Navy is preparing to conduct a major fleet operation in the Pacific soon. They want war correspondents to go with them and have asked to send our best available reporters, so I am sending Marcy... and we also are sending you. Provided, you think you're up to it."

Pamela looked at him in shock, and her feeling of annoyed levity fled. A feeling of deep fear filled her.

"Sure Bernie, I'm up for it..." she heard herself say.

"Are you sure?"

"Yes..."

**\*\*\*\***

300

Pamela walked through the doors into the CNS office complex to a tumultuous welcome. She was wearing a dark blue tight-fitting pantsuit, showing everyone she was back in spades. Everyone was there to hug her and a cake was brought out and pieces of cake, carefully measured in Pamela's case, were portioned out. Marcy Braxton and Madihira Kapoor were there , back from the Aleutians, and greeted her with shrieks of delight.

"Too bad Cassie couldn't be here," said Darlene, sadly, "And coming from me that means a lot." As the festivities died down, Manny Berkowitz called her into his office overlooking the Capitol on the other side of the Potomac.

"So how is Cassie, where is she and how do I get ahold of her?" demanded Pamela as soon as the office door closed behind them. Pamela planted herself defiantly in front of Berkowitz as he took his seat.

"She is off someplace quiet getting some rest. This town was driving her crazy." said Berkowitz, sitting down to face Pamela behind the fortified position of his large desk. *God, she looks like a million dollars,* thought Berkowitz. *How does she do it?*

"Well, I want to talk to her and see how she is doing, so how do I do that?" said Pamela insistently.

"I don't know, we arranged it so she would be incommunicado and at an unknown location," said Berkowitz. "Look, we want her to get well, and she has to find someplace where all the people who blame her for this war can't find her. You would not believe the hate mail we have gotten here for her! Someone even sent her a live rattlesnake! We have an arrangement now to lock up everything in a bombproof pen now for a week and everything to be opened by robots." said Berkowitz vehemently. "And the insurance rates for the robots themselves are astronomical!" he added.

"So, they blame her for the war! That is so unfair Manny!"

"I know, Pam, but this is not a rational situation. It's a lunatic fringe! This war, it's a 1950's sci-fi horror movie but with social media! It's like

301

opening Pandora's box!" said Berkowitz, shaking his head ruefully. "They have wartime censorship in place, but nobody can control what happens on the net! The government people who come here to give us our guidelines, they tell us it's impossible to control the net!"

"I mean it's unfair because I deserve some credit too!" said Pamela with a smirk. "And I think it's time I got some recognition!"

****

"Good evening friends, yes, it's me, Pamela Monroe," said Pamela appearing with the stars as a background. She was smiling in a slightly sad way. "I am out of the hospital and strutting around again causing trouble. Yes, it's true, I am the 'other woman' who started the war. Yes, even in this instance there was an 'other woman." she laughed. "Cassandra Chen, whose memorable broadcast from Devil's Mesa after she had been held captive and tortured there, which warned the U.S. government of a planned Unash attack at the end of their Ultimatum expiration. She is still recovering from the wounds, both psychic and physical of her ordeal. If you are listening to this broadcast Cassandra, we all send our love and prayers for your speedy recovery. However, the idea that Cassandra or even little old me, started this war is an outrageous and childish fantasy. It is like someone blaming the weather-girl for the hurricane she warned about .

"The idea that I or any other human being started this war, is ridiculous. The extraterrestrial people known as the Unash began this war by coming here and trying to take over this planet using terror and treachery. They have failed, the human race is now alerted and united against them, but the Unash will not admit failure, and so the war continues until they withdraw from the Solar system and return to their home worlds. What was intended to be a quiet little murder in a house at night has now turned into a knife fight in the galactic street, with everyone else in the stellar neighborhood watching. We already have evidence that other neighboring peoples, such as the Pleiadians, who are apparently our genetic cousins, are applying pressure on the Unash to end this war and go home. If this sounds like a 1950's science fiction movie that is because the U.S. government has known since the early 1950's that the Unash were here and their intentions were hostile, and therefore the government purposefully bankrolled many Hollywood movies to prepare the people for the very possibility we are facing today. You may remember some of the bigger ones, such as **War of the Worlds** and **Earth Versus the Flying Saucers**, or even my personal favorite, **Mars Needs Women.** That possibility, war with aliens from outer space, which the US government tried to prepare for, with some mistakes, is the same open warfare with the Unash we now face.

"So this war started with the Unash coming here over many light years with the intention to take over this planet. It is as simple as that, they are not from here, and the Unash can end this war, their war of aggression, here anytime they wish, by simply returning home. As for the opinion that they were here even before the human race or somehow created us on Earth so we should do their bidding, is a possibility being proposed by various bootlicking clowns in this city. The facts expose this claim as a lie cooked up by the Unash's psychological warfare ministry and propagated by the remaining Unash sympathizers on Earth, who apparently missed out on the attempted coup." An image of troops in black surrendering in the ruins of Georgetown, along with E.G. Miller of the Magi, meekly surrendering to Army troops in West Virginia, flashed on the screen, beside Pamela as she spoke.

"The Unash are genetically much different than us, being closer to insects, and this fact caused them to go to a great deal of effort to create a race of sickly hybrids to replace the human race on this planet." An image flashed behind her of grotesque sickly and deformed hybrid children being cared for at Morningstar. Genetic studies have found that the Unash share only genetic material of the most primitive kind with us, which is now believed to be common to all primitive bacteria found to have spread life from planet to planet throughout the universe in a phenomena called panspermia."

"Some people have asked us why we should continue to fight a war with someone who is superior to us in technology, and who can obviously travel between stars. As a graduate from the Naval Academy in Annapolis and now an Ensign in the naval reserves, I can tell you what any student of warfare will tell you, that technology is only one of many factors in

303

warfare. Both the French and Americans lost wars in Indochina despite having superior technology in all categories as did the Russians in Afghanistan. What really matters most in war is whose side God is on. And He is clearly on our side in this war."

As for those who propose we seek a negotiated settlement with the Unash that allows them to remain in the Solar system, I can tell you from meeting the Unash first hand, that they will never give up their ambition to take this Planet and replace the human race here with beings of their own primary heritage, unless forced to. Peace is a wonderful thing, but like freedom, it is not free. No, peace has always been bought by strength, on this planet and every other planet in this Cosmos. No amount of wishful thinking can change that. If there is anything we have learned in the past few months, it is that peace and freedom are bought by able men and women willing to lay their lives on the line for it. The roll call of those who have died in this war includes Lt. Thomas Mantel of the Us. Air Force, who was it turned out, shot out of the sky by the alien craft he was pursuing over Fort Knox Kentucky in 1948. So the war, even if at slow smolder, has been going on that long. We have had, at last count almost 40, 000 combat deaths in this war so far, and that figure does not include the dead still being counted in the 'boneyard' found under the former secret Unash base at Morningstar." An image of the vast sea of human skulls and bones filling vast underground vaults filled the screen. "Yes, it is hard to look at this picture, these piles of human remains, believed to be from approximately 2.5 million human beings. And even once you see it, you do not want to keep this image in your memory. However, this image is part of the reality of this war and a reminder of what we are fighting against. I challenge those in this town who advocate peace at any price with the Unash to go to Morningstar and see these works of the Unash for themselves. This challenge is especially for the Bozo in Chief, Senator Tunney, and his fellow Magi auxiliary members!"

****

Senator Tunney rose shaking with rage and took the podium in the U.S. Senate. The Senate chamber was mostly deserted, except for cameras of various news media. Pamela's broadcast was only a few hours old.

"I speak to defend the right of dissent in this country! This Senator has been labeled a traitor for advocating alternatives to war! This is not an attack just on me but on all voices of dissent in this civilization! I therefore condemn Pamela Monroe, former weather girl from Cleveland as being a crypto-fascist bent on establishing a military dictatorship in this country, and bent on continuing this suicidal war for the purposes of wartime profits for the aerospace and arms industries in this country, who hope to become rich while the human race is destroyed!" he yelled into the microphones. "I declare I will not waver, I will not be dissuaded by slander or scare tactics! I will continue to advocate that we find a negotiated peace with the Unash! This is the best course for human survival! And no one will silence me!"

****

Well , you certainly stirred up a hornets nest Pam! Good job, viewership was 90% for you broadcast last night! Phone calls and emails are running 95% in support for your point of view!" laughed Berkowitz.

"You will also be happy to know that the post office intercepted a rattlesnake of some kind mailed to you by overnight delivery!"

"What type?" asked Pamela happily.

"I think it was FedEx," said Berkowitz

"No! What kind of snake?" she asked sharply.

"I think it was a Sidewinder."

"Excellent! The one mailed to Cassie was a Western Diamondback! If this was a Sidewinder, then the lunatic snake handler has to live in Southern California near the Mojave. That's the only place he could catch both species easily!" laughed Pamela. "I hope the idiot likes prison food!"

"OK now, back to business, we are sending you out to Dr. Malvik's clinic to get your scars looked at," Pamela grinned and looked down at the long scar on her sternum, between her breasts.

"Great I can start wearing low cut blouses again," said Pamela.

305

"That treatment should take two weeks, they think. Then you are to report to Long Beach Navy Yard for transport to meet with the Fleet. They are flying Marcy out to San Francisco and then to Pearl Harbor via Navy transport, that's all they will tell us."

Berkowitz looked suddenly pained, and looked down at his desk.

"Are you absolutely sure you are ready for this? I mean they lost five ships including an aircraft carrier up in the Aleutians. These battles are either walkovers or blood baths. You were completely on the front lines with Cassie for the downfall of the Cover-up, nobody questions that, don't you think you might want to sit out this battle behind the lines?"

"Manny, the Unash could drop a hydrogen bomb on this city any day," said Pamela rising from her chair and looking out the window. "Of course, we could vaporize their Moon bases in response, so we have good reason to think they won't do that. But no one on this Earth is safe right now, there are no rear areas. There never were." she said.

"Well, please be careful," said Manny looking sad, as she picked up her package of tickets and reservations , and blowing him a kiss as she walked out the door of his office. After a while, a knock came on the door, and he invited the person in.

Darlene entered, looking devastated, she sat down and wept in front of his desk.

Manny turned and looked out the window, wiped his eyes. A feeling of overwhelming grief moved through him.

"I am afraid she is going to die out there with the Navy someday, I know this..." said Darlene. Berkowitz looked at her and offered her a box of Kleenex. He then looked at the cloudy, cold sky over the Capitol dome.

"I know this, Manny, but I let her go anyway." sobbed Darlene. "As for Cassandra, I saw the scars on her wrists, we could receive notice of her suicide someplace, isolated, alone, any day now, and it wouldn't be a surprise." Manny turned to Darlene and shook his head.

"Don't say that, Darlene, we did what we could," he said quietly. "I could have had Cassie committed, but I think that would have destroyed what was left of her…" He stared out the window for a long while then rose and looked squarely at Darlene. "No, she will recover from what happened to her, and come back here, stronger than ever. So will Pamela. You just watch." he said looking out the window to hide the sorrow on his face. Darlene seemed to take encouragement from this.

"I'm sorry Manny, I guess I am just tired."

"It's OK, why don't you take the rest of the day off.," he said turning and smiling as best he could. She rose smiling and wiping her eyes and left. He was alone with his thoughts.

*Is there any hope for any of us?* Manny wondered. *Yes, there is hope for Jerusalem! Jerusalem must stand, Jerusalem must see the coming of the Messiah! Yes, Jerusalem will be my hope. Next year Jerusalem…*

****

"Oh yes!" began Pamela smiling brightly in the broadcast," I have had the honor today of being attacked, by name, from the floor of the U.S. Senate by Peace-at –any-Price, Bozo in Chief, Senator Tunney. He seems to think I am trying to take away the right of dissent in this country! Who? Little old me!? I am just a former weather girl from Cleveland!

"For the record, I am fine with dissent, in fact I reserve the right to dissent from the idiocies and delusional nonsense proposed by Senator Tunney, who seems to believe if we surrender to the grey aliens they will be nicer to us than they have been over last forty years when they secretly abducted and murdered an estimated two million people! Their bones are at Morningstar, and I urge Senator Tunney to go look at them! Yes, I dissent with this view of Senator Tunney, and by this dissent, I honor the idea of dissent. If I was actually against the gentleman from Massachusetts right of dissent, I would not have called him Bozo in Chief, but instead called him a cowardly, imbecilic, lickspittle… But let the record show I restrained myself!"

"I am now headed off to the war front, to cover this war. I know I helped to start; a war being fought for that most fundamental of human rights, the right to life. You might say I am going out, like thousands of other war correspondents, to put my money,  and my sweet behind,  where my mouth is, concerning this war.  My next report will be from the front lines until then be brave and God Bless you all."

Pam looked around the studio after the camera light went out.  She smiled, keeping her face controlled. Everyone in the studio rose and applauded her as she exited the sound stage, and took the elevator downstairs where her bags awaited her in a limousine to  take her to Andrews Air Force Base, and a waiting military transport West.

****

The two Samaran bodyguards for the ambassador entered the room, their faces stoic and relaxed looking. Both wore swords and light armor.  The Chief of Protocol entered, garbed in a long dark brown robe with gold disks everywhere on it.  Finally, the Samaran ambassador entered,  Krayus of Rigel of the house of Mirzam,  sword and gold-hilted dagger on his belt, a gold chain with an eight-pointed silver star emblem with a large blue sapphire in its center.  He was a powerfully built man, with reddish hair, obviously a seasoned warrior and knight of the Samaran empire.  His family had served also as diplomats and mediators among its clans for generations, and so it was said 'Mirzam by Rigel and the Throne by Mirzam.' He had a wide face with a well-trimmed reddish brown beard tinged with grey and a bald head.  His green eyes looked steadily ahead as he took his seat.

"You requested a meeting with me, great Lord of the Vikhelm." said the Lord Protector,  himself  wearing  his  sword,  nodded  wordlessly. Surrounding the Lord Protector were four bodyguards, bearded and armored, with swords and daggers on their belts,  gazing ahead stoically.

"Yes, what does the Samaran Empire do in the Quzrada?  We have heard reports of fleets of ships entering and leaving the Quzrada. We have heard that there is now war at Erra, in the heart of the Quzrada.  We have heard the Errans fight now against the Unash, who are your servants.  We have a

308

treaty, that states no fleet of war may enter the Quzrada unless the peace is broken. This situation presents great danger to the peace."

"I can assure you, great Lord, that the Samaran empire wishes only peace and tranquility in the Quzrada, and that we are in complete compliance with the Neutral Zone Treaty. There has been, however, some trouble in the Quzrada that has required, in some cases, our fleets to move temporarily through the Neutral Zone." answered Krayus.

"The Unash, who are not treaty signatories, and are of course, of little consequence to anyone, are in the process of colonizing Erra, which is a situation not anticipated in the Treaty, but should be therefore of no concern to either The Samaran Empire or the Vikhelm. After all, when the Quzrada treaty was signed, the Errans were believed to be extinct. But the Errans have resisted this effort by the Unash, but their resistance is futile, as it turns out. Since the Errans are doomed were believed wiped out during the great war, and only recently seemed to have returned to life, this colonization by the Unash can only be regarded as a restoration of former simplicities in the Quzrada. The situation has been complicated by the Unull, also not treaty signatories, who have been at war with the Unash for many decades, and have also been interfering in the Unash colonization effort. So we have the situation of the Unash-Unull war spilling into the Quzrada and the Errans attaching themselves like fleas to this conflict. We of the Samar have merely tried to keep the Unull-Unash war from disturbing the peace in the Quzrada and tried to keep it away from our own borders. So our fleets have patrolled, sometimes in the outer districts of the Quzrada, as they secure our frontiers. That is why you may have heard reports of Samaran fleets in the Quzrada. But these are only brief transits of the Quzrada, at its boundary region, nothing more. We have no presence at Erra and no involvement in the trouble there. We uphold the Quzrada treaty."

"So there is war at Erra, in the heart of the Quzrada, between the Errans and Unash?" asked The lord Protector. He stared at the Samaran ambassador intently. "So there is war on its frontiers and also its heart?"

"That struggle at Erra can hardly be called a war my Lord. The Errans are being crushed as we speak. It is like the struggles of a mouse seized by a serpent, momentary and useless.   Likewise, the conflict of the Unash and the Unull  is merely the war of two minor powers that has spilled into the Quzrada neutral zone.   Are lions disturbed, when termites fight nearby? So it is that these conflicts need not concern either Empire nor disturb the great peace of the Quzrada.   The Errans are a primitive people, and the Unash have moved a space platform to restrict the sunlight reaching Erra, cutting off both their warmth and food supplies. The Errans are helpless in the face of this. Even now the high councilors of the Errans plead with their leaders for them to beg for peace with the Unash.  So this business at Erra is finished.   Soon you will hear of no more trouble at Erra and there will be tranquility in the Quzrada again.  The Samaran ambassador noticed this latter news produced no reaction in the Lord Protector. *Ah yes, you have eyes at Erra, as I guessed.* He thought. *Important I eyes, I think.*

To ensure that this matter need not concern you further,  we have granted the counselor among you , Karlac of Delphin, the privilege to transit the Quzrada to see this colonization of Erra  first hand, and also to recover a Vikhelm citizen, who seems to have gotten himself stranded on Erra in the middle of this trouble. We have no objection to this if you have no objection.  Would not recovery of this Vikhelmian traveler on Erra, and the report of Karlac of the restoration of peace on Erra, give you confidence in the security of the Neutral Zone Treaty?" asked the Samaran Ambassador.  He smiled inwardly and the long silence of the Vikhelmian lord protector. *We have you now Vikhelm!*

The Lord protector nodded slowly and spoke.

"Yes, the mission of Karlac to Erra and his safe return with our stranded citizen would be of great benefit in this situation.  As would the quick resolution of the problems at Erra," he said gravely.

*Yes, let this matter be resolved quickly,* thought the Samaran ambassador gravely, *before things become more stirred up...He wants plainly what we desire also! We all want a quick end to this thing! The Unash must move quickly! With things going badly with the Tlaxin in the galactic outer regions, we cannot afford trouble with the Vikhelm! Neither do Vikhelm, who face the Xix from the galactic core, seek trouble with us...In the Great*

*Game of the Stars, alas, Erra is in the way of things and will be crushed as if by the wheels of the great war chariots of old..."*

"Therefore, I am satisfied Lord Krayus, and bid peace unto you and the Samaran Empire." said the Lord Protector rising. Lord Krayus rose and bowed, and the Lord protector turned and left the room followed by his bodyguards. Krayus and his attendants also rose and filed out , returned to their airship. Soon they were cruising back to their embassy compound.

"Dispatch a letter to the Palace of Rigel,"  said Krayus to his chief of protocol, who stood ready with light pen and lector-tablet. "Tell the Palace: Have had an audience with Lord Protector, he is satisfied that the Unash will soon colonize Erra and that troubles there will then cease. We have provided safe conduct pass to Karlac of Delphin to come to Erra and see for himself that things are concluded there. and to recover a Vikhelm spy stranded by the fighting on Erra. This spy is  apparently someone of importance  to the Lord Protector.  We are not to disturb him.  These things, the colonization and the return of this spy unharmed, should be accomplished quickly to ensure no further frictions with the Vikhelm over the Quzrada.  Also, the Unash laziness and lack of stomach for this fight has caused these problems and they must finish this thing at Erra as soon as possible.  They must be told to finish this thing at Erra quickly,  at all costs!"

With that Krayus of Mirzam relaxed in his chair as they rode through the clouds. *Ah, to serve the Throne of Rigel in the Great Game of Stars , and ride in the game's great chariots... What heady wine I drink.*

"I should like to have some of the maidens of Erra saved from the Unash," said Theon, his chief of protocol. "It is said their embraces are like no other woman's.   They fetch a high price in the slave markets on Belletran, I hear!"

Krayus laughed at this.  *Hah, it is a pity to destroy such beauty, but necessary none the less,* he thought.

"Yes, I have heard this also of the maidens of  Erra, Lord Theon, but, they are simply in the way..." said Krayus, smiling.  "They are simply an obstruction in the path of great plans..."

311

****

In the heart of the Palace at Vale, the Lord Protector lay down his sword carefully. Lord Ragnar stood close by.

"I think this Erran thing is basically finished business, Lord Ragnar. So we must look for the evacuation of our agent from Erra."

"Your grandson my Lord?"

"Yes, we must fetch him back here and stick him someplace safe from the Bloodaxe clan. We must notify Karlac he is to go to Erra and bring Vikor home."

"It's a pity, my Lord, Erra was the perfect place to send him. The Bloodaxe sought him everywhere but there."

"Yes, tis a pity, in more ways than one. But we must see to the Xix now, and be grateful this matter in Quzrada will soon pass. It is a distraction from more serious matters."

****

Krayus entered his ornate quarters in the Embassy compound and noted a curious silence. He had expected his wife and her attendants to greet him. Instead, Takaan , chief of the guards at the embassy stood with his lieutenant. His face was grim. Takaan stood by an ornate wooden table. Krayus, froze at the sight of him, then marched resolutely forward towards him. Takaan and his attendant bowed their heads, and Takaan pointed to a black envelope on the fine polished wood of the table.

Krayus, stepped forward stoically and took the envelope in his strong hands and opened it . He read its contents.

"Samus! My Son! DEAD AT ERRA!?" Krayus exclaimed wide-eyed, now staring at Takaan. "THIS IS NOT POSSIBLE!"

"Yes my Lord, we have confirmed the message. It is from the Palace, and they sent it three times under code channel...at our request," said Takaan , his head still bowed. "Our Lord Dakon sends also his condolence."

Krayus stared at Takaan, his face now twisting in grief. Krayus began to shake.

"NO! NO! HE WAS MY LAST SON!" cried out Krayus, as he drew his sword and brought it down on the envelope, cutting deeply into the table. "FOUR SONS BEFORE HIM DIED FOR THE EMPIRE!!!" Krayus collapsed and his retainers ran to help him as he fell to the floor tearing his clothes in grief and wept like a child. "SAMUS! SAMUS! MY SON! MY SON! I SENT HIM TO ERRA TO KEEP HIM SAFE!!!! " he screamed.

****

## Chapter 7: Crush Depth

Pamela boarded the Guided Missile Frigate USS Collins as it rode in the grey water of the harbor at Midway island. In the lagoon at Midway, several other ships, all grey like the Collins, heaved in the grey water against the dark grey sky. A cold wet wind blew. Pamela wore a dark blue heavy Navy jacket and a dark blue beret, as she bounded up the gangplank from the dock. A sailor carried her sea-bag. The ship was crowded with weapons and its deck space crowded with orange flying saucer shaped arctic life pods called K-4s, open lifeboats being an oxymoron in the cold Pacific to the north of them. In that cold subarctic ocean, freezing rain and cold ocean waves resulted in death from exposure within days in an open boat. Pamela noted that a tall magnetometer mast had obviously been retrofitted above the bridge of the Collins, and two others slung out from the sides of the stern. *We are going hunting for Greys and vice versa,* she thought grimly. *This is not going to be any pleasure cruise,* thought Pamela with sudden dread. Large silver steel tanks with hemispherical ends, 1000 gallon propane tanks, were strapped to the side of the ship by heavy metal straps, two on each side of the ship, covered with red warning signs, gave another fearsome sight. Pamela knew these had been converted into super depth charges called S-42s, and each contained 42 tons of Alumanol: a high explosive mixture of ammonium nitrate, fuel oil, and powdered aluminum. They were intended to be dropped on the undersea alien base when it was located, two miles down it was said.

To prepare for the trip Pamela had worked out furiously and had practiced swimming in the cold water of the Northern California coast. At San Francisco, she had gone out deep sea fishing for four days in a row in heavy seas to get used to sea duty. She had only caught a small Grouper but had overcome seasickness. She looked at the grey sea and sky and thanked herself for having prepared.

"Permission to come aboard Sir?" said Pamela saluting the sailors standing by the gangplank and a marine in full combat gear with an M-16. To her surprise, they all returned her salute smartly. She was required to salute even though her commission in the Navy was reserve. *A small price for walking again.*

"Permission granted Ensign Monroe!" said a tall Officer in a khaki dress uniform. He had dark hair and movie-star handsome face. His nametag said, Di Franco. "The captain requests you report to the bridge at once." His face became serious "Chief Roberts, we are to cast off at once!" said Di Franco to a sailor nearby. "The Captain wants us underway immediately." He turned back to Pamela, his eyes danced all over her.

"I am chief executive officer  Di Franco, follow me, " He said with a bewitching smile.  Pamela walked hurriedly to keep up with his long strides. The deck was moving. *Got to get my sea legs as quick as possible* she thought. They climbed two flights of grey steel stairs to the bridge. *Glad I'm not wearing heels.* A cold wind blew her neck length  blonde hair into her face. The ship was pulling away from the dock swiftly now. They entered the bridge via a hatchway.  It was cramped with barely room for the helmsman a chief engineer and the captain to stand. Captain Matsuga, a stocky Japanese-American smiled at her as she stepped in, and everyone exchanged salutes.  He motioned for her and Di Franco to step back in the CIC or Combat  Information Center, behind the bridge where sonar, radar and magnetometer data was analyzed and exploited. The fire control panel was also manned and ready. Sailors, some female, sat at the consoles and did not notice their entrance.  Captain Matsuga smiled graciously.

"It is such an honor to have you on my ship Ensign Monroe.  I want you to know I consider you and your colleague Cassandra to be heroes for what you did.  His face became serious, "I also want you to consider yourself an active duty officer on my ship, and I also want you to wear a navy uniform, despite being a correspondent.  Commander Di Franco here will get you a uniform from the ship's stores."  *Manny won't like this,* thought Pamela, *but he's not here,* she thought with a mental laugh. *What a shame!* "Did you have a good trip out from Pearl?"  he asked.

"Yes, Captain, a little bumpy, but fine."

"Good,"  he said.  *Here it comes*, she thought bracing herself, *the detail.*

"I am detailing you," he began looking stern, "as someone who is both a Naval officer and also a correspondent,  to take our group of correspondents on board in tow and keep them from getting underfoot here, as this task force is headed into combat operations. I cannot spare any of my regular officers for this duty. You are also detailed to making sure the other correspondents all wear helmets and lifejackets on deck and are always near a life-pod if things get difficult. Do you understand these orders, Ensign Monroe?"

"Yes, Captain"

"Excellent, Commander Di Franco here will give you a tour of the ship, get you a uniform and show you to your quarters. Won't you Commander?" Matsuga turned to Di Franco.

"Yes Captain," said Di Franco, beaming.

****

Far to south on Maui, Hawaiian drums beat out a staccato rhythm, as Cassandra, clad in a grass skirt with a wreath of flowers around her head and black silk shirt they had let her wear because of her scarred back, was dancing the hula furiously in dance school with a line of other women. She had tied up the shirt on the bottom to expose her now well-trimmed midriff and navel, which gyrated in incredible circles as she danced in near ecstasy. She knew she was now within the dancing elite, not just a student or haumana, but an 'olapa' -a true dancer at the school, and she had practiced relentlessly off hours on the beach at the exclusive resort hotel she stayed at when on-shore. She left her room only to swim in a wetsuit or dance. No one seemed to recognize her at the exclusive dance school, or if they did, no one said anything. She was just one more attractive Asian woman with long black hair dancing, *And a damn good dancer,* she thought. She had danced herself to exhaustion several nights on the beach as if dancing would expel the demons that haunted her. After two weeks of hula and a week of belly dancing thrown in, plus swimming in the surf and snorkeling off the Mirage for hours every day, she felt incredibly strong and physically healthy again. Liani Kawai, the dance school director or Kumu, a lovely native Hawaiian, danced past her as she moved down the row. She smiled and winked at Cassandra as she did, provoking Cassandra to dance even harder. It was warm, the first warm day in a week, and Cassandra and the other women were dancing furiously, now feeling waves of perspiration even as a gentle ocean breeze

317

refreshed them. Liani, trim and strong with hips that rocked like a precise machine, turned away to the ocean, and with her gently moving arms beckoned them to follow her movements, as the native Hawaiian drummers picked up the tempo of the native drums they beat relentlessly with a seemingly endless supply of energy. *I have become the dance!* thought Cassandra in triumph.

****

The tour of the ship was both fascinating and exhausting for Pamela. The Navy did not put elevators on Frigates in this war, so every change of deck had its stairs or ladders. *Good thing I have been working out a lot* thought Pamela. The ship was new, being finished in two months as the Navy replaced losses. Some bays still smelled of fresh paint. The ship was also cramped and filled with obvious last minute modifications. EMP generators and forty millimeter automatic cannons firing magneto-proximity shells had been hastily added and had become standard fixtures. Pamela noted an obvious extension to the radar-radio mast, a spherical superconducting magnetometer high above the steel hull to improve its sensitivity, as well as a pair of similar ones hanging off the stern of the ship on long masts. She saw the ship from the cave-like engine room with its massive marine gas turbines singing far below the water line, all the way up to the observation deck above the bridge where sailors in warm coats still braved the wind and spray to scan the horizon with night vision equipped binoculars - a precaution against alien craft sneaking up on the ship with radar cloaking. They were now out of sight of Midway island, and catching up to a squadron of other warships, moving through heavy grey seas topped with white caps under a grey sky, part of a task force called Typhoon. A woman petty officer issued her a surprisingly well fitting khaki uniform and then Di Franco took her to her quarters, which she shared with two other women officers on the ship, a redhead named Kirkland and a brunette named Vasquez. Di Franco conducted Pamela to the door of their quarters, somewhere in the forecastle of the ship, a room with small portals viewing the grey sea. The two women welcomed her and dismissed Di Franco with surprising coolness. Pam looked at them with puzzlement as she held her gear and the ship rolled and yawed with increasing amplitude.

318

"We both know Lt. Commander Di Franco, let's leave it at that," said Vasquez with a knowing glance at the redhead, then both laughed wickedly. Pamela noted there were only two bunks in the crowded quarters.

"Here ensign, we'll have to hot bunk, I have night duty , so you can use my bed." said Kirkland.

**** 

Cassandra was swimming with Liani the mother humpback whale, now accompanied by her calf, who Cassandra had named Li Li. The sun danced on them below the water, and Cassandra, wearing a black wetsuit swam strongly in her snorkeling outfit alongside them.

"Oh I love you little Li Li," Cassandra bubbled in the water. Liani and Li Li seemed completely at ease with her presence and Li Li would draw near to be stroked by Cassandra. Dolphins would swim by in swarms and make chortling noises as they swam off of Maui under the blue sky and golden Sun. Li Li would soon be large enough to cross the Pacific to the fall feeding grounds of the pod in the gulf of Alaska. Soon, within days, the Mirage would depart to await the whales up in Alaska.

****

After another long day on the rolling ship, Pamela went to the officer's mess and sat down to sea rations served on a rolling and yawing table. Four other correspondents were sitting nearby enjoying themselves with coffee and conversation in the officer's mess. One of them greeted her and invited her to join them. Megan Strand of the Washington Post, an attractive older brunette, Carl Levy, a short former sailor, bald with a trim grey mustache and a happy-go-lucky attitude was there from the New York Times. Eloise Harper from the Boston Globe was also there. She seemed an unlikely person to send to sea, and looked like an out-of-shape suburban housewife and was mostly quiet. Another fellow named Ethan Miller was sitting at another table, a tall awkward looking man with a dark well-trimmed beard and short hair, listening intently to an IPod, apparently oblivious to the rolling ship and the others in the room.

319

"Where is he from," asked Pamela, motioning with her head as she shipped her rich Navy coffee.

"He's from Buzz magazine," said Meg with a chuckle, "also known as 'Buzzed'." Pamela felt included in the circle of correspondents, one of the things she had always cherished about the news business: the comradery of intelligent news people. She enjoyed being around a group of people who knew everything before anyone else. Both Carl and Meg seemed to look on her with admiration. The conversation was mostly centered on the Operation Typhoon they were headed into.

"The Skipper told me he considers me active Navy on this ship. They had to declare me official Navy at Annapolis so I could get treatments for my legs in the hospital, so this is the payback. The Captain then ordered me you to make sure you guys stay out of trouble on the ship and are first into the life pods if we have "difficulties" as he put it. So don't get mad at me if I start ordering you around in an emergency."

"What are our chances of seeing some real action on this voyage?" asked Meg.

"The way the Captain talked about my life pod duty, my guess is our chances of some real excitement are good. Then again, except for the fights at Morningstar and Adak, most of the base elimination operations have been either minor skirmishes or the bases were found abandoned. So this could be just a luxury cruise, to a spot in the ocean to drop a bunch of ordinance on an undersea base to implode it, then cruise back to Pearl. However, there is some concern they may have evacuated a lot of personnel from other bases to this base because they thought it was safer. So they may put up a big fight here."

"Why would the aliens put up so many bases and then abandon them without a fight?" asked Levy. He continued, "Why come here from 100 light years and pour concrete bunkers then abandon them. And why put this big fancy base on the bottom of the ocean that must be close to imploding all the time, where we can find it? I read about undersea habitats that humans experimented with, people hated them, they were cold wet, and all you could see outside the windows was darkness. People said it was like living in a dungeon. And a base like that is so vulnerable

320

once we find it, you can't move it! Once we find it, we don't even need depth charges like they have on the sides of this ship. We can just drop rocks on it!"

"Well I have actually met these people," said Pamela. Meg looked sad at this, but Pamela went on. "A lot of what they do doesn't make sense to us. One pattern is recognizable, though, and that is a very aggressive sort of bluffing behavior. They seem to have established more bases than they could really support because their strategy was to establish bases everywhere and improve them later, a sort of establish lots of footholds, and use them when more troops arrived. They were even trying to recruit me and other abductees to be a fifth column. One abductee we talked with told the Greys she would rather commit suicide than betray her people, they responded by offering her the chance to be a suicide bomber. So looking back on it, their strategy makes sense in an extremely aggressive, almost reckless way. But some things they do make no sense, or are just miscalculations, like coming all this way here and actually having no idea how to inspire real loyalty in normal human beings." Pamela paused, "Aside from terror that is."

"I want you to know I think you and Cassandra Chen did humanity a great service in breaking up the UFO Cover-up," said Megan. "I must say that I didn't pay much attention to you girl's story at first, then when I saw what you had uncovered, it was unspeakable."

"Yes, unspeakably hideous," said Carl, "like the holocaust almost." Eloise nodded in frightened agreement.

"Where is Cassandra Chen?" asked Eloise, both Carl and Meg looked embarrassed by the directness of the question.

Pamela took a deep breath, blinked.

"I don't know," Pamela said sadly. "She was the point person on the Star Gate story, and things that happened to her when they captured her, she hasn't recovered from them yet." Pamela looked off into space. "They tortured her, you know, and she can't even force herself to remember everything they did to her. She said it was just a black abyss in her memory." Pamela looked at Megan, Carl and Eloise, who now looked

321

down at the table." God, who would want to remember something like that?" Pamela looked away from them all. "She also knows some people blame her for the war. That's an additional burden she has to carry where ever she goes, even if it's not true." Pam looked at Meg and Carl, who met her eyes and shook their heads in disagreement with that opinion.

"She just did what an investigative journalist was supposed to do!" said Megan. "Just because somebody finds a fire burning in the basement and calls 911, this doesn't make them an arsonist!"

"Yeah, she did what any of us would do! The fact it caused a war, well it's like spotting the Japanese planes on radar just before Pearl harbor, so the war starts an hour early, that makes her a hero in my book!" said Levy. Pamela felt better hearing this.

Eloise was silent and looked away. Pamela ignored this.

"What was it like? Working on the Star Gate story before it broke," asked Megan, her eyes large.

"Well Cassie was point, and it was like she was captain of a battleship in the lead and I was following directly behind her ship in my own battleship to support her, moving across some dark ocean, with every gun and missile ready, looking for the enemy, looking for a battle. We knew we were powerful. She sort of radiated power, and confidence, and it made all of us feel powerful too. We were on a mission for God!" she said laughingly. "I still don't know how we did it. They tried to kill her three times. The aliens came after me, and let's not forget the part where they dug up my rather colorful and supposedly sealed divorce files from Cleveland and dumped them on stage during the debate I had with that Harvard professor..." Pamela laughed. "It was a sort of a wild, strange adventure, and though we warned everyone this could lead to a war with the aliens, I must admit Cassandra and I completely underestimated the abruptness and magnitude of violence that was unleashed when the cover-up finally collapsed. We thought the President would just resign like Nixon did and there would be a bunch of sensational trials. So we miscalculated big-time, and I have the scars to prove it too."

322

"Well, we not only miscalculated Pamela, we ignored the fire alarms when they sounded. All of a sudden we went from debating whether Stargate was real to watching fighters and saucers dogfighting over Washington DC and tanks fight in the streets. Part of what happened Pam, is that this whole thing hit us in the rest of the news media like an invisible train at a railway crossing," said Meg. "I mean, most of us were simply not paying attention. I know we were warned. So, the lights were flashing at the crossing, but we didn't see any freaking train! There was no time for debate or analysis, just boom! Suddenly there's tanks fighting on the Capitol mall, there was Cassandra on the TV screen in weird space-queen eyeshadow, and then U.S. military is freaking attacking a base full of outer-space aliens! I mean to say it, was confusing and bizarre is a cosmic understatement. There was just no time to process it all!"

"But we talked about it for months on CNS! We had a big UFO special," protested Pamela.

"Yes, you certainly did," said Carl Levy, to Pamela, with a twinkle in his eye, "But you forgot the near infinite supply of hubris that resides in the press. The fifth estate is a palace of conceit! We are a shameless bunch of know-it-alls, and we all know it! I remember my editor going around the conference room like a crazy man, tieless, with his shirt sleeves rolled up, yelling at everyone in a meeting the morning after you girl's Stargate special. He was saying over and over again 'the Government can't keep secrets like this! Those two bimbos are simply delusional!' He even turned to me and demanded 'Carl would the government be in bed with little grey aliens and letting them kidnap people to secret bases in Colorado and the Times not know about it?'," Carl reported with a laugh. "So, I answered him dutifully and said 'of course not chief, that question is too ridiculous to even ask'. Then he makes this frenzied emphatic speech to all of us waving his arms. He says, 'I know everything that happens in DC, it's a goldfish bowl to me'! He yells, 'I know which senator is sleeping with which staffer and who refuses to carry a pooper scooper when they walk their dog! I know which Congressman is ardently anti-gay and also in the closet, and I know which Senator is ardently pro-environment but whose wife wears real fur and drives a Humvee for god sake! Therefore, this Stargate thing can't be true! BECAUSE IF IT WAS TRUE I WOULD FUCKING ALREADY KNOW IT'!" then Carl laughed heartily. "So your girl's

323

careful tutorial to everyone was unfortunately wasted on most of us fellow members of the press. Because we were too fucking smart to believe the truth when it was shown to us!" With that, he laughed until he began to cry and looked away.

"So we, just freaking ignored it for the most part!" said Meg laughing. "We just thought, 'Oh my god CNS has finally done it this time!' We really did admire you girls, secretly, but it was like, 'what's next a Big Foot movie?' Then in about a week, all in the press suddenly went from thinking this was the mother of all internet conspiracy theories, on steroids, or as one of my colleagues put it, 'a magical witch's brew of the two most beautiful witches of the East'." said Megan, laughing. Pamela even laughed at this description. She imagined her and Cassandra wearing clingy black witch's outfits and peaked hats and cackling as they happily stirred a huge pot of magical brew. She then imagined them in some powerful castle guarded by hunky guards and flying monkeys. Megan was now becoming somber and continued. "So, we went from witch's brew and bigfoot, bemused disbelief in a few days, to the stage of: 'What in The Freaking Hell is going on?' when the Joint Congressional hearing started and they blew up Cassandra's car. Then we went to the 'Oh-My-God-This-IS-REAL' stage, of shock and horror when in more than two days the attempted coup happened and then Cassandra with her alien eye-makeup broadcast, and then... being suddenly at war with people from outer space!" She looked off into space blankly. "So a lot of us have never really digested it all, and some of us even blame the messengers, you girls, even though in our heart of hearts, we know we simply let ourselves be completely blindsided."

"Well that's actually a testament to the UFO cover-up people and their incredibly, fiendishly clever disinformation campaign." said Pamela, without really believing her own words. *We all rationalize, she thought, it's that or insanity sometimes...* "They had the most clever liars imaginable working overtime for decades on it." *You were all so good at seeing through lies, though, why couldn't you see through this one? It was because no one wanted to believe it..."*

"To answer your original question, Eloise, Cassandra has sort of disappeared, " said Pamela, and then continued. "Cassie told me she would be back when she got well. She didn't tell me where she was going so if anyone asked me, I would not have to lie. I even asked our news chief Manny Berkowitz, and he said CNS had arranged it so nobody would know where she was, and that was the  way she wanted it. So she has gone someplace to heal herself. *Somewhere out in the dark world, in some place of sanctuary. Trying to find peace of mind,  in the middle of a war."* I know she will return someday, as her familiar,  preposterously, superhuman self," said Pamela  forcing a smile. Pamela then thought of the cyanide capsule Cassandra had carried between her breasts during the Stargate story, and what had happened afterward at the hospital..." But sometimes,  I wonder if I will ever see her alive again." Tears fell down Pamela's cheeks. She wiped her face in irritation. "Let's talk about something else now. Shall we?" she sniffed.

"How about those New York Giants?" said Carl in helpless embarrassment. Meg and even Pamela smiled. The conversation changed to sports but dragged after that.  Finally, everyone agreed that the next day might be momentous and they should all get some sleep.

The next day was stormy like the previous one, the Frigate Collins had joined a large task force of grey ships plowing across the dark grey sea  in a fleet that stretched to the horizon. Destroyers and frigates predominated but also there were fast container ships, hastily painted grey and their cargo decks piled high with S-42 depth charges all painted silver. Apparently, these S-42s were mass produced in Bremerton, Washington, from old propane tanks, equipped with moveable fins, a magnetic guidance system, and a simple mechanical depth gauge for detonation. You could fire computer viruses at them all day, and they wouldn't care. 'Stupid is smart in this war,' Pamela had heard several military people confide. It had quickly been established that the more sophisticated the device was, the simpler it was for the Greys to disable it. Hence, the military had gone as much as possible to man-operated and man aimed weapons. Pamela stood on the deck with her fellow correspondents looking around at the task force with compact binoculars. Flight after flight of F-18 hornets and F-35 Lightnings flew over, and then A -26 Intruders - all weather fighters - so an aircraft carrier, or several, was obviously part of the task force.  Pamela knew that nuclear attack submarines prowled everywhere beneath the grey sea around the Task

325

Force. The Task Force seemed to be headed north at high speed. This was about all they could report. *Power and brute force, incredible violence about to be unleashed,* thought Pamela as she scanned the fleet plowing through the cold waves.

"It's really cold, you notice, I've heard reports that temperatures are dropping all over the world much more rapidly than normal. It's going to be a really cold winter." yelled Carl over the roaring waves and cold wind. "In World War Two it was colder than normal also. It's like the industrial output pattern changes and so does the weather." The grey sea was now topped with whitecaps, the Frigate rolled and rocked with the sea around it.

"My people are from Ukraine," yelled Pamela, laughing. "We have antifreeze for blood, that and vodka!" she was scanning the sea, thinking of a story to file. "Pammy goes to sea!" she muttered. *It is getting cold, too cold, what does it mean?* She pushed the thought aside.

Despite the fact that all they did was look around and try to stay out of the way of the sailors rushing around the wave washed decks, the day was exhausting. As the frigate closed in on the region of the ocean that was its target, standing around on the deck of a frigate in stormy seas was increasingly hard work. The task of keeping your balance, being doused with cold waves and being blown about by the wind caused everyone to retreat back the officer's mess. The correspondents all turned in early after their observations and slept deeply.

****

The Mirage had departed Maui and its warm sun-kissed waves, now they drove North-East through a cold ocean under a grey sky. Liani and the other Humpbacks, their calves born and nourished, were now journeying north to the Gulf of Alaska. Cassandra stood on the deck in her wetsuit, trying to get used to the colder water temperature. She went down to the sonar room on the ship and listened to the faraway voices of the humpbacks in the wide grey ocean. Mathew Renoir was the chief operator of the sonar and happily pointed out the hydrophone signature of Liani and Li Li on a large computer screen. The sophisticated computers on the ship, all of French design, could recognize the 'voice print' of the

326

various whales and their offspring from their calls. Mathew was the only member of the crew who was friendly, the rest keeping a respectful distance. Dr. Renoir had long since adopted an aloof, professorial disdain for her, apparently, because of her bonding with some of the subjects of his research program. Genevieve, his wife, was polite in a guarded way. Cassandra respected this and was silent for the most part at their shared dinners.

The Mirage was a portable kingdom-of-the-sea, propelled by massive German diesel engines. The food was the catch-of-the-day, supplemented by vegetables and pasta. The news was the call of the seabirds near land and the crash of the waves on the open sea. The scenery was the ever changing sea and sky, formerly sun-drenched and blue, now grey and stormy.

Of the crew, only a salty, older, pug of a man, known as 'Creol' would smile at her and occasionally help her back onto the boat, when she went over the side to snorkel. She would do this when the Mirage stopped to silence the engines and listen to the sounds of the sea, and when the sea was calm enough. To dive into the cold grey-green abyss of the deep ocean was something she had never imagined to do before, but now she was drawn to it. To imagine the ocean floor in the cold darkness miles below as she snorkeled around a few feet below its surface made her feel somehow at home. It was as if to glide above the abyss was her role in life, and now she was acting it out in metaphor. She would sometimes imagine coming to the surface and finding herself alone in the grey ocean, with the ship vanished like a mirage that was its namesake. She would feel at peace when she imagined this.

****

In the morning they were obviously in the combat zone. The sea and sky were a darker grey. The rest of task force was nowhere to be seen. Only one destroyer was visible in the far distance. Pamela could see tension everywhere on the faces of the crew. The losses at Adak and the loss of the USS Monterey weighed on all of them. Shortly after lunch, the Captain called her to the CIC behind the Bridge. He had assembled all the senior officers there. Captain Matsuga looked over his men. His face was like

327

iron. Di Franco, Kirkland, and Vasquez stood with faces without expression. Pamela stood with them in her Navy uniform. On a chart table, Matsuga motioned with his strong hands.

"Here is the main body of Task Force Typhoon, 100 miles to the south-south-west of us. Here is the location of the alien base. It has the approximate shape of a dome and is four kilometers underwater on the bottom, It's directly between us of the North squadron and the main task force. A strong deep sea current flows towards us from the main task force so they will begin releasing their mines and have the current carry them to the alien base where the mines magnetic guidance will provide terminal targeting on the magnetic field of the base. They will begin to lay depth charge patterns at 1600 hours to commence the attack on the base. We estimate the first depth charges should impact on the base and detonate at approximately 1700 hours.

"How many depth charges will they be releasing," asked one of the officers. It was Kirkland. Matsuga looked at her grimly.

"5000 S-42 depth charges will be released in a pattern calculated to do maximum damage. Admiral Jenkins, the Task Force Commander, said he wants a 'warm feeling' about the results." said Matsuga with a slight smile. Some muted laughter followed this statement.

In Pamela's heart, something trembled at these words. She thought of the aliens trapped in the dome down in the darkness of the cold ocean depths. *Shouldn't we give them a chance to surrender?* She thought. A deep sense of foreboding filled her, and then almost a sense of sorrow. *No, No, get a grip! She suddenly thought. Be tough! You are at war and you are in the Navy!*

"No alien activity in the air or undersea has been detected," continued Matsuga. " But we anticipate this will change once the charges begin to detonate on the sea floor. We must be prepared for possible alien craft trying to escape or attack, and rising up from the base in our area. Previous attacks on US and allied warship have involved attacks from directly below, a surface ship's most vulnerable angle. So, if we detect any alien craft rising we will take evasive action, launch torpedoes downwards, and as a last resort, we will deploy the S-42s we carry from

328

the side of the ship. As you know they will be deployed by firing explosive bolts, so shrapnel will be a hazard for anyone on deck." Captain Matsuga looked straight at Pamela when he said this. "So look sharp!"

"Also, the S-42s, if they detonate too close to the surface, may damage our hull and so we need to be ready to man life pods. Pamela absorbed the words and felt a renewed chill run through her.

"I expect every officer and sailor on this ship to perform their duty in this battle to the utmost of their ability. Now, to your posts!" With that, every officer departed to their cabins to don combat gear and helmets. The Captain looked at Pamela.

"Take care of your detail, Ensign," he then saluted her and turned away to the communications console where coded messages were now flying across the task force, now spread across thousands of miles of grey ocean. Pamela, feeling faint, returned his salute and rushed down and donned her fatigue uniform, helmet, flak jacket and life vest. Vasquez was doing the same wordlessly, with a distant blank look. Pamela checked her 38 snub-nose to make sure it was loaded, then dropped it in a plastic sealable sack to keep in dry. She then put it in her jacket pocket. She said a prayer and then checked her eye makeup. Pamela walked out into the hall, found the correspondents gathered in the officer's mess helping each other on with flak vests and helmet straps. Sailors and officers rushed by in combat gear, their faces were calm but with a faraway look.

****

*Dusk was falling and the sky had cleared. A cold wind was blowing from the North and Cassandra retreated from the deck into the sonar room. Mathew smiled at her entrance, and she sat beside him at the console.*

*"I am picking up lots of sounds like deep ocean sonar from the North East of us, many miles away." Cassandra looked at him with slight alarm. "Your Navy is looking for something," he added grimly.* Suddenly all feeling that Cassandra had cultivated about being on another planet called Pacifica vanished. She was back on Earth, it was like awakening from a dream.

329

*Pamela* thought Cassandra suddenly, *She is up there with the Navy! God, keep her safe! A feeling of utterly helpless anguish filled her.*

Cassandra went to her cabin and got down on her knees to pray by her bed that Pamela would be safe, finally after what seemed like hours, she felt a modicum of peace. She lay her head on the bed and wept. Then heard voices and footsteps. She rose and went down the hall back to the sonar room. It was now night outside, in the sonar room Dr. Renoir and Genevieve stood illuminated by the lights of the sonar consoles and their faces were masks of dread. Dr. Renoir angrily motioned to Cassandra to be quiet as she came in the door. Mathew had his headphones on and another sonar expert on the crew was also listening intently to a speaker output. Strange haunting gonging noises were issuing from the speaker. Suddenly a series of noises came in quick succession like large gongs, finally merging into a chorus of strange, distorted roaring.

"Explosions, father, there are large explosions in the deep ocean," said Mathew to his father. Dr. Renoir looked at Cassandra as if he wanted to cry. "There is a battle, a large battle to the northeast of us," continued Mathew.

"The Fools! Don't they know what this will do to the sea life!!" exclaimed Dr. Renoir in anguish, before his wife clung to his arm and he lapsed into sorrowful silence. Cassandra turned and headed for the deck outside.

It was a cold clear night, the stars hung brilliantly over the dark ocean and a cold breeze blew. Several other crewmen stood on the deck gazing to the northeast. Aurora now hung flickering in the dark sky to the North. Suddenly Casandra saw a flicker of light on the horizon in the far distance, white then fading to blood red. The crew reacted with an outpouring of oaths and obscenities in French. Then a bright flash came then another, like faraway lightning, then a flickering light of white orange and blood red, spreading along the horizon. A horrible feeling of fear and longing rose up in Cassandra. Then after another large flash a ghostly speck of light rose above the horizon, was then chased by other specks of light. They moved north into the aurora, then seemed to turn and head straight for them in the sky. Suddenly other points of light moved across the sky from the south and one of the lights seemed to merge with another speck

330

of light from the Northeast over their heads and then they disappeared as the other specks dispersed across the sky. A shower of what appeared to be meteors flashed across the sky to the south-west of them. A sharp crack of thunder followed, then there was a faint rumbling like distant thunder. The northeast horizon was now flickering with red and white light. Cassandra could not watch anymore. Dread and horror filled her and she fled back to her cabin to lie on her bed and pray before troubled dreams of being alone, floating in the grey sea, filled her sleep.

**** 

Marcy Braxton stood on the dark, wave washed deck, in a helmet and lifejacket. She saw the container ship beside them lit with flashes as explosive bolts fired and released a cascade of silver cylinders into the dark sea. Onward they rolled like an endless sparkling avalanche. Then suddenly the whole sky lit up like daylight. *Where is my cameraman?* She thought and began to curse.

****

"You guys ready?" asked Pamela. They were now sitting in the officer's mess. The nearby reporter's faces were masks of stoic calm. She could sense that the battle had already begun to the south and was briefing the other journalists on the worst possible scenarios, at the same time hoping that the most they would see were some flashes on the horizon. Everyone was nodding grimly to her instructions  but Ethan, who was sitting looking as if in a daze listening to his Ipod. Pamela leaned over  to him and pulled the earplug out  of his right ear.  He looked it her in stunned irritation. "Do you know what do if this ship starts to sink?" she asked. He nodded in annoyance. She smiled back at him. "Now stick with me when we go to general quarters and stay out everyone's way. The best place for us if the shit starts going down is right here, in officer's mess, because it's above deck. Now if the hull ruptures, you follow me through that door," she pointed to the hatchway leading to starboard, "out to the deck to K-4 Lifepod # 3, it holds six people. If things go South I am going to tell you to open its hatch and get in. Then we will pull a lever to drop it off the side of the ship. So I repeat, you follow me through that door if

331

things go south, to Lifepod #3, and if I tell you to get in, you get your asses in there and hang on to the ropes inside, because it's a twenty-foot drop to the ocean surface." She looked around, trying to appear calm. "It's something like a carnival water ride," Pamela added to try to calm the rising fear she saw in their eyes.

Suddenly the general quarters sounded and a group of marines in full combat gear ran through the officer's mess carrying Stringer missiles and a 50 caliber machine gun, obviously to set up on deck. The marines barely noticed them. The dull rumble of the engine now picked up intensity and the ship lurched as it picked up speed. *Oh no, we are going to be part of this battle after all!* she thought grimly. Despite her fear , Pamela felt a sense of power and elation at this sound of the ship going to full power and lurching forward in speed.

"Battle stations all hands to battle stations!" came a command across the loudspeakers and a ringing alarm sounded, as the ship increased speed. Standby to engage submerged hostile vessel!' Pamela looked out the porthole, darkness had fallen early this far north but the south horizon was flickering with light - blue and orange.

Suddenly the ship shook as vertical launch anti-submarine missiles roared out of their launching tubes. Each burned out their motors and released a torpedo straight down into the ocean, where it ignited its own rocket engine and dived down into the dark depths below. She watched stunned out of a portal as the rocket engines lit the deep ocean beneath them with a ghostly diffuse light. Megan and Eloise cried out in fear, Carl stood still hanging on to the table grimacing. Ethan simply sat at the table in shock. The ship was now zig sagging at high speed. "Standby to deploy S-42 mines, all decks take cover. Tremendous bangs sounded as the huge mines deployed. The ship was heeling to the left and right as it plowed through the sea in its zig-zag course, now lighter because of the mines being deployed. Suddenly Pamela realized, *this ship is evading something, it's fighting for its life!* Suddenly the zig-zagging stopped and instead the ship's engines began to race, higher and higher the turbines began to scream. *They have stopped evading they are now just running! They are running in a straight line for maximum possible speed!* Came the thought to her with crystal clarity.

332

"FOLLOW ME!" yelled Pamela. And the petrified correspondents rushed after her as she wretched open the hatch leading to the port deck. Water and cold ocean spray flew in their faces. Outside a flickering light filled their eyes. The whole southern horizon was a mass of flickering blue and orange light. The #3 Lifepod was next to her now. Then blinding white light lit up the ship as another antisubmarine rocket flew from the bow vertical launch tubes then arced directly over the ship and plunged into the sea behind it. "They were not zig-zagging anymore. The Frigate is now running in a straight line to achieve maximum speed," said Pamela as she looked at the exhaust stacks where blue fire was now coming out of them. They were running at full military power, the turbines screaming as they wound higher and higher in speed, they were now a deafening scream. `They are burning out the engines to gain speed!' The sea behind them was suddenly convulsed with a brilliant blue light, and the whole ship shuddered as the shock wave from 42 tons of high explosive struck it, then again the sea was convulsed this time almost beneath them. Then a suddenly a strange shrill siren a whooping sound . Instinctively she reached over to the life pod hatch and yanked it open. She suddenly realized what the shrill whooping sound was, *Collision warning!*

Suddenly the whole ship behind them was twisted away from the part they were standing on, Pamela hung frantically on to the railing as the other correspondents fell over on the deck . With a scream of tortured steel the entire aft end of the ship from twenty feet behind them sheared off the front. Flame from ruptured fuel tanks now splattered across the ship and onto the ocean, making a sea of flame. A blinding white light filled her eyes.

*"GET IN THE POD! GET IN THE POD!"* Pamela screamed. She grabbed Carl Levy and with astonishing strength threw him up through the hatch, Megan was next as she climbed in helped by a final shove from Pamela. She had to pick up Eloise, as she struggled to her feet and threw her in also then she grabbed Ethan who had the sense to jump in head first. Two sailors, a tall black man and short, stocky white man came running up. The deck was tilting now at a steeper and steeper angle. *Oh God help us!* Pamela screamed mentally.

"CAPTAIN ORDERS ABANDON SHIP! ABANDON SHIP!" the sailors were yelling and dived into the pod one after the other head first. A blinding light then filled Pamela's eyes as she followed them into the life-pod, she saw the sailors both pulling with all their strength inside the pod on the lever that would free them from the ship. Suddenly a last man dived into the pod, in the flash of white light that then filled the pod as they slammed shut the hatch, Pamela recognized it was executive officer Di Franco, as the ship lurched and began to sink and now cold sea water exploded into the pod hatchway as they tried to close the hatch. The pod, with the women all screaming , then by some miracle now floated free as the Frigate Collins deck sank beneath them. Pamela was floating in the icy water, struggling with the others to keep the hatch pulled shut. Finally they sensed the pod was floating free and floating in the water, where the ship's deck had been moments earlier. It had all happened in less than a minute.

"Get your helmets off and bail! or the next wave will swamp us!" Di Franco was yelling. Now he opened the hatch and they all began bailing water out of the pod with their helmets, buckets, even cupped hands to try to get the hundreds gallons or more of water filling the pod, out into the ocean. They bailed desperately as the waves washed over them, refilling the pod, finally after a few minutes of frantic bailing they seeming to clear away some of the water when a deafening crash sounded and a spear-point of metal slammed down on the top of the pod and through it, impaling Di Franco as he tried to bail water at the hatch with his helmet. Pamela and other woman screamed in terror and pity. He turned in the flickering light and looked at Pamela dully, blood exploding from his mouth, as suddenly the metal spike wretched out of him and yanked off the hatch and part of the shattered plastic roof with it. Pamela saw fire outside, burning oil on the sea, and in the light of the burning sea surface she saw that the ship's tall magnetometer mast had fallen on them as the front half of the ship sank.

Without thinking, they pulled Di Franco's body away from where the hatch had been and began bailing desperately again. The black sailor was holding Di Franco's upper body out of the water. The water was now full of blood. Finally, after many exhausting minutes, the pod was less full of water and the fires went out. There was only darkness and exhausted

334

sleep, punctuated by someone sobbing uncontrollably, as the cold waves pushed the pod to and fro on the dark sea.

"Stanny! Get some light and the medical kit for Di Franco!" yelled the black sailor cradling Di Franco. Pamela stood by the hatchway, now with no door and bailed with her helmet as waves washed more water into the pod. She remembered a faint light filling the pod and hushed voices as she bailed and bailed until the sea calmed it seemed and she fell into an exhausted sleep.

Pamela awoke at dawn on the sea. It grew lighter as Pamela scanned the horizon for any signs of rescue or other survivors. She was afraid to turn and see how badly Di Franco was injured, she realized. All she saw outside was debris and corpses of sailors and marines floating in the waves. In stunned reflex she counted at least eight bodies then quit counting. She was freezing in the cold water. The hatch and part of the roof had been lost when Di Franco was impaled by the toppling magnetometer mast. On the hatch had been several packages of survival gear. The gear was gone, and so was half the dome roof that was supposed to shelter them. Other survival packages had jarred loose apparently when the mast hit them, and they had floated out of the open hatch or been inadvertently thrown out during the frantic bailing. . The pod was still partly full of bloody water and listed. Two feet of water was on one side but only a few inches on the other. Many survival food and water packages and other things had floated loose in the water in the pod, some had broken open to be spoiled by sea water. Pamela finally steeled herself and turned to look at Di Franco, being cared for by the two sailors. Franco had been impaled through the abdomen. The two sailors tried to keep him mostly out of the water, forcing the others in the pod into the side of the pod where water was deepest. Ethan complained bitterly about this.

"Where is the medical kit?" asked Pamela as the sailors, the older black man named Gordon, his hair streaked with grey and who was obviously a Navy Chief by his uniform, and the young white man named Stanfield, with a dark mustache and who was a Torpedoman's Mate, tried to help the injured officer. Di Franco was fortunately unconscious, but his wounds were obviously mortal unless they were rescued soon.

335

"I don't know!" said Chief Gordon looking around desperately. "Stanny try and find the medical kit," he said. "We got to give him some morphine before he wakes up." Stanfield dutifully began looking through the water and around on the top of the domed roof of the pod, where most of the survival goods were latched.

"Here!" he yelled in triumph, as he pulled a plastic box with a red cross on it from the deepest part of the bloody water.

"Here Chief!" Stanfield handed the box eagerly to Gordon who was now cradling Di Franco's head on his lap, trying to keep it out of the water.

Chief Gordon suddenly exploded in rage as he looked desperately through the box.

"There's no morphine or syringes in here Stanny! Somebody stripped it all out!" he yelled. He looked at Pamela incredulously. Pamela took the box, looked inside. It held only bandages, burn cream, sutures and a needle, some antibiotics and some aspirin. It was dry inside. A space marked painkiller was empty. Pamela fought panic. She opened a fresh water bottle, found a cup and ground up some aspirin in the fresh water, gave the cup to Gordon, who tried to have Di Franco drink it. Instead he began to cough up blood. Stansfield was looking at Di Franco's abdomen wound grimly..

"Oh Jesus, Gordo" said Stanny. Looking first to Gordon then to Pamela. "Gordo, his guts is coming out. We got to get him to doctor quick!"

"Radio, is there a radio anywhere?" queried Pamela. Gordon and Stan looked around desperately. Finally they found a smashed radio in the salt water at the bottom of the pod. Chief Gordon shook his head miserably.

"Flare Gun then!" Pamela looked around and found one still latched to the domed roof.

"That won't do us any good unless there's a plane looking for us!" said Gordon sharply.

"Well a plane, or a helicopter is coming soon!" said Pamela, "and we're all going to be OK"

336

"How soon will help come?" asked Eloise.

"It's light, it will come soon. The Captain would have put out a distress call when the ship broke in two. It's standard procedure!"

"Are you sure?" asked Eloise.

"Yes!"

Suddenly a large wave sloshed through the hatchway and something flopped into the pod. I t was a fish.

Megan screamed as it swam around in the water near her. It was hideous and glowing in the dim light and had long needlelike teeth. Pamela moved swiftly and scooped it up in her helmet. She sat looking amazed at it. Stanny looked at it amazement. Pamela handed him  her helmet in revulsion so he could hold it.

"Gordo it's radioactive or something. Look it's glowing!" said Stanfield. Chief Gordon looked at it incredulously. Pamela leaned over and looked in horrified curiosity. It was obviously a deep, deep,  sea fish. She took the helmet from Stan, now fascinated.

"It's some really deep sea  fish, frightened up to the surface by the explosions  down below," said Pamela. She offered Megan and Carl a look. They looked at it amazed. *Distraction, an essential  tool of command,* thought Pamela.

"Well get it out of here!" said Chief Gordon crossly. "This ain't no fucking science expedition! We got get this man some help." Di Franco began to groan, coughed up more blood, and opened his eyes. He was bleeding steadily from his abdomen. The water in the bottom of the pod was now full of blood. Di Franco grimaced in pain. Pamela noticed Ethan drinking something out of a hip flask.  Pamela quickly dumped the fish over the side of pod through the hatch, being careful to dump it when the waves would carry it away from the pod. She put her helmet back on, it kept her head warmer.

"That's whiskey right? Give me that!" demanded Pamela, turning back to Ethan. "It will ease his pain!" Ethan looked at her defiantly but saw the steely glare of both Stanny and Gordon directed at him. He meekly surrendered the flask of whiskey. Pamela took it and put it to Di Franco's mouth as Gordon cradled his head. Di Franco smelled it, drank several sips, and grimaced in pain.

"Let's get this place empty of water while the sea is reasonably calm," said Pamela. "Carl, Megan, help me bail." Ethan, she had already written off, Eloise looked like she was in shock. Megan and Carl pitched in, and after a while, the pod was mostly empty of water. *Progress.* The pod was made of heavy orange plastic and appeared to have ten-foot diameter flotation ring of rigid foam in which a tube with ballast weights at the bottom was tied. The weights were heavy steel and tied with rope so they could be released. *Why would they do that?* wondered Pamela. The roof was an orange dome above them, half shattered and gone. Survival packages were fastened to the underside of the now half-destroyed roof with heavy plastic latches, many now shattered and empty. Other survival packages and gear was stowed in latched in positions around the inside of the flotation ring. Pamela stood up in the hatch in the cold wind. The sea and sky were grey as before but reasonably calm. Nothing could be seen for miles, except for debris and occasional lifeless bodies. Near the pod, she noticed what looked like a large fish thrashing in the water. It looked like a swordfish, apparently stunned in the fighting of the previous night. It was swimming weakly and rolling over and over in the water. *Its swim bladder must be damaged,* she thought, remembering from a course how fish reacted to high explosives at sea. *Sharks tolerate shock waves that kill other fish* she thought fearfully. *In fact, explosions attract them.*

"Chief! Have we got a gaff or pole on this boat?" she asked. Stan found a telescoping aluminum pole attached to the pod roof. It had a blunt hook on the small end. He was deploying it, it extended in sections with threaded rings to secure it.

"What do you see Ensign?" asked Chief Gordon.

"Food, maybe! gimme it Stanny!" She motioned for the pole. Suddenly the biggest shark she had ever seen, white as a ghost, engulfed the stricken swordfish whole in an enormous mouth full of enormous teeth, as it stuck its head up out of the water to what Pamela estimated was 10

338

feet. The mouth appeared 5 feet across. Pamela screamed in terror. The enormous shark's head then disappeared beneath the waves , in its place, and the place where the stricken swordfish had been, was only a whirlpool of dark grey sea water.

"Jesus!" yelled Gordon. "Did you see that?" Pamela turned trembling and looked at them all amazed. She nodded spastically. She turned back and saw, perhaps forty feet away, a greyish dorsal fin of a shark, that was perhaps six feet tall appear out of the water as the gigantic shark apparently chomped down on some floating debris, then the terrible apparition disappeared.

"All right, everybody be quiet, nobody move!" yelled Pamela carefully easing back down into the pod. "That thing may come back and take a bite out of this pod if we attract its attention!" She set down the telescoping pole with trembling hands. She scanned the faces in the pod, Di Franco, near death, Chief Gordon, Stan, masks of wary courage, Megan, and Carl strong and miserable, Eloise catatonic, and Ethan, who was trying to ask her something.

"Can I have my flask back?" he asked quietly. Pamela felt a flash of rage.

"NO DAMMIT! It's the only painkiller we have here for Di Franco!"

"We better give him another dose, he is starting to move again," said the Chief.

Pamela pulled the flask out of her pocket and slid over to Di Franco, his head still cradled in Gordon's lap. As gently as she could, she put the now open flask up to his lips. Di Franco, she noticed now, had a bad head wound bruise, as well as a stomach wound. The head wound was not bleeding much at all but was wide and now blue and swollen. He looked pale as death, and he seemed to be unresponsive. She reached over and checked his pulse on his neck. He had none. She opened one of his eyes. It was dilated wide and did not respond to the light.

"Chief, check his pulse on his wrist," she said sadly and looked away over the grey sea. Chief Gordon checked his pulse, looked at Pamela, and shook his head sadly.

"Can I have my flask back now?" asked Ethan again.

"Yeah Ethan, Di Franco doesn't need it anymore," she said disgust. *Some people respond well in a crisis, others...not so much,* thought Pamela, eyeing Ethan.

Pamela put the flask to her own lips and took a swig, she then handed it to Gordon who did likewise, then it was passed to Stanfield who took a swig also. He put the cap back on it and tossed it at Ethan, who eagerly scooped it up and began drinking it. *Mental log note, grog ration issued to the Navy personnel,* she thought in misery. The whiskey burned her throat and made her feel momentarily warm. *I better get that thing back from him,* she thought, *we may need it again later.* From the roar of the waves and dark sky outside, it began to sink into her that rescue could be hours, or even days, away.

"We best put him over the side Ensign," said Chief Gordon.

"Yes, Chief," said Pamela sadly.

"You're ranking officer on this boat Ensign... As CO you should say some words over him," said Chief Gordon grimly. He was easing him into the water to move him over to the hatchway. Pamela felt a deep sinking feeling. *Am I responsible for this lifeboat?*

"OK, let's do this thing." she said grimly.

"We gotta put some weights on him, if we don't , he'll come floating up in a day or so, I saw it happen," said the Chief. "You don't wanna see that" he added.

Stanny pried two ballast weights loose in the bottom of the pod and they tied them to Di Franco around his waist using his belt. They stripped off Di Franco's life jacket from his now rag-like body. She could see the wound in his abdomen was very deep. She wanted to use more weights than two but feared for the stability of the pod in the waves if they took more. *Now I know what the detachable weights in this pod are for.* The two sailors and Pamela mournfully lifted Di Franco's body to the open hatchway, his corpse now bleeding profusely into the bottom of the pod. Pam took off

340

her helmet and stood unsteadily. She was trying to remember what the sea traditions course at Annapolis, which she had attended on weekends, had said about sea funerals.

" Dear Lord, please take the remains of our able shipmate Lt. Commander Di Franco, who served his country bravely as a Naval officer and tried to see ably to the safety of his ships company... We now consign his body to the sea." She couldn't think of anything else to say.  Chief Gordon sat stoically and Stanfield wept openly. They had apparently served with Di Franco at sea many months and regarded him as a good officer at sea, and, as Pamela had learned from the women officers  over coffee on the Collins, he was a good-hearted cad on shore leave.  She nodded, and the two sailors and she then pushed his body overboard, she watched it sink out of sight in the grey-green waves.  Tears rolled down her cheeks, but she caught herself. *NO, NO, NO weakness! You are CO on this boat now! Keep everyone busy.*

"OK let's bail this bloody water out of the boat, get this place cleaned up and the gear stowed, we want it to look orderly when we get rescued. And Ethan,  give us back that flask, it's the only strong medicine we have on this boat!"

Ethan looked at her defiantly.

"Ethan, I am ranking Navy officer on this boat, and mister,  I have just given you an order!"  she yelled. The whiskey was giving her a feeling of seriousness. Chief Gordon and Stan were now looking at him in cold rage. Ethan took out the flask, took one last long drink and tossed it at her. She angrily scooped it up floating in the bloody water, saw that he had drunk the last drops." She angrily threw it over the side.

"Under the law of the sea, you're  gonna be next thing that goes over the side, asshole, if you don't start acting better on this boat!" she snapped.

Ethan folded his arms and looked away.

"You watch your ass Ethan!" yelled the Chief. "She is in command here! She is a Navy Ensign and this shit bucket  is a NAVY boat!" *Thank you Chief, she thought.*

341

"Alright, everybody! Let's get this boat cleaned up and as dry as we can make it," said Pamela. "Chief, can you figure out what's left on this boat of our survival gear and you and Stanny get it stowed. I am going to try and rig a distress flag on this pole so we are more visible. We are gonna have to post watches too with the flare gun in case any rescue shows up." *Keep the crew busy at all times...*

"How soon can we expect rescue?" asked Megan, she was tearful from the burial. Carl looked somber and miserable. Eloise still looked in shock, she was looking out the hatchway with glassy eyes. Pamela motioned to Carl, who was sitting beside her to check on her. They had more room now but were huddled close for mutual warmth. The wind was low but cold, and blowing through a hatchway that no longer had a hatch.

"Soon. Rescue will come soon," said Pamela, "very soon I think. Now let's get this water out of the boat." *Thank God the sea is fairly calm, thank God Di Franco died without ever fully regaining consciousness, thank God we have some supplies...*she thought. *God, please help us! God, please send a rescue soon!*

In a while, they had the horrid bloody water out of the boat and had even washed it down, so the remaining water was clear faint green. The Chief methodically organized the remaining survival gear. Pamela waited dutifully for his report, she stared out the open hatchway at the grey sea and sky, hoping for a rescue aircraft.

****

Marcy Braxton was huddling on the deck of the supply ship shivering, wet, and exhausted. She was helping sailors pull people on board who had been rescued from the stormy sea . Several ships had gone down in the battle the night before. The sea around them was covered with debris, bodies and flaming oil. The fleet had dispersed in every direction. F-18 fighters flew over on constant patrol.

Marcy was helped a civilian woman with dark blond hair, either another correspondent like her, or a technician, off the deck and then led her to the sailor's mess and got her a hot cup of coffee, which she held in her

342

hands for several minutes shivering, apparently to warm herself, before drinking it.

"What ship were you on?" asked Marcy. Trying to get a response from the trembling woman.

The woman simply stared straight ahead speechless as a Medical Corpsman came over and put a blanket around her.

****

"Ok, here is our supply and survival gear situation. We got five gallons of fresh water, and we got twelve survival granola bars," began Chief Gordon. So that's a pint a day for each of us for two days, which I know is minimum from survival school. We can have survival a bar each a day for two days, or four days if we go to half a bar a day." Pamela listened to the Chief's report on survival gear with a soggy and cold satisfaction.

"The medical kit has a dozen bandages," the Chief continued, "some antibiotics for infections, some suntan lotion," he grinned slightly at this since the Sun had been missing for days. *Oh the chief does have a sense of humor, after all,* thought Pamela. "We got 50 aspirins for pain. The radio is iced, but we got a flare gun with three regular flares and one radar chaff-flare. And we got an axe for firewood," he added with another slight grin. "We got a two hundred foot rope and a telescoping pole ten feet long with a hook on it, which we can rig a distress flag to, so somebody will see us. That's it, and that is enough, I think, to see us through. Help should show up soon. We're not in bad shape here."

"Thank you Chief," said Pamela. "So we are fine on supplies, until we get rescued, which will be soon." She noticed that the Chief now a day's stubble on his chin that was white and light grey, making him look like an old man.

They had gotten the pod cleaned up and organized and reasonably dry, except for an occasional big wave that would slosh through the open hatchway and missing area of the roof. They even had designated two bailing buckets for waste disposal, one for civilians one for the Navy. Torpedo mate Stanfield had demonstrated the proper way to dump a

343

waste bucket over the side, once one had used it. The civilians looked on this with sharp interest. One did this chore by checking the wind and waves to prevent what Stanfield euphemistically called : 'flush back'. They then all watched newswoman Eloise douse herself attempting to follow this careful Navy advice. Eloise had finally lost her stunned look when this happened and had burst into tears, and continued in that state as the rest of the crew cleaned up the resulting mess and washed out the hold. Having demonstrated her incompetence to empty her own waste bucket, she was relieved of that duty. *Well played,* thought Pamela in seething anger. Eloise had then resumed her nearly catatonic, silent state.

They were now all crowded together for warmth under the half -roof that remained, with Pamela and the two sailors rotating who got to sit in the warm middle. The news people somehow, after some nasty argument, managed to rotate who would sit on the end of the row and be coldest.

"Thank you Chief, I am detailing you and Stan here to distribute rations. I think we should go to half rations beginning now. She was sitting in between the two sailors and almost felt comfortable, despite being soaking wet, because of the warm of their bodies and reasonably calm sea.

"But were going to run out of water in two days anyway!" said Ethan helpfully. Why not eat the food up at the same time, while we have water?"

"Because it's going to rain soon and we are going to have plenty of fresh water Mister Ethan, so we will most likely run out of food before water," said Pam with a forced smile looking up at the grey sky. She was hoping a plane would fly over any moment, and they had the flare gun loaded and within easy reach because of this possibility.

"I thought you said we were going to be rescued soon!" said Eloise with sudden animation.

"We are at war Eloise, just after a battle. It typically takes a few days to recover from the chaos and tie up loose ends," said Pamela idly. She felt like drifting off to sleep. Eloise suddenly exploded in anger.

344

"This war is all your fault! If you and Cassandra Chen had just left things alone we wouldn't be in this mess, floating in this boat with no rescue!" Eloise shrieked.

"Yeah your friend, the war-whore, started this damn war!" shouted Ethan. Pamela bolted upright and her blue eyes flashed like two acetylene welding torch flames.

"The fucking aliens started this war when they came here to conquer this place and make sausage out of people like you! The  aliens can fucking leave anytime they want to! That will end the war!  In fact, you can go with them when they leave!

"No! You started this war!" shrieked Eloise,  beginning to cry.

"You started this war so, you could establish a dictatorship  and so you could play dictator here in this fucking boat! Giving orders to us! Hah! You aren't a Navy officer! You aren't even a real journalist! You're just a shill for this war!" shouted Ethan.

"My only regret is saving your limp asses! And I am not a dictator you fucking idiots! You don't have a fucking conception of a dictatorship! If I was a  real dictator you two would be the last people I would tolerate on this boat!" retorted Pamela.

"Dictator! DICTATOR! IF THE SHOE FITS WEAR IT!" screamed Eloise.

"Listen you assholes! You are living proof that ignorance is bliss, in your cases ignorance is nothing but a big cock to suck on!" screamed Pamela back, rising to face Eloise and Ethan.

 "Everybody shut the fuck up!" yelled Chief Gordon rising angrily.  He turned to Pamela looking serious, almost pleading.

"Don't talk that shit with these people skipper, you're the CO here. It ain't becoming."  At this, Pamela regained her composure. She had reached into her pocket and felt her 38 snub nose, enclosed in its plastic sandwich bag. She now let go of it. Calmed herself. *He's right,* she thought as her rage cooled. She felt better . Gordon leaned close.

"Skipper, the task force maybe got the shit kicked out of it down south," he said quietly. "We were watching the flashes on deck. Last news we heard was a destroyer and container ship was going down. Whatever happened, it wasn't a case of them just dropping those S-42s and heading back to Pearl..." he paused. "So what I am sayin is it may be a long time before they find us. They maybe got bigger fish to fry." Pamela absorbed all this, nodded slowly. A deep feeling of mute despair began to fill the lifeboat. It was impossible to have a private conversation in the pod, everyone had apparently heard the Chief's assessment. Pam saw black hopelessness now growing on every face. *Even my own,* she thought. Gloom settled in the pod for hours. Finally, Chief Gordon issued half a survival bar along with a cup of fresh water to everyone. Despite themselves, people seemed to perk up at this.

"Let me tell you all a story of the sea I learned at Annapolis," said Pamela breaking the silence. *Distraction.*

"It is the story of the FOO bird" she began with a smile, thinking of happier times. To her amazement, everyone in the pod looked suddenly transfixed, even Ethan and Eloise.

"There was this group of three college professors who heard about a legend of this big exotic bird that lives on an isolated island in the middle of the sea. It's called the FOO bird, and it had never been discovered before. So this first professor rents a motor boat and goes out to sea, to this island and camps out, and then the next morning he sees this big bird with bright feathers flying towards his camp, going 'FOO! FOO!' as it flies straight for him. He records all this in his logbook, then he looks up and the bird flies right over him, and it shits right on him!" everyone laughed at this. *Laughter in this place!* thought Pam in triumph. *My gig in infotainment is useful even here.* "So he notes this in his logbook as a 'territorial threat display', and writes that he is going to wash off the bird shit in the surf. Well as soon as he washes off the bird shit, he falls over dead," More laughter, eerie now, followed. *Di Franco would be laughing too if he were still here.*

"So, his two buddies fly a floatplane to the isolated island to find out what happen to their friend, and they find him dead on the beach with his logbook. Then after they read about his last moments, they look up and

346

here comes the big FOO bird. The big bird flies straight at them and goes 'FOO! FOO!'"

Pamela was flapping her arms as everyone laughed, "and then, just like before, it shits on both of them. So these two professors stand there and one says to the other, 'well his bird obviously doesn't like being spied on, but we have enough data to publish an article, so let's wash this shit off and get back to civilization before he comes back.' And the other professor, says 'hold on, you know what happened to our colleague. We should leave this shit alone." The Chief and Stanny laughed loud and hard at this.

"That man is Chief Petty Officer Material!" laughed the Chief.

"Yes, but before he can stop the other professor, the poor guy goes down to the surf and starts washing himself off, and sure enough, he falls over dead too! It was some sort of poison in it!

So the last professor hurriedly packs up all his gear and high-tails it out of there on the float plane, only by the time he reaches civilization, this shit is really ripe. So he thinks, it's been a week, I can get rid of this shit! But as soon as he steps into the shower, boom, he falls over dead!" Her audience looked at her in shock.

"The moral of this story being: 'If the FOO shits, wear it!'" There followed several minutes of raucous laughter, even Eloise laughed hysterically. *Oh, laughter is a survival tool, for sure,* she thought happily. Finally, everyone grew silent and Pamela was scanning the horizon. The smiles began to fade and began to be replaced by grim stares. Eloise now looked catatonic again, but also like she wanted desperately to say something.

"I need my medications..." said Eloise abruptly.

"What medications?" said Pamela in disbelief. *Psychiatric?*

"Insulin, I'm diabetic" gasped Eloise. "My muscles are starting to cramp really bad," her voice became raw.

"Mam, you got no business being on a warship in a combat zone and being diabetic!" exploded Chief Gordon. "We got no fucking insulin on this boat!"

347

"I need my insulin," Eloise said vacantly.

"You should've fucking brought some then!" retorted the Chief in helpless anger. He shot Pamela a look of horror. She felt a chill on seeing his look.

"Chief, give her some aspirin," said Pamela shaking her head in disbelief. Pamela felt a deep sadness strike her. *Radio, we need to get her help soon! She'll die too, soon.*

"We need to post watches to look for a rescue then, I will stand first watch, then you Chief, then Stanny. "She rose and took her place standing in the cold wind. The anger had made her feel warm. But it was slipping away.

The wind was now rising. She was looking around and spotted another orange life-pod. Unlike theirs, it appeared intact. Her heart leaped when she realized, after staring at it for several minutes , that it was drifting towards them in the wind. After a while,  as they all watched mesmerized with hope, it was about 100 yards away.

"Chief, Stanny,   a life pod, its drifting closer to us." She pointed at it.  The Chief rose, he was tall and thin and older. His face broke into a smile.

"Yeah, and it's riding high in the water too. It's got less people in it. We can swap supplies with them.  Swap out some people too." *I can think of two candidates right off the bat,* she thought angrily. The wind was blowing now, and the waves becoming higher. The lifepod continued to move closer. Obviously, it was lighter and being blown more by the wind than their heavily loaded lifepod.  Pamela was doing calculus in her head to figure out what the distance of closest approach would be.  She estimated it would pass within a hundred feet of them as it moved.  She arrived at a decision instantly.

"Chief, I am a good swimmer, I am going to try to swim to it and attach our rope to it. We can them pull the pods together and offload some people and get some medical supplies and a radio if they haven't used it already."  The Chief suddenly looked dubious.

"You ever swam in this water skipper? It's too damn cold. We got enough supplies, and a plane will fly over any moment. This is a crazy-ass idea." Pam was watching the pod slowly get closer. It would pass close by in about a half hour she estimated. If they let it pass they might never get another chance at more supplies and a radio. *Unless that big shark shows up,* she thought, but she suppressed the idea. *Naw, It's long gone.*

"Yeah, we got enough supplies for two days for us, but Eloise there needs some medicine, and if she needs insulin we can't wait two days, we need a radio or at least morphine for her. I am going to try. I'll have the rope if it's too hard you can pull me back on board. We'll have to cut our time in the cold water to a minimum, so we have to just be able to swim to it when passes closest. *Thank you calculus course!* She thought as she steeled herself for what was coming. *At least I am used to being cold and wet now*, she thought. *I can do it!*

"Stanny can you swim well? She asked. Stanfield grinned bravely.

"Sure skipper, I'll go with you. We can't wear life jackets, they'll slow us down, we have to dive in soon and swim with the rope as fast as we can to reach it when it gets close. We can tie life jackets on the rope in case we need them." said Stanny staring off into space as he did mental calculations.

Pamela began pulling off her wet clothes. The cold wind hit her bare skin like ice as she stripped down to her panties and bra, Stanny, was stripping down to a pair of boxers. He was powerfully built and looked able to do the job. She had been working out furiously and suddenly realized her life was now on the line because of it. That if she hadn't felt so fit she would never even have considered what she was preparing to do now. The chief was frowning as he tied the rope securely to the side of the life-pod , the rope was at least two hundred feet. He looked like he wanted to say more but couldn't. *This may be it,* she thought *my last grand gesture.* He tied two lifejackets to the end of the rope with some slack rope on the end so they could tie it to the other pod. They tied the end of the rope to Pamela's waist. She was priming herself mentally for the swim. She peeled off her bra, covering her breasts with her right arm. *A bra will slow me down,* she thought desperately, *survival trumps modesty in this case!* She

349

prepared herself for what was coming. *You can do it! You can do it!* She calculated the closure rate by dead reckoning, *jump in too soon and arrive early with too much time in the water, jump in too late and miss the pod as it passes by! Now!* she thought, *the time is now!* Pamela and Stanny now rose in the hatch out into the full wind and then both dove into the water. Pamela cried out as the cold hit her but began to swim as fast as she could with Stanny swimming along beside her, the cold was paralyzing but the burning desire to reach the other pod was stronger. It was life now and their hope of rescue. *Radio, radio* was all she thought as she swam as hard as she could hoping to generate enough body heat to keep warm.

After what seemed like an endless struggle they drew near to the pod. For a moment she felt her muscles failing and freezing up, she began to sink, *Oh God help me!* She somehow renewed her struggles and closed to within six feet of it. *Almost within reach.*

"Help! Anybody in there!" gasped Pamela.

"Yo! anybody in there! Open up and help us." Yelled Stanny who was now six feet behind her.

The pod was silent and motionless except for its relentless drift before the wind. Finally, with what seemed a superhuman effort Pamela grabbed on to a rope loop on the pod and with numb fingers tied the end of her own rope to it. She could hear the people in her pod break into cheers. She could barely move her fingers but Stanny helped her tie the rope. Soon the Chief's strong arms were pulling the pods together. She then threw her leg up over the side and managed to climb up to where the hatch was. *I have to get out of the water! I am getting this thing done!* She banged on the hatch and then opened it. She then recoiled in horror.

Three corpses floated inside, two sailors and a marine, it appeared. A one-foot hole with melted edges was burned into the roof on the side not visible to them as they had swum. The bodies were charred and the pod held an overwhelming stench of rotting, burned, flesh that assailed her nostrils. The floatation ring on the pod had kept it afloat despite the water inside, where the bottom was punctured. That, and the natural flotation of rotting bodies. Stanny pulled himself out of the water as Pamela began to shiver uncontrollably. Without hesitating, he went inside and pulled a slightly burned blanket out of a storage bracket on the roof away from the burned area. She joined him then in wading through the hideous water festooned with charred bodies. The other crew was busily hauling on the rope, even Ethan was helping. Soon the two pods were side by side. Despite the hideous nature of the pod's contents, the supplies were mostly good, once washed off. This did wonders for morale on the pod of survivors. *We have Booty!* Thought Pam in exhausted joy, without thinking about the bodies. They now had five days rations of food and water, blankets, more rope. The medical kit on this pod had not been stripped of narcotics. However the radio's electronics had been burned up by the alien proton beam, so it was useless. The GPS unit was also fried, but GPS had not worked since the war began, so this was tossed overboard without comment. Soon Chief Gordon was injecting Eloise with morphine to ease her agony from her muscle spasms. Pamela, finally washed herself off in cold water and jumped back into to the original pod , and wrapped herself in a blanket. The men seemed mostly oblivious to her topless form moving around, only Megan starred at her as if stunned. They even found hot packs, on the other pod, that could be filled with sea water and which then released heat. Pamela exhausted beyond all understanding, wrapped herself in a blanket with a hot pack and lay down and lost consciousness, in the bottom of the pod.

She awoke with the other pod gone, they had ripped the hatch off to help cover their own damaged roof and cast it adrift. She was lying between the two warm bodies of the Chief and Stanny both also asleep. Nobody had enough energy to stand watch. The stars were now visible through the remaining hatchway. Northern lights flickered and danced over the stars as she watched them. It was a dead calm outside. Pamela felt suddenly happy. She fell back again into an exhausted sleep.

She dreamed she saw Cassandra and her dressed in black witches costumes with the fabric clinging tightly to their dangerous curves. Cassandra was smiling wickedly underneath her black peaked witches hat. Cassandra looked fabulous and had a confident smile of power, her dark eyes flashing. Full of plots and intrigues!

*"The time comes soon to prepare our great cosmic spell Pammy!" she said laughing. "A spell so powerful it will change the orbit of the Moon and Mars! It will shake the stars and the galaxy will tremble on its axis!"* Cassandra was waving her hands at the stars, and making incantations and magic. *"Because of our magic spell, Moonbeam, the very cosmos will suffer a great sea change!"* Then both she and Cassandra became luminous blue stars of blinding light amid the other stars.

"Oh you're alive my friend, you are alive and getting stronger!" she gasped to herself. *"You're alive and well, That's what this dream means! Oh, Thank God."* The stars, brilliant, still drifted above her in the cold sky, with occasional aurora flicking past them blue-green, pink and blue. She felt strengthened by the dream, the surreal beauty of the stars and aurora, then sleep overwhelmed her again as she lay between the two sailors, wet but warm.

She found herself awake and looking at the stars and the aurora again. Soon the lifepod lifted out of the water and began to sail amid the stars, it was their own flying saucer. She looked around incredulously at the sleeping forms of the rest of pod's occupants and realized they represented the human race, the good, the bad, and the clueless, but they were all each other had. Soon they were flying amid the stars of the Milky Way galaxy light years in the future and she was looking down seeing the human race expand amid the stars, this filled her with joy. Their human race was going to survive this war, and be victorious and expand out into the stars itself. She saw the whole galaxy as a giant flying saucer-like her pod. She saw a great space-warship. It had a functionally torpedo-looking shape. She was its captain. She saw herself on the bridge looking serious, she was wearing a skin-tight spacesuit, and she was in great shape. Then she took off her helmet, and her hair was short in a pixie cut. Her eye makeup was fabulous. She was talking to this group of young brave and handsome officers on the ship about something. Then she turned and looked at herself, and Pamela-in-the-future saluted Pamela in the cold wet life pod. Then she saw herself knocking on a great silver door, and it opened and there was blinding light.

Pamela suddenly was awakened by screams, something was now blocking the stars in the hatchway. Chief Gordo and Stan awoke and sprang into action, the turned on flashlights and saw to their horror a tentacle of something like an octopus was wrapped around Eloise's arm. Pamela grabbed a flashlight and turned the beam on the hatchway and saw an enormous single eye staring back at her, whose pupil contracted when the flashlight hit. The Chief and Stanny, with a cloud of sailor's curses, were attacking the tentacle with an axe and the retractable rod and suddenly it was severed and withdrawn. The massive eye had disappeared from the hatchway and stars were visible again. Eloise was screaming in agony as Gordon tried to peel the remains of the tentacle off her. It was covered with sucker disks but each disk had six catlike claws that had sunk into her flesh. Chief Gordon pulled them all out and washed the wound with rubbing alcohol, as Pamela put her bra and wet clothes back on, and kept watch while Stanny helped Chief. She kept her hand on her gun now. Eloise's arm was a bloody mess. Finally, with the chief giving her more morphine, the pod grew quiet and, its occupants lay awake fearfully until dawn.

Dawn, so longed for, came brilliantly. The sky was a deep sad blue.

"Hey! You didn't empty the bucket after you used it! YOU DUMB SHIT!" It was Carl; he was sitting up glaring at Ethan. Who looked back at him in disdain.

"You can't prove it was me!" growled Ethan.

"Yes I can, your shit smells worse than anybody else's on this boat!"

"Yea, and I saw him use the bucket this morning!" said Stanny rising "FUCKHEAD!" he added glaring at Ethan.

Pamela wearily rose, *Oh God, now what?* she struggled groggily to understand what they were squabbling about. Finally, she stood unsteadily in the wind.

"Ethan you are SO on report for your conduct on this boat..." said Pamela seething, pointing a delicate finger at him. "When we get rescued, I am going to have you court-martialed!" *Mental log entry, the affair of the shit bucket.*

"I am going to report your conduct on this boat BITCH, you run this place like your own private dictatorship! Nobody elected you!"

"YOU STOW THAT SHIT!" yelled the Chief, waving his fist at Ethan. "AND DUMP YOUR OWN SHIT BUCKET! NOW!" Stanny moved closer to Ethan with a murderous look in his eye.

"I AM GOING TO TELL THE WHOLE WORLD ABOUT THIS FASCIST DICTATORSHIP!" said Ethan rising and dumping the bucket over the side. They all watched him carefully, to see if could do so efficiently. In the pod sheer hatred was now so thick, it weighed down even the air. Ethan then turned back from washing out the bucket in the sea and glared at Pamela.

"I will report all of you," he hissed.

*A lost man* thought Pamela sadly. *Lost at sea.*

"You go right ahead and report all of this shit Ethan - make my millennium," said Pamela coolly. "And by the way, you can chew those funny medical cigarettes of yours, if they've gotten too soggy to smoke. It might put you in a better mood..." The Chief looked at her, caught her eyes, and shook his head, as Pamela was going to continue with her list of ironies. She saw his look, nodded, and fell silent. *My quick tongue has always gotten me in trouble, one way or the other,* she thought as she tried to calm herself. Ethan lay down and turned his face away from everyone.

Pamela sadly turned and looked out the hatchway. She froze in astonishment. What she suddenly saw now, and recognized, was even more horrifying than the terror of the middle of the night, or the grim contents of the pod the day before.

As far as the eye could see under a calm, cold, blue sky the surface of the ocean was covered with dead grey aliens, Greys, bobbing lifelessly in the water. She was stricken with stupefying horror and turned speechless to look inside the pod. Megan was trying to rouse Eloise. It was a futile effort, it became evident. Megan cried silently as the Chief reached over and checked the pulse on Eloise's wrist and throat.

354

"Skipper, could you come here please and double-check this woman's pulse," he said quietly. Pamela numbly reached over and sadly felt for a pulse, felt only cold inert flesh. She then pointed mutely out the hatchway.

"Oh my God Skipper! Look at what's in the water! Exclaimed Stanny as he noticed the scene outside on calm ocean. Everyone was now looking. Carl Levy rose and looked wide eyed at the scene,

"We didn't just win a victory... It was a massacre" said Carl in horrified astonishment. Megan looked up from poor Eloise and covered her mouth with her hand in wide-eyed shock.

" You started this war!" cried Ethan rising and looking around as he burst into tears. "Is this what you wanted?" Pam's shock was instantly replaced by burning rage.

" I DIDN'T WANT THIS YOU MOTHERFUCKER! THEY SANK OUR SHIP! THEY KILLED MILLIONS AT MORNINGSTAR!" screamed Pamela. She turned and looked at the alien bodies, whitish grey and floating limply everywhere, most were naked, some wore silver garments and equipment belts. "This is what a war looks like! I suppose you didn't notice the bodies of our own people floating in the ocean the other day! No! You were too busy sucking on your whiskey bottle!"

" It seems so disproportionate," said Carl in horrified awe.

"War is never proportionate," said Pamela bitterly, remembering her Grandmother fighting the SS with the Red partisans in the Ukraine in WWII, while looking out at the floating masses of death. This memory steeled her. *Better to be pissed off, than pissed on,* she thought.

"It is totally disproportionate! This is mass murder," wept Ethan. Pamela snapped at this and fell apart.

"I WARNED THEM! I WARNED THEM THAT IF THEY STAYED THEY WOULD BE DESTROYED! I WARNED THEM, I WARNED THEM!" wailed Pamela now crying. "THIS IS NOT MY FAULT!" she screamed. IT'S THEIR OWN

FUCKING FAULT! Chief Gordon reached up and took her trembling hand gently.

"Skipper, you got to get a grip..." he said firmly, "We got to get that poor woman's body over the side, and say some words over her." She looked down at him looking at her calmly. She nodded trembling. Wiped her face. They silently tied weights on her body, weights brought over from the other pod of the day before, by the chief for this very purpose. *Gordo knew she wouldn't last much longer - Good planning, Chief.* And with that, Stanny and the Chief pulled her body up the hatchway. *Distraction, how sweet.*

"Dear Lord, please take our fellow news person, who has served as well as possible in this crisis." she wept," and please take all these other unfortunate children of yours also who are floating around us!" She then helped the sailors push her body over the side. It sank quickly beneath the now green water. Pamela looked away. *One way or another the sea wanted her,* she thought sadly. *God, please let us be rescued soon, I don't think I can handle this much longer...,* she thought desperately. All she could think of now was death. It almost seemed kind to her now. Like the sea, beckoning. But then she remembered seeing herself on the bridge of the spaceship, she was the Captain.

*I am going to believe that is somehow going to be all true, clingy spacesuit, great eye makeup, everything.* She made a decision to hope.

Her thoughts were abruptly interrupted by a sharp sonic boom, followed by the roar of a distant jet fighter.

"Chief! Load the radar chaff flare and fire it! she instantly exclaimed, looking widely up in the sky for a sign of the plane that was making the noise. The Chief sprang into action and fumbled with the flare gun, loading the radar chaff shell. Raised it on his long arm high above the boat and fired it straight up. The flare rose high in the clear blue sky and exploded into sparkling glitter. "There it is, way over there!" She pointed at a small grey speck far away in the sky.

"Gordy, Should we fire a regular flare?" she asked as he stared at the faraway plane. The Chief reacted by methodically loading a regular flare, then he stopped and stared off into the sky. He turned with his face a mask of terror.

*"GET DOWN ! ITS AN ALIEN!" he bellowed. ITS COMING OUR WAY!"*

Pamela gasped a prayer and ducked down. She pulled out her snub nose and made sure it was loaded. *The last bullet is for me , she thought calmly, under the chin, straight up.* Then she saw it out the hatchway,  a dull eyeless silver saucer plowing along at what seemed like 500 knots  from the South at about  1000 feet. She braced herself for a proton beam strike on the pod. *Oh Lord..* she began to pray mentally.

Suddenly Ethan sprang up in the hatchway waving his coat.

"GET DOWN! They'll KILL US!" Pamela yelled. She had her gun raised at him. "GET DOWN OR I'LL SHOOT!" Ethan waved his jacket. She fired just as the Chief and Stanny pulled him down like a rag doll and began pummeling him relentless with their fists. He was screaming.

"SHE SHOT ME! SHE SHOT ME!"  he wailed as the saucer flew nearby  with a dull vibration in the air.  Ethan was making muffled animal noises as the pummeling continued with the Chief holding his hand over Ethan's mouth. Pamela wheeled with her gun raised tracking the saucer. *A single bullet has brought down a saucer before,*  she thought with determination. *I'll wait till it gets close and try and hit the  EM drives on its  underside.* But instead of vaporizing them or wheeling around the saucer bore on at high speed apparently not noticing them.  It soon became apparent why the saucer had paid so little attention to them. The Chief rose and grabbed the flare gun frantically and pointed it straight up and fired a red flare.

"GORDY!  WHAT ARE YOU DOING!" she yelled as she wheeled to face him but his face was now  just one big grin, and he then pulled her down with her with a long powerful arm to the bottom me of the pad.  She saw Stanny delivering one last punch to  Ethan's face as five US NAVY F-18 Super-Hornets flew over from  the South on full afterburner.

The whole life pod seemed ready to come apart as a deafening sonic boom shook the life pod and it seemed to leave the water completely and crash down into it again. The wonderful smell of burned jet fuel filled the

357

pod. A wave of green water poured into the pod as Pamela realized her hearing was temporarily gone, and only recovered with buzzing noises and then finally voices as she raised her head to see the fighters chasing after the saucer in a cloud of jet fuel smoke and bright flaming exhaust, and shock diamonds from the afterburners.   Everyone was cheering and shouting.  Chief Gordon swept her up in his long strong  arms and hugged her as she put her gun carefully back in its plastic bag for another day, and her hearing returned.

"Do you think one of them saw the flare?" she asked looking after them.

"Yeah they saw it. I looked over and saw them coming after that saucer and fired while they were still a mile away, then I saw the shock waves hitting the ocean surface behind them, they were all doing Mach 2 at least, so I figured we better all get our asses down as deep in this boat as possible."

They looked at the northern horizon, pensively. Then suddenly a lone F-18 appeared and flew over them wagging its wings and thunderously fired a burst of  yellow tracers into the sea.

"Good Job Gordy!" exclaimed Pamela laughing.  They gagged and tied up Ethan, who wept profusely and seemed to have lost his mind. Pamela's lone bullet had apparently  shot off his earing, causing  Ethan great pain but little injury. Soon a sleek and powerful Navy P-3 Orion  four engine turboprop roared  over and dropped flares and wagged its wings at them. Everyone but Ethan was waving and cheering back.  Megan and Carl both lunged over the center of the pod and began hugging her.

****

"Number 4 has failed me utterly!" cried out Sadok Sar. "Where is he?"

"His ship was lost my Lord, over Moscow." said one of the lesser officers fearfully.

"Number 2, you will assume command of the space forces!"

*Out of the bottom of the sea to the Moon and now commander of space forces,* thought Number 7 in wonder,  grateful he had not been chosen.

358

****

*Pamela shakily scaled the ladder to the deck of the Destroyer USS Cranston. Chief Gordon and Torpedo mate Stanfield followed, the Sun was bright but a cold wind blew.*

"Captain sir, that man we got tied up in the boat is guilty of disobeying orders in a war zone from a commanding officer on a Navy vessel, and his ass should be thrown in the Brig!" said Chief Gordon emphatically to the captain of the Cranston who looked on incredulously. Stanny nodded in vigorous agreement. "This woman Ensign here, she did a fine job as skipper of our boat sir, and me and Stanny say she should get a medal!" added the Chief.

Pamela stood in exhausted shock at this, was asked to lay down on a stretcher, and was taken by a stretcher to sick bay and a warm shower. Task Force Typhoon had lost five ships and over 2,000 men, but had achieved its mission objectives, Pamela filed her story with CNS a few days late.

****

Pamela dressed in a bathrobe and with her hair wrapped in a towel, came to the door of her Hilton Hotel suite. She had just enjoyed another long hot bath and felt like a human being again. To her surprise, Megan Strand was there. Megan smiled asked if she could come in. Pamela, slightly surprised, invited her in and closed the door. Megan produced a bottle of white wine and two glasses.

"I wanted to come up and talk with you one last time about what you did for us on the lifeboat. My flight leaves in the morning. So this was my last chance." said Megan seriously. Pamela smiled and sat on the bed. Pulled the towel off her head and began drying her hair.

"Well, Megan ..."

"Please call me Meg," said Megan quickly, popping the top of the wine bottle and pouring two glasses. She had a serious look that Pamela did not understand. She handed Pamela a glass then stood and offered a

359

toast. She had long brown hair framing a face combining attractiveness and great intelligence. She was older and slightly overweight in a curvy way. She was wearing a casual dark blue blouse and short skirt.

"To our careers as journalists! May they be very long and successful!" said Megan laughing and drank her glass in one long drink. Pamela followed suit, the wine was a slightly sweet Riesling. Megan then refilled Pamela's glass and her own.

"Now you toast..." said Megan.

"Oh..." said Pamela helplessly. Her mind was blank. "To the many stories we will file covering our victorious war effort!" said Pamela finally with an impish grin. Megan smiled and then drank her glass again quickly. She motioned to Pamela to follow. Pamela complied, the wine tasted wonderful. Only when she had emptied her glass did Pamela realize she was getting tipsy.

"Megan, I probably better not have any more tonight. I have to catch a flight back to Washington at Noon." said Pamela. Megan smiled warmly.

"Please call me Meg. I just wanted to say thank you for saving my life and the lives of everyone else on the life pod. When you swam out to that other pod full of supplies, I was so afraid that giant shark was going to come back and get you... I knew you were going to try and save Eloise ... It was the bravest thing I ever saw anyone do in my life..."

"No, Meg, I just was doing..." Megan leaned over and kissed her on the lips. Pamela greeted the kiss with a look of surprise. Megan then kissed her again. This time more deeply and passionately. Pamela found herself responding. Then broke the kiss.

"You know, I don't do this sort of thing ... anymore" said Pamela looking slightly dreamy. Megan stood back and rapidly shed her clothes. She then stood naked in front of Pamela, then leaned over and embraced her on the bed. She was voluptuously beautiful. Pamela looked at her in mild surprise as she kissed Pamela deeply.

"Don't you know, that I know everything about you?" said Megan. She then rose and untied Pamela's bathrobe, pushing it down over her bare shoulders, baring her lovely torso. She then softly kissed both Pamela's erect nipples. Pamela leaned back on the bed on her arms in pleasure.

"I have followed everything you have done since you began the Stargate story, everything. I thought 'this chick is crazy, but boy is she hot…' I envied Cassandra Chen, more than anyone on Earth."

"I thought you were married…" gasped Pamela as Megan began kissing her neck.

"Yes, but this war, and, you know Pammy, in a war, anyone more than a hundred miles from their spouse in a war, is single…" she kissed Pamela passionately. Pamela now wound her arms around Megan tightly and wiggled out of her bathrobe. "So I'm not married, not tonight," said Megan licking her lips between sucking kisses. "Tonight I am just a sophomore back at Brown University, and you are just a freshman girl just out of high school."

****

Pamela awoke in the bed, naked and alone. Megan was gone.

"Alone in the morning, just like always," she said to herself remorsefully. *"Why can't my life be simple, like a normal person's. Why couldn't I just have been a suburban housewife, back in Cleveland? With a yard with a white picket fence? A husband who loves me, children…Why couldn't I just be back in the hospital, paralyzed from the waist down again?"* She cringed at her own thoughts and wiped her eyes. She arose and found her bathrobe and put it on, looked at the clock. She still had a few hours to get to the airport. *I wonder how Cassie is doing?* This last thought made her happy because she sensed Cassandra was happy someplace.

She checked her email and found to her delight that Michael had broken his long silence. The Message read:

Dear Pamela,

Let's get married! I have wrangled a plum Navy assignment at Norfolk in Virginia for a few months for some new training. We could rent a cottage on the beach!

Love Michael XOXOXOXO

Pamela exploded into tears of joy at this message and wrote quickly back.

YES, YES, YES!!!!

I am headed back to DC! Call me there!

Love Pammy XOXOXOX OXOXOXOX

She then rushed into the bathroom and took a hot long shower, singing to herself.

****

## Chapter 8: Sitka

After a week at sea, they pulled into Crescent Bay at Sitka, Alaska, to wait for the pod of whales that Liani and Li Li belonged to. It was now late September. Dr. Renoir had become slightly more friendly after a week and a half at sea, perhaps because Cassandra was not swimming regularly with his research subjects. Perhaps it was just because staying angry with someone on the confines of a ship was just too much work. Cassandra noted a great sadness in him, especially after hearing and seeing the battle far off in the Northeast. They had sighted several more military ships as they neared Sitka, and several times jet fighters, their wings covered with missiles, overflew the ship at low altitude. Grey military jet transports were a frequent sight at high altitude moving north and south.

The weather was calm, they anchored out the bay. The Zodiac fast motor launch was winched from the deck into the water by the crew and made multiple rapid runs into the docks several miles away. The boat was very fast, with a powerful outboard engine, and made the trip in a few minutes. Cassandra mostly kept to the yacht and contented herself with snorkeling in the cold water in a wetsuit. The abundance of sea life was dazzling in the clear water. Large numbers of dolphins and seals frolicked in the water near the shoreline rocks and fed on abundant smaller fish and shrimp. Large numbers of seals sat on the rocks nearby. The diet on the ship developed some welcome variety from the deep sea fish that had been their staple during the transit from Hawaii. Above the small sea town of Sitka, to the East rose spectacular forested mountains called `The Sisters', and to the west on a small island was a dormant volcano sat called Edgecombe, its gaping crater bespeaking hellish violence in the past. Cassandra acclimated quickly to the cold still water of the bay and regularly dove in her wetsuit with only her snorkel and face mask on head, relying on her long thick hair to keep her head warm. In the clear cold water, swimming alone except for an occasional dolphin or seal, she recovered a sense of peace she had lost in the days after the sea battle to the north. Added to this was the feeling that wherever Pamela was out in the Pacific, she was now safe and sound. So Cassandra returned to the planet Pacifica that had been her sanctuary before. On one trip to the shore she had found herself staring at an aquarium tank full of crabs without flinching. It was outside a seafood restaurant by the harbor. She had stared at the large crabs in fascination, comparing them carefully to the rat-crabs of her hallucinations, noting differences and similarities as if she was a zoologist, while Mathew, who had accompanied her onshore, watched her in bemused curiosity from a distance.

One night she found herself despondent and wandering the decks late at night.

"Why am I alive? What could I possibly hope for in the future?" she asked herself. She imagined herself as an elegant wine glass, now marred with cracks. "I have started a war I can't win, and become an emotional cripple in the process..." she said to herself.

The lights of Sitka shone in the distance. The night was clear and cold, and the stars shone brightly, she had wrapped herself in a warm coat. The aurora flicked in the north, beautiful, but now a nightly occurrence.

She stood at the deck railing looking at the dark water. The thought occurred to her to simply jump in, sink, and end the whole drama. But she resisted it.

"No, I will see this life through," she said to herself. "I am alive for a reason, I will find out what it is and accomplish it..." Suddenly, as if in response, the aurora flared brightly and turned pink, and seemed to reach across the sky from the north and turn a beautiful magenta above her.

"Oh, you like that attitude..." she said aloud, and a smile came to her face. Then she sensed someone was near her and turned and saw an unfamiliar woman standing on the deck, she was attractive with light brown hair parted in the middle. Cassandra stared at her in surprise. *You're not Lauren Hill, at least,* she thought, *so you're probably not a hallucination.*

"So, who are you?" asked Cassandra quietly.

" A friend of a friend," replied the woman.

"But you have a name, then?" asked Cassandra nervously.

"Call me Semjase," said the woman smiling. "Come with me, I can help you." The women offered Cassandra her hand. Cassandra surprised

366

herself and reached out and took the woman's hand. It was warm. Suddenly they were on Semjase's spaceship in orbit. Cassandra let go of Semjases's hand in surprise and looked around . Sanjeed the medical technician, was standing there and bowed his head slightly in greeting. Tam was sitting at the controls of the ship and looked at Cassandra with amusement.

"Let us look at your back, Sanjeed here can help with the scaring there. We are Pleiadian and have treatments for this type of injury." said Semjase smiling, and gesturing to Sanjeed, who smiled dutifully.

"Tam, please monitor the sensor panel, while she is being treated." said Semjase with a slight smile and edge in her voice. "Could you take off your coat and top, so we can look at your back. We don't have a lot of time, only one orbit of 90 minutes."

Cassandra, looked at him in bewilderment, then, took off her warm coat and then her blouse and bra, covering her breasts with her arms, and then turned to show them her back, pulling up her long black hair with one arm.

"You are extraterrestrials then, aren't you?" said Cassandra quietly. "This happened to my back because of some different extraterrestrials who have come here." Sanjeed touched her back gently, running his hands over her scars, she sensed sorrow and horror from him, and desire to help, she felt suddenly reassured.

"Please lay down on your stomach on this table." said Semjase gently. She was beside her motioning to a small medical table. Cassandra, feeling like she was in a dream, stepped over to the table and lay down on it. "Put your arms above your head please and please relax your back." The table was smooth and seemed warm to her breasts as she lay still. She heard a quiet whirring sound and sensed a warm comfortable feeling like a massage on her back, and around to her side ribs where the burning high voltage wire had wrapped around her partially when they were flogging her with it at Devil's Mesa. Now she sensed a wonderful healing feeling. She felt the one named Sanjeed was moving a cylindrical object over the skin of her back and it was creating a feeling of soothing warmth.

Semjase's, smiling face appeared beside her head.

"We are smoothing out the scar tissue so it will be smooth with rest of your skin," said Semjase looking at her back as she talked. "And it is the same color, but you must avoid direct sunlight on your back because the scar tissue is still there and is still sensitive to ultra-violet. We are using electromagnetic waves at a special frequency that make the cells let go of each other and move easily and mix and repair themselves, so the skin becomes plastic and can lie smooth." said Semjase. "Can you tell things are better?"

"Yes it does feel better," said Cassandra. *This is a wonderful dream, what can I do but flow along with it?*

"Well we are very sorry this happened to you, but we have tried to make things better for you."

"Thank you..." said Cassandra in wonderment.

"Now we are soon coming around in free orbit over the place where we met, and we will have to send you back to your vessel. I wish we could talk more but as you know, the situation at your planet is dangerous, and we must limit ourselves to this one free orbit."

Casandra nodded and looked at the woman in amazement. Cassandra felt the object touching her back be withdrawn. She back felt soothed and relaxed.

"Sanjeed has finished the treatment. Now you must put your garments back on so I can send you back." said Semjase hurriedly. Cassandra sat up on the table and replaced her bra and blouse and finally put on her coat. She reached over to Sanjeed's hand and shook it. He looked at her and smiled.

"Thank you for helping, my back feels much better," said Cassandra. She slid off the table to the deck of the spaceship. "I also have some more questions..." said Cassandra.

"OK, now take my hand," said Semjase looking distracted. Cassandra numbly offered her hand. Semjase took it, seemed to close her eyes in

368

concentration and suddenly Cassandra was standing on the deck of the Mirage in a cold breeze again. She thought she saw Semjase for in instant beside her but then she was gone. The aurora flickered brightly above Cassandra's head in the sky and then retreated  back to the Northern sky. She looked around and then down at the dark water at a splashing noise. Several dolphins were poking their heads out of the water and watching her, a seal joined then and barked at her playfully.  She turned in bewilderment and found herself alone on the deck. *I must have fallen asleep standing at the railing,* she thought in amazement. She felt very weary and went down to her cabin and fell into her bunk and slept dreamlessly until morning.

In the morning she went for her customary swim in her wetsuit. She then went in the swim locker area in the ship and washed the salt water off herself in the warm shower. That was when she discovered the scars on her back had disappeared.

She stood in the shower, running her hands over her back in astonishment. The skin of her back was now as smooth as silk. She hastily toweled off and went back to her cabin, where she stood topless next to a mirror holding a hand mirror and painstakingly examined her now clear smooth bronze colored back, all the while shaking her head in amazement. Tears came to her eyes.

"I got abducted by aliens, and they fixed my back..." she gasped in astonishment. She then looked at her wrist holding the mirror. The traces of scars from when she had slashed them, still remained. The aliens had missed them.   Cassandra nodded to herself sat down on her bunk, wept and uttered a prayer of thanks. *Now I am whole again...*she thought, *at least physically.* She rubbed her back again, felt its smoothness, rubbed the only partly erased scars on her wrists, the remnants after Doctor Malvik's treatments, felt their roughness.  She put on her bra and French tee shirt. *They repaired what others did to me, leaving only what I have done to myself.* She stood and looked in the mirror again.

"What does this mean?" she asked herself, looking now in the mirror and smoothing her hair. "It means I am a remarkable person, to whom both remarkably bad,  and remarkably good,  things happen...  That means I have remarkable responsibilities..." She pondered this as she looked in her own large dark eyes.

"It means I must rejoin the war effort soon," she said to herself in the mirror. But then a thought came suddenly and urgently. *No! Not yet, it's not time yet!* she shook her head and eyes filled with tears, bewildered at where the thought came from. *But Why? Why? I want to help!*

She was bursting to tell someone on the ship about what had happened to her. But instead, she stayed in her cabin until the feeling passed. *Let us keep this simple for now. Next, I will be telling people who I really am, and this ship could start feeling really tiny if that happens.* She decided to go for another swim after enjoying a simple breakfast in the galley. She encountered Mathew, while dressed in her wetsuit and holding her snorkeling gear, in the passageway on the ship. He looked worried.

"What is wrong Mathew?" she asked him.

"Oh nothing , but there is good news, we now hear the pod of whales nearby. They all made the crossing from Hawaii apparently." Her heart leaped at this news. *Liani and Li Li!*

"Oh that's wonderful news!" she said and then hugged him. She rushed off eagerly to get into the water. It was a beautiful crisp cool day with a light wind. Small waves filled the harbor. She paused at the stern of the ship by the ladder to the water and put on her snorkeling mask, and looked out to sea happily. The whole scene was happy and bright to her. The French Flag fluttered merrily from its spear pointed mast on the stern of the ship. The fast Zodiac boat bobbed in the low waves on its rope tying it to the stern. *Thank you for this beautiful day!* she thought. *Maybe if I get in the water, I will hear their calls!* She donned her swim fins and mask and snorkel and slid down the aluminum ladder into the cold water. She swam back and forth under the water beside the Mirage, thinking of the wide oceans on the planet of peace called Pacifica. Then she suddenly returned in her thoughts to Mathew's worried look. *Something is wrong.* She suddenly noticed that no dolphins or seals, her usual company in the sea, had appeared. *The sea is silent. Why is the sea so silent!?* She turned and swam back to the ship, clambered quickly up the ladder to the deck and quickly doffed her swimming fins and pushed her swim mask back on her head. She quickly doused herself off from seawater on the deck. She looked around, no one was on the deck. On the rocks, all the seals sat silently as if waiting for something. A deep chill of fear suddenly ran through her. *The sonar room!*

She ran down the passageway to the sonar room. It was crowded with the crew. Dr. Renoir stood in the middle of the room looking grim. Genevieve at his side was clinging to his arm and looked in anguish at Cassandra as she entered. In the silence, Cassandra heard strange whale noises coming from the speaker. Mathew was wearing his headphones and staring intently at the computer screens.

"It is the one named Liani, she is making distress calls," said Mathew soberly. "By stereo-sonic ranging, she is three, maybe four kilometers from here." Then, across the speakers, came a strange loud solitary click. *Oh my God! What was that?* Thought Cassandra fearfully.

"Orcas! Flesh eaters! " exclaimed Mathew looking at the screens . "That was their ranging click!" At this Doctor, Renoir and the others walked quickly out of the sonar room. *Liani , Li Li! No! NO!* She thought as she followed them helplessly. They were all on the outside of the bridge. Everyone looked grim as binoculars were passed out. Doctor Renoir scanned the sea to the West pointed mutely at what looked like an area of choppy white water. Creol, the older sailor, sadly passed Cassandra a pair of binoculars, she pressed them to her now tear-filled eyes and blinked. Her heart sank into an abyss as she saw in the middle of the white turbulent water the large mass of a humpback whale, and on it back a baby whale frantically trying to stay out of the water. Then, around them circled the black fins of killer whales circling in a pack. She handed the binocular back to Creol wordlessly, and he took them and resumed his own sad observations. Others of the crew departed and went about their duties.

"It is the drama of life and death in the sea," commented Doctor Renoir sadly as he watched the circle of orcas tighten around the helpless mother whale and her calf. "We are here to observe, we cannot interfere. It is the way of the sea," continued Renoir." This is why, in our studies, we normally never give our whales names," he said soberly as he suddenly

371

looked away from his binoculars and looked to see Cassandra's reaction. Suddenly the silence was interrupted by the mighty roar of the engine of the Zodiac, and Renoir and the rest of the crew watched in amazement as the Cassandra waving the spear mounted flag of France roared past the prow of the Mirage wearing her wetsuit and diving mask pushed back on her head like a helmet. Her thick, long black hair streaming in the wind. She was tearing across the choppy waters of Crescent bay with the Zodiac leaving the water as it hit the waves. She was headed straight for the patch of white water containing Liani and Li Li.

Cassandra pushed the throttle forward as far as she dared. She then pulled out her flashing steel diving knife and pinned the French flag to the steering wheel of the Zodiac as she cut the flag from the spear topped pole. Then she replaced the flag with her black skull and crossbones scarf tied onto the top fastening rope.

"I christen this ship the Black Swan!" she cried to the wind as, she raised the black pirate flag on its spear to the sky, and now being able to concentrate on steering the high-speed boat in the choppy water, she pushed the throttle forward as far as it would, go. The boat was careening through the waves, the bronze spinning propeller singing as it left the water on each bounce into the air. *YES! MY SINGING SWORD!*

"THAT'S RIGHT YOU BASTARDS! THIS IS THE SOUND OF DEATH COMING FOR YOU!" Cassandra yelled." IT IS THE SOUND OF THE BLACK SWAN COMING TO TEAR YOU TO PIECES IF YOU DON"T GET OUT OF HERE, NOW!" she screamed into the wind. She was nearing the white water, she could see clearly now the tall black fins moving in a circle around the mother whale and her baby. She noted with satisfaction the circling motion stop and disintegrate into frantic milling around in the water! The sight filled her with fierce joy.

"THAT'S RIGHT! BONNY JONES, THE PIRATE QUEEN HAS ARRIVED!" Suddenly the black fins broke into a mob, scattering in confusion, going in every direction as the orcas fled in apparent panic. She steered the boat to the side, skidding across the water in a wide circle around Liani and Li Li, whom she recognized joyously by the marks on their flukes. She slowed the boat abruptly to a trolling speed as she shot past them, to avoid terrifying them. The Orcas had disappeared. *Hah! You are intelligent after all!* Cassandra did one slow circle around the two whales and noted that the whale calf had slid off its mothers back into the sea again. After idling in the water for several minutes, Cassandra turned off the boat engine and threw out a sea anchor. Then she donned her face mask, snorkel , and fins. Then, grasping the spear mounted flag, she jumped into the cold water near the obviously shocked whales.

"Liani , Li Li, it's me, Cassandra," she said under water. The whales seemed to move closer to her. She pulled out her bright-bladed diving knife and banged it several times on the aluminum spear bearing her black pirate flag, now streaming under water. After what seemed like an eternity, a large bull orca approached her out of the underwater dimness. She tapped her knife blade on the flag shaft, making a metallic ring and flashed it in the sunlight underwater. *Yes. Think it over!* she thought as the bull orca slowly turned and seemed to be eyeing her. She braced the spear against her side in case the orca decided to make a run at her. But he simply moved on majestically into the dim depths. *Yes, go find something else to eat that is less trouble!* She thought emphatically. The male orca did not reappear after several minutes. She bobbed to the surface and cast the spear into the boat. Then feeling that the Orcas had departed for good, she swam next to Liani and stroked her and then moved close to Li Li. *This day you live, child.* After a while, they swam away to the West and she was left alone with her thoughts in the deep blue sea. *Thus ends Pacifica, my beautiful little world where nothing bad happens,* thought Cassandra sadly. *Time to return to planet Earth.*

It was early afternoon when she pulled the Zodiac up to the Mirage. She held her head high in defiance. She had washed the French Flag carefully and replaced it on its staff, so it was wet but bright like before. Creol , looking sober and slightly embarrassed, caught the mooring rope as she tossed it and helped her up the ladder to the deck. She handed him the French flag on it staff and he mutely replaced it. The ship was silent. She went down to the locker room and showered and donned her customary bra, French tee shirt, and Levi trousers and went to her cabin. She decided to pack her things. *I think my voyage on the Mirage is over.* Then she did her makeup perfectly and showed up for dinner. *Everyone needs their say about today's events. I will not hide from this.*

Dinner was coldly cordial to her surprise, with the Doctor, Genève, Mathew and the first mate, all sitting silently. She gratefully poured herself some white wine and sipped it quietly. She tried her best to keep her face solemn. The dinner was fresh shrimp with vegetables and pasta, all in a delicately flavored sauce. *A tasty last supper.*

Finally, after everyone had eaten. She cleared her throat and took a sip of wine, then spoke.

"I want to thank you for your hospitality on the Mirage, Dr. and Madam Renoir, but now that we have made landfall here in Alaska, I think I should depart," Genève smiled graciously. Mathew smiled warmly. The first mate looked warily at Dr. Renoir. Finally, Renoir spoke.

"What you have done today, Jian is inexcusable. You have destroyed an entire summer's research!" he said angrily. Cassandra motioned for the wine and poured herself a new glass as he said this. She then took a sip, while she thought of how to respond. Then, looked at him squarely with a delicate frown.

"I am sorry Doctor Renoir," she began. "But surely at this point in this war, the fact that big fish eat little fish in this cosmos, can hardly be considered a major scientific discovery. Oui?"

Renoir responded by throwing down his napkin on the table, rising , and leaving the dining room in an angry huff. *Certainly civilized, and better than being keelhauled,* she thought with some amusement. The first mate rose and departed after Renoir. She thought she saw a twinkle in his eye as he did so. She rose and bid Genève and Mathew good night. Their eyes were both downcast, and they looked torn. Cassandra went back to her cabin and sat sadly watching the sunset out her cabin window as she lay on her bed. *So, there was a cost. But if I had let the child die, I would have never forgiven myself.* She thought.

Later, she walked the deck alone at the last glow of twilight. She looked in vain in the south for the southern cross and golden brilliance of Alpha Centauri, around which orbited her own little blue planet of Pacifica. But she realized they were too far north to see it. The aurora was dancing in the north amid the stars and this comforted her. She imagined herself belly dancing amid the northern lights, with sparkling jewels like stars on her bracelets and bra, then breaking into a gentle hula.

She noticed suddenly that Mathew was standing next to her, leaning on the railing.

"Oh," she said in surprise.

"You must forgive my father and mother, for them, their scientific detachment is a sacred thing," he said with a smile. "Actually, my father's anger was very mild. I think everyone looked upon what you did with admiration, grudging admiration, but admiration none the less. We were relieved that you saved the little child of the sea and the fact that we beat our chests in scholarly indignation, well, that is only to be expected."

Cassandra sighed with relief at hearing this.

"Oh, that makes me feel so much better," she said embracing his muscular arm. "I am used to doing things that I believe are right, and then causing a train wreck. I just can't be an innocent bystander in life. I see things happening and I join the battle, and that makes me guilty sometimes. I have never been accused of being cowardly or indifferent."

"I am sorry you are leaving. You really did brighten the voyage for my father and the rest of us, even if he seemed to regard your antics as an annoyance. You provided, a lovely distraction from the drama of the sea when we needed it."

"Oh, that's very sweet. I wish I could stay too. But after today, I have to get back on shore and resume my life. I can't remain lost at sea." She hugged his arm again and turned to him, looking him in his gentle blue eyes and then kissed him on the lips. They both laughed after this.

"I do have a fine bottle of champagne in my cabin, which I had been saving for some auspicious moment, such as the last night on the Mirage of an honored, but mutinous, guest." She looked at him and barely suppressed a laugh.

"But of course," she said, and they merrily walked down to his cabin. She sat on his bed as he pulled the bottle out his small refrigerator. "Lorraine

Vineyards 1959," he said with a smile, holding up the bottle for her. "A very good year they say." He produced two elegant blue glasses and popped the cork and poured, then sat down beside her. After several toasts, she began kissing him all over.

Later as they relaxed in bed naked together. She emptied the bottle of champagne into her elegant blue glass.

"Thank you for being so relaxed and gentle with me. I haven't been with a man in a long time," she said after emptying her glass. He held her closely in his muscular swimmer's arms.

"Think nothing of it. The thanks are mine. I have been pretty much stuck on this boat since April."

"How is that?" she asked.

"Oh, my mother pleaded with me to come on this voyage for my father's sake. My girlfriend refused to come along. It was a big mess. But, you must ask why does a scientist like my father go out to study whales, when the world is at war with aliens from outer space? He does it to escape. You see the sea has always been his mistress, and he has escaped into her arms," said Mathew sadly shaking his head. "That and my father is convinced this war is suicide for the human race, and he and my mother were afraid that I would join the armed forces. I am there only son. You see France has done badly in most of its wars, so we French have a different attitude about war than Americans."

"What do you think. I mean, about this war?" she asked.

"Oh, like most French people I think we have no choice but to fight! I mean, they have come here 100 parsecs, not the other way around, yes? Also, we remember the Nazi occupation. So I wanted to join the French army and be in an antiaircraft regiment. But I made the mistake of saying so in my father's house." laughed Mathew. "So off to sea we went."

Cassandra, paused, afraid to say anything else that might reveal her identity. *I want so much to speak freely*, she thought, *but I cannot.*

"Oh, and you might like to see this ," said Mathew. "I was going to show you these before you left." He reached over with a mischievous smile and pulled out a plastic sack full of small electronic parts and wires.

"Some people from the French national intelligence came and put these listening devices in your cabin, while you were away visiting Pearl Harbor. It was some Horse's ass Colonel named Duvalier, he told us it was our patriotic duty to cooperate in this. But I am the master of electronics on this boat, so I jammed them with interference while we were in port and ripped them all out when we put out to sea."

She looked at the bag full of listening devices in astonishment. Put her hand over her face.

"You know who I am then," she said in embarrassment, snuggling deeper into his arms.

"Of course, I figured it out from your pictures after Duvalier left, but your finding sanctuary here on the Mirage at sea, it is very French. Because of our history, because it is so complex, many people in French history have tried to lose themselves, lose their identity, and find asylum someplace, join the Foreign Legion or something. But you must know that you are considered a great heroine in France and every Frenchman adores you. They know you speak French, and were a summer student in Paris." He paused and looked puzzled.

"In fact, one of your greatest admirer's is my second cousin. Claude Gavin, that is very strange."

"Why is that strange?" she asked.

"Oh, because he is crazy." laughed Mathew. "It is actually very sad, he graduated from the Ecole Polytechnic as an electrical engineer and seemed to have bright future. Then he went to work for the government in the Vaucluse, which is a mountainous region in France where we kept all our nuclear weapons. They have big underground facilities there. But after being gone for two years he returned, with no explanation, to his parent's home in Paris and was completely changed. He barely spoke, and when anyone asked where he had been or what he had been working on

377

for the previous two years, he would get this terrible look of horror on his face and be unable to speak for about an hour. It was terrible because it was as if the government had done something to his mind, to prevent him from remembering. But, he got disability checks from the government and helped in his family's pastry shop in Paris. It is near the Cathedral on the Mont de Sacre' Cour, so it gets a lot of business. So the tragedy was lessened."

"Oh, I spent part of my summer in Paris in a youth hostel on the Mont de Sacre' Cour. You could see all of Paris from it," said Cassandra happily. "That was such a pleasant time. The Cold War had ended, and the future seemed impossibly bright then."

"Perhaps you remember the shop, it is called the Le Bon Paine, it has been there forever."

"Yes," she stared off into the distance trying to remember it. "I think I do remember it. We American French students joked that it meant 'the good pain' instead of 'the good bread.' I may have even been there for a croissant or something. The good pain, it's like when a foot was injured and gets better, and you walk on it for the first time again, and it hurts, but it's a good pain because it means it is healing."

"Well the strange thing," continued Mathew, "was that my cousin, he was very quiet and would never speak about what he did for the government until he saw you on the news talking about UFO cover up after someone tried to kill you by blowing up your car. This became big news in France, partly because the French press loves American government scandals and also because this was so dramatic. And suddenly, my cousin became mesmerized by you and said that he knew that what you were saying was true. He became himself again for a few days. He didn't say anything else, but he suddenly got much better and has your picture up everyplace in the shop and where he lives."

"So, do you think he worked with aliens in the Vaucluse?" she asked, "for the French Government?" *The rascals!* she thought. *The bastards!*

"I don't know," said Mathew. "But the idea of you pursuing this scandal even when your life was threatened by being caught between different

378

factions of a secret government, makes you seem very French. And we know that you model yourself after Joan of Arc and that like her, you are consumed with your great cause."

"Some people have said that I am crazy..."

"Well so was Joan of Arc. Everyone who gets wrapped up in great cause must sacrifice part of their sanity. These things we French understand maybe better than Americans, because your history is much different." On hearing these words she wept, and smothered him with kisses and rolled over on top of him.

"So, you know who I am, but I will purchase your silence then for this last night..." she said as they embraced again.

****

Cassandra was riding a fast hydrofoil ferry up the island channels to Juneau, the Captain of the craft was an older man, an obvious veteran of many Alaskan winters and ice jams. The day was beautiful. Few people were on the boat, and the Captain seemed to be running it with only two crewmen. Cassandra stood in a windbreaker on the deck wearing dark glasses. She had managed with Manny's help to get an airline ticket from Juneau to Seattle. Airline flights were now scarce and very expensive due mostly to the diversion of all jet fuel to the Air Force and Navy, and the fact that airliners flew only during daylight, often with fighter escort.

She was looking over the railing at the beautiful mountains, which had acquired snow during the night somehow when the Captain approached her smiling. A crescent Moon, pearly white, floated in the blue sky.

"I noticed your last name is Chen, you wouldn't by chance be Cassandra Chen?" he asked, bowing his head slightly. She laughed merrily at this.

"Captain, do you know how many people there are in the world with the last name of Chen?" she laughed.

He looked embarrassed but then leaned on the railing beside her.

"Well, I am a Vietnam combat veteran, and if you were Cassandra Chen, I would say that you are a real hero for what you did, war or no war. It's an honor to have you on my boat." With that, he smiled, turned, and walked back to the main cabin of the boat.

****

## Chapter 9: The Abyss

On interstate 10 in Texas between Houston and San Antonio on a cold night with high overcast, on September 4, all traffic was blocked except for military convoys. On the dark freeway between Flatonia and Katy at regular intervals of a mile, military trailers were parked between green camouflaged wedge-nosed HVAC heavy military trucks and tankers full of caustic and highly explosive Hydrazine. Other heavy tanker trucks were full of Nitrogen Tetroxide, pure anhydrous nitric acid, that would ignite human flesh on contact. Patriot missile batteries, armed with magneto warheads and cortex fragmentation warheads had already deployed. At 100 yard intervals, the crews of quad-50 caliber anti-aircraft and quad 40-millimeter antiaircraft guns, all with magneto proximity ammunition and magnetic detection, scanned the skies warily. Carbon monoxide laser batteries had been set up at the rest areas. Above in the sky, squadrons of F-51 Griffins flew in constant NICAP or Night Combat Air Patrol.

In a military trailer, Colonel Patrick "Blue" Steel, USMC, a veteran fighter pilot and astronaut veteran of the Sepulveda Asteroid interception, stood in his close-fitting space suit covered with blue-black carbon-fiber armor-fabric holding his Mercury style space helmet of titanium alloy, also painted blue-black, and stared out at the 20 other astronauts crowded into the trailer, all similarly garbed and holding their helmets. His face was grim.

"The goal of tonight's operation, code named Bannockburn," began Steel, "is to seize and hold an orbital position in Low-Earth-Orbit. You have all been trained extensively for this operation in the last weeks in space simulators. The Human Alliance is now carrying the war to the enemy in space." They would be launched in arrow-head shaped, Super-Hellcat, trans-atmospheric fighters, developed and flown in space under the latter stages of the UFO cover-up. They would be launched by the mobile Titan II launchers dispersed along this highway, which are now being fueled. "After launch, we will form up our squadron in space, in orbit, and be joined by MIG 100 TAV fighters, launched by the Russians on converted SS-18 launchers as well as orbital refueling tanks and armored habitats orbited by both us and the Russians. The goal of the operation is to establish and maintain a position in space at all costs. We of the first wave will be expected to stay up for 25 orbits each, before being relieved; however, relief from the second wave may not arrive on time, depending on alien counterattacks in which case we will simply hold and fight in space until relieved. We expect this to be an intense combat operation with high casualties. So, we are going to chew their asses and take some too." Blue scanned the room, most the men were former Shuttle astronauts that he knew. Most of them had been in space numerous times. Some like "Roy" Rodgers and Robert Forrester were veterans of space combat with the Greys. He felt filled with pride as scanned the lean, hard faces staring back at him. Each face encircled by an alloy neck ring on their spacesuits where their helmets attached. "It goes without saying gentlemen, that failure is not an option on this operation," said Steel stabbing the air for emphasis. Everyone knew he had basically returned from the dead, after flying the 'Doomsday Special ' during the Sepulveda Asteroid intercept. "We will begin launching in 30 minutes." He looked at his watch on the wrist of his space suit, looked back at the men's faces.

"Any questions?"

There was silence in the trailer.

"I'll see you men in space then," said Blue, and snapped a salute as all the men stood at attention and returned the salute. He then left the trailer and marched out under the overcast sky, lit dully by the lights of Houston in the distance. The Moon had set shortly after sundown. The air was cold, but blue was enjoying it as he marched up to the Humvee that would take him straight to his mobile erector- launcher. Soon he was flying down the dark highway to his launcher. He put on his helmet and turned the portable air-conditioning unit for his spacesuit on high as he studied a picture of Alicia and their son in his gloved hand.

****

At 100,000 feet and moving at Mach 5, Tiger Forrester sat in the cockpit of his F-71 Scorpion fighter and looked at the stars shining brightly above him. The curvature of the dark Earth below him was clearly visible, along with green airglow on the horizon. Except for the fact that he had to fly the airplane, he felt like an astronaut. But below him were, he knew,

382

numerous night combat dogfights. The Air Force was now mounting a maximum sustained effort to regain the night sky from the Greys over the CONUS or Continental U.S., flying now thousands of sorties. Gray losses had mounted, as well as their own. He had been moved from flying an F-51 Griffin now to an F-71 Scorpion, a long glossy black, needle shaped aircraft, with two enormous turbo-scram jets boosting it through the sky so high and fast that orbit seemed only a few inches above his cockpit. He was waiting for any grey craft rising from the battles at lower altitude. He now had four kills in this war, one more and he would be considered an ace.

Suddenly he received a radio alert.

"Tiger this is Topcat, descend to 80,000 feet and engage possible bogey over South Texas, come to bearing O 5 4 Niner..."

"Rodger Tiger copies," he responded, his whole body tensing as he pushed the nose down and armed his cannon and missiles. "Down into the soup I go," he muttered as the atmospheric density rose dramatically. He knew the sonic boom he would soon be inflicting on those below would be horrific. "I hope everyone taped their windows." he muttered, referring to the now standard practice of putting clear plastic tape on household windows to prevent cuts from shattered glass. He was scanning his radar screen for contact, the magneto sensor was already picking up a magnetic source. *They need strong pulsating magnetism to make anti-gravity, which tells everyone where they are. If I was a grey, I would try to put my ship into a simple aerodynamic glide just to be stealthy.* But if the Greys had thought of it this tactic, he had never heard of it. His chief worry was that the grey ship would detect him coming and simply dart straight upwards and escape. Nothing the humans had, aside from a captured "Foxtrot" saucer, could match the climb rate of a fleeing grey ship, *yet*, he thought. He descended down through a thin high overcast. Suddenly his keen eyes saw a faint glow due to the grey's antigravity drives breaking down the air at high altitude. *Corona!* he thought. He was closing rapidly on the grey craft just 10 kilometers ahead of him and apparently not seeing him. He picked a super-ARAM missile from his list weapons and armed it. It would be ejected by a cannon style launcher through the hypersonic shock envelope enclosing his craft and then ignite its engine and deploy control fins. He waited for the targeting computer to produce a solution for the intercept, and reflexively pushed the fire control button on his control stick as soon as the solution light appeared. The missile departed with a bright blue flash that he tried to avert his eyes from and then watched out the cockpit as the missile raced away. He then glanced at the head-up display in front of him as the missile closed on the magnetic source, he then saw the missile merge with the target symbol and saw a bright flash in the sky below lighting up the overcast.

"We have confirmed kill of seagull type 2 craft, with fragments and thermal signature. Good shooting Tiger, return to cruise altitude and continue patrol." came NICOM.

"Well, that was easy. I am now an ace! Wait until I tell Veronica about this!" he said to himself happily, as he threw the throttles forward and climbed back to 100,000 feet.

****

As Blue climbed into the cockpit of his Super-Hellcat trans-atmospheric fighter while the ground crew was topping off the Titan II rocket with hydrazine and NTO, the sky suddenly was rent by an earsplitting crack of thunder followed by a roar. Blue glanced around nervously, but saw no balls of fire rising from the highway in the distance either east or west. He signaled for them to lower the canopy and seal the clamshell aero-shroud in place around his craft on the top of the Titan II missile. Soon they were erecting the missile, he could see out only through a small window in the aero-shroud. It reminded him of riding on a carnival ride at night. He turned on his ejection seat button just in case the launch aborted. The button would blast the shroud clamshells apart and eject him out of the craft if the Titian failed on launch. He knew that he was riding on 100 tons plus of anhydrous red fuming nitric acid and hydrazine, that would explode on contact should anything go wrong. *Rocket Science!*

10, 9, 8, 7... Blue braced himself, muttered a prayer. Took a look at Alicia and Bobby's picture taped up on the crowded instrument console, 3, 2, 1, 0 ignition. He was slammed back in his seat as the mighty Titian II engines on the 1st stage ignited and moved him up into the dark sky. Soon he was feeling seven g's as the rocket tore up through the night sky.

A tremendous shock hit him as the first stage ran out of fuel and the second stage ignited and blasted it away. The Titan II was designed to boost nuclear warheads to their targets, not people, and was a known as a 'rough ride' among the astronauts, having been the basic booster for the Gemini program in the Moon race. Soon the rocket upper stage was pushing him deep into his pilot's couch. Then, to his relief, the clamshells of the aero-shroud flew off with the flash and boom of explosive bolts firing, and his fighter was riding free and clear on the top of the second stage over the gulf of Mexico, he could see the blue-green airglow wrapping the curvature of the Earth now below him, and the bright stars of space above him.

The arc of the night side of the Earth, wrapped in green airglow, now stretched beneath him. White and yellow lighting flashes raged below him in a chain of thunderstorms stretching across the Southern U.S. Beyond the massive curve of the Earth, lay the stars like jewels on ebony. Stars impossibly brilliant, blue, red, and yellow. The deep sense of joy and awe that Blue had always felt upon entering space returned to him, as weightlessness hit him.

*What a beautiful place to die,* he thought. *It's a lucky thing I'm Irish, and seeing this.*

"It's damn good to back in space!" he exulted, as much for himself as for anyone listening. "Now let me get some greys!" But he remembered seeing the grey ships moving effortlessly around them during his shuttle flights, during the days of the cover-up when he and the rest of the astronauts were sworn to secrecy about what they would see in space. This remembrance, gave him a deep feeling of apprehension and foreboding. He knew the grey ships were vastly more maneuverable than the trans-atmospheric fighters they were flying. The second stage engine cut off and his fighter was forcefully ejected from its second stage booster and its own engine ignited to boost him into orbit. Soon he was flying into a brilliant sunrise. The earth below him was breathtakingly beautiful.

"This is havoc squadron leader, sound off you killers!"

" This is samurai, flying in orbit with you!"

"This is Assassin! on orbit and in formation.

"This is Grim Reaper on orbit and in formation …"

Everyone had launched and achieved orbit successfully. The sound design of the Titan II had triumphed again. Now they waited tensely for any grey reaction while a white refueling pod was launched below them and rose to take up formation robotically with them. It carried more hypergolic fuel for their engines and magazines of twenty-millimeter magneto cannon ammunition. They were all flying now in a loose formation, 1 kilometer apart. One by one the fighters closed with a Russian fuel pod already in orbit and topped off their tanks by connecting with a fuel probe. The tension was palpable, for while this refueling was being done, one proton beam from the Greys and both the fuel pod and fighter would both go up in a ball of flame. However, the operation proceeded without mishap, and after a few orbits everyone had topped off their tanks. Now several arrow-head shaped Russian MIG 100s, launched from mobile launchers in India, rose and joined the formation. Now an orbital habitat joined them, launched from Kennedy Space Center. They could dock with it using a side hatch on the fighters and go inside for a meal and shower once things settled down.

*This is going a lot better than I expected,* thought Blue. *We are claiming a chunk of near-Earth space and the Greys don't even seem to have noticed.* Down below, however, several battles had apparently occurred in the atmosphere in the night skies over the CONUS. The blue earth, now in daylight, graced by brilliant white clouds, rolled beneath them on the day side and on the night side a blue-green sheen of airglow wrapped the dark Earth, and lightning from thunderstorms painted the dark clouds below them while the stars shown down unblinkingly.

One Russian fighter docked with the habitat briefly to verify the docking mechanisms and then disconnected. *So far so good,* thought Blue. *We expected a battle and instead we have a victory parade!*

"Houston this is Havoc Squadron leader, we are beginning 10th orbit, we have link up with Red Squadron and have topped off tanks on refueling pod, one member of Red Squadron has successfully docked with orbital

386

habitat and departed... " Suddenly a bright glint appeared in the distance in space near the Earth's dark limb and Blue, tensed.

"Havoc leader, this is Assassin. I have magnetic contact, bearing 00-Niner!"

"This is Samurai, I copy assassin on magnetic contact 00-Niner and closing!"

"This is Havoc Leader. All fighters arm weapons and prepare to engage hostiles! Go and get kills!"

*Here it comes*, thought Blue, as he armed the missiles and twenty-millimeter cannon on his fighter.

Suddenly the lead fighter opened fire with blue tracers and began maneuvering before exploding into an orange fireball. Blue threw forward the throttles on his rocket engines and darted ahead to where the lead fighter had been and only a phosphorescent cloud of expanding gas now remained. Then he saw a flight of four seagull-2, grey craft closing with the squadron at several kilometers distance . He opened fire at a range of 300 yards with missiles as the four saucers opened up with blue beams of what he knew were high energy protons, the protons ionizing the thin gas of low earth orbit into faintly glowing plasma. Two more fighters exploded. Now everyone was moving and firing, and blue tracers from the American craft and red tracers from the Russians were flying all around him. Missile trails sprayed off into infinity, most missing their targets. He was maneuvering his fighter as fast as he could in a sinuous helical path, never flying straight for more than a second at a time as the flight of four saucers flew past them. One other fighter then exploded. One of the saucers flew away rapidly from the other three up into the darkness of space. The fighters swarmed after the other three, who now turned agilely and flew through the squadron again claiming two more fighters as blue and red tracers and now missiles streaked wildly in every direction. Suddenly one of the saucers exploded into a cloud of glinting fragments. The remaining two saucers now darted away into space. They were emerging out of night now into brilliant sunlight from the Earth's shadow. Blue maneuvered back to near the habitat and fuel pod, that had been spared in the fighting. They had apparently killed one seagull-2 and damaged another  for a loss of six fighters, four American and two Russian. *They flew rings around us,* thought Blue, *but it doesn't matter, we are still here, and so is the fuel pod and hab.*

****

Tiger looked up from the cockpit of his F-71 scorpion, still flying NICAP back and forth over the southern CONUS, and  saw a shower of shooting stars. He guessed these were the remains of  a human fighter spacecraft and its pilot,  grey ships tended to give a fierce blue light when they exploded due to their magnesium-aluminum alloy hulls, but these shooting stars were white. *Soon I'll be up there,* he thought grimly, *flying faster and higher, and getting kills.*

****

In the White House Situation room, Secretary of Defense Clayton Thomas looked haggard and weary as night fell. The president sat at a desk in his shirt sleeves, listening to the radio traffic between Houston and the havoc squadron, now two days in space. James Bergman, the Deputy Secretary of Defense, stood watching the computer screens. The Greys had now attacked the squadron with its habitat and refueling pods four times and each time they had been driven off.  But the toll of fighter pilots was dreadful,  fourteen had been lost, while three grey ships had been destroyed with another two damaged. However, the squadron had been reinforced and three fuel pods  were now in orbit with two habitats surviving.   The human race had now grabbed a tenuous bridgehead in space and was defending it successfully, if bloodily.  In contrast, the Air Force "Surge" in the airspace over the CONUS had flown four thousand sorties and claimed 10 grey spacecraft in two nights of battles in the dark skies,  only 10 fighter aircraft had been lost.

"I think the strategy of the Air Force Surge down in atmosphere has been entirely successful, Mr. President," said Bergman, "our air surge seems to have pulled all the grey space strength down into the atmosphere, where we have overwhelming numbers of jet fighters, and we can assign five fighters to each grey ship.  That's why the exchange numbers are nearly even now!"

388

"In the meantime the Greys seem stretched in resources by the air surge, and they have not attacked our Havoc Squadron in low orbit with more than six ships at a time. So our space forces have been able to hold despite our losses. It is possible the Greys simply do not have the reserves to contest air and space supremacy at the same time. And it is also possible they view their terror attacks on our cities at night as so important they cannot stop them to concentrate forces into space"

"OK, then when will we be able to launch operation Archangel? Does this mean we can move up our timelines?" asked the President.

"It's too early to say, Mr. President, but I think we can launch Archangel, in two months assuming we can keep building up strength in Low Earth Orbit." said General Standish.

****

Cassandra found herself in the bathroom on the airliner cutting her hair short and donning dark glasses as she neared SEATAC Airport. Her worst fear now was that she would be recognized as she got off the plane. Fortunately, the crowded flight was uneventful as was getting off the plane into the nearly empty airport. She quickly caught a cab to a nearby Hilton Hotel and plotted her next moves. She noted a flyer at the front desk advertising jobs in a nearby defense plant. Taking out her contacts and going to a nearby Walmart, she was fitted with a pair of eyeglasses. She went to a jewelry store and bought a fancy diamond wedding ring. *I want no male supervisors harassing me on the assembly line,* she thought. *If they do I'll tell them my husband is a green beret and a jealous man to boot!* She noted happily that there were lots of Asians in the local population so she was able to blend in easily. The next day she showed up at the main gate of the plant and was ushered in with a large group of other prospective workers. Inside the fence, they were led to another fenced area which was obviously full of activity. In the large building in front of them, a production line was churning out F-51 Griffin Fighter planes, a fact that was emphasized when a flight of 4 Griffins took off over their heads with a roar and departed to the South. However, this was not their destination. They were lead to a newer building and sent inside where a production line for Super–Hellcat, trans-atmospheric

389

fighters was being started up. The applicants were asked to stand in line according to height and then Casandra was sent with the taller half of the workers to the tail end of the line where a massive three-D printer was printing out the basic frame of the fighter in titanium-aluminum alloy, and where the final wiring harness was being placed on the fighters prior to outer plating being spot welded to the frame by a line of industrial robots.

In twenty minutes, Cassandra and two other women had been instructed on how to attach the ends of bundles of wires of various colors into color coded sockets, to lay the wire harness across the side of the fighter, and screw the bundles down with an electric screwdriver. Soon she was wiring Super–Hellcat fighters and attaching the resulting wiring by a plug into a computer that verified all the connections were solid. She would then give a thumbs up sign to pass the fighter chassis on to the next stage of the assembly line. She estimated she was wiring one assembly every 40 minutes. She learned to crave lunch hour and breaks. As she left the plant exhausted at the end of the day, she noted a series of falling stars in the darkening sky. *Boosters burning up, or Greys, or people…* she thought.

She got herself a small furnished apartment near the plant and her life became an endless series of bus rides, days of labor, followed by bus rides back to her apartment. This life was not without its simple joys. For every time she heard the roar of jet fighters departing the plant, she rejoiced inwardly every time the wiring harness she had done passed its computer check. She took pride in her work. She learned to glory in small achievements, the first paycheck, the run to the grocery store. Learning the bus routes well enough to get to a museum. Being asked to join part of the crew to get a beer after work. Gradually, a feeling that she could deal with reality on its own terms returned to her. In fact, she realized that for the first time in her life, she was holding a job that she had gotten not for her looks or family name, but just because she had shown up. No one seemed to recognize her, or if they did, they said nothing. She was aware of the war going on in the heavens every night, and acknowledged it as she said to herself, "by doing what I can …"

**\*\*\*\***

390

"I want a panel of experts read into this program, Alicia, to see if we have missed anything..." said Goldberg looking haggard. "We need four or five good people we trust with this thing. Winter is coming, and temperatures are already 1 to 2 degrees below normal in the North, and near the equator, we have a spreading drought, with rainfall 20% below normal. This is going to be a real disaster..."

"How soon can we launch an attack on the platform at the libration point?" asked Alicia, almost afraid to hear the answer, she knew Blue would probably help lead it. Goldberg shook his head wearily.

"They are hanging on to a position in LEO by their fingernails. We have lost over a hundred space fighters," said Goldberg , but he smiled weakly. "But it's been three weeks and our strength there has grown, we haven't been dislodged, and reportedly the Greys have lost twenty ships. We need that place to be secure... "

"OK, I'll try to get a list of names we can trust," said Alicia rising slowly from her chair. She was starting to feel her new pregnancy. She walked down the busy hall in the Pentagon, now a beehive of activity 24/7. She realized she had somehow decided to keep the child.

****

Samurai Nakajima, lowered the visors on his windshield to protect the glass, he was powering up the backup APUs. The blue-white limb of the Earth rolled beneath him as he and the rest of the squadron prepared to meet a new flight of grey ships. The APUs were turbo-alternators driven by hydrazine that supplied power to the new laser weapons in the nose of his super-hellcat. The Greys had now changed tactics and were engaging them at longer ranges so that 20-millimeter cannon were no longer effective. The fighters had received weapons upgrade packages to oxygen-iodine lasers, a bright blue laser spotlight acted as the targeting laser. Samurai was now a hardened space veteran with twelve space missions and two space kills. He had been promoted to Squadron Commander after the death of his previous wingman. The radar and magnetometer data fixed the enemy in the distant blackness and he

391

engaged his rocket engines, now augmented with rest mass reduction gear to help his fighter move more agilely .

"Alright Leopard Squadron, on me!" he yelled into the radio and gunned his craft into the blackness on a tail of flame.

****

"Kenneth Forrester, with Bonny in the car with him and his foreman, raced the car down the road to the fire burning in the distance in the forest near Roxy Anne mountain. The clear autumn sky was full of shooting stars, and thunderous sonic booms, with many brilliant fragments impacting in the distance. A particularly large and bright falling star had crashed in the distance. Several cars full of men with guns, and carrying shovels and axes to put out the fire in the woods were racing ahead of them. Many cars followed them.

Soon they reached a place on the road where several cars had stopped and men were piling out running into the woods near where the fire raged. The woods were dry and if the fire was not put out quickly it could spread rapidly. Kenneth was now running through the woods with his shovel and flashlight.

"I see him in his cockpit! You can tell he's an alien by his big head!" somebody was yelling and a shot rang out. Kenneth however, was now staring at a charred piece of sheet metal stuck in a tree, despite the discoloration , he could make out clear "AIR FORCE" and a charred star symbol under the light of his flashlight. At the sight of this, his heart sank. Another rifle shot rang out.

" Stop Shooting! It's one of ours!" he yelled and ran over to where the main debris pile was burning. In the flames, he saw what he recognized as the charred remains of a space-suited pilot in his space helmet. Bewildered men lowered their guns and looked at him.

No, No, Lord Please, he thought.

"This thing is US Air Force ..." Kenneth gasped out pointing at the dead pilot in the shattered cockpit . *And that might be one of my sons..."*

392

"This is the augmented version of the Saturn V with a bigger upper stage using hypergolics so we can store it in orbit until we want to use it," said Bergen Holm to Alicia, both standing in hard hats with obvious pride as the giant crawler moved the huge white and black booster to the launch pad. "The two big solid boosters on each side use ADN, that's Ammonium Dinitramine. It's like ammonium nitrate on steroids, gives better performance per kilo than ammonium perchlorate and won't hurt the ozone layer over the cape. So we can launch these babies all day. With is this new Saturn V Mark IV We can now put 200 tons in orbit or 75 tons on the lunar surface. Once we have LEO secure, we can build out and prepare for the Lunar phase of this war." He motioned out to the sea in bright sunlight. A line of supertankers and cargo ships carrying Saturn V tank sections stretched to the far horizon.

"We have 50 tankers out there full of RP1, high-grade kerosene for the lower stages, and we have 1 million tons of LOX, liquid oxygen, in underground tanks here, ready for surge launches." He looked at Alicia, his neatly trimmed beard now tinged with grey.

"You know me, Alicia, I am all about unified field and antigravity, that's what I thought would win this war for us. But right now, I would say what is going to win this war is sheer space lift, LOX- kerosene and ADN. Once we gain space superiority, we can put more hardware in space and on the Moon than the greys can move here from 100 light years away."

"Good, excellent, Bill, but we need your expert eye on another problem," said Alicia, trying not to let her despair show. "We want you to come up to DC for a meeting and look at some contingency plans, so we can get your opinion."

Just then, with a thunder that grew to shake the air around them like Jell-O, a mighty Saturn V upgrade lifted off a launch pad in the distance and joined a swirling halo of fighter escorts as it carried its load of 150 tons of supplies up to the war front in low-Earth-orbit. Few people around them seemed to notice.  Launches were now routine, at five a day, of various boosters.

****

In the great council chamber, the Unash commander of space forces, Number 2 waited impatiently for the arrival of Sadok Sar.  Number 7, with his aid, another Idelkite, tried to think of other things.  But every thought proceeded around to the council room again.

"Number 7, we need all qualified Unash personnel not needed for work in your sector to be reassigned to the ships at Erra.  There has been much loss of personnel," said Number 2, angrily.  Number 7 knew, with relief, that the anger was not directed at him, but worried that if unabated, that Number 2 might kill him or one of his staff as a "statement" to Sadok Sar, who could not be contradicted directly.  The door opened and Sadok Sar entered, looking dour and distracted as usual.

"My Lord Sadok Sar, I have bad news!" began Number 2. "Our losses on recent missions of the terror have been grievous, with ten ships lost at Erra and three more so damaged they were picked off by the Unull on their way back to Una. That is thirteen lost in one night out of thirty!  My Lord also knows the Errans are now established in space above their atmosphere. We must redeploy our ships from terror operations in the atmosphere and concentrate them against the Erran space operations."

"NO! The Yoke of fear must be reestablished upon the Errans! That is the way to win this war! FEAR! Do you not realize that if we cease our terror operations, the Errans will draw encouragement from this! They will think we are retreating! No! They must fear the night! That is the theory of this whole effort.  Soon the dust blockage of their sunlight will take effect as the Solar disturbances ease, it will be winter in their northern regions of the planet and this will bring them to their knees. So the terror must be unrelenting.  However, I want you to direct your terror attacks upon the industrial regions making their spacecraft." With that, Sadok Sar turned and left the council room .  Number 2 covered his eyes as he did so.

****

394

Tiger Forester, settled back in his seat as the Titan II erected and the powder blue sky filled his one view portal. Once the Titan booster reached zenith in elevation, the countdown began at 30 seconds. *No horsing around.* He had gone through this process 40 times in high-quality simulations, but now it was, as they said, *the highest quality simulation of all the ones that you could die in.* How many pilots had died trying to carve out a piece of space and hold it, was classified, Tiger knew. But the rumors said it was hundreds of deaths now, and he noted they were now advertising for volunteers, never a good sign. He watched impassively as the countdown appeared on the main viewscreen in the middle of his control console. All the lights were green for the spacecraft systems. *Go for launch.* He braced himself against the seat and positioned his arms on the armrests. They had gravity compensation on board, but it took power, and that took fuel, so they had told him and other pilots to "tough it out" through the high g's on ascent to save fuel and power for fighting in orbit.

3, 2, 1, 0, the spacecraft shuddered then began to climb as the Titan booster engines swallowed tons of red fuming anhydrous nitric acid and poisonous hydrazine every second being shoved into the engines to ignite on contact with high-speed pumps spun by turbines, that themselves ran on rocket fuel. He was launching out of Florida from a mobile pad near Titusville. Soon he felt the crushing weight of 7 g's and the view of the blue sky turned dark violet as the first stage dropped away and the second stage ignited with a tremendous jolt. The clamshell atmospheric fairing blew apart and he could see the brilliant curving limb of the Earth. In a few minutes he was in space, and the other members of his squadron were sounding off. *So I am finally an astronaut,* he thought briefly but had no time to savor the fact. Tiger was arming his missiles and laser cannon. They were flying right into a battle in space.

****

Cassandra was trying to ignore the thunderous explosions and sonic booms in the sky above the factory roof. When she had arrived for her rotation onto night shift on a bus the sky in the distance had been lit up with rocket trails and streams of tracers. The crew boss had told them all to ignore it, and get to work.

395

"I don't need to tell you all there's a war on," he said crossly. Cassandra had seen the fear in his eyes, however, as they walked across the snow into the main assembly hangar. Cassandra passed the crew getting off work, most of them too weary to speak. It had begun to snow now, even though it was only October. *Something has gone very wrong with the weather...* she thought, *it's obvious now.* She remembered the look of despair in the President's eyes when he had put a medal around her neck. *I think I know what that was about now.* But all she knew to do was assemble wire harnesses on Super-Hellcat fighters, endlessly, for pilots whose lives she knew would depend on her doing her job well. So she was now part of the machinery of the plant.

****

"You want to negotiate with the people who did this?" asked Pamela to the viewers as they were treated to a visit to the New York City Morgue where bodies of the night's victims were being brought in.

"Never give in to terror! And ask those who do want negotiations with the Greys, why?"

****

Cassandra sat in her apartment listing to the thunder of the battles overhead in the sky. The light of tracers and flashes of explosions lit the curtains over the sink as she sat and read the bible. It was the only thing she could read that would stop the hallucinations of Lauren Hill from emerging from the shadows and standing over her, or seeming waking dreams of rat crabs clambering across the walls. She had volunteered for a longer night shift rotation at the plant, but everyone wanted night shift now so they could sleep during the day. Every night featured battles in the sky, so much so no one paid any attention anymore. The days were now becoming colder and an icy winter was descending on them even in November.

****

"We have now sustained a human presence in space continually for 30 days Mr. President. We are now expanding our presence to include more small space stations and refueling depots." reported General Burnham, his hair now completely grey.

"What are our losses"

"They are severe, Mr. President. We are basically putting men into space faster than they can be killed." said Burnham grimly. "However, we have also taken a heavy toll on the enemy, they have lost 29 ships in space combat as confirmed kills, and since we began our space operations they have lost 35 ships down in the atmosphere, some even from ground fire. Curiously, they seem to have reacted to our operations in space by increasing their operations at night over our cities. This has played to our strength, we have 300 fighters to every one of their ships that flies over our cities in the atmosphere.

"There is a saying in war, Mr. President, *that quantity has a quality all its own. We* are proving that saying. We are overwhelming them with sheer numbers of men and machines."

"Who came up with that saying?" asked the President smiling, as he looked around the conference table at the White House.

"I believe it was Joseph Stalin, Mr. President, he said it after Stalingrad," said Burnham grimly.

"I see," said the President nodding somberly. "Very good, keep it up! Prepare for Archangel. It must succeed!"

**\*\*\*\***

Tiger Forrester, now on his 14th space mission pushed forward the throttles on his Super-Hellcat space fighter as it tore after a grey ship trying to escape up to higher altitude out of the melee of laser beams, tracers rocket trails and explosions. He was now looking high above the blue horizon of the earth into the black abyss of space, flowing the ship as it tried to flee. The ship was obviously damaged and having difficulty climbing as he caught up with it, locked two missiles onto it, and let them fly. But he was too close, and when the missiles impacted the fireball swelled to engulf his fighter and he heard many shrapnel impacts.

He cursed himself in dismay as he watched red warning lights flare on the control console in front of him. Finally, he noted the console became mostly green again as the ship stabilized itself. However, one light kept blinking red. It was one of his APUs, the hydrazine-fueled turbo generators that supplied his craft with power. He looked at the radar and realized he was too far from the space station to try and get back. He watched the power drop as the APU failed, leaving him with ½ power as he was shutting down optional systems.

"May day! May day Falcon leader. This is Tiger. I have lost starboard APU!"

"Tiger this is falcon leader, we copy, you may have to deorbit..."

**\*\*\*\***

Cassandra was at the church where her friends from the plant had invited her. She was in the center of a prayer group being prayed over.

*Now we will see if God is the God of unreal as well as the real...*she thought.

After that, they all boarded the company snowcat for a ride back to their apartments.

**\*\*\*\***

The massive Saturn V, Mark II, ignited its two massive strap-on solid boosters whose white flames lit up the night sky like dawn. The five main lox-kerosene engines than ignited, built up thrust, and then the whole rocket carrying 200 tons into orbit lifted off as Griffin fighters circled and missile battery commanders scanned their radar screens warily. The orange flame of the lox-kerosene temporarily overwhelmed the brilliant blue-white flame of the ADN rubber and aluminum fueled boosters as it rose flawlessly into the sky, dwarfing the Titan II boosters sitting in rows on their launch pads . Above them, faint sparks of light paraded by in orbit. They were space fighters and support platforms for refueling, repair, and rest for pilots. 500 men now were permanently stationed in orbit, Americans, Russian, British, Japanese, and French. The Saturn V arced over into the night sky over the sea to join them in orbit. The payload

398

carried four new fully supplied habitats, 50 tons of rocket propellants, and 10 spare fighters to replace damaged ones in space. The two solid boosters flamed out, fell away, and the first stage continued to burn until it too burned out and fell away. The second stage ignited like a sparkler in the sky and poured on thrust to increase speed until finally the payload was in orbit and began to deploy its subcomponents like a delivery truck driving through town. The Earth had a new surface now, where humans dwelt, up above the atmosphere on the edge of the abyss.

****

"I'm crazy, I really am, and I don't think I will ever get well…" gasped Cassandra as another cold night fell. "Please help me." She was on her knees praying by her bed. She then got into bed wearily and put her bible by her head and the big brass cross under her pillow. Distant thunder told her the night's battles were beginning, even as her dream battles would begin.

****

"She's fine, she checked in and says, "hi". She is just laying low! She is working in a war plant to stay busy!" said Berkowitz

"Why won't you tell me where she is?" demanded Pamela.

"Because if I do you'll send her messages," said Berkowitz angrily, "and people who are hacking our email and phone systems will track her down! Do you think that idiot snake rancher they arrested for sending you the Sidewinder is the only nutcase out there who wants to kill both of you? The FBI says they have lists of thousands of people posting messages all over the dark-net saying they want to kill both of you! Some of them may even actually mean it!"

"What are the stats then? How many threats for me versus her?" said Pamela with a sudden smirk.

"I'd estimate she still is in the lead for threats, 2 to 1. So get to work girl!" said Berkowitz breaking into a smile. "Let's get those stats even by next week!"

399

My Lord, our losses are severe, we must pull our ships out of the atmosphere, and concentrate them to eliminate their space bridgehead," said Number 2 .

"NO, NO, it is retreat! There must be NO RETREAT from the skies over Erra. If you were truly a master of war you would know that all victory in war is achieved psychologically! It is in the minds of the Errans that victory will be achieved! You must attack their factories and rocket fuel supplies!

Cassandra sat at her kitchen table waiting at 3 AM for Lauren Hills ghost to appear. Outside the sky flicked with the light of high altitude explosions. The roar of jet fighters flying high above was constant. She had failed again to get night shift, it was rumored only sex could buy those coveted shifts now.

Right on schedule, Lauren appeared, and Cassandra suddenly pulled out from under her Bible a large brass cross and held it up. Lauren stopped and stared at Cassandra.

"Ah, so I have gotten your attention. Why don't you sit down and talk for once, since you obviously have something you want to say to me," Cassandra said with a shaking voice and shoved Lauren the other kitchen chair. To Cassandra's surprise, she was not nude, as was usually the case, but was wearing a dark green blouse and skirt.

"I like your outfit tonight," said Cassandra as Lauren Hill sat down and looked at her blankly. Lauren then bared her vampire fangs at Cassandra, but Cassandra held up the cross in her face.

"Oh, let's keep this encounter polite..." said Cassandra.

Lauren Hill faded away.

Cassandra woke up shaking, she had fallen asleep at the kitchen table reading her Bible, the cross was where she had left it, underneath the bible. The kitchen was as she had left it.

"I call that encounter a draw..." said Cassandra with satisfaction. She then picked up her Bible and cross and carried them back to bed. She lay down then saw a tiny golden spark in the room.

She stared at the spark of light in wonder. Then she held out her hand. The tiny spark of light seemed to approach her. Then touch her hand as she stared at it in amazement. She felt instantly comforted and went to sleep, and slept soundly, even as distant thunder of the night battle in the sky echoed in the distance.

****

"Mr. president, we have prepared five million tents and 3 million portable latrines for evacuation camps. We have managed to stockpile 200, million emergency rations meals and water . The railroads will become the major vehicle for evacuation of those cities above the 40$^{th}$ parallel. We anticipate 50 million people will have to be moved. We have 40 million diesel generator sets each capable of supplying 500kW continuously to keep people warm.

We have now completed preliminary evacuation plans with the Canadian government and also plans for the evacuation of the U.S. and Canadian Capitols to Atlanta Georgia if it should become necessary.

"I thought we were moving it to Jacksonville, Florida"

"Yes sir, but some of the weather models predicted an increase in hurricane activity, so we were advised to move the location inland," said General Prescott. He continued "We also have now a new technology: hybrid fusion-fission nuclear power plants that are mobile and consist of three tractor-trailer rigs, one for steam turbines and heat exchangers, one carrying electric power transformers and switching to allow power coupling into local substations, and finally a semi-trailer containing three modular fusion-fission hybrid reactors and their containment vessels. The reactors consist of an electrostatic fusion neutron source core that creates neutrons and a shell of thorium and uranium alloy with water cooling. The fusion neutron sources provide seed neutrons to activate and control the fission reactions. Because the fusion supplies the neutrons the reactor can be controlled electronically and can be more compact and cannot melt down. We have now field tested three of these units and they can provide 5 Megawatts of electric power each. We are now in mass production of these units and expect to have 20 units by the end of the month for deployment anywhere a railroad or highway can run."

What about Africa and India, the possibility of drought there while we freeze," asked the President.

"We have worked with the Indian government to create food stockpiles and to pre-deploy reverse osmosis water purification units to both coasts," said Prescott. "No one should go thirsty."

"What about Africa?"

"We have much less to work with there, sir, particularly in regards to security. If the local government disintegrates we will have to commit major ground forces to maintain order at any aid camps."

"Well, I want provision made for an African drought, I want desalination units placed on ships for rapid deployment, and I want local food stockpiled plus as many tents as we can spare. I don't want anybody saying we abandoned Africa!" said the President angrily.

"Mr. President, we only have so many resources to respond to this crisis..." said Prescott.

"Dr. Sepulveda, how long can we expect this current series of solar mass ejections to continue," asked the President, seemingly ignoring Prescott.

"We project the current series should last for another month but then subside. All the models seem to say that Sir," said Alicia with her voice trembling slightly.

"Damn!" said the President. "How long before we can launch operation Archangel?"

"Two months sir, minimum," said General Standish. "We will only get one chance at this Mr. President, and we have to do it right. We have to emplace the space assets and prepare the diversion operation. We are working non-stop sir"

"That means we have a one month gap …" said the President in resignation.

"Yes sir, if the CMEs don't continue…" said Standish.

****

Cassandra was working the evening shift again, many workers had protested and the rotation was restarted. It was midnight when the thundering in the sky, usually far away, became louder and sharper. Suddenly a blue-white ball of fire burst through the high factory ceiling and crashed into the factory floor, burning fiercely with a stunning roar. Cassandra felt the fierce heat on her face and calmly turned to escape out the side door of the construction hanger, joining a panic-stricken stream of workers. The factory sprinkler system turned on just as she got out the door into the snowy tarmac outside. The shift was sent home, they returned the next night as usual with huge electric fans blowing to dry out everything and production continued. The factory proudly displayed a downed saucer symbol on the exterior walls to claim credit for the antiaircraft crews.

****

"It's the curse of this age that the internet provides everyone with a soapbox, whether they know what they are talking about or not." said Pamela smiling. "Hence the opinion that has been widely circulated that I, in fact, am responsible for this war occurring." She made her eyes large. "That is an amazing opinion. Let me give a tutorial about war that I learned while getting my degree at the Naval Academy, a place where they know something about wars."

403

"Wars," began Pamela writhing sensuously behind her desk," are the extension of politics by other means, that is, they are part of the struggle for power or vital resources. Somebody wants something from someone else, and that someone refuses to give it to them peacefully, so the somebody tries to take it by force. This is called attempted robbery when it occurs on the street between two people; this is called a war of aggression when it occurs in this cosmos.

"In the case of a war between the human race and aliens from outer space that we find ourselves in," continued Pamela, "the struggle is over which species will enjoy the resources of this planet. Yours truly has no desire to control this planet or its people, except for some small amount of beachfront property in a warm climate with a good hotel staff. I did not bring the aliens here; all I did, in fact, was be abducted and raped by them at 15 years old, and complain about it." Pamela stared at the camera blankly after she said this.

"The sad fact is that we are in a war with people who desire to exterminate humanity as we know it, and assume this planet for their own progeny," continued Pamela. "And we, the human race, have resisted this. Those who suggest that this is about tungsten deposits on the Moon, or my wanting my tech-heavy stock portfolio to increase in value, or even that I wanted to bring about the end of the world to increase CNS ratings, are sadly mistaken. Nothing will make this war end except the aliens' departure. There is no quick fix for this, there is no magic formula, there is only a bloody and bitter struggle. I recognize, that many in a generation most known for its love of instant gratification, find this situation shockingly at variance with the rest of their comfortable past lives. But you got lucky so far, note it is time for real struggle and endurance. So quit asking me how to fix this problem, it can't be fixed, it must be battled."

"One might instead inquire into the motivations of those like Senator Tunney of Massachusetts, who want us to negotiate some sort of peace with aliens." Pamela's face became a mask of disdain. "Hah! You might as well be a mullet negotiating with a great white shark. These people did not come 400 light years to Earth to settle for half the planet. They will not rest until they get the whole thing, no matter what senator Tunney

404

believes. No, I think the motivations of these people urging negotiations are just the common impulses of all yellow belly cowards who would rather live as slaves than die as free people..."

****

They were in Goldberg's temporary office in a sea of trailers now occupying the Capitol Mall. Where tanks had dueled the night of the attempted coup, now thousands of technicians, clerks, engineers and scientists labored to coordinate the vast war effort that had sprung from that attempted coup.

"The solar irradiance reaching this planet has now declined by half a percent," said Alicia, trying to be as unemotional as possible, "and global temperatures are down by an average of a third of a degree. We believe more CMEs will come and blow the dust out of libration zone, but the Sun has already passed through the peak of expected activity. Without more CMEs, we will lose three-quarters of a degree per percent drop in solar radiance. This temperature drop will fall disproportionately on the northern hemisphere this winter. The oceans will remain warm, and this will help the coastal regions, however, it will also mean that the oceans will shed moisture and this will go north to result in catastrophic snowfalls and flooding. While the disruption of global moisture circulation caused by this northward flow will cause severe drought conditions to occur in the tropics. In other words, the cold northern regions will act like a moisture magnet for off-ocean moist air flow. That is the projection based on numerous weather codes we have been running to simulate this crisis."

"We have adopted an emergency plan to deal with both crises," continued Alicia, seeing the faces in the room become grim. "This emergency plan is called Plan Joseph. We have been aided in this by a bumper wheat and corn crop this year due in part to the abundant rains this summer. We are stockpiling this bumper crop as an emergency food reserve. We have also converted 4,000 armored personnel carriers to be snow transport vehicles, we have converted 4,000 tanks into snow plows. These are being distributed to northern population centers. We are preparing 5,000 300 kW diesel gen-sets, and we have stockpiled 5 million

405

gallons of diesel oil to supply emergency power into the grid. We have also prepared and tested 20 new 5-megawatt fusion-fission hybrid mobile power plants and we are prepositioning them also in the northern tier of the country. The nuclear aircraft carriers Nimitz, Forrestal and Saratoga are also being prepared to serve as emergency power plants for northern coastal cities."

"These preparations appear massive. But what are the projections of the magnitude of the disaster if the libration zone occultation is not halted?" asked Bergenholm.

"They are very bad, doctor Bergenholm," interjected Goldberg. "We are projecting millions of deaths this winter if these preparations are inadequate , and the occultation is not stopped. Does that answer your question?"

"Yes," said Bergenholm soberly.

"What are the estimated chances of the success of operation Archangel? Which I gather is the military operation to stop the occultation" asked Dr. Patel.

"Good, as long as we don't talk about the plans," said Goldberg with a smile.

"By order of the President, extensive planning is also being made to aid the tropical zone countries in case of the expected drought. Food is being stockpiled, 1,000 diesel gen-sets are being positioned to run pumps for well water, and 100 drill rigs have been positioned to begin drilling new water wells. Fortunately, the rains have been good during the summer, perhaps an unintended effect of the occultation and the aquifers should be full even if the rains fail. So we are hoping that water shortages can be circumvented if the occultation is ended quickly... Again our most serious threat is the killing cold and heavy snowfalls in the north this winter."

A stunned silence followed the talk with no questions.

Later in Goldberg's office, Alicia sat down, exhausted, in a large comfy chair while Goldberg pulled out a bottle of tequila and poured two shot glasses.

"Here I got this especially for you for after this briefing," said Goldberg offering a glass, which she took eagerly. She sniffed it fondly, and then thinking of her unborn child, pushed it away.

"How did I do?" she asked.

"Great, you were the perfect person to deliver the news that doomsday is upon us. Why do you think I sent you out during the asteroid crisis, to talk to the press."

"I thought you did that because I discovered the asteroid and you thought I was a genius!" she said, feeling a craving for the tequila burn inside her and shutting her eyes momentarily. *Plenty of time for that later...*

"Nah, it's because you're a babe, and if you've got to tell people bad news, it's always better to send a pretty woman to deliver it. It reassures people for some reason."

"Thanks, Abe," she said sarcastically. Handing him back the full shot glass. He took it with a smile and drank it. Outside, dusk was falling over Washington DC.

"You know until this Lagrange point occultation, I thought we had this war won. It looked like the Greys simply didn't have enough hardware or personnel here to do anything, short of a nuclear war. But, now I see that this night-terror stuff may simply have been a diversion. They really do have the resources to destroy us..."

"Yeah, but we are going to stop them," said Goldberg with seemly utter certainty.

"You think Archangel will succeed?" she asked plaintively, rubbing her belly.

"Projecting space power out four times farther out than the Moon: piece of cake..." he laughed. "We've sent probes to Neptune and everywhere else in the Solar System remember."

"Abe, I think Blue is part of Archangel." she said suddenly. Her dark eyes looked at him desperately.

Goldberg paused in pouring another drink. He looked at her grimly, then resumed pouring.

"Well, that's good then. Then I am even more certain the operation will succeed..."

****

Schwartzman, clad in a suffocating bio-isolation suit and helmet walked slowly through the Indian village called Sana, on the neat streets, dead bodies were everywhere. He gripped his M-4 carbine tightly, having no idea what to expect next. But all there was, was silence, not even the call of a bird. The bodies were covered with red blotches and in some cases the skin blotches had ruptured into bloody hemorrhages, leaving pools of blood stained earth beside where they fell. Arizona, also clad in a bio-suit walked with him filming everything. To their relief, they passed through the mass of dead villagers to where the crashed alien craft lay in the distance outside the village. A body in an Indian Army uniform lay by the road, he had been carrying water filled canteens towards the spacecraft. Several military vehicles lay beyond, full of dead. In one place beside an ambulance, a cluster of bodies in uniform lay, and beside them two medics, also dead the same way, their bodies covered with hemorrhages below and above the skin. Medical gear, including several vials of blood samples, lay around them.

"Arizona, get those blood samples," said Schwartzman pointing at the sample case. "Stow them in the pack." Arizona carefully picked up the vials and put them in a special sealable backpack.

Soon they approached the crashed alien vessel. It was a large manta shaped type called a Scarab-4, in terminology developed during the Cover-up. it was as large as a jet airliner. Several dead Indian military personnel

408

lay beside it near an open hatchway.   A dead grey alien lay beside them, with black blotches covering its face. The black areas being regions of decayed liquefied flesh.   In the hatchway, a pile of alien bodies, all showing a similar mode of death,  lay still.  Flies were now buzzing over the bodies as the Sun rose higher and warmed the landscape. Even through their air filters, the stench of rotting squid was getting stronger.

"Stay here," said Schwartzman handing his carbine to Arizona and pulling out his pistol.  He then climbed gingerly over the pile of dead alien bodies, apparently dying in panicked flight from inside  the craft.  Inside, he walked down a passage way with ribbed walls familiar to Schwartzman, whose floor was littered with alien bodies, some of whom were wearing spacesuits without helmets. There was an open hatchway. It led to a large control room.  Red liquid was leaking from a hole in one wall, and pooling in the floor,  aliens lay dead at control consoles, but on the other side of the room was a blasted hole in the bulkhead with blackened edges. Schwartzman passed by the end of a bulkhead and saw the leaking red liquid was coming from a large tank.  He walked back and carefully opened a sample vial from his belt and scooped up some of the red liquid. He then rose, looked around, and stored the vial with its precious sample in a sealed pouch.   A noise disturbed the silence and he pulled out his pistol and froze.

Suddenly a hatchway into the room opened and a short figure in a full space suit stepped into the room, holding a pistol. He turned slowly and faced Schwartzman.

Schwartzman shot the alien right through the faceplate three times. The alien, looking startled, fell forward, as Schwartzman heard the shell casings rattle off the wall and on the floor.

*Time to go,* thought Schwartzman.  He carefully stepped around the now dead alien, lying halfway in the pool of red liquid on the floor, with his pistol still held in his hand. He knew that if he pierced his  bio-suit, he would probably be dead within an hour, so virulent was the disease the alien ship was carrying and so loaded was the air around him with its agent. After a few minutes of careful egress. He stood outside the vessel beside a relieved looking Arizona.

"Looks like it was carrying tanks of bacterial warfare agent, but took a rocket out in space, and the stuff got loose on the ship and nailed the crew," said Schwartzman. "This stuff is designed to kill humans but is apparently deadly to any flesh and blood in high enough concentration. We have to get this thing isolated and burned." Schwartzman then smiled.

"Creeping around in that ship, it was just like old times in the Carney" added Schwartzman. Arizona grinned.

"Rock and roll, Boss!" said Arizona.

They then trudged back to the heavily armed Indian Army cordon, ordered to shoot anyone who tried to break out, that had been put around the area. They were hosed off thoroughly with formaldehyde and alcohol and handed off their blood and agent samples to an American team.

*Where angels fear to tread, they send us in,* Schwartzman thought with satisfaction. *I did my job and lived another day.*

****

Cassandra passed cold beers out across her dinner table in her simple apartment for Angie and Leticia, two of the girls from the production line at the plant. It was wonderful to have human company in her lonely apartment. They both eagerly grabbed the beers and began drinking them as Cassandra waved her arms around the simple apartment.

"Well, as you can see, I like things simple here," said Cassandra after a drink of beer. "So I told my interior decorator to adopt a minimalist approach." Both women laughed as they looked around with great curiosity. Angie immediately went over to Cassandra's picture of Bob Schwartzman in his green beret dress uniform in her living room. Cassandra had carefully taped all the pieces of his picture back together after ripping it up in an angry episode.

"Wow what a hunk!" said Angie with obvious envy. " So this is your jealous husband you threaten the shift boss with?" Latecia was now also looking at the picture.

410

"I see you posted this picture back together, looks like you have a had a stormy relationship!" said Laticia with a wide grin.

"Yeah, I get mad at him sometimes!" said Cassandra after taking a long drink of beer. "The son-of-a-bitch never writes!" she said indignantly.

"What's he like on leave?" asked Angie. "Is he all polite, mister officer, or a 'rip your clothes off 'sort of guy." Both women turned and looked at Cassandra smiling.

"Oh he's definitely a bodice ripper!" said Cassandra with a big smile, remembering their nights together. I think he was some sort of pirate in a previous life, kidnapping young maidens like me, and then lowering his big Captain's boom on me that night in his cabin." sighed Cassandra happily, waving her sparkling wedding ring around in the kitchen light.

**\*\*\*\***

## Chapter 10: Archangel

"The infectious agent is a rickettsia type bacteria similar to the Rocky Mountain Spotted Fever bacterium. Only it is amazingly more lethal and aggressive. Its code name is XSF standing for X-ray Spotted Fever, a name chosen to sound fairly harmless in order to reduce the possibility of panic. It kills its victims within hours and spreads by aerosol; it is also very contagious." began the lead scientist, Doctor Miller, from the Centers for Disease Control. Alicia, Abe Goldberg, and the other War Science Board members sat listening in the highly classified conference room deep within the Pentagon, the fear in the room was palpable.

"We have its genome mapped and it clearly shows signs of being a genetically modified and a weaponized version of Spotted Fever. It causes breakdown of the blood circulation system leading to hemorrhages, and for this reason, it is being called the Red Death by the Indian authorities. They said the village of Sana, with 554 people was wiped out within hours of the vehicle crash. Fortunately, the village was isolated and the progress of the disease was so rapid that no one was even able to carry the infection to any nearby villages. They report that standard formaldehyde ethanol solution is effective as a disinfectant." the scientist continued, trying to sound confident. "The genetic link to Rocky Mountain Spotted Fever would make sense since the aliens occupied a base at Morningstar Colorado, where Spotted Fever is endemic. However, we have a vaccine already in production, and though the agent is resistant to tetracycline and many other common antibiotics, it responds well to Amonataxafil, also known as Amonafil, if administered early. Unlike spotted fever, it spreads by air exposure and is very contagious. It is lethal to humans and many other animals, hence our ability to study it in animals, especially rabbits. It is very aggressive and kills its victims within hours of exposure. That includes apparently, and somewhat surprisingly to us at the CDC, Unash aliens. We have instigated a crash production program for the vaccine and also for Amonafil. Until we get these remedies in full production, for emergencies it responds somewhat to the sulfa drug Torine. And we have found the standard vaccine for Spotted Fever to be partially effective."

413

"Thank you, Dr. Miller," said Goldberg. He then blew his nose loudly. "Colonel Paulson of the Army Bio-warfare Center at Fort Dietrich will now speak on contingency planning for any mass urban outbreaks of the Red Death." Goldberg paused. "I mean XSF." he corrected himself.

"Pardon, me I seem to have picked up a cold," said Goldberg looking weary. Given the subject of the emergency briefing, everyone tensed as he paused and blew his nose again. Colonel Paulson took the podium; he was wearing an Army dress uniform. A power point slide appeared on the screen beside him, marked Top Secret, Special Access. In large black letters, it read

**Contingency Plan Alpha: Emergency Quarantine and Martial Law Procedures for Large Urban XSF Outbreaks.**

"Briefly ladies and gentleman, the view at Fort Dietrich, which has been communicated to the Joint Chiefs of Staff and adopted by them, is that the XSF agent presents a grave threat to urban centers due to its ability to spread through the air, extreme contagiousness and lethality, and lack of vaccine or effective antibiotics in any quantity for the next months. Therefore we are putting in place the following contingency plans should mass outbreaks occur in any urban centers. Step 1: Martial law will be immediately declared in the affected areas. Step 2: Cordons immediately established around the affected areas by police and national guard and paratroops who are now being given full bio-warfare gear. These cordon-forces will have orders to shoot to kill anyone attempting to leave the affected areas. Step 3: All supplies of vaccine, Amonafil and Torine will be diverted to surrounding areas where the population will be ordered to undergo mass inoculation. Anyone refusing will be deemed a public heath menace, and will be shot.

"What about the people in the cordoned areas?" asked Alicia, feeling sick.

"Until we have sufficient stockpiles of Amonafil and Torine to combat outbreaks medically. We will have to let the disease run its course in the affected areas. We will basically take advantage of the fact that whoever concocted this agent was too focused on it creating terror to make it spread effectively. XSF basically is so aggressive that it weakens and kills

414

its victims before they can travel and spread it to others. Also, the red hemorrhages appear within an hour of infection making it victims easy to identify and isolate… "

****

In space above the blue arc of the Earth, Tiger lined his cross hairs up on a large Manta shaped craft as it maneuvered sluggishly to try to escape, and streams of blue tracers flew from his Super Hellcat to strike it. Explosions erupted on it as the twenty-millimeter cannon shells struck, many others penetrating its hull. Suddenly it exploded into a ball of blue-white flame, and he flew through the fireball and out the other side, hearing debris rattle off the outer titanium skin of his craft as he eagerly sought another target in a sea of battle. He quickly lined up on another Manta shaped craft but a rocket struck it before he could get target lock and the craft fell with blue-white flames pouring out of a massive hole in its hull . Already below him, he could see countless ships and large pieces of debris hitting the atmosphere and burning like meteors.

"Damn !" he yelled and sought another quarry.

****

The enormous Blackhawk helicopter flew swiftly across the snow covered fields under a leaden sky, as Schwartzman, wearing full chem-bio warfare fatigues leaned out the doorway into the frigid wind, which was studded with occasional snowflakes. Suddenly the Helicopter crossed a major, snow covered highway and banked sharply to follow it North, being followed by four more helicopters full of airborne Rangers. It would not be long now. *Hours late!* Thought Schwartzman in a rage. His men had been mobilized from Fort Bragg at midnight, but endless delays had slowed their arrival.

He turned and waved three fingers at the assembled Rangers, all in full winter white camouflage chem-bio suits and cradling their M-4 carbines. This was the standard three-minute warning before a combat drop and he could see the men steeling themselves for what was coming. They were to relieve a thrown together contingency force of state police, sheriff's deputies and national guard troops manning a roadblock outside of

415

Dyersville Ohio, North of Cincinnati, a small city of 50,000 people. They had flown from the national guard airfield at Cincinnati and were now passing swiftly over the small town of Weaverville. The roadblock was 5 miles north. Schwartzman tried to harden himself for what they might confront on the highway. He felt for his berretta pistol in its holster, was reassured by its heft and feel to his gloved hand. Suddenly they were dropping sharply. He looked down the road in alarm. A cluster of police cars with blue and red lights flashing and armored personnel carriers with quad-50 caliber turrets on their tops, plus several Humvees with 50 caliber machine gun mounts, was strewn across the highway blocking it in both directions. The guns faced north. He glanced quickly at the map, saw the roadblock below was several miles south of where it was supposed to be. They were dropping quickly to land the helicopters, and soon hit the ground with a jolt near the cluster of vehicles and flashing red and blue lights, brilliant in the dim light.

"DEPLOY! DEPLOY!" sergeants were yelling as Schwartzman leaped out of the helicopter on the snow swirled highway. He was running up to what looked like the Command Post at an Armored personnel Carrier or APC parked by the road with no armament on the top. He heard the pounding of boots behind him as his Ranger Battalion followed him out of the helicopters. He saw a man in desert camouflaged fatigues sitting in the back hatch of the APC, the man looked up as he approached with a vacant stare. He had Captain's insignia on his uniform.

"Captain, I am Colonel Schwartzman of the 42nd Ranger Battalion and we are your relief. Where is your CO?"

"He's up there," said the man waving his arm vacantly towards the line of armored vehicles. Schwartzman saw, in the flashing blue and red lights, that the man was not looking at him, but staring at the ground.

"We were told your position was three miles north of here Captain, why did you relocate?"

"We got overrun...the people from the town, they came out in a mob," said the Captain looking at the ground. "All their faces covered with blood, screaming, they wanted us to let them out of the cordon, we told them to go back. Women, women were holding up their children. The men wouldn't shoot…"

He shook his head and stared at the ground. Lt. Colonel Jason Parker, a powerfully built black man with a trim mustache, ran up with several more rifle platoons.

"Jason, get these men deployed and get every man here vaccinated and dosed up with Torine. Some of these men may have been exposed. I want our Battalion CP set up here at this APC." said Schwartzman waving his hand at it.

Suddenly there was a single pistol shot in the snowy air. Schwartzman and everyone else ducked down instinctively. The shot came from the direction of the two APCs with the quad 50 caliber turrets. Schwartzman looked up with apprehension and motioned for Parker to remain with the morose captain. Schwartzman marched quickly up to the line of Humvees with 50 caliber mounts and the quad mounted APCs. As he walked forward he passed a line of state police, sheriff's deputies and national guardsmen in winter uniforms coming from the other direction and headed back to the helicopters. All of their faces wore a look of horror and fatigue, all avoided his eyes.

He saw his own fresh Army Rangers manning the line of vehicles, as the light snow fell. *My men will hold this line.* He thought with grim satisfaction. He noted that the ground was increasing strewn with brass shell casings, glittering in the flashing red and blue light as he got nearer to the APCs. Near the APCs , painted unaccountably in desert camouflage, the ground was completely covered with 50 caliber casings. Schwartzman steeled himself for what lay beyond on the highway in front of the APCs. He passed beyond the last Humvee and beheld a pile of snow covered dead laying across the highway. He unconsciously estimated that perhaps a thousand bodies of men women and children lay there dusted with snow. He turned away, saw Arizona and several other Rangers standing in the snow beside a blood splattered body in National Guard fatigues, and Schwartzman strode up to them.

Arizona looked up grimly, his own face and snow camouflage fatigues spattered with blood.

417

"Arizona, what happened?" asked Schwartzman.

"This was Major Stoughton," said Arizona levelly. "I told him we were his relief. He just looked at me, said 'the men wouldn't open fire until I fired first,' and then he shot himself in the head before I could stop him."

Schwartzman nodded grimly.

"Go get yourself cleaned up back at the CP.," said Schwartzman patting him on the shoulder and motioning him back towards it. Schwartzman then turned and looked at the snowy highway and its horrid burden.

"Alright, you Rangers!" yelled Schwartzman to the grim-faced Rangers now manning the roadblock. "Our orders are to hold this cordon to enforce the quarantine !" Schwartzman pulled out his pistol. "No one passes! Medical teams are going in soon to help the survivors, but our job is to contain the Red Death so it can't spread!" *Survivors, who could survive this?*

Lt. Colonel Parker walked up swiftly and saluted. His face was grim.

"Colonel the APC was full of men with the Red Death," said Parker quickly. "They got exposed when the first roadblock was overrun. Most of them are dead. This stuff is lethal in a few hours and contagious as hell!" *God help us, what a nightmare,* thought Schwartzman.

"It looks like they hit this town with Red Death because we have good fighter cover over the major cities. It was a soft target," said Schwartzman looking down the road towards Dyersville. He noticed what looked like a figure walking in the snow-misted distance.

"One good thing, though, they found the ship that spread the stuff crashed North of Dyersville. It was light seagull type, and all the crew was dead because of the plague," said Parker incredulously.

"The stupid little shits, they made a plague that kills their own people!" said Schwartzman in amazement. But now he was looking at a figure walking slowly down the highway. A dog, perhaps a K-9 unit, walked slowly beside the figure.

"YOU! STOP! YOUR UNDER QUARANTINE!" bellowed Schwartzman. The figure continued to walk towards them. It was a national guardsman in desert fatigues, and his face was covered with blood. The figure raised it arms. The dog beside him opened its mouth and let out a pathetic bark, it exposed a mouth that was red with blood.

"STOP!" yelled Schwartzman and raised his pistol. Around him, all the Rangers raised their M-4 carbines and were priming them. The figure continued to stagger forward. Suddenly gunfire exploded across the roadblock, Schwartzman was firing too. The figure and its pathetic companion collapsed onto the snow covered highway. A thought came to Schwartzman, clear as crystal, *If this plague gets loose in a major city, we won't be able to contain it.*

****

Alicia and Goldberg walked on a snowplowed sidewalk in the center of the Pentagon. Overhead the sky was a sad blue , the Sun was reddish and weak above the horizon.

"Abe if you have a cold, you should go back indoors!" said Alicia. He looked at her with a frown.

"I have to get some fresh air, right now Alicia," he said mournfully, turning to face her. "I felt like I was going to suffocate in there. After that Martial Law briefing." Suddenly he lost his balance, fell into the snow beside the sidewalk, and then vomited.

Alicia screamed and guards began running towards them to help. In a moment military medics arrived and they were carrying him inside on a stretcher. Alicia was holding his hand.

"This is a catastrophe, I wish I had never been born..." he gasped to her and then lost consciousness.

****

Number 7 followed the large ship closely, as it raced across the starry gulf back to the Moon. Soon it was rounding the curve of the Moon to Mare Moscoviense , where the main base was.

419

"Flight 12, you are to dock only at Bay 4 for decontamination! Do you understand? Please acknowledge!" demanded Number 7 into the radio as the large ship ahead of them flew swiftly. Space static was the only response. Number 7 was in an impossible position. He was an Idelkite trying to give orders to a ship full of Unash. A slave trying to give directions to masters. The large ship, however, had dropped its deadly load of Red Plague serum in space, far above the atmosphere at Erra, where the bacteria would die instantly from dehydration and the ultraviolet of space. Number 7 knew the commander of the ship would face death for this act of insubordination. However, the cowardly act had had one benefit, it was the only plague dispersal ship that had survived the mission. The craft swiftly dropped out of space toward the nearest docking bay, which was Bay 5. Below them, the vast complex that was the Unash base in Mare Moscoviense was spread below them.

"Commander! They head for Bay 5, should we open fire on them?" asked Number 7's second in command. But the errant ship was piloted by Unash, and Number 7 and his crew were only Idelkite, of lower caste, so this was not possible.

"No! Follow them into the bay! It is all we can do!" snapped Number 7 helplessly. "Where are the other ships of the Unash!?" Number 7 then realized his own and the plague ship were they only ships returning from the mission to Erra. "Call the base command! Tell them the ship is contaminated and is headed for docking Bay 5! Ask them for permission to open fire!" ordered Number 7. He looked about his ship, fear gripped the faces of his crew.

The ship swiftly glided into the cavernous white docking bay, followed by Number 7 in his smaller Seagull-class ship. The larger ship put down its landing legs and skidded to a halt in the docking bay, and one of its landing legs collapsed. Number 7's ship landed nearby. "The landing was done badly. Perhaps the plague is loose on the ship?" wondered the first officer aloud. The massive doors of the docking bay closed behind them and the bay filled rapidly with breathable air. Number 7 watched in horror as a group of four Toman Daz security guards approached the large tilted ship with weapons drawn. They were not wearing space suits.

"Should we assist them, commander? I do not think they know the ship may be contaminated." asked his first officer.

"No! Keep the ship sealed, do not open the hatches!" cried Number 7, as he stared helplessly at the view screen as the Toman Daz guards stopped beside the main hatchway of the large ship. Suddenly the hatchway opened and out of it spilled dozens of Unash crewmen, some in spacesuits, with or without helmets. Some simply fell out of the ship or slumped in the hatchway. Some had guns and a firefight developed with the four Toman Daz guards being cut down by blue beams as the Unash from the ship began running wildly about the bay in seeming panic. One ran directly by Number 7's ship, his face covered with bluish black blotches and bleeding wounds. He was carrying a gun in his hand. He was screaming as he ran. Number 7 watched in horror as the bloody Unash ran towards one of the open hatchways from the docking bay into the rest of the base, running past a work crew of puzzled looking blue-skinned Oyans.

"Get me the Base Central Command!" yelled Number 7 as he watched more panic stricken Unash running wildly away from the ship hatchway in every direction, seemingly driven by one emotion - a hysterical desire to get away from the plague loaded ship.

"EMERGENCY, EMERGENCY! I MUST ADVISE THAT SPACE DOCKING BAY NUMBER 5 MUST BE SEALED OFF!" Number 7 was yelling into the communicator.

****

"The crews refuse to fly with the plague created by this fool!" shouted Number 2 at the cowering figure of Dr. Acra. "The carrying of many tons of this liquid plague slows down our ships, making them more vulnerable to attack, and any spillage or punctures of the plague serum tanks on the ships spreads death among our crews! They should have given us dry spores! Dr. Acra also told us the procedures for handling the serum would protect us! He told us the plague would not attack out own people! Both

421

of these were lies! This Dr. Acra should suffer a thousand deaths for his incompetence!"

Number 7 looked on past Dr. Acra, standing naked and in chains in the center of the council room, illuminated by a beam of light in the otherwise dark chamber. Number 7 and everyone else looked to Sadok Sar. Sadok Sar sat in a clear crystal booth, protecting him against death ray, and several Toman Daz guards armed and in armor stood next to him.

"My Lords, the procedures we assigned to the crews were poorly implemented! The crews were careless!" pleaded Acra "The mutation gene caused the plague to evade the immunity of the Unash!" Acra covered his eyes. "It was the mutation gene which you ordered me to apply, my Lord , that caused this to occur!" he pleaded.

"SILENCE!" shouted Sadok Sar. "Put this fool into a dark cell until we can think of an appropriate punishment for his crimes." Acra was led away roughly by several Toman Daz guards. Sadok Sar was silent for a long period. None dared speak.

"Let us now look forward to our next operations against Erra, " said Sadok Sar, looking around the dark council chamber. "Number 2 , report on our next operations against Erra!" he ordered.

****

"Do you think he can still do his job? " asked Bergman, a tinge of desperation was in his voice. He was facing Alicia at Bethesda Naval Hospital in the hallway outside Abe Goldberg's room.

"Yes, he's got the flu and is suffering from exhaustion! But he'll be fine!" said Alicia. Bergman was now acting Secretary of Defense, Clayton Thomas had suffered a massive stroke after hearing about the village of Sana, and lay in the same hospital near death.

"If he can't do it anymore, I want you to take over the War Sciences Board," said Bergman. Alicia looked at him gravely. Bergman's face was now deeply lined after eight months of war. She nodded, turned and walked in the door of Abe Goldberg's room.   Abe lay in his bed looking annoyed and uncomfortable.

"Alicia!" Abe said sharply. "I want you to help me get out of here so I can go home," Alicia smiled broadly at this  as she waltzed over to the chair by his bed and sat down.

"Feeling better are we?" she said cheerfully.

"No,  I feel like baked-over shit, but I'll feel a lot better once I get out of here!  I need a few days to get well, and I want you to take over for me until I get better." She nodded.

"Of course Abe."

"How many doses of Amonafil have we got now?"

"Two million Abe, we are in surge production and every major city has at least 300 doses, we also have the Sulfa drug, Torine, in surge production, and we have 10 million doses now."

"What about the vaccine?" he demanded

"They have a dead cell vaccine in surge production Abe, we will have a million does in a week. They are also developing a better one."

Goldberg starred off into space, he seemed to be mentally calculating.

"Good! Excellent!" he said  "I am guessing that the ship that crashed was an alien  test mission to see if the Red Plague actually works  since somebody nailed it,  it  didn't return,  and the Indians have kept a complete lid on this thing, this may be a lucky break. The Greys may think the plague wasn't effective.  The fact that crew got infected is another lucky break, the Greys may not have dealt with communicable diseases like this for a thousand years, and they may barely know what they are doing."

" Yes Abe, you may be right,"  said Alicia nodding.  She decided not to tell him about Clayton Thomas.

423

"Yeah, a piece of cake," he said nodding to himself. "It reminds me of the Japanese trying to use Bubonic Plague on the Chinese in World War Two. It ended up killing thousands of their own troops." He then paused. "Now help me get out of here Alicia,  so I can get some home-cooked chicken noodle soup from my wife!"

****

"You may have heard of rumors of the aliens attempting bacteriological warfare against us, Pamela?" said the President smoking Cuban cigar. They were sitting in the Oval office, it was snowing outside.  The President tipped back his head and blew a smoke ring, that floated gracefully up to the high ceiling.  She was dressed in a black clingy turtleneck and grey slacks.  He was dressed in a suit and tie.

"We have heard rumors of this, yes,"  she said writing in her notebook. *We heard they wiped out a village in India and a town in Ohio.* A terrible chill filled her. *It must be true.*

"Well, I can tell you on background that we captured an alien ship full of a bacteriological agent, and we have analyzed it, produced a vaccine, and identified several antibiotics that are effective against it.  We are presently stockpiling the drugs and vaccines in case they are needed. "

"Yes, so we are prepared?"   asked Pamela nodding her head and scribbling on her notepad.

"Yes, we are well prepared,  but we are not going to publicize this unless we deem it absolutely necessary.  It's clearly designed to be a terror weapon, so in order to prevent it from causing terror, we are keeping a lid on it.  That,  and increasing out air and space patrols to shoot down anything that might be carrying the stuff."

"So you don't think this will be a problem?"

"No," said the President putting down his cigar and looking at her with a smile. "That's why this is on deep background. We got a 'lucky break' in capturing that ship,  as one of our scientists said. But I like to keep you informed.  It just shows again the sort of enemy we are dealing with.  You

424

might also know that when we captured the ship, most of the crew was infected by their own plague, so these people obviously have problems with trying to wage this sort of warfare. I've dealt with geniuses all my life Pamela, and one thing they all had in common was that they thought they could do anything! So these aliens actually fit that pattern! We also know from testing that the bacteria dies in cold weather, so we have another lucky break." He motioned to the snow outside. "Oh, we shot down five ships last night also," he added taking up is cigar again.

Later, Pamela was sitting in Manny Berkowitz's office at CNS drinking some coffee, she had her feet up on the coffee table and was trying to relax.

" So everything is going fine with the war? I mean according to the President?"

"Oh yes!" said Pamela feigning happiness. "According to the President, we just had two towns wiped by some sort of Red Death, which the Greys can deliver over our cities anytime they want, but other than that the war is going fine!"

" So the rumors are true?"

"Yes, Manny, if they weren't I wouldn't have been invited to the Oval office to receive a pep talk. Things are going so perfectly well, they are stockpiling vaccines and drugs against this plague as fast as they can, and we have been asked not to talk about it."

"So they want us to keep quiet about it? Even the vaccine and drug stockpiles?" asked Manny in disappointment. Pamela put down her coffee and stood and went to the window and looked at the swirling snow.

"Yes, I am afraid so, Manny. Just because I get to sit in the Oval office and listen to glowing reports doesn't mean we get scoops every week. But I have learned one important new thing."

"What's that, Pam." She turned and her beautiful blues eyes fastened on him, mesmerizing him despite himself.

"I have learned the wonderful power of denial and wishful thinking to sustain oneself in a disaster," she said smiling. "I never realized before that denial was such an essential human ability," she added.

****

Schwartzman, Arizona, and Jason Parker sat in the headquarters office of the 42nd Ranger Battalion at Fort Bragg, staring at the phone that they hoped would never ring. They had received new bio suits, thousands of doses of Tamozone and Torine, and been vaccinated with what was called a "new and improved vaccine". *All I know is, that I am still alive, and so are all my troops. Nothing else matters,* thought Schwartzman.

In the darkness, the hours crept by, but the phone did not ring.

****

Abe Goldberg, Alicia and a team of Army officers from Fort Dietrich sat in the special "Red Death" command post in the Pentagon, waiting for any alerts as the midnight approached. If a new outbreak was reported they would throw into action thousands of soldiers, planes, and medical personnel.

Goldberg was well again and looked relaxed. Alicia was a nervous wreck, worrying about everything, including Blue, who was off going through crash astronaut training.

"Alicia , how is your kid doing in preschool," asked Goldberg suddenly.

"Oh, he's doing really well Abe. He can add and subtract now."

"Good, sounds like a future rocket scientist," he said happily. "You should be teaching him Bergenholm's unified field theory next."

The vigil continued until Alicia slipped into her office and lay down on a cot and went to sleep.

****

426

Number 7 looked on blankly as a large self-propelled death ray projector rolled up on motive screws and lowered the muzzle of its death ray projector down the wide hallway. Hundreds of Toman Daz warriors in full armor stood beside it, fully armed and looked determined. At the sight of this, Number 7 commanded his company of lightly armed Idelkite warriors to retire behind them. They were in the main passageway connecting the western space dockyards to the core of the base in Mare Moscoviense. A high caste Unash officer stood in armor with a death ray carbine held at the ready. Number 7 approached him and bowed low.

"I yield this position, my Lord, to your august unit! What are your further orders?"

"Remove your troops to the main hatchway and seal us in! Then KILL THAT FOOL, SADOK SAR!" spat the officer. Number 7 was stunned at this statement and bowed lower in confusion. "He has ordered this section to be vented to space if we cannot hold back the plague infected ones!" yelled the officer. "We have been given no spacesuits for protection, no respirators, nothing! So we are already dead if they come down this passage! So we are dead by plague exposure or dead by being vented to space! HOW ARE THE BRAVE WARRIORS OF THE GENSPORE WASTED BY SADOK SAR'S STUPIDITY!"

Number 7 looked at the brave faces of the other Toman Daz looking on grimly. Waved his own troops back down the passageway.

"Yes, my Lord!" said Number 7, helplessly and bowing low. Soon they were running down the passage to the great main hatchway. Only when they were safely through it and it was closed and sealed, did he feel safe? More Toman Daz warriors in armor and with death ray carbines stood at the ready.

"You! Idelkite!" shouted an Unash officer in armor at him. "What was the status of the last barricade when you left?"

"It was well and peaceful my Lord," said Number 7 bowing low.

"How can you say anything is well, in the middle of this shitstorm?" asked the Unash officer angrily . Number 7 stared at him, not knowing how to

427

answer." Set up your line behind us then dungeater! And hope the plague victims have not the sense to operate the controls to this hatch from the passageway!"

"yes my Lord!" said Number 7. The deep voices of the Toman Daz shouted, and Number 7 looked up at a view screen. Blue death rays were mowing down crowds of plague victims and others simply fleeing the plague in the passageway he and his men had just occupied minutes before. He looked on in horrified fascination and saw that despite the rapid firing of even the large self-propelled death ray projector, the line of Toman Daz warriors in armor was being overrun. Suddenly, there were loud booming noises and Number 7's eyes darted to the large crystal viewport to the vacuum outside. The entire west dockyard area was being vented to the vacuum of space by means of large remotely operated ports, with large plumes of water vapor and debris spewing out into the vacuum beneath the cold unblinking stars and forbidding lunar mountains beyond. He now recognized that mixed with the debris flying out of the hatches as the dockyards were depressurized, were countless bodies.

****

Nora Goldberg walked slowly into the dimly lit room wearing a loose fitting blue robe. Tears were streaming down her face. In the room were a bed and a table with an open bottle of wine and two plastic glasses. A handsome and muscular young man with sandy blonde hair and also wearing a blue robe sat on the bed. He only looked up when she had approached closely to him. He smiled at first, then looked away. They were on Nashan, the home world of the Unash.

"Hello," he said. "Do you want some wine?" He turned to look at her. She was quite pretty but crying now.

"No," she gasped.

"It's not that bad. They have tried to copy some cheap fruity wine from Earth."

"What's your name." she wept.

"Joseph Forrester. What is your name?"

"Nora, Nora Goldberg"

"Well, Nora, you and I are supposed to make a child tonight. If we do not make love tonight, we will both be punished," he said looking at the wall.

"I know, they told me." she gasped. "They say I am at my most fertile now."

"Why are you crying? It will be OK," he said gently to her.

"I'm scared you'll hurt me. The last time this happened to me was two years ago on the Moon. I was fifteen, and I was raped by an alien hybrid, in a room like this." she wept, and she was trembling. He reached up and took her hand, it was trembling. He gently pulled her down to sit beside him.

"I won't hurt you. I promise I will be gentle."

"What do you think will happen to the child we conceive tonight?" she asked.

"I try not to think, Nora. I just live moment to moment, try to make Doctor Vasa happy."

"Vasa, is he a nice person?"

"He can be, all I know is that everyone around here, human and Unash, wants to make him happy."

"He is friends with doctor Ukla, I know. Doctor Ukla is nice. He brought me and Doctor Rosen here from the Moon to save us, he said."

"He did?"

"Yes, I saw him and doctor Vasa talking. They seemed like they were friends."

"Well, we had best make them all happy then."

"There is war back at Earth and on the Moon; the United States and the Russians, they are at war with the Unash now," Nora said quickly. At this report, Joseph suddenly stood up and stared off into space in the dimly lit room. He seemed deep in thought.

"Earth, that is 400 light years from here," he said finally. "That is no longer part of our reality here."

"Don't you have family back on Earth? Don't you care about what happens to them?" she asked. He slowly sat down beside her.

"Yes, I have a family back on Earth. I have two brothers, a sister, and a mother and father."

"Don't you ever think about them?" she asked. "I think about my family all the time."

" You'll quit thinking about them after a few years here," he said.

"I have an uncle Abe who is a scientist, and I have another uncle Avram, he's a commando in the Israeli Army. I keep thinking he will come and rescue me someday."

"You have to quit thinking that, it's bad mental health here, " said Joseph " It makes you sad. If you get sad here you tend to disappear. They like their lab rats happy here."

"God has not forgotten us, I will see Earth again," she said.

"Who says that?" said Joseph with irritation.

"Doctor Rosen, he taught us to pray and gave us lessons from the Talmud," she leaned close to him and he gently put his arm around her.

"I have quit praying to God here. He might as well not exist."

"You used to pray?" she kissed him on the cheek, and she felt the wetness of tears.

"I got brought here when I was sixteen, that was three years ago. I used to pray that God would bring me back to Earth so I could see my family again...But I learned I had to focus on the here and now, that is mental survival and that is physical survival."

"What do you do here?" she asked vacantly.

"I demonstrate that human beings are not animals. That's what I decided my role was here. That's what Doctor Vasa wants. They taught me Archmetan, which is a sort of common galactic language, and lots of physics and literature and Vasa has me go to universities around here on this planet and give speeches, and I dance with a dance group, just like trained monkeys, to impress Unash students. But we quit doing that a few months ago. Now, I know why."

"I am going to pray, will you pray with me?" asked Nora, she leaned forward and kissed him on the lips. She slipped off her robe. He kissed her in return and they embraced.

"OK, you pray, I will agree." He said, slipping off his robe.

"We are going to pray that the child we conceive tonight is going to grow up on Earth and be free..." she gasped as she began kissing him again.

****

Tatiana and Amber were preparing emergency medical kits for the crews of the spacecraft when they looked up in the medical lab and saw Oyka glaring at them from the doorway.

"You dung eaters are the cause of all my misery on this rock!" he said loudly. He approached them and pulled out his pain wand. "Because of you, I get no promotions! I GET ONLY REPRIMANDS!" he screamed.

Tatiana stood up from the medical kit she was working on, as did Amber, and both began to retreat from him. Tatiana glanced behind them, the doorway to the out area was sealed, a precaution since painkillers had been disappearing from the medical kits. Suddenly Number 7 appeared in the doorway.

"Unit Oyka! Why are you not at your appointed post?"

431

Oyka froze, and turned.

"I do not have to take orders from you, Idelkite!"  But a medicast Unash appeared beside Number 7.

"Unit Oyka! You must accompany us! INSTANTLY!"

Oyka wilted and sheathed his pain wand.  He then turned and slowly walked out of the medical lab and disappeared from the doorway with the medicast Unash.

The idea of more emergency medical kits for missions to Erra had been the suggestion of Number 7, and he had been commended for this idea by several Unash commanders, and as a result, he watched over their preparation carefully.

Number 7 lingered in the doorway watching the two women return to work. He nodded at them.

"Carry on with your work," he said  quietly, then disappeared.

Later at the main space docking by Number 3,  the crews were lining up to make another terror mission to Erra.

"Unit Okla, here," began Number 7, "has shown by his righteous hatred of the Errans  by interfering with the Errans on the  medical staff, who have been helping us recently. "A chorus of jeers and curses  arose from the assembled  crews. "Number 18 has therefore honored Unit Oyka  by assigning him the role  of ship's  mutilator on terror missions."

The assembled Unash and Idelkite crewmen cheered.

So Oyka departed with an Unash crew to Erra, and neither he or the crew was ever seen again.

****

Joseph and Nora stood facing each other wearing beige coveralls  of handsome silky material; they were in the main room of a mansion of an important personage Grand Marshall  Skana, in the City of Nashan.

Marshal Skana and his wife, both elderly, sat with blank expressions as Dr. Ukla motioned to Joseph and Nora to begin.

**The Song of Erra, first chapter**

Oh hark, the beautiful light with which the universe began, shining from one end to the other and banishing the darkness!

Oh, light like a rainbow full of colors! Light brilliant! And from this light, the angels were born so the heavens were full of song! Oh, wondrous life made of light!

Then from the light came dazzling lighting both blue, red and yellow like gold, the stars were born and the from the rainbow hues, planets, no two being alike and all in many colors.

Oh behold, then was born Erra, called most beautiful of the worlds, with blue oceans vast and verdant mountains high, crowned with brilliant snows. Deep forests covered her and grassy plains, green and sweet, and all manner of life. For the seas thronged with silver-scaled fish and whales, and likewise, the land was filled with beauteous life, of deer and birds of lovely plumage, so like the beauty of Erra amid the stars were the children of Erra beauteous, and of as many colors of the rainbow.

Then came brave Arik of the Vikhelm, who first set foot on Erra. For he said, I saw its fair light, and was drawn like a moth to a candle.

He stood in an emerald green place by the ship where it had landed and saw a beautiful woman with hair of fine copper polished, so it shown.

He inquired of her, what was the name of the place, waving his hands to four winds, and she replied with a smile that the place was called Erra. So was it that this globe of beauty received its name among all the stars, meaning sphere of beauty and fair one, fairest of all known worlds.

**Second chapter of the Song of Erra verses one through four**

Because of the beauty of Erra, that fair jewel among the stars, and the beauty of its daughters, came many who journeyed far to behold her.

433

There came the Vikhelm and the Samar and bold Pleiadians from across the stars to see if the tales of Erra's beauty were true. And all who saw her and her children carried word to the farthest stars, of her bounty and fair light. All loved her, and all desired her.

But then came those who were not content to behold the beauty of Erra and its daughters, but said in their hearts, I shall not only behold, but touch and possess.

So by of the beauty of Erra, were her sorrows multiplied.

**Third chapter of Erra , verses 20 – 25**

Alas, and alas, my ear is torn asunder for the travail of Erra, who is called most beautiful of worlds!

For the takers have come to Erra, and they seize of the beautiful daughters of Erra whomever they choose and serve death to any who oppose them.

So by your beauty are your sorrows multiplied, of Erra, most fair of worlds, for the planet is ravished along with its daughters, so the villages are full of fatherless children, and the earth is raped to yield gold and other metals. So are the children of Erra enslaved to serve those of the stars, how is the fair world ravaged, so that the cosmos cannot bear it. For they have not picked them a few of the choice wildflowers of Erra, they have picked them everyone, so the villages are full of the fatherless. So the cry of this came up into the Heaven of Heavens , and God looked down to see if the transgressions of those of the stars were according to the cry of it. And He became very Angry.

Avert not your eyes from Erra, say not, that we did not know what transpired there.

Avert not your eyes, but behold the reasons for the things to come.

*Song of Erra chapter 7 verses 10-17*

Alas and woe, my heart is broken by travail! For after the battle over the fair daughter of Erra, Geeanne fairest of a thousand of her daughters, they buried her beside the brave knight of the Samar, Tonkaal son of Tawn, who had been her protector against Bursus of the Vikhelm. For he said to Bursus, let her alone, that this further sin be not added to us all.

They also buried many of the brave companions of Tonkaal, and of the brave knights of the Vikhelm, in the same field, for there were many fallen in the battle, over the fair daughter of Erra, Geeanne.

The dead were so many, that they buried them in the same field, for those left alive were too few to move them.

And when Lord Tallus of the Samar heard of the battle and the many fallen of the Samar, he said

We shall avenge the glorious dead of the Samar seven fold!

Then said the brothers of Bursus of the Vikhelm, who had desired Geeanne

We shall be avenged of our brothers upon the Samar to seventy times seventy!

So there was war at Erra spreading from one end to another, and into its skies and seas.

War spread from the Erra to the very heavens. For they said, we will take Erra, the fair, for our own possession!

Now was their war at Erra and the brave sons of Erra were made to serve in the armies of the Samaran and the Vikhelm and Pleiadians, now was fair Erra a battlefield and its children welcomed into the embrace of it earth, so there were too few left alive to bury the dead.

Then there was war in heaven, and Erra and spreading like a fire to the stars surrounding her, for God had determined to avenge Erra and her daughters, of the evil that had been done to her.

Now is their war at Erra, called the beautiful one, and now no star will know peace.

Woe to all stars and those who dwell in them! The daughters of the Samar go about in black, because their men are gone, never to return! Behold in Vale of the Vikhelm the funeral pyres burn until the forests can no longer give wood for them. So in the entire Echelon, there is sorrow. To the Pleiadian, there is shame of face and blue robes of mourning in every house.

And like a beautiful flower torn,when strong men strive over her, avert not your eyes! Nor say, we did not know, for the stars bear witness to all things. So was Erra destroyed by the war.

For some said, if we cannot possess Erra , let none have her!

So nova weapons were used by the Vikhelm and Samaran and even the Pleiadian on the white polar caps of Erra, to flood the planet and drown all its life, for they said, we will destroy all the camps of our enemies in the valleys of the lands.

So great was the destruction, that when those faraway heard the tale of it, their ears tingled at the hearing of it, and they wept at the terribleness of the account.

Oh Erra, your beauty is now wrapped in the white clouds of death, like a beautiful pearl You are fair even in death, where before you were like a beautiful blue sapphire.

Avert not your eyes! Nor say, we did not know, for the stars bear witness to all things

Oh let it be recorded forever, that myself and my companions of the Vikhelm repented of the evil that our people had done, and searched below the clouds for any alive, of the children of Erra,

But we found only bare mountains and storms . None remained alive, though we looked for many days in the rains and lightning.

Found we only dead, floating in the waves of the storm.

So was the light of Erra snuffed out like a candle and its fair children destroyed.

Like a beautiful flower when strong men strive over it.

But the war continued, like an unquenchable fire, to all stars after that, for many years, so no place was left untouched, and in no house was their not mourning. For nova weapons, first used on the beautiful world, were then used against many fair worlds, like they had been used against Erra.

I, the recorder of this terrible tale, lost my wife and children and four brothers, so I alone am left of my house to tell this tale.

Thus did the Father of All Stars avenge himself for the children of Erra, so that for the ravishing of the daughters of Erra we are dishonored, and for the destruction of Erra we are destroyed.

Oh, Erra blessed be those who bless you and cursed be those who curse you.

Avert not your eyes! Nor say, we did not know, for the stars bear witness to all things.

But behold I will show you a wonderment! I will show you a miracle like the dawn of the stars, for Erra will be reborn to her former beauty and fullness.

Her blue oceans will once again throng with life, her forests be filled with deer and birds.

The skies of Erra will return to azure blueness with clouds of white.

Behold the children of Erra will again walk the deep forests and emerald plains, and her beauty will be restored.

So they will say Erra has risen from the dead with her children.

Those whom the stars counted dead will rise, and sing, and their sign shall be the rainbow of bright colors!

For behold God will do a wondrous thing at Erra, so her beauty and life will be restored.

And the house of Batelgeen of the Samar, God will remember, because of their help to Erra, and by a daughter of Erra, a daughter of two mothers, will the throne be restored to Batelgeen, so will the fair stars of the Echelon be saved by the strength of Erra.

And it shall be written, at the end of time, that the ruler the Cosmos shall be called the Child of Erra.

****

Marshall Skana closed his eyes at this account, and his wife covered hers in sorrow.

"So is the reading of portions of the Song of Erra, my Lord," said Dr. Ukla, motioning to Joseph and Nora to retire.

"Please let these beautiful children go enjoy our gardens outside." said the wife of Marshall Skana as she rose to pour tea. She then also retired so the Dr. Ukla could speak privately with the Marshall.

Joseph and Nora went outside and sat on a beautifully carved stone bench, in the garden above the mansion. There they could see the whole city of Nashan, under a blue sky, with the mighty river Ushan flowing out to the sea beyond the hills. Joseph put his arm around Nora and held her close. The city below them was made of glittering metal buildings, but also was largely composed of dwellings and shops carved from a soft volcanic rock found in the area. It was the first time either of them had been allowed above ground in all their time there.

"It looks so much like Earth," said Nora sadly. Joseph turned to kiss her as they sat, feeling the cool breeze from the sea, amid the garden.

Inside Dr. Ukla leaned close to Marshal Skana and spoke.

"My Lord, forgive me for my forthrightness, but as you are aware there is a crisis at Erra in the Quzrada, and the threat of a second war of the Quzrada if this crisis is not addressed.

"Stay on, Dr. Ukla, as a member of the high council," said Marshall Skana. This has lately been of concern to us. You are one of the few who has

438

been to Erra in the Quzrada and can give a firsthand account. So you words are valuable to me."

"My Lord, if one analyzes the larger picture of our people in the cosmos you see that our problem is that we have no friends or allies. Whereas the Vikhelm are part of a strong alliance, and even seek an alliance with the Anak and Pleiadians against the Samar, whereas we are alone."

"We have the Haddan Daz and Oyan, as allies, Dr, Ukla."

"But they are only servants, they can give us no insights or advice, they only tell us what they are ordered to tell us."

"Have we not the Samar as our allies in the Quzrada?" asked Skana.

"My Lord the Samar are not our friends, they despise us and are only using the blood of our brave warriors to advance their own interests. I have seen this at Erra. I believe they want Erra for themselves."

"Well, the high council considers them allies, but I would agree we can do better. So how do you propose to remedy this problem?" asked the Marshall.

"We should make peace with the Errans and become friends with them!" said Dr. Ukla. "They are poorly developed, but with our help, they would become mighty, like Pleiadians and even the Samar. From my dealings with the captive Errans, I am convinced we can earn their friendship, and they can learn to appreciate our wisdom and culture. Just as you saw in the recitation of our two young captives, the Errans can be taught high civilization. But if the crisis at Erra continues, I see only disaster for our people. We must make peace before this war involves other peoples and spreads to become another war of the Quzrada.

"You call this crisis a war? How does this war go so far? I have heard several reports, but I am curious to hear a firsthand account of this crisis. "

"My Lord, the war goes badly at Erra! The Errans discovered our plot to subvert their government, and now they fight with great bravery, even though their weapons are inferior to ours. Compounding this problem, our commander at Erra is a fool and should be replaced. We must send a true commander of war to stabilize the situation, and then negotiate a peace! This must be done quickly before the Errans invade Una!"

"Are they capable of such a feat? I had heard that they were quite primitive."

"Yes, they are capable of it, and they have captured much of our technology and have begun to duplicate it. So, my lord, we must seek peace with them and trade with them rather than fight. I believe that we can make peace with them.

"I think that the course of action you suggest is not possible because of our agreements with the Samar," said Skana levelly. "Is this not the theory of this whole operation at Erra; that we should have coition at Erra and merge with their genome? Then we should have them as allies, in a manner of speaking. Has this not been successful?"

"No, my Lord, it has not been. The theory of coition at Erra was that the Errans, being genetically mixed people containing Samaran, Pleiadian, and Vikhelm genetic materials would be a central genome that we could fuse more easily with than any other Archmetan genes, but alas, the hybrid beings are sickly and weak and do not live long. As is well known, the major problem is that the blood of the Errans is iron- based, whereas ours and the rest of our servants use hemocyanin which is copper or hemosphorin which is copper and manganese based. This was known from the beginning to be a grave difficulty existing at Erra, but the project was pressed ahead despite this because of its importance. However, several clever attempts to bypass this problem have failed, and so the hybrids who live, have weak blood. This failure was predicted by Dr. Tunal many decades ago, who first studied the Errans. As he said, 'a worm and a serpent look similar and both dwell in the dirt, but their physiology is completely different and one cannot mate with the other'."

"So this is a crisis," continued Dr. Ukla, and we should make a peace settlement with the Errans and quit fighting them. Are we not already fighting the Unull?"

440

"Our war with the Unull progresses well, you should not be concerned about it," said the Marshall quickly.

"Yes, my lord, but the crisis at Erra?"

"We have heard of only slight difficulties at Erra, and that these do not constitute a crisis, and will be resolved quickly. However, I will discuss your proposal with my fellows in the high council. Such a change of policy would have to be taken to the Genspore himself, however, I think that our policies cannot be changed without also consulting the Samar, who are our sole friends in this matter. "

"My Lord, there is saying among the Errans, that with friends such as the Samar, one has no need for enemies"

"Do not ask me to quote sayings of the Errans to the council, good Doctor," scolded the Marshall. "However, I am very grateful for your reports, and I will enquire further concerning the situation at Erra.

****

At night over the British midlands, near Lincolnshire, Number 7 and his crew of Idelkite hovered at high altitude. They were Flight 16, supporting a terror mission, waiting for the return from lower altitude of several Unash ships. They were startled by a break in radio silence.

"Emergency! Emergency! Flight 16 descend and help us! Two ships are damaged!" the message was followed by a blast of static.

"Descend! Descend! Arm all weapons! Prepare for battle!" barked Number 7 to his crew. "Tell the others to follow us!" He remembered thinking , *our ships are more lightly armed than the Unash, yet they call for help from us?*

They descended many thousands of feet to find a raging battle. British Typhoon fighters were swarming around a group of rising Unash seagull ships , trying to escort two ships damaged by ground fire. The Unash had apparently been ambushed on their terror and mutilation mission. Number 7 looked in awe at the sky around them, now filled with fire explosions, red tracers bullets, and glowing missile trails. Suddenly, a

441

Typhoon fighter appeared flying straight at them and opened fire with red tracer shells. The view screen became a cloud of brilliant red lights. Number 7 heard a deafening sound and felt a great impact on his space suit.

Number 7 awoke, an Idelkite crewman was bent over him in a space suit. The crewman was placing tape over the chest plate of his space suit. He tried to rise but felt an awful pain.

"Lie still oh Captain! You are badly wounded!" said the crewman winding the tape around him to seal the breach in his spacesuit. "We are safe in deep space now and returning to our base! Lie still!" The crewman took a syrette of pain killer and stabbed it through Number 7's suit, causing him to fall into a sweet mental fog. "I serve the Genspore!" he gasped as he lost consciousness.

He awoke being carried off his ship. The interior of the ship was covered with splattered blood and what he recognized as lumps of flesh. He then recognized the ceiling of the space docking bay.

"He has a shell in him! It must be removed!" he heard one of his crew crying out to someone.

*Poor fellow* thought Number 7 *I hope he can be saved . I hope it is not another member of my own crew.*

He was now involved in a confused jumble of movement and noise. An Unash was screaming in agony. He heard also hushed voices of Unash and Idelkite . He saw he was in a space docking bay medical area as he looked up at its familiar ceiling metal plates. Two Unash dressed in medical suits were now above him, he felt them removing the chest plate on his spacesuit.

"HE HAS AN EXPLOSIVE SHELL STUCK IN HIS CHEST!!!" one of the medicast faces screamed and both faces disappeared. "EVACUATE THE AREA!" Number 7 heard a jumble of feet and sounds of things being dragged then, suddenly all was silent except for distant sounds and cries, and he realized he was alone, laying on the floor, staring up at the ceiling of the space bay.

After a moment a strange thing began to happen to him. He began to see many memories, his time in the nurseries with the other children, his favorite nurse, then harsh days in school with Unash schoolmasters and their harsh discipline, then the spaceflight academy, the joy of comradeship with his fellow Idelkites, by far the most talented of all the slave species of the Unash. *We serve the Genspore.* Then he remembered the happy memories, of flying through space amid the endless stars. Then, he saw a great gentle light approaching him. It was made of many colors, all beautiful. It was, he sensed, the source of all good in the stars coming for him.

Suddenly Tatiana's face was over him, ending his beautiful vision. He tried to speak to her of the vision.

"Lie still!" she snapped and he felt a painful tugging in his chest. She then disappeared. *Come back! I must tell you of my vision!* He thought dreamily, and then an Unash face was above him and he lost consciousness.

Tatiana, dressed in white medical coveralls, splattered with blue blood, was walking carefully towards the explosive disposal chamber clasping the 27 mm explosive shell, slick with blue blood, in a pair of surgical tongs, normally used for removing shrapnel from bodies. She stepped carefully to avoid slipping in the pools of blue blood on the floor. Everyone else had fled in terror leaving Number 7 lying alone and dying in the medical area of the space docking bay. Even the wounded had been picked up and frantically moved away from him. They had left him lying alone on the floor of the cavernous docking bay, with only dead bodies lying near him.

But Tatiana had recognized him and rushed over to him as everyone fled. *If he dies, we will all die here,* she thought. *He is the only one here who cares for us.*

Everyone was running from her as she carefully approached a nearby disposal chamber, a heavy cylindrical metal chamber with a heavy alloy funnel on the top. It had been installed since many ships now returned with unexploded shells embedded in their hulls or crew.

She carefully dropped the shell, covered with blue blood, into the funnel, so that it slid down the side and into the chamber, and then she leaped way as it exploded when it hit the bottom, with a deafening metallic clang. Acrid smoke arose from the funnel. She coughed and waved at the medical crews to resume their work. Amber and Kathy were helping the wounded as were several other women, for the regular medical Unash medical staff had been seriously depleted during the plague outbreak, now even Errans like her with medical training were being pressed into service to take care of the tide of wounded returning from Erran missions.

She walked carefully over to where Number 7 lay. He had become an important person of late, and she saw that several senior Unash were attending to his injuries. She then went over to the nearest unattended wounded and tried to help them .

****

Qwami Howsa, his large afro bobbing as he vigorously emphasized each point, summarized his briefing on his and Dr. Levine's analysis on Unash flight control systems. He was the picture of a young, enthusiastic scientist.

"What we see in the Unash craft, is best described as a copying of biological systems, using a control system that is best described as a "super analog" without a digital language. This is not a new observation we realize, but what we have found in our research is that this neural net can now be mapped extensively in terms of topology and functionality using this model. One obvious advantage of this system is that it is much more difficult to "hack" by exterior signals than a language based system, and also that it does not rely on data buses but instead on distributed, almost holographic, structures that are robust to damage. Signals are processed in terms of a cascade of multiplex nodes which respond to control voltages by sending out other preset voltage signals. It is basically a network of multiplex input-output nodes. The system, which includes even the skin of the craft, resembles a biological nerve net in a complex animal. In general, the Unash seem to have largely avoided computers in the sense that we use them, instead, they make the entire control system a sort of supercomputer integrating signals and functions. This is

444

particularly true of control voltages controlled in turn by proportional light signals in the layered skin of the craft. Our colleague, Josh Resnick, will now discuss how this active skin is used in the control of the Poynting vector boundary layer of the gravitic drive."

"So they don't use processors or computers in their control system?" asked Alicia.

"Not in the sense we use them. In fact, we cannot find a central flight computer that controls the craft in the sense of flight computers in our own craft. We see in the Unash craft that we have recovered, a very different design philosophy from human technology. Humans tend to centralize control and computation. In the Unash systems, we see, we have found and what appears to be an aversion to central processing or computation. We are trying figure out the motivation for it."

Abe Goldberg then stood up, looked at his watch.

"We'll have to save further discussion on this subject for later. We are behind schedule." Abe then turned to Joshua Resnick and Richard Mathews, two eager young students, and motioned them to the podium.

The first viewgraph of their presentation appeared: 'Spacetime/Fluid Dynamics Duality and Computational Models of Geometro-Electromagneto-Dynamic Vacuum Bulk and Boundary Layer Flows'

Alicia was watching spellbound. *The finest minds we have, now, unleashed...*

Later, the briefings from the Prometheus group were over, and everyone was relaxing over dinner. Still, a great sense of optimism and excitement hung over the room. Abe Goldberg and Alicia were sitting next to Josh Resnick and Quami Howsa, obviously the shining stars of the group.

"The biggest puzzle we have uncovered is the lack of real supercomputers on the crafts, at least that we can identify. Everything we find so far in the neural maps seems to be quite localized and specific in function, like a neural concentration to control the electromagnetic gravity flight systems or one to control life support. The ship's controls are very much hands-on

445

also, they relied on the crew to fly the craft most of the time, not an autopilot. It's driving the hardcore cyber guys in the group crazy. They want to find the main computer and unravel its operating system, but it's like they're looking for the wrong thing. Instead, we have them making algorithms mimic the neural net digitally.

"Yes, it's almost like the Unash viewed themselves as part of the computing architecture. Like they viewed their own crew as automatons. It is also like they were afraid of powerful computers. I talked to one of the Air force officers about recovered ships from other cultures that they have, and he said they saw the same thing, ships flown by flesh and blood with no central flight computers. It's especially baffling because these people are a hundred years ahead of us supposedly, and yet they are still flying the craft with biological crews. The cyber people say that any truly advanced culture would consist only of machines, yet here we are looking at control panels with knobs and switches for manual control."

"Yeah, I noticed that too. It's a paradox. You would have thought all these cultures would have gone through some technological singularity and replaced themselves with computers." said Quasi.

"Singularity? I have never believed in that concept," laughed Goldberg, nursing a glass of wine. "Asking people to engineer their own genocide? Hah! Ever since I was a graduate student at MIT, the computer science experts have been rushing up to me and telling me humanity will be replaced by computers. Back at MIT when I was in grad school in the 1970's, the comp science majors said to me, `Abe! AI will make the human race obsolete by 1980! And extinct by the year 2000!' "He then added, "of course these same guys were telling me to try this new drug called cocaine, that wasn't addictive, they insisted." Everyone at the corner of the table near Abe laughed at his comment. "Actually, never took those projections seriously then, I figured then we would be extinct from a nuclear war long before 2000. Now, that talk of singularity and computers being the next stage of evolution, instead, kind of reminds me of all the talk about eugenics before World War Two. Scientists, then, talked about producing a new superior breed of human being by selective breeding. What they ended up producing instead was the Waffen SS and the Holocaust." He paused and drained his wineglass. Abe then added,

446

"So there was lots of talk about eugenics before World War Two, afterward... not so much. The Singularity will be the same way, I think."

"I haven't heard much talk of the Singularity lately, thank God." said Alicia feeling the child inside her womb suddenly kicking her. "It always seemed implausible to me, and right now we see the human race engaged in a massive struggle to head off the possibility of a real extinction. So, the idea that people are going to cooperate in their own extinction sometime in the future seems pretty absurd."

"I would like to also say" Alicia continued holding aloft her fruit juice, "that you Prometheans have convinced me, just this afternoon, that the human race is not going anywhere, that instead, we humans are a fairly permanent fixture of the universe, as annoying as that is apparently to some people." *La Raza Cosmica, it will endure...*she thought *somehow...*

****

Cassandra sat in the main office at the Aircraft Plant in Wichita Kansas. Several somber FBI agents sat looking at her. Two were men, one was a women. They looked at her with what she recognized as grudging respect. The chief of the plant was standing beside her. She glanced out the window and saw the Sun high in the clear cold sky. It was reddish and weak. *Why?*

She had been transferred to Wichita from Seattle, ostensibly because she was a top performer on the assembly line, with fewer faults wiring space-fighters reported than anyone in the plant. But now Cassandra wondered if that had all been a ploy to get her out of Seattle, where she had sensed danger. She knew she was good at her job but now realized that her conceit at not being recognized was actually a farce. The authorities had known her every footstep all along.

"So Miss Chen," began the senior FBI agent. "I think you understand that we can't protect you here. You have to be transferred to a government facility, preferably a military base where the Men in Black or alien sympathizers can't get to you. Do you understand?"

447

"Yes," she said somberly. *I guess this little adventure as part of the proletariat is over. It was getting old anyway.* She admitted to herself. *Time to move on.*

"We are trying to set up a secure place for you at Fort Sill, but if that falls through we'll have to send you to the most secure facility in the vicinity, which is at Morningstar Colorado," said the senior agent.

The words hit her like a physical blow. *No, NO...* she thought while keeping her face controlled. *But I have to live to accomplish my mission. It would be embarrassing at this point, after all, these warnings, to have some idiot shoot me on a bus.*

"I understand, if that's where I have to go, I understand." she said with a trembling voice, she was now looking at the floor.

"We understand, given your background, that this is probably the last place on Earth you would like to go, Miss Chen but we can't find anywhere else where you can go and be incognito, which we know you want, and which we feel is necessary for your safety," said the senior FBI agent.

"I will go," she said standing up, her voice strong. *Somehow, it is fate.*

****

Pamela was standing by Hans Bergenholm at Kennedy Space Center, in her tailored combat fatigues, watching a Saturn V, Mark III rise off the pad on a tower of blinding radiance. The cold air around her shook and she felt her body shaking with it. The Saturn V, Mark III was a heavy lifter, a standard Saturn V core with two solid-fuel strap-on boosters that had blinding white hot exhaust.

"That's two hundred and fifty tons into low earth orbit or 100 tons to the Moon in one pop!" yelled Bergenholm over the snapping roar of the shockwaves washing over them "The strap-on solids use reformulated fuel with ADN, rubber and aluminum, and no chlorine. We can launch these guys all day and they won't hurt the ozone layer!" Pamela watched now with binoculars as the Saturn V, Mark III arced over in the cold blue sky and dropped its solid boosters. They deployed parachutes. Ships waited offshore to recover the solid booster casings for reuse. The thunder and cracking of shock waves abated as the mighty booster became a spark in the deep blue sky. She glanced over and saw two more S5-3's, the common term for the booster, being readied for launch.

"The gang up in space, they are hanging on. The aliens can't dislodge them from low-Earth-orbit. We have a firm beachhead in space now. They tell us every time they see us make one of these big launches it does wonders for morale. They know it means more ammo and more groceries." said Bergenholm, waving his gloved hands at the cold sky. She mustered a brave smile. *I notice no one talks about how cold it is,* she thought. Bergenholm put down his binoculars and answered his ringing cell phone.

"Oh, good," said Bergenholm happily. "Grubenard is flying in with his saucer," he said turning to Pamela. "He's landing down by the Vehicle Assembly Building."

"His saucer?" asked Pamela, as they both ran to the nearby dull blue Humvee and jumped in the front seat. Soon Bergenholm was driving swiftly down the road, a dull blue Humvee full of armed guards was following them closely. Pamela was riding beside Bergenholm and scribbling notes on a notepad, the only recording device she was allowed to use. They were driving back to the massive Vehicle Assembly Buildings looming white in the distance. They passed a massive crawler carrying another Saturn V, Mark III to the launch pad area. By the side of the road, at regular intervals anti-aircraft guns and missile emplacements sprouted, manned by wary-eyed soldiers in fatigues, who watched them drive by grimly.

"You've got to see this!" said Bergenholm as he drove swiftly. "I write the theory, this guy makes it fly!"

"He has a flying saucer?" asked Pamela incredulously

"Yep!" said Bergenholm happily. "He sure does!"

"Captured?"

"No, he built it himself!" said Bergenholm as the Humvee turned into a large empty parking lot and abruptly stopped. The Humvee fill of guards pulled up beside them. "Of course, its design is not exactly an original invention," laughed Bergenholm.

"Can I get some pictures?" asked Pamela cautiously. They had told her she 'would be shot immediately' if she took any pictures in the launch pad area.

She and Bergenholm went out into the cold crisp air. Pamela followed Bergenholm's gaze up into the sky.

A silver speck was high in the dark blue sky; it was growing in size. Pamela was shielding her eyes from the cold sun and fighting a small twinge of fear as the round silver object descended towards them. Soon the whine of a jet turbine was audible. The silver disc now was deploying three slender landing legs. From its center was a faint orange flame pointing down towards them.

"Here he comes again!" laughed Bergenholm. Pamela looked at the nearby guards, all with M-4 carbines on their shoulders standing nearby beside their Humvee, they were all grinning ear to ear and looking up at the now quickly descending saucer. This reassured her and she returned to studying the descending saucer with intense curiosity. It was now clearly visible in detail, three slender landing legs of dark bronze metal sprouted from doors on the underside and in the center of the disk what looked like an orange jet exhaust was shooting down. A clear dome was in the center of the craft on top, catching the sun, the disk was lens shaped, being thicker in the middle, and there was a small triangular stabilizing fin on the top side near the edge of the disk, which appeared to be constructed of standard-looking aluminum aircraft sheeting, with small rivets in neat rows. It had a large American flag emblazoned on the edge of the disk with some dark lettering. The smell of burned jet fuel washed over them as Pamela felt a warm gust of downdraft as the disk slowed near the ground, wavered slightly as it hovered. A strange feeling of being lighter was apparent, then ebbed as the craft moved away. The craft then gracefully came down to a gentle landing forty yards from them, with dust and leaves blowing in all directions. The whine of the jet engine

450

dropped, ebbed, then idled.  It was roughly fifteen yards across and bright and shiny in the cold sun.  In the central dome of the cockpit, a figure in a spacesuit moved, then disappeared, as the jet engine shut down completely.  The craft sat roughly six feet off the ground on its three legs and was a graceful lens shaped disk roughly 3 yards thick in the center where the dome was.  A hatch opened on the bottom and rope ladder descended followed by a man in a silver spacesuit and space helmet with the visor pushed up.  A grinning face beamed out from the helmet as the figure quickly walked in a crouch from under the saucer towards Bergenholm and Pamela. He stood tall once out from under the saucer and waved at them as he walked towards them.

" Yo John! How was outer-space?" bellowed Bergenholm.

"Scenic, the launch looked great as I was coming in,  who's this?" said the space-suited figure as he walked up. He twisted off his helmet to reveal a handsome balding  head with slightly greying hair.

"John I'd like you to meet Pamela Monroe of CNS News, our honored guest here at the Cape," said Hans, turning to Pamela.

"Dr. John Grubenard," said the man beaming at Pamela, as his eyes danced all over her and he extended his hand.

"Oh very glad to meet you!"  gushed Pamela as she stepped forward to shake his gloved hand. "If you don't mind, I have a just a few questions." laughed Pamela. "Could you show me this fancy ride of yours and tell me how it works?" She paused and turned to Bergenholm who was grinning broadly. "If that's OK of course?" she added.

"Why of course Ms. Monroe!" said Grubenard, with a wink at Bergenholm. He then turned and she followed him eagerly back to the craft.  The smell of hot metal and jet fuel greeted them as they approached.

"Well, Ms. Monroe..."

"Pamela please call me Pamela," Pam said happily, looking at the craft.

451

"Yes, Pamela, this craft has just returned from low Earth orbit. The Air Force has had this technology flying since the 1980's actually. It uses electrogravitics powered by lithium ion batteries in space and a jet turbine-alternator down in the atmosphere." He motioned to the shape of the craft. "In the atmosphere, we make maximum use of ordinary aerodynamics, so its lift is roughly 70 percent aero and 30 percent gravitic in the air. The Greys fly the same way in the atmosphere, that's why most of their ships we bring down are so streamlined." Pamela was staring at the name in bold blue letters on the edge of the disk, beside a large American flag. Pamela fought a twinge of jealousy, the name on the side read "Cassandra II"

"You named this after Cassandra Chen?"

"Sure did, I met her once down here before the war started..." said Grubenard smiling. "I found her courage was quite inspiring."

"Yes! I was wondering John if we could get ahold of some space suits, is their room in this thing for you to maybe give Cassie and me a ride into space? I mean I am sure I could get her down here for that," said Pamela eyeing the craft in wonder. *It's so amazing but yet looks so familiar...*

"Oh, I am sure we could arrange something ...It can carry a copilot and a passenger" beamed Grubenard. Pamela suddenly began to scheme, as the tour around the outside of the craft continued. *Copilot.*


****


Cassandra Chen stared out the window of the armored Humvee, part of a long column of trucks and other Humvees. They had passed out of Dodge City many hours before and since then, the landscape was only a snowy wasteland and abandoned ruins. *The world is dying*, she thought, *dying of cold.*

Finally, they passed a snow drifted sign in the middle of the arctic expanse, "Welcome to Colorado" it read. She was suddenly overcome with laughter.

452

"We're not in Kansas anymore!" she laughed out loud, causing her bodyguard in the front seat to turn and look at her nervously. The bodyguard and the driver exchanged nervous glances.

"Sorry," she said trying to be sober.

\*\*\*\*

Blue looked down at the blue luminous, curve of the Earth below him as he went quickly through the final checklist for the third time. "Mac, how is it looking?" Blue glanced at a picture of his two children with Alicia, at the edge of the cockpit.

"AOK Blue," we are ready to rock and roll. We are minutes before main booster ignition.

"Houston, this is Soccer Coach. We are go for booster burn with T-minus 2 minutes and counting. What do you say muchachos, shall we light this candle?"

"Coach, this is Firefly 1, we are good to go!"

"Firefly 2, let's do this thing!"

"Firefly 3, good to go!"

One by one the rest of the squadron reported in, all good to go.

Blue, took one last long look at Earth from low-Earth-orbit.

"This is Hatchetman, head of Eagle Squadron, wishing you guys bon voyage and happy hunting!

By the numbers, the Titan 5 hypergolic upper stages lit, like clockwork. Around him in space, puffs of flame erupted, and Blue was slammed back into his seat as his and thirty other spacecraft, surrounded by a cloud of unmanned vehicles, now ignited their boosters for their journey to the Moon. Operation Green Cheese, as it was known, had now begun. After cruising pressure, the jolt of the main engine cutoff and explosive bolts

453

firing to free them from the booster was felt. They were now flying out across the black abyss to the beckoning Moon. The war had entered a new phase, in return for ice, they were going to visit Moon with a little fire.

"Oh, there was a young cougar not keen,

Who sought rabbit for his cuisine,

He looked first  and pounced

But off the hares back  he did bounce

For its hair was in fact wolverine!"

said MacClintok from the rear seat, who was found of limericks.

"That's good Mac, just keep those limericks coming," said Blue, as his eyes roved over the spacecraft systems. The simple mechanisms mostly modeled after the old Apollo capsule, where performing perfectly. Having discovered early in the war, that the Greys could hack into any digital system, no matter how supposedly encrypted, old analog logic designs with high redundancy and simplicity of design were now standard for all warcraft. This had apparently been quite successful, as one officer had told Blue, `you can't play mind games with somebody who is a crafty ignoramus.' Blue looked out and saw a few metal glints from the cloud of standard bombardment warheads they were being accompanied by to the Moon.

"This bunch of warheads is going to be surprisingly vindictive" he muttered to himself.  They had been ordered to, if possible, pursue selected spacecraft and even individuals across the lunar surface and destroy them. The goal of their mission, he had been told,  was to hopefully, effect enemy moral, possibly to do some damage, and if possible return home alive. He and the others were all volunteers.

Mac, after going through his checklists, reported the ships systems nominal and announced his desire to get some sleep. Blue's shift was beginning. Mac did let fly with another happy limerick as he dozed off.

"Oh my friends went to Tokyo to play the fiddle

Some asked why go so far when you can't do diddle?

But by light of Pearl Harbor funeral pyres

They sailed boldly to Tojo to make some fires

Saying if you can't do much then you can at least Dolittle"

"Good night Mac," said Blue.

There was a young woman named Mankowitz... Macs voice trailed off.

**\*\*\*\***

Four, six-wheeled Light Armored Vehicles, or LAVs, mounting quad 50 teardrop turrets carrying magneto ammunition preceded the column through the arctic landscape on highway 112, they passed abandoned and collapsed buildings under snowdrifts everywhere under the grey frigid sky. Cassandra, riding in an armored Humvee in the middle of the column, contemplated the ironies of her fate, as she sipped hot coffee in the seat behind the driver and bodyguard. She was going back Morningstar, the only accessible place the government could think of to keep her safe.

*The last place on Earth I want to go to, and it's my only sanctuary...*thought Cassandra as she studied the desolate landscape flying by. She was wearing a white winter-warfare parka, ski pants over long johns and snow boots. Despite her warm clothes, the bleakness of the landscape made coldness enter her eyes and chill her soul. They had entered the foothills of the Rockies on Highway 112 and were deep in the Winter Emergency Evacuation Zone, a region the government had conceded to the Winter and ordered all population evacuated to the South to Texas and Arkansas, in vast refugee tent cities which were now full of the displaced; and beside them relocated war-plants had sprung up, out of the necessity of the requirement to give the displaced populations something to do. *Helplessness leads to despair, despair is our most mortal enemy now...*

"You know how to handle a gun right?" asked a handsome dark haired soldier named Nordgren, her bodyguard, from the front seat, disturbing her thoughts. He and the driver also wore winter warfare gear.

"Yes," she said dully. Reality then sank into her. *I am in danger, we all are,* she suddenly thought. *The armored vehicles in this convoy are not just for show.*

"Here is a 9 mm Berretta. It loaded with D-Sap rounds just in case this convoy gets attacked. The other clip on the holster is regular ammunition." he said, handing a black leather pistol belt back to her. The words sank into her. D-sap, made to go through alien body armor, tended to go right through human beings without stopping. The regular ammunition was obviously intended for her to use on herself if the situation required.

"Thank you, Lieutenant," she said, trying to muster a brave smile. She put the pistol belt on around her waist, it was cold and uncomfortable, but she was glad to be wearing it. She carefully pulled out the pistol, felt its cold heft. *Thank you, Pammy,* she thought studying the safety, remembering how Pamela had taught her to shoot a pistol and also an Uzi submachine gun. *Now I can kill as well as be killed,* she remembered thinking. Then, she heard the sound of one of their Apache helicopter gunship escorts fly over them. *I can kill ...*

But then a sudden realization hit her, clear as crystal, as she stared out at the abandoned buildings in the snow by the road. *The world is dying... The cold ...It is the Greys.* She was suddenly seized with the impulse to kill herself, then and there, with the gun. *This is all my fault...I started a fight we cannot finish.* She stared down at the dark steel of the gun mesmerized. *What have I got to live for, what does anyone have any more?* she cried out mentally. But then something reacted from deep within her.

"No, we will get victory...In the end, we will get victory, just like Pammy said" she blurted out, defying the despair within her. She put the gun back in its holster. She looked up and saw Nordgren looking at her attentively. She smiled as warmly as possible at him. His face broke into a smile in response.

456

"Sorry, I've lived alone for a while and I talk to myself sometimes."

"How are the conversations?" he asked.

"Oh scintillating and occasionally sensuous," she said teasing him. *He is cute, a nice distraction.* He smiled more warmly. "Have any of these convoys been attacked before?" she returned the conversation to the road, after a pause.

"No, but they were buzzed once by a saucer, a few months ago," he said. "It was some real fireworks I hear. Everybody in the column opened up on it with rockets and tracers. It just scooted out of there." he laughed. A chill entered her at these words. *We will be traversing territory where human control is precarious...* she thought. *Especially now.*

"Thanks for the update," she said and resumed looking out the window. They had begun to climb noticeably, around them the forests were now snow-clad pine trees. *We're definitely not in Kansas anymore. Too bad I didn't bring my snow skis,* she thought defiantly, feeling the gun on her hip. Snow had begun to fall, not rapidly, but in a thin curtain that wrapped the distance in a mist, she felt the cold through her eyes. She noticed the Apache gunships were now absent. *They must have turned back due to the snow,* she thought, with sudden concern. *Yes, but the Greys will have limited visibility also, they are trapped in this situation as much as I am,* came a thought. *We are all alike slaves of this fate.* This thought steeled her, and she began to pray. *Lord, let me live to fulfill my mission here.*

After an hour, they were entering some sort of pass through the mountains, whose peaks rose up around them into the snowy darkness above. She saw another armored column pulled up on a side road with big snowplows. A large radar antenna and some "fly's eye" EMP domes sprouted from the top of military trucks, along with the now familiar 'quad-50'-teardrop turrets on top of several armored vehicles. This made her feel braver. *They have special units guarding the pass. These people know what the hell they are doing here,* Cassandra noted with satisfaction.

They rolled on through the snow, after a while, Cassandra sensed they were crossing the summit of the pass. She noted that the driver and her

457

bodyguard had fallen into silence. She calmly tightened her seat belt and adjusted her pistol belt. Suddenly the radio crackled to life.

"X-ray Tango, repeat, we have X-ray Tango Charlie! Go to India Alpha India, ALPHA INDIA! She saw Lt. Nordgren turning to look at her with a faint smile, as he grabbed his M-4 Carbine off a rack in the front seat.

"Cassie, just stick by me ..." he said. What happened then all seemed to be occurring in slow motion. There was a blinding flash, freezing every snowflake in midair outside the Humvee. Then all hell broke loose.

A tremendous explosion lifted the Humvee and it sailed through the air into the drifted snow beside the highway. She felt the impact of the snow embracing the Humvee and then they were tumbling over and over with snow and darkness hitting her in the face. For a moment, she sensed her consciousness slipping away as they rolled down a slope, but she hung on to consciousness by screaming as loud as she could.

"God help me!" she screamed. Suddenly they came to a stop. Cold darkness filled the Humvee. They were upside down. Straining to keep calm she unsnapped her seat belt and fell into snow that had invaded the Humvee. She heard the sound of someone kicking open a door. It was Nordgren; more snow blew in as the door flew open. A flashlight was lit with curses, dazzling her. She was aware of the sound of a barrage of gunfire above them. A strong arm was grabbing her leg, pulling her out into the snowy dimness. She looked, it was not human. It was a short being in grey body armor. With a calmness that amazed her, she deftly kicked it in the face as hard as she could with her other snow-booted foot, causing it to let go of her. She had her gun out, and now, somehow flicked off the safety by reflex and blasted away at the being with D-sap rounds. Part of its head disintegrated, with its helmet and it bounced around in convulsions, she was firing at another figure beyond, who fell struggling into the snow. She was thrashing herself out into the snow. She saw two figures in grey armor lying in the snow beside her surrounded by greenish-blue blood in the dim flickering light. The thunder of gunfire and flashes of light came from above. Tracer bullets, blue and yellow were slashing across the sky, brilliant in the dull light. *Three, there would be a team of three,* she thought suddenly and rolled suddenly in the snow to

458

face a third grey figure and shoot her last remaining shots into it as it jumped on her. It screamed pathetically and rolled off of her jerking in spasms of death. She rose quickly and put a fresh clip in the pistol, then turning swiftly to look at the wrecked Humvee, she noted both the driver and her bodyguard were dead. So she holstered her gun and grabbed the M-4 carbine held in Nordgren's lifeless hand and primed it, flicking off the safety. She turned and swung the carbine around her, the snowy landscape illuminated now with the flickering light of blue and yellow tracer bullets arcing everywhere across the dark sky. She was acting on reflex without thinking. She moved to get around the Humvee and suddenly was confronted by the edge of steep chasm where the Humvee had come to rest, just before it would have plunged down thousands of feet to a river below. She turned waving the carbine, began to climbed back up through the snow drifts toward the edge of the road above, now lit by the red of flames, explosions, and waves of tracer bullets. She was getting colder as she struggled through the snow drifts and rapidly becoming exhausted. The snow was inside her parka and freezing her face and body. She was perhaps halfway up the snow bank to the edge of the road. Suddenly a rocket trail flashed across the sky and there was a tremendous explosion, then an avalanche of snow fell on her from the slope she was trying to climb.

"Help me! Help me!" she gasped, as she tumbled in the snow and darkness down the slope, cringing at the thought of going over the lip of the cliff. She was suddenly stopped by a blow to the head, and for a moment she lost consciousness. She awoke choking on snow, frantically flailed her arms to get out of the snowdrift she was in, losing her grip on the carbine. She struggled furiously and through the snow covering her, she now could see the light of the battle above her still being waged furiously. She had come to rest against a pine tree wreathed in snow. She struggled to move against the snow around her, but could make no progress. It was hopeless. She was trapped, imprisoned in tons of snow. She was now feeling overwhelmed with cold and utter exhaustion. Her hands were numb, the numbness spreading up her arms, and to her face. Her legs also were now feeling like slabs of rubber. She felt herself becoming sleepy, wanting to just lie still and quit struggling. The sound of the battle around her was now just a distant continual roar. Cold, like all the cold of the world, soaked into her. She felt like she was falling now, like she had fallen over the chasm near her, weightless. *I die like the world dies now...*

She suddenly realized she was dying. She could no longer move, all her strength was gone. She heard her heart beating slower and slower. But she could do nothing. She saw her life passing before her eyes, a long slow movie, people she knew, people she loved, were urging her to get up and move. "No , I'm finished...this is the end" she said to them. Then everything grew dark and still. She made one last effort and got her face to the surface of the snow drift, caught a glimpse of the cold snowy sky, then lay still. She could no longer move.

Then a small golden light appeared in the dark grey sky. It was a beautiful baby girl with dark hair, she was wearing glowing gold clothes, like royalty.

"MAMA!" the child screamed at her in alarm. "MAMA PLEASE DON'T DIE!" and touched her face, with her tiny hand. "IF YOU DIE, I DIE! YOU HAVE TO SAVE MEEEE!" Her voice was a shriek.

Suddenly Cassandra was wide awake in the snow, the battle raged thunderously around her, tracer bullets and rocket trails, burning wreckage falling from the snowy sky. She could see blood in the snow around her, it was her own.

"Got to move" she gasped. By some superhuman power she did not comprehend, she began moving her numb arms and legs and struggled to half way out of the snow pile she was in. Summoning every last ounce of strength within her, she wrenched herself free of the snow bank, flailing her numb arms, and flopped on top of the snowy slope. She rose and struggled through the snow, crawling upwards again, the burning fires and tracers lit the edge of the road above. Now she was struggling up the snowy slope again. It looked impossible to climb. Despair gripped her heart. She could barely move.

Then she remembered Pamela battling in the Snow in Siberia, *she did not give up!* With her numb hands useless she wrapped her arms around small tree trunks and pulled herself upward. Finally, after what seemed like an eternity of mindless exertion, she fell over the top of the snowdrift on the edge of the road, into the fiery hell of the battle on the highway. She

460

caught the glimpse of one huge metallic shape looming over her as it suddenly exploded into brilliant blue streamers in the sky. Streams of blue and yellow tracers and now red ones hammered away at the large fragments they fell flaming into the chasm she had just escaped from.

Her legs too numb for her to stand, she rolled across the snow frantically, moving now by sheer willpower to seek shelter by a burning 5-ton truck rolled over on its side. Bodies of soldiers in snow parkas and wreckage littered the road. She rolled as close as she could to the fire on the truck, trying to regain some sort of warmth. Suddenly there was a crash of a sonic boom and a jet fighter flew over on full afterburner. She lay near the fire trying to sense feeling come back to her numb face. She was looking up, now so exhausted she could only lay still and pray while the battle raged around her and in the sky. She saw a jet fighter explode in mid-air into a ball of burning jet fuel and blackened wreckage. Then something moving across the sky, flaming, tracked by streams of tracers, and then crashed with a tremendous explosion into a distant snow wrapped mountainside with a brilliant blue ball of fire. She was dully aware of the thunder and brilliance of the battle ebbing. She sensed herself falling asleep again. But her legs were now warmer, and she could feel her feet!

"NO! NO!" she gasped, and somehow struggled to her feet on partly numb legs. *This battle was not over some supplies for the facility at Morningstar-This battle is over me!* She gasped mentally. *My life is still important! People are dying because of me!* She tottered to her feet and staggered down the road past a score of burning and overturned vehicles. Her numb arms flopped uselessly beside her as she tried to wave for help. Her face was covered in frozen blood from a cut on her forehead. She was too exhausted and cold to think; all she could do was stagger on her half-numb legs one step after another.

"HELP ME! HELP ME!" she was crying out hoarsely as she staggered down the snowy road.

Suddenly, a bunch of soldiers in snow parkas carrying M-4 carbines ran up and carried her down the road to where a mass of armored vehicles, ablaze with outgoing tracers and earsplitting heavy automatic gunfire, still fought.  She was carried to makeshift medical shelter and left there with the wounded and dying. They laid her in the hot exhaust of a diesel engine cooling fan and she gradually regained full feeling in her arms and legs. The battle faded as she experienced welcome agony, and cried out as her frozen feet were removed from her boots.

****

## Chapter 11: The Dead of Winter

In the snowbound railway station, half collapsed from the weight of the snow on its roof, Colonel Yuri Ivanovich Korkorin, of the Russian Spetznatz, with a scarred cheek, and massive frame, stood shouting orders to the forty assembled troops in full winter combat gear bearing Kalashnikovs. About two dozen heavily bundled-up, half-frozen people stood nearby, the only survivors of the town of Katyia, once holding 3 thousand people. Korkorin was ordering them to conduct a search of the outlying buildings of the train station. The rest of the town was buried under 50 feet of snow. General Vitaly Gregorovich Samarsky, of the Russian, or Red Army, as it was now called, stood beside a massive rotary snowplow in the front of an equally massive diesel locomotive that had cleared the track from the last town south of Norakova. Behind the diesel locomotive, stood another and another after that, and behind that tanks of diesel to feed them, some box cars full of more troops and then another two diesel locomotives with massive rotary snow plows. This was viewed as necessary if the train was to make it back from Katyia to Norakova as the killing snow continued to fall relentlessly. In the two weeks since the snows had started, 20 feet had fallen in Moscow, grinding the city almost to a halt until tanks equipped with 4-ton snowplow attachments had been used to clear the streets. Four thousand people had died in Moscow alone due to collapsed buildings and cold. North of Moscow, in Kirov, 40 feet of snow had fallen, and the death toll was unknown, 100,000 people of a city of one million had been evacuated by trains running around the clock to keep the rails clear of snow. Across the North of Russia, the coldest harshest, and deadliest winter in its history had fallen and everyone north of 70 N was being evacuated South in the most massive and desperate evacuation effort in history.

They were north of Kirov now, and Katyia, like Norakova, had been cut off for a month.

"Do you know if there are any others who have survived?" was Samarsky's relentless question, as he moved among the survivors. They all shook their heads silently with a desperate look of horror. The 'killing snow' had taken even hardened Russians by surprise. Men, women and haunted-looking children, stood around in shock. "Have you heard any communications from the towns north of here?" was his second question.

"A train will be coming to take you south where you will be well taken care of! There will be food and warm shelter," yelled Samarsky to the two dozen survivors, who looked at him listlessly. He knew better, they would be taken south in boxcars and dumped on the Steppes in makeshift tent cities south of Volgograd where hopefully the supplies of food the Americans had promised would be waiting for them. No food or even potable water was available now, except for snow melted in former diesel barrels heated by coal and frozen firewood. The magnitude of the suffering and death in the catastrophe was beyond Samarsky's comprehension, so he had ceased to think about it. He concentrated on the problems before him in immediate space-time, the here and now. He caught Korkorin's attention, waved him over with a heavily gloved hand. The cold was penetrating even his electrically heated suit, with batteries in a small backpack, which was now standard issue to the Red Army in the emergency. It was an unnatural killing cold in an unnatural winter. The temperature was forty below zero, supposedly too cold for it to even snow, but down the snow was coming to immobilize, freeze, and crush. Korkorin in his ushanka of winter white camouflage, with its earflaps, pulled down for warmth, walked over warily. Like Samarsky he had quit thinking about anything except the next survivor, and the next town north on the railway.

"Where is the other train!?" Samarsky demanded in hushed tones.

"It should be here in an hour, they say on the radio," said Korkorin grimly.

"Let us load them up and get out of here then! We have to return to Norakova before we get trapped here!" said Samarsky. "I think it is poorly advised to go further North in the dark. Recall your men!" Korkorin turned and bellowed for the men to return to the train. Suddenly another train approached throwing a geyser of snow out from the rapidly covered tracks. It shut off its rotary plow as it rolled into the station. Out from the engine poured fresh troops in great coats and ushokas, all carried Kalashnikovs, one squat figure was in the lead.

464

"I am General Babayev of the Interior Ministry!  Who is in charge here?" Korkorin and Samarsky looked at each other in grim amazement. They thought that Babayev had been stripped of rank and banished to North Sakalin Island after the 'Moscow Incident.' In that infamous encounter, he had tried to arrest Pamela Monroe, then an honored guest of the Russian Defense Ministry.

"I am in charge General," said Samarsky as he and Korkorin reluctantly exchanged salutes with Babayev.

 "I am here to investigate reports of cannibalism  among the survivors," said Babayev waving a sheet of paper enclosed in plastic.  He turned and yelled orders to the soldiers behind him who fanned out looking through the abandoned, half collapsed,  and frozen railway station.  Korkorin's troops were returning from their attempts to move across the snow to the other buildings, some only visible as bumps in the snow.

"Have you seen any signs of cannibalism here?" he asked. Samarsky shook his head. Babayev looked over to the group of survivors. He walked over to one woman and roughly pulled off her hat and head scarf; her hair was brown and her face appeared swollen.

"Look at that fat round face!" exclaimed Babayev. "What have you lived on for a month here?" he demanded.

The women merely trembled and looked at the ground.

"Answer me!" yelled Babayev.

"MY ORDERS ARE TO LOCATE EVACUATE SURVIVORS!"  yelled Samarsky at Babayev.  I WILL CARRY OUT THESE ORDERS!  He turned to Korkorin, "Colonel, get these survivors on our train, let these vultures continue the search here, he added grimly. He turned back to Babayev, "you yourself look very well fed General. Don't you know in a catastrophe like this, with millions going without bread, that it is a sin to be fat in Russia?" Babayev paid no attention to him but walked away, as one of his soldiers waved to him out of the doorway in a dark corner of the partly collapsed station. Samarsky walked after him on the frozen concrete cursing.  Babayev followed the grim-faced soldier into the darkened doorway and Samarsky followed, drawing his pistol as he did. Down a hallway, they went into a room now illuminated only by powerful LED flashlights.

It was a butcher shop for human beings. A pile of naked corpses missing arms and legs lay frozen on the floor. Several half-butchered bodies hung naked from the wooden beams on the ceiling. Several of the corpses had obviously died of gunshots or having their throats cut. Samarsky holstered his pistol, looked around.

"You see the swine took only the best cuts of meat! In this crisis, this is doubly heinous!" said Babayev gesturing at the corpses.

"Yes, I see this, let us deal with this situation then so we can both follow our orders," said Samarsky grimly. *Awful times sometimes require awful people.* thought Samarsky in resignation.

They marched out together; Korkorin was herding the survivors onto a box car. Samarsky pulled out his pistol and picked out three of the largest and strongest looking men, and ordered them back onto the platform where Babayev and his soldiers waited.

"General Babayev here, of the interior Ministry, wishes to speak to you three men to gain knowledge on your survival procedures during this emergency. Please cooperate with him," said Samarsky smiling. The men complied dully. *If Moscow had stockpiled supplies at the train stations, this would not have happened! The fools ignored all the warnings from the Americans!* He thought angrily.

Samarsky pulled out a map and called Korkorin over to him. They were two hundred miles south of the large city of Pechora, now also cut off for a month.

"Yuri Ivanovich, I think we should declare victory on this expedition or today and get back to Norakova before night falls and the snow increases." A barrage of gunfire and screams exploded from the far end of the railway station, it was followed by three single pistol shots in succession. Samarsky glanced up at the other survivors. They cringed in the box car silently.

466

"I think that the Interior Ministry can handle finding any further survivors in this area, don't you think?"

Korkorin nodded and motioned for his troops to board the train.

"Just when things were becoming simple, Babayev shows up again, like a bad kopeck..." said Samarsky as they jumped into the boxcar and the diesel engines roared to full power and the train rolled south clearing the tracks of fresh snow again.

An officer approached them as the train began to move slowly south, he handed Samarsky a printed message. Samarsky read it with some amusement. He turned to Korkorin.

"Congratulations, my friend! You have just achieved the dream of every red-blooded young man in Russia!" Korkorin looked at him warily.

"What has happened? Am I to become Pamela Monroe's bodyguard?" asked Korkorin.

"No, my friend! You are ordered to report to Star City immediately! You are becoming a Cosmonaut!" said Samarsky laughing as he handed the printed orders to Korkorin. "At least I hear the spacesuits are warm!"

****

Cassandra awoke to thunder in the distance and trucks full of troops rushing past them in the opposite lane. The sky was full of scattered clouds.

"Wow! Look at them plaster the side of Mount Blanca!" yelled someone, and let out a war-whoop. "Arc lights! Those are B52 arc lights! They must have found an alien nest there! Wow! Look at the strings of bombs light it up!" continued the soldier in the front seat. She struggled to rise from the stretcher she was lying on to see what was going on. But suddenly a nurse's face appeared above her.

"Get the fuck down!" yelled the woman. "Lie still, you're still hypothermic!" said the nurse, looking exhausted and careworn. More trucks and armored vehicles roared past going the other way. The fields beside them were snowy.

"Where am I?"

"We're north of Alamosa, we'll be at the base in about a half hour, just lie still." said the nurse, wearing military fatigues, and put another blanket over Cassandra. Casandra listened to the roar of the passing vehicles and the distinct thunder. She glanced down at the army fatigues she was now wearing. The name tag said, Rodriguez. She had an IV in her left arm.

"How did I get these on?" she asked dully.

"Your clothes were wet and full of snow; we had to put you into something warm and dry. We bagged your clothes for you, you can get them cleaned and dried at the facility.

"Facility?"

The AIAI Facility at Morningstar. You'll be safe there. Now be quiet and rest."

"Who's Rodriguez?" asked Cassandra, fingering the name tag.

"She didn't need her fatigues so we put them on you."

"Tell her thank you..."

"YOU CAN'T! SHE'S DEAD NOW!" the nurse snapped. "Now, shut up and sleep!" And motioning to someone else, another nurse did something to the IV line. "Cassandra felt suddenly overwhelmed by sleep.

She awoke, startled, as she was being carried on a stretcher, to a small room. The room was warm. She was put on a bed, a doctor pulled open her fatigues and checked her heartbeat, with a cold stethoscope, then they left, turned out the lights, and she slept.

Cassandra awoke coughing wretchedly; she stumbled out of bed and blew her nose painfully. She obviously now had a cold. Her arm hurt and she pulled up her sleeve, a ball of cotton was taped the inside of her elbow.

468

She washed her face and tried to straighten her hair. She had a bruise on her forehead and small cut with a bandage on it. *It's good I'm not doing the news tonight* she thought. Then she looked down at the bloodstained combat fatigues she was wearing, with the name Rodriguez on the nametag, and began to tremble uncontrollably. Suddenly the scenes of death and mortal struggle she had seen yesterday flooded back into her mind. Tears flowed down her cheeks. *No, NO! No crying!* She forced herself to become calm. She looked around for her clothes, her purse was there on the floor by the bed, but her clothes were gone. She blew her nose again and washed her face, wiped her eyes. She starred at her beautiful face framed by her raven black hair.

"You can do this Cassie, I know you can. You're on a mission from God," she whispered to herself hoarsely.

She turned and marched out of the small room, she held her head high. She was in some sort of officer's quarters; a break room was outside the door. Everyone turned and looked at her and stood and saluted by reflex. Rodriguez had been a First Lieutenant.

After a pause, she returned their salutes awkwardly by reflex. She was too tired to explain anything.

"Where is the CO of this facility?" she asked in a deep hoarse voice. She liked her husky voice, it made her sound tough as nails. *I am. I just killed three Greys face-to-face.* A woman officer in a tee shirt pointed mutely down the hallway. Cassandra turned and walked down the hall in her combat boots with determined strides. She followed the signs. People were saluting her as she passed them in the hall, she returned their salutes, too exhausted to explain she wearing a dead woman's uniform. Soon she stood at the door of an office marked Base Commander. She marched in, two enlisted staffers, wearing Army uniforms, leaped to attention, and saluted her.

"At ease, she croaked. "I need to see the Commander here, I am Cassandra Chen."

"Do you have an appointment Lieutenant?" asked a woman sergeant.

"Yes," said Cassandra and marched abruptly past the two office workers and up to the door marked base Commander and opened it.

Inside, the base commander, wearing a dark blue navy Captain's uniform was talking on the phone as she entered. He looked up and suddenly flashed a warm smile. He had a strong face and a dark mustache. Cassandra froze in shock as she looked at him. He rose painfully and put down his phone. It was John Badgio, of the Carney; he was obviously now out of the Bethesda naval hospital.

"Well Cassandra Chen, it's a small universe!" he laughed. "I heard you were sick and we wouldn't see you for days!"

"Captain Badgio! You're out of the hospital!" she exclaimed happily, she ran over and embraced him.

"Sit down Cassie! You're looking great, beautiful as ever! I want to hear how you ended up here." said Badgio, sitting down painfully. She could see his legs were still not fully healed, perhaps they never would. He sat down and smiled at her, motioning her to sit down. She found a comfortable looking leather chair and sat down in it smiling.

"Oh," she said smiling helplessly and smoothed her long raven hair. "I guess I am sort of 'on the lam' so to speak. The FBI told me I have people after me, either men in black or alien sympathizers, so they said I should hang out here for a while. I was working in a war plant in Wichita, and they sent me here..." her voice trailed off. "I'm really not well yet after what happened to me, here, before you guys rescued me.." her smile faded. "You should know that..." she said intently. Badge nodded thoughtfully. "But I am much better!" she added with a brave smile.

"Well you seem to be getting around well, and I hear you had quite a battle getting here! In fact, we found out there was a nest of Greys under Mont Blanca because of you. We have troops mopping up the tunnels today. They have apparently been laying low ever since the war started eight months ago, and came out just to ambush your convoy. So you helped us find them. Good work!"

"Yeah, I actually shot three of them...One of them actually grabbed my leg, so I kicked his face in, then shot him, "she said, recalling it in wonderment. She stared at him wide-eyed to see his reaction.

"Yes! Good work!" said Badgio. "You could join the Carney!" he laughed.

"Yeah, so I guess I did OK," she said to herself in puzzlement. "Since this is a war, and shooting people is what I am supposed to do in such situations." she nodded to herself. "Yes...highly appropriate." She turned to him and looked puzzled.

"Well, you've had a rough trip and I think you could use a drink!" said Badgio. Pulling out a bottle of Bacardi rum and a bottle of coke from a small refrigerator behind his desk. "Provided of course that you don't throw it at me, like at the airport when we first met."

"Oh, that. Yes, well, I was upset then." She said breaking into a smile as he poured two drink glasses half full of coke and then filled them the rest of the way with rum. *Murray had just been killed,* she remembered, *one of the early casualties in this war.* She leaned over and took a drink from his hand. It was cold and the cold burned her hand. They both raised them in a toast.

"To your safe arrival here Cassie," said Badgio. "And to victory!" he added.

"Yes, victory!" she added vacantly and drank down the rum and coke, it burned marvelously. She hadn't had a drink in several weeks.

"I spent some time on the lam too," said Badgio, looking at his drink. "It was when this thing first started, just before you and that blonde made this whole thing blow up." Badgio said smiling. "I had the snakes, the Magi's people, after me because I tried to go to the Chief of Naval Intelligence about what the Magi were doing. So they were after me and I went to New York City and hid out with my cousin Gino," Badge broke into a laugh, "who is in the mob." Cassandra laughed at this and held out her glass for a refill, which Badge quickly took care of. She was drinking from the fresh glass as he continued. "So Gino, he's close family. I mean half my family was in the mob, and half not. It made for really interesting family get-togethers when I was a kid. I sort had a choice of joining the

471

mob or the Navy when I got out of high school. My pop says, 'son, live the good life!', so I chose the Navy. So anyways, Gino is a good guy and takes me in. He brings me along on some debt collections, cuz he runs a loan business down on the docks in the city and in Jersey. Gino tells me, 'just come along and stand there and don't say nuttin, and you'll be a big help, Giovanni.' He calls me Giovanni cuz that what everybody called me in the old neighborhood in Brooklyn. So it's OK for a few weeks. I help him with the 'looking-like-the-muscle' bit on a few collections, and I'm staying in his guest room. Then one morning he takes me down to Jersey,  to a wrecking yard, just across the Hudson, and there's this brown car there." Badgio paused and looked pained.

"Gino says to me, 'Giovanni, go, get in this car' and he hands me ten-grand in a big roll of bills. The car has the keys in it and a full tank of gas. My cousin Gino says to me, ' Giovanni , you got every bounty hunter in the Five Boroughs looking for you now, they got a price on your head of a cool million, so you got to get in this car and drive as far away as you can, then leave the car with the keys in it and walk away. You got that, and I don't even know where you're goin, capuche?' Cuz it ain't safe for you here in the city anymore. My cousin is starting to choke up when he says this. Then he hugs me and I get in the car. Then I ask him "whose car is this?" and then Gino just laughs and waves goodbye. "He says 'Giovanni, the guy who owns it don't need it no more , he's gone deep sea fishing,' then he says again, 'GO!'"

"So I go."

"Where did you go?"

"Well, I heard there were more saucer sightings in the place call Xenia, Ohio, it was a regular spot because the greys  were building a secret base there underground. So I head there, figuring the Carney will be there and I'll join back up with them. But I also know the snakes will be there too. So I'm careful. Finally, I get to about ten miles outside of Xenia and stop to take a leak, and these two snake bounty hunters tried to nail me, but I got both of them. That's where I got this, he unbuttoned and pulled open his collar and showed a wide scar on the muscle on top of his hairy shoulder. Cassandra was mesmerized and felt pain just looking at the thick scar, where a bullet had plowed through his flesh. "I got em with this, he pulled open his uniform jacket and she saw he a had a 9 mm Berretta in a shoulder holster. I call her Gina, cuz I sleep with her every night." His brown eyes looked haunted. "So I ended their snake careers and they grazed me pretty bad, so I slapped some folded paper towels on it and taped them down and kept driving to Xenia. And it was in the morning. So I just stood at the corner of Main and First street with my gun in my coat pocket." He paused.

"I guess I had decided I was done running, because I had lost a lot of blood, but couldn't go to a hospital, and so I just stood there leaning against light-post, and figured that either the Carney or the snakes were going to see me there, and if the Carney found me that would be good, and if the snakes found me first that would be OK too, because I would take a bunch of them with me and at least I would die in the light. That's how a lot of us was thinking then. So what do you know? Schwartz and a bunch of Carney men drive right up to me at the corner where I am standing and Schwartz says to me 'what the fuck are you doing here Badge?' Get the fuck in the car!' So they took me to a safe house they had in Xenia and patched me up. Then we went out hunting snakes that night and men in black! And I tell you we had a royal good time doing it. Then we ditched our cars and bought a bunch of Harleys and rode back to Washington DC, as a motorcycle club just in time for you girls to make the shit hit the fan!" Badge laughed at the memories, as he leaned back in his chair behind his desk.

"What do you think of this place?" asked Badgio leaning back in his chair. "The good ship AIAI! You know I've only been here running this place for two weeks! The Navy decided to send me here and put me in charge, me!' he laughed. "The biggest thing I've ever commanded in the Navy was a dinghy full of Seals!"

"Oh!" exclaimed Cassandra "Your scar remedied me of something! I have been dying to tell somebody about this!" She suddenly rose, putting down her drink on his desk, and quickly turned and took off her combat fatigue blouse, realizing as she was doing it that she was not wearing underwear. She didn't care, she was trembling with excitement. She covered her bare breasts with her left arm and pushed up her long hair off her back with

473

her right hand, and showed him her back, as Badge looked on smiling genially and sipped his rum and coke.

"I got beamed up to this Pleiadian ship by this Pleiadian woman, her name was Semjase or something, and they smoothed out all my scars! Look! My back was all scarred and now it's smooth as silk! "Badge looked on in amused fascination. "I have the pictures from before to prove it! This doctor in Hollywood he tried the best he could but still looked horrible from when they flogged me. It looked like my back was welded together. Now it's all smooth again!' her voice cracked. "But then one night in Alaska this woman just appears while I am walking on the deck of this yacht and whoose! I am on her ship and her doctor uses this wand on my back. It feels warm and they say it just uses radio waves tuned to make the skin layers liquefy and smooth out!" She was looking over her bare shoulder at him. Tears were flowing down her cheeks. Suddenly the woman sergeant came in through the door, and looked at her and then at Captain Badgio with an amazed look. Badge simply smiled at her pleasantly.

"Please put the daily reports on my desk, for now, Sergeant." She put down the papers and stood looking at Cassandra standing naked from the waist up, with her back turned.

"Ms. Chen is showing me the results of her back surgery, could you please go call the chief medical officer, sergeant, I think he should see this too." said Badge, motioning  for the woman to leave. She did promptly and closed the door behind her.

"Cassie, would you mind being debriefed on this encounter? The Pleiadian's posture in this war and any new medical technologies we can gain from the aliens are of high priority, especially here on this base."

Cassandra, feeling slightly embarrassed, put her fatigue blouse back on and buttoned it up to the collar, before turning around and facing Badge.

"Sure, it's the least I can do. But getting those scars fixed, it really has helped my confidence."

"I can see that, " said Badge sipping his drink and smiling broadly. She suddenly felt exhausted and sat down in the leather chair.

"Maybe, on second thought we should help you back to your quarters Cassie, and let you rest some more, right now?" said Badgio looking at her carefully. "You look really tired."

"Sure," she said, feeling incredibly exhausted. "How did you end up here, Badge?"

"Oh, they needed to put me someplace so the French wouldn't get me. So some genius said, well he's a Captain and this is technically a classified naval facility, a boat, so let's make him a skipper of it. So here I am, Captain of the good ship AIAI, the Alien Isolation, and Analysis Intelligence Facility." The medical officer arrived and looked in the office; Cassandra was deeply asleep in the leather chair. They helped her back to her room and she slept dreamlessly.

****

Down in the near darkness under mount Blanca Jessie Baxter, a corporal in the Colorado National Guard braced himself and pulled the stock of the M-60 Machine gun close to his shoulder as they heard a hoarse shout of the Toman Daz warriors charging down the tunnel in a last desperate assault. He pulled the trigger, and even with earplugs the tunnel echoed with a deafening staccato roar of the machine gun and the fully automatic fire of the guardsmen around him, and the metallic sound of the armor piercing bullets and D-SAP rounds striking the Toman Daz armor as they charged suicidally. It was the apparently the last tunnel to be cleared, and surviving aliens had sought refuge there, and there was no exit. So they had turned and were now making a last charge.

****

Pamela stood in the dreary coldness that was the White House. She was wearing heavy clothes and a furry Russian style round hat. The polar vortex had shifted down wreathing the Capitol in unbearable cold. There was one respite however, the snow had moved further south after depositing 5 feet . Several buildings had collapsed due to the weight, but

475

the end of snow meant the rest would hold.   The President was looking grim and haggard as he sat behind his desk in the oval office.

"Ms. Monroe, thank you for coming here to see me." he said wearily.  He looked like he had aged ten years since the war had started.  "Please sit down," he motioned to a large leather chair. She sat down and she took off her hat and unzipped her coat.

"I thought it would be good to talk to you Pamela, today, because I have to meet with a delegation of Congressmen and Senators later today, and you are one of the few people who has actually met one of the chief aliens here in this solar system and actually talked to him."

"That's true, but I don't see..."

"This delegation is going to present a petition to me calling for me to sue for peace." said the President. "Because of the cold..."  A cold chill passed through Pamela when he said this; this was followed by a surge of hot anger.

"Mister President, we cannot make peace with these people, they intend to destroy us and take this planet for their own spawn.  They intend for us to go extinct. The chief alien told me this ..." said Pamela firmly.

"I know..." said the President smiling. "That is also the best estimate of alien intentions the Joint Chiefs of Staff across the river in the Pentagon can give me, based on everything they know now, from downed craft, interrogations of prisoners, the files of the MAGI, even alien plans captured by the Russians, when they overran an alien base in Siberia, and from captured documents at Morningstar."

"Well, why meet with this delegation then?"

"Because I have to keep the gears of democracy turning here, even if some of them are free-wheeling without any connection to reality.  But I wanted you to come here and discuss this with me anyway. Even I sometimes can't be absolutely sure of what I am doing."

\*\*\*\*

476

"Deploy into box formation, we are two minutes from Earth radio blackout." said Blue as the harsh lunar surface wheeled below them. The had succeeded detection, apparently, by being immersed in a swarm of ballistic bombardment warheads that were headed for the back of the Moon. Blues squadron of fighter-bombers now began to deploy away from them as their trajectories were bent by the Moon's gravity to whip around the far side. At earth-radio-occultation, as they whipped around the far side in formation with the swarm of unmanned drones of death, they would maneuver onto trajectories for the twin bases at Crater Daedalus and Mare Moscoviense, just as the drone warheads received their last commands from Earth and fired maneuvering thrusters to follow ballistic trajectories to the same targets. They would draw fire from the aliens, while the manned light bombers dove below the drones and followed the curve of the lunar surface at only a 1,000-meter altitude.

****

The President opened the door to the oval office and in marched several Senators and Congressmen. Senator Tunney of Massachusetts led the group. The men looked somber, Tunney was also angry.

"Please sit down gentlemen," said the President, and he resumed his seat behind his desk.

"Mr. President, I think I speak for most men here when I tell you that we must sue for peace with the aliens at this point. We simply cannot fight the kind of technology they are employing; it is a futile waste of human life."

"I see." said the President. "I am sure you understand that if we sue for peace with the grey aliens at this point, Senator Tunney, they may require our abject surrender and the armed occupation of this planet as the price for peace... They have committed many atrocities here, both before the war began and since then, and I am sure you are aware of this also. I think we should consider that as a context for this situation."

"Yes, though we ourselves think they will be willing to discuss peace under terms that we can accept. I think we can understand the atrocities if we have a dialogue with them. It could be that these actions are actually their

477

way of trying to initiate a more enlightened dialogue. I myself believe we could negotiate peace on terms far more favorable to us than those you have just mentioned. I see no harm in asking the grey aliens what sort of terms they are seeking. We can at least, if we sue for peace, begin a dialogue with them, the killing and cold will end."

"I will consider it." said the President, looking around the room at the somber and frightened faces.

"Mr. President, this delegation asks that you do not just consider it, but that you sue for peace immediately, in the name of all human decency!" exclaimed Tunney.

****

It was night on the far side of the Moon and stars shown unblinkingly like jewels on black velvet. The comforting blue crescent of the Earth was nowhere to be found. Blue watched tensely as his ship passed over the lip of the enormous crater holding the sprawling grey alien base at Mare Moscoviense. He gasped in astonishment at the vast city complex, consisting mostly of two and three story grey-white sections radiating from a central core, far away in the center of the crater. Occasional towers of grey-white with hexagonal cross sections rose above the surrounding buildings. The city seemed to cover hundreds of square miles below him. His ship glided over it in a tight orbit of the Moon at a few kilometers a second. They were observing complete radio silence, hoping the Greys were watching the cloud of small warheads coming in at higher altitude. The scene was dreamlike. The sprawling city was dark, with only faint, blue and white lights shining from numerous small windows as it passed slowly beneath him. *There must be millions of aliens living there, above ground, and even more below, he thought with astonishment. These guys are seriously pouring concrete.* However, he then saw before him the dark Central Tower of the city, a thick spire rising almost two kilometers from the center of the city, blocking the light of the stars as he approached it. At this sight, his astonishment was replaced by anger and grim determination. The tower was a giant directed-energy, beam director that controlled a large region of space above the Lunar far-side.

"Mac, button up, we have target in sight, beginning final approach, the show starts as soon as I get a firing solution," said Blue before closing his space helmet visor. Blue then wordlessly armed the craft's weapons systems, then waited for the binocular optical range finder to give him a range readout. The dreamlike character of the scene was shattered as he pressed the trigger on the control stick unleashing an avalanche of missiles carrying high explosive and armor piercing warheads. He watched with satisfaction the missile exhausts streak towards the tall beam director, itself apparently engaging large warheads hundreds of kilometers away. Blue could see missile trails from several other ships in the squadron. Suddenly, the beam director tower lit up brilliantly with dozens of impacts from his and other missiles, it lit up brilliantly with blue-white flames and then noiselessly shattered, and slowly fell to incandescent pieces in the weak Lunar gravity. Blue looked on in astonishment as they flew through the cloud of falling debris. *We have achieved complete surprise...*

"Ooh Rah!" Blue bellowed. "TARGET DESTROYED!"

**\*\*\*\***

Tatiana awoke to screams filling the human women's quarters as thunderous explosions echoed in the halls. She pulled on her coveralls beside her bed over her naked body and bolted through the open doorway. Kathy and Amber were both standing naked in the hall and screaming as the lights dimmed.

"The door! The door is sealed, we can't open it! WE ARE TRAPPED!" Amber was screaming. The door out of the women's quarters was sealed and they could not open it. Other women in various states of undress were pouring out of their rooms.

"BE QUIET! QUIT SCREAMING! GET THE EMERGENCY BREATHING GEAR ON!" Tatiana was yelling, for she felt her ears pop, indicating a drop in air pressure as outside the hallway lost its air to the Lunar night.

**\*\*\*\***

"NUMBER SEVEN! NUMBER SEVEN!" a Medicast was yelling as he ran down the passageway on the mammoth Moondust dispensing platform at the Earth-Sun Lagrange point.  Number Seven reacted coolly and rose from his seat in the conference room, where he had been conferring with his Idelkite colleagues.  His squadron had been assigned to guard the massive space platform from attack by the Unull. He stepped out of the conference room to confront the terrified Unash officer.

"The Prime Base is under attack! Number one orders your squadron to return to base immediately!"

"But the Unull, they are near here, we believe."

"YOU ARE ORDERED TO TAKE YOUR SQUADRON BACK TO THE PRIME BASE IMMEDIATELY! THE BASE IS UNDER HEAVY ATTACK!"  wailed the officer. Without thinking, Number Seven turned to his colleagues.

"EMERGENCY LAUNCH PROCEDURES! EVERYONE TO THEIR SHIPS NOW! THE PRIME BASE IS UNDER ATTACK!" shouted Number Seven, as alarms began to wail throughout the space station and his fellow Haden Daz began to run for the launch bay.

**** 

Captain Robert Forrester, in his spacesuit with his helmet visor up,  on the US Navy ship USS Dahlgren, watched calmly as the space platform in the distance amid the stars, a huge grey hexagon, three kilometers on each edge, now suddenly erupted with a series of space launches. The space suited helmsman tensed visibly.

"Steady at the helm…" said Forrester slowly.  *We have either been discovered or the raid on the Lunar far side has begun,* he thought calmly. The series of sparkling lights streaking away from the massive space station suggested to him that they were headed for the Moon, not for them. As the Dahlgren  and the other Navy assault ships, now closing on the station at a kilometer a second.

"I think we did it gentlemen," said Forrester levelly over the voice tube. "They have no idea we are here," as the light grey station loomed large in

480

the viewports. "Arm grappling charges, and tell the Marines in the boarding tunnel to stand by for boarding," said Forrester. "Range to station hull?"

*"800 meters Captain and closing at 60 meters a second"* They were now slowing down with jets of cold hydrogen gas. Everything possible had been done to suppress infrared and electromagnetic emissions from the assault ships. "500 meters, 380 meters, closing now at 20 meters a second, 300 meters!" called out a sailor.

"Standby by to fire grappling charges, brace for impact, inform Captain Madsen, his Marines may board and storm on my word. Tell ship's crew to prepare for follow-on boarding," commanded Forrester as he lowered his space helmet visor as did the sailors around him.

"100 meters! Closing at 5 meters a second." The hull of the space station loomed in front of them filling the viewport. He could make out seams and plates on it as they closed with it.

"All hands secure for collision! Fire grappling charges!" yelled Forrester. The ship suddenly shuddered and thundered as seven special shaped-charged warheads were explosively launched from mortar tubes on the front of the long cylindrical ship. On they flew, playing out carbon nanotube cables, before impacting on the grey hull in front of them. The viewport suddenly light up with blinding flashes as explosive shaped charges detonated driving Tallin alloy spikes through the thin metal of the space station hull. The flat end of the cylindrical ship then smashed into the punctured hull, rebounded, then slammed into the hull again with the scream of tortured metal as the carbon nanotube cables were reeled in, pulling the Dahlgren into a death grip on the station hull. A thunderous explosion sounded as a massive shaped charge on the front of the hull fired at point blank range to tear a wide hole in the space station hull, to make way for the Marines. Forrester saw another flash in the viewport as another ship, the USS Farragut fired its grappling charges at 100 meters away then pulled itself in tight to pierce the hull also with a brilliant explosion.

"Captain Madsen! Begin your board and storm operation!" Forrester commanded the Marines. "All hands standby to commence board and storm operations! Turrets deploy!" yelled Forrester and grabbed his own AK 74 and plunged down a passage behind the bridge to boarding tunnel, following a dozen armed sailors all in armored space suits. They were now sailing weightless through the boarding bay, into the airless tunnel now leading into the enemy space station. The Marines were already deploying inside.

\*\*\*\*

Blue starred at the lunar terrain below him trying to estimate his speed. Their ship had been hit by ground fire or debris of some kind, almost nothing worked on the instrument board. They were flying homeward, however, on a free-return ballistic trajectory back to Earth. He glanced ahead. To his joy the Earth was rising above the horizon, soon they would be plunging into deep space for the return journey on a vast figure 8 trajectory that had wrapped them around the moon.

"Mac we did it! We hit those bastards hard and now we're going home!" All he heard was tapping from the back cockpit, obviously with the intercom out, Mac was signaling the only way he could.

\*\*\*\*

At a massive bulkhead inside the station, the Marines and sailors in armored spacesuits jetted to the cover of a series of large cylinders, while Marines attached a string of C-5 charges to the bulkhead and then jetted away to cover themselves. Captain Forrester saw one of the Marines twist a detonator handle, and the next instant a brilliant welding-arc blue light filled the dark bay and even in the vacuum a bone-numbing concussion shook him in his armored space suit. From the now ruptured bulkhead spewed a stream of debris, water vapor, and to Forrester's astonishment, a dozen or so grey aliens, none of them even wearing space suits. All bore a look of surprise and despair as they were sucked into the vacuum of the bay. Marines hurled grenades into the breach to kill anything that remained alive, exploding with brilliant electric flashes, before the Marines poured into the ten-yard wide hull-breach with guns blazing.

"Follow me!" yelled Forrester as he led the sailors in their spacesuits into the now flickering breach following the Marines. *We have achieved*

482

*complete surprise. We are going to take this space platform,* he suddenly thought.

****

The phone on the President's desk rang. He motioned for the Senators to quit speaking. He put the phone to his ear.

"Mr. President, this is General Burnham, we have a touchdown, repeat we have touchdown..." said Burnham's voice. It was shaking with excitement.

"Thank you, how soon can I be briefed." said the president calmly. *THANK GOD, THANK GOD, THANK YOU GOD! IT'S A MIRACLE,* the President thought desperately. He calmed himself. *Of course it worked, God is on our side.*

"I will have Col. DiMaggio over in 10 minutes Mr. President, with a preliminary briefing"

"Very Good." The President put down the phone. He surveyed the group of defeated looking men sitting in front of him. Senator Tunney of Massachusetts sat glaring at him.

"Gentlemen, I get the gist of your request, so this meeting is over. I will consider your petition." The President rose from his desk. The Senators looked at him uncomfortably, then rose and filed out.

"Lickspittles," he muttered, "ass kissers...." He pulled open a desk drawer. Pulled a large Cuban cigar out of a box, lit it with a lighter and sat down, put his feet up on his desk, and pushed a button on the intercom.

"Ms. Baxter, could you send in Pamela Monroe, to see me now."

Pamela, who had been asked to wait in another room with some Secret Service agents, drinking coffee, came walking in. She smiled at seeing the President looking so relaxed and grinning. She coughed slightly at the cigar smoke in the office.

"Ms. Monroe, I wish you to be the first to know we have just scored an enormous victory in deep space. The aliens had a platform positioned at

483

the Earth-Lagrange point and were injecting Moondust into the Lagrange point to block Sunlight from reaching here. That's why the weather has been so cold. The U.S. Navy and Marines have just captured it intact, and have stopped the dust injection."

"Oh My God! That's wonderful! Can we broadcast that?" she exclaimed. She felt faint and sat down in a chair. She stared at him in wonder.

"Sure! We'll give you a briefing packet, in a few minutes."  said the President between puffs. "Just wanted you to know that I appreciated your pep talk an hour ago. I wanted to talk to you before meeting with Senator Tunney and his posse of ass kissers."

"Sure..." she said.  *"How did they do it,"* the Sun-Earth Lagrange point is *four times farther out than the Moon*...she thought in amazement.

"You know, we know Tunney is talking to a lot of people in the peace movement, and we suspect some of them are hard X-rays.  They have infiltrated the Peace Movement."

"Oh, nothing would surprise me at this point..." Pamela was staring out into space. "Does this victory mean we are now operating in deep space?"

"Yes, you could say that. Just wait around a few minutes; we'll get you a briefing packet. I hope you'll run this big on your network." The President blew a big smoke ring up towards the ceiling. "Normally the whole White House is a no smoking area, but I though this news called for a cigar..."

"Oh yes..." said Pamela nodding.  *Deep space*, she thought in astonishment, seeing stars.

"You want a cigar?" asked the President, with a chuckle. Pamela coughed and shook her head smiling, as Colonel DiMaggio entered the office with several staff officers from the Navy Marines and Air Force.

****

Cassandra awoke. Someone was knocking on the door to her room.

484

"Just a minute! Who is it?" she called out hoarsely. She rose painfully, feeling like every muscle in her body had been strained by the battle the day before.

"It's Captain Badgio" came a deep voice.

"OK, I'll be ready in a minute!" she said. She flipped on the light, pulled on her dead person's uniform, brushed her teeth and her hair quickly, before opening the door to receive the Captain. He stood at the door smiling beside his wheel chair, then limped in, slowly and in obvious pain. She offered him her only chair and she sat on her bed. He sat slowly. Cassandra could see he was in near agony.

"Cassie, I have a big favor to ask you," he said looking at her with a pale controlled face.

"Yes?" she said somewhat fearfully.

"I need you to be my ADC, my Aid De Camp, my administrative assistant." he gasped.

"What am I supposed to do for you?" she asked in puzzlement. *Coffee, I need some coffee...* she thought. She suddenly regarded him with suspicion. Her eyes narrowed.

"Relax, it's not what you may think," he said with a grin. She smiled also, despite herself.

"I am about a year from any activity like that anyway, so they tell me..." he said with a wink. "I have heard some Admiral is coming around soon for an inspection of this place. So what I need right now is your beautiful eyes around this place. I need you to check up on things for me. I mean this place is really big, and it's full of stairs, and I'll be damned if I am going to have people carry me around or ride around on a scooter. I need you to walk around this place and find out what in hell is going on here for me! I can't do it, not until my legs heal up more..." he paused. "This is the first time I have walked more than 50 yards from my office in the place since I got here." Then he spoke in low tones, "I mean, I don't really trust anybody here. They put me in charge of this enormous place, and I can't

485

really figure out what they are doing here... But I'm the skipper here, at least on paper, of this vessel, and that means I am technically responsible for everything that happens here..." His face was calm as ice but his eyes were pleading. "So you'll do this for me, right? Be my eyes?"

"Don't you have an assistant commander or something? " she asked groggily.

"Ha! My assistant is Colonel Desmond of the U.S. Army!" retorted Badgio. "He don't even know the first thing about this place! He never leaves his office! He just sits in there and reads memos! I have to have people check on him twice a day to see if he's still alive! He don't even realize this Navy facility at Morningstar is A SHIP! "

She looked at him and laughed helplessly.

"Well it does seem to be rolling with the waves, a little, " she laughed weakly.

"So you'll help me, right?" Badge insisted.

"Of course, I will," she said nodding. She really did want to help him.

"Fabulous! You are now my official ADC!" he said with visible relief. "Get some rest then. You look like you still need it. I'll send some people over tomorrow, with a new official uniform for you, and I will get you better quarters. I also want you to debrief with the medical officer on your encounter about your back." He rose in pain, but now obviously happy, and limped out of her room. She sat in shock for a few minutes, then fell back onto her cot and slept dreamlessly.

****

Captain Robert Forrester stood in the command center of the captured space station, surveying the damaged consoles. Technical teams from Foxtrot squadron were hurriedly fitting the one intact set of controls with Shoemaker-Yang translator heads, to allow human control of the alien systems. The technology for this had been developed during the UFO Cover-up to allow human pilots to fly captured alien saucers. Dead aliens, most of whom died of asphyxiation when the Marines had blown open

486

the bulkheads, lay all over the floor. Captain Kerrigan, the commander of the USS Farragut, stood nearby. The technicians were giving him the thumbs up sign, meaning they had successfully gained control of the alien systems and shut down the deployment of Moondust into the Earth-Sun Lagrange point. Kerrigan then was looking out the windows at the Earth, farther away than any human had even seen her before. The Earth and Moon were in a vista that lay over a flat landscape of moon dust, estimated to be 500 yards deep, and stretching kilometers into the distance. It was estimated the platform held a billion tons of raw moon dust, all full of helium 3, and rich in aluminum and titanium. In parts of the vast space platform, fighting was still occurring, Forrester knew, and a steady procession of Foxtrot squadron ships, captured grey ships being flown by humans, was ferrying in more Marines, a platoon at a time.

"OK, we did it! Now let's move this son of a bitch to Key West before the Greys can figure out what has happened!" Key West was the L-5 stable Lagrange point in the Earth-Moon system. Outside, on the surface of the Moon dust, Forrester watched a squad of Marines erect an American flag while in the distance, a missile system was being set up to defend the platform against the expected counterattack.

Forrester and Kerrigan both snapped to attention and saluted as the Marines, having finished their task outside the window, lined up and saluted the flag. It was a surreal yet stirring scene, with the blue Earth in the background and the grey Moon and the flag hanging in the airless star-studded sky.

Soon the vast station was moving to a much deeper gravitational embrace in the Earth-Moon system.

An hour later a huge coronal mass ejection erupted on the Sun and in 24 hours after that, a blast of Solar wind blew all the dust out of the Lagrange point and Sunlight level returned to normal for the first time in 5 months. The long and terrible winter was over.

****

The next day Cassandra went through a two-hour long debrief with the chief medical officer and his assistant and explained her encounter with

487

the Pleiadians on board their ship. She then had her back looked at with an MRI. This revealed that the scars were still present beneath the skin, but had been smoothed out cosmetically. Cassandra was then confronted with a seamstress, measuring her for a uniform of some sort. She stripped to a tee shirt and panties and gladly gave up the uniform of the dead Lieutenant, and was given some fresh combat fatigues in the interim.

The next day, resplendent in a green military looking uniform with shoulder boards with the letters DARC, emblazoned on them in bold black and white and trimmed in gold. It had a tight fitting blouse and a name tag on her left breast saying Chen. And a tight dark green skirt that ended above her knees. A dark green beret was also provided. *What idiot designed this getup,* she thought in irritation as she put it on under the seamstress's watchful eyes. *I feel like a girl scout!* But she decided it was acceptable. *This job will keep me busy, at least,* she thought as she walked quickly to the Captain's office and noted the stunned looks from the military personnel. They looked like they did not know whether to stand at attention when she entered the room or sit still. *I see, it looks military even if it isn't. We are cultivating ambiguity here*, she thought with sudden satisfaction. *Ambiguity is good for a reporter!* Suddenly she felt a feeling of being herself again, at the center of attention.

Captain Badgio rose and saluted her as she entered his office. He looked immensely pleased with himself.

"Excellent!" he said beaming. "Do you like your uniform? I designed it myself!" Cassandra cringed mentally at the memory of her previous thoughts. "I saw a Thai woman Army officer in a uniform like this once. So I copied it from memory," continued Badgio. *He probably saw her without it on too, knowing the company he keeps,* she thought as he motioned for her to turn around. She suddenly was carried away by a flood of seeming memories of seeing Special Forces operating in the jungle as she slowly turned. "Good, excellent! It looks just military looking enough to intimidate people around here, without being regulation!" he said as he motioned for her to sit down. Badgio seemed more confident and moved more easily than the previous day. *Hope heals,* she realized. She suddenly realized that she also missed Robert Schwartzman. *No!*

"Is that my job then, to intimidate people here?" she asked, with a faint smile.

"Yes, as a matter of fact, it is. I live in fear that an Admiral is going to fly in here any day and do a snap inspection of this place! I want you to spread that fear around! Share the fear, Cassie! You're my designated ADC, an actual military rank. People are supposed to salute you and you should return their salute. You are supposed to be my eyes. Anything in this place that doesn't look right to you, you report it to me. You're a reporter again, right? Got that? I want this place ship-shape." she nodded worriedly in response. *Ship-shape, Pammy would be pleased!* "Now, let's see your salute." She saluted the best she could. He frowned. "Well, we'll work on that later. He handed her a military e-pad with keyboard." Right now, we need to go to a meeting with the department heads. I am going to introduce you and tell everyone you are carrying out an inspection of each department and further, that I have a high-speed reamer reserved for any department head who either gives you trouble or doesn't have their department ship-shape! Rodger that?" She nodded and managed a weak smile at this news. "Come on Cassie!" he responded, "You're a tough as nails reporter, and your job is now to snoop around here for me and report." He put on his Captain's hat and motioned to the door with a strong hand and she followed him. She noticed that he walked more firmly now, seemingly with less pain. He had discarded his wheel chair, apparently. As they marched down the hall everyone was snapping to attention and standing aside. He was returning their salutes smartly. She did the same as best she could.

"By the way," said Badgio turning with a big smile, as he walked down the hall. "The U.S. Navy and Marines just took control of a big alien space station out past the Moon. It's a military miracle! This platform has been blocking the sunlight and causing this big winter we've been having. So it's going to warm up soon. Apparently, we kicked some royal ass in deep space!"

****

In muggy Lagos Nigeria, near the airport, with military turboprops and jet transports landing and taking off constantly, in a crowded bar,

489

Schwartzman sat in jungle fatigues and took a tall drink from a shapely Nigerian waitress with ritual scars on her cheeks and brilliant smile. Beside him sat at a crowded table, Arizona, and a Russian Spetznatz Colonel named Andrie Smirnov, a tough-faced man in Russian jungle camouflage, who downed his drink of Nigerian Vodka in one quick gulp, as the waitress handed out the rest of drinks to an assortment of soldiers and jungle mercenaries at the table. They were all handing various types of money to the waitress, who stood counting it happily.

"Ah, Africa!" shouted the Russian. Rising and wrapping his muscular arms around the waitress and kissed her on the cheek, as she laughed and wiggled out of his grasp. "It's good to be back in Africa! It's warm here for one thing! I served here in the 80's as a young recruit, in Angola! He roared to the rest of the table. "We fought you South Africans then!" He motioned to two mercenaries, who laughed as they drank their drinks. "Ah, that was a fight! The Cubans manned our tanks, the East Germans ran our antiaircraft batteries, and we Russians advised the Angolan infantry."

"So how did that turn out for you, Andrie Ivanovich?" asked Schwartzman laughing, sorry he had missed out on this particular episode of the Cold War.

"They threshed us like wheat!" laughed Smirnov. "Their troops and tactics were far superior. But we had one advantage the South Africans did not possess. We had time! So, soon they had to pull back into Namibia. Sometimes that is how victory is made, by outlasting your enemy! Girl, another vodka!"

Ten hours later Schwartzman was riding in a motor launch up the mighty Congo River as a thunderstorm gathered. The boat was crowded with US Army Special forces and Mercenaries, and elite Nigerian Marines. A fifty-caliber machine gun sprouted from the prow of the boat, full of hard-faced men. A green beret stood in the middle of the boat with a Stinger missile on his shoulder, scanning the leaden skies. On the banks of the river fifty kilometers north of Kadula, crocodiles lounged on the jungled banks, and ferocious man-eating Tiger Fish roamed the deep muddy water beneath them. An alien base had been located in the upper Congo basin, and whatever had passed for government in the region before this discovery had disintegrated. Behind them on the river, a fleet of armed motor launches carried more Special Forces, Nigerian Marines, and Congolese Army troops. Schwartzman's orders were to find the base and destroy it. *Simple enough orders,* thought Schwartzman.

"Well boss, they must think you can do anything now, after that fight on Adak!" said Arizona beside him, reading their unsealed orders. "But this Op, I have never seen an operation launched with such poor intel! They don't know where the base is exactly, and they don't know how big it is! This operation has been thrown together in a few days, by the looks of it."

"Yeah, we are supposed to gather the Intel by finding the base and attacking it," said Schwartzman, putting on his wide-brimmed jungle camouflage hat as the first heavy raindrops of a jungle cloudburst began to fall. "But at least it's warm here!" he shouted, grinning above the rumbling thunder. The boat simply churned on up the river in the center on the channel, as the view of the banks was soon obscured by a torrential downpour. With the roar of thunder and descending rain, Schwartzman was alone with his thoughts.

*We are just throwing men at whatever we find right now, hoping the Greys will stay even more disorganized than we are right now*, he thought, *and that's the perfect place for me right now, in the heart of this dark chaos, where no one can find me.* With everyone distracted, he pulled the plastic sealed photograph of Cassandra Chen from his chest pocket, looked at her fondly, then placed it back his now soaked uniform pocket. *I wonder how Cassie is?*

****

Escorted by a young male Navy Lieutenant named Fred Jenkins, Cassandra walked into the biological labs next to the base infirmary. An older lady doctor, Army Captain Adams, with stunning platinum hair, in full dress uniform, stood stiffly with her staff of nurses and technicians. Cassandra saluted as best she could. *I will get better at saluting; in the meantime, I have to report something.*

*The lab area looks clean at least.* She thought as they went into a conference room. The woman doctor seemed to be sizing her up and did not like what she saw apparently. *Fine, we can do this the hard way.* Thought Cassandra as she sat down, steeling herself for an inevitable confrontation. *But I am the queen bee here, so mind my sting...* Someone who was obviously a deputy manager got up and began a long droning report on how many bioassays and DNA tests they were doing each week for the "bone yard " nearby. The boneyard was the major activity at the base as far as she could tell, the President having ordered that every bone fragment found under the now captured alien base be DNA tested and identified. It was reported that they had identified 100,000 dead by matching them with DNA samples from families with missing relatives, and had only two million more or so remaining to be identified.

"So you are now identifying approximately 10 people a week?" asked Cassandra politely. *How many years will it take then to identify two million remains? I wished I had brought a calculator.*

"Pardon me, I hardly think that is a relevant number in this situation," said the chief of the lab crossly. "We have a lot of other things to do also. It is simply not a priority here."

"Oh I think it is a priority," said Cassandra. "Let me help, there are 54 weeks in a year, so that is 540 a year...

"Could I talk with you in private Ms. Chen?" said the platinum-haired doctor icily.

"Certainly," said Cassandra pleasantly. They both rose and stepped outside into the now empty lab as everyone in the lab looked around nervously. Lt. Jenkins looked at her desperately, not knowing what to do, but she just smiled sweetly and motioned for him to stay in his chair. Outside, in the empty lab, the woman turned on her angrily.

"Ms. Chen, I know some of the staff are polite enough to take this farcical spectacle of an inspection you are making here seriously, but I am not one of them! You are not a military officer! You have no claim to be doing inspections here or making reports to anyone!"

"Farce is not a word I would be bandying about here Captain, by my calculations you are going to take 400 years to work through this bone pile!" replied Cassandra coolly. "That defines farcical..."

"It's 4000 years! You can't even do math right!"

"So! It's even worse then! Shocking! This war is going to be over long before that, Captain Adams, so I would get my people's asses in gear and boost that fucking rate!" shot back Cassandra. "Make it four fucking years! That means 10,000 fucking IDs a week!"

"I happen to know you only got this position because you're giving the Captain services other than clerical, and I am going to file a report on this whole episode!"

"Go right ahead bitch! Then I can report your insubordination to the designated representative of the Base Commander, and I can also report how you are attempting to undermine his lawful command authority by spreading false reports!"

"You can't fool me , you don't know anything about military regulations!" said the woman contemptuously.

"I STARTED THIS FUCKING WAR BITCH!! I FOUND THIS HUMAN BONEYARD! I MOWED DOWN TEN GREYS WITH AN UZZIE, WHILE DOING IT! I KILLED THREE OF THEM GETTING HERE TO THIS ASSHOLE OF THE UNIVERSE! THOSE ARE MY MILITARY CREDENTIALS! BODY COUNT IS PART OF THIS WAR EFFORT! SO GET THIS LAB PRODUCING OR CAPTAIN BADGIO WILL HOBBLE DOWN HERE HIMSELF WITH HIS HIGH-SPEED NAVY REAMER AND FIND SOMEONE WHO CAN!"

The woman stared at her stunned and blinked.

"I think my inspection of this section is over..." added Cassandra calmly, trying to keep from trembling, "and I can tell you, Captain, that if Captain Badgio has to come down here on those combat wounded half titanium legs of his, he is going to be in a really bad mood...I might also add, I am engaged to Captain Badgio's former CO, who also happens to be the only

493

human being on this planet that Captain Badgio is afraid of." She flashed her faux wedding ring from Washington State.

"Well, I suppose we could figure out how to streamline the DNA matching process and automate it. We could offer a plan..." the woman said, now looking petrified.

"A plan? I would love to hear such a plan Captain, and report it to the Skipper, together with target rates of DNA matches... target rates like ten thousand a week..." Cassandra calmed herself, became like ice.

"Yes, we can give a plan, I have one in my office, I can present it in a half hour..."

"That would be excellent Captain, just enough time for me to enjoy a coffee break..." said Cassandra "You do have some coffee around here? Maybe with some cream and sugar? "

"Yes, Ms. Chen!"

Cassandra smiled.

****

Cassie, I just wanted you to know," began Badgio gravely, "that I have received several complaints about you for being rude and demanding."

Cassandra was standing in her uniform in front of Badgio's desk in his office holding an e-tablet and an electronic pen. She looked at him frowning. He then broke into a broad smile. She looked at him in a puzzled way.

"Cassie, this means you're doing an excellent job!" said Badgio beaming. "I couldn't be doing a better job myself!" he added as her face broke into a smile. "Admit it, you enjoy terrorizing people!"

"No skipper I don't, I am just trying to get the place ship-shape." she protested. "I thought that is what you wanted?"

"It is what I wanted! You are doing a great job!" he laughed. "But now I need you to change your procedures. I notice you've been going down through the list alphabetically. I need you to concentrate on some high priority departments first."

"Captain, I am doing this alphabetically because I don't even know what half of these acronyms even stand for!" protested Cassandra. "I mean, I have gotten down to the 'D' departments. Yesterday, I inspected the DPRA offices. I asked Lieutenant Jenkins while we are going there, 'what does DPRA do? He says he thinks it's the Department of Personnel Records. We get there, and it's the damned department of Disposal Protocols, Recycling, and Analysis. I mean it's the trash disposal people! So there I am looking at the landfill, and it smells to high heaven! I asked the person in charge, who is Navy Chief Cramer, ' where is the recycling and analysis part of this operation? All I see here is you burying everything!' " said Cassandra waving her pen emphatically. "And he says, I quote, 'we're burying everything so it's safe to be   recycled and being analyzed later after we get our recycling and lab equipment! If we don't bury it someone might steal it!' says the Chief."

"Well that's the Navy," sighed Badgio. "I am just glad were not far out at sea. But I need you to get over to Isolation and Analysis today. I have reports things are not good there. I need you to go over there, find out what the hell is going on, and put the fear of God in that place!" Casandra was working her e- tablet, with her long fingers with their regrown fingernails. She looked up in puzzlement.

"Skipper, I can't find any Isolation and Analysis Department in the directory!"

He looked at her in puzzled annoyance. He pulled up a map of the base on his computer screen.

"There it is on the map, it's a big square building." said Badgio.   The building had the acronym IA on it.

"OK, I'll go right over there with Jenkins. Could you tell me what it is they do there?"

495

"No! I can't! That's why I am sending you!" he said with a wide grin. "All I know is that one of the nurses treating my legs says the place is being run very badly." said Badgio. "I want a report this afternoon about what you find and how to improve it."

****

Cassandra, wearing a heavy winter parka over her uniform approached the stark, nearly windowless, concrete grey building through a barbed wire tunnel. Lieutenant Jenkins followed her likewise garbed. Despite being in the middle of the AIAI complex, the IA building was not connected to the rest of the compound and was surrounded by a triple fence topped with razor wire gleaming in the weak winter Sun. Cassandra felt herself fighting panic as she looked at the tiny windows covered with steel bars. She now understood the IA building was some sort of prison, and her every instinct was to turn and run away from it. But she forced herself to be grimly determined. *I have to do this for the skipper.*

Soon they stood at a pair of massive steel doors and they rang the intercom on the outside wall by the door.

"Who is it?" came a voice from a speaker grill. Instinctively, Cassandra looked up and found a TV camera looking at her, and forced a smile.

"We're from Captain Badgio's office for a snap inspection. I am his Aid de Camp!"

"This is a highly classified facility, we can't admit you without a clearance!" came the voice from the speaker.

"Clear it with the Skippers office then! You're part of the AIAI, and the Skipper sent us here!" yelled Cassandra feeling sudden anger. "I am the ADC!" *she added angrily. Good, anger trumps fear any day,* she thought.

There was a long pause, then suddenly the steel doors opened, and Cassandra and Jenkins rushed inside out of the cold. The building was basically a hollow shell inside with two stories of dark looking cells on open terraces overlooking a courtyard. Cassandra felt a wave of revulsion and sadness at the sight. Several grim looking US Army soldiers in green

496

fatigues and fatigue caps stood confronting them. A rather frazzled looking Army Captain rushed up in khaki uniform. His name was Peterson.

"I am Captain Peterson, and I am acting commandant here." said the officer crossly. "We were not told about this inspection, and we are not sure you have authorization to conduct it." Cassandra felt a grim smile cross her face as she pulled off her parka.

"Well, I can assure you, Captain, that if you refuse this inspection, Caption Badgio is going to come right down here himself with a company of Marines and conduct the inspection himself, and he will bring his high-speed Navy reamer with him."

"Well … this is highly irregular" he muttered frowning.

"Yes, please proceed then Captain," said Cassandra icily, pulling out her e-tablet and electronic pen. "I want to see your prisoners here."

"Yes, we have a high-value prisoner here."

"Good let us begin with him." said Cassandra. Captain Peterson turned and took Cassandra and Jenkins to a cell near an office. The cell had an outer door, followed by a dim entryway and then a second door. The doors had multiple locks and the guards were rattling keys on large rings to open them. Cassandra felt the oppression of the dimly lit entryway and the heavy steel of the locks and doors.

"We use mechanical locks to thwart any computer hacking of the security system." said Peterson

The door swung open. The cell inside was windowless and dimly lit. A figure rose from a chair at a table.

The figure had white hair and a pale haggard face.

"VIRGIL!" Cassandra exclaimed and rushed forward to embrace him. The gaunt figure of Virgil Jackson looked startled, then his face broke into a warm smile.

"Baby doll! I was just thinking of you yesterday." He embraced her warmly. "I was thinking, `I'll bet Cassandra Chen will come and get me out of this hellhole.'"

"Lieutenant Jenkins! This is Virgil Jackson who rescued me from certain death when I was held captive!" said Cassandra ecstatically and turned to present Virgil to Donald Jenkins.

"Captain, I want this man moved out of this cell to a cell with windows immediately!" said Cassandra sharply, as she turned to Captain Peterson, who looked at her angrily.

"Ms. Chen, you can't give me orders here in my own facility!"

"Your right Captain, but I can call Captain Badgio down here and tell him you are treating your prisoners here inhumanly! Then he can replace you with one of your able subordinates here." she said through clenched teeth. She was now staring at Peterson who was looking very uncomfortable.

"Lieutenant Jenkins, go check the other cells and then report to me the welfare of the other prisoners." She said without taking her eyes off of Peterson.

The Captain and his men looked frozen as Jenkins rushed off to look into the other cells on the ground floor. Cassandra noted this paralysis with alarm. But she turned back smiling to Virgil.

"Where is the other guy who helped me, McCaffey?"

"Oh, he's dead. They tell me he was in the next cell over." said Virgil pointing at the wall. "He kept back his dental floss and wove himself a rope and hung himself a few months back." said Virgil smiling matter of factly at Captain Peterson. "Ain't that right Captain?"

Cassandra spun and looked at the Captain, who lowered his eyes.

"Pretty damn clever. Actually, McCaffey always was a bright boy" said Virgil with a slight laugh.

"Is this true Captain?" demanded Cassandra "How many other prisoners have committed suicide here?"

"Well, we can't watch everyone all the time here! We are short staffed!" said the Captain defensively.

Jenkins rushed up.

"Cassie! All the other cells are empty!"

"Captain, how many other prisoners do you have here in this place?"

"We have 25 other prisoners..."

"Captain, where are they?" she asked in mounting horror.

The Captain merely looked at her. She looked at the other guards, one of whom looked down at the floor. She stared at them in disbelief.

"Major Taryton, who was the commandant here until three months ago, ordered all the other prisoners confined in the lower levels for security reasons!" stammered Captain Peterson. "Those were his last orders!"

"Lieutenant," she said icily as she turned to Jenkins. "I need you to contact Captain Badgio's office right now, and tell him to send a squad of Marines and a medical team here immediately."

**** 

On the dimly lit first subterranean floor, the stench of backed up toilets and unwashed human bodies was heavy in the air as Cassandra, accompanied by a frantic looking guard with rings of keys, several Marines and nurses and a medical corpsman. Cassandra walked swiftly down the narrow steel stairs. The guard opened the first cell. The stench of rotting flesh assailed them as they turned on a flashlight and saw a rotting corpse, laying on the floor in the dark. Cassandra with tears flowing down her face grabbed the keys from the guard and began opening prison cell doors.

"THIS IS CASSANDRA CHEN ! WE ARE HERE TO GET YOU OUT!!!" she yelled. To her joy, she heard hoarse cries and banging of cell doors down the darkened corridor of cell doors. Pale, emaciated people began to be pulled out of the cells, some too weak to move under their own power. Cassandra realized they were all technicians and nurses from the former Morningstar facility. Finally, in the last cell on that floor, she pulled nurse, Becky, who had treated her wounds after Cassandra was rescued from the torture chamber. Becky's hair had turned white. She looked at Cassandra in astonishment, then her face melted into tears. "I always knew you would come back for us ... to rescue us" gasped Becky as Cassandra rushed to embrace her and Becky collapsed to the floor in her filthy cell.

****

As Cassandra watched, weeping, the grey alien named Howie was brought up on a stretcher from the horrid lowest level of the prison with the other alien prisoners. Jenkins, looking pale and dumbstruck with horror at what he had seen, stood before Cassandra to report on the clearing of the last cells on the lowest levels. Cassandra had tried to go down to the lowest level but had been emotionally unable to. Six alien prisoners had been held there, and three had been found dead in their cells. Of the 25 other prisoners Captain Peterson had reported at the prison besides Virgil Jackson, only twenty were actually alive. The rest had died of infections or other untreated medical conditions. Apparently, the high classification of the facility had been interpreted by Major Taryton, its former commandant, as preventing medical attention or sanitary cells to its inmates.

Cassandra had the only window in the place uncovered, which held a view of the snowy mountains. She ordered Howie laid near it so he could look at the sky, as the rest of the prisoners, those who could walk, were given showers and fresh clothes to wear. Nurse Becky now clean and in fresh clothes immediately went to Howie, the alien, and examined him; the other medical personnel being baffled by his alien physiology.

Cassandra walked up to where Howie lay as Becky looked up from the stricken alien. He lay on a mat on the floor. Another alien who was apparently his friend, stood nearby covering his own eyes in a sign of grief.

Cassandra looked on hopefully at Becky as she rose up from beside Howie. Becky looked at Cassandra and shook her head.

"He has bad infections in his abdomen; I can't even figure out why he is still alive..." said Becky sadly. "All of the aliens I have seen before, who were this sick, didn't make it." Cassandra absorbed these words and wiped her eyes and knelt beside Howie. It was now twilight outside, and the first stars were becoming visible in the dark blue sky over the mountains.

"Oh, how long I have wished to see the stars again." gasped Howie.

"Howie, do you remember me, it's me, Cassandra, and we met before the battle..." Cassandra wept and held his delicate hand between her hands.

"Oh yes, I remember you, lady Cassandra, it is so good to see you again," gasped Howie. "I have often thought of our nice conversation. Can you bring my friend Gintusk close to me so I can see him?

Cassandra motioned to the aliens standing nearby to come closer.

"Gintusk my friend, I told you Lady Cassandra would not forget us here, but would help us." said Howie with apparent great effort. Howie's turned to look at Cassandra. "I want you to meet my friend Gintusk, who is a good fellow, and who comes from the same planet as I, and like me, shared the misfortune of volunteering to come here...." Cassandra looked up and smiled at Gintusk who now knelt by the dying Howie.

"You have got to hang on Howie, we are bringing more help for you," wept Cassandra. But Howie turned away slowly and looked at the stars outside the window.

"Oh, you have already helped me much lady Cassandra. I now have found more goodness here, than on my own world..."

Howie then shut his eyes and his breaths slowed and stopped. Cassandra wept for a moment then lowered Howie's limp hand to his side. She looked up at Becky, who shook her head. Cassandra rose.

Captain Badgio had arrived with his aides and was looking around with a mixture of anger and sorrow on his face. He walked painfully over to Cassandra.

"Well, Skipper, I can report things here in IA department have been run very badly," she said with a trembling voice, looking down at Howie's dead form as she did. Nurse Becky covered his body with a sheet. "I would also recommend a court-martial for the men in charge here, especially a Major Taryton."

****

## Chapter 12: Cosplay

"The situation is complex; it is partly real and partly imaginary"

Pamela Monroe

"This victory as permanently changed the calculus of power in the Earth-Moon system..."

Lt. General Standish, CINC Space

****

Cheers were ringing out as the staff in the AIAI main office stood in the crowded conference room, stared at the big conference room presentation screen, and watched Admiral Haynes of the Navy and General Standish of Space Command deliver a press briefing on the spectacular victory the Navy and Marines had achieved at the Earth–Sun Lagrange point. Under the bright lights, the gold braid and brass on their uniforms shown brilliantly. Behind them, on the stage, several other admirals and generals smiled confidently. Cassandra was sitting beside Captain Badgio in the front row of chairs in the conference room. Despite feeling exhausted and slightly ill, she was beside herself with joy as Admiral Haynes, Chief of Naval Operations, described the diversion attack on the Moon followed by the stealthy and surprise attack on the alien space platform, its capture largely intact, and then its movement to the L-5 Lagrange point in the Earth-Moon system where it was now being turned into a heavily fortified allied forces `Space Platform Lagrange' or ASL.

"My God, we are going to win this thing after all!" exclaimed Cassandra happily wiping her eyes.

"I never doubted it!" said Badgio, grinning. "But remember me and the boys have been fighting the Greys for years. They muffed their big chance in 1947. If they had tried then, with everything they had, they might have taken the place. But they didn't because they were cowards..."

As the Pentagon briefing ended the President appeared with a brief message of thanks to the Navy and other space personnel involved in the

503

operation. He then proclaimed a National Day of thanksgiving and prayer for the next day. When he was done, there were deafening cheers, and Badgio rose and began belting out the Navy Hymn "Anchors Aweigh." And everyone, including Cassandra, rose to their feet and joined in the singing.

"All hands are to report to the rec center where all drinks will be on the House!" shouted Badgio, and the entire group began marching down to the rec center on the base. Badgio was walking vigorously and Casandra had to walk quickly to keep up with him.

The inject of Lunar dust into the Sun–Earth Lagrange point was now over, and thanks to one last massive solar outburst, the dust had been cleared out and the Sun shown brilliantly in the middle of the clear sky for the first time in months . Cassandra had even walked outside to bask in it with a large crowd of others.

****

"He says what?" asked the President in disbelief.

"He says he is Karlac of Delpin and he wants to negotiate a peaceful resolution of this conflict. He is talking to us by radio on an open channel; we have a fix on his ship. It's coming from the outer solar system, and he is now within the orbit of Mars. He says he wants to land here and talk with our representatives. What should we do?" asked Bergman. He was now full secretary of Defense, Clayton Thomas having resigned due to his stroke. "This could be some sort of ruse, Mister President. He is flying here in a spaceship at fairly rapid speed. It could be a cover for some sort of intelligence gathering. He should be here tomorrow."

"Well, we'll have to take the chance," said the President. "Only don't let him land here in Washington, that would create a frenzy and be dangerous as well. Tell him to land at Morningstar where the Boneyard is, I want him to see it for one thing. If anybody is going to negotiate an end to this war, they should see why it started." continued the President looking reflective. "Yes Jim, and I want you to go out there to meet him, get NATO and Russians to send somebody, let's present a united front. I want you to leave for Morningstar immediately. "Bergman turned to

504

leave. "And for God's sake be nice to him!" exclaimed the President. James Bergman nodded and left.

**** 

"Cassie," said Badgio in great pain. "We got some galactic peace emissary coming here, tomorrow, I mean here to Morningstar. I banged up my right leg dancing yesterday; the surgeon says I may have popped a rivet or something." Badgio rolled his eyes and flashed a pained grin. Badgio was lying in a bed in the sick bay with his right leg raised. Cassie and Lt. Col. Desmond of the Army, his second in command, stood beside the bed. "In any case, you're going to have to go meet this emissary for me and bring him here until some Alliance representatives can talk to him." Cassandra nodded in amazement at this.

"And Cassie, be real nice to him!" said Badgio, "this could be a lucky break for us!"

**** 

Karlac's small spacecraft landed near Alamosa, in a snowy field by highway 11 where the snow was three feet deep. Chief Deputy, Toby Clemens, was first on the scene and pulled up to the silver spacecraft in his SUV just as Karlac was climbing down the ladder in his silver space suit.

It had been a hard winter since the battle on Manzano crest, and Deputy Toby had recovered from his wounds but not his bitterness. His first impulse was to kill anyone or anything from outer space.

Karlac had landed just beside the snow plowed road and stepped down onto the road surface. Toby watched incredulously, with his hand on his gun as Karlac waved at him and then took off his helmet. Karlac was very human looking with a full head of white hair and well-trimmed white beard on a genial, middle-aged looking face. Karlac sensed great sorrow in the place, far more than he had ever experienced before. However, he reacted by trying to be even more cheerful and friendly. He turned on his voice translator as Toby looked on incredulously. Toby was amazed that he hadn't ignored his orders and shot the man already, but he was stopped from doing this by an overwhelming feeling that the personage

505

seemed to intend no harm and seemed so completely clueless. *We've had no shortage of killing here in these parts, so a little less would do no harm, maybe,* thought Toby as he relaxed and took his hand away from his gun. *Maybe he actually is a peace emissary...*

"Can you understand me?" asked Karlac.

"Yes, I can understand what you're saying. You understand me?" replied Toby. "I am just a deputy sheriff here, and I am told important federal Government people are coming here to talk to you, so I would just stay put if I was you."

"How soon will they be here, do you estimate" asked Karlac cheerfully. He was looking around smiling, holding his space helmet. The air of the planet smelled sweet and was fresh and good after months on his spaceship.

"Ah, they will be here...directly..." said Toby nodding to himself, hearing the throbbing of a helicopter approaching. *This fellow is either very important or very stupid,* thought Toby in amazement. He pulled out an e-cig and primed it and began to smoke it. He then leaned back on the fender of his SUV. It was a beautiful day. It was actually warm.

"This is a really nice planet you have here," said Karlac beaming at Toby.

"We'll mister, that's a really nice spaceship you got there..." said Toby with a broad smile, and waving his e-cig at the spaceship.

Cassandra rode in a Blackhawk helicopter towards the field where the silvery spaceship had landed. She had carefully combed her hair, only to have the helicopter rotor wash blow it all into disarray. She could see the ship, it was silvery white and lozenge shaped, with stabilizer fins. It dwarfed the sheriff's SUV beside it, being roughly the size of a greyhound bus.

The helicopter landed about 30 yards from the spaceship, and she and the others leaped out as soon as it was in contact with the road. The rotor wash again put her long hair into disarray but mercifully the dust from the moist road was minimal.

506

Karlac looked up at the strange craft landing. Was struck by its primitive yet effective propulsion, but quickly his eyes fastened on Cassandra walking towards him at the head of a party of several human in military uniforms. Her long black hair, bronze skin, beautiful face, and statuesque body mesmerized him. He had heard of the beautiful women of Earth. Now for the first time, he saw the rumors were true. Despite his vow of chastity, he fought a feeling of overwhelming passion for her. He suddenly realized she was the woman he had seen in his dreams calling for help.

*I must save this people,* he cried out mentally. *Somehow, I must do it!*

She was now standing in front of him, pushing her long black hair out of her face. She was dressed in her ADC uniform with jade green slacks. She smiled nervously held out her bronze colored hand.

"Welcome to Earth Mr. Karlac. I am Cassandra and I will be your host."

He held out his hand and grasped hers with a broad smile. He hoped this meant she would be his guide during his sojourn on Erra.

"Thank you," he said with a slight bow. She bowed her head and smiled nervously.

"Our commander requests you follow us in your ship to a meeting place, where emissaries of our government wish to speak with you about your mission here," she said with large eyes. "Do you understand ?" she nodded smiling.

"Yes, I understand you," he said smiling.

*He is so human, even the way he looks at me is human...*Cassandra thought in astonishment, remembering Semjase and their crew on their ship, risking their lives to help her. *The universe must be full of other humans... We, therefore, do have hope, like Pammy said.*

\*\*\*\*

507

Doug and the rest of his squadron were now flying like the wind to Key West, the code name for the L-5 Lagrange point, to rendezvous with the new space station there.

"Oh my God! Look at the size of this thing," yelled Doug over the squadron frequency, as they approached. It was a huge grey hexagon, 2 kilometers on each side and a kilometer thick. And judging by the large American and Alliance flags now spread out on its sides, it was thoroughly owned by the humans. He was guided by a flashing blue beacon to a landing bay in the side. A crudely painted sign was hung above the entrance "UNDER NEW MANAGEMENT"

****

"You're late!" said Tatiana sharply, pointing at Amber. They were in the medical lab, now sparsely staffed. Amber looked at Tatiana speechlessly. "I've had my period since the Samarans visited, so has Katherine here, but you're a week late now! I also heard you were throwing up this morning! We have to do something before they take you away to Daedalus!" Amber simply looked at Tatiana in silence. "Cathy get the hydrazine!" yelled Tatiana, her blue eyes blazing. Kathy stood paralyzed. Hydrazine, an extremely toxic chemical, was used by the humans on the Moon to induce abortions. "Get it!" said Tatiana turning and glared at Kathy. "The syringe is over there!" she motioned fiercely. Amber stood shaking in front of Tatiana. Suddenly a group of Unash, with two armed guards, entered the lab. It was Doctor Okoha, a high caste Unash, and notorious experimenter on humans at Daedalus. At this sight, Tatiana froze.

"One of you is with child," hissed Okoha, "We know this from the hormones in the waste water. This child belongs to the experimental section..." He took a scanner from his belt, and lifted it to one of his eyes; his gaze swept the room. "It is you!" said Okoha pointing at Amber.

"Oh God, please," whispered Kathy helplessly. Okoha shifted his malevolent gaze to her.

"What did you say?" Okoha demanded.

508

Abruptly, a group of four Samarans entered the room in armor and bearing guns and swords. Zomal of Alnik led them.

"You!" said Zomal pointing at Amber. "Are you with child?" he asked. She nodded slowly.

"Good!" said Zomal smiling broadly. "You must come with us to be a guest in our quarters, for the child you carry is a high-born Samaran."

"This is no concern of yours, Samaran; the child is our property, like all of these women, are our property." hissed Okoha.

"Yes, and we own you Monchkini!" sneered Zomal. He pulled out his heavy laser pistol and pointed it at Okoha. His companions instantly leveled their weapons at the remaining Unash.

Zomal smiled fiercely. He pulled out an order from his belt. "This woman and the child she bears are the property of the House of Krayus of Mirzam, the high Ambassador of the Samarans to the Vikhelm." Zomal threw the paper onto a table beside Okoha. Okoha looked at it, and then suddenly left in a rage, followed by the rest of his group of Unash.

"You have not heard the last of this Zomal!" said Okoha loudly as he left the room.

"Nor you of me … Dr. Okoha," said Zomal with a smirk. He turned to face Amber.

"Get your things, and come with us, and do not worry about them. You shall be our honored guest." His voice was gentle.

Amber looked at Tatiana with amazed eyes, then turned and followed the Samarans out the doorway. She gave one last fond look to the Tatiana and Kathy before leaving.

"Thank God!" exploded Kathy.

"No, thank Zomal. He asked me yesterday if Amber might be pregnant. I told him I thought it was likely, because of the last set of Samaran visitors we entertained." said Tatiana looking relieved. "But I confess, I did not think this would be his reaction." Tatiana looked deep in thought.

"With Amber gone and half of us gone for that experiment, we are really shorthanded," Tatiana announced.

"What will happen to her now?" asked Kathy, wiping her eyes.

"Slavery, a thousand light years from here, most likely. She'll be a chambermaid if she is lucky. If she minds her manners, she will probably outlive both of us here," answered Tatiana looked somber, and she then became more animated.

"We have to get Christina out of the hybrid nursery to replace Amber. I mean, we are really shorthanded here now! " said Tatiana nodding to herself.

****

Robert Forester was walking on the Moondust, 500 meters deep, with Captain Jeffers of the USMC on the vast upper surface of the ASL Key West, the Allied Space Lagrange station, as it was now termed.

They both looked at the frenzied activity in the distance, rank upon rank of missile systems being set up by the Marines to prepare for what they all knew would be the alien counterattack to try and retake the platform. They looked at a group of supply and fighter spacecraft approaching to dock at the station. "Good, more groceries," said Captain Jeffers. "My Marines were worried we might have to eat some of that canned cow rectum we found in the alien stores."

They looked out into the abyss above the grey surface, at the huge bright Earth in the distance and then to the equidistant Moon.

"Skipper, we now got those bastards flanked!" said Jeffers waving his space gloved hand at the Moon.

****

In the landing bay at space station Sophia, one of five now orbiting the Earth to service the growing fleet of space fighters, cargo craft and space Corvettes run by the Navy.   Patrick Steel tore off his space helmet and was helped out of the cockpit of the space fighter-bomber, still feeling dizzy from the feeling of gravity in the bay. The look on the Marine ground crew beside the craft told him what he had guessed on the way back from the Moon, that "limerick MacClintok" was dead in the back cockpit.

"How is he?" asked Steel.

The Marine sergeant simply shook his head.

"He's hamburger," he said.  Steel paused, fingered the gold crucifix around his neck, then turned and trudged in the unfamiliar gravity to the locker room.  A bright yellow stripe on the floor led to the locker room.  In the large bay, painted light space-gray, ground crews were fueling and arming fighters feverishly.  Outside a window in the bay doors, Steel could see the brilliant blue edge of the Earth as the station road in orbit.

A Marine Colonel met him on the way, dressed in the standard space 'pajamas', a blue coverall.

"Congratulations Captain, you and your men just won the war. Your diversion operation was successful. We going to give you a full debrief so you can see what it was you bought us." said the Colonel.

 "How many of the squadron made it back?  My radio was out for most of the trip back."

"You and three other ships made it back." said the Colonel looking more grim. "We have a full debrief on the operation for you after the flight surgeon checks you out." Steel got a deep sinking feeling. *Four ships came back out of 20.*

"Colonel, with all due respect, what need now most  is a shave and a hot shower," said Steel  with a salute," the Colonel smiled, "and some shore leave..." added Steel with a grin. *I wonder if Chiquita misses me as much as I miss her?* The Colonel returned his salute and motioned in the direction of the lockers.  He had been wearing space diapers for a week. *A nice long hot shower...*

**\*\*\*\***

Karlac  stood in front of the blackboard.  James Bergman, Anton Tikonov, and Charles Harrison, the British emissary for the EU, sat waiting expectantly.   Cassandra Chen sat near the board; she saw in the faces of the humans, guarded hope.   In Karlac's face, she saw good will and optimism.

*Is there any hope this could actually lead to a truce in this war?* She wondered. *This is such a disconnect with everything else that has happened... But we have to try.*

"Thank you , good people of Erra, for agreeing to meet with me.  We have no time to lose, I am sure you will agree, and so I ask you to agree to terms for a truce between you and Unash.  I have mediated many disputes among peoples of different stars. It all begins with a dialogue between the parties. I have clear lines of communication with the Unash commander on the Moon, and you I understand,  can communicate with your Allied governments.

"I wish you to know that the war you are having at Erra is of great concern to other peoples in the Cosmos, and they all want it to end quickly.  Please also know that the safety of Erra and its people is also of great concern to other peoples," said Karlac.  *Yes, I am lying now, but what I say will be reality later,* thought Karlac with determination. *I will make it a reality. These people will not be forgotten!* He turned and smiled at Cassandra.

"They have a strange way of showing their concern," said Bergman incredulously.

"Ahem, let the gentleman finish, shall we James," said Harrison with a forced smile.  Tikonov merely looked on deep in thought.

**\*\*\*\***

In desperation, Vikor put on his clothes and a wide-brimmed hat over his long blonde hair.  He looked at his still slightly bruised face in a mirror for a last time, stuffed a laser pistol into his coat and left the spacecraft as the helicopters seemed to move closer.

*They have detected my ship somehow, he thought. It kept me alive through the winter, but I must abandon it. I must find a road and go to the town where it will be harder to find me. Where is Semjase? Why can't she come and get me out of here?* He found himself near a paved road with traffic. He began to walk along it. He was trying to remember the procedure that humans used to flag down a ride. The snow had melted, and the Sun shone brightly. He instinctively waved as people drove by. It was a cold afternoon. Finally, a dark blue pickup truck pulled over and offered him a ride in the back. He found himself riding with several Mexicans and a bunch of muddy farm tools in the back of the truck. The Mexicans were chattering away in Spanish as he pulled his jacket close to him against the cold. They were headed into Medford, and houses became more frequent beside the road. Vikor noted the large freeway running in the distance, with heavy traffic.

*If I can get to that highway and catch a ride I can get far from here easily,* he thought hopefully. But suddenly the truck slowed. A wall of traffic lay ahead of them and a helicopter was circling overhead. It had green camouflage.

*Roadblock!* he thought desperately. *They are looking for me!* He bounded over the side of the truck and began to walk along the side of the road. *A tall fence bordered the road. If I turn and run away or climb the fence they will see me. What can I do?* He found himself walking along the road. Police cars and military Humvees blocked the road ahead, but he noticed the fence ended before the roadblock in a residential neighborhood. *If I can get past the end of this fence without them noticing.* Large numbers of people, police and deputy sheriffs, and what looked like military personnel milled around ahead and were letting cars through. A large number of young people stood by watching. *Good! Confusion.* He tried to walk nonchalantly up to where the fence ended and the crowd of gawkers stood watching.

He drew near to the group of police cars, blue and red lights flashing and military Humvees blocked the road and were letting only single lines of cars pass after being checked.    Suddenly he caught a glimpse of something out of the corner of his eye that filled him with fear.   A soldier in camouflage had a German shepherd beside him on a lease.   He looked up carefully as he got closer to the road block; he was fifty feet from him and only thirty feet from the end of the fence.

Suddenly the German Shepard looked straight at him and began barking furiously.  *Damn! He smells me!*   *Vikor now* broke into a full sprint, straight for the end of the fence.  He pulled out his laser pistol and fired a warning shot into the sky.  The girls in the crowd of young people broke into screams and the crowd scattered, running away from him.  Vikor was now running as fast as he could down a residential street waving his pistol. Behind him, sirens burst into wailing and engines roared to life. He made a beeline for the largest close building he saw.  *I must find someplace to make a stand, he* thought grimly.  It was a church.   He ran up the steps to the front door and wrenched it open.  He ran into a large room with a tall ceiling and beautiful glass panes of many colors.  Several people were having a meeting with their chairs in a circle.  The people were looking at him and rising, he pointed his pistol at them. Several women screamed.  *NOW WHAT!* he thought in a panic.

"HELP ME! HELP ME!"  he yelled in confusion.  "People are chasing after me! They want to kill me!"

Kenneth Forester, the head of the Thursday afternoon prayer group, motioned for everyone in the group to be quiet.  He waved his hand to the man to point the strange looking pistol someplace else.  The frantic looking man complied and pointed the gun away from them.

The older man with grey hair smiled at him, Vikor, his heart racing and the fatigue of the sprint down the street on his half-healed body now caught up with him, tried to smile back. He pointed his gun at the floor.

Kenneth Forester, muttering a prayer, looked at the strange design of the laser pistol, and his blood ran cold. *Man in Black*, he thought, Alien. *That's what all this police activity has been about! They have been looking for an alien, not an escaped convict, as they said!* He decided to approach the man slowly.  Outside the church, Forester heard sirens and police and

514

military vehicles and running booted feet. *They are surrounding the building.*

"Here Young Man, calm down, I will help you, I will stand beside you. They will not hurt you if I am standing beside you..." *Sanctuary I will declare Sanctuary for him until we can calm down the situation.*

"I AM NOT YOUR ENEMY! I AM A FRIEND TO THE HUMANS!" the man suddenly said to the other people in the church. "My people do not make war here against your people! I am here to watch and report what happens here! Do you believe me?" the man asked Forester. His eyes bespoke desperation. Forester muttered a prayer.

"Yes I believe you," said Forester. *Please, God let him be telling the truth.*

"I believe you too," said a woman named Rosa. She smiled tearfully at the man. The man seemed to relax and put his gun back in his coat. The man lost his frantic look and managed a nervous smile. Forester reached out and shook the man's sweaty hand.

"Rosa, go outside and the tell the men out there that the man is a stranger here and has asked for sanctuary. Tell them we think he is not an enemy alien but maybe a friend who is trapped here by the war," said Forester quickly. "Go! I will stay here with him," said Forester insistently and motioned everyone in the room out .

"The soldiers outside want to shoot me, but I am a friend to the humans! I swear it!" said the man to Forester, as the rest of the people quickly left. Rosa led them out.

"I am Ken Forester, I live near here. Where are you from?" said Forester as pleasantly as he could manage.

"Oh I have been living on the side of the mountain over there," said Vikor with a helpless smile. "My ship crashed, and I was living in it." He gave an embarrassed smile.

"Oh, I meant, where did you come from originally?" said Forester with a warm smile.

515

"Oh yes." The man looked slightly embarrassed." I come from a long way from here, from a star in what you call Sagittarius. We are friends to the humans!" *I am a spy, and a spy is supposed to be a good liar,* thought Vikor desperately, *my people could actually not care less about this place or its people...*

Vikor sensed his fate was being discussed outside in the front of the building. He looked around, the older man was smiling at him reassuringly. This made him have hope that he would somehow get out of this alive. He looked around idly, his eyes fastened on a pot of black roses on a table that someone had brought to the church as a decoration.

Forester could here Rosa arguing with the police and soldiers outside. Suddenly the sirens stopped wailing outside. Forester heard Rosa talking calmly. Suddenly, everything was peaceful.

He found himself looking at Vikor, who was staring at a glass container full of black roses. It was a death memorial for someone's son at the church who had been killed recently in the Pacific. Forrester looked at Vikor with a mixture of wonder and pity.

*He must know so much more than we do, but he is lost just like we are,* thought Forester

**** 

"He says he is a friendly alien? I mean does that check out? Have you done an earwax test on him? " Bergman was on the phone as Harrison was listening.

"Ok so the dogs say he is ET and his laser pistol is obviously ET. He says he's a what? A Vikhelm? Oh this is marvelous!" said Bergman ginning. "Good! Good, I will tell this Karlac fellow. For God's sake be nice to this new person! Treat him like visiting royalty... I don't know; take him out for a steak dinner or something!"

He hung up the phone, turned and smiled at Harrison.

"We may have just had two lucky breaks!" said Bergman.

"It's about bloody time!" said Harrison. He went to a wet bar and poured himself a cognac.

"Also, Lao Tzu, the Chinese Foreign minister, is en-route to join us here," said Bergman

"Splendid, James, it shall be a grand tea party here!" responded Harrison.

**** 

"Here are the terms we have asked for, that are agreed upon by our governments," said Anton Tikonov handing the paper to Karlac. Karlac looked at them awkwardly. "Here, I will read them to you," said Tikonov shooting a knowing glance at Bergman and Harrison. The Chinese foreign minister Lao Tzu had agreed to them and was en route. The Indian government had also agreed.

"The Unash will immediately cease attacks upon Earth; they will return all ships to their bases on the Moon. We will declare an armistice when this done."

"The Unash will then evacuate any remaining bases on Earth and release all human prisoners. Once this is done the Unash will evacuate their lunar bases and all other bases in the Solar system and depart."

"The Unash government will also undertake to pay reparations and damages to the governments of Earth and to persons they have abducted."

"These are our conditions for an armistice and permanent peace. We urge the Unash to agree to these terms immediately."

Karlac nodded. *The Errans should speak more respectfully to the Unash...*

"I will convey this to the Unash commander on your Moon, and urge him to respond so negotiations can begin. Be prepared for him to respond with slightly different conditions. This is the negotiating process." said Karlac. *I hope the Unash will not be offended by the tone of the Errans. They obviously expect to be treated as equals by the Unash,* worried

Karlac. *May the Creator bless my efforts and not make me look like a fool for even attempting this.*

Tikonov nodded. Bergman approached Karlac.

"Also, Honorable Karlac, we have received word that another person, not Erran, claiming to be a Vikhelm has become the guest of our people here. He says his name is Vikor of Vale. When informed that you were also here he said he wished to speak to you, and said you could transport him home." said Bergman. "We are treating this person with the utmost courtesy."

Karlac nodded. *It is very good that I am here. This is very fortitudinous.*

"Can you arrange for me to have a communications link with him so I may see him and speak with him?"

Bergman nodded.

"Yes, we can arrange that within a few hours I think.

"Good let me convey these terms to the Unash, and let us see how they respond. For this, I must go to my ship."

Karlac bowed slightly, turned to Cassandra, and smiled. She rose, smiled, and bowed slightly. He then turned and left to the passageway to his ship, now parked in the AIAI facility.

****

"Very Good! Vikor, I can return you to Vale. I have a safe-conduct pass from the Samara and from the Echalon Alliance. Tell the Errans to transport you here, while I continue with negotiations for an armistice." said Karlac on the video link.

"You are here attempting to negotiate an armistice in this war?" asked Vikor incredulously. *He is obviously is a fool!* thought Vikor sadly. *This is no trade dispute over nectar wine or chambermaids from Elsung...One might as well try to arrange a truce here as between lions and sheep! I*

518

*only hope he realizes how hopeless the situation is soon, and gets us both out of this doomed place!*

"Of Course, I am trying to negotiate a peace here. You know that is what I do..." replied Karlac with a confident smile, but Karlac read Vikor's face, and his heart sank.

"Very good!" said Karlac turning to Bergman and Harrison. "I will transport him home when these armistice negotiations are concluded. That should take several days. Can you transport him here in that time?"

"Certainly, we can have him here as a guest in this facility in a day's time if you wish." Karlac nodded and turned. Could I have the pleasure of your presence Lady Cassandra, on my ship for tea?" Casandra smiled and rose from her chair. Cassandra followed him down the passageway to his ship. She turned and winked happily at Bergman, then disappeared.

"He takes his tea with honey perhaps?" asked Harrison turning to Bergman with a smile. Tikonov went to the wet bar and poured himself a tall glass of vodka.

"Not really," said Bergman also heading for the bar at the end of the conference room. "Ms. Chen has spoken to him extensively over the last few days. She says he belongs to some sort of Monastic Order, no marriage or touching a woman."

"Well he certainly seems taken by her," said Harrison.

"Yes, her presence here is very fortuitous and unlikely." said Bergman, selecting a bottle of Southern Comfort and opening it. He poured himself a glass, went looking for some ice. He noted Tikonov had downed his glass of vodka and was now pouring another. "You know she was held prisoner here for about three days. She told me this is the last place on Earth she would have wanted to return to. But here she is. Then this Karlac fellow turns up here and now, soon this Vikhelm fellow. So we have had a string of good luck. Perhaps, a breakthrough is possible." he noted Anton Tikonov shaking his head grimly and downing another glass of Vodka.

"No, I expect no breakthrough," said Tikonov with a slight look of merriment. "This Karlac is a fool. I think he has no idea what has occurred in this place, or what he is doing here. He's what you Americans call a "do-gooder, a wandering galactic naïf." Tikonov smiled. "Of course, I will be most happy if I am mistaken."

"Anton, on what do you base this assessment?" asked Harrison.

"He could not read the message I handed him. He understands our speech. That is some sort of translator hardware he carries. Anyone with a radio could do this, from our broadcasts. But to read, he would have had to deal with the Unash, and learn this about us from them, or at least get a scanner. He has apparently not dealt with them much. Therefore, he does not know even half of what this situation here consists of." Tikonov downed another drink of Vodka. "He is like Napoleon paying a visit to Moscow, without bringing winter clothing. You see, I have visited the alien base we Russians captured in Siberia, on the Lena River, at Tsungaya." Tikonov sat down wearily. "I have seen what the grey aliens did there," his face took on a look of grim horror. "Therefore, I believe, he knows nothing about this war, or what goes on here, and therefore, these negotiations will conclude quickly. "His face lit up in a now drunken smile. "Again, I will be most happy if I am mistaken."

In Karlac's ship, he poured a cup of green steaming tea for Cassandra. She took the cup, which had two opposing handles and sipped some of it. Leaves of some succulent plant floated in the tea. It tasted marvelous.

"Oh this is very good!" she said smiling. Karlac smiled, but looked troubled and sipped some tea from his cup. Behind him on the console of the ships controls a light flashed and a small electronic note sounded. He paused, set down his cup, and rose from his chair. His face looked troubled as he looked at the flashing light.

"That is strange." said Karlac, "The Unash commander has apparently responded very quickly to the terms your people have offered. "Karlac looked at the message that printed out on a strip of paper like substance. His face fell. Cassandra felt a deep cold fill her. She set down her tea. "I would have expected a response after a day or two, after some thought and consultation with his home-world"

"Is the response positive?" she asked.

Karlac, turned, his face troubled, and punched several buttons on the console.

"I am requesting them to resend the message, to verify it." The light flashed again like before. This time, he merely looked at it on the screen, comparing it to the printout.

He then turned and looked at her sadly; there was something else in his expression. Despite his alien origins, Cassandra recognized the expression as abject horror and incomprehension.

"No, the response is not positive," he said looking at the floor. "I am sorry..."

"I am amazed, that the Unash commander would respond so quickly and in this manner," said Karlac with a look of embarrassed confusion. "Normally, people take longer to respond and respond more positively..."

Cassandra looked at him and her eyes began to fill with tears. Then she caught herself, and her sorrow was replaced by white hot anger.

"If you knew these people like we did, you would not be amazed!" she yelled at him. "We have suspended military operations so you could do these negotiations! The whole fucking Alliance is in stand down!"

"I am sorry. Perhaps if the terms offered by your side were less confrontational," said Karlac looking contrite.

"They are the only terms we can offer!" she exploded. "These are the same terms we have always offered! WE WILL LIVE AND DIE AS A FREE PEOPLE! YOU TELL THAT TO THE WHOLE FUCKING COSMOS!" she yelled. Tears ran down her cheeks. She paused and regained control of herself. *All of this, for nothing...* "You fool!" she said wiping her face. "Why do you think we are at war with these people!" She then caught herself. Karlac looked at her deep sorrow as if it was too much to bear. She bowed her head, reached out her hand across the table to grasp his.

"I am sorry Karlac...," she said fighting back tears. "I had hoped you could work a miracle here, and get us a just peace. A peace we could live with. That's all I ever wanted in this, I swear to God." He squeezed her hand in response. She blinked and looked back up at him. He smiled weakly back at her. She managed a weak smile. "What was the Unash commander's response, exactly?" she asked, her voice gaining strength.

"He said that you Errans must surrender immediately without conditions," he then paused, "but only after you each plucked out your right eyes, and presented them to the Unash as a peace gesture." Cassandra stared at him, a feeling of fear and revulsion swept through her, and then despair. But she fought this feeling.

"I might have expected this," she said coldly. "After all, I have dealt with these people and their enablers before." She smiled and nodded to herself. Karlac looked devastated and despondent.

"It appears my journey here has been for nothing. I had no conception that the Unash would behave like this."

"No, your trip has not been for nothing. You have obviously learned something new here," said Cassandra thinking deeply. "Would you not agree?" she added. Karlac nodded dejectedly. *What can I report to the negotiators in the officer's club?* thought Cassandra. *That this whole exercise has been an absurd waste of precious time? No, this is like a news story. We have to frame this, get a story together and quickly.* She thought feverishly.

"Karlac, it is very important to me that you don't just walk back to the other negotiators and tell them this has all been for nothing. For one thing, this war has to end eventually with you, or someone like you, coming here and negotiating some sort of peace between us and Unash. I truly believe that will happen someday," she smiled. He seemed to straighten up and smiled back. "We have always believed that the universe as a whole means the human race no harm, that we will eventually join a community of peoples of the Cosmos, and that we will even find friends in this community. So...," she picked up her tea and drank a sip to give herself more time to think. "Yes, we have to present this to my colleagues honestly, as a setback. But also as a first step. We want everyone to believe that you can eventually negotiate a peace, do you agree? I mean, I have total confidence in you to do this, even if it takes more time. " *Please Lord let my words be prophetic*...thought Cassandra.

Karlac smiled and nodded, looked less discouraged. "Good," she beamed at him. "So I am going to rehearse a little speech with you that will make my own people not lose hope in an eventual peace process, so they will have confidence in you as the able negotiator that you are.   But, I am going to ask you a favor in return, so that you can learn a lot more about what is happening here at Erra and as a result make yourself a better negotiator here." She stared at him making her eyes as big as possible. He nodded and smiled at this.  "And also, so you can bring back some more of this excellent tea from your home-world."

An hour later, Cassandra entered the conference room ahead of Karlac with her dark eyes sweeping the faces of the emissaries of the Alliance. Her eyes and expression were not despondent but conveyed a mixture of disappointment and barely suppressed anger. The initial smiles of the emissaries vanished.  Bergman, Harrison, and Tikonov stood and looked back at her soberly.

Karlac followed and stood before them, looking sober and slightly annoyed, he bowed his head slightly to them.

"My lords, I bring bad news.  The Unash have completely rejected my attempt at opening negotiations.  I would, therefore, end the cease fire you have declared and resume your military operations immediately. We must look upon this as merely a first attempt at negotiations and not their end."

"What did they say exactly?" asked Bergman.

"They said they wanted you to surrender unconditionally, and,"  Karlac spoke with effort, "They said you should all pluck out your right eyes as a peace offering." Cassandra could feel  a chill enter the room when these words were spoken.  Bergman looked at Harrison and Tikonov. Harrison looked stunned at this report. Tikonov merely shrugged with a slight smile.

"This is a negotiating tactic. I have seen this when I was in Afghanistan," said Tikonov with a slight laugh. " They hope to gain a psychological advantage in this."

"Yes, I think this is how it should be interpreted," said Karlac. "Eventually, someday, they will negotiate seriously and this war will end. However, I wish to apologize to you all for raising false hopes. I simply did not understand this situation well enough."

"That is quite all right Old boy," said Harrison with a smile. "You are to be commended for trying to do something. We understand that you come from a place of high civilization, and may not fully grasp the barbarities of this situation here." Bergman nodded in agreement, and Tikonov simply smiled. *Thank you, God*, thought Cassandra. *They accept his apology. He has won them over.*

"Yes," continued Karlac. "In the region of the galaxy where I live, such things as the Unash have said, are unheard of,  and only recall times long forgotten among our people.  At the same time, please understand, my people know very little of what is going on here.   I confess I came here in haste,  without learning more about this conflict. I was hoping to stop it as quickly as possible.  To make up for this,  Lady Cassandra has suggested that I take a tour of the Unash base that was in operation here. Would such a tour be possible?"

Bergman looked at Harrison and Tikonov, who looked back in surprised assent, and then turned to Karlac.

"Yes, we can arrange this. You will have to wear  a bio-isolation suit."

"I will come also," said Cassandra, but inside she felt herself shaking with fear and horror.

****

"We should hurry Mr. Ambassador if we want to be done by nightfall," Cassandra said trying to urge herself ahead. Karlac was obviously not eager to do the tour. Inside her, she was beginning to tremble. *NO! I have to show him what they did here! I have to show him what happened to me here! The naïve fool, he doesn't understand! I have to make him understand! It will help end the war!* They were walking to the entrance to the mesa with Lt. Jenkins, Karlac followed dutifully. Casandra suddenly stopped. Karlac stopped and looked at her in puzzlement. She was trembling, tears began to flow down her cheeks.

"I can't go in there Karlac...I am sorry" she gasped.

"You will not be giving me the tour of the former Unash base? I was so hoping you would do so. Your presence is very pleasant to me." responded Karlac. Cassandra was shaking. *No, No, I can't* a voice screamed within her.

"No, I cannot accompany you ." She looked at him, her eyes pleading with him to understand. "You see they took me there before. They tortured me there, and they raped me." she blurted out tearfully. She looked at him with tear filled eyes. "I am sorry. It is too soon. I thought I was strong enough to do it, but I am not." she gasped. Karlac looked at her deeply taken aback, immense sadness suddenly filled his kind eyes.

Karlac felt the pain within her in that instant, like a white hot iron through his soul. He blocked it out.

*What did I just say? I just said it to him! Did they rape me here? THEY RAPED ME!,* she cried out mentally in disbelief, *IS IT TRUE?* She tried to keep her face calm as inwardly she was screaming. *Have I been blocking it out all these months? Was I raped here too?*

"I understand," he said, then turned, his face now very calm and followed after the Lt Jenkins into the large steel doorway. He turned as he went inside and looked sadly at her one last time. The door shut, and she collapsed in a sobbing heap on the gravel walkway as two soldiers rushed up to help her back into the Humvee, and took her back to the main base.

*They raped me! They raped me! It happened. I have been blocking it out all this time, until today,* she thought as she wept and the Humvee took her back to the base. She felt sick and began to tremble.

525

"I couldn't tell anyone, not even myself, and I just told a man from outer space," she muttered tearfully to herself as they rolled down the gravel road. It was noticeably warm and the spring Sun was bright, but to her, all she could see now was shadows and darkness.

****

Kenneth Forester rode in the seat beside Vikor, in the military cargo jet, the last words of his wife still ringing in his head. Outside he could see several jet fighters flying along as escorts. He had been asked by the military commander to fly with Vikor to Morningstar to keep Vikor calm since he had refused to surrender his laser pistol.

Vikor sat beside him staring straight ahead. He was holding a black rose blossom. Vikor had asked for one, and they had clipped him one. Forester did not have the heart to tell him what it meant. Finally, Forester cleared his throat.

"Vikor, my wife asked me to make a request of you, for when you get back home which I know is many light years from here."

"Yes?" asked Vikor, he seemed relieved to be engaging in conversation.

"My son is named Joseph, Joseph Forester, and he was kidnapped by the grey aliens. My wife has asked that, could somehow try to bring him back to us, when you get home.

Vikor stared at him in deep thought. *I cannot refuse, this man has saved my life. But I cannot tell him the truth, that it is probably hopeless.* Vikor nodded gravely in response.

"I will try to find your son, and return him," said Vikor. "I am in your debt, it is the least I can do in return."

"Is there any hope, that you will find him?" asked Forester.

"The night sky, it is very vast, with many stars," said Vikor, staring off into space, "but I will try." *Liar* thought Vikor to himself, *why do you lie to everyone? It is hopeless here! If this son is alive someplace better he never returns to this doomed place!*

526

Kenneth, perhaps sensing the inner conflict in Vikor, turned and simply stared forward and prayed.

*Please, Lord, let this man be successful and return our son safely to us …*

****

"This was a combination execution chamber and biowaste disposal room. Many people were apparently fed alive into these chambers and dissolved with enzymes," said Jenkins pointing at the huge hourglass chambers. Jenkins had been on tours of the place before, still, it filled him with blood-curdling horror. The room was still blood splattered, from the battle and body outlines were still marked on the floor. The decision had been made to leave them there until after the investigation. "Cassandra Chen was rescued from one of these chambers before her execution could be carried out." Jenkins motioned to some plastic sealed images taped to the chamber. "This is a picture here of what she looked like when she was rescued. Here is a picture of her back, in particular, the staples are holding together gashes in her back inflicted by an electrified whip." Jenkins looked at Karlac, he looked as though he was in a trance. His face fixed in a look of frozen amazement.

After Cassandra Chen was rescued here, the special forces team decided to escape with her by going down into the depths of the mesa, since intense fighting and fires were above them. So we will follow their approximate route, that will lead us to the chamber of the dead, where all the bones were found, and the place of the Unash massacre of many alien workers. We believe they massacred them so they could not surrender to our forces." Karlac nodded knowingly, and the tour continued.

*Uakal Dum korel nach Uakal Dum korel nach,* Karlac was praying *"Oh God protect me from evil,"* he said mentally over and over as they led him from one terrible sight to another.

He had seen some evil things in the Echalon while trying to mediate disputes there, but everything he had seen before now was trivial compared to the stark evil and cruelty evidenced around him.

*And lovely Cassandra, they treated her horrifically here, in this awful place,* Karlac thought for a deeply sad moment, pausing in his endless mental prayer. *Yet she is so fair, even after surviving this place.* He blinked back tears at this thought and forced himself to resume the endless mental prayer. The thought of her suffering here was almost more than he could bear. Karlac was now deeply afraid if he did not fill his mind with that prayer of protection, he would lose his mind in that place.

****

"You must launch your attack in 20 hours to regain the space platform at all costs. If it cannot be retaken it must be destroyed! Is this clear!" said Sadok Sar to the assembled Unash commanders.

"We must make maximum effort!" he added. Number 7 sensed resistance from the Unash commanders.

Number Seven stood near the conference table, he felt a terrible tension in the air.

"But our fleet of ships is very much depleted by recent combat operations." said Number 2 , "We must wait for reinforcements!"

"NO! We must attack immediately while the Errans respect the truce they have called! I knew that fool Karlac would be useful to us! Now it is proven. We must attack while he still negotiates!"

****

Vikor, looking grim and somber stood beside Karlac beside the boarding ramp to Karlac's spaceship. Vikor's eyes were fastened on Cassandra. *She is the one who started this war. The Black Rose of Erra. Truly, beauty is power.* Her long black hair framing her face fascinated him, for such hair color was extremely rare among the Vikhelm and usually meant the woman was a prophetess. *There are some things I will miss about this place,* he thought sadly, *women like her will be one of them.* He turned and looked sadly at Kenneth Forester, who was standing beside Cassandra . *But we must get out of here quickly ...*

528

Everything had fallen apart in the past hours. The negotiations had failed, and now the Errans had informed him that the Unash were preparing for an attack on the Lagrange point station and that Karlac and Vikor should leave immediately for their own safety. Cassandra stood in front of Karlac and embraced him goodbye tearfully. Kenneth Forester shook hands with Vikor a final time. James Bergman, Harrison, and Tikonov stood by stoically. Captain Badgio stood painfully behind them resplendent in his dress uniform.

Karlac made one last gesture of peace, the raised open hand, showing it carried no weapon. He gave one last look at fair Cassandra, who looked down at the ground tearfully. He then turned, and walked into his ship followed by Vikor. In the ship, he immediately sat down at the controls and buckled his safety straps. His passenger followed him and sat in the copilot's seat, and buckled himself in. They had barely spoken since Vikor had arrived , there had been no time in the emergency that was unfolding.

"Buckle yourself in tightly, we must leave quickly," said Karlac.

****

The ship lifted off and Cassandra wept as it rose into the blue sky and disappeared, she then walked past the somber group of Bergman, Harrison, and Tikonov; she tried to mustered a brave smile as she walked past them. She stopped by Captain Badgio. Kenneth Forester, a tall grey eminence, stood beside Badgio looking at the sky in exhaustion. He looked at Cassandra, recognized her from the news.

"Do you think this helped?" he asked her. He was a head taller than she was.

"Yes, I think this helped," she said as bravely as possible. "The longest journey begins with a single step. Maybe this won't end this war in the next month but it is the beginning. The Cosmos is apparently very complex, as we would expect, so this is progress." she said as confidently as she could muster. Inwardly, she felt overcome with despair. "I understand you helped get the other alien to come here, that will help too. The more people we can send back to the galactic community after seeing what is going on here the quicker this will end." Kenneth Forester nodded gravely.

"I am Kenneth Forester,    I understand you are Cassandra Chen…" He offered his large hand.

"Yes, I guess I started this war. I was hoping I could help end it here," she said as she shook his hand in return.

"You didn't start this war , miss,  the Greys started it when they took my son, many years ago," he said smiling weakly. "I see you tried, though, to end the war."

"Yes," she nodded tearfully.  "All I ever wanted was a peace we could live with."

He looked up and motioned to Devil's Mesa, looming in the distance, to her, still a pit of horrors.

"I think making peace with that will be hard.  I helped the other alien in the hopes of merely getting my child back." She hugged him when he said this and was overcome with an emotion of loss and despair.

*My child, my child,* she thought , *I have a child*, suddenly afraid she was losing her grip on her sanity.

The Chinese Foreign minister, Lao Tzu, a late arriver to the conference stood nearby with his aides.   He was a short greying man with a look of stoic endurance.  His eyes caught hers as she passed and she went over to him and bowed slightly. He offered his hand and they shook hands. He surveyed her with wizened eyes.

"I am sorry the negotiations had to be cut short, but the emissary advised us to end the armistice," she said.  "I am sorry your trip here was for nothing, Mr. Minister."

"Oh, no,  Ms. Chen it was not for nothing. I have met and talked with the emissary and shared our views with him, this was most enlightening. And now I have  met you, the courageous daughter of China, who saved the whole world." He said with a guarded smile.

"Oh thank you, but I don't feel very courageous right now Minister, in fact, I think I am going to faint," she said.

"You must endure, it is your heritage," said Lao Tzu firmly. He then bowed slightly to excuse her, as Bergman was approaching to speak with the Minister.

She then turned and walked over to Captain Badgio.

"Skipper" she gasped to him looking faint. "I have to leave here. If I don't, I think this place will kill me…" she stammered to him. He looked at her with deep concern, then motioned for Jenkins to escort her away. They led her to her quarters, where she collapsed into her bed and lay there unconscious, tears streaming down her cheeks. Jenkins and the nurse with him withdrew and shut her door. Not knowing what else to do.

****

"What course are we taking out of here?" asked Vikor as they flew above the brilliant blue arc of the Earth, they were headed for the Earth's Moon in the distance.

"I must pass near the Moon, it is the quickest way, but I must also consult with the Unash commander on a tight communications link, so the Errans will not be able to intercept our conversation. I must inquire of him why the negotiations have been cut short and why he gave such a rude response," said Karlac. He was feeling suddenly weak and dizzy.

"I do not think that is a good idea," said Vikor. "We should get the hell out of this place as soon as possible. Every heartbeat we remain in the Solera system and in the Quzrada itself is dangerous."

Karlac looked at Vikor incredulously.

"I have letters of safe passage from the Samaran Empire and from the Unash." "The Samarans said you also have safe conduct."

"You believe them?"

"Yes."

"You do not look well," said Vikor looking at Karlac closely.

"I am well enough, and you are my honored guest, so be quiet please," said Karlac in irritation. "I am on a mission of peace, and taking you out of here is just a helpful gesture." Karlac programmed the ship's flight computer for a course towards the Moon.

"You will not bring peace to this place, the Unash are determined to take this planet for themselves, and the Samar back them. So you are wasting your time," said Vikor. "You might as well try to hold back a mighty river with your hands!"

"You are a spy, and I am a peacemaker, I think we view the universe differently. You look on this place as merely a zone of conflict. I view it as a place full of people who deserve to be saved."

Vikor laughed at this. "If you are really interested in making peace, you should first seek the advice of spies, then you would know who is worth saving and who is not. For me, sentient beings, Archmetan or not, they are just tools." He looked out the cockpit in the blackness of space studded with stars. The Earth was receding from them. The Moon loomed ahead. "These Errans, they are just people like any other Archmetan people. They are as rare and valuable as common stones on a beach."

The dark-haired woman who stood by us when we left, is she is not worth saving?" asked Karlac as he adjusted the dials on the ship's navigation computer. "I saw you staring at her."

"Oh, I recognized her. She is a rare flower, indeed. She started this war." said Vikor smiling. "She discovered the plots of the Unash and the human traitors who supported them, and exposed them. Everyone believed her because she is beautiful." he laughed. "Beauty adds the great force of logic to a woman's words, this I know." he laughed, then became more sober. "The fighting began soon after she did this. I wrote a long report about her for my superiors, and I found it impossible to explain how this war began here without discussing her central role in it. Leave it to a beautiful woman to start great trouble." he laughed.

"She is trying to save her people, I do not consider that merely causing trouble," said Karlac angrily making further adjustments to the navigation computer.

"They cannot be saved, Karlac," said Vikor soberly. "The best that can be hoped for is that the Echalon does not get dragged into this. We face the Xix towards the galactic core. This thing in the Quzrada, it is just one of those sad things one can do nothing about. It is fate." Vikor paused, looked sadly at the stars. "I am just a lowly spy, and even I can see this."

Karlac stared out at the stars , he felt exhausted.

"Well your fate, Vikor, was just fate until I got sent here and got you out. What is the death of a spy, in the grand scheme of things? Yet you were not abandoned, I got you out." said Karlac . "Think about that."

"Who sent you here?" asked Vikor.

"I, I am not feeling well," said Karlac, unsnapping his safety harness and rising unsteadily. I came here in great haste, and I did not get any inoculations against common illnesses on Erra. I did not even enquire of the Unash concerning this. Apparently an unfortunate oversight." He looked around, squinted. "I am going to lay down for a while. Awaken me when we go into orbit around Luna." Karlac went back to his small sleeping compartment and fell upon his bed.

Vikor sat then alone with his thoughts as the ship dove through space, propelled by gravitic drives. It was good to see the unblinking stardust of space again. Despite his unease at their course towards Luna, he allowed himself the comfort of hope. He then reached into his coat pocket and pulled out the Black Rose, and studied it.

*You started this war beautiful one. But will you live to see its finish?* Vikor thought as studied the rose in his hand and thought of Cassandra standing in front of him. *Oh, how I will miss the fair women of Erra,* he thought with sadness.

**** 

"I don' t know if we accomplished much here," said Bergman to Lao Tzu.

"Oh we must be patient, I think this is a positive development. This war is now waged on a larger chessboard than before," said Lao Tzu. "This fellow may not command fleets of spaceships, but he may command something else more powerful."

"What would that be?" asked Bergman.

"The opinions of others in the larger Cosmos," said Lao Tzu. "That is where the ultimate battle of this war may be won, I think."

**** 

Admiral Hodges, a tough fireplug of a man, stood at the end of the control room in his space suit. He faced a group of grim-faced officers, also in spacesuits. He had just arrived at the Alliance Space Platform head of a squadron of what were called Fast Space Frigates. His eyes were like flaming coals under his dark brows.

"We expect the Greys to launch an attack to try to recover or destroy this space platform at any time!" I have been placed in command here. Captain Forester, you are relieved of your command here and transferred to command of the Fast frigate Elgin, which I just arrived on. Now, Report to me on the platform defensive status."

"Yes, Admiral! We have the 5 space frigates you have just brought. We have 50 U.S. Navy and 20 U.S. Air Force space interceptors here, 20 Royal Navy, and 35 Russian. We have two battalions of Space Marines readying the platform for defensive action with long-range missiles and laser cannon and we have two rifle companies of Russian Marines doing the same."

"How is coordination with Russians going?"

Suddenly, a series of sharp explosions sounded in the distance. The whole structure of the space platform shuddered and vibrated.

"Yes, admiral, it's not going well." began Forester. "As you just heard, the Russians, under the command of one Colonel Orgarkov, are right now blowing holes in the outer shell of the platform rim near here with shape charges, sir, to make gun ports they say. We have mounted our guns and

534

missile batteries on the outside for better visibility, but they wanted theirs shooting out of ports," said Forester. The Admiral nodded frowning.

"I see," said the Admiral, as another series of distant explosions sounded. "Do we have a com line to Orgarkov?"

"Yes, Admiral, but I got into a big argument with him over blowing trench lines in the Moondust on the upper surface. It makes too much dust and limits visibility."

"Admiral sir," said Colonel Girard of the Marines. The Russians are digging trenches now, trenches in the Moon dust to guard the East flank of this com center. We were planning on fighting any boarding party here inside the platform, but the Russian plan looks good, so we want to dig some trenches too."

Forrester sighed at this last comment from the Colonel. He figured if the Greys got to the platform and landed on it, his orders were to blow it up. A one megaton hydrogen bomb had been given to his command for this purpose. Admiral Hodges considered all this with a deep frown and then nodded.

"Well, Captain Forester, good job!" said Admiral Hodges. "Leave this situation to me now, and report to the Elgin. The exec officer is Jim Hudson and he is a good man. He'll get you familiar with the ship. I want you to take command of the Frigate squadron and immediately depart. I want you to position yourself in a halo orbit around the Lagrange point at 500-kilometer radius from the station and await my orders there. As I said, Space Command expects an enemy attack at any moment."

****

Cassandra lay in her bed, she had tried to sleep but now lay awake trembling. She was looking out her small window at the cold stars over the mountains.

"No peace, no end to this war," she began to cry, "I failed."

"I was raped while I was held prisoner here, they raped me." she wept. But then in her despair, she saw the little golden spark, like Tinkerbell, in

535

the dark room. She blinked to make sure she was not dreaming. She held out her hand to it in wonder, it looked so beautiful. To her surprise, it seemed to come closer and finally cautiously settled on her open palm. It seemed smaller and dimmer than she remembered it.

"Here baby, don't be afraid... she gasped in amazement, forgetting her sorrows for a moment. She slowly pulled her hand closer, it was a little golden spark of light. Then she slowly cupped her hand around it and brought up her other hand. It seemed to want to be held. Then suddenly she felt it, overwhelming sorrow, a sense of complete abandonment and despair.

"No, Nooo" Cassandra wept, almost overwhelmed with a feeling of abandonment. "I still love you, I will love you if no one else does." She grasped the little spark close to her and held it close to her chest. She felt herself pouring every atom of love into the little spark as if it was her child. "I love, I love you, I love you," she gasped over and over as she wept.

Cassandra dreamed she was some sort of lioness, powerful, in the prime of her life, and she was leaving her litter of cubs safe in her den and swiftly running across the sparsely treed wilderness at night. She was answering a cry of some child-thing, following an overwhelming motherly instinct. It was cold and she was now slowing warily, as she approached a place of sharp cliffs. She heard the abandoned child wailing. She then heard and could see two upright beings moving toward the child-thing . She sensed they meant to do it harm as it cried, so she glided forward carefully and powerfully and leap on the nearest one. She felt with satisfaction as its salty neck snapped in her jaws and then she tossed it aside with the flip of her head and bore down on the other one, near the edge of the cliff. The other one saw her approach and screamed and leaped back, falling over the cliff crying out in a long wail until she heard its body impact on the rocks far below. She listened intently but could only hear the babble of a small stream at the bottom of the chasm, before she turned to the small child-thing on the ground near the cliff's edge.

She came up and sniffed it, and then sensing it was cold and in distress licked the top of its furry head with her large soft tongue. She felt and

536

overwhelming instinct to care for the child-thing and lay down and curled her large furry body around it and offered her warm teats to it . The child thing snuggled close and began to nurse. Sensing all was well, the lioness blissfully curled tighter around the child-thing, covering it with her long furry tail, and kept it warm and protected until dawn came.

At dawn, the lioness sensed more upright beings approaching but sensed they meant well towards the child by the tone of their voices. She uncurled herself gently from around the sleeping child and stood watching as the upright ones approached. With a low warning growl, she turned and left the child-thing. The child-thing had now awakened and was crying again. But she sensed it true mother was nearby and the child-thing was safe, so she swiftly ran off, to rejoin her cubs, making sure no one was following.

Cassandra awoke with a start in her bed. She felt her blouse, it was wet with some liquid. She sat up , felt the dampness and then brought her fingertips to her mouth. It was milk, her own.

"The dream, it was so real," she said to herself in astonishment as she rose and took off her top  and bra and washed herself.

"I took care of my child," she said to herself in wonder.

"Someday I will understand..." she said stepping into her small shower.

****

On the fourth world of Amalon, a star near Bellatrix, and the home-world of the Beltran clan.  Reya the chief maidservant and now chief nurse to princess Nori, ran up to her naked form on the ground and with tears of joy lifted up the child in her strong hands and held her close to her warm bosom, kissing it on the top of her warm head. She tore open her blouse and began to nurse the child. Another maid servant came up to here and draped a warm shawl around her and the child.

"The child lives! She lives and was nursed and protected by a lioness!" called out Reya  to the others rushing up. "Go, go quickly and tell our

537

mistress the child lives!" Reya yelled at a younger serving girl who rushed off with tears of joy to bear the happy news.   Even the white-bearded Elder of the Beltranian clan looked happy and amazed.  He was standing over the corpse of one of the men lying dead with his neck mangled. Others looked over the cliff where another body lay smashed at its base.

"These men are strangers by their dress.   And the one killed by the lioness, behold,  she did not feast on his flesh but only left him lying here. It is a great omen.  This child is favored of the gods." said the Elder in amazement, now leaning on his staff.  Henceforth, this child shall be called Amagur, 'mothered by a lioness'

****

Number Seven, stared into the view screen as his squadron of twelve ships bore relentlessly through space towards the space platform at the Earth-Moon Lagrange point.  The Lunar far side receded behind them. About him in space, he could see the rest of the task force. There were only 45 ships in all, 41 fighters and four cargo ships hastily converted into troop landing ships and crammed now with thousands of Toman Daz and Hadden Daz warriors, now sworn to retake the platform or embrace death in the attempt.  This small fleet represented half of their remaining space forces, depleted after nearly a year of relentless combat at Erra.  Half the pilots, were newly trained and had never flown in combat before against the Errans, and clearly to Number Seven, they had no conception of what awaited them.   Many of the new pilots had, in mindless bravery, volunteered to  be in the lead group of spaceships. Despair tore at Number 7's heart even as he tried to put on a braver front.   The Errans had many fighting ships at the platform and hundreds were now streaming towards them from Erra.  He surveyed the brave  Idelikites beside him. Heavy in the air of the cockpit, as they sped into battle, were the unspeakable words, *Sadok Sar is a fool, and the attack to retake the platform is doomed.*

****

Captain Robert Forester watched intently as flight after flight of space interceptors took off from the mammoth space platform, a platform they had not built but was none-the-less theirs now.   He was sitting on the

538

bridge of the Elgin, a ship almost completely unfamiliar to him, that made his previous command, the Jones, look like a space lifeboat. He sat in the center chair of the bridge in his space suit with helmet sitting on a "tree" on the right armrest of his command chair. The bridge looked like a dead ended tunnel dominated by a large view screen on the front bulkhead and whose walls were covered with electronic panels of flashing indicator lights. The weapons officer and the helmsman sat in front of this at consoles. Sensor and communications officers sat at consoles on the side walls ahead of him, his executive officer, a person he relied on heavily now, sat beside him. They all wore space suits with their helmets stowed within easy reach on 'trees' next to their consoles. Forester had been reading technical reports on his new command feverishly as they orbited, at a 500-kilometer radius, around the space platform. His ship was powered and propelled by a compact fusion reactor fueled by He-3 and deuterium, and mounted high energy lasers, proton beams, and missiles. Out of a porthole, the space platform looked like merely a bright speck amid the stars, but on the main view screen with magnification, it was now a beehive of activity, with wave after wave of chemically propelled interceptors flying off it into space using disposable solid boosters to conserve fuel for the coming battle in deep space. He punched a button on his console.

"Crew this is your Captain, prepare the ship for rapid maneuver and combat, all hands to battle stations." With that command, the Frigate Elgin came to life with red flashing lights and ringing of Battle alarms. On cue, the fusion power plant flared into increased output and a wailing chorus of siren sounds filled the ship as rotating inertial energy stores spun up to ever higher rpm's, storing energy for the coming battle, energy to be released as laser and proton beam pulses against the four large alien targets now headed towards them. It was these targets that Forester was to stop in the coming action, as the Elgin and her three sister ships now moved out of orbit around the L-5 Lagrange point one kilometer, with long flares of blue hydrogen plasma, and bore on toward the approached alien formation.

"Lord God, may we be victorious!" prayed Forester in a low voice.

****

Douglas Forester, despite the gravity compensation in his cockpit, was slammed back into his seat as his new Space Eagle fighter shot across the dull grey Moondust that covered the top surface of the Allied Space Platform.  With a metallic clanging noise the four solid boosters, still trailing blue flame ejected from their hard-point attachments on his spacecraft.  He was now commander of the U.S. Air Force Squadron based on the ASL.

"Emerald Squadron, we make  three groups of hostiles ten minutes away and closing.  We will engage Earthward  group of hostiles,  Gold Squadron you will engage center group,  Silver Squadron you will engage spaceward group of hostiles, is that a confirm on battle assignments?"

"Roger that Emerald, this is Gold squadron!" Rang back the Navy Squadron.

Roger that Emerald, this  is Silver Squadron! Let us destroy them!" rang back the Russian Squadron, whom Forester now watched incredulously on his radar pulling ahead of the two American squadrons.  He knew the Russians had lost two million people in the horrid winter caused by the Unash Solar-Lagrange point dust operation. So he decided not to protest.

Another group of  bright triangles was on his screen and was approaching the battle space. This was a large Air Force squadron that had boosted out of low Earth orbit hours before and was now closing on the battle area. However, Tiger knew they would not arrive for 40 minutes and,  that until then,  the battle with the alien formation was their mission.

Tiger was now looking carefully at the Moon ahead of him, looking for bright moving specks in space or shadows against the lunar disk.

The seconds flew by.

"Emerald squadron! Arm Firefox 1's and standby to launch. Open up our formation to engage–two formations!"

A chorus of acknowledgments  from his squadron rang back on the radio.

He saw the seekers on his four long-range missiles were getting locks on the leading alien targets, now two minutes away and closing.

540

His space-suited hands flew over the control stick arming his 20 millimeter Webber cannon and short range missiles fire-fox 2.

"Standby to fire Firefox 1's on command!"

He saw a bright speck ahead of him moving against the stars.

"Fire Firefox 1's!" he yelled and pressed the fire control button on the stick, and his fighter shuddered and was engulfed in blue flame as the four rockets flew off the sides of the space frame and streaked away. Around him, space exploded with blue fire as rockets flew off the other fighters, and streaked ahead like a shower of meteors.

"Emerald squadron. Break, break, break!" he yelled as the squadron now flew in every direction to evade return fire.

An explosion of blue flame expanding and turning yellow and then red blossomed in space head of him, and then another.

"Got one! Got two!" someone was yelling.

**** 

"Why don't they open fire?" a crew member was yelling at Number 7, and he realized that the Unash squadron leader's ship had been hit and now no one could give the order to open fire. He stood stunned at the control console watching ship after ship in the leading edge of their task force being blown out of space.

"Open fire. Open fire all ships!" screamed Number 7 on the open channels.

**** 

Tiger watched incredulously as twelve of the Unash ships in the leading part of their formation blew up and disappeared from the radar. But then two fighters in his squadron exploded in balls of orange fire as their tanks

541

of hydrazine and NTO mixed and ignited. He was now weaving all over space and his wing man's fighter then exploded behind him. He now was focusing on a bright speck ahead of him and getting target lock for his short range hypervelocity rockets. His hand flew across the control stick and he fired two of them, he then darted away and the bright speck exploded ahead of them.

"God! They aren't jinking! They're just flying in straight lines all of them!" he exclaimed, and eagerly sought another target." Emerald squadron! Enemy ships not jinking, swarm in on them! Swarm into them!" he yelled as another speck of light appeared in his viewfinder, and he launched another pair of hypervelocity rockets.

****

"Wake up Karlac! Wake up," yelled Vikor shaking Karlac's comatose form on the bed. The autopilot has us flying into a battle! Let me fly the ship on manual!" Karlac, dreaming of piles dead bodies in Devil's Mesa, awoke deliriously. He looked around in confusion. Just then the ship shuddered with an impact.

"Paradise!" Karlac gasped. "This universe... so rich ... so beautiful ... It should be paradise for everyone who dwells in it!" Vikor looked at him incredulously.

"You have to let me fly the ship on manual! We're flying into the middle of a space battle!" yelled Vikor

"Why? why can't it be paradise?" wept Karlac. Vikor grasped the front of his shirt and pulled him up out of the bed.

"MANUAL CONTROL! I HAVE TO HAVE MANUAL CONTROL OR WE'LL BE DESTROYED!" Vikor bellowed as he hauled Karlac's limp form across the cabin floor, and pulled him up into his pilot's seat. He buckled him in so he wouldn't fall out of the chair and took his seat in the copilot's chair.

Outside the cockpit window, the expanse of stars was covered with blue flashes and blossoming fireballs. The Moon loomed out the window to their left. Karlac looked in horror at the scene outside and finally seemed to become fully conscious. He reached down and flipped several switches on the navigation computer.

"Can I fly on manual control now?" exclaimed Vikor frantically. Karlac looked at him and nodded weakly, then slumped over in his chair as Vikor eagerly took the barely comprehensible controls and tried to make the ship go faster and weave a sinuous path so no one could hit them. Soon the Moon's disk was dancing randomly across the cockpit window as Vikor desperately tried to guide the ship away from the battle in front of them and at the same time not present a predictable moving target. Karlac stared out the window in transfixed horror.

"Paradise... we all have everything we could possibly want..., this universe should be paradise..." Karlac gasped sorrowfully. Suddenly, surreally , a human body in space suit but missing a leg flew by the cockpit window.

****

The Frigate Elgin, having lost all three of its sister ships, pulled up within point-blank range of a large alien cargo ship and began pounding it with lasers and proton beams. Its magazines now empty of missiles. The alien ship appeared helpless as laser beams from the Elgin blasted holes in its hull and bodies of Toman Daz infantry poured out into space in silver space suits. Inside the Elgin there was a bedlam of space suited corpses, screaming wounded and the wails of spinning inertial energy stores spinning down to dump their energy into laser and proton beams. Forester sat alone with the replacement helmsman and the weapons officer. The executive officer was dead, and Forester was issuing orders on instinct.

"HAMMER THEM, HAMMER THEM!" he was yelling. "Don't let them catch their breath!"

Finally, after several proton beams hit the alien ship, it managed one last proton beam hit on the Elgin. It cut through the hull near engineering and hit a fully spun up inertial energy store, which exploded, sending shrapnel through the thin bulkheads like they were paper and killing ten of the remaining crew. The Elgin lost all power except emergency batteries and

543

delivered the last contents of its last remaining inertial energy store to blow the alien into two pieces with one last salvo of proton beams. A cascade of silver-suited bodies poured out of it into space when they did this.

****

On the ASL, Admiral Hodges watched in disbelief as one lone alien ship staggered through a barrage of missiles, laser and proton beams, and automatic cannons firing tracer rounds, taking multiple hits and trailing bodies and debris It managed to crash land on the top of the ASL in the Moon dust. It had crashed near the command center of the platform and Hodges cringed, waiting for a titanic explosion. Instead out of the wreck poured a wave of silver-suited Toman Daz warriors running blindly towards the edge of the platform and right into a crossfire of American and Russian Marines dug into the moon dust. In a barrage of tracer bullets of green and red, the charging mass of Toman Daz was cut down. Soon from the trenches the American and Russian Marines rose and charged the wrecked alien ship, and were soon lobbing grenades into its hatches and spraying gunfire into the many holes in its structure. After this last crescendo of action, the alien ships near the ASL withdrew.

****

Vikor grimly steered the ship into the cover of a field of debris and floating bodies, both human and Unash, near two wrecks in space. Bodies in space suits, parts of bodies and bodies without space suits were floating by the window, all alien and Erran alike seemed to have the same frozen look of horror and anguish on their dead faces. Karlac looked on this scene outside of the cockpit in stupefied horror and finally lost consciousness.

****

"Withdraw back to our base ! Abandon the damaged vessel! We are ordered to return to base with our remaining fighters without delay!" shouted Number 7. A vast wall of Erran fighting ships was arriving from Earth now, in overwhelming numbers. The battle was lost, and with it,

544

they had lost three-quarters  of the ships that had started out from the Moon.

 He saw the last remaining cargo vessel receding rapidly behind them, still full of helpless infantry . He turned away and could not look as they abandoned it and all its occupants to its fate. *Oh, they are the lucky ones,* thought number seven bitterly, *their life of terror and waiting for death will soon be over.*

****

"We are friendly aliens! Friendly, we were here on a peace mission, do not shoot!" Vikor was shouting endlessly into the radio and he guided the ship away from the shelter of the horrid debris field. It seemed to work, for none of the Erran fighters pursued them. Karlac slumped in the safety straps beside him,  unconscious as he drove on into deep space beyond the Moon as fast as he could make the ship go.

****

Douglass Forester watched in horrified satisfaction as the newly arrived ships from Earth hammered the remaining Unash troopship, apparently abandoned by the faster warships with all its pathetic cargo,  by the fleeing Unash. Soon  the hapless ship exploded into sparkling fragments as he flew past, his pursuit of the fleeing Unash ships now impossible due to low fuel and ammunition. He was now headed back, with the two surviving members of his squadron, back to the ASL.

****

Karlac awoke groggily. He rose from his  bed with effort, went to the sink and washed his face. Vikor was sitting in a chair looking at him drinking from a bottle of nectar wine.

"How long have I been unconscious?"

"Three days," said  Vikor grimly. Karlac looked outside, only the sea of stars was visible. They were not pointed towards Sagittarius, he noted. He looked at the half empty bottle of nectar wine in Vikor's hand.  Vikor was unshaven and still wearing the same clothes as before.

545

"I was saving that wine for a special occasion," said Karlac in annoyance.

"This is a special occasion, the ship is damaged and can't make the jump to light speed."

"Where are we?" asked Karlac in alarm.

"We are in the outer solar system, beyond the orbit of Jupiter, still in normal space. The navigation system appeared to try to go to tach space several times but failed," said Vikor with a stone face. "So, I drink to our doom here."

Karlac looked in dumb horror at the navigation computer on the control board. Several blood-red lights were blinking.

"We will fix it then," said Karlac firmly. "Right after you take a bath and get a fresh change of clothes. Cleansing the body clears the mind."

"My mind is clear enough, it's yours that's been delirious for the past few days. You kept talking about that dark haired Erran, Cassandra" said Vikor with a snicker. "I think you are in love with her." Vikor drank another sip from the bottle. "From my experience on Erra, she would probably break your heart after one night in bed." He added with a big grin.

"You know the vows of my religious order!" said Karlac angrily. *First this failed mission to Erra, now am I condemned to spend my last days in the company of this uncouth lout? Why?*

"I can't find a space pressure suit in this ship that fits me," said Vikor now looking serious. "Tell me where one is and I will go out and find the damage. Who knows, perhaps the gods have been careless and the damage can be fixed," said Vikor looking at him intently.

"There is no other space suit. I have never needed another."

"Can you got out and fix the hyperdrive then?" asked Vikor.

"No, I don't know anything about such things. I am a peace emissary. I am used to being the guest of various governments."

546

Vikor responded to this statement by staring at him intently and then taking another long drink of wine from the bottle.

"I told you I was saving that for a memorable occasion," said Karlac angrily

"From what you just told me, this occasion is especially memorable!" said Vikor bitterly looking out of the cockpit into the stars. "To quote a saying of the Errans, my friend: we are fucked!"

****

Zomal of Bellatrix stood in his armor, speaking with his vice commander Tankos, a swarthy, dark-bearded man, who stood also in armor. Behind them was the main relaxation or 'pleasant' room, adorned with fine pillows with some of the men playing music on their mandolins, Amber was chatting and laughing with some of the men at a table. Tankos, like Zomal, showed the strain of the prolonged dispute with the Unash at the base.

"The gods have been gracious Tankos," "We have distress signal from the ship of Karlac of Delpin. His ship was damaged in the recent battle."

"He was involved in the battle? What is that meddling fool trying to do now?" asked Tankos.

"Apparently, they blundered into the battle. Demonstrating again, his lack of understanding of war. He was trying to come here to speak with that fool Sadok Sar. But the gods willed that this parley of fools was prevented."

"More is the pity he was not destroyed! I tell you, he was sent here to spy out the place for the Vikhelm," said Tankos.

"Yes but this works to our good fortune, Tankos . Tell me, is the scow in good operating order?"

"Yes my Lord ," said Tankos.

"Excellent, we shall solve several problems at once here," said Zomal, turning to look at Amber laughing with the men as they sat around a table in the pleasant room.

"We have to get her out of here," said Zomal starring at her. "Once she is gone, the Unash will turn their attention to other pressing matters, of which they have no shortage. Now with the space platform at the stable Libration point, under control of the Errans, and the attempt to retake it having failed most disgracefully, even Sadok Sar, despite being a prince of fools, will see that his situation here is critical and ask for major forces to be sent here," said Zomal with a smirk. "Do you know, Tankos, their space fighter craft were ordered to retreat in the face of the Errans, and to abandon their own troop ships in the battle, so many fine Toman Daz battalions were slaughtered in their troop ships like helpless cattle?"

Tankos nodded grimly .

"I had heard this, my Lord. This was a waste of fine soldiers! Sadok Sar holds the bravery of his own people in contempt."

"Yes, he does. I find him completely without honor," said Zomal. "Do you know also, he has not even requested that major reinforcements be sent here, even now when the Errans may invade this ball of slag? He told me he sees no need to declare an emergency here. He wishes to hide his failures from his superiors. That is why we must move quickly to get this woman out of here and off to Vale because his folly is profound and therefore unpredictable."

"Surely, my Lord, the Errans cannot invade this place now! said Tankos in astonishment. "They would not dare!"

"Oh yes, they would dare," said Zomal turning again to look at Amber. "The Errans landed here unarmed six times before, remember, in the face of the Unash! Tankos, my brave friend, they are our cousins, the blood of the Samar is in their veins, the blood of the Pleiadian and the Vikhelm as well. So their blood has no shortage of daring. They will invade this ball of lava to impress women like that." Zomal pointed at Amber. She turned and smiled at him. He smiled back. He turned once again to Tankos. "Get the scow ready and find some of the men who know how to make repairs

548

on the hyperdrives in space.  We are going to repair that ship and send it on its way, and Amber and her child with it."

"This will anger the Monchkini further, my Lord," said Tankos.

"Yes! It will!" laughed Zomal. "But they have many other issues to deal with now, and they will soon forget this trifle over a woman.  They know the Errans are coming here also, and soon."  Zomal looked thoughtful. "There is another reason I want her on that ship and out of this system."

"What is that my Lord," asked Tankos, as a chorus of laughter came from the pleasant room nearby.

"Having here in our quarters is making the men soft, and homesick.  I want them hard, hard as ty-alloy and sharp as razors.  I want them hard and sharp because of what is coming."

"Yes my Lord," nodded Tankos ruefully.

"Besides, having a woman here always leads to trouble, especially Erran women, who excel  at causing trouble ever since Gee-Anne started the great war here.  That is why Koton is dead on Erra.

"Because of an Erran woman?"

"Yes, by the gods," said Zomal looking grim.

"My Lord, how will we get this Erran woman on the scow?" The Unash have guards all around our compound here?" asked Tankos, eager to change the subject.

"Oh, I have already thought of that," said Zomal looking at Amber again and smiling.

****

Cassandra dressed in her Aid-de-Camp uniform and walked into the nursery. She had thrown herself back into the routine of inspections, now that Karlac and  Vikor  had departed. She did not know what else to do. She recognized nurse Becky from Devil's Mesa standing in the center of

549

the nursery smiling in a nurse's uniform. The children were hybrid children, rescued from the wreckage of the mesa, they looked like normal children except their eyes were larger and black, and their heads had only sparse hair on them. Becky, her hair now dyed brown, stood smiling and looking well in the middle of a bunch of happily playing hybrid children. The children were dressed in 'footie' pajamas, playing with blocks and dolls. The children were quieter than human children, but otherwise seem to be playing normally.

"Becky, it's good to see you here," said Cassandra. Becky smiled and walked over to her.

"Yeah, they let us all out of detention if they could place us in a job around here. So I'm doing what I used to do. It's not freedom, none of us can leave this place, but it's a major improvement." She then added: "Thank you for getting us out. I just wanted to say that."

"Oh, I'm sort of prisoner here myself, still," said Cassandra helplessly. "I want to leave, but don't know where to go." She surveyed the neat clean nursery with satisfaction. Large windows looked out on the mountains, still capped with snow. Everywhere else, the snow was rapidly melting, however.

"So how are things going here?" Cassandra looked around at the strange children.

"Oh about as well as can be expected. The hybrid children you see here are the healthy ones. We have about half of them in another ward under special care. Those ones are dying off. We lose about one a month. They don't live long mostly. Their blood systems are all screwed up, they use hemoglobin, red blood, for their bodies but have a separate blood system, complete with a separate heart chamber, and an oxygen exchange organ, thrown in, to supply hemocyanin, that's blue, for their brains and spinal cords."

Cassandra absorbed this and shook her head in disbelief.

"I'm not a biologist, but that sounds crazy. How could that possibly work?" asked Cassandra looking at the children playing.

550

"It doesn't, at least not very well," said Becky looking around at the children sadly. "It was a compromise between the grey and human physiology, apparently worked out by some committee on dope." she added with a hint of sarcasm." The problem is that it's backward, the brain needs more oxygen than the body, but the blue blood doesn't carry oxygen as well as red blood, so the brains tend to run oxygen starved as the hybrids get older."

"Well, other than that inherited disaster, how are things going around here," asked Cassandra?

"Actually, fairly well," said Becky. "They actually put me in charge. The children are happy and well cared for, at least as well as we can take care of them. However, this morning, we are missing three of the high caste hybrids, the type with the bigger heads. They sometimes hide in the mornings. So we have several nurses looking in their usual hiding places. The high caste hybrids seem to recognize that they are different from us humans very early and, no pun intended, they begin to feel alienated." Cassandra typed in a brief report on her e-pad as she looked around. Everything looked clean and happy, and if you ignored the large, sparsely haired heads of the children, it looked like a normal well–run nursery.

"Well this all looks fine," said Cassandra wearily. "Good."

"How did the meeting with the humanoid aliens go? Everyone has been talking about it," asked Becky.

"Oh, I don't know," Cassandra said sadly. "I dealt with the peace emissary, but he seemed completely lost here, and I don't even know if he represents any sort of authority in the larger cosmos at all. He may have been just an emissary for himself and his idealism. He may have been just a 'galactic do-gooder.' That's what the Russian representative called him. That's the problem with dealing with human beings from other planets, you can read them, and the emissary's case he couldn't hide the fact that he was clueless. The other alien looked like a blonde heavyweight wrestler, kept a laser gun stuck in his belt at all times, and looked at me like he only cared about getting into my pants." said Cassandra shaking her head. "So it's not clear we accomplished much, except to learn that there are other, basically human, beings elsewhere in the stars, with all

551

that implies. It means the cosmos is complex, really complex." Becky looked bewildered and sad at this report.

"But the emissary was horrified by his tour of the mesa," added Cassandra trying to smile bravely. "So that is progress. One person from the outer cosmos received some education about this pit of horrors. That gives me hope."

"It does?" asked Becky.

"Hope is a decision," said Cassandra nodding to herself. She then looked off at the mountains through the wide windows. "I was wondering Becky," asked Cassandra, " if you can remember much about what happened to me when I was being held at the mesa. I can't remember a lot of it." Becky looked at her sadly.

"I won't be much help to you, Cassie. I can't remember any of it what happened in those last days at the facility in the mesa." Becky's eyes filled with tears. She stared off into space. "The last thing I remember clearly was we received a lot of wounded guards in the infirmary, from the battle on the Manzano Crest," said Becky, her voice shaking, "and we were trying to take care of them. Then an announcement came over the PA system from the base commander, saying that the guards were ordered to kill all the staff if the base security was breached, because of op-sec." Becky was now staring wide-eyed out the window at the mountains with her arms folded. She turned back to Cassandra and spoke levelly. "That's the last thing I remember, or would ever want to remember."

Suddenly another nurse rushed up to Becky and Cassandra. Her face bore a look of horror.

"Becky, we found the three missing children." said the nurse gravely, motioning towards a corridor. Becky suddenly lost her sad look and it was replaced with a look of intense concern, the nurse and Becky walked off quickly and Cassandra followed them, steeling herself for what they might find. They went down a clean shiny corridor, to a closet with an open door where several nurses were standing by it sadly.

552

Becky and Cassandra both swung the door wide and recoiled in horror at what they saw.

Three children lay together in the bottom of the closet, with their heads fused together, blood, red blood, was coming out of their mouths and eyes. The fusion had not occurred symmetrically but had contorted the faces of two of the children horribly.

"Oh, my God!" exclaimed Becky. Shaking her head in disbelief. She turned and looked at Cassandra in speechless horror. "I wouldn't have thought this was possible!" she gasped.

"Have you ever seen this before?" asked Cassandra. She forced herself to look at the fused bodies. Then shut her eyes, a horrid chill passed through her. *I have seen this before.*

"No, no, never," said Becky now leaning down to look at the inert bodies in wonder. "Look, the blood coming out of the eyes is red, that means the blood stream separation failed when they fused their heads." Becky looked at Cassandra and motioned at the dead hybrids. "The eyes are holes in the brain case in the Greys and hybrids, There's no optic nerve like in humans, and the retinas are simply part of the optic lobes of the brain. So the red blood has to be coming from the brain cases," she said in wonder, shaking her head. "What in hell were they trying to do?" she gasped. Becky looked again at Cassandra, then her face adopted a look of sad endurance. She turned to the other nurses.

"OK, girls let's get this mess cleaned up and get these bodies covered up and out of her so the other children won't see this."

"Where should we take the bodies?" asked the nurse who had led them to the closet.

"God. Take them to the bio lab," said Becky with resignation, shaking her head.

****

Petrosian and Fitzgerald were studying the pictures of Cassandra Chen and the results of her medical exam, immediately after her rescue.

"Aside from her fingernails and back, she was in remarkably good health when they got here out. Traumatized yes. But healthy. No sign of concussion or head trauma that could lead to physically induced amnesia."

"Yeah but look at this. The medics were thorough, they didn't just do a vaginal exam on her, they did a swab," said Petrosian. He was looking at an asterisk by the summary of the exam.

"Yeah George, but it didn't show anything. It's the first thing I looked at," said Fitzgerald. "No forced entry, no semen. She wasn't raped. Which makes her a rare exception to a woman in that place. At least she was spared that."

"No, we can't actually say that." Petrosian was reading the notation of the asterisk at the bottom of the page. "They found signs of menstrual blood and lots of some sort of vegetable oil on the swab. Her vagina was also dilated. The oil was scented. Some sort of sex lubricant?" Petrosian handed the report to Fitzgerald, who studied it.

"She may have had consensual sex with someone while she was there?" said Fitzgerald in wonder. "Someone wearing a condom?" He shook his head. "But they looked, there were no signs of that."

"In a situation like she was in, the line between rape and consent really disappears. She may have traded sex to avoid death."

"But with who?" asked Fitzgerald.

****

The scow, as it was called, was a short-range ferry ship without hyperdrive that the Samaran garrison maintained at the main base at Mars Moscoviense, its own private dock.

Zomal marched on board with his cohorts, themselves bearing a large coffin-shaped box of tools and hyperdrive components. Several of the men wore heavy armored spacesuits. They sat in their seats and buckled in as the ship undocked and headed out over the stark lunar mountains and into the starry sky. Soon they were deep in space. *So far so good,*

554

thought Zomal. He knew they were flying into a war zone, in a ship that was lightly armed and unarmored. *But this is just brazen enough to work, no one would expect it, it is so foolhardy!*

He turned, and saw Amber tearing off her fake beard and wig, and stripping off the armored space suit to reveal her comely form.

"I thought we were dead, my Lord when the Monchkini demanded to check the big toolbox," said Tankos, I am glad you did not tell us where she was hiding. "

"Yes, I knew they would dare only to search one thing. When they found nothing in the box, after much dispute, they were humiliated. I know these people well," laughed Zomal.

****

Hontal awoke from a troubled sleep in his cabin.

"My Lord, the Captain wishes to speak with you. It is most urgent." The first officer of the ship stood in the doorway, Hontal's retainer stood near to him.

Hontal arose quickly and put on his armored space suit. They were still in the Quzrada, having taken a roundabout path to Samaran space in order to avoid the Unull–Unash fighting near Batelgeen space. They were traveling slowly to avoid detection, for, as the Captain had said, "there are things now prowling about in the Quzrada whose attention we do not wish to attract."

Hontal looked at the half completed report he was preparing for the Palace. He quickly folded it up and stuck in a pocket on his spacesuit. He was increasingly aware that eyes were watching him on board the Tlakmar, and that the contents of his report could cost him his life if they fell into the wrong hands. The words of Bekar of Batelgeen returned to him: 'make sure your report is pleasing to Betelgeuse' but he was determined to write an honest report for the palace, and deal with its consequences afterward. Soon he was walking down the corridors of the starship followed by two guards, sent by the Captain. The sense that bad news had arrived was thick in the air of the ship and on the faces of the crew.

The Captain awaited him, in full armor, in the communications room adjoining the bridge. As he entered the room, the Captain, looking grim, motioned to a large view screen. The face of Zomal of Bellatrix, the acting commander of the Samaran garrison on the Moon, appeared on the screen. His face was stoic.

"My Lord Hontal, as the emissary of the palace, I must inform you of recent events in the Soleran system since you left. I serve the Throne of Rigel, therefore I make this urgent report."

"The Errans have now struck at the primary base of the Unash on Una, causing some damage, but this attack was a diversion. The Errans have then struck far into space, using this diversion, far beyond Una, and captured the Unash space platform that was creating a dust cloud to freeze Erra and force its submission. In this, the Errans have demonstrated far greater skill and boldness than we thought possible. They are children of virtue indeed. The Unash have now attempted to regain the platform, but their attack has failed. The platform has now been moved close to Una to a Libration point and is rapidly being converted into and Erran fortress. The Unash have thus suffered a disastrous defeat in space in addition to the destruction of their bases on Erra, which now fall like ripe fruit. Thus the 'cow mounts the bull' at Erra, and something must be done immediately to turn this situation from its present course. In my view, the Unash commander is a fool and must be replaced. As everyone knows, one can have a fine starship with an able crew, but it all matters little if its captain is a fool.  So are the treasures of the Samar being wasted here. This situation must be remedied or all will be lost.  I request that this garrison be evacuated if things cannot be remedied. Why should the lives of more good Samarans be wasted for the honor of fools?"

The transmission then ended.

Hontal was stunned,  he turned to the Captain. Who looked back with a grim face.

"We received this transmission an hour ago. It took  this long for it to be decoded." said the Captain dourly. "The dickless ones are making a mess of things at Erra. I have seen this coming for a long time. The Unash  have not fought a worthy foe for centuries, and they are not fighting some bugs like themselves. No,  they are fighting the Errans who are children of the Samar and the Pleiadian."   The Captain's face took on a  look of amazement. "I have just heard what I would have thought was impossible, that an officer of the Samaran Empire would request a retreat from a place once we have occupied it. Truly, he feels they are but fleas trapped on a drowning dog, and that there is no honor in enduring this."

Hontal nodded gravely. *Tatiana, she is also trapped there* he suddenly thought desperately. He fought to keep his face calm. *But I can save her.*

"Then it is a good thing that I have been sent here to make a report," said Hontal. "A squadron of Samaran cruisers can be dispatched here and settle this thing in an hour."

The Captain shook his head.

"I don't know what you have been told brave Hontal, but sending a fleet into this place will lead to a war with the other treaty powers.  It cannot be done."

"What are the treaty powers to the Samar?" said Hontal with contempt.

"Combined against us, they are more powerful than the Tlax." said the Captain. "Surely you know better than most, by your scars earned bravely in battle, that  the Tlax are worthy foes to us. I want you to understand Hontal, from one who has cruised the Quzrada and all the frontiers of the Samaran empire since you were a child, that the things they taught you in the academy, that the Samarans  will conquer the whole universe, are but tales told to little children. Forget them, instead, open your eyes." The Captain paused his eyes became wide. "The Cosmos is a boundless sea of stardust, and the far distant galaxies as snowflakes in a snowstorm, merging into a blue haze, and even we,  brave Hontal, the Great Samar, as powerful as we are, as full of virtue as we are, we ourselves  are but a speck of stardust."

557

Hontal absorbed these words and felt sudden despair. *But I must save Tatiana*, he thought desperately. He nodded and gave his fist over his heart salute to the Captain, then turned and left the communications room.

****

The large ship approached out of the stars near Jupiter in the distance and docked with the Peace Song in deep space.

Karlac looked at the Samaran ship happily, even Vikor seemed pleased, though he was careful not to show it.

Zomal entered through the hatch with Amber and a small bag of clothing.

"Karlac of Janus, I am Zomal of Bellatrix, we heard your distress call and received your technical readout, and are here to repair your ship, and to send you on your way. "Zomal smiled. He noted Vikor reacted to this by dropping his hands to his sides and acquiring a blank look. *A true son of the Vikhelm, this one,* thought Zomal, *too bad he is not carrying a sword, we could settle some old scores.* Zomal knew immediately that the Vikhelm was preparing to reach for some sort of weapon, but it did not concern him. Rules of chivalry, common to both Samaran and Vikhelm cultures, required that sword be met with sword and gun be met with gun. It was the concept of 'paray' in old galactic or 'appropriateness' apparently inherited from the old Archmetan culture that had seeded the galaxy long before. So Zomal, with characteristic bravado, assumed the Vikhelm would not draw a gun on him since he himself was not displaying one.

"Thank you Noble Zomal," said Karlac, who smiled and then looked at Amber in puzzlement. Amber managed a weak smile. Zomal took off his fine leather jacket and gave it to her.

"In return for this favor, I request you take this woman," said Zomal speaking to Karlac, "who is with child, to Vale. She and her child must be presented to Krayus of Rigel, of the House of Mirzam, who is the high Ambassador of The Samarans to the Vikhelm. Vikor stared at her and rolled his eyes and gave a noise of derision.

558

"Did you say something Viker?" said Zomal putting his hand to his sword. Vikor tensed.

"He said nothing!" answered Karlac quickly. "And of course we shall convey this lady to Vale, as you require," said Karlac as he shot an angry look to Vikor.

"If you are impertinent further with me Viker, I will lift your head off your shoulders with this sword."

"Then fetch me a good sword also, Samar, and we will see whose head goes where." replied Vikor calmly with the same blank look.

"STOP! Both of you! This is a diplomatic mission guaranteeing him safe passage, and we must be about it! We will also be delighted to transport this woman to Vale and deliver her wherever you wish."

Zomal and Vikor stared at each other for a long moment, then Zomal turned to Karlac and smiled.

"Excellent, most noble Karlac, I knew you would agree to this exchange of favors." said Zomal. Amber walked over to the table in the middle of the ship and sat down wearily.

"Oh yes, the lady is with child by brave Samus of Bellatron, last son of Krayus of Bellatron , son of the high Ambassador of the Samar to the court of Vale of the Vikhelm. Please accord her every courtesy."

Karlac looked at Amber with amazement. She responded with a weak smile.

"Yes, of course! We shall treat here as an honored guest, as much as is possible on this small ship."

"Excellent! I have heard you're a noble person, now I can report this as truth! Now forgive my abruptness, but this is a war zone and we have begun repairs outside and must get you on your way before our good fortune runs out! Good bye lady Amber!" he said waving to Amber with a broad smile. Amber waved at him weakly.

Zomal then bowed with great flourish turned and left out the hatchway, and closed it behind him.

Karlac looked around the ship in amazement. Then went and sat at the controls of the ship and stared outside at the unblinking stars, as they heard a thumping noise from the outer hull.

They were all silent in apprehension as the repairs were completed outside in space and soon they were flying again rapidly away from Erra and Una, and then into hyperspace to leave the Solar system.

****

The door opened to Virgil Jacksons spacious new cell, on the top floor of the detention center, he even had a barred window with a nice view of the southern San Luis Valley. Virgil was sitting at a desk with his reading glasses, on studying the Groveland report on the UFO Cover-up, with a look of shocked amazement.

Cassandra Chen entered and he rose and embraced her, taking off his reading glasses and wiping his eyes.

"Baby Doll! It's sure good to see you!" he said pulling up a simple wooden chair for her and then resuming to his seat. She was a vision of loveliness wiping her eyes. She was wearing her usual uniform.

"Virgil, how are things, I see at least you have a nice view." said Cassandra looking around with satisfaction at his spacious cell with wide windows.

"A lot better, Baby Doll. Thanks to you. I have to keep reminding myself that I am not the base commander here." he said smiling. "I also want to mention, I have been reading this big official report about the UFO Cover-up. I was never good at big–picture stuff, in fact, that sort of thinking was discouraged where I come from. So this is really interesting. You and your blonde cutie pie friend are even bigger hero's than I thought you were! As for myself, now I understand what the housefly said after landing on a big dunghill, just before somebody dynamited it, to spread over a farm field." said Virgil grinning.

Cassandra looked at him in confusion.

560

"So what did the housefly say, exactly?" she asked him in bewilderment. *That's me too.*

"Says the housefly, 'Next time I will be more particular about which shit-pile I land on...'" laughed Virgil. He then looked at her carefully and his smile faded.

"So how are you doing baby Doll? You look a little down," he asked.

"Virgil I need to ask you something about when I was a prisoner here at Devil's Mesa," she said quietly. She was trembling.

"Sure Baby Doll," said Virgil sadly. "I'll do my best."

"Was I raped, while I was there?"

"No," he said in amazement. "Not that I ever saw," said Virgil shaking his head sadly. "We were trying to watch over you as best we could. I thought we saved you from that in the torture chamber. Oh Baby Doll, I and my men, we did everything we could to protect you, baby, in that awful place," said Virgil in wonder. "We all knew, my men, that you were our ticket out, our savior." Then his face changed to become more sad.

"But it was such a nightmare," said Virgil looking at her. "I couldn't watch over you all the time. I had to go fight to try to regain control of the place for the Wizard. He put me in charge. So I had Johnson, my best man, guarding you. He was my best man, and he swore he'd keep you safe." He paused and looked curious. "Who did this to you? Can you remember?"

"I don't know," her eyes welled up with tears. "I just know it happened, I remember it happening. I had my eyes closed I think, but I can remember it happening now," she said. "I have had trouble remembering a lot of what happened there. But it's coming back slowly. Now I can remember this part, but I can't connect to anything else."

Virgil looked away sadly, shook his head.

"We'll I am so sorry, Baby Doll. Like I said, my men and I did everything we could to protect you in that nightmare place. We were fighting Dr. Pain's people, people who were just running wild on drugs, or just out of their

561

minds. I must have killed a hundred men that day, some just three feet away, and I saw a thousand people die. But I couldn't be there all the time, beside you, I mean, because the Wizard wanted me in charge of everything. I was his trouble shooter, literally, that was the only hope I had of saving you and the rest of my people. I had to keep his confidence." He picked up an e-cigarette, primed it, drew in a deep breath of vapor while looking out the window. He then looked at her sadly, "Like I said, doll, I tried, God knows I did, and I'm sorry. I know you don't feel this way, but you're actually lucky if you can't remember everything, Baby Doll because I can't forget anything that I saw."

"I understand Virgil,  you did the best you could." she looked out the barred window. "It was like you said, a nightmare. But you kept me alive." She managed a weak smile.

She leaned over and kissed him on the cheek, then stood and left his cell.

"I am going to get you out here Virgil," she said to him as she turned to leave.

"I have never doubted it," said Virgil nodding somberly.  "But, you watch out for yourself, Baby Doll," he said as she left and door to his cell shut behind her.

****

## Chapter 13: Kotanga

"My Lord Dakon, I had thought I was to deliver my report in person to you at the palace," said Hontal in astonishment. He stood with the Captain, both in fully armored spacesuits, as was their standard garb in the Quzrada, The Captain's first officer, also stood close by. They were still a week from Samaran space on their slow and careful journey out of the Quzrada. Hontal could hear the power plant of the ship roaring , obviously putting out as much power as possible, to support the communication he was now witnessing. On the large view screen in the communications room of the ship, was the grim face of Dakon, sitting in the same room in the palace where Hontal had been assigned his mission.

"Events have changed our plans, I need your report, in summary, at this instant," said Dakon,

"May I remind my lord Dakon, that this two-way instantaneous transmission requires high levels of power, and minimal coding," said Captain Qinton.

"Yes, Captain, so let our brave knight Hontal give his summary report quickly, so we may be done with this business!" said Dakon sharply. Hontal felt fear creep into him, his report was not good, he knew. He would have present it as a fine tale, as was his talent.

"My Lord said Hontal. Things have not gone well in the Quzrada. In summary, the Monchkini had hoped to gain control of Erra by means of a cadre of traitors within the principle government of Erra, called America. But this woman, a picture of Cassandra Chen appeared on the view screen beside Hontal, discovered this treason." Cassandra wore a tight fitting deep purple dress and had stars in the background, it was an image from the UFO Cover-up special the year before. She was an image of loveliness, but her face was serious. Her long raven hair wave waved and expertly combed.

Hontal noted a slight smile cross Dakon's face at the sight of Cassandra. This reassured him. He did not want Dakon to become angry at his report. "She discovered this treason within the government," continued Hontal, "and alerted the patriotic men of war of Erra. She led them to fight a great battle with the traitors and defeated them. She led her forces boldly in battle."

"So she is like the warrior queen Xenoba?" said Dakon with a slight laugh.

"Yes, my Lord," said Hontal relaxing slightly. Bearers of bad tidings did not fare well in Samaran history. Often they had been executed to demonstrate the gravity of their tidings and the displeasure of their superiors with those tidings. "The traitors captured her in the battle and retreated to a great secret base of the Unash on Erra, but her men of war stormed the fortress and rescued her. Now the Errans have destroyed all but a few of the Unash bases and the Monchkini are in disgraceful retreat, they tried to block sunlight to Erra from space to freeze the planet, with a great space platform, but the Errans attacked boldly far into space and took the platform for their own. They have made it a fortress near Una my Lord, and the Unash seem helpless to recapture it. Truly my Lord the cow mounts the bull at Erra."

Dakon smiled grimly at this and laughed slightly.

"So the Errans have found a queen Xenoba to rally themselves and fight courageously, and the Monchkini are put to the worst before them?" Queen Xenoba was a raven haired warrior queen of legendary beauty, who had heroically led her armies in battle in Samaran history. She had died bravely in a final battle as her kingdom was conquered.

"Yes my Lord" Hontal hesitated. "Also the Monchkini want more money because they say things have become more complicated, I told their commander they would have to send a special emissary to the Palace for this request." Dakon looked annoyed at this report.

"Do not include that impertinent request in your report!" said Dakon abruptly. He then smiled cruelly" I will deal with this haggling by the Monchkini myself," said Dakon, He then smiled again in a friendly fashion.

"What is your recommendation for this situation, brave knight?"

"A fleet must be dispatched to Erra and the Errans must be crushed my Lord before they can attack the Monchkini great base on Una. No

Archmetan power can be allowed to rise in the Quzrada!" answered Hontal, with finely chosen words.

"Very good brave Hontal, this is a grave report and bold counsel," said Dakon. "The question will be, whose fleet should be sent? But never mind, we will sort this out here. Therefore, Hontal, prepare a more extensive report, with many pictures, for you must present this tale of queen Xenoba of Erra and the great battles on Erra and in space, and of the Erran cow mounting the Monchkini bull...at the palace to the royal council." said Dakon. Hontal felt a mixture of fear and excitement fill him. *The Royal Council...* "Make a fine tale of it Hontal!" added Dakon with a smile. The transmission then ended. Dakon obviously was himself worried about reception in the Palace of this news of the catastrophe at Erra.

As he heard the ship's power plant powering down. Hontal turned with a smile to the Captain, who looked at him dourly.

"It appears news of the space battles near Erra has reached the palace," said the Captain. "You have done it now, brave Hontal. The fat is in the fire!" The Captain then paused "But cleverly told, brave Hontal, cleverly told, instead of the fumbling's of the dickless ones, you tell them of a Queen Xenoba leading her brave armies in battle!"

"I have done my duty to the palace, Captain Quinton," said Hontal levelly.

"So you have, brave knight, and this has become a great affair of the palace! The Quzrada has become the center of the universe! And at its heart is Erra! So rest assured, many eyes and ears in the Quzrada, and all the way to Rigel, have seen this same transmission!" Captain Quinton turned to the first officer.

"Quantal! Prepare a course to the Donastad system in Samaran space! Maximum hyper-speed! Place the ship at battle stations! "Donastad was a star system on the frontier of Samaran space with the Quzrada. It was not in Batelgeen clan space, however, but Belltrean. The Captain then turned again to Hontal.

"Take my advice brave one, and wear a mail shirt under your tunic at all times!" said the Captain emphatically. "I will post a guard at your door, for when your own guard sleeps." Hontal nodded, he sensed danger around him now. "Sleep with your mail shirt on!" added the Captain. "Even as you dream of your golden haired dancer of Erra." Hontal looked back at him narrowly.

"Oh yes, as I have said, the Quzrada is full of eyes and ears, brave Hontal." said the Captain patting him on the shoulder with a faint smile. "But I have been charged with bringing you to the palace in one piece with your report." The ship was roaring as its systems were prepared for battle and for maximum hyper-speed. "So go to your cabin and make a fine tale of your report!"

****

Pamela sat in Bernie Mankowitz's office, looking stunning. She was wearing silver sunglasses; she had just arrived at the office, and the sun was shining brightly outside with the snow melting everywhere. She had on a light blue blouse, a navy blue dress jacket and dark blue skirt with glossy red high heels. Her blonde hair was still cut fairly short. She was laughing. She took off her sunglasses and looked at Berkowitz with smiling eyes.

"So when did Cassie say she was coming back?" asked Pamela.

"She didn't." She says she's been working at a war plant wiring space fighters. But now they are moving her someplace else because she is a star worker."

"That sounds like she is getting better! She's a brave one! What a hero!" exclaimed Pamela wiping her eyes.

"You also got a special delivery package."

"It's not a long skinny box is it?" laughed Pamela. "I thought we nailed mister 'snake-in-the mail'"

"No, it's from a Commander Michael Donnelly, we ran chemical tests on it, found no poisons or explosives, and we X-rayed it, it's safe."

566

"Oh, wonderful! Michael, he's alive and safe!" she exclaimed with tears in her eyes. "What's in it?" she then asked eagerly.

"See for yourself," said Berkowitz beaming, her perfume was intoxicating. He pulled out the post-marked package and handed it to her. She tore it open carefully with her well-manicured pink nails. *This Michael is one lucky bastard...*thought Berkowitz, as Pamela pulled out a beautiful gold engagement ring with a sparkling small diamond. She slipped it on her ring finger, it fit perfectly. She held it up in the light beaming, turning it and watching it sparkle. Her beautiful face was filled with relaxed bliss.

"Congratulations Pam," said Berkowitz. He rose and extended is hand. Pam rose and embraced him tearfully over the top of his desk. Berkowitz then sat down. "I hate to cut this short, but I have to talk to Madihira and Marcy on the cable," said Berkowitz.

"Where are they?" asked Pam still standing, vacantly holding up her ring and admiring it in the light.

"Maddy is in India, near Kashmir, the Chinese and the Indians just had a skirmish up in the Himalayas, so we sent her out with a film crew."

"What?" said Pamela incredulously. "We are fighting aliens from outer space, and the border in the Himalayas must be still under 100 yards of snow! What could they possibly find to fight about up there?" she said finally looking at Berkowitz with a look of exasperation.

"I don't know, but several soldiers were killed on both sides, so, you know what we say in the news business: if it bleeds it leads."

"Where's Marcy?" said Pamela resuming her pose of admiring her ring.

"She's in in the middle of the Congo, at Brazzaville, covering Operation Black Magic, but she made the mistake of visiting the Slave Coast of Sierra Leon first. I told her not to go there. Most black people I've known who went there, come back angry and depressed. So, as I expected, she has been really bummed out ever since. It would be like me visiting Auschwitz. "Berkowitz leaned forward and looked at Pamela intently. "In

567

fact, I am a little worried about her. If I decide to pull her out of there will you go instead?"

"Sure!" said Pamela, holding up her engagement ring and admiring it again. "But give her a chance, I know her. She is a tough cookie. She'll snap out of it."

"Well its bad place, I know, they were fighting another tribal war upriver from Brazzaville, before this outer space war started, but it is what it is," he said regretfully. "OK then, now scoot, I have to talk to both of them," said Berkowitz rising and looking at the clock. "War with outer space aliens or not, we need to worry about market share here at CNS."

Pamela departed, making a bee-line for Darlene's office to show off her engagement ring.

****

An eerie silence hung over the morning on the outskirts of the village of Kjabi on highway 8 in the Congo, on the banks of the Shaba river. As the Spearhead of the 29th U.S. Army Division approached. It was misty and silent. The familiar odor of death hung in the air. At the head of the spear, Colonel Robert Schwartzman, commander of the 42nd Army Ranger Battalion, scanned the village fruitlessly with his range finding binoculars. He was now the commander of the Spearhead of Operation Black Magic. He was dressed in full jungle camouflage as were his men and wore a fatigue camouflage cap. Standing near him were Macmillan and Krueger, two mercenaries experienced in fighting in Central Africa, in camouflage uniforms of a slightly lighter shade of green. Standing also nearby was Major Muhammed Kwango in jungle camouflage fatigues, commander of several companies of elite Nigerian Army troops. The common emotion on the faces of all the men was wary determination.

"Alright, Kroog, Mac," said Schwartzman putting down his binoculars and turning to the men. "I want you to take two squads of your men and scout ahead into the center of the town." He pulled up a satellite image of the town on a camouflaged e-tablet, motioned with a strong finger, "I'd send one squad up the main street here, another around the town to the north and come in on this avenue here. I want regular reports. The two

568

mercenaries, both tall, extremely muscular men with several days growth of beard on their cheeks, nodded grimly.

"Looks good Swartz," said Kruger nodding, MacMillan also nodded grimly. This was a totally different jungle than Schwartzman was used to dealing with, and in the few days since the operation had begun he had come to trust Kruger and Macmillan implicitly. They knew the ways of Africa and its snakes.

"We will form up the battalion here, with the mortars to give you immediate fire support, if you need it" continued Schwartzman, pointing to their location of the satellite map, "and we and your men, Mohamed," he motioned to the Nigerian commander, "in place, will advance up the highway into town, once the advance teams can give us a report of conditions there."

The two mercenaries walked off and began shouting orders to their men, a mixed group of Africans and Europeans, all in South African camouflage and all obviously jaded veterans of years of jungle fighting. The mercenaries split into two groups and moved off into the town. Schwartzman noted that the cocky self-assurance of the mercenaries had vanished the day before, and been replaced by a grim wariness as they had encountered a mass of terrified refugees streaming down the highway as they had approached Kjabi. The mercenaries had men who spoke the local languages, and after hearing the account of the refugees, they reported horrific accounts of terror and horror to Schwartzman.

Bands of `Goohabis', demon possessed men, and `Shabas'-demons in the local tongue, had reportedly taken several towns on the highway ahead and were killing everything that breathed. Schwartzman noted that even the two mercenary commanders, both acclimated to the usual atrocities that accompanied central African wars, seemed shocked by the reported scale and ferocity of the reported massacres.

"These are some bloody bad bastards, we are dealing with up there," said Kruger vehemently. "The refugees report some of the men have large black eyes. They call them `mouse eyes' so these may be Greys or grey-human hybrids."

569

Schwartzman called Arizona, resplendent in his green beret and camouflaged fatigues, over to his side.

"Arizona, I want you to take your rifle company in an arc around to the North if the Mercs say the village is safe to enter. I want flank protection to the jungle frontage up North there." Arizona, now a Captain in the 42nd Rangers, nodded gravely.

" Well boss, I guess this op ain't gonna be a cake-walk after all," said Arizona with a weak smile.

"No, but the cake is up there," said Schwartzman smiling grimly. "They are defending something, and clearing out the locals out to deny us good intel, that much is clear. There is an alien base up here." Schwartzman paused, a look of utter determination came across his face. "And I am going to find that cake and eat it too," he said nodding to himself.

****

In the desert afternoon near Las Vegas,  Abe Goldberg, and Alicia Sepulveda-Steel stood with several other scientists in a concrete lined trench wearing heavy goggles.  A mile from where they stood in the trench, a three-inch thick steel plate stood upright on a concrete pad. Near them a pair of Army 5-ton trucks were parked, one held a new powerful laser based on oxygen impregnated diamond crystals, a yard tall and half a yard thick  enclosed in circulating fluorocarbon coolant. Besides the laser and its beam director, on the other 5-ton truck was its portable fusion power supply burning polarized helium-3 and deuterium.

Abe pulled a rectangular-shaped synthetic diamond as big as a brick out of his pocket.

"Here Alicia, want a diamond?"  he said and handed it to her. It was deep blue due to heavy oxygen doping and perfectly clear.

 A siren sounded, then a horn sounded three times.  A piercing whine split the desert air as the fusion power supply ignited and idled, a spinning vortex of magnetized plasma inside it spinning ever faster.  Then it howled, and a beam of blue-green light too bright to look upon appeared

570

from the laser beam director and struck the center of the steel plate. In a split second, the plate vanished into a fireball of white hot burning steel. The laser shut off and the fusion power plant quieted before turning off. From both the power plant and the laser, one could see heat waves rising.

Alice looked at the steel plate, now with a blackened hole a yard wide though it and bright silver, splattered molten metal droplets were everywhere. She could see the desert beyond through the hole. She had stood beside the plate only twenty minutes before, verifying its strength and bulk.

"Wow," Alicia exclaimed, "So that's what a ten-megawatt laser looks like in action!" Goldberg grinned in response.

"This laser can do the same thing to targets 1,000-kilometers away in space, which is its ideal environment of operation. Everything has to be super-efficient, so they don't have to dump any waste heat in space," said Goldberg, as a breeze brought a cloud of thin white smoke mixed with the smell of ozone and hot steel. "The diamond matrix oxygen laser operated at 95% efficiency using power from the fusion power plant, which itself captured 99% of its fusion power as electricity," said Goldberg in awe. "Until now, I never thought the human mind could invent machines of such precision and efficiency. Necessity is truly the mother of invention."

Goldberg looked at what was left of the target and grinned.

"Oh by the way, the Navy liason office just told me why none of the torpedos worked in that battle up in the North Pacific." said Goldberg, turning to look at Alica. " They recovered a saucer on the ocean floor near the remains of the base. The saucer had an exploded torpedo stuck right though its hull. The found out the warhead computer had been hacked by the greys so it wouldn't detonate the warhead."

"I thought everyone fixed those problems! Why didn't it have a contact detonators for backup like everything else?" exclaimed Alica. " I thought the Navy was better prepared than that!"

"Well Admiral Smoot said, 'nobody thought we'd end up shooting torpedos at flying saucers' so nobody issued orders for a retrofit like they

571

did for all the missiles. He said it just got overlooked in the confusion when the war started." Goldberg shook his head ruefully. " A statement which I don't understand, given the histories of all of this. "

"Well, I guess it is not a scenario you'd think of immediately. Its sort of like carrying shark repellent in the desert." said Alicia smiling as the all-clear sounded and they began to file from the trench.

****

"Skipper, I have to go. I have to get away from here," said Cassandra to Captain Badgio. They were in his office, and he was sitting behind his desk looking at her with concern. "I feel like I was supposed to be here, to help you, and to meet with the peace emissary, to try and make an armistice. I mean, for a while, I was so hopeful, that we could make a just peace. That would have been so wonderful."

"And also," she continued "It was really good for me to help you get things ship-shape at the facility here, especially to free all those prisoners and help them. So I have done that. I feel really good about that." Her voice began to crack. "Yes, so I have to go now." she sniffed. Badgio absorbed theses words with a look of deep regret.

"Well you have done a great job here, Cassie," said Badgio pushing a box of Kleenex over to where she sat in front of his desk as she wept. "I know Jenkins and the others can take over, now that the place is running pretty well." He looked at her with a frown. "I know some of the staff here have not always been helpful, is that part of it?"

"No, no. You've been great Skipper, your staff has been great here too." she protested tearfully. She then laughed momentarily, "Mostly." She then looked at him with a fixed gaze. To Badgio she suddenly appeared to be the most beautiful woman alive.

"It's something else. It's something in the stars at night here," she said with a haunted look in her eyes.

"You know, I came here because the FBI thought it would be safest for me here." she continued. "It wasn't my idea. Even so, I hoped I would get

572

healing in this place and from what happened to me here. But instead, it's like the wound reopened here. It's bleeding again and I can't stop it!" she gasped.

Badgio looked at her sadly, nodded.

"I can arrange an armed escort for you, Cassie, back to Colorado Springs, then air transport anywhere you want."

"The wound just bleeds and bleeds now." she continued with a shaking voice. "I, I discovered something terrible here. Something I couldn't remember before."

"Oh well...that happens," said Badgio helplessly. He was now looking down at the desk.

"I was raped here... when they were holding me, prisoner, here," she whispered.

Badgio nodded regretfully, looking at her.

"And as a result of what they did to me here," she paused with her voice shaking, "I know now...somehow, I will now have a child someplace, someplace out there in the stars, my child." she whispered. Then buried her face in her hands and wept.

**** 

"OK, OK, you're bummed out and having nightmares about being in a slave prison awaiting transfer to a slave ship! I understand, but your also a star anchor person at CNS, and a former NFL cheerleader for God's sake! I sent you there to get us good footage of a war!" said Berkowitz with annoyance. He stared at Marcy Braxtons' lovely but exhausted looking dark face on the com-screen. Here hair was cut short because of the heat. They were talking via undersea optical cable, the highest bandwidth means of communication since satellite communications had gone down at the beginning of the war.

"I'm sorry, it was just so shattering to see the cells in the slave prison, the chains, at Badagry on the Coast., ...and to realize the tour guides were all

573

descendants of tribes that sold my people into slavery," she said with shaking voice. "I hate them! I wanted to kill them all right there!" said Marcy angrily. "I haven't been able to sleep since then," she added dejectedly.

"I know! I know! So get some sleeping pills! You got to go out and look good on camera!" said Berkowitz. "Everyone one of the other networks had footage from the Congo yesterday but us!" He added in exasperation.

"I'm sorry, " said Marcy tearfully. "I just hate this place, Bernie, it's the heat, it's the flies! The flies don't just sting you here! They stab you!"

"Don't cry!" urged Berkowitz. "You got to be tough to be in this business! Look at Pamela, they sunk a destroyer right out from under her, she still filed a story as soon as she was rescued! And she looked like a million dollars when she did it too!" said Berkowitz pleadingly. "Now, did you get your press credentials from Mr. Tsango at the Ministry of Information Office in Brazzaville? Atkins told me Tsango can get you up river to near the fighting with an escort of Army troops. This little service cost us a considerable sum too, I don't mind telling you!" continued Berkowitz becoming more angry. *War with outer space aliens or not, nothing changes in the Congo,* thought Berkowitz.

"You mean you bribed that son of a bitch?" said Marcy suddenly becoming angry.

"We are calling it a special fee for expedited paperwork! You think the other networks didn't pay? Everybody has to pay!" retorted Berkowitz. "It's the Congo! And everyone else is upriver now, reporting!"

"Tsango wanted me to go to bed with him!" said Marcy angrily.

"So now you don't have to do that, do you!" said Berkowitz. "So get down there with Atkins, with your crew, and get your paperwork and your escort, and get your lovely ass upriver and on the front line!" shouted Berkowitz. "Now, let me hear a 'can do!' out of you Marcy!" he added.

"I don't like Tsango! And the armed escort, if it's anything like the so-called Army of the Congo, it will be just an armed gang! I have seen Rent–a-Cops with more sense of duty! I mean who is guarding the fucking guards?" said Marcy coldly. "There is no government here! There is no front line! It's a complete cluster-fuck here! Nobody knows where the fucking aliens are! Nobody even knows where the fucking US Army is, the fucking US consulate won't tell us! I don't think they even know! The mother fuckers! Bernie, I have never seen such a fucked-up situation run by such a bunch of fucked up Motherfuckers in my life! This place gives chaos a bad name!" she shouted angrily.

*Well, at least she is not crying anymore...*thought Berkowitz. *Progress.*

"If you can't handle this assignment, Marcy," said Berkowitz icily, after a pause. "We can bring you home and send somebody else. I mean this is Africa, you're Black, you're an Army veteran, you seemed the perfect fit to lead on this story. So, are you telling me I made a mistake?" asked Berkowitz calmly. "I mean the other networks are on the same ground you are, and they are up-river reporting."

"No dammit!" she said angrily. She became icily calm. She looked down at the floor. "I'll do it, Bernie, I'll go upriver. 'Can do' Bernie," she said with a quivering voice.

"Good! That's my tough girl," said Berkowitz. "Now go get me some footage upriver near the fighting, and let me see you looking your beautiful self doing it, OK"

"Yes Bernie," she sniffed. Her finely formed chocolate features now staring at him. He cut the connection, sighed deeply, and looked out the window in the brilliant morning in Washington DC where snow was now melting everywhere, flowing in rivers down the streets to the river and then to the sea. *The world goes on, it could all end tomorrow but business is still business.*

**\*\*\*\***

The Tlakmar descended through the clouds accompanied by its escorts into the spaceport of the palace at Alkmar. Hontal stood in polished armor, as did Captain Quinton of Rigel, who had been also ordered to also make his report. Soon they both marched, accompanied by heavily armed guards in armor, into the Palace. Its perfumed air, smelling also of the sea, was a welcome refreshment from the stale air of the Tlakmar that he had breathed for months. Through a huge jeweled door, Hontal and the Captain were led to a royal council chamber whose walls were polished white stone inlaid with golden stars. A long table of fine dark wood polished and shining was before them, lined on its far side with high back chairs of similar dark polished wood. Above them, the high ceiling was white and studded with bluish silver stars, and at it zenith a depiction of mighty Rigel. Grave-looking and bearded, the Council sat in the chairs clothed in fine robes, except for Dakon, who sat nearly facing Hontal and the Captain, and who wore polished armor. Hontal and the Captain had to stand at two dark wooden lecterns facing the table. Hontal handed a data disk to an aid in a red robe who hurried off to load it into a computer projector. Suddenly, the bearded elder, in the central chair, rose. It was Sontal, the chief minister of the Emperor. At this recognition, Hontal's heart raced, but he quieted himself. *I will deliver my fine tale of Erra in the heart of the Quzrada, as is my solemn charge.*

An aide in long red robe stood forth, holding the Banner of the Samaran Empire, a Red flag with a black winged dragon rampant, and before the dragon, a light blue seven pointed star.

"Hear one and all," said the aide in a loud voice. "This room is now sealed, and the reports now to be given are henceforth high secrets of the Palace."

Abruptly, there was a disturbance in the side of the room, and everyone suddenly rose from their chairs and bowed, as did Hontal and the Captain by reflex.

"His majesty the Crown Prince had now entered the chamber!" Everyone bowed still lower, as the Crown Prince took his place at the table. Dakon himself gave up his seat and everyone moved down one seat, dislodging a lesser official at the end, who was then swiftly brought another chair. The Crown Prince was a handsome bearded man in armor, who was the only

576

one smiling in the room. He carried a large goblet of red wine and had obviously been drinking from it.

"So, let us hear the great report of the Quzrada, especially let us hear of the brave Queen Xenoba of raven hair, who leads the brave Errans in battle!" said the Crown Prince loudly as he lay down his wine goblet and took his seat. The First Minister smiled awkwardly, took his seat as everyone else sat down, and waved at Hontal to begin.

Hontal, feeling slightly giddy at the presence of the Crown Prince, cleared his throat and began making his voice as deep and grave as possible. He then began his tale of the great doings in the Quzrada, at Erra.

**** 

Schwartzman stood in the street surveying the carnage. Men women, children, the old, the young, had been hacked to pieces and filled the street as far as he could see into the mist. Most had died by machete, some by gunfire, others clearly by death ray - it left a blotchy-gray burn mark on the Africans. The dead were all civilians, only one Congolese policeman lay among the fallen, gun still in his hand, its magazine emptied of bullets. *A good way to die in this place,* thought Schwartzman.

Krueger was pointing out, with clinical detachment, a Z-shaped mark carved deeply in the foreheads of several dead children.

"That's the mark of Costos Zarkomedis, Swartz. We call him "Zarko;" he is a merc like us, who has done much business before here in the Congo," said Krueger looking at the child's head intently and pointing at it with the barrel of his gun. A formation of American jet fighters flew over at high altitude.

Flies swarmed everywhere, and huge black spiders had set up shop immediately, spinning webs from the trees, lampposts, and building fronts and catching flies and feasting on hordes of them. It looked like Hell on Earth. MacMillan came down the street with several grim looking mercenaries. A group of screaming and crying children, many horribly wounded, followed them. The children had apparently taken shelter by instinct in the jungle at the town outskirts and now emerged at the sight

577

of what looked like government soldiers. Arizona and Lt Colonel Jason Parker, a tall muscular black man with a well-trimmed mustache, stood beside him, the expression on all the men, all combat veterans, was stony calm.

"You mean this merc is working for the Greys?" said Schwartzman with murderous rage creeping into his voice.

"Oh! Zarko, was known for things like this, Swartz, " said Krueger looking up calmly at Schwartzman, his dark blue eyes like steel rivets." He gives us fellow mercs a bad name. He often told us, 'the worse his employer, the better he liked his work.' " said Kruger with icy determination. "We take him alive, then you leave him to us, Colonel," he added. Macmillan now stood by and nodded fiercely.

"The band went straight North, through the jungle," said MacMillan. "They didn't take the highway. Probably afraid of the allied air cover, so they are staying under the jungle canopy. They are about a day's journey ahead, perhaps fifty men, by the tracks they left." reported MacMillan. Schwartzman noted one of the medics treating the wounded children, was starting to weep.

"Jason! Send that man to the rear! And get us a fit replacement, and get an evac for these children, ASAP!" snapped Schwartzman angrily, pointing out the medic to Parker, who walked down the street with several rangers to replace the man. Schwartzman looked at the huge spiders devouring flies, at the already rotting bodies piled high everywhere, and heard the cries of the children, he felt his sanity slipping for a second.

"What's due north of here?" he demanded of Kruger.

"Kotanga on Ubangi River, Colonel," said Kruger with a fierce joy in his eyes. "If they are hacking a path through the jungle, they will have to go slow -we can catch them! Zarko would not be so stupid to travel this way, so the commander must be alien, a "nuudos", a novice at fighting here in the Congo." Schwartzman smiled and nodded. *Every smart guy looks at a situation and imagines he is master of it,* thought Schwartzman with satisfaction.

578

"Arizona!" yelled Schwartzman. "I want a rifle company, all volunteers, to follow after this bunch of maggots! We leave in five minutes, carry only food, water, and ammo! We travel light! We travel fast!" he roared. He turned to face Lt. Colonel Parker, who had returned, and waved his hand at the street full of bodies.

"Jason, I am leaving you in charge. I need you to form a blocking force here, so no one can follow us." Parker looked disappointed.

"Let me lead this mission chief! I'll catch those bastards!" protested Jason angrily.

"Don't worry Jason! You'll get your shot at point!" responded Schwartzman. "This one is mine! Now, you will observe complete radio silence concerning this operation. Hopefully, we can surprise these mother fuckers and get some good intel out of them. I also want you to get some trenches blasted with C-4 , up north of the town near the jungle. I want you to requisition some vehicles and transport these bodies there and get them all in the ground, ASAP." Schwartzman paused pointed, at the dead policeman. "And I want that one brave one over there buried in a separate grave from the rest. He died like a soldier, and I want his body treated with respect." Jason nodded regretfully and saluted.

"Yes sir!" said Jason as he turned and began shouting orders.

The men of the pursuit team were gathering by the mercs, Arizona's hand-picked US Army Rangers, and Mohamed with a dozen of his toughest Nigerians, 70 men. In a few minutes they were off at a run for the jungle with Schwartzman in the lead, carrying an M-4 carbine with a sheathed machete on his back. Task force Vengeance was now moving.

**** 

Marcy Braxton stood, clad in her well-tailored Army jungle fatigues showing off her cheerleader curves, at the prow of the powerful motor launch carrying her and some cargo upriver. The breeze was cool on her chocolate skin. Atkins her editor, her Congolese film crew, Mr. Tsango,

579

and squad of 10 nervous looking Congolese Army troops rode in the boat with her. The powerful diesel engine of the launch filled the air with a deep rhythmic rumble. The wrinkled Congolese Captain manned the wheel, resplendent in a battered captain's cap, and smoked a pipe stoically. A formation of jet fighters flew over, high in the sky, too high for good footage, she realized with disappointment. Then, they were gone, leaving her feeling alone and vulnerable again.

She stood at prow of the boat because she was afraid she would glimpse naked captives chained beneath the decks of the boat, if she stood anywhere else. Human trafficking was still a lucrative business in the Congo, especially now, with so much foreign military in-country. Marcy wore a broad brimmed jungle fatigue hat and silver sunglasses to ward off the brilliant Sun. They were plowing through the muddy water of the Ubangl River, a tributary of the mighty Congo. Fishermen and merchants rowed or motored by in brightly painted craft. War with aliens from outer space or not, life went on in the Congo. Mr. Tsango, in a blue suit and tie and white fedora, stood near her. Since they had left Brazzaville hours before, she sensed he represented the only functioning government existing for a hundred miles.

"Well Yankee girl" said Tsango smiling. "What do you think of our arrangements?"

"Good, Good!" said Marcy nodding without looking at him. Several shades lighter than her African counterparts, she was no longer amazed that she was treated like any white person. They did not even ask her what tribe she was from. Her people were Fulani, but to the Africans, she was from America, therefore, she was American. *There are no Africans in Africa,* she thought sadly, *Only tribes-people.*

"How long before we get to Kotanga?" she asked warily.

"Oh we get there in a few hours; my brother is chief of police there and he will give you Yankee VIP treatment!"

*Now I know why we are going to Kotanga,* she thought with resignation.

Lamar Atkins, her ruggedly handsome, sandy haired editor, clad also in jungle camouflaged fatigues, walked up to her. He was American, and had been a freelance journalist and whatever else, in Africa for years. He was obviously an adrenaline junkie, a lost soul in a lost continent, attracted to the Congo by its series of wars. She was reassured by his happy-go-lucky presence. He was her emotional lifeline now.

"Mr. Tsango's brother runs the police station at Kotanga," she said shaking her head.

"Well, that solves that mystery, then," he replied, smiling.

"What mystery is that?" she replied. *There are so many mysteries here.*

"The mystery of why we are going to Kotanga on the Ubangi river, rather than going up the Kotto river where the fighting has been mostly reported," he said with a shrug. "But the fighting has been everywhere upriver of Brazzaville, and so is the chaos, so our chances getting footage of terrified refugees is good. Besides, with Tsango's brother as the local police chief, I now know who I am paying dash to and what to expect."

"dash?" she asked vacantly

"A local I term for bribe money," he said smiling. "Think of it as a tip for good service, before the service is received."

"This whole operation is paved with money! Doesn't anyone just do their job in this place? We can't even check out of the hotel without an extra tip, so they call it!" she said bitterly. "I want out of this fucked up place!" she said in a low voice, leaning close to Atkins. "Get me out of here Lamar," she said pleadingly.

"Well the locals figure that just because there's a war with aliens from outer space, this is no reason to change local customs," he said with a laugh. "They tell me, in fact, this war has been really good for business in Brazzaville. A dash here and dash there! So the locals consider this war a real business opportunity. A bonanza!"

"Well then, let's get some footage at Kotanga and get back down to Brazzaville then!" she retorted. "I have a bad feeling about this trip. I want

581

to go home," she said looking at him and lifting her sunglasses to bore into his blue eyes with her chocolate brown eyes.

Atkins grinned in response and nodded.

"Well cutie-pie, just trust old Lamar to get you home safe with some good footage. We find some scared refugees, of which we have no shortage here, never mind what they are fleeing, we make our brave escort here look like the whole Congolese Army, and pay them a little extra to look brave. Presto! We have footage for Bernie! Piece of Cake!" he laughed. "Marcy, trust me, I know this place like the back of my hand. I am part of this place."

****

Hontal finished his long account, lasting an hour and a half, punctuated by many images, of the recent events at Erra. He then gratefully accepted a goblet of wine to quench his dry throat.

"So Your Majesty, and my Lords, to summarize my report, the Unash, had hoped to subjugate Erra by stealth and treachery, rather than all-out war, and thereby secure the center of the Quzrada without disturbing the peace of that region. Such plans were well known to our officials and had our approval. However, because this treachery was discovered by the dark-haired maiden, and the Erran patriotic forces alerted, whom she led in battle against the traitors in her government, this scheme of the Unash has failed utterly. Now there is war at Erra both in space and on the ground, and the Unash have suffered many defeats by the Errans, whom despite their inferior weapons and space technology have fought with great boldness and ferocity so that the Unash have fainted before them.

I have asked Zomal of Bellatrix, who is acting commander of our garrison on Una, the reason for this disgraceful set of defeats, and he replied that the Unash thought to enter Erra as thieves enter a house at night, armed only with daggers, and were then confronted by a brave homeowner banishing a sword and shield. He also said that because of the dark-haired woman, the men of war of Erra fight with great virtue, but the Unash are much wantin in virtue, because they were expecting no resistance. They have no stomach for this fight or armaments for the battle they find

582

themselves in. So it is because of this raven haired woman that the cow now mounts the bull at Erra.

This last phrase caused the Crown Prince to laugh heartily, and he was then joined nervously by many others.

"Well, this seems simple enough! Kill this witch! Kill her and then crush the Errans! Their virtue will count for nothing if a fleet is sent, and we glass their planet!" said one councilor loudly. He was Travon of Batelgeen.

"Ah, but it seems a shame to make ashes of such fine flesh!" answered the Crown Prince. "Better yet, she should be brought here in golden chains to be our guest at the palace." he laughed. He suddenly leaned forward with a broad smile. "Let me also see more pictures of her companion and helper in this war, the golden-haired wench who was the armor bearer for the dark haired one." Hontal, using controls of the lectern called up images of Pamela. In some cases standing beside Cassandra, in other cases standing alone. Hontal tried to control his heart. *She looks just like my Tatia.*

"Yes, have a set of silver chains forged for this one." said the Crown prince whimsically.

"Captain Zomal, you were also there, what say you to this report of Hontal." said the Chief Minister grimly.

"I agree with it, my Lord. The account of Hontal is altogether true as I saw it. The Unash are put to the worst before the Errans, despite all expectations otherwise. I have observed the battles in space between Errans and Unash from a distance. The Unash have no stomach for this fight, whereas the Errans fight as if they have contempt for death. The more advanced weapons of the Unash cannot make up for this deficit in virtue."

"What is your recommendation Hontal of Alnilam"

"Your Majesty and My Lords, I recommend a fleet be dispatched at once to rectify this situation in the Quzrada. The Errans must be crushed with overwhelming force if they will not surrender."

"Yes, but whose fleet?" asked Dakon. He looked around the table, "This a delicate matter..."

"Your recommendation then, is that we burn the planet to a cinder if they do not yield ?" answered the first minister, seemly ignoring Dakon's question.

"Yes, my Lord. We cannot allow an Archmetan power to arise in the Quzrada," said Hontal, hoping his decisiveness would please the council. He saw Dakon nod in agreement. But part of him felt revulsion at what he had just uttered.

"But of course we can preserve some of their women alive as prizes of war," said the Crown Prince.

*Yes,* thought Hontal with sudden desperation.

"Thank you for you good report and bold counsel, Hontal of Alnilam, and also you Captain, for your brave service to the realm." The First Minister said as he rose. "The council will now meet in private session. You are excused, my two brave knights," said the First Minister waving his hand at Hontal and Captain Quinton, who bowed low, and then they were led out.

"How do you think this went, my Captain?" asked Hontal once they were outside and the door was shut.

"Well , we have just told the Royal council that things go badly in the Quzrada, and yet we both have our heads still on our shoulders. So that is good." said the Captain happily as they walked out of the palace.

****

Schwartzman, his fatigues sodden with sweat, followed MacMillan off the trail, to where and several other mercs stood in the jungle. He had paused from leading the men at a murderous pace, down the jungle trail hacked by their fleeing enemy. He was drawing strength and endurance from places he did not know. Now he stood in a cloud of flies, the smell of rotting flesh was suffocating. The familiar smell of rotting squid assailed his nostrils-dead alien flesh. Two short, scrawny, human-alien hybrids lay dead. Their uniforms were composed of a dull green tattered plastic membrane, with a camouflage pattern, with fine holes in it to make it porous. Like a garbage sack with fine perforations. They wore wide brimmed jungle camouflaged hats of similar material. Their greyish skull-like faces had pure black eyes and were covered with red boils, as were their bodies. The skulls both bore bullet wounds. Their shoes consisted of shredded camouflaged plastic boots, like galoshes, with soles worn out completely. The soles of their feet were masses of pestilent infection. The hybrids' every step for the last few miles must have been agony.

"These two look like they fell behind, so they were shot," said Krueger. "There footwear and uniforms look like they were issued for duty on a golf course, not for here in the Congo. Krueger looked at Schwartzman in puzzlement. "Colonel, it looks like these people did not plan very well for this war."

"No, I think a real war in a jungle was the last thing they expected here," panted Schwartzman. "They are space people."

"Another thing Swartz, the people wielding machetes at the front of their column," continued Krueger. "They are hacking through tree branches as thick as my thumb without slacking. Normally people steer the head of the trail for thinner brush. Not these ones, they are plowing through it in almost a straight line. The bush-whackers in the lead are either incredibly strong or on drugs to travel this way. We noticed this also with the bodies back at Ndali, lots of the machete work was done by men of great strength, they chopped through legs and skulls like they were paper. "

"Not these, then? " said Schwartzman, pointing at the two emaciated looking dead hybrids with his M-4 carbine. Kruger shook his head. "No, they must have special hybrids of some type at the head of their column. Another good thing, they seem to be moving too fast to lay any booby traps on the trail. I don't think they know anyone is following them."

"All right then men saddle up! Let's move!" yelled Schwartzman. In a moment the Task Force Vengeance was plunging down the hacked out trail through the jungle again in the gloom of the gathering thunderstorm."

****

On the river, the sun was disappearing behind black thunderclouds of afternoon. The river suddenly was full of debris and floating bodies. One was a dead Congolese sailor, tangled in a rope with a life ring from a Congolese river-patrol gunboat. This was surveyed with growing unease by the troops on the boat. The boat's Captain simply reloaded his pipe with tobacco and motored on. Encouraged by Atkins, Marcy managed to get some footage of herself commenting on the grim tableau floating by.

After several hours and with the first raindrops of what promised to be a downpour, they motored into the small dock area of the town of Kotanga. Kotanga looked like a small sleepy river town with dirt streets lined with trees. Scores of frightened people waited on the docks for them. They included what was apparently the local police chief and his second in command, standing resplendent in blue uniforms and red berets. They looked grim and impatient and exchanged only brief and tense greetings with Mr. Tsango as he got off the boat at the dock.

"If these guys are brothers, they must be from a troubled family," commented Lamar to Marcy as they watched the two men seeming to argue on the dock. "Leave this to me, we'll get some footage and then get ourselves headed back downriver before this rain hits." He turned and shouted some orders to the Congolese camera crew, who nervously began getting the camera and sound equipment out. Atkins got out of the boat and the police chief turned to him angrily.

"You there Yankee!" he motioned to Atkins, "I have kept watch here for you to be safe! You have put me to extra trouble!" Marcy, the film crew and very nervous looking troops got off the boat and walked off the dock onto dry land. On the land, a small group of villagers gathered around her and the crew eyeing them with frightened curiosity. Fear hung over the village like the rumbling thunderclouds above them.

Atkins suddenly came walking up.

"OK Marcy, let's get some footage and get out of here before it starts raining. She quickly was in character as the seasoned cosmopolitan newswoman, talking about cosmic war and the local tribal war that had

586

scarred the area just a few months before, as the camera's red light gleamed, with the soldiers lined up behind her in the background being sold things by the townspeople. Atkins produced a frightened townswoman who spoke in the local tribal language to a translator who reported to Marcy that the 'devils' had come to the town the night before riding on lights in the sky and left a dead body in a tree to scare them all. It had apparently worked.

They followed the woman a block down the dirt street into the town, to a town square area, where, in a large tree, a dead body bleached grey by the alien death ray, hung naked from the tree limbs. It stank horribly.

"Why doesn't someone take it down?" asked Marcy in horror.

"They are scared to," said Atkins grimly. They say it's 'bad Ju Ju', that it's guarded by spirits. They won't touch it."

"Got shots of this?" said Atkins tuning to the terrified looking cameraman, who nodded.

"Then Marcy, let's get out of here. I think we have captured all that is newsworthy here in Kotanga," he said with a wry smile.

The terror tactic had apparently worked so well that people were crowding the dock with bundles of pathetic possessions. Tsango, the boat Captain, and the Police chief brother were near the dock and Atkins motioned for Marcy and film crew to wait while he went and negotiated. Marcy watched as he spoke to them and handed them all bundles of money, which they took grudgingly.

He came back looking grim.

"They say the river boats won't travel at night, because of spirits on the river. Apparently, the aliens sank some boats last night," said Atkins with frustration. "So we have to spend the night here." He paused. "They say we can stay with our crew at the police station over there, and leave at dawn. He pointed to a small, sturdy looking, grey concrete building by the river, with a dock beside it.

"What about the police?" asked Marcy.

"They're gone. That's why the police chief wanted more money. He says he stayed even after his men deserted. So I paid him. I promised the boat Captain more money back at Brazzaville once he got us and the crew home. So at least our way back is ensured."

Rain started to come down so they all ran to the police station. Inside were a dozen or so frightened young children. One girl, called Mambi by the other children, was the oldest of the group at 9 years old. They managed to learn from her that the children were orphans from the tribal wars up-river, who had been brought to Kotanga and apparently abandoned. Marcy was overcome with emotion and promptly began scrounging through the kitchen area for some food for them, as a torrential rainstorm began outside, and lighting crashed. She found a bag of rice and some dried beans, soon the children each had a bowl of food and despite the crashing thunder, things settled down for a while and became almost happy. The rain ebbed, and the night became full of fearful sounds, the children went to sleep on blankets on the floor in the mess area. But to Marcy and Atkins fear had returned.

"I'm sorry I got you into this mess. I am used to working in the Congo, but this situation is a lot worse and lot more unpredictable than I expected," he said regretfully.

"That's Ok Lamar, you can buy me a drink in Brazzaville tomorrow night when we get back," she said as brightly as she could muster. He smiled gratefully. "I'll sleep out in the front office, to stand guard. You watch these kids. "

She found an office littered with papers with a cot in it, off the mess area. She noticed also that Atkins was now wearing a pistol, so she looked and found a Sten 1960's vintage submachine gun hanging on a wall and took it with a bandolier of several clips of ammunition. The police had apparently felt it was useless for what they were facing and had left it behind.

The rain had stopped and she looked out of the window and saw strange red lights in the distance over the river.

"Helicopters come to rescue us," she told herself hopefully, too tired to think about them any more deeply, she lay down on the cot, pulled the Sten gun on top of her, and fell into an exhausted sleep.

****

Cassandra , clad in an Army winter jacket stood up joyfully in the hatchway of the Armored Personnel Carrier as the sun shown strongly down on her. It was a perfectly warm day. She had left Morningstar. The armored column taking her and some other personnel on rotation had arrived at the base of the rocky mountains after passing out of the San Luis Valley. It was spring everywhere, and everywhere along their route they could see houses being reoccupied by families who had fled south during the killing Winter. Snow was melting everywhere and the creeks were full. The armored column was paused at a railway crossing, and a huge train carrying strange armored vehicles with a multi-shaded, grey, camouflage pattern were hurtling past. Also on the train were trucks and antiaircraft missile batteries. All of this was rolling south.

"What is that grey pattern camouflage for, Antarctica?" Cassandra asked an Army officer watching the train, from the hatch next to hers.

"No, it's for Lunar operations, " he said matter-of-factly. She stared at him incredulously. But soon her thoughts were only of flying back to Washington DC. To home. She felt stronger now, more determined. "I must tell Pammy about all of my adventures," she said to herself happily. Then her thoughts became sad. "And I must tell Dr. Petrosian what I have discovered."

"I swear to God I am going to march back into the studio and do the news!" she said to herself, as the endless train covered with lunar camouflaged equipment hurtled past.

****

Marcy awoke with a start. It was morning, but it was silent as death outside. She glanced at the doorway, Mambi and some other children were looking at her apprehensively. She rose holding her submachine gun and walked out into the mess area where the children now cowered as Atkins, holding his pistol, looked out the windows at the town.

"The town appears deserted and all the boats are gone, " he said grimly over his shoulder as he scanned the town riverfront. "And so is our film crew," he added. "At least I have a copy of our footage on a thumb drive. Here, I feel better if you keep it." he handed it to her.

"But the Captain of the boat..." she stammered fearfully as she tucked the chip into her bra.

"He's dead, he's floating in the water by the dock." Suddenly Marcy's knees felt like rubber. She quickly regained control of herself. *Straighten up Lieutenant!* she thought fiercely, her old army instincts kicking in.

"So this is not good, Marcy."

"Yes, but I saw a radio in the front office! Surely, we can..."

"Yes! I managed to raise the police headquarters at Brazzaville, but they say they may not get a boat here for two days. You notice it's real quiet out there too."

"Yes," said Marcy apprehensively.

"That's not good either!" he whispered emphatically. "Look, I am going to scout around. If I can find a boat or dinghy, we'll just float downriver with the current."

"What about these children? We can't just leave them here!" cried Marcy.

"Alright a raft then, of planks!" he muttered angrily.

"Lamar, what does it mean here when it's really quiet like this?"

"In the Congo, it usually means something really bad is about to happen! That's why we have to get out of here!" he said turning to her. "Now you get these children some breakfast and I'll find a raft or a wooden awning we can use as a raft, for us to float down river on. That's all we need, we'll just float down river. And be out of here." He then checked his Berretta 9 mm pistol, squared his shoulders and left out of the mess area and then out the front door of the police station. She watched out the window as he walked up the deserted street of the town, towards the main square. The eerie silence was deafening. She busied herself dishing out cold rice and beans from a pot into the bowls of the children as she stole glances out the window. She ate several mouthfuls herself still cradling her gun. She noted it looked well-oiled despite being of an older vintage. The clips were full of 9 mm pistol cartridges. She had four curved clips of 30 rounds each. The children ate silently, pensively. She took a clue from them and began scanning the riverfront buildings of the town, listening.

Suddenly an explosion of noise erupted, as a flock of frightened birds flew up from the far side of town squawking. She jumped at the sound, undid the safety of the submachine gun, and took up a position in the front office by a window. Several of the children began to whimper piteously. They somehow knew what was coming next. They had grown up here.

An explosion of gunfire came from the distance and screaming.

"Oh shit." she gasped.

People were running down the street towards the police station, their faces were mostly masks of pathetic terror. Among them she saw Lamar, his face was determined as he ran with his pistol in his hand. Instinctively, she rammed the muzzle of the submachine gun through the glass of the window pane shattering it. She drew the submachine gun up to her cheek, drew back the bolt. She was aiming over Lamar's head, at whatever was coming down the street after him. The sound of fully automatic gunfire grew louder. He and the others were nearing the waterfront area. People were falling. Then Lamar stopped as the others still able ran past, he raised his pistol and was firing back down the street from where he had just run. The pistol making flares of orange flame in the shadows under the tree lined street. He was like a man shooting at a tidal wave, however. He then fell, as did the others around him. What she saw next almost made her lose her sanity.

591

Bounding down the street hacking at the bodies fallen or standing with long machetes, came several enormous grey creatures like a cross between a man and a gorilla . They rushed up to Lamar's body and began hacking it to pieces and then turned their eyes to her, their faces were like lions, with enormous fangs. They seemed to see her with their coal-black eyes and screamed a high-pitched wailing cry that froze her soul. They were hideous chimeras, a terror weapon, part man, part several species of animal. But she suddenly felt a wave of anger that overcame her terror as the creatures bounded after the remaining running people, instantly overtaking them  and hewed them down as they screamed their lives away at the waterfront in front of her. She lined up the nearest chimera in the sights and pulled the trigger. The submachine gun barked deafeningly in her strong dark arms, clouds of dust flew out of its mechanism, and the creature fell screaming, his long machete flying from his clawed hand, his body did not lie still but convulsed and leaped about in spasms. She lined up on another one and the submachine gun barked anew. Her years in the Army were now kicking in as she carefully limited her firing to short bursts. To keep the submachine gun muzzle from climbing above her target, she aimed low now.  Children had run into the room and were now grasping her legs and screaming, her ears were ringing. Suddenly bullets began to hit the concrete around her and she felt a bullet go past her ear. The gun quit shooting, jammed. She ducked behind the concrete wall framing the window and tried to work the jammed gun so it would shoot again, screaming obscenities to keep herself from being overwhelmed by fear.  The gun would not work now, it had apparently overheated and was searing hot. She exploded into tears as she tried to work the bolt to free the mechanism. The strength in her legs vanished and she slid to the floor on her knees. She looked outside saw a group of figures in camouflage and broad-brimmed hats cautiously approaching the police station, she could barely see them with her tear filled eyes. Her mind was freezing up now as she heard footsteps on the front walkway of the police building and the sound of the children screaming in terror merged with the screaming in her mind. She dropped the useless gun and covered her weeping face with her hands helplessly.

Suddenly, a deafening barrage of automatic gunfire and several sharp explosions sounded. There was piteous screaming outside the building both human and animal, bullets, and shrapnel bounced off the concrete outside like rain amid the deafening gunfire and explosions that went on seemingly for eternity.

Suddenly it stopped and was replaced by occasional shots and piteous screams and pleas for mercy followed by more shots and the sound of machetes impacting flesh. Then there was silence, except for the ringing in her ears, the children still clutched at her, but even they were silent. She heard heavy footsteps. Outside she heard barked orders in... English.

"Miss?" came a deep voice. She continued to cover her face and sob.

"Miss, I'm Colonel Schwartzman, US Army Rangers, it's OK now. The bad guys outside, well, we have dealt with them. It's Ok now." said the voice more reassuringly. She still heard one voice pathetically pleading for its life outside in some foreign language. Trembling uncontrollably, she lowered her hands slightly and looked up. Schwartzman and several other Rangers, plus Krueger stood there grinning. Schwartzman was holding a bloody machete and had an M-4 carbine slung over his shoulder reeking of cordite. He wiped the bloody machete on the leg of his fatigues and sheathed it as he saw her looking at in horror. She stared at them silently trembling.

"Can I help you up Miss?" Schwartzman said offering a strong sweat-soaked hand. Arizona poked his head into the doorway.

"Chief! looks like we bagged their whole force! MacMillan says they got Zarko too, and he's still alive!" Schwartzman smiled at this. Numbly, Marcy took his hand, and with his help rose on her wobbly legs. Krueger produced a small bottle of South African whiskey and offered her a drink. She took it and drank a gulp, as she leaned against the concrete wall by the window. It burned her throat satisfyingly. A cooling morning breeze was now blowing through the shattered windows.

"Good work you clowns," said Schwartzman to Arizona. "Nice deployment." He then turned to Marcy, smiling reassuringly.

"Miss, are you hurt?"

593

"No, I don't think so." Her whole body felt numb. Schwartzman swept his eyes over her lovely form, nodded approvingly. *She looks in good shape,* he thought.

"Miss could we have your name, I mean, what are you doing here in this hellhole?" His tone was slightly scolding.

"I'm Marcy Braxton, from CNS news" she stammered tearfully.

"Oh my God!" he laughed looking at Arizona grinning. "Yeah, I recognize you, now. I might have figured CNS would send somebody like you into this mess," laughed Schwartzman. "I mean, who else sends their Hollywood people into situations like this, absolutely clueless!" He looked at her carefully. "Just my luck to rescue a news reporter too," he frowned.

"Miss Braxton," began Arizona sternly. "We are part of a classified military operation, so I'm going to have to ask you not to report our presence or operation here. Got that? Now we are going to evac you ASAP back to Brazzaville in the rear. But 'it's loose lips sinks ships,' about us and our op here, OK? Unless you want a trip to Kwajalein in the Pacific for the rest of the war."

"Arizona," said Schwartzman scoldingly. "Miss Braxton is our honored guest, and of course, she'll keep us out of headlines, right?" he said gazing at her. She nodded fearfully, the whiskey was at least making her feel calmer.

"Actually, your lovely presence here, without knowing what you're doing, is in the highest mindless traditions of CNS reporting on sensitive national security matters." chuckled Schwartzman, grinning at Arizona.

"Now Ms. Braxton, who do these children belong to, and do they need any food or medical care?" he asked, surveying the now smiling children.

She then rushed over and hugged him tearfully.

\*\*\*\*

Dakon sat at his desk, trying to write a detailed recommendation of action for the Royal Council. Janek, his deputy stood by him when Hontal was ushered in. Dakon looked up and smiled at him as he entered. Janek also smiled heartily.

"Well done Hontal of Alnilam. You managed to coat the bitter medicine from the Quzrada with honey. It is said even the Emperor was seen to smile at hearing of this. For nothing so entertains a Samar as a tale of fierce battles and fair women," said Dakon himself relieved that the bad news had been delivered, and no one had been executed as a result.

"For this good service, I raise you in rank to First Knight of the Realm, and I give you command of your own starship," said Dakon rising. Hontal stood tall with pride at this.

"I know you must return to your household now, but return here quickly, once you have set your house in order, for I have a new assignment for you." Dakon looked then deep in thought. "Wear your Imperial pendant at all times, it marks you as an agent of the Palace and keep your bodyguard close. I can also offer you a special guard detail."

"That should not be necessary, my Lord," said Hontal confidently. He felt like a prince of the realm now. Dakon nodded at this response thoughtfully.

"Yes, but be watchful, not everyone in the palace is as pleased with your report as I am."

"If I may ask my Lord, what did the council decide concerning the situation in the Quzrada?"

Dakon frowned at this question. Then nodded, as if to himself.

"Well, this bumbling by the Monchkini changes nothing, brave Hontal. No Archmetan power can arise in the Quzrada, full of virtue or not, raven-haired Queen Xenoba leading them or not," said Dakon gravely. "Such things make fine tale in a tavern, but this is a grave matter of the Palace. Therefore, that is what was decided, and it is the only opinion the council could arrive at." Dakon looked to the star map on the wall.

"Erra must be crushed or destroyed," Dakon continued. "That is the edict of the palace that was decided upon decades ago. The only thing this new information adds is complications. It makes complicated a thing that should have been simple. The Monchkini will simply have to put their backs into this task and finish it." said Dakon grimly.

Suddenly a knock came on the chamber door.

"We are in conference!" roared Dakon angrily.

"My Lord, it is a gift from the Crown Prince." came the voice of a guard. Dakon cast a bewildered look at Janek.

"Then, bring it in!" roared Dakon looking down at his desk in exasperation and waving for Janek to attend to it at the door.

Janek returned with a member of the royal guard bearing two boxes of fine scented wood, one inlaid with gold and the other with silver. Janek was looking puzzled. Dakon motioned for them to be placed on the desk and opened their lids as Hontal and Janek watched. The gold inlaid box contained a set of shining gold chains and manacles, and the other box chains and manacles of finely polished silver. Both apparently sized for women. A note was in the gold inlaid box from the Crown Prince. Dakon opened it and read it aloud.

"To my most excellent Lord Dakon, receive these gifts to inspire you in resolving the situation in the Quzrada." he recited gravely.

Dakon looked up at Janek glowering. He then calmed himself and looked at Hontal.

"Yes, my brave Hontal, there are complications. But to you, a safe journey home, to return quickly. I will soon have other tasks for you concerning these matters," said Dakon looking perplexed. Hontal saluted and then turned and left.

Dakon slowly shut the lids on the two boxes. He rose and turned to the royal guardsman, who stood impassively.

"Tell the Crown Prince my heart is moved with gratitude at these gifts, and I am inspired to bold actions in the service of the throne of Rigel by them," said Dakon slowly. Then he motioned for the guard to depart. He sat down heavily at his desk as the door closed. Janek stood before him. Dakon shook his head wearily.

"The galaxy trembles on its axis!" muttered Dakon, "which runs now right through the heart of the Quzrada! To solve this crisis I must either send our own fleet, and risk a Second War of the Quzrada, or watch a bunch of incompetent dickless pygmies attempt to wage war against men full of virtue such as ourselves! And risk watching these Monchkini continuing their train of defeats!" Dakon paused. "And in the middle of this, the Crown Prince sends me jeweled fetters for two women!" said Dakon trembling in rage. "Janek is it not said of old that by a woman, all troubles entered the world!" continued Dakon looking at Janek. "So, you see it proven here!" he motioned with his hand at the gold inlaid box and its contents.

****

Schwartzman stood, clad only in pistol belt as the tropical downpour washed over him. He soaped up and let himself be rinsed off by the cool rain. He then retreated inside and put on his still filthy fatigues in an abandoned office in the police building. He had assigned half the men to set up a perimeter for the night, and half to sleep. The mercs, he knew, had taken Zarko and several other wounded prisoners into the largely abandoned town for interrogation. He shaved, then began feeling like a human being for the first time in days. He then sat down at a desk with a combat laptop computer and began to write an after-action report on Task Force Vengeance and its success, as the rain continued outside.

"Task Force Vengeance was able to overtake a mixed mercenary and alien raiding party as they were raiding Kotanga. We were able to deploy behind them as they engaged armed parties near the riverfront and attack. The surprise was complete and no casualties were sustained by the Task Force, as it annihilated the enemy force. *No letters home, excellent.*

A knock came on the door

"Come in," he said picking up his pistol and holding it as he turned to face the door. It was Arizona. They exchanged casual salutes as Arizona stepped in and shut the door.

"Boss, we got the riverfront area secure for the night. We got the children fed and bedded down. The men who are off guard duty also. The CNS reporter, we are giving the luxury suite facing the river, complete with her own private bath. But she says she wants to talk to you, 'on deep background' she says." Arizona looked at Schwartzman worriedly. "Also, Colonel we just heard the French are airlifting a light division into Chad and are going to come sweeping south. Division HQ says intel places the alien base somewhere north of here, that means the French are hoping to find it first. General Alvarez wants us to move North as soon as we can to find that base," Arizona paused.

"Permission to speak freely, Boss?"

"Yes Arizona, permission granted," said Schwartzman wearily.

"Boss, you can't go around introducing yourself to news people in the middle of the Congo! You got to start using a Nom de guerre or something. Our previous operations have been in exclusively American theaters, now we're out in the wide world, so you got to be more careful. That goes double with the French now starting operations in- theater. So I wouldn't go talking to that woman, anymore, in fact, I say she goes to Kwajalein!"

"Nah, she'll keep quiet, she's former Army," said Schwartzman putting his pistol back down on the desk. "But I do want her and those kids evacuated out of here tomorrow at dawn on the first boat." And, you're right, of course, Arizona, I will pick a nom de guerre, and we will start using it." said Schwartzman looking chagrined. He was silent for a moment." I must confess that I have been so buried in the mechanics of these operations, I forgot that important little detail. I have been having too good a time!" he grinned. Arizona nodded and looked more relaxed. Arizona produced a pint bottle of Bacardi Rum from his fatigue jacket pocket.

"Here chief, we liberated this from a store down the street. I know it's your favorite." Schwartzman reached for it eagerly and took it. He opened it and took a swallow, handed it back to Arizona, who also took a swallow before putting it down on Schwartzman's desk.

"Fer de Lance," said Schwartzman, as the rum burned his throat. "That's my new name. It means `head of the spear.` It's also an absolutely memorable poisonous snake down in South America. That thing can kill you just by looking at you."

"Sounds good chief!" said Arizona. "We can call you Colonel Lance, for short. The men will like it."

"Yeah, and the French will understand it too," said Schwartzman with a smile, taking another swig of rum. He then held up his Berretta pistol and smiled at it. "By the way, it is not my intention to be taken alive by the French or anybody else. You make sure of that Arizona if it should come down to it."

"Yes sir"

"Alright I better finish this after-action-report for Alvarez, just because we have a war with aliens from outer space doesn't mean Army paperwork stops flowing. Particularly since this op went down so sweetly. I can't remember an op going down this smooth. No letters home."

"Yes sir," said Arizona smiling, as they exchanged salutes and Arizona turned and left. Outside, the rain had stopped, and the sounds of the Congolese jungle at night began to resume their usual chorus. In the middle of that cacophony, Schwartzman could make out pathetic human screams coming from somewhere in the abandoned town. He took off his fatigue jacket and shirt as the cooler air of the rain was replaced now with the oppressive steam-bath heat of the night.

After a while, he had nearly finished the brief report and there was a knock on the door.

"Who is it," said Schwartzman in irritation.

"It's Marcy Braxton, Colonel." said a female voice.

"I'm busy," said Schwartzman.

She came in anyway. He reflexively grabbed his pistol and pointed it at her. She froze in terror and held up her hands.

She had obviously bathed and changed clothes into a khaki tank top and pants. She was still holding her hands up.

"All right, come in!" he snapped impatiently, putting down his pistol. She found a chair and sat down looking at him. She was transfixed by his trim and very muscular frame and massive arms as he sat shirtless at the desk. His chest hair was black speckled with grey.  He looked at her in annoyance.

"What is it Ms. Braxton?"

"I can't sleep, I keep hearing someone screaming out there," she said in a trembling voice.

"That's just some night bird or something, don't worry about it," he said turning back to his desk. "You had a pretty bad scare today, you should get some sleep. Also, we're all sorry about your colleague Atkins, but at least he died quickly and honorably. That's exceptional around here." He paused. "We buried him with the other dead town's people."

"I saw your people took some prisoners."

"Ms. Braxton, we are 'in country' here, do you know what means?" he said with anger creeping into his voice. He turned to face her.

"No," she said with quavering voice.

"It's an expression from the Vietnam war. It means you're in another country and you have to adjust your attitudes accordingly. You have to flow with the local culture."  He stared at her intently. A faint scream was audible above the night jungle chorus. Tears started running down her face.

"If me and my people had arrived an hour late, that would be you out there." he added.  She rose, and walked towards him tearfully, he rose uncomfortably. She pulled her tank top up showing off her deep brown nipples, pulled the tank top over her head, let it fall to the floor and put her arms around him. He felt her warm soft breasts pressing against his bare chest and her erect nipples pressing into his flesh. She then kissed him.

"Colonel, I just wanted to say thank you for saving me," she said kissing him again, he wrapped his strong arms around her. They kissed again.

"Well, your very welcome." he said smiling.

Later he left her sleeping in his cot and went outside in his fatigues to inspect the perimeter. A half-Moon was overhead in the sky. A fire was burning, and some of his men were nearby it on the waterfront area. Several civilians, mostly very old, had clustered around the fire. As he approached the fire, and old woman near it turned and looked at him.

"You are the commander of this group of men who saved us?" she asked staring at him as behind her sparks leaped upward.

"Then, I will tell your fortune, for no charge," she announced. The other civilians looked upon her with reverence and some fear. He decided not to protest as she moved towards him and sat down, then produced a set of bones and threw them in the dust beside the fire. The bones made jagged shadows in the light of the fire. She studied the bones, then looked up at him in amazement.

"You are a great man, you will not die a common death." she pointed up at the Moon above them. "You no die on earth, you will die on the Moon." He looked up, looked back down at her, nodded with satisfaction.

"We must all die someplace, a death on the Moon suits me just fine, old lady," he said with satisfaction. "Thank you."

He noted a faint glow in the East, dawn was coming.

****

In a tavern at the spaceport, Hontal, still wearing his jeweled pendant sat at a table with Captain Quinton, and they both drank good ale from large

601

mugs. The talk in the tavern was subdued. A great battle had occurred on the Tlaxian front, and despite the brave talk, 'that the Samar had inflicted great losses on the Tlax,' Hontal could tell that things had not gone well for the Samar. He himself felt this was an evil omen. The Captain merely nodded thoughtfully and sighed at the news from a serving girl. Hontal decided to push the thoughts of the Tlaxian war out of his head. *It will be well, in the end, has it not always been so?*

"Thank you, my friend, Captain Quinton of Rigel," said Hontal to the Captain. "For your testimony and my safe passage. I have truly gained much wisdom serving with you in this venture."

"Well young lion, I apologize if my manner was sometimes harsh," said Quinton. "But know truly, we were being followed in the Quzrada by warships on several occasions. I did not want to distract you by informing you. I was the Captain, and you but my honored passenger. But know now, brave Hontal, the Quzrada is a place of death."

"Whose warships?" asked Hontal. The Captain shrugged and shook his head. "Every ship in that place masks its identity," he said. And the cost of getting close enough to another ship, so as to identify it, brave Hontal, can sometimes be very dear. Take my advice, if you ever find yourself in the Quzrada again, never approach any other ship there unless you intend to vaporize it instantly if it be found a foe."

The Captain looked at the clock on the wall.

"I must take my leave of you brave Hontal, with the hopes we will serve again at each other side." The Captain rose and drained his mug of ale.

"Where do you go now, brave Captain?" Hontal asked.

"On the business of the Palace," he said smiling, "and home, to visit the wife and sons so they won't forget my face."

He suddenly looked at Hontal with concern.

"Know this last thing, brave Hontal. Methinks more is afoot in the Quzrada than a scuffle of two minor peoples, so remember, a mail shirt at all times under your tunic, and keep your bodyguard and sword close." Hontal rose and saluted  Captain Quinton, who returned the salute and then turned and left.

****

Schwartzman felt the comforting blast of wind from the open helicopter doorway while he and the rest of the 29th ID spearhead, a phalanx of heavy Sikorsky  Black Hawk helicopters, raced at tree top level across the African Savanna beneath them, consisting of grassland and widely spread apart trees. They had left the jungle canopy behind a few minutes ago and were now racing for a designated landing zone, 5 kilometers  south of an isolated island of jungle called the Juba Hills. For Zarko had revealed, before he died, the location of the alien base in the Congo Basin. This had been confirmed by ultra-sensitive magnetometer readings. It was in the Juba hills.  Now every allied military force was converging on the area.

Soon they were descending and he was leaping out of the helicopter into clouds of red dust.

Schwartzman was now assembling his command teams at the edge of the landing area as he clutched a map display and was shouting orders and pointing to locations for fortifications to be built. Soon teams were assembling to move north 1 kilometer and establish a front line as more Blackhawks in an endless stream from the south began lowering lightweight airmobile 155 mm artillery pieces and ammunition.

*Soon, we will bring the hammer down. Then all the terror you tried to create, will become your own.* He thought as the artillery was quickly set up and dug in by soldiers caked in red dust.

****

"Manny, can I have some time off?" asked Pamela with suppressed excitement. She was standing in Manny's office. It was a golden afternoon. The cherry blossoms had begun to appear.

603

Manny looked up from watching Marcy's coverage from Africa on his computer screen. In a few carefully edited minutes she had managed to convey the confusion and horror she had seen going up the river and at Katanga. He gathered from talking to her that what she had captured on tape, conveyed only the tip of the iceberg of the horrors she had seen there. Lamar was dead and she was lucky to be alive, that much Manny also understood. He had commended her. Marcy's coverage was adequate, in his opinion, since no other network was allowed near any real fighting, or could show the real horrors of the Congo. He had decided to be pleased with her. Manny now looked up a Pamela, who looked radiant and beside herself with joy.

"Vacation? Sure, when?" asked Manny

"Right now!" said Pamela with excitement. "Michael just called me, he popped up in Norfolk on leave. He wants me to come down so we can get married before he ships out again!" Manny rose happily, hugged her across his desk.

"Sure! But can you wait till Marcy and Cassandra get here?" he then countered. "I mean you're our star right now."

"Marcy will be here next morning, right? So let me do the 6 to 8 PM slot tonight and Marcy can cover tomorrow night!"

Manny nodded then received another hug from her again before she flew out of the office.

****

Cassandra, waited for Marcy to emerge from the dressing room. Pamela was off at Norfolk with her Navy Doctor. Cassandra had therefore immediately accepted Marcy's invitation to join her for a drink downstairs at "Nicky's", the bar and restaurant downstairs in the newly rebuilt CNS building. Marcy emerged looking fabulous in a black pantsuit. She had obviously matured professionally in the time Cassandra had been away. They quickly were in the bar downstairs sitting in a booth. Outside deep darkness had fallen.

604

"You look fabulous Cassie!" said Marcy as they began downing their drinks. Marcy was drinking Jack Daniels , Cassie was drinking a Cuba Libré. "So do you, girl," said Cassie. In the hyper-competitive world of television news, Cassandra had never felt close to Marcy before, but now she saw beyond the makeup and brilliant smile, the familiar pain of experienced horror.

"So how was Africa? I mean your coverage looked great. You looked great doing it too!" said Cassandra, sensing that this was what Marcy wanted to talk about. Marcy had only been back a day.

"Oh, let me have a few more of these first," said Marcy waving down the waiter and ordering two more drinks.  They arrived and she downed one immediately then sipped from the other. Marcy's face became pained. "You know my editor got killed there. Lamar Atkins, he was just some freelancer-adrenaline junkie like me. But he was a good man."

Cassandra saw horror in Marcy's eyes, the horror of remembrance. Cassandra ordered another drink herself, mentally braced herself.

"I mean he thought he knew the Congo,"  said Marcy looking far away. But he got in over his head there this time. Me too." she said.  "I grew up here in Anacostia  near the Navy Yard, crack, bullets, funerals, everything. I thought I would be tough enough to go into Africa and not let it get me." She was silent for a long time.

"Cassie do you know who to see, I mean  when you have seen stuff  you want to forget and you can't?" she asked, still looking far away.

"Yes, I am seeing this psychiatrist  named Petrosian. He has helped me a lot. He helped Pam too," said Cassandra cheerfully, trying to be helpful. She also ordered another drink.

"If  I go see him too, maybe Manny can get us all a group discount!" said Marcy with a bitter laugh. "I know you saw a lot of terrible things, it does things to you , doesn't it?" she said, with tears appearing in her eyes.

"Yes, but you can overcome it. Pam and I, we have overcome it," said Cassandra, feeling overwhelming sadness suddenly. *She wants to tell me something, something secret.*

"I saw him there," gasped Marcy, tears flowing down her cheeks.

"Who?" asked Cassandra. *Bob?*

"Your ex-boyfriend, the one you told to go to hell at the hospital."

Cassandra suddenly felt ice pierce her soul.

"Well, how was he?" asked Cassandra, as coldly as she could muster, taking a long drink.

"Oh, he was fine," said Marcy with a quivering voice. "I mean he saved me when Lamar got killed," said Marcy shutting her tear filled eyes. "He told me I wasn't supposed to talk about it. It was a classified mission. When they rescued me." she whispered. "They saved me, and it was this close." Marcy held up her thumb and index finger together. Something in the way she said this made Cassandra fill with rage.

Cassandra's eyes narrowed.

"So, you mean, he was fine in bed?" asked Cassandra staring Marcy in the face. Marcy looked down at the table.

"I think I better call you a cab Marcy," said Cassandra coldly. She fumbled in her purse found a card for Doctor Petrosian, and laid it carefully next to Marcy who was now quietly sobbing.

"It's OK Marcy," said Cassandra coldly, stroking Marcy's shoulder. "He's moved on, so have I," she said sadly. *The universe moves on, c'est la guerre...*

After calling Marcy a cab, Cassandra was riding the elevator up to the CNS offices, her mind was blank. She walked in past security, managing only a momentary smile until she got to the sanctuary of her office , sat down at her desk and exploded into tears. She covered her face with her hands.

606

"Bob? How could you!" she cried. "How could you be so cruel to me?"

****

Hontal left the ship with Gamal his bodyguard going before him. Hontal happily breathed the air of Tocon, his home planet near the star Alnilam. He was in the spaceport of Altok, a day's journey from his family's estate. But he noticed suddenly the chief servant of his household, waiting for him by the embarkation ramp, wearing a black cloak. Hontal's heart suddenly froze at this sight. The servant saw him and bowed his head silently in a sign of sorrow. Hontal rushed down the ramp to meet him.

"My Lord, your mother sends greetings and urges you to rush home," the servant, an old man in long service to the House of Lancom, bowed his head and wept. "My Lord, Mara, the goddess of sorrow now resides at your father's house."

"What has happened?" demanded Hontal.

"My Lord, your bride and your son, have both died as she was to bear him. Your mother craves you to come swiftly to your father's house to mourn with her." The news fell upon Hontal like a great stone falling from the sky, staggering him as he stood. He barely controlled his face, for a knight of the realm was supposed to bear all news, both good and bad, with public stoicism.

"I have brought steeds, my Lord, to bring you and your guard swiftly on your way.

Hontal then found himself riding through the dusty streets of Altok, lined with buildings of brick and wood, with his servant and guard Gamal. They did not speak to him, for they could see that his grief was very great. 'Women console each other, but a man bears sorrow alone,' was the saying of the Samar. The sun shone and in the streets children played; in the distance, white clouds rose, telling of a thunderstorm later that day. But to Hontal the world was black as night.

He also saw at the wall of a constable's office, many women and men gathered in the black of mourning. They were reading the list of the dead. For two starships crewed by men of Altok had been lost in the recent battle at Takgosh. So it seemed the whole world was caught up in tragedy to Hontal that day. He saw also further down the street where they rode, a group of young men was marching with their rucksacks, led by an officer of the fleet, many of them with only the faint beginnings of beards on their faces. Following after them was a group of weeping young girls. He knew the young men were headed for the spaceport to train for the fleet and the Tlaxian war.

*More cattle for the slaughter,* Hontal found himself thinking, shocked at his thoughts.

Around him Hontal saw a simple agrarian society, still using the ox for plowing and the steel sickle for mowing. No aircraft graced the skies over Altok, except the occasional starships coming and going, nor did motorized vehicles move on the street. The Samaran empire, and the aristocracy that ruled it, flew starships of super alloys faster than light, and employed nuclear weapons and powerful laser cannon in battle in the interstellar reaches, but that same aristocracy had banned such technologies on all but a few worlds of its vast realms, on the theory that such inventions would lead to the "decrease of virtue" among the common people. The Samarans wanted their people accustomed to hardship, so they would remain hard.

A long days ride down tree–lined, dusty, wagon roads found them at the Tavern of the Three Sisters, in Wagondell, a few hours ride from the great estate of Lacom. There, Hontal told his servants to go on, as he desired to be alone. In truth, he could not face seeing this mother's grief that night. His guard Gamal had protested, but to no avail. Well within the boundaries of his families fiefdom, Hontal wanted to manage his grief in solitude and thought of little else.

He took a room for the night at the tavern, hiding his royal pendant and its chain so as not to attract attention. He went up to the simple room and lay on the bed exhausted as night fell. He thought of his great journey and testimony at the Palace, his promotion to high knight, but all of that seemed useless and vain now. Only one thought comforted him, thoughts of Tatia on Una so far away, but thoughts of her filled him with such apprehension for her future that he finally rose from his bed and went downstairs to the main room of the tavern. The tavern had a large stone fireplace in which a merry fire burned, and a pot of fragrant oxen stew boiled. Several other men sat at the table talking and drinking ale or eating. He saw the owner of the tavern, a long-time resident of Wagondell, who knew Hontal and his family well.

"My Lord Hontal, I offer my condolences at you families sorrow." said tavern owner bowing his head. His attractive daughter stood near as well with her head bowed and sadness on her face.

"Yes," he sighed. "He laid down his cloak at a table, and the tavern owner brought him a mug of honey ale. "Some of your savory stew will also do me well," said Hontal, he had not eaten all day. The tavern owners daughter turned and got him a large bowl and spoon, and then he followed her to the stewpot on the fire and she served him a full bowl of the good oxen stew with spices and poached grain. She then gave him a chunk of freshly baked bread. He walked back to his table with this and sat down heavily after thanking the girl.

However, at his table beside his mug of ale was now someone's hat. It was a grey peaked hat with wide brim and a long feather in it. Hontal looked around for its owner in mild annoyance, and then pushed it aside and had a drink of ale and spoonful of stew.

Suddenly a bearded, strong looking man appeared in front of where he sat.

"Sir , you have moved my hat." said the man with a smirk.

"It was placed on my table."

"You have insulted my hat. You have moved it from its prominent place."

Hontal then realized that he was not wearing his royal pendant, it was up in his room with his clothes.

"I meant no offense to your hat, sir, you merely foolishly mislaid it on my table. So I moved it," said Hontal with menace in his voice.

"If you insult my hat, you insult the head that wears it," said the man moving closer.

Hontal rose from behind his table, placed his hand on his sword hilt. He saw the tavern owner's daughter standing nearby, in his peripheral vision.

"Good, sir, know that I am a knight of the realm, and my blade is ty-alloy, and if you continue to trifle with me, I will lift off your insulted head with it."

"I invite you then to step outside in the alley with me, so-called knight and try to remove my head from its appointed place. " The man then turned and waved his hand at the side door, and raised his cloak to reveal a fine sword.

Hontal turned to the serving girl, who looked petrified.

"Keep this stew warm for me, this will take but a moment," he said angrily. He then strode after the man through the side door. He was seething with anger, and not thinking.

He walked out into the dark drawing his sword when suddenly he felt a crushing pain in his chest and fell backward against the stone wall of the tavern feebly trying to hold his sword up and thrust it against whomever had hit him.

"Finish him! Earn your gold!" yelled someone. But then came the rush of feet out the tavern door. It was the tavern keeper swinging an axe. Gamal, his bodyguard flew past. Then came the cry of "Constable! Constable! The Constable is here!"

He felt strong arms lift him and carry him inside. His chest felt as though it had been crushed and he reached up with his remaining strength and felt blood pouring from a wound. Then blackness.

**\*\*\*\***

Hontal became aware of voices. Someone was talking right above him. 'a poison blade', his mail shirt saved him," said the voice. He could not even open his eyes. He felt intense cold spreading over his body. He heard his mother's voice weeping. *My father's house, it perishes with me, I am last of his sons...*he sensed his life slipping away and his father's house with it. *My own son is dead.*

"My sword, give me my sword." he gasped with all his strength. Suddenly his mother's voice broke into sobs. Like any good knight of the Samar he wanted to die 'sword in hand.' Strong hands put the hilt of his sword in his hands and laid it on his chest. He now awaited death as the unbearable cold spread through him to every limb.

Unbearable sadness overwhelmed him as he slipped into blackness. The gods of the Samar did not receive prayers from knights, except prayers for victory, every other request to the gods was handled by women, for even the gods of the Samar delighted in hardiness. He thought of Tatiana, and for one last moment he saw light, he cried out in complete desperation , *God of gods, God of Erra, save my house, let my father's house not die...I pledge my sword to thy service...Tatiana.* Then blackness overwhelmed him.

****

"I am being deployed again. I may not be back for several months," said Captain Robert Forrester.

"You didn't volunteer for another secret mission? HAVEN'T YOU DONE ENOUGH?" cried his wife Deidre. It was late at night in Cocoa Beach, Florida. The stars shone brightly. The children were asleep, the house was silent, but the night of love they had planned was now empty.

"Where this time? Mars?" she wept. He was silent. "Beyond Mars?" she demanded tearfully. He was silent. He tried to embrace her but she pushed him away. "Don't you realize that when you go away part of me dies!"

611

"When you come back, the children and I, we won't be here." she wept. He stood facing her without emotion.

****

"Jason, what the fuck is going on?" demanded Schwartzman, as he stumbled out of his dugout quarters in the battalion CP. He was wearing his fatigue pants and a green tee shirt. He watched in confusion as several Black Hawk helicopters, lowered large containers of what looked like a communications trailer to the ground amid clouds of dust.

"Where's our two other rifle companies?" he asked turning to Lt. Colonel Parker.

"Change in orders Colonel! General Alvarez says we have to run a classified technology op!" said Parker shaking his head. He handed Schwartzman a printed set of orders. "They want to fly some new high-tech classified drone, they call it operation Wizard. Some young major named Taryton is in charge.

"Get me Alvarez on the horn! We got them unprepared if we hit them now! Today, with a reinforced. battalion! I know it! We got no time for this Mr. Science bullshit!" roared Schwartzman. He whirled and stalked back into the dugout. He went to the radio man and grabbed the headset and put it on.

"Mike! Is that you? General, with all due respect, what the hell are we doing here? We have these maggots if we hit them now! We got them with their pants down! We see no preparations for ground defense here at all!"

"Yeah, I know Lance!" came General Miguel Alvarez deep voice from the headphones. They were all using his nom de guerre now. "This op has been ordered from the top. It's a new armed drone with a supposedly unbreakable encryption com link. We have orders to stand down for two days so they can run this op and test this new technology."

"That's crazy, General! That gives those motherfuckers up in that sand pile two days to prepare for our assault! If we hit them today we can take this

612

place easy! I know it! Besides, you know what happed the last time they tried flying an armed drone against the Greys. They hacked into the come link, turned it around on the unit flying it, and they lost forty men!"

"Yeah, I know, but this comes down from the Joint Chiefs. They want to get armed drones flying because they have lost so many fighter pilots. They say this is a direct order, Colonel. So you get this operation run, and then get me a report. I'll use these two days to get more troops and artillery up there and more air support for an attack two days from now. "

"General, What about the French? In two days they will be here. If I attack today we can keep them out of this!"

"Colonel, you run this op like we are supposed to! That's an order! We have established unit boundaries so the French have to stay north of parallel 3, North 55 50. If you have any trouble from them you call me!"

"Yes General!" said Schwartzman snapping to attention. He put down the headset and yelled obscenities for several minutes.

Jason stood near him.

"They're turning this thing into a science project!" said Schwartzman angrily to Jason. They then made arrangements to meet with the Operation Wizard team.

****

Major Steven Taryton, a short, stocky young man with an aura of intense self-importance led the briefing in the dugout of the Battalion Command Post. The portable computer projector shown its image on a bedsheet hung from the wooden tree-trunks making up the ceiling of the dugout. They were denuding the Savanna of trees in the area as more troops, a Nigerian Special forces battalion, arrived and was digging in. Schwartzman, Lt. Colonel Parker, Arizona, Taryton and a short scrawny civilian, with his brown hair in a ponytail and with a goatee named Linus Quisling. He was wearing simple green fatigues. Krueger and Macmillan, the mercenaries, also sat by, looking on with interest. *The problem of having a military in wartime is that it attracts both men of nobility and*

613

*men of shameless self-advancement, like this asshole...*thought Schwartzman.

"Gentlemen, operation Wizard uses the combination of a revolutionary new computer processor design with a new double encrypted data link system to achieve what we believe will be a nearly automatous drone controlled by an absolutely secure comlink." began Taryton. "Basically, the drone thinks on its own, and therefore, needs almost no communications to do its job of surveillance, target acquisition, and attack. When it does communicate, it does so by a revolutionary new system of doubly encrypted data streams." The image shown on the screen was of a fairly conventional, propeller driven, high endurance drone carrying four hellfire missiles under its wings. Schwartzman winced at the sight of the missiles, was filled with grave misgivings, but remembered he was under orders to carry out the operation. So he sat quietly. "I will now let Dr. Quisling speak about the drone computer and comlink," continued Taryton. Quisling rose. He was a dour pale individual who looked like he was having a bad bout of Congolese Revenge. *What is this ponytailed geek doing here on the frontlines of this war?* thought Schwartzman, suppressing feelings of rage as he watched Quisling walk to the position beside the screen.

"Thank you, Major, I want you all to know that you are participating in not just a first frontline test of a new weapons technology but also a transformative event in human evolution . The drone we will launch contains the first conscious computer, a fully independent actor, fully integrating all its sensor inputs to make rational decisions and carry out orders. This means the human side of this war is now a human-cyber alliance! For this reason, it needs almost no communication with us to perform its mission, which will be to scout the alien installation, locate targets there and attack them." Quisling showed a series of nearly incomprehensible slides showing what appeared to be the sensor systems, a complex diagram of the computer and double encryption system. Schwartzman shot an amused glance at Arizona, who smiled and shook his head. This reminded him of the periodic pep talks from the Magi during the UFO Cover-up days.

"We call this drone the "Demon" because of the automatous conscious computer which guides it." continued Quisling. Schwartzman acquired a look of impatience.

"Pardon me Doctor, but demon isn't a term we go throwing around here in the Congo. It makes our native troops superstitious. So I request you stow that name for this op." said Schwartzman as pleasantly as he could muster.

"Well it shouldn't be a problem Colonel, it's only written on the tail and the wings."

"Well, paint it over then," said Schwartzman coldly.

"Why should it be a problem, most of the natives here can't read," said Quisling indignantly.

"The Nigerians read English just fine Doctor. Now find some paint and paint over that name. Or there's no op," said Schwartzman sharply, shooting an angry glance to Major Taryton. Taryton looked properly terrorized and immediately spoke up.

"Linus, tell the Colonel the name will be painted over."

"OK, we'll paint over the name." said Quisling grudgingly.

"I want this op launched at 0500 tomorrow. Is that going to be a problem?" asked Schwartzman rising from his chair. "No Colonel, everything looks nominal for 0500." said Taryton.

"I also want a flight plan for this drone when it's within one kilometer of our lines."

"Colonel you don't understand, the Demon has a mind of its own. It is supposed to intelligently figure out which route to fly," said Quisling.

"Well, if your drone is truly intelligent," said Schwartzman smiling, "then you should explain to it clearly, that if it deviates from the flight plan within one kilometer of our lines, or begins flying back towards our lines while still carrying those Hellfire missiles, then we will shoot it down."

This prospect seemed to fill Quisling with enough terror that Schwartzman felt he was being taken seriously.

"So a flight plan at O-500 tomorrow," said Schwartzman now looking at Major Taryton, who saluted nervously.

He shot a glance at Parker who was barely suppressing laughter.

"Yes Colonel!" said Taryton.

"Good, see you in the morning then," said Schwartzman smiling. Taryton and Quisling picked up their computer projector and filed out into the darkness. When they had left. Schwartzman turned to Jason Parker.

"Jason, I want every soldier on alert for this test tomorrow and want every piece of ordinance we have, tracking that drone, especially that new 1-megawatt laser. If it begins deviating from the prescribed flight path, or you see me fire a red flare indicating its comlink has been compromised, I want you to light it up with everything you have," said Schwartzman. "Understood?" Everyone nodded. He turned to Arizona. "Arizona, I want you to set up a temporary CP a hundred meters back from this one and evacuate this CP during the test. You are all dismissed, get some sack time." The men filed out except for Arizona.

"I have a really bad feeling about this op Arizona," said Schwartzman with a laugh. "For one thing, I don't think I have ever met a bigger idiot masquerading as a scientist than this fuck-wit Quisling. And unless the Greys are a lot stupider than I thought, it will take them less than a heartbeat to break any encryption technique this asshole can write."

****

The morning was sunny and still when at 0500 Operation Wizard was launched. The Drone, a now painted dull grey, to Schwartzman's satisfaction, launched perfectly, boosted into the air with rockets. It flew north over them gracefully. It was being monitored from a dull green electronics trailer partly dug in 30 meters behind them near the launcher. Schwartzman watched it fly over warily, noting four deadly Hellfire Missiles under its wings. He had two flare guns loaded with red flares, in case the aliens hacked into the drone's control circuits and sent it back at them. He noted happily that a nearby 50 caliber machine gun mounted on a stand was tracking the drone as it flew over.

Schwartzman stood in a trench near the now evacuated Battalion CP, standing next to Arizona and Krueger and Macmillan, who had deployed their mercenaries further down the trench line. Schwartzman now regarded their presence and advice as indispensable. The fact that they seemed nervous about the whole Wizard operation did nothing to help his mood. Lt. Colonel Parker was 1,000 meters to the south in the temporary CP.

"I notice our young Major Taryton is not here in the front trenches," said Arizona to Schwartzman with a grin.

"Yeah he's back with Parker at the secondary CP." retorted Schwartzman acidly, as he watched the drone fly north through his range finding binoculars. "Not a great sign of confidence in our Doctor Quisling's creation, me thinks. "

"So far, so good. It's out past a kilometer," said Schwartzman. He was watching the range finder readout display inside the binoculars below the image. In the misty distance, some 3 kilometers beyond, he could see the dark mass of the Juba Hills, an island of jungle in the Savanna several kilometers across. The drone was now just a grey dot in the morning haze even in his binoculars. He blinked suddenly. The range readout suddenly quit changing and held steady, then started decreasing. The drone had turned around and was now coming back at them. For an instant, he was mesmerized by the dark grey dot now growing larger in the binoculars.

Suddenly the door on the electronic trailer flew open and Linus Quisling leaped out screaming and running toward Schwartzman and the others. Schwartzman whirled around to face him.

"COLONEL! COLONEL! WE HAVE AN ANOMALY!" Quisling was screaming frantically.

Schwartzman spun around and again found the drone in the binoculars, it was now speeding towards them.

Spastically he grabbed a flare gun, with obscenities spewing from his mouth, and pointed it up in the sky. Just then the first Hellfire missile ignited under drones wing, he pulled the trigger and with a loud bang a red flare went up.

"NO! NO! DON"T SHOOT IT!" Quisling was screaming as he ran towards him.

"LIGHT IT UP! MEN! OPEN FIRE! OPEN FIRE!" Schwartzman yelled as he and the others ducked into the trench and a Hellfire missile screamed past them and hit the electronics trailer with a deafening explosion and a thunderous fusillade of gunfire erupted all along the front line . The explosion of the electronic trailer blew the hapless Quisling into the trench with them, as every automatic weapon on the line poured tracers into the morning sky at the oncoming drone, now definitely trying to kill them all.

A second Hellfire missile now hit the abandoned CP near them filling the air with choking red dust and the smell of cordite. As Schwartzman's ears quit ringing he heard a chorus of automatic gun and cannon fire and 50 caliber machine guns blazing away. The dust hid everything, but soon the barrage of gunfire ended and Schwartzman rejoiced inwardly as he heard war whoops of triumph, indicating the homicidal drone had been shot down. He jumped out of the trench and ran clear of the dust cloud to survey the scene. The drone had flown over them and crashed in flames two hundred meters behind them, fortunately not being able to fire its remaining Hellfire missiles, whose warheads were now exploded in the fire, flinging flaming wreckage all over the landscape. Schwartzman, now shaking with rage, surveyed the destroyed electronics trailer and the smoking crater that had been his CP and spun around and walked rapidly back to the trench where Quisling had now risen and was wailing like a child over his destroyed creation. As the dust settled Schwartzman launched himself at Quisling as Arizona and Krueger tried to stop him. Quisling fell after two punches to the face and Schwartzman was now kicking him viscously in the stomach in the bottom of the trench as Quisling screamed for help. Arizona managed to pull Schwartzman away from Quisling.

"YOU DUMB FUCK I"LL KILL YOU! "Schwartzman was yelling. Schwartzman pulled out his pistol and aimed it at Quisling's head as he screamed and cowered on the floor of the trench.

"NO BOSS, HE AIN"T WORTH KILLING!" Arizona was yelling. "HE AIN"T WORTH THE BULLET!" Arizona paused breathlessly. Schwartzman regained his senses. "BOSS YOU"RE IN ENOUGH TROUBLE ALREADY!"

Schwartzman, still pointing the gun at Quisling, looked at Arizona dully. Schwartzman was still shaking with rage.

"WHAT ARE OUR CASUALTIES!!? " he demanded hoarsely.

"NO CAUSULTIES FOR OUR PEOPLE REPORTED SIR! EVERYBODY WAS DUG IN AS PER YOUR ORDERS! IT FLEW IN STRAIGHT AND LEVEL AND WE KNOCKED IT DOWN, SIR!" yelled Arizona frantically. Schwartzman looked at Krueger and MacMillan, both covered with red dust, looking at him nodding. Both men smiled weakly. Schwartzman hesitated, then, abruptly lowered his pistol, then put it back in its holster.

"The Wizard people, they lost two people in the electronics support trailer," said Arizona quietly after Schwartzman holstered his pistol. Schwartzman nodded and looked contemptuously at Quisling.

"Get this piece of shit out of my sight and out of my perimeter," he snapped to Arizona, motioning backward at Quisling, still who lay weeping in the trench. Schwartzman turned and walked back up the trench line to where the radio was. Arizona, Krueger, and MacMillan followed him. The drone, with its still full fuel tanks, was burning fiercely, sending a column of black smoke into the blue morning sky, as he saw soldiers emerging from their fox holes and trenches to watch it burn. They were all smiling with relief and waving their guns and shouting in triumph. A wave of relief overcame him at this sight of everyone moving around freely. No medics or stretcher bearers, just joyful milling around.

"Those clowns!" he said to Arizona, then nodded. "A modest victory, but still a victory of sorts," he laughed. "Look at them. Happy about shooting down our own fucking drone!" He laughed despite himself. "WHAT A GREAT DAY FOR SCIENCE!" he laughed loudly. He then sat down in

619

exhaustion at the edge of the trench and watched the drone burn. He began thinking of what to say in his after-action report about Operation Wizard. *Except for the assassination of her husband, Mrs. Lincoln thoroughly enjoyed the play,* he thought as he pondered how to begin the after-action report.

****

The next morning, with Operation Wizard concluded, dawn broke over the African Savanna. Schwartzman had been able to move two more batteries of air portable M777 155 mm Howitzers up in the night, and more ammunition for all of them. He now had a reinforced battalion of two thousand men, including 3 companies of Nigerian Army Rangers. Krueger and MacMillan were up near the Juba Hills in the distance with their teams of mercenaries. They had reported a vast number of African game, everything from Zebras to Wildebeest had taken shelter in the small patch of forest that covered the Juba Hills. Adding to the complications, the French had arrived the previous night and had announced they would to attack the alien base from the North the next day. Relations between the French and American task forces were not cordial. The liaison on the French side, only known as a voice on the radio, was some annoying officer named Captain Duvalier, whom Parker insisted on calling Pierre, apparently much to Duvalier's annoyance.

"Look at this operational goat fuck!" said Schwartzman in disgust pointing at the map in the newly dug out Battalion CP. The French zone of operation now bisected the Juba Hills with a line running east-west on parallel 54 22, dividing the postulated underground alien base into two sectors, North and South. The southern portion of the hills was theirs, the North was the French operation zone. "I just hope the southern part of that base has the latrines in it! Now we have to worry about friendly fire from the French down in the tunnels once we penetrate the base! If had just attacked two days ago, I know we would have had the Greys with their pants down! It would have been a cakewalk! Now the Greys are ready for us and we have the French to worry about also." roared Schwartzman as parker and Arizona listened patiently.

620

"Well boss, maybe the Greys will decide the French are more dangerous, and they'll get all the letters home." said Parker with a grin. Schwartzman frowned, then laughed.

"Are Krueger and Mac's people dug in up there?" asked Schwartzman. "How about Alpha Company, do we positively know where everyone is, so we can start the bombardment?"

"Yes sir, Russgovic's people are dug in here a thousand yards from the hills to the East, and Krueger and Mac's people are dug in a thousand yards to the south also but to the West." Schwartzman nodded.

"Tell the artillery to open fire," said Schwartzman tersely, as he stepped outside the CP looked through the binoculars. To the South of them, three batteries of 155 mm Howitzers had lifted their muzzles skyward at high elevation to lob shells onto the Juba Hills. Lt Colonel George Parker, at his side, barked orders into his radio. The guns now lit up with huge yellow muzzle flashes as the bombardment began and soon the thunder of 155 mm artillery swept across the plain. In Schwartzman's binoculars, the forested hills of Juba erupted in fire and explosions. As he expected, a stampeding mob of African livestock exploded out of the forest's edge in terror.

He looked with a moment of pity at several of the animals running wounded, then hardened his heart. Soon, the forest had emptied of whatever livestock could still run and Schwartzman ordered the artillery fire intensified. He then readied the rest of the battalion to begin moving forward.

Suddenly, a frantic radio call came in. Parker, given the French presence, was now taking in the radio calls.

"What!" Parker yelled. He then exploded into obscenities.

" What's going on!" demanded Schwartzman.

'It's Captain Russgovic from Alpha company! He says a bunch of French Foreign Legion armored cars just rolled through his position from the North, headed due south! He wants to know if he should open fire on

621

them?" Arizona, manning the other radio, suddenly yelled" Colonel! Krueger reports French armored cars rolling south past his position!

"What the Hell!" exclaimed Schwartzman. Then suddenly a terrible realization hit him. *I am now the objective of the French operation here.*

"Pierre, Pierre! We have spotted your forces South of the 54 22 parallel! Tell your forces to stop and retreat North of the line! Now!" Parker was yelling on the French radio frequency.

Parker threw down the headset and picked up the com-link to the 155mm batteries.

"Crawford! Crawford! Stop the bombardment of the Juba Hills! We need you to drop smoke on a parallel North 500 yards from of our lines and standby on my orders for a walking bombardment with HE north from that new line!"

Schwartzman felt suddenly sick. He reached for his pistol, gripped it.

"Colonel I think you need to direct this battle from the backup Command Post back by the battery," said Parker grimly, turning to Schwartzman. "You leave the French to us and concentrate on the Greys." Just then a series of white phosphorus shells impacted in a line 500 yards to the North. White smoke now obscured everything. There was a new radio message.

"A Colonel Duvalier needs to speak with you, Colonel Parker! He says it's an emergency." said the radio operator.

"Well roll me in flour, and call me a biscuit!" laughed Parker taking the phone. "Bon Jour Pierre!" Parker listened intently, then smiled broadly. "Well, you better get your French asses back north of the unit boundary we agreed on Colonel!" Schwartzman, sensing he was now a distraction, boarded a Humvee and was swiftly taken South to the backup CP near the 155 mm gun batteries. The guns were firing with barrels at high elevation, to make for plunging shells land on target. However, they were now falling silent as the French vehicles were reported to be withdrawing.

622

"What a goat fuck!" muttered Schwartzman as he was scanning the now smoke-filled battlefield with his binoculars, several staff officers stood beside him in a trench. Suddenly he saw brilliant flashes. He then saw several French armored cars emerge from the smoke, headed towards their lines, he then saw one of them disintegrate into a ball of fire and molten steel.

"What the Hell?" he muttered to himself in confusion as he scanned the clearing clouds of smoke. "Who's firing at who now?"

"Sir! Colonel Parker reports enemy vehicles have come out of the forest!" said a nearby Lieutenant.

He looked and saw several silver manta shaped vehicles floating above the ground coming out of the smoke. A brilliant blue beam of light come from one of them and hit two of the other French armored cars causing them to explode into white hot fireballs.

*Oh my God! The Greys are coming out of their holes after us!* thought Schwartzman in sudden fear.

"Chadwick! Shift fire to Antitank! Antitank!" he turned and saw the 155 mm guns now lowering to fire flat-trajectory hypervelocity armor-piercing rounds. In a few seconds, the air was rent by the scream of high-velocity anti-tank shells flying over the savannah a few feet over the heads of the men in the forward trenches. The shells had red tracer charges in them shining brilliantly as they few. Schwartzman now watched with mounting desperation as the armor piercing shells ricocheted off the silver craft in the distance, as they now raked the nearby ground with the blue death rays, igniting the grass of the Savanna and, as Schwartzman now saw, running figures of men on fire.

"Use Teflon antiforce-field rounds! Load with Russian Teflon rounds! TEFLON ROUNDS!" ordered Schwartzman. In an instant, blue tracer rounds were snapping across the Savanna towards the manta-shaped ships. He was only guessing that the craft, which looked like standard "seagull" type grey craft, had been modified to be hovercraft with force fields, as had happened on one occasion before. He watched with astonished fascination as a blue tracer shell seemed to explode in mid-air

623

near one of the craft and project a beam of white hot material into the silver craft, causing it to explode in flames. Within seconds he watched two more blue tracer shells explode and then impale two silver craft which then erupted into flames. The shells, developed by the Russians, exploded on contact with the electromagnet force fields around the manta-shaped ships, and explosively formed and launched a projectile of pure diamond-hard cross-branched Teflon to hit the ship itself. Teflon having the ability to cross powerful EM fields with no effect.

Now all three silver ships were burning brilliantly on the Savanna putting out clouds of white smoke as their magnesium aluminum alloy hulls burned. The 155 mm guns fell silent, having run out of targets, and the battlefield fell silent. Schwartzman scanned the scene with utter relief.

"Now Chadwick! Hit the hills with high explosive! Pound them!" Schwartzman yelled into the radio. He picked up the other radio.

Col Parker! I want bravo Charlie and the Nigerian companies to move forward as we bombard the hills! I want them to find exposed entrances and storm the base!"

**\*\*\*\***

Pamela had walked with Michael into the cottage that he had rented on the beach near Norfolk and began unbuttoning his Navy Khaki uniform shirt. He looked devilishly handsome, and leaner, more muscular.

"Oh I have missed you so much!" she wept as she began smothering him with kisses. She was pushing him into the bedroom as she pulled his shirt off his powerful frame. He was trying to say something but she was kissing him so much he finally gave up as they rolled on the bed, and she was shedding her clothes.

"I love you! I love you, Michael!" she was crying"

**\*\*\*\***

On the C-17 flying back to the United States, a bottle of Bacardi Rum was being passed around as Schwartzman, Arizona, and Lt. Col Parker sat in the passenger area near the wounded.

624

Schwartzman, still in his jungle fatigues and green beret, was grim, as he took a large swallow from the rum bottle and passed it to Parker. Parker and Arizona were in a festive mood, however.

"Well chief, that's three alien bases under your belt now," said Arizona. "I hear General Alvarez is putting you in for a Silver Star and were headed back to the states to prepare for lunar operations.

"We lost too many men," said Schwartzman somberly. Most of Alpha company, the mercs, Mac and Krueger, those were all good men. He was staring at the deck of the transport shaking his head, cradling the bottle. Parker and Arizona looked on him sadly.

"Chief, it was a hard fight," said Parker. "That and the French screwing up the assault, but we overran the base anyway. They were ready for us this time."

"Yeah, but that screw up here was because of me. Because I was here," responded Schwartzman. He looked up wearily, took another long drink.

"The French got their ass kicked really bad, though, they maybe lost a whole battalion," said Parker trying to sound encouraging. "So they paid for it. We also saw where they massacred a bunch of Greys who wanted to surrender at the end, down in the tunnels. We just figured it was their sector, they can do what they want with the Greys there. It wasn't pretty, but we got the job done, Chief." continued Parker. "The tech people are going crazy over those three seagull craft modified to be hovercraft, the hypervelocity Teflon slugs went right through their force fields, but they said there was enough left of one of them to get good technical intel. This is the second time they have used modified seagull type craft as ground vehicles, so they are clearly shifting tactics, Chief. The other time was down in Patagonia in Chile, the tech people said. The Chileans simply retreated and took out the craft out with land mines, but you showed we could get them with these Teflon rounds. Most of the other bases they either abandoned or just fought it out in the tunnels before this. This is the only second time they have come out looking for a fight."

"Yeah, I didn't expect a big fight," said Schwartzman with regret. "But, why should they change tactics now?"

"Good question," said Arizona. "When this war started there were at least 100 alien bases identified. This was the last known base on Earth. The only base we know of now is up on the Lunar far side, and that's our next stop."

"What was in the base that you could see, Arizona?" asked Schwartzman suddenly. He had been forced to stay back because of the French. Arizona, whose identity was untraceable in the Carny, was considered safe enough to send in after the base was taken.

"It was a butcher shop like all the others Boss, you didn't miss nothing by not going in there. I saw one room that must have had a pile of bones of a thousand people or more. Other rooms were full of fresh bodies."

"Why do they hate us so much?" asked Jason Parker vacantly, as he listened holding the half empty rum bottle. "What did we ever do to them, that they would come 400 light years to butcher people like this."

"I wondered about that a long time, during the cover-up, Jason, I never understood it then," said Schwartzman. "Now after seeing everything, I think it's because they sense that we are already what they can never be. It's like an old blind man hating a child who can see. They are a ruined people somehow, the Greys, a shadow of what once was somebody. Now they are the lost children of the cosmos somehow, grown old and hard, and we, despite our numerous flaws, are princes and princesses to them. They envy and hate us because they are already destroyed somehow, and we are fresh and new." Schwartzman paused. "Just like I envy other people, who never even heard of the UFO cover up except what they read in the tabloids in a grocery store checkout line. I envy people who aren't dodging warrants from the French for crimes against humanity."

"Boss, you're really tired and not thinking straight," said Arizona looking nervously at Parker and then back at Schwartzman. "You know that French thing is chicken-shit, you got a pardon and medal from the US government for your service. But you been up 48 hours straight. You ought to get some sack time in."

"I want to sleep. I wanted the big sleep many times, during the cover-up," said Schwartzman drunkenly. "I thought 'I will never be able to get myself

626

out of this, I'm trapped', but something made me keep going. 'In honor there is hope' is an old Roman Army saying, and I hung on to that. Then she came along," Schwartzman produced a plastic enclosed picture of Cassandra from his fatigue pocket. It was a picture of her face smiling pleasantly. Arizona recognized it from the rescue operation at Morningstar, when everyone was given her picture to identify her. Arizona stared at her picture transfixed. "She gave me hope," said Schwartzman. "I mean hope like I was a dead man, and she brought me back to life." He took the rum bottle from Parker and held it then took a long drink from it. It eased his pain.

"She gave me hope too boss. The other Carny men too," said Arizona quickly.

"Yeah, when we got her out of that hell hole at Morningstar, we came to that room full of bones, and I remember like in a dream pulling out my Berretta and putting it to my head, because I thought, I feared this was happening. And now, here I am face to face with it, and I'll never get clean of my role in this horror story as long as I live. It's over. And I was going to pull the trigger, but she was there crying, saying 'no you have to get me out of here, you can't leave me here', and I guess I decided to err on the side of duty instead of ending it there. And for a while in the hospital, when we got out of the place, when I didn't know what was going to happen to me, I actually hated her for stopping me from killing myself, then and there, back under that Mesa, and dying honorably. But then I thought, no, that if it wasn't for her, I would be dead in that place, and the whole human race with us. Because I know nothing short of a miracle could change the course we were all on. With the Greys and the Magi taking over the government, nothing but a pair of archangels straight out of the sky carrying flaming swords could change the course we were on. And suddenly there they were. I mean Arizona, you were there, how did you do it? I faced such black despair sometimes...black despair"

Arizona took the bottle from him, grinned and took a long drink.

"Easy Boss, I guess I just thought, you and General Trenton had some secret plan to get us out of that jam we were in. I mean we all knew we

627

were up shit creek, but we thought, you and General Trenton will get us out of here." Arizona smiled and nodded, handed the bottle to Parker, who took a drink and handed it back to Schwartzman. "That's what the rest of the men thought too sir. And admit it, you got us all out with honor!"

"You dumb clowns!" laughed Schwartzman sadly. "Trenton and I, we didn't know what the fuck we were doing! We felt utterly helpless. We were like on a big train rolled towards a cliff, and we all knew where it was going, but all we could do was ride it." Schwartzman looked down in anguish, then forced himself to smile. "But then her and the blonde," he waved Cassandra's picture, "they pulled bobby pins out of their hair, stuck them on the tracks or something, and derailed the whole fucking train! I still wonder at it, how they managed to pull it off. It was a miracle, like the parting of the Red Sea." Schwartzman slumped down on the hard metal deck of the jet transport. Arizona took the rum bottle out of his hand and slid a folded blanket under his head.

"They both paid the price for it, though, the blonde stopped a bullet, almost got killed. Cassie got captured, I rescued her, but she probably won't ever be the same. I couldn't really save her in the end." murmured Schwartzman, as Arizona and Parker spread a blanket over him. He was soon dead asleep.

"With all due respect Colonel, I notice you asked for a transfer to keep serving under Colonel Schwartz, as his unit vice," said Arizona to Parker, and he prepared to lay down on one of the aluminum benches in the hold of the jet transport. Parker was also preparing for sleep. "I figured they were gonna give you the 44th Ranger Battalion with a promotion to full bird Colonel after this op. I just hope you know that the Boss is probably stuck at Colonel for the duration because Congress has to OK his promotion to General officer, and I hear they can't do it with this French thing hanging over his head. So we here in the 42nd; we're stuck in a holding pattern with him."

"Yeah, well Major, I sure don't want to miss out on this next big op," said Parker wearily. "Call me crazy, but I figure wherever the action is, old Colonel Schwartz will find his way right to the middle of it. The man obviously has a widely recognized genius for finding trouble and dealing with it. So I figured all I need to do is stay right by his side, and I'd be on the far side of the Moon before you know it. That may not be a regular Army promotion, but it sure beats shining my boots on Earth for the rest of this war. " Parker then seemed to doze off, but then spoke groggily, " So goodnight Major..."

**\*\*\*\***

## Chapter 14: Beaches

Cassandra looked through tear filled eyes at the CNS staff assembled in the main break room and the glorious "welcome back" banner. It was noon. Her official return to the office from Morningstar had been sudden, but the crew at CNS had thrown together a joyous celebration in any case. Cassie's tears were tears of joy. She had never felt so physically strong and fit in her life, so full of confidence. Everyone was there, and cheering her, Manny, Bob, Darleen, a score of new young faces, mixed with old veterans still bearing scars from the night of the coup. Marcy Braxton appeared looking radiant, came up and hugged her, barely meeting her eyes, then quickly disappeared to do the morning news. *Awkward but still nice,* thought Cassandra. *What does it mean? Someday I'll understand, I'll sit down and think about all this sometime and make sense out of it. She had been telling this to herself for weeks now.*

"Thank you, thank you!" Cassandra yelled above the applause and turned to cut the glorious cake, slicing off a tiny piece for herself to uproarious laughter. *The last thing I want to do is gain weight now,* she thought. Manny, himself looking fit and trim took a more generous slice, to everyone's delight, and Cassandra beamed beside him. She was wearing a dark red dress, clinging deliciously to her well-toned statuesque frame. Cassandra beamed as she scanned the room hopefully, for Pamela, knowing Pam was on vacation, but hoping she would appear anyway.

"Where is Pammy taking her vacation anyway?" she asked Manny, as he washed down some vanilla frosted chocolate cake with some champagne. "Virginia Beach with her boyfriend Michael," said Manny with a broad smile. "She deserves it too, after what she went through, out in the North Pacific"

"What happened, I heard about the naval battle, the destruction of the alien undersea base, and that she was there, but I haven't had time to learn anything more," said Cassandra.

"I am not going to spoil her telling you the salty sea tale herself," said Manny as he beamed at her and clapped Cassie on the shoulder. "But she ended up getting a Navy medal and command of her own ship, so to speak, she also got us some good footage!" She did great!" Despite herself, Cassie felt a slight tinge of competitive envy. *Oh well*, she thought, *that's my girl. But I am back now! Information overload...so much to sort out.*

Darlene walked up smiling and hugged her, then pulled her aside, her face suddenly clouded.

"Pam is on the phone for you, Cassie, she's on hold in your office," said Darlene motioning to Cassie's office door down the hall. "She sounded upset," Darlene added, looking seriously at Cassandra. Cassandra, her heart leaping with delight and concern, set down her champagne quickly, and with a smile at everyone dashed off down the hall to her office.

Cassandra noted with satisfaction that her office was as she had left it, and had been regularly dusted in her absence. She kicked the door shut deftly with one of her high heels while grabbing the phone and hitting the blinking line.

"Pam it's Cassie! Are you there! "Cassie heard only a gasp of breath at the other end of the line.

"Cassie," she heard a trembling voice, "could you come down to see me...here?" said Pamela

Cassandra felt her heart suddenly feel like breaking.

"Sure Pammy, I can come down right now." said Cassandra in her most reassuring voice" what's wrong baby?"

"Can you come down, like now." Pam's voice faltered. "I'll send you a map, I need you to come down...as soon as you can..."

"Sure Pammy, I will come down right now. My bags are still in the car! What's wrong, can you talk about it?"

"It's Michael,"... Pam's voice cracked, "they took him away!"

Cassie was quickly then was flying down the freeway to the South in her rented red Ferrari.

****

Dr. Petrosian  sat in his car at Arlington Hospital, bracing himself for the arduous process of getting out of his car and into his wheelchair. He had been offered an assistant but had refused,  as he waited to start the process of his wheelchair being deployed robotically outside his driver seat.  The temperatures were warm that day. He noticed a minor drama occurring in the parking lot.  Someone, a young East Asian woman, with long black hair, was being arrested. Several military police stood by.  A regular policewoman was putting handcuffs on the woman's wrists, behind her back. The Asian woman  was crying stoically  and was being led away.   Getting arrested near the hospital, a wellspring of drugs and the focus of military activity took no great talent.  All one needed apparently was to look suspicious and be uncooperative.

The policewoman was a striking young brunette with mirrored sunglasses. She was leading the Asian woman to a police van.  The policewoman had a utility belt with a large nightstick and a gun.  Petrosian found himself transfixed as he watched the young girl put into the van that then sped off.  The policewoman paused writing down something on a notepad.  She then looked up and stared at Petrosian.  A chill went through Petrosian. *How could I have been so stupid,*  he thought and began to deploy his wheelchair.

****

On the Moon, things in the Samaran garrison had slipped back into an arduous routine of constant training with weapons, particularly the sword. Zomal had his men train constantly in order to fight boredom.

Zomal and Tankos, themselves covered with sweat from training, looked with satisfaction on the  men training.  They then departed for the baths. As they walked they talked.

"Do you think the Errans will come here and meet us sword to sword," asked Tankos smiling.

"No, I think they will blast this place to dust," said Zomal grimly. There will be little honor in it. The Errans fight the Unash, who have no honor, so the Errans will give none. We will die with the Unash unless fortune changes."

"Then, I envy Koton, my Lord, and his honorable death," said Tankos.

"Honor? I can tell you now since you are now my second in command Tankos, that Koton went to Erra to cleanse his honor. It was because of the golden-haired Erran woman Tatiana."

"How my Lord? I never saw her with him."

"It was because when Bekar of Batelgeen and that witch, Nor of Bellatrix, came here."

"What?"

"They demanded war-custom," said Zomal with a frown. "The woman, Nor of Bellatrix, wanted Tatiana, the golden-haired Erran, and took her for the night." Tankos looked at him in horror. Though the Samaran society gave broad latitude for men's behavior, women were expected to remain chaste, and sex between women, or any sex not connected to making children, was considered unspeakable. "Koton asked me afterward," continued Zomal, "'Am I a Papa-don of a whorehouse here?' He then said to me after they were gone, 'This place is my house! Bekar has defiled it! I am completely dishonored!'"

"My Lord, this is a shameful thing, and abuse of custom, it is in passing, very sad..." said Tankos, shaking his head. "I did not know..." added Tankos.

"It was kept very close," said Zomal grimly. "I told Koton, 'My Lord, we all know that the *powerful may do as they please, and it has ever been thus.* So this black mark is therefore upon them, not you... ' But he would not listen to me. He said 'you are young, Zomal, and I am old. I have given everything to the Empire except my honor'" Zomal paused sadly. "Yes Tankos, so the brave Koton, our commander, like a father to us, no longer wanted to live, and sought out a battlefield to die on. He found it on Erra."

Zomal paused and gave a brave smile.

"But brave Tankos,  the gods favor the bold, so we shall yet escape out of this death trap, with luck and with honor," he said.

****

Cassandra made the drive to Virginia beach in record time, flying down the freeway and out onto a long barrier island studded with beautiful cottages. Despite her concern for her friend, she looked with admiration at the beautiful resort cottage #14 as she pulled into the long driveway. Pam's electric blue corvette was parked there.  To the East was the ocean and a wide sandy beach.  And to the South, the sprawling Naval Base at Norfolk. This sight filled Cassandra with foreboding. *Why can't things ever work out for Pammy and the men in her life?* She paused at the thought, *Or me either?* she thought fiercely. She launched herself out the door of her rented Ferrari. Pulling her dark glasses up on her head as she walked up to the front door, in her new high heeled boots.

The cottage appeared dark, and Cassandra sensed deep pain inside. Despite this, she admired herself in the reflection on the dark window and adjusted her hair. "Got to look good for Pammy after all these months, I can't disappoint," she said to herself.

"Pammy,  it's me, Cassie!" she yelled as she knocked. To her surprise, the door instantly flew open and Pamela, looking sad and hurt but otherwise immaculate, appeared framed in the doorway.  Pamela had her hair slightly short framing her lovely but sad face, she was wearing a windbreaker over an electric blue, two piece bikini that clung to her lovely figure like it was sprayed on. She had makeup on. *Atta girl*  thought Cassie. Pamela's face broke into a sad smile, then beamed as she looked Cassandra up and down. She then embraced her, as they wrapped their arms around each other.

"Oh look at you, you look fabulous," Pam wept happily.

*"Oh,  so do you, Pammy! Sea duty obviously agrees with you," wept Casandra. As Pam pulled her into the cottage and shut the door. "I'm so happy, you look so well."*

635

"it's so good you're here Cassie," said Pamela sadly. "So good," she said as she broke her embrace but still held her arm around Cassie's waist as she guided her into the kitchen.

"And where did you get that jacket? It looks marvelous!" exclaimed Pamela looking at Cassandra's new light coat.

"Denver!" said Cassandra, triumphantly. "I went on a real shopping spree there!"

A bottle of rum sat on the counter with two glasses, a plate of cut limes sat nearby and a bottle of Coke. Pam broke away and quickly poured two drinks. She poured in some coke quickly, and then pushed a glass to Cassie while grabbing hers and drinking it. Pam poured herself another.

'What happened?"

"The Navy keeps a harsh household, Cassie, always remember that."

"Where's Michael?"

"They took him, the Navy. He traded volunteering for a secret mission, for extra leave so we could get married...he got a promotion too." Pamela paused. "He tells me about this sweet deal as their taking him away," her face filled with anguish. "But the Navy, they cut his leave short by a week! Because of new orders! So A Humvee full of Marines showed up and took him away! Just like that! SO MUCH FOR THE DEAL! SO MUCH FOR THE BIG LONG JUICY PROMOTION!" Pamela wailed. "THE MOTHERFUCKERS! The mother fuckers!" her voice trailed off to nothing. Suddenly her blue eyes flashed. "To lovers torn apart! To war and its confusions, and war's stinking bullshit." She finished her glass, then grabbed the bottle and drank a big swallow of rum. "I AM DONE WITH MEN!!!!" she yelled.

Cassie swallowed her drink, nodded, pulled the bottle away from Pamela and drank a big swallow herself. "To fate!" Cassandra said vehemently, holding up the bottle. "Bitter fate," she said putting the bottle down out of Pamela's reach. Cassie's face was now grim.

Pamela waltzed over to the couch in the living room near the kitchen grabbed a large pillow and held it to herself. She then flopped down on the couch, buried her face into the pillow and burst into wretched tears. Cassandra sat down beside her, pulled off her boots and held Pamela, pressing her cheek into her soft mop of blonde hair, and wept silently.

****

At the White House, with the public military ceremonies concluded, President Petrov and President Martel chaired a meeting of military and defense officials regarding the planning for the invasion of the Moon.

General Suvurov, the commander of Russian space forces, had concluded his report, concerning moving three elite guard divisions to the Moon, in a parallel effort to the American invasion. He had pointed out the requirement for American space lift to assist in the Russian deployment.

"Mr. President," began President Petrov. "My country has lost, in our best estimates, 2.8 million people due to cold and starvation in the recent alien–induced severe Winter. We know also that your nation lost approximately 100,000 in the same way. So, in return for your help to supplement our space lift capacities by approximately 50 percent, which is basically asking for sheet metal and rocket propellants , we offer our own flesh and blood to go to the Moon and fight. Like your own soldiers and cosmonauts, these soldiers of Russia will fight hard, and many will die. That is the truth. We have no illusions concerning this fact. As your own General Burnham has said, `the easy part of this war is ending, and its most difficult phase is just beginning'."

"So, we offer, in return for help with space transport, an equal share of the sacrifices to come. This is no time to think about future territorial claims on the Moon which, in any case, are covered by the Outer Space Treaty of 1967. Rather this us a time when we must engage in an all-out effort to achieve victory and secure the existence of a human future when such trivial matters can be settled at a conference table set up on the ruins of the alien base in Mare Moscoviense."

****

They were walking on the beach in their bare feet. It was near sundown and warm, with a slight breeze from the ocean. The sky was clear as

637

crystal over the sea. Cassandra had changed into a Maroon French tee shirt and black shorts and was wearing a blue baseball cap. Pamela, still wearing her windbreaker over her bikini, seemed to have recovered after her long crying session and was even smiling and joking. She had entertainingly told Cassandra about her adventures at sea in command of a lifeboat. Cassandra wanted her to talk, feeling it would keep Pam's mind off of her loss.

"I can tell you the worst form of hell imaginable is to be in command of a lifeboat of soggy, cold reporters running short of liquor. But it was my first command."

"Since you got a medal, do you think the Navy will give you a big promotion too?" asked Cassandra with a girlish smirk.

"I already got one!" laughed Pamela hilariously. "Michael got it for me! He said no skipper of a ship was complete without one!" Pamela was momentarily overcome with laughter. "It's this big strap-on dildo!" she giggled and motioned with her hands to indicate its size. "It's detachable, so he said it was for when he was gone. He said it was to make me think of him!" Pamela's voice trailed off and her eyes grew sad, she was staring at the full Moon rising.

A steady procession of sleek Navy ships, frigates, and cargo ships mostly, was gliding along the horizon , going to and from the big Naval base at Norfolk in the distance.

The Moon rose, yellow and huge on the horizon, a destroyer of rakish design moved across it on the horizon. It bristled with guns, missile batteries and dome antennas, which Cassie recognized as the Naval version of the "Flies Eye" EMP projector to disrupt saucer drives.

"That's a new one, a Dahlgren class, they put more guns back on them, along with above deck launching rails for the missiles," instructed Pamela. "They like direct fire weapons now against saucers, less time for the shorts to react when the rockets and shells are launched straight at them."

"Shorts?" asked Cassandra.

"Yeah, or shorty's, that what everybody calls them now. It's because of the Russians, in Russian "short" means 'devil or goblin'. The Russians kept referring to them as shorty, which is plural, so we picked it up because the Greys are short."

"Oh, Pammy! I love it when you explain things! You sound so technical now!" laughed Cassandra.

Deep twilight came as they walked. The Moon rose higher and went from yellow to bluish white.

Soon it was becoming darker and cooler, the Moonlight bluer and more frigid as it rose beyond the dust band on the horizon. The first stars began to appear in the twilight over the ocean. Cassandra stared also and she pulled her arm around Pamela as she began to cry again. The breeze rose and began to feel cold so Cassandra clung to Pamela's soft warm shoulders to keep warm.

"I love him, Cassie," said Pamela with sudden seriousness. "I love him more than I have ever loved a man. It's so strange that I would finally find true love, now ,... in this wasteland that we call war. But I suppose we all live life more strongly, in a war, when we are all torn apart and death is so near. We love more sincerely and passionately when the cosmos is now animated by hate. When even the stars themselves shed darkness more than light, and go about to slay us."

"He'll be out there soon, in space. I am guessing that's where they're sending him." Pamela gasped as she stared out at the rising Moon, her face solemn and beautiful, her eyes electric blue in the now blue moonlight, and her blonde hair moving gently in the evening breeze. "Michael told me what he had traded for our few precious hours together, as they took him. When he blurted it out, what he had signed up for in order for us to have time together before his deployment, I want you to know Cassie, that part of me suddenly hated him. Part of me suddenly hated him as he drove away in the green Humvee because I understood that if we had gotten married next week like we had planned, then I would have become not only a wife but widow, in that same moment. I literally saw myself wearing a black gown instead of white, as they drove him away."

639

So I loved and hated him at the same time at that instant, Cassie, I hated him for being a fool for love, in a cosmos where fools perish, and even the wisest of us, fear for next year's existence. "

So, Starbuck, I'll probably never see him again, which is why I am done with men now…". Cassandra held her in the mounting cold breeze, and steered her back to the cottage, feeling her warmth beside her.

Back in the cottage, they turned on the gas fireplace to warm the room, and Pam microwaved some frozen Chinese food, and they ate it. Finally, it was warm, Pamela shed her jacket, and was resplendent in her two piece bikini. Cassandra had never seen her in such good shape, and she told further tales of the sharks and squid she saw in the Pacific as the rum bottle reappeared. Pam took her seat on a barstool beside the counter and motioned to Cassandra to join her there as Pam poured two shot glasses half full then poured coke into them, and with great flourish dropped slices of lime into them as Casandra watched, now also sitting on a barstool beside the kitchen counter. Pam and Cassie both raised their shot glasses.

"So Starbuck, my old friend," began Pamela with a solemn face. "Let us now discourse again on the world's great systems… on the great clockwork, that is the heavens. Let us speak of the true faces we wear behind our brave masks, in this vast cosplay we call fate… on this wide stage, we call the cosmos." They then drank their drinks. Cassandra pushed her empty glass back to Pamela, who refilled both of them. Cassandra took hers and then they both held their drinks again. Cassandra laughed for a moment then struggled to regain her dignity.

"Aye, Captain Pammy… let us speak of eternal truths," began Cassandra, staring off into space. "Truths, that will be spoken long after the stars have faded into darkness, of how we walking wounded of this epic struggle called life, stagger across the darkling plain, where our every breath and movement is pain…with only love and sweet friendship." She turned and motioned with her glass to Pamela, who blinked but smiled, "to comfort us on our journey…" Cassandra blinked back tears from her dark eyes, made them wide. "Where what was lost, and what was gained, we see only through a shattered glass darkly… as we sail across the dark sea in our tiny junk called a galaxy. Yes, let us speak of the great mystery of our being and movement and underneath the stardust, across the deep black sea, in our tiny craft, her name is My Song, and it's all that I have left..." Cassandra then paused, her face covered with wide-eyed amazement, "and so I raise my black banner and sail on a dark tide with every weapon armed, sail to rescue my beloved mortal enemy who lies trapped on a dark crag rising lonely from the battering sea... chained in the shards of a broken mirror... Cassandra then drank the drink down in one gulp, and Pamela did the same. Then they both threw their glasses across the room into the fireplace. Cassandra wiped her eyes and then beamed at Pamela who looked more beautiful than she had ever seen her. Pamela smiled bravely and pulled two more glasses from across the counter.

"Oh! Yes! I must give you a brief report of my own great adventure on the deep sea!" exclaimed Cassandra suddenly. "I am not only a salty veteran of sea duty, but I am a vile mutineer and buccaneer as well!"

"YOU WERE PART OF A MUTINY?!" exclaimed Pamela laughing. "Wait, if I know my Starbuck, you probably were chief mutineer! "Cassandra looked off in mock defiance as Pamela poured two more drinks of straight rum. "You know that mutiny is the most serious crime you can commit on a ship. I would have clapped you in irons and thrown you naked into the brig!" she added pushing now a full glass of rum back to Cassandra.

"One must take account of extenuating circumstances and fullest contexts," said Cassandra with her nose in the air, sipping the drink delicately.

"Which would be?"

"First! I did it to save a baby whale!" exclaimed Cassandra indignantly.

"Even worse! Starbuck! I would have had you flogged also, then tossed in the brig!" said Pamela drinking down her drink in one gulp. She suddenly winced, thinking of Cassandra's scarred back, and looked at Cassandra in apology, but Cassandra merely smiled back and patted her on the hand.

"Secondly, and most important in terms of the fullest context of this mutiny, it was a French Ship! With a salty French Captain and First Mate!" exclaimed Cassandra drinking down her drink and handing Pamela the empty glass as she refilled her own. Pamela paused and looked at Cassandra with tipsy incredulousness. Pam's face broke into a wide smile.

"A French First Mate?" she laughed.

"Oui!" exclaimed Cassandra, taking her now refilled drink. "I was technically serving in the French navy!" She threw her shoulders back and saluted the air. "Viva la France!" she then drank her drink in one gulp.

"The French Navy! Well that changes everything!" said Pamela beaming. "I will return to only having you in irons and thrown naked into the brig! However, since it was the French Navy, I will also give you a double ration of grog in my cabin!"

"I do feel badly about it, truly!" said Cassandra staring off into space. "But I did save the baby whale!" She moved her hands up and down as if to try and balance the two acts morally.

"Starbuck, honestly, I have never met anyone who enjoys being bad more than you, while also enjoying feeling bad about it later," said Pamela smiling. Pamela reached over and patted her on the shoulder as Cassandra continued to stare off into space.

Cassandra suddenly turned grinning, handed Pamela her empty glass. Pamela took a drink straight from the bottle and handed it to Cassandra.

"So, Blondie girlfriend, how big was this big shark you saw from the lifeboat, really?" asked Cassandra after taking a drink. "I think you should report on this as an interesting science note as the mighty ace reporter and now veteran war correspondent that you most certainly are!"

"Oh, Cassie! I swear it was this BIG!" laughed Pamela, standing up by the barstool by the kitchen counter and stretching her arms wide above her head.

"But I saw a big bull killer whale that was BIGGER!" said Cassandra standing and handing the bottle back to Pamela. "I was in the water with him, and I swear he could have eaten me in one bite!"

"Sounds delightful." cooed Pamela with raised eyebrows. "Did he have a big promotion?" she passed the bottle back to Cassandra after a drink.

"YES!" said Cassie after another drink and setting down the bottle, then standing and motioning frantically with her arms above her head. "Oh! OH! And I have to show you something Pammy, you're not going to believe this! I have been dying to tell someone! Is my big secret" Cassandra suddenly took off her baseball cap, reached up behind her back under her tee shirt and unsnapped her bra, then turned and pulled both her bra and tee shirt off over her head, and pulled up her long black hair off her back with both hands, piling it on top of her head to show Pamela her now perfectly smooth honey-colored back.

"Those awful scars …They're gone!" exclaimed Pamela. "How? Was it the Martek Clinic in Hollywood?"

Cassandra shook her head. "Feel it, the skin is smooth like silk again." Pamela drew closer and ran her warm hands down Cassandra's back, as Cassandra leaned against the wall with her elbows. Cassandra felt suddenly warm at Pamela's touch. Pamela withdrew her hands, Cassandra put her French tee shirt back on and turned to face Pamela. Pamela had tears in her eyes.

"That is so wonderful!" said Pamela. She cast her eyes down to her breasts. "They did a good job on my scar too, you can barely see it." It was true, the long scar that had formerly run up Pamela's sternum between her breasts was now almost invisible. "They say I have to keep it out of the Sun, though." She looked up at Cassandra's dark eyes, blue eyes met brown eyes and locked.

Cassandra suddenly leaned over and kissed Pamela on the lips. Pamela then kissed her back, a long lingering kiss. Pamela then wrapped her arms around Cassandra and pushed her hands up under the back of her tee shirt.

Pamela pushed Cassandra back into the wall by the kitchen, her hands now caressed Cassandra's swelling bare breasts under her tee shirt. Cassandra broke the kiss and with tears in her eyes and unstrapped Pamela's bikini top and saw Pamela's large white breasts grow naked with her wide pink areola and erect pink nipples. Cassandra lowered her head and kissed Pamela's pink nipples. Cassie then blinked back tears and looked her in the face.

"Pam, I want to pretend I'm Barbarella, and you are the great Tyrant holding me prisoner in the city of darkness," Pamela nodded woozily.

Casandra, pulled off her tee shirt over her head and embraced Pamela and kissed her deeply. Pamela's body was warming, and she was comfort personified. Cassandra then slid out of her shorts and panties and stood naked before Pamela. *I need her, to comfort my secret pain,* thought Cassandra drunkenly.

"Could you do that for me...play the great Dictator?" asked Cassandra. Pamela nodded dreamily. Cassandra kissed her again, a long deep kiss with Pamela's soft mouth now wide open. "I promise to make it worth your while," said Cassandra. Cassandra then knelt at Pamela's feet and kissed her warmly just below her navel. Cassandra could feel Pamela's body flash into heat. Pamela gently pulled Cassandra up off her knees. Pamela kissed her deeply then slid off her bikini bottoms and Cassandra put her arms on top of her head in surrender.

"So lead me to the dungeon, oh great Dictator...you can loosen my tongue there... and milk me for information..." gasped Cassandra motioning her head to the open bedroom, it was dark and moonlight was now streaming through the windows. On the bed, the night dissolved into hot lingering kisses.

Cassandra awoke next to Pamela's naked form on the bed. Full Moonlight filled the room with bluish white radiance. Cassandra and Pamela were entangled in each other's arms. Cassandra felt waves of pleasure oozing around in her body, then a moment of shock and disorientation and wave of dizziness. She noted an empty rum bottle on the bed stand.

644

*Oh no...* she thought. She had something around her waist –she put her hand down and felt a soaking wet protuberance. She looked down and saw it was a strap-on dildo. "Oh my God ," she gasped mentally, felt a wave of panicked confusion. She calmed herself, then kissed Pamela on her warm cheek and Pamela smiled in her sleep and moved closer. *Someday I'll understand,* Cassandra thought desperately. She looked down again at the large dildo strapped to her waist.

"One thing is certain, I am not in Kansas anymore," Cassandra said to herself in wonderment, shaking her now aching head. She carefully pulled her arm out from under Pam so as not to awaken her, slid out of bed, fumbled with the strap-on, unfastened it from her waist and gingerly let it slip to the floor. She felt utterly confused. She went into the bathroom, ran some cold water and washed her face. She found a bottle of aspirin in the medicine cabinet and washed down four of them with cold water. She felt even more confused,  but calmer. *Well, I certainly got Pam's mind off of Michael!* she thought, feeling better.

"Why am I doing these things?" she asked her reflection in the Moonlit mirror. "Why ask why?" she answered herself.

She quickly showered and dried her hair with a towel , putting on Pamela's  electric blue bathrobe. Cassandra felt her body aching with pleasure, then noticed a stream of lubricating jelly was emptying from her vagina. *Oh No*, she gasped mentally holding her shaking head. *This just keeps on getting better...* she fought a feeling of being violated, let it slip away into a pleasant feeling of pleasure, then nothing. She  looked in the mirror blinked, then rolled her eyes at herself, bit her lip pensively, then smiled slightly. *Instead of my friend committing suicide I let her ravish me...* Cassandra  felt better at this thought. *This was just another Crazy Cassie incident...that's all.* She then went out and pulled up an overstuffed chair and sat down looking over Pamela's lovely and shapely form on the bed. *This is merely the Mother of all Crazy Cassie-Bad Pammy incidents, happening in juxtaposition... on the night of a Blue Moon,* Cassandra rationalized.

Pamela had moved over into the spot Cassandra had been in on the sheets and was in a near fetal position. Cassandra leaned over the bed and kissed Pamela on her warm cheek, then pulled the covers gently over Pam and tucked her in, then put her own feet up on the bed and resumed her deep thoughts in the Moonlight as she surveyed Pamela's sleeping form. She was then seeing things, she was trapped in a dark tower, by a wicked witch, a flurry of images flickered through her mind, the policewoman with sunglasses, the nightstick, being naked, and repeatedly hit with the nightstick. Then it was Pamela wearing the strap-on, Cassandra kneeling in front of her, Cassie was performing slow fellatio on her, then looked up, and it was not Pamela. It was the policewoman with dark brown hair. It was Lauren Davis from the White House, long dead. Cassandra then had an orgasm. Cassandra forced herself to awaken, tears were streaming down her cheeks, she could not awaken. She was dreaming of Pamela. Pamela was delightfully sucking her breasts, then Pam was a baby, Cassandra was holding a beautiful baby and pouring love into it like a star burning brilliantly pouring out light, *I love you hamster, I love you hamster...*she was cooing to it as they whirled around and the baby laughed Then she was awake again, sitting in the chair in the Moonlight. She felt she was losing her mind again. *No, No!* she fought to calm herself. *You will understand this someday... you will understand...*she promised herself as she wept. *But this is all so confusing. Like sitting in the middle of a kaleidoscope of hallucinations.*

Suddenly a tremendous and deafening crack of thunder sounded, and the whole cottage shook.

"Oh my God!" Cassandra yelled and instinctively rolled out of the chair onto the floor. Pamela rose screaming on the bed. A second crack of thunder sounded, and several jet fighters flew right over the cottage. The roar of jet fighters and more sonic booms shook the cottage as Cassandra frantically pulled Pamela out of the bed onto the floor, screaming. Cassandra covered her mouth with her hand, and Pamela was trembling like a leaf.

"My gun! my gun! It's on the nightstand!' yelled Pamela as a tremendous blue flash filled the cottage, followed by the sound of a sharp explosion. Pamela jumped up and dived across the bed and then rolled back off it with a pair of pistols, a .38 snub-nose and a 9 mm Berretta. She checked the snub nose muttering obscenities and shoved the Berretta into

Cassandra's hand. Cassandra grabbed it and primed it, and felt it comforting her. A series of sonic booms, sharp bright flashes and thunderous explosions in the sky followed. They both crouched there beside the bed, Cassandra wrapped her arm around Pamela's naked form and pulled her close to her, feeling her tremble, she held her, as the battle in the sky intensified, and then slowly became only a flickering light in the distance and muffled thunder.

"I knew I should have brought my magnetometer!" yelled Pamela angrily, as dawn finally began to glow in the window. Pamela rose angrily and walked into the bathroom. Cassandra still crouched warily on the floor cradling her pistol, realizing only when dawn was arriving how terrified she had been. She heard Pamela brushing her teeth, and showering, then the toilet flushing several times. Finally, Pamela, a vision of annoyed beauty, came out of the bathroom wrapped in a towel as dawn filled the room.

Pamela sat down on the bed in front of Cassandra and laid down her gun. The powerful turbines of a fast patrol boat sounded as it thundered by outside, then passed. Waves from its powerful wake could be heard crashing on the beach.

"The shorts tried to get me again! RIGHT BY A NAVAL BASE! It's this damn implant in my nose! I have got to get this thing yanked out!" said Pamela in frustration. Cassandra rose on unsteady legs and tried to stop trembling.

"I say we go into town and have nice jade and Blondie breakfast!" said Pamela suddenly beaming. "Starbuck, it's a good day to be alive and hung over!" said Pamela throwing a pillow at her gleefully.

"Sure ," said Cassandra picking up the strap-on dildo and throwing it on the bed beside Pamela with a troubled look. "As long as it's someplace quiet."

Pamela looked at the strap-on on the bed, still covered with lubricant. Pam smiled weakly.

"It would appear that unintended levels of absurdity were achieved last night. This I will admit." said Pamela looking at Cassandra with a vulnerable smile. Cassandra was staring at the empty rum bottle on the nightstand, held her head in both hands as if in pain with closed eyes. She then opened her dark eyes and looked at Pamela, smiled back weakly.

"I told you it was big," said Pamela.

"I was warned..., I must admit," said Cassandra staring off into space, then sitting down beside Pamela on the bed. Cassandra then kissed Pamela on the lips, a kiss that grew deeper and longer, and Pamela let go of her towel and embraced her giggling.

Later they were walking on the beach again after breakfast in town. Apparently, a sharp battle in the sky over the Chesapeake Bay had occurred the previous night, with one alien craft downed, and a Navy jet fighter lost as well, the pilot dead. The restaurant just buzzed about it.

Pamela was wearing shorts and a tank top with a jacket, Cassandra was wearing her black shorts and a long sleeve shirt as they strolled down the beach. Cassandra was also wearing her blue baseball cap from Alaska.

"It couldn't have been too bad last night, there're no bodies floating in the surf." said Pamela. "The battle I mean," she added with a whimsical look at Cassandra. Two Navy patrol boats were cruising off shore as if they were looking for debris, cruising back and forth with a muffled roar and whine of turbines. They were battleship grey and bristled with weapons, guns, missile tubes and EMP projectors. Further out to sea, helicopters were cruising low over the ocean. Cassandra noted a pair of handcuffs was in her pocket from the night before. She could not remember how they got there.

"About last night," said Cassandra looking around at the sky with a trembling voice and stroking her hair with her hand. "I was wondering if we could forget that all happened..."

Pamela looked at her, shrugged. The wind blew her blonde locks across her face. Cassandra could not tell if Pam was smiling or looking hurt. Cassandra put her arm around Pam's shoulders. Pam moved closer to her.

648

"I am working through some things, baby, and I honestly don't know what I am doing sometimes. "said Cassandra with a trembling voice. "All I can say is I am better than I was last year. I am stronger. I can truly say that back then, for a while, I was mad as a hatter." Her voice gained strength. "I was seeing things, hearing voices back then. I knew enough not to tell anyone and gradually the stuff went away. I keep telling myself someday I'll understand all of this. That's my mantra now. I can't understand how going through something bad like I did, can affect you like a hallucinogenic drug almost. All I can say is that the drug is wearing off." She looked at Pamela sadly. "I also hope I didn't take advantage of you last night, in your distraught condition," said Cassandra, after a pause. Pamela exploded into helpless laughter at this.

"I should be distraught more often," said Pamela, giving Cassandra a reassuring hug. "I, in turn, hope I didn't take advantage of your present mental craziness. You are mentally competent Cassie? Right? But I hope you have another bout of being unhinged soon." Pamela then sighed and looked at sea. "Like I said, I am through with men now... and I am on the market." She stopped and looked deeply into Cassandra eyes.

"So, you know me well enough Cassie, to know that you weren't taking advantage of me. You just want to hear me say it, don't you." she said, looking now at Cassandra narrowly. Cassandra nodded, smiled and felt better. Pam smiled. Cassandra pulled the handcuffs out of her pocket and pitched them into the surf.

"I hope those weren't valuable." she said in sudden remorse.

"I have two other pairs in drawer someplace," laughed Pamela. Her face then clouded. "Don't you have to go see Doctor Petrosian tomorrow? I mean it might be good to talk to him about your recent shocking behavior, Starbuck. I mean, strange things happen when one of us is crazy, and the other is distraught, and both of us are drunk. That's how I would summarize it to Petrosian."

"Yes." said Cassandra frantically. "I must report on my latest solid steps toward mental health!" They turned and walked back towards the cottage. They walked by another cottage. A lonely-looking young oriental

649

man sat smoking a cigarette on the back porch. Both women waved at him and smiled. He waved back weakly.

"He looks lonely, " said Cassandra.

"He looks hunky," said Pamela. "He looks like a fighter pilot."

They went over, smiling sweetly,  and sat by him for a while. He was a rugged-looking man, with an eye patch.

"I got this in a space battle," he motioned to his patched eye. "Now I can't be fighter pilot anymore, just a cargo pilot." he said  sadly. "They say I'm well enough for duty, so I ship out tonight." Both Pamela and Cassandra did their best to cheer him up.

"Oh, I'm Captain George Nakajima, US Air Force." he said.

"Oh I'm Pamela Jones," said  Pamela, edging Cassandra with her foot as she shook Nakajima's hand.

"Oh, and I am Jennifer Shimada," said Cassandra, quickly  trying to string together a Japanese sounding name, and leaned forward to shake his hand also.  Nakajima smiled at this slightly.  Cassandra then glanced down the beach at their cottage.

"Oh my God, look!" exclaimed Cassandra pointing at the cottage down the beach where they were staying. A Marine Humvee had just pulled up into the driveway.  Several men in uniform were getting out. One tall figure was wearing a white dress naval uniform, the rest were in fatigues.

"MICHEAL!" Pamela screamed, "OH MY GOD!" and got up and ran frantically toward the cottage.

Cassandra rose from her chair, beside Nakajima.  She suddenly, on impulse, kissed him warmly on the cheek and hugged him.  Then stammering an apology, she ran off after Pamela.

Cassandra now ran down the beach as the figure in white ran out to meet Pamela and embraced her. He then got down on his knees and pulled out a big diamond ring as Cassandra ran up in amazement.

650

"Yes!" said Pamela. Whereupon Michael Donnelly rose, and they kissed deeply. Cassandra suppressed a sudden flash of jealousy and instead smiled sweetly. *Where would we all be, without a sense of irony,* Cassandra thought with resignation.

A frantic looking Marine Captain jogged up in fatigues. He had a dark mustache.

"Commander! We haven't got much time, so let's move this operation right along, the Chaplain's waiting to get this thing done! Then your ass needs to be back on base ASAP!"

"Thank you, Captain Garza," said Michael looking resplendent in his dress whites. Pamela clung to his arm ecstatically as they walked up to where a Navy Chaplain stood in fatigues. Two other Marines, a Sergeant, and a Corporal stood grinning. The Corporal was holding a bouquet of flowers. He smiled in embarrassment.

Cassie, could you stand beside Captain Garza here, he has graciously agreed to be the best man, and you are obviously my maid of honor. The corporal, looking transfixed at Cassandra, handed her the flowers. "Let's get this thing done!" exclaimed the Chaplin. Pamela taking her position beside Lt Commander Michael Donnelley.

In a few minutes Michael was kissing Pamela, and they were man and wife on the doorstep of the cottage. Cassandra then kissed Captain Garza quickly on the lips which seemed to put him in a better mood for a moment, then a look of frantic exasperation returned to his face. Pamela turned and tossed the bouquet of flowers at Cassandra who caught them with helpless laughter. Then everyone moved to the Humvee and Michael got in with some last long kisses with Pamela and Captain Garza having to frantically remind everyone that they had to go.

"You two already had your honeymoon, Commander! So let's roll!" shouted Garza.

The Humvee departed in a cloud of dusty sand.

The apparition faded. Pamela stood staring at the road trembling after the Humvee disappeared in the distance. Pam then turned in shock to Cassandra, held up her huge diamond ring in the sunlight watched it sparkle. Pam's blue eyes were wide, and several emotions, merriment, sorrow and confusion danced across her lovely face.

"Did that just happen?" said Pamela turning to Cassandra in confusion. She then beamed, "I guess you can call me Mrs. Donnelly now," said Pamela in amazement.

"I am just glad they decided to have the wedding on the doorstep rather than inside," said Cassandra with a sly smile. "We are talking dodging a major bullet of awkwardness here!" she said waving her hand.

"Your right Starbuck! Of course! The place is a mess!" said Pamela, looking down the road, squinting. "You're most surely right Starbuck! Major, major, awkwardness was avoided, I must admit. Things lying around that should be concealed in drawers! I mean the furniture kind! You are also correct in your earlier comment about last night's kerfuffle, which, given my new circumstances, should remain an absurd, drunken, riddle wrapped in an enigma."

"I guess I should also be glad the Greys decided to come around last night," continued Pamela, "because of them Michael's flight was grounded! So they gave him an hour's leave this morning!" said Pamela now ecstatically looking at her ring sparkling. She was dancing now in a circle looking at it.

"Truly, we will have to remember this one good deed of the Greys when the final accounting is made..." said Cassandra staring off into the blue sky. Then she turned and looked at Pamela sadly.

"Pam, I need you to come back with me to Morningstar and do a tour of the alien base with me," said Cassandra quickly.

"God Cassie, are you sure?"

"Yes," said Cassandra as tears ran down her cheeks. "I am ready now..."

"Sure baby," said Pamela, and hugged her.

****

Near Houston, Texas, in  a vast new Army Camp,  Colonel Robert Schwartzman ran at the head of his Battalion as they jogged three miles on a road for their morning physical training. They all wore mottled grey lunar camouflage fatigues, to accustom themselves to the Lunar environment, and to make it seem as natural as Earth.  They were singing old war songs as they ran.  In the distance, a Saturn VII, Mark III was lifting off from its launch pad on Padre Island.  The first of three such launches scheduled for that day.  Each boosting 300 tons into orbit.

*Soon these men will be sharp as razors,* thought Schwartzman, looking up at the Moon in the blue morning sky.  *Soon I am leaving Earth, never to return.*

****

Trembling, Cassandra put on the orange bio-isolation suit and stood looking at Pamela as they tightened the straps to make it fit more tightly around their bodies.  They were in the ready room on top of Devil's Mesa on a gloomy morning at the facility at Morningstar.  They were tightening the suit so it  was less likely to snag and tear on some of the wreckage downstairs. Lt. Jenkins stood by them in his suit, looking grim. Pamela's eyes were deep blue, but her face was resolute, and this gave Cassandra strength as they all put on their clear plastic dome helmets and snapped them into tight seals.  Jenkins stepped into the elevator, and Cassandra and Pamela followed. Cassandra could hear the battery powered fan in the air conditioning unit begin to whir as the elevator shot down into the bowels of the mesa.

They got out down in the bio-disposal level, and as the elevator door opened they were met with another lieutenant in a bio-suit named Dalton, he carried an MP-5 submachine gun.  Lieutenants Jenkins and Dalton exchanged salutes.  Jenkins turned to the women and gave a thumb's up sign. Cassandra stepped out into the dimly lit corridor lined with square glassine ceramic tile on the ceiling, walls, and floors. Cassandra felt panic and terror suddenly seize her, but she grasped Pamela's gloved hand and Pamela's hand strengthened her. *Can I really do this? Am I really capable of it?* Cassandra gasped mentally.  *Yes, yes, I can do it. I have to do it!* she thought fiercely and stepped forward out of the elevator as strongly as she could, towing Pamela along. *I have to get well!* She knew where they were going, to the bio-disposal units, where she had been rescued. She had gone over the places she wanted to visit with Petrosian. He had agreed reluctantly with helping on the tour planning and had recommended beginning with the rescue site first.

The wall where still heavily scarred by bullets in places as they walked and the floor was still bloodstained.

"Sorry, the place is still a mess," said Dalton matter-of-factly. "We basically just picked up the bodies and mopped up the worst of the blood. We are still finding bodies and old ordinance. That, and trying to control the vermin here."

Cassandra shot a look to Pamela. Pamela was striding along strongly, her face determined, but she managed a faint smile for Cassandra.

*Pammy, my brave little trooper, what have I gotten you into here? What would I do without you?* thought Cassandra. *Why am I inflicting this little tour of Hell on you also?*

They came to the doorway of the bio-disposal unit, went through it, past the control room, into the area where she had faced death. The three huge clear plastic hourglasses of the bio-disposal units were there. The walls were still partly bloodstained in places, as was the floor. Pictures of her naked were taped on the center heavy plastic chamber, taken by a helmet cam on one of the special forces when she was rescued. Jenkins looked slightly embarrassed. But Cassandra waved to him that it was OK, and looked at the pictures with obsessive curiosity. She could see her heavily gashed back, held together by staples.

"This is where Bob and the Carney, rescued me. "rambled Cassandra. Her voice at once trembling and forceful. "Before they did that, they massacred a bunch of Bremer's guards here. I remember stripping off parts of their uniforms after Bob got me out, so I could wear something. The guards had divided up my clothes here when they stripped me before they put me in there. So I even got my famous white thong panties out of one of their shirt pockets afterward. And just as I thought the acid enzyme was going to flood my chamber, you showed up Pammy, standing right beside me. You were made of golden light." Cassandra began to cry but stopped herself. Pamela smiled at her bravely.

"OK! Let's go up to the next place," said Cassandra firmly.

Soon they were on a level higher than before. They soon stood next to a bashed-in metal door. The chamber inside was dimly lit, so Jenkins and Dalton turned on flashlights. Inside was a horrid room full of abandoned instruments of torture and dirty, bloodstained, tile walls. A sudden movement caught Cassandra's eye, and she recoiled in horror. It was a rat crab scampering along the floor. Instantly two deafening shots rang out, and Cassandra grasped Pamela closely and closed her eyes. Pamela was holding her tightly also and trembling. Cassandra opened her eyes, looked at Jenkins poking the now dead rat crab with his bio-suit boot and putting his pistol back in its holster. Dalton was panning the flashlight around, nothing else moved. The place seemed clear.

Pamela was staring at the rat crab with huge eyes and a look of disbelief. Cassandra maintained her grasp on Pamela's gloved hand and looked around the desolate chamber with its still bloodstained floor and bullet pock-marked walls. She saw the cross-shaped table where she had been stretched out on her stomach and been shocked and flogged. The electric cables still lay there and led to a small evil looking console. She stepped away from Pamela and walked over to the table.

"This is where they worked me over with the whip and the high voltage," said Cassandra matter-of-factly, as Pamela looked on in horror. Cassandra felt stronger, almost numb. *But they didn't break me, by some miracle, by the slimmest of margins, God got me through what happened here.* She shook her head in disbelief. *Thank you , thank you...* "Then Virgil Jackson and his two men came in and got me out, just before they could break me."

She grasped Pamela's gloved hand, and they turned back to the two guards. Both Jenkins and Dalton were still looking at the rat crab, engaged in an intense discussion about it and then talked on walkie-talkies. *I did it, I survived this place, and they didn't break me...*tears came anew to Cassandra's eyes. But she blinked them back.

"Sorry girls," said Jenkins turning back to the women. "We thought this level was clear of these things, but we have had a real problem with these little bastards," said Jenkins, waving the antenna of the walkie- talkie at the rat crab corpse. "We have literally tried everything to get rid of them." He looked around. "We should probably be moving along before any others show up." Cassandra saw something else on the floor, reached down and picked it up, to the obvious discomfort of Jenkins and Dalton.

"Ms. Chen! The first rule around this place is, 'IF YOU DIDN'T DROP IT, DON'T PICK IT UP'." said Dalton crossly. "We still find live ordinance around here, and some even embedded in the walls!"

Cassandra coldly turned it over in her gloved hand. It looked like a heavy pair of pliers.

"What is it Cassie?" asked Pamela fearfully.

"It's a fingernail extractor, Pammy, Russian apparently," Cassandra said, noting the Cyrillic writing on the handle. "It's probably the same one they used on me." Pamela's face trembled and tears rolled down her cheeks, as she stared at it. "No baby it's OK now, they've grown back now, good as new!" said Cassandra hugging Pamela. She then turned to Jenkins, holding out the horrid device. "I want this thing bagged as evidence, just in case anybody wants to enquire about what happened to me here! Can you do that? " Jenkins and Dalton both nodded, looking grim.

"Also, I have an idea," said Cassandra stepping over to the dead rat crab. She picked it up by one of its crablike legs and held it up in front of the horrified faces of Pamela and two officers. Jenkins was angrily mouthing obscenities as he looked at Cassandra holding the thing up. "I think this thing looks actually pretty interesting, and pretty tasty!" said Cassandra brightly.

"Jesus, Cassie!" exclaimed Pamela. "Put that thing down!" Pamela turned to Jenkins and Dalton, and said, "pardon my friend, she's really not right in the head you know..." with a helpless smile.

"I would think it was tasty, IF!" said Cassandra loudly, holding it up higher and waving it side to side. "IF I WAS A JUNK YARD RAT!" she then dropped the rat crab carcass in an awful heap on the floor. "On to our next stop Lt. Jenkins, I think I am done here." she then said with a smile, and walked towards the door.

"Cassie! you pull one more stunt like that again, and this tour will be over!" sputtered Jenkins. Cassandra merely marched out the door, turning to only give a wicked smile to a still horrified Pamela. Pamela looked at Cassandra worriedly, ran up next to her.

"Cassie! Are you Ok!" she demanded. "I think maybe we should stop this tour!"

"Pammy, I have never felt more sane than I feel now! And I promise to behave for the rest of the tour," said Cassandra marching along. "Back there, that misbehavior was just my way of saying, 'I have triumphed over what happened to me back in there'. " She then gave Pamela's hand a squeeze and marched on. Pamela turned and tried to give Jenkins and Dalton are reassuring smile, but managed only a worried one. *She always was a little crazy... even in normal times,* thought Pamela.

Finally, they came to the detention section. Here Cassandra's attitude of merriment and triumph ended. She went to the narrow corridor, to the cell where she had been held for several hours when she had first been brought to the mesa. She opened the heavy door and looked inside at the simple bed, sink and toilet. She walked in, looking subdued, with Pamela and the two officers standing in the doorway. She felt waves of incredible sadness washing over her. She turned to Pamela tearfully, motioned to her to come into the cell. She then sat down on the floor with her back leaning on the bed and stared straight up at the ceiling blinking back tears. Pamela sat down beside her and clasped her hand tightly.

"Could you leave us alone here , for a few moments," asked Cassandra to the two lieutenants still standing at the door. Pamela sadly waved at them that it would be OK. The two men walked back down the corridor, leaving Cassandra and Pamela alone. Cassandra was now staring straight ahead at the wall. Her eyes became wide.

"Oh God !" she gasped. "It was  here, in this cell... This is where it happened." She clasped Pamela's hand tightly, her hand trembling. "Oh God!" she shut her eyes.  Then suddenly, she rose up from the floor. She helped Pamela up, smiled bravely, then they walked arm and arm out of the cell. Cassandra said nothing  until they reached the surface on top of the mesa, they had walked through a curtain of disinfectant liquid and then a corridor of blowers to dry their bio-suits.  Finally, Cassandra took off her helmet, turned and thanked Lt. Jenkins, who still looked slightly annoyed, and smiled sadly at Pamela before walking out into the sunlight of the late afternoon. The sun was near to setting and lighting everything with  a beautiful golden light as Cassandra stared at the mountains and then ran her hand through her dark rich hair. A gentle breeze was blowing her hair, and the rich golden light was lighting up her golden skin.  She starred off into the sunset with wide eyes. *Now I remember everything...I am free now...*

On the flight to Denver  that evening,  Cassandra said almost nothing.  She simply stared off into the distance.  In the hotel by the airport  that night , they  shared  a  room,  and  Cassandra ,  wearing  a  tee  shirt  and  panties wordlessly pulled Pamela into bed in her bathrobe after they had both taken long hot showers.  They  hugged each other then both  fell into an exhausted sleep.  Cassandra had arranged to  see Doctor Petrosian the next  morning at a military hospital there.

****

In the smaller Lunar Environment Training Facility, a concrete dome enclosing a 100 yard diameter area of simulated lunar dust, in lunar vacuum, on a six foot surface of specially treated volcanic ash simulating lunar dust, a brilliant flash occurred, and a curtain  of dust covered three men in combat Moon suits, complete with mottled grey lunar  camouflage coveralls. The men rose and dove into piles of lunar dust simulant , each pulling out an automatic rifle, and attempted to clear it and open fire at a nearby target. Of the three rifles, only the modified Kalashnikov AK Luna fired instantly and accurately,  though lunar dust sprayed out of it, as it fired its initial bursts.

Schwartzman stood stoically in the control room with his massive arms folded, along with Lt. Col Parker nearby, watching the test.

"I don't care what they say, the AK Luna is the gun we are using on the Moon." said Schwartzman. "It shoots even when it's full of Moondust, for one thing, and it shoots straight, for another."

"Right Chief, but General Collins ain't gonna like it."

"I'll make him like it." said Schwartzman nodding with a faint smile.

****

In the psychiatric ward of the hospital, in a private office, Doctor Petrosian sat in his wheelchair, none the worse for wear after a trip on a military transport plane from D.C. *Being important has its occasional perks*, thought Cassandra. *My doctor will make house calls, for one thing.* Casandra and Pamela walked slowly through the wards full of horribly wounded men and women, finally into the psychiatric ward full of people wounded in both mind and body. Some of the men, a nurse explained, had been there since the battle at Morningstar. One man simply sat in his bed staring ahead with a look of speechless horror as they passed.

Soon they sat in chairs in a large office with the blinds drawn on its windows. Cassandra had wanted no distractions as she discussed what had happened to her. She had also pleaded to have Pamela present for this session. Petrosian sat in his wheelchair, Cassandra sat facing him in an overstuffed leather chair, she was wearing a maroon bathrobe. Pamela sat in a similar chair off to Cassandra's right.

"You're both looking well Cassandra, Pamela. And I want you especially to know, Pamela, that I am getting an evaluation for an arm and leg graft, as you suggested. *She looks pretty well for somebody who has just taken a tour of Hell*, thought Petrosian looking at Cassandra. *In fact, they both look fabulous. Everyone else seems to have aged ten years since this war began; they seem to have gotten younger,* he thought with astonishment.

"I am going to take off my robe now Doctor," said Cassandra firmly. They had discussed it that morning, Petrosian had protested to no avail. *She is*

659

*running this show, and she knows she can*, he had thought when the conversation ended. Petrosian now looked at Pamela, who merely looked at him and nodded. Pamela moved her chair closer as Cassandra stood and doffed her bathrobe, letting it fall back on the chair. She then sat down naked in the chair. Cassandra then began her account.

"I am in the cell, I am alone, I try to sleep because I haven't slept in two days with the coup and everything. There is shooting and screaming elsewhere in the place. Then women guards come, they take me to a shower, and I get to shower, but they take my clothes to clean them. They tell me I have to meet the Big Boss, and that this is Virgil's idea. They won't tell me anything else. They give me a clean white lab coat to wear after I dry off until my clothes get cleaned. So then they take me back to the cell. I see some other guards make somebody kneel down in the hallway, then they shoot him in the back of the head as I am being taken back to my cell. One of the guards, a black man named Johnson comes with us everywhere to protect me. I feel safe with him there. He sits down on a chair outside my cell with a machine gun and is smoking a cigarette when they shut the door. I feel strangely rested and clean, and I just stand there in the lab coat facing the door. I am praying , "Please help me God, Please don't let them break me here..." over and over. I am afraid they want me to do something for them, and if I don't do it they will torture me to death. So I just stand there waiting, listening to shooting in the distance, explosions, screams... My mind sort of goes blank after a while. The suddenly the door opens, and it's this woman guard in her black uniform, and she has short length brown hair and mirror colored glasses on. She has my clothes all folded on her arms in front of her. She has this belt all covered with equipment, like a policeman. Then she just stands there in the doorway and smiles at me in this strange way.

And suddenly I am really afraid of her. Because she looks so happy, and nobody looks happy in that place. But here she is beaming at me. And I see the guard, Johnson, sitting behind her, and he looks like he is asleep with his eyes open, just staring and holding his cigarette like he is in a trance. And suddenly I am too frightened to move or speak and the door shuts, behind her. She then goes over and puts the clothes on the bed, by the pillow. Then she looks at me smiling and takes off her glasses.

660

"YOU!" blurted out Cassandra. It was the Mediterranean woman who had been stalking her in DC. "Why!?...how are you here?" she stammered.

"Take off your coat." said the woman smiling. The woman was slightly shorter the Cassandra and curvaceous and muscular. Cassandra in desperation lunged at her with all her strength. But the woman had something in her hand, and hit Cassandra in the throat with it, with a paralyzing sting, and Cassandra could not even cry out because her vocal cords seemed paralyzed. A feeling of dizziness and intoxication filled her. Then the woman deftly grabbed her wrists and suddenly pushed her against the wall in an excruciating pain-hold.

Suddenly agony, like she had never felt her life, overwhelmed her, agony so terrible she could not even scream,

"You do what I want!" the woman demanded, then the agony came again. It felt like her body was being torn apart by metal hooks.

"You do what I tell you!" said the woman again.

"Yes, yes, I'll do anything you want..." gasped Cassandra. "Please don't hurt me anymore!" she sobbed.

"Silence," the woman said sharply as she forced Cassandra down immediately on her knees facing the wall. Cassandra trembling with terror and feeling like she could barely think, suddenly quit struggling. The woman somehow stripped Casandra's lab coat off her and Cassandra was naked, then Cassandra felt the coldness of handcuffs on her wrists behind her back. Then the woman pulled her up to her feet, stilling smiling and threw Cassandra down on the bed.

"What do you want?" asked Cassandra her voice sounded slurred and she felt she was speaking in slow motion. The woman merely continued to smile then began to strip off her uniform. She stripped to her waist as Cassandra looked on in groggy un-comprehension, revealing an athletic and buxom torso. She took off her boots and socks lithely, then stood still.

661

"I am Nor of Rigel, Cassandra. I am important here, and I want you to be cooperative. I actually want to save you from being tortured to death here... Are you interested?" said the woman precisely.

Then the woman then took off her pants revealing a large and erect penis.

"Then I knew," said Cassandra, "I knew I was going to be raped."

"Then she cupped my boobs together with her hands and slid the penis between them from below. It was covered with some sort of sweet smelling oil," Cassandra paused looked off into space, "and I did what I was told after that... she didn't just want me, she wanted me to perform oral sex on her ... ," said Cassandra holding herself and staring off into space in the psychiatric office. She reached out and Pamela clasped her hand. "Everything she wanted me to do, or, to do to me...I acquiesced... I was like groggy like I was half asleep and dreaming. Then it was like I started to wake up... I suddenly realized I was wide awake and this was happening to me, and I was sucking her boobs, and I had no dreamlike excuse anymore! I was mentally naked." Tears flowed down her cheeks. Finally, she was on top of me and inside me, pushing over and over, kissing me, and I was kissing her in return. Because I wanted her to save me." Cassandra paused and drew a deep breath. Then she broke me... I felt myself break... I broke... I felt whatever will I had left break into a million pieces. I folded like paper for her, with her dick deep inside me, I became her slave."

"I told her I loved her... I surrendered to her," Cassandra said lowering her eyes to the floor. "I suddenly felt like I truly loved her, that she truly was going to save me, and I should love her for saving me. I felt I lost total control of my mind, my emotions, my body." Cassandra then looked up with a look of horror. "Then something horrible happened," she said. Cassandra bowed her head. Petrosian and Pamela both looked at her transfixed. Cassandra trembled and grasped Pamela's hand tightly.

"You don't have to tell us anymore baby," said Pamela.

"Then I had an orgasm," wept Cassandra. "Then another... I was just her whore by then... a slave, she raped my soul."

Cassandra awoke naked in the bed, with her hands still cuffed behind her back. Nor of Rigel was fast asleep beside her naked. Her face was lovely and composed. Cassandra shook her head in disbelief at this sight. She looked down, the penis was lying dis-attached near the edge of the bed- it had been some sort of strap-on. Cassandra gingerly picked it up and dropped it closer to Nor's stomach. Nor was obviously now just a normal women anatomically. It had obviously gone deep inside Nor also. Cassandra felt suddenly filled with rage. She quickly pulled up her legs up tightly to her stomach and pushed her cuffed hands below her feet so they were in front of her body.

Then, she raised both cuffed hands together to bash in Nor's face with all her strength. But she could not do it, she lowered her arms trembling and began to cry. But caught herself. *No, No! So she ravished me! Now I have to live! I did this so I could live!* Cassandra jostled Nor's now soft shoulder.

"Wake up Nor! You have to wake up!" said Cassandra softly. *Idiot! If we get killed now over this, it will all be a waste!* Nor smiled groggily, then looked startled, and rose up on the bed. She immediately looked down and grabbed the penis and then reached down to her utility belt on the floor and brought up a plastic canister. With great care, she put the penis in the canister and carefully sealed it. The canister rim lit up with small multicolored lights when she did it, and Nor looked on it with apparent relief and then satisfaction. She then kissed the black canister and refastened it to her belt. She then rose and quickly put her uniform and belt back on, as Cassandra watched in confusion and mounting despair from the bed. Cassandra rose. Nor combed her hair in the mirror, put on her cap, then turned to Cassandra. She smiled warmly.

"You had better get dressed Cassandra," they will be coming soon for you," said Nor. She reached down, unlocked the handcuffs on Cassandra's wrists, and took the handcuffs. Attaching them back on her belt. Cassandra began putting on her underwear and quickly put on her clothes and jacket. Her clothes were slightly damp. *But clean at least!*

"I have to go now. I will do what I can for you to save you," said Nor.

"What am I supposed to do now?" asked Cassandra standing and facing her, forcing herself to have a soft soothing voice. "Do want to see me again? Alive? We could do that."

"Of course. Just be cooperative, like you just were, and everything will be fine, I am sure. A woman in your position can do little else but be cooperative in a situation like this. Am I correct?" Nor reached up and stroked Cassandra's cheek.

Cassandra nodded. Nor then came close and Cassandra forced herself to kiss her passionately. *This kiss may save my life.* Nor then broke the kiss, put on her mirrored glasses with a smile, and motioned for Cassandra to lay down on the bed. Nor then followed her back to the bed and sat down on the bed as Cassandra lay on it. Cassandra was hoping Nor of Rigel would say something else to reassure her. Nor then, took off her glasses and cap and kissed Cassandra passionately and deeply again. *Good, she wants to see me again. Alive.* Nor, looking dreamy, then put her glasses back on and left the cell putting on her cap as the door slammed behind her. Cassandra rose trembling from the bed. She went to the bars on the window in the cell door and looked out. The guard Johnson sat staring ahead, asleep or unconscious with is eyes open. Two inches of cigarette ash was on the end of his cigarette. It had been like a dream. *Did this thing actually just really happen to me?* Cassandra went back and lay back on the bed. *Sleep, I need to sleep.* She fought the desire to begin screaming hysterically. *Am I losing my mind? Did I hallucinate this whole thing?* She forced herself not to think but lay still.

In the office, Cassandra slowly slid out of the chair in the office to kneel on the floor in a sobbing heap, she was holding herself and wailing. Pamela came and hugged her, and she held her for many minutes until she quit sobbing. Then she simply wept quietly. Petrosian handed Pamela a box of Kleenex for Cassandra, then looked away. *Now we know,* he thought with grim satisfaction, *now, hopefully, the healing can really begin.*

\*\*\*\*

High above the Earth, amid a cloud of projectiles and empty boosters headed for the Moon, rode the U.S. Navy Space Frigate Dauntless. It had

664

been thrown into an escape trajectory from Earth's gravity by a massive S4B-III booster. On board, Captain Robert Forester unbuckled himself from his chair and lifted the visor on his space helmet. All around him, his crew began to unbuckle themselves and to check the ship's systems. They were headed for deep space.

****

Cassandra sat in the psychiatric office at Arlington, doctor Petrosian sat opposite her in his usual wheelchair. She was dressed to kill, and her makeup was perfect. She cleared her throat, primed her e-cigarette and inhaled, releasing a stream of vapor.

"So now you know the dirty little secret I have been hiding Doctor. I managed to hide it from everyone, including myself."

"What is that secret?" asked Petrosian quietly. *You hid it well, but I saw it finally...*thought Petrosian with satisfaction, *because I a damn good doctor.*

"THAT I BROKE! I BROKE IN THAT CELL!" Tears filled her eyes. "I prayed to God, don't let them break me! I told him I wanted to die there rather than break! Then I broke! HE LET ME BREAK!"

"But who did you betray in that cell, your country, your people?"

"I BETRAYED MYSELF!!!" she screamed. She then covered her face with her hands.

"As we have explored, Cassandra, earlier," began Petrosian, you were asked to do a broadcast supporting the secret government, you refused and were tortured because you refused. You did not break then, you did not make the broadcast they wanted. You instead turned the tables completely on the traitors and aliens, leading to their downfall that day. I have spoken to several military officials, and they tell me that you are universally regarded as a hero in their circles. The preemptive attack that they launched because of your broadcast resulted in a disaster for the Greys and their collaborators. Instead of this war beginning with an alien victory, we had a stupendous victory on the first day."

665

"They think I am a hero because they don't know anything! They don't know that an alien woman raped me, and she didn't just rape my body, SHE RAPED MY SOUL!   AND I LET HER! IN THE END, I LOVED HER FOR IT!" she grabbed a box of Kleenex and wiped her eyes. "And as for the torture chamber," she continued quietly, "that barely counts. I would have broken there too if I hadn't been rescued...It was this close..." she held up her thumb and index finger a millimeter apart.

"Yes, it was close, but you didn't break, and you turned the tables on them, didn't you? That's  a lot better than most people have done, in similar situations."

"Yes, I suppose...It resulted in a truly fine first day of this little war of mine." she laughed slightly despite herself.  "I accomplished my mission, the first part of anyway. I guess I got a little payback too."

"What is your mission now?"

"Oh, I want to see the Greys driven out of here … and I want there to be some sort of peace  afterward. Real peace with the stars.  We are at war with them now, but we cannot defeat the whole cosmos. "Monkey has made havoc in heaven, but she wants to make peace there eventually… I want to create conditions for a just peace between Heaven and Earth, unfortunately,  the road to that peace lies through this dirty little war."

"All wars are dirty Cassandra , but this one, there is nothing little about it. Normally I don't bring  the bigger picture into the therapy session.  It is normally just about the patient and their inner struggles.  But you are not any patient, and you didn't end up here because you  didn't get into Yale, and feel you let down your parents.  No, you are here because of a war. And not just any war."

"Normally we in the  helping professions are great skeptics of war in all its forms," continued Petrosian.  "In this profession, we see clearly that  war is normally really  over penis envy, started by middle-aged boys,  eager to kill off their sons, so they can have more women for themselves."

 Cassandra looked at him with wide-eyed surprise at these words . *What an interesting theory of war,* She thought. *I must tell Pammy!*

"Yes, we get cynical about war very quickly in this profession." continued Petrosian. He shook his head. "We in the helping professions normally see only the tragedy and human damage of wars and conclude that none of it was worth the cost. However, this war is different. It is a war for the survival of humanity in the cosmos. At least from our point of view. It is not so much a war, as a mortal struggle. Life and death. That is why I signed on for this war on the night of the coup. So I own it too Cassandra. This war has already cost me an arm and leg, and below us are five floors of human beings, who have given almost everything. It is their war too, so you have no real claim to exclusive ownership. That is bogus. It is as bogus as saying you caused a hurricane by flapping sheets at the sky, and you know it."

*Bogus?* she thought, *Could I, Cassandra Jian Chen, be possibly a victim of bogus thinking?*

"Just so you know, I would make that charge across the 14th street bridge in a heartbeat again, because I am Armenian, and because I understand what you and Pamela were doing. This is a war we have chosen for the sake of human survival. So, many others have made that choice in this war and paid the consequences. So don't tell me this is your little war, Cassandra, it's everybody's."

"I know that. You know I do! Pam warned me from the beginning that ending the cover-up might start a war, might end our lives, might result is hospitals full of shattered human beings and piles of dead, MIGHT DESTROY EVERYTHING! Strange, but I finally understand what the Magi, the masters of the UFO cover-up were afraid of. They were afraid of what we are facing now. But Pam and I both went ahead anyway. Pam laid it all out for us at the beginning, and we all agreed. We had no choice but the one we chose."

"But doctor, as for the people in this hospital, all five floors, that is their pain and ruination, here in this office, I feel only my own..." she wept.

****

Under the massive concrete dome of the Large Lunar Simulation Facility, Alpha Company of the 44<sup>th</sup> Ranger Battalion, under Lunar vacuum and marching on simulated Moondust, marched endlessly in a large circle, all wearing Lunar Combat Suits with lunar camouflaged coveralls, and all carrying new AK Luna 7.62 rifles. Schwartzman, clad similarly, marched in their lead. They had been marching for three hours, so far only one suit had malfunctioned and the Ranger had managed to get out an airlock safely to get it repaired. They had discovered that everything and everyone marching across the lunar surface, was getting covered with Moondust, sticking to them by static electricity.

****

"You said last time that you betrayed yourself, Cassandra. Let us explore this." She looked at him somberly. She was dressed comfortably this time, in French tee shirt and jeans.

"I meant I betrayed my oath to myself not to break. Yet there I was performing fellatio on this woman or man, or I didn't know what. I mean I figured she was going to molest me when she took off her top and there I was naked on the bed in handcuffs, but when she took off her pants. I guess I was in shock after that, or drugged or both. My mind sort of went blank for a minute."

"Why were you behaving that way?"

"Because she said she could help me… and I believed her. I knew she was important once I recognized her and she acted like she owned the place. I was really afraid they were just going to take revenge on me for the collapse of the cover-up and the failure of the coup. I thought that Bremer, the Wizard, was going to have me tortured to death in front of him. So I had no hope, then she comes into my cell, and says she can help me if I cooperated while she raped me." Cassandra paused, "so I did what she wanted, only I was only pretending to cooperate. But, I then suddenly I broke and I was feeling like I was in love with her.."

"Cassandra, this happens to a lot of people, especially women in situations like you went through. I have treated women who got pregnant like you reported, and they don't even snap out of it, they even wanted to reunite the children with their rapist fathers."

"That's another weird thing about this doctor, I had these weird feeling and dreams like we conceived a child in that cell. That is why she put the thing in the canister so carefully when she was done. It was like she harvested an egg from my ovaries and took it, maybe even joined it to one of her own eggs. At one point I wanted to bash her face in, but I couldn't. For one thing, I felt for her, and another I still thought I needed her good will to give me hope of getting out of there alive. There was also this feeling like we had something between us, something that was also going to survive and be meaningful to us. I am convinced now we somehow conceived a child with that alien technology. Is that possible?" she asked.

"There have been a lot of reports of such things," said Petrosian. "But let us explore that later. Right now, I want you to know that your reported behavior was normal, normal for the extremely abnormal situation you were trapped in."

"So you should not be ashamed." he continued. "This happens to a lot of people in situations like you survived. Some call it Stockholm syndrome, I just call it human survival behavior in extreme situations. Women are especially susceptible, because as the weaker sex they were always being abducted or enslaved in ancient times, and they had to be able to fall in love with their captors or new masters in order to survive. It's embedded in a woman's genes, but it happens to men also, in prison and wartime...so it is a sense universal. Giving sex to buy survival or good treatment when you are in extreme fear, and finally falling in love with your captor can be said to be ingrained in human genes. It is behavior that lies latent in all of us and only surfaces in situations far removed from normal modern life. It is a throw-back survival behavior from a violent and oppressive human past. A past we can barely imagine under normal modern circumstances, but you experienced it and lived through it. So you have nothing to be ashamed of. You didn't betray anyone in that cell, not even yourself. You simply offered your body with all sincerity to someone who seemed powerful and offered to help you. From your

669

account and the other things you have said. Your ploy worked. They didn't simply execute you for show; they gave you a chance to live, and you turned it back on them. Given that this encounter was with the extraterrestrial and resembles some abduction accounts, this princess, as you call her, sounds like what we are calling an extraterrestrial human, and many people have reported encounters with them. A lot of those encounters were similar to yours and involved rape. Also, your belief that a child resulted from this has also been reported, so it all makes sense."

"So you are telling me I wasn't a traitoress or a crazy bad person, after all, doctor? I was just a poor frightened woman trying to survive in a place where nearly everyone else got killed?"

"Yes," he said gently. "You didn't do anything except what any human would have done, you tried to do more than most actually..."

Cassandra sat feeling exhausted, staring at the doctor, but she felt the knot in her soul was now gone. She smiled, then wept tears of relief for several minutes.

****

General Burnham rose to the podium in the conference deep within the Pentagon. He was chairing a massive meeting of allied space commanders, going into every detail of the pending Lunar invasion.

"General Standish," began General Burnham. "I wish to commend you and your staff for achieving space superiority from the Earth to Lunar nearside. I believe this creates conditions whereby Operation Watchtower can move forward to advanced planning. However, I would like to see heavier surface bombing to neutralize all grey surface installations associated with the Kepler Crater, which remains our objective for D-Day plus one. I would also like to see more emphasis on Operation Bullhorn, the jamming of all alien electromagnetic and gravitic spectrum signatures of the invasion force assembly and launch..."

670

\*\*\*\*

"Let's go over this one more time Cassandra, from last time. You were in mortal fear for your life and death by torture by people that had captured you and who wanted revenge on you. Then someone comes into your cell, tells you they can save you, then forces themselves on you and you cooperate because you believed they could help you escape an awful death." Cassandra nodded at this.

"Only I cooperated much more than I wanted to... I got carried away sort of, with my cooperation ...I was entirely too cooperative in the end." she said somberly.

"Yes, and have you ever experienced anything like that before? When maybe you went to bed with somebody because you wanted them to help you with something, only you found yourself having emotional feelings for that person that you didn't plan on? Maybe in college when you wanted somebody to help with studying for an exam? My goodness, I have even heard of journalists going to bed with somebody occasionally to get information for a story."

"Ah yes, the journalist part," said Cassandra sitting upright. "Yes, I have heard of that happening sometimes." She looked uncomfortable. She suddenly brightened. "But I certainly remember going to bed with a good looking somebody to try and help Pammy get out of trouble once, up in Canada, and I certainly was very cooperative then. I sort of fell in love with the guy. In fact, it was the most enjoyable, necessary, desperate thing I have ever done. The helpful person was this very hunky Canadian Army officer, and I kept seeing him for years afterward when he would turn up in DC..." Cassandra smiled, looked more relaxed. "So I guess what I experienced was an extreme case of the same thing. Only instead to offering my body to somebody important to get Pammy out of jail, I was trying to get myself out of jail... or worse."

"Yes, that's what I want you to understand. You were only doing what people do, especially women when they are in situations like you were in," said Petrosian. But Cassandra's face fell and she began to cry again.

"What's wrong, I thought we agreed you had nothing to be ashamed of."

671

"The child I think we conceived. It's a rape child...a little girl, she is beautiful. I call her Hamster. But I have heard that being a rape child is not good for a child."

"Cassandra, that's not really true. Let us say, as you believe and feel, that you really did conceive a child with the other woman, as part of some experiment on human-alien hybridization, in this case with basically an extraterrestrial human. Let us say it happened; then how did you feel towards the woman when this happened."

"I felt I loved her, at that moment," said Cassandra looking at the floor, tears were falling from her face.

"And I know you felt that emotion with all sincerity, at that moment in that cell. To the extent of being surprised by that emotion. Am I right?"

"Yes," said Cassandra softly still looking at the floor. Tears were coursing down her cheeks.

"So what you are saying was that you, without intending it, conceived a love child in that cell."

"Oh, Hamster..." Casandra sobbed. "I love you..." She covered her face with her hands.

****

"Like I told you, Pammy, I thought I had a child because of what happened in the cell at Morningstar," said Cassandra back at their apartment. She had poured a tall glass of red wine with shaking hands. She was weeping. Pamela had just gotten out of the shower and sat across from her with a blue towel wrapped around her head, wearing a blue bathrobe. Pamela looked at her; she was now crying also. Cassandra downed the glass of wine in one gulp.

"Like you Pammy, my baby it was taken away from me. I am convinced of it now...I have seen her..." Cassandra looked at Pamela, a vision of sorrowful loveliness, with tears pouring down her cheeks. "Oh Pam, how do you do it...How do you stand the pain? " Cassandra exploded into

672

sobs.  Pamela moved to her side of the table and held her as they wept together.

"We will see our babies again, I know it. God will make it possible somehow... I know it, Cassie ...I swear it..." wept Pamela as she held Cassandra.

****

"Now that you have recovered physically and understand why you were so conflicted, and can look at the whole thing that happened to you, are you pleased with the outcome?"

"Pleased is not the word I would choose doctor. I would say, I am Ok with it now. I am very grateful to you for that. I understand what happened to me now, and what I did, and why I did it. And I even have a feeling that I accomplished things, but it all cost me and everyone else far more than I thought it would, far more. But I even understand that is what happens sometimes when you attack a big problem, and instead of collapsing, it blows up in your face far bigger and far worse than you imagined. But I am OK with all that now." she said slowly.

"So I say thank you for that." she continued. "For helping me to understand everything. I even sometimes think what happened in the cell, the worse part of what happened to me, it seemed to me at first had some sort of deeper meaning. Perhaps I was supposed to come there and help conceive a child. Conceived in a moment of love even if it was deranged and coerced. A child born later, who I believe will accomplish great things." Her eyes welled with tears.

"My child," continued Cassandra staring out the window. "A child, who can be a bridge between this place and the stars. A child who can bring peace to the stars..." She wept for a long time, then seemed to regain her composure. She wiped her eyes and cheeks.

So thank you, doctor, I understand, and consider the costs to have been, worth what we gained from them. I now have an unfinished task, a war... A war everyone blames me for starting."

"Who is everyone? I know most people think you are a hero."

"Some people then..."

"Let me tell you something about the human race Cassandra. From a psychiatrist's perspective, a sizeable fraction of the human race is quite neurotic. They blame everyone else for problems they create and they, interpret every bad thing that happens to them as part of a conspiracy to make them miserable. They are mad at you because they have been inconvenienced by this war."

Cassandra laughed despite herself.

"Yes , they are inconvenienced and they are mad as hell about it!" laughed Petrosian. "Some of them have sat in the same chair you're sitting in, and told me so! And just like Roosevelt arranged Pearl Harbor in their minds , you Cassandra Chen have arranged this war so they can't go about their normal daily routine of seeking pleasure and avoiding pain. They are mad at you in one instance, and I am not making this up, because you have caused noisy air raids that have caused their dog to lose weight so they can't win the next American Kennel Club dog show!"

Cassandra laughed merrily at this.

" So the whole constitutional crisis, stealthy alien invasion thing went right past them?" asked Cassandra.

"Absolutely! Even the mention of these things will cause them confusion or to accuse me of changing the subject from the real issues, which how to get their dog to gain weight for the upcoming dog show! These people do not think about the Big Picture, in fact, they don't even think about their own picture, " said Petrosian smiling. "For them, the war is just a disruption of their life caused by other human beings. Human beings like the human beings who have always caused them trouble in the past.

"So this is a war, that most thinking people understand could end instantly, the moment the Greys decide to leave and go back where they came from. Yet this other group of people you worry about, people who believe it was caused by you, Cassandra Chen, to create more news, so you could report on it and make their lives miserable! The sad truth is , Cassie, a significant fraction of the human race is itself almost certifiable, and they desperately need therapy, but they won't get it! "

"So, I am telling you not to pay any attention to this group of people. They are the same bunch who still blame the 911 attacks on Bank of America because they are mad at them already. If these people they had been with Moses as part of Exodus , after one day in the desert with Moses, they would return to being slaves in Egypt. If you pay attention to these people's opinions they will drive you as crazy as they are!"

Cassandra nodded.

"Now , you mentioned Cassandra, that you wanted to die when you were first brought to the mesa at Morningstar. You mentioned this once before when you said that you began this whole UFO investigation with a sort of death wish. So, why did you want to die? "

" Oh I had my reasons," she said with a mischievous smile.

"I am curious, as to what they are. I mean before this whole thing started you had a great job and career. You were a star. Why would somebody in your position want to end your life? "

" Doctor," she said smiling. " I am very grateful for your help, and I Pammy and I are going out to San Diego, for a vacation and so I can reconnect with my parents. So I am going to defer discussion of my mental state before monkey began to make havoc in heaven for another time. "

"Are you sure?"

"Absolutely, that is one arrow struck in me, we are going to leave alone for now..."

****

"Good evening my fellow Americans and Allies," said Cassandra staring at the camera, she was luminously beautiful in a black dress. Her hair in

675

luxurious tresses  framing her face and falling across her shoulders. Behind her was a field of stars.

"Yes, it's me again,  Cassandra Chen."

**** 

In the White House, the President and wife watched the image of Cassandra Chen television screen spell- bound.  The President's wife wept.

"How did she do it, Charles?  How did she recover? She looks as beautiful as ever."

**** 

"It's  good to talk to you all again," continued Cassandra. "It has been a little over a year since your nightmare began, with President Taylor's declaration of emergency, the attempted coup and then the attack on the alien base at Morningstar and the beginning of this war.  For me, it has been a year of recovery from what happened to me when I was taken captive by the forces of the secret government.  I was their prisoner for forty-eight hours before I was rescued.  I   understand now the US government had given the grey aliens an ultimatum of 48 hours to release me and the other captives they  held at the Devil's Mesa. During that time I was tortured and was then rescued before I died  by some mutinous guards at the base, and in order to try to save the hundreds of innocent people held at the base, I agreed to make a propaganda broadcast for the secret government. I managed in the broadcast, to warn the government of the alien intention,  to launch a massive attack on the Earth at the end of the ultimatum period.   I knew this was the alien intention because the secret government officials bragged about it to me before the broadcast. Right, not very clever of them considering my job is to report things. Fortunately, the US government was able to understand my warnings and launch their own attack ahead of the deadline, throwing the aliens plans into confusion."

"What is the origin of this  terrible war we are fighting?  It is a lie. It was originally a lie told by the aliens to themselves, that the human race was nothing in the universe, just a tool to be used and then thrown away.  Not

676

surprisingly some human beings in the government, the treasonous Magi, came to believe this lie also, and in order to be on the winning side were willing to sell the human race for a few crumbs of power in the new order they hoped to establish. The origin of the violence of this war was a lie, the lie that you, the human race are nothing, when in fact, you are one of the most valuable things in the cosmos. My friends, always remember."

*"Lies beget violence, and the magnitude of that violence is directly proportional to the greatness of the lies being told.."*

****

In the Pentagon James Bergman, General Burnham, and several staffers had interrupted their meeting on the lunar invasion planning to watch Cassandra Chen on television. They all watched mesmerized.

****

"We have now been at war for a year," said Cassandra. "In this time our military have suffered terrible casualties. However, the alien's causalities have also been terrible. They began this war with approximately 100 bases that the US and allied governments knew about . At this time 125 alien bases have been captured or destroyed, and no confirmed bases remain on Earth. 2,532 alien spacecraft have been shot down. Reported abductions and mutilations have dropped from hundreds a week to now only two a week worldwide. Those who appealed for peace at any price with the aliens, and who said that the aliens would crush us in a week, have been proved wrong. We are now preparing to invade the Moon, the only confirmed location of alien fortifications that remains near the Earth, and we are fully capable now of pushing the aliens out of the Solar system. If you ask when this war can end, the answer to that is simple. The war will end when the aliens give up their now hopeless ambitions to conquer the Earth and enslave its people and return to their home. That is, all that is required for peace, is for the aliens to leave here and return to their home worlds and leave us alone."

She paused and smiled whimsically.

"This sounds very simple, and some people in Washington here are now giddy with optimism and have told me breathlessly that the resistance of the Greys here is collapsing and that they will decide to leave soon without any further trouble. The Greys, see the quote "inevitable logic" unquote of simply pulling out and going home; one of these breathless characters told me. These same people are already preparing to flip real estate on the lunar far side, and hoping to auction off thousands of square miles of helium-rich Lunar Maria. However, "inevitable logic" in war seldom becomes apparent without crushing military defeats and great loss of life. No sentient being changes its mind easily. Determination and perseverance are not just human quantities."

"So please be skeptical, of these people, my friends, who tell you this war is nearly over. Instead, I tell you this war will probably last many more years, and we may see several more dark days before we achieve final victory. I wish I could tell you something different, but my encounters with aliens and those who served them argue otherwise.

I can tell you now that a peace emissary from a group of extremely human aliens arrived on Earth and met with representatives of the alliance, hoping to negotiate a truce and alien evacuation from the solar system.

****

Kenneth Forester held his wife tightly as they watched Cassandra Chen on television.

"If she can come back, so will our son... I know it," said his wife trembling.

****

"Alien evacuation from the Solar System, release and return of any human captives, and payment of reparations to their victims and their survivors was the Allied terms that he passed on the aliens on the Moon. To the great disappointment of the extraterrestrial emissary, these demands were utterly rejected by the grey aliens, who responded by demanding our unconditional surrender."

I was honored to be able to assist in these negotiations, and I was bitterly disappointed when they were ended. The emissary agreed also, to take a tour of the captured alien base at Morningstar to understand firsthand the crimes against humanity committed by the aliens here. As we expected he was horrified by what he saw there. As he left to return to the stars, he told me personally that he would tell the rest of the interstellar community of these crimes and try to get us help. So as we speak, a larger community of peoples in the Cosmos is now being told of our situation and the crimes committed against us. I know this fact will one day lead to the just end of this war."

"I am a much better now, much stronger, and much wiser." she paused and smiled, "well a little wiser. But you also have endured, with admirable courage and endurance, the onslaught of the aliens and their attempts to win this war by terror and attacking our climate. Our brave airmen, soldiers, sailors, and astronauts have now carried the war to the aliens and even now are bombarding their bases on the Moon."

****

Lao Tzu sat in the foreign ministry in Beijing with his staff, staring intently at the image of Cassandra Chen on the television screen. His face broke into a rare smile. At this, the entire staff began to smile broadly.

****

"I can tell you that for me and my colleagues at CNS, this war began many months before it began for you all when we began to investigate the crimes of the aliens and their human minions. I can tell you now, that I would do everything again in a heartbeat. Every suspicion we held regarding the genocidal ambitions of the aliens against the human race has been confirmed. We thus can have no primary hope for the future but to force aliens to abandon the Solar system. It is true now that the Greys are not the only extraterrestrial species nearby, and that some of these peoples find the grey activities here as horrifying as we do.

679

Therefore, we must move forward in hope, hope that with God's help, our war effort will continue to be successful, hope that we will eventually be able to join a community of like-minded peoples in the cosmos, and together with them will deter any further aggression by the greys here. So may God keep you and bless you all, and may God preserved his children here on earth."

"I am now going on a small vacation, but I will be back doing my job of reporting our war of deliverance to you very soon. My friends, never give up hope in God's help, never give up hope that with His help, we will get victory and secure a just peace in the end. God bless you all, and God bless and preserve America and its allies.

****

Patrick Steel, sat with several other officers in the bar on a space station orbiting the Earth, watching Cassandra Chen on a large screen TV. At her last words, the bar erupted into wild cheering, whistles, and war whoops. Everyone rushed to the bar and began ordering more drinks and laughing.

"She'll be waiting for us up on the Moon!" yelled one Marine.

****

Pamela rushed up and hugged Cassandra she as rose from her anchor desk, and everyone in the studio applauded.

"What is more powerful than fusion energy or unified fields; stronger than the latest super-alloy in this war, Cassie, is hope. And that is what you have given us all tonight by your recovery and by your brave speech" said Pamela.

****

Pamela was sitting in her office drinking coffee and getting ready for her 10-midnight news anchor spot. She was watching a recording of Cassandra delivering her address with approval when a knock came on her office door.

To her amazement, Madihira Kapoor stepped in. She was fabulously dressed in a gold pantsuit. She was beaming a sad smile as she sat down in front of Pamela's desk. Her makeup was flawless and her hair at shoulder length was rich and dark, framing her glamorous Brahmin face.

"Maddy!" we didn't expect you for a week!" exclaimed Pamela as she rose to give Madihira a warm hug.

"I know. I decided to report in early because I need to ask Manny for some time off," she said sadly.

"What's wrong?" asked Pamela with sudden caution.

"Oh, nothing, I am getting married," said Madihira.

"Oh, that's wonderful! Who is the lucky guy?" said Pamela beaming. She was waving her own wedding ring, hoping Madihira would notice it. But Madihira seemed sad and distant.

"I don't know... it's an arranged marriage, you know, a traditional thing," said Madihira in resignation.

She looked at Pamela, sad brown eyes met Pamela's now wide blue eyes.

"Are you sure this is a good idea Madihira?" asked Pamela cautiously. "I mean you're an international news correspondent, you've been living in the United States as an American girl! How are you going to be happy as an Indian Housewife?"

"I guess I wanted to reconcile with my family, especially my father, and this is the price."

"Why now?" asked Pamela in mounting horror.

"I was up in the Himalayas covering the fighting between India and the Chinese, in this desert valley two miles up. It's all very confused and stupid because we should be concentrating on defeating the aliens instead of who owns a few kilometers of high altitude desert. And I am sad because my people, the Indians, obviously are no match for the Chinese. Just like the first time they fought in the 60's. I mean yes, we're much stronger than before, but the Chinese are much, much, stronger now." She paused. "I mean my people think time is a wheel, but the Chinese think like Westerners, that time is an arrow. If there is anything I've learned it's that conceiving of time as an arrow makes one a lot more motivated than thinking of time as a wheel." She looked at Pamela sadly. So I am barely acclimated to the altitude and sick, but I am there to cover this tragi-comedy I am seeing."

Pamela looked on in deepening concern.

"I was in this trench watching this firefight down near the valley with Indian Army officers on either side of me. We were all watching the battle with binoculars, and then I bent down to get a camera attachment for the binoculars." she paused, her large brown eyes became glassy. "Then there was a big explosion. And when I got back on my feet in the trench I saw that a shell, it's called a 'daisy cutter, had landed in front of the trench and the officers on either side of me were all without their heads any longer, just fountains of blood." Madihira's face dissolved into a look of horror.

"So, I decided that life was short after that and that I had to try to make peace with my family. So I went to see them in New Delhi, and before you know it , my father is planning my wedding. He works for the government you see, as a deputy minister of the Capitol district, and I am his oldest daughter. So I must be married off if proper procedure is to be followed."

Pamela absorbed this account in shock. Finally, she nodded helplessly.

Madihira looked at her with a look of sad strength and resolve.

"I see, Maddy," said Pamela searching for words to respond properly. Suddenly, her face brightened.

"So, what you need Maddy, is a real bachelorette's party!"

Madihira smiled sadly at this, then laughed slightly.

"Yes, guess so," said Maddy.

****

682

Later, at Pamela's house, Madihira, Pamela, Cassandra and Marcy all sat around the kitchen table pouring drinks for each other. They had been drinking concoctions of Sloe Gin and orange juice, called a "Sloe Screw", for some time.

"Alright, it's time for the great questions of the evening," said Pamela woozily. " Madihira gets to answer the first question."

"Oh, question," exclaimed Cassandra waving her hand above her head and giggling.

Pamela, who was sitting beside her, turned and asked her what her question was.

"I was going to ask her if marrying this guy she's never met is a good idea?"

"That not a good question Cassie!" said Pamela in a scolding tone. "I have a better question!"

"Let's hear it then!" said Cassandra in mock annoyance, looking at Pamela with big eyes.

"The question of the evening is: Who was the best person we ever went to bed with?"

"Oh! Good question!" Madihira laughed. Cassandra clapped her hands and laughed.

"The best lover I ever had was this Muslim student from Pakistan when I was doing my undergraduate at Ohio State! His name was Mohamed something!" laughed Madihira. "I lost my virginity with him, then he had the nerve to be mad at me the next morning, claiming I had lied about being a virgin!"

"Boooooo!" said Marcy, Cassandra, and Pamela in unison.

"He sounds like a complete jerk!" said Pamela.

683

"Yeah well he was a jerk, but he was great in bed! I went out with him for a month before his Imam threatened to write a fatwa against him!"

"Aren't Pakistan and India enemies of something?" said Cassandra.

"That would be correct!" said Madihira smiling. "We called our nights together 'undercover peace negotiations'!"

"Now, it's your turn Marcy!" said Pamela.

Marcy grinned widely. "The best lover I ever had was Lionel Gregson when I was a cheerleader for the then Redskins."

"Didn't somebody named Gregson go to jail for embezzling DC government funds?" asked Cassandra.

"Hey! I didn't say he was good! I just said he was great in bed!" said Marcy. "I remember him giving me this gold necklace one night, and I wore it and nothing else later with him in bed. Later, after he went back to his wife, The FBI came to my place and asked me if he had given the necklace to me, I said sure, and then they asked me how he had paid for it, and I said 'do I look like an accountant?' The women all laughed uproariously at this for no apparent reason. Finally, Marcy pointed at Pamela.

"Your turn Pammy and the question of the night concerns only male lovers!" said Marcy grinning.

Pamela stood unsteadily and smiled serenely.

"Well I have a tie, one lover was this black dude named Abdul at Cuyahoga Community College. He was on the football team..."

"Once you go black you never going back!" laughed Marcy.

"Then after him, there was this other guy named Bill who was on the debate team," said Pamela looking deep in thought.

"Let me guess, one had a fabulous dick and the other a fabulous tongue!" laughed Cassandra "you're damn close!" said Pamela laughing. "Now it's your turn, Cassie!"

Cassandra stared at Pamela in glassy-eyed shock as everyone looked at her.

She then held up her right hand and grinned sheepishly. Everyone around the table, including Cassandra, collapsed in helpless laughter.

"It is war after all!" said Pamela. "So let morals be low so that morale can be high!"

Pamela continued. "What do you call it when a black person, a white person and an Asian all go to bed together?"

"An argument over positions?" asked Cassandra.

"No, when a black person , a white person and an Asian all go to bed together, it called a Planet Earth!"

The women  exploded into drunken laughter.

Finally, Madahira stood dizzily.

"My friends, normally in my community in India, I would have to do this for my in-laws.  It's called Varaha Grhyasutra Nagnika," said Madahira, but instead I am doing this in front of you all, my friends.  In translation it's called  the 'presentation of the goods'!  It is to make sure everything that is standard equipment  is all in its proper place!" she then stripped off her blouse and slacks. Then took a long drink from her glass and peeled off her bra and panties, standing before them gloriously nude.  She raised her arms over her head and swayed as her dark nipples jiggled.

"The goods are fabulous!" exclaimed Pamela and with everyone else applauded while  Madahira danced briefly in the nude in front of them. Finally she paused and put her clothes back on somewhat haphazardly and then sat down pouring herself another drink.

"The truth! I'm only doing this to make my parents happy!" said Madahira and downed the drink looking serious.

685

"To your parents happiness!" said Pamela holding up her drink, everyone raised theirs.

"To your happiness Maddy!" offered up Cassandra.

Finally, after many more toasts everyone nodded off to sleep in various overstuffed chairs and on various couches, and did not awaken until the Sun shone brightly the next morning.

****

In the second Black Hawk helicopter carrying highly sensitive superconducting magnetometers, Mongoose glanced at Lt. Werner Muller of the Luftwaffe, who was running the ultrasensitive, German- made, magnetometer system. They were flying just after midnight near Mount Fuji in Japan, near a mountain lake that shown beautifully in the moonlight.

"Contact!, Contact!" shouted Mongoose as the magnetometers suddenly picked up variations in the local magnetic field. They had just discovered a hidden alien base. And as the helicopters turned rapidly and sped away, it was apparent to Mongoose that the base was large, larger than any others seen before.

****

"Congratulations Maddy, on your upcoming wedding, but I am going to have ask you to cut short your honeymoon afterwards and go to Japan. They have just found a big alien, hidden base near Mount Fujiyama, and you're our Asian correspondent."

Madihira, her head pounding from the previous night's bachelorette's party, tried to muster a smile and nod.

****

Cassandra was hugging her father tightly as he paused at the door to go to the hospital in the bright San Diego morning.

"Drive safely father, I love you," she said, and kissed his cheek. Her father turned looking slightly embarrassed and left out the door to go do surgeries on war casualties at the Naval Hospital. Cassie turned and walked back in from the kitchen and then hugged her mother who was cooking scrambled eggs and ham at the stove. Pamela, clad in a French tee shirt and sweat pants looked on smiling and drank her coffee.

"I love you Mom," said Cassandra desperately, as she hugged her and then let her get back to her cooking. Cassandra and Pamela had been there several days, relaxing during the rainy weather, and Cassandra reestablishing her relationship, long tense, with her parents. Today was the first morning of clear sunny weather.

Cassandra consulted her I-phone as her mother, now smiling happily, resumed her cooking. Cassandra was consulting the surf report.

"Oh my God! Pammy! Surfs up!" Cassandra exclaimed and rushed off to change into her surfing outfit.

"What about your breakfast?" asked her mother turning. But Cassandra had already raced out of the room. Her mother sighed, and looked at Pamela smiling. Pam smiled back.

"You know her father and I are really grateful Cassie has somebody stable like you to be her friend."

Pamela suppressed her urge to laugh hilariously at this statement, and responded by drinking some coffee and nodding her head.

"Thank you Mrs. Chen. Cassie helps me stay sane too. We work in a really crazy business."

"Yes, but I should also thank you for giving us back our daughter. She was always the one we worried about most in the family. She always seemed to be the one child who was most flighty and dared to do the biggest things. Then this happened to her, but now she seems to be healing."

**** 

687

Don't you understand father, I have been living in the United states since I was 19 , no women in the United States is a virgin after 21 , it just isn't done and I am nearly thirty-two." said Madahira with a quavering voice. They were all seated in her father's private study, full of bookshelves. Her grey haired father, looked at her and frowning. Her mother looked at the floor. "So you tell the groom's family I am not a virgin, and that if this is problem then the wedding must be called off."

Madahira leaned forward and held her father's hand in both of her hands. She starred at him, searching his face. He would not meet her eyes.

"So this must be made clear, transparent," she repeated . "Do you understand father, otherwise I cannot go through with this." Finally, he nodded his head.

"Good," said Madihira, leaning back in her chair. "I'm so glad this matter is settled." Night had fallen in New Delhi outside as she looked out the window sadly.

****

On the beach, Pamela was wearing a dark blue two-piece bikini but stayed safely out of the sun under a big umbrella. Cassandra was out surfing the waves. Finally, about noon, she rode a magnificent wave right up to the beach. A bunch of very athletic young men had by coincidence put a beach volleyball net in front of Pamela's umbrella and were having a furious game. Pamela was wearing a huge pink beach hat and sunglasses as she signed some autographs for some teenage girls as Cassandra walked up in her black surfing suit. She stripped it off, revealing a tight black two piece bikini, the volleyball game proceeded to have more errors.

The volleyball team was a bunch of Marine Corps officers, who then invited both Cassandra and Pamela to a party at a local nightspot on the bay called Pirate's Cove.

****

Madihira had enjoyed the wedding ceremony, the groom was a handsome, rugged officer in the Indian Army, a Captain in his mid-thirties.

They now sat in a luxurious honeymoon suite in the Hilton, tired after the long ceremonies and dinner. He sat with shirt off looking at her from across the bed as she filed her nails and prepared for bed. She was wearing a bathrobe over a sheer negligee. She turned to him in her chair smiling.

"I am very pleased to meet you, Captain Roy," she said with a twinkle in her eye. She was a vision of loveliness. He looked at her strangely.

"They tell me you are a virgin. Is that really true?" he asked skeptically. The words hit her like an electric shock. Her smile faded. She rose, pulled back the bed covers, extended a slender arm from her bathrobe over the exposed sheets and plunged the nail file into her forearm, letting the blood drip on the sheets as she stared at him blankly.

"There, your honor is safe Captain," she said levelly, pressing some Kleenex against her bleeding arm. He starred at her in shock.

"I have decided we shall observe the custom of Chaturthikarma, meaning I am a virgin and shall remain one this night," she said as he rose from his chair. She held up the razor sharp nail file. "Let us not have any unpleasantness about this." He looked at her in confusion. She turned and swept her makeup kit off the table and into her airline bag. Then walked out of the room pulling it behind her as he stood speechless.

"Can't we talk about this?" he asked loudly as the door shut behind her. She stepped into an elevator to the lobby and quickly changed in a woman's room, then caught a cab to the airport.

In an hour she was in a jetliner on her way to Japan. She stared out of the window into the darkness and quietly wept.

"Now I can say, I was married ...once," she said to herself sadly.

**** 

689

Cassandra and Pamela danced the night away deliriously with young marine officers at the Pirate's Cove and were invited by General Turkovich to the 1st Marine Division review the next day.

"It would be a great honor and good for my Marine's unit morale if you two ladies could join us in the reviewing stand, " he said. The First Marine Division was deploying. Where they were going, they would not say, but the deployment would begin the morning after the review.

****

The next day Cassandra and Pamela were sitting in the reviewing stand at the El Toro Marine Base. They both wore big floppy sunhats and mirrored sunglasses as the review began with thousands of young trim Marines marching by in mottled grey camouflage fatigues, snapping to eyes right as they paraded by. This was followed by a procession of armored vehicles also painted a mottled grey, followed by more troops.

"Why is everything painted grey Colonel?" asked Cassandra to a Colonel standing next to her.

"We are training to deploy to a grey place Ms. Chen."

"Where would that be?"

"That is classified, Ms. Chen, all I can say, is when we get there, we promise to turn around and wave." said the Colonel with a grin, as another sea of hard young faces snapped to eyes right as they paraded past.

****

*At the Sheraton Fujiyama, Madihira, her story of the frantic military preparations filed, sat in front of* her mirror sadly . They were preparing for a military assault on the newly discovered alien base within days.

A knock came to her hotel room door. She rose with some annoyance and opened the door. It was her husband, resplendent in his Indian Army officer's uniform.

690

She stood paralyzed in shock. He smiled warmly.

"Would you like to join me for a cup of coffee, in the restaurant?" he asked warmly.

"Yes," she heard herself say, and soon she was sitting across from him in a private booth in the restaurant.

She found herself admiring him sadly across the table, he was a big strong man, ruggedly handsome and smooth shaven. She admired him as coffee was served to them. There they were the two most dark-skinned people in a sea of pale East Asians and Westerners.

"Here by way of apology for my rudeness the other night, is a gift." He handed her a gift box with a pink ribbon.

She numbly opened it; a beautiful gold necklace studded with rubies was inside.

"Oh my God ! It's beautiful," she exclaimed clutching it to herself. Thank you Captain Roy

"Please call me Jay."

"Jay then," she said, then after a pause added. "Apology accepted Jay, she smiled. He returned her smile helplessly." Now, may I ask, what are you doing here?"

"Oh, that. Yes, I managed to trace your airline ticket here to Japan, and then volunteered to observe the Japanese–American assault on the alien base here for the General Staff. I must admit I called in a few favors to be sent here and fortunately, things are moving quickly here so they sent me out on the next flight."

"So you here to see the battle I suppose?" her face clouded and she looked away from the necklace at him with sad eyes.

"No! No! Actually, I am actually her in the hopes we could have a cup of coffee. You know, I can take you out to dinner and we could get to know each other. Like normal people." he laughed helplessly.

Later, she lay her head on his bare chest in the bed in his room. The sound of jet fighters flying overhead filled the sky.

"When will they attack the base, do you think?"

"Oh, I think tomorrow. The Japanese are frantic that an attack be made as soon as possible. I was down at headquarters before I came to the hotel. The Japanese Colonel I spoke to said that with land so scarce in Japan, letting the aliens possess one square centimeter for one more day was intolerable. The Americans, whom I would have expected to be more patient, agree with the Japanese, so they have airlifted in a Brigade of armored infantry to help in the assault. The Japanese are sending in a whole division."

"What do you think will happen?" she asked curling her naked body around his comfortably and kissing his cheek.

"Oh, I think it will be OK , like the other bases. Most of them were not much of a battle. The Americans said they will blast it with artillery and a massive B-52 strike from Guam, then storm what is left of it. So I asked the American Colonel, how big is this base, what are its defenses and how many aliens are inside it. And the American I was speaking with said he didn't know, but he thought it is like the others. He said they are moving quickly on the theory that the aliens will have no time to prepare proper defenses."

"Oh, that is good Jay!"

"What is good?"

"That they have a theory!" she laughed "And your questions, beloved husband, they are so insightful. You should be a reporter like me!" she laughed. "I just hope they know what they are doing," she said with a sigh.

"Are you going to be there observing?"

"Yes, all us visiting Allied officers will get a ringside seat."

"Beloved, can you get me a place near you?"

692

"Yes, my darling, I will get you a pass as my special press assistant."

"I want to be close to you tomorrow, Jay, if something happens," said Madihira, as they began to kiss again.

****

Tatiana, Kathy, and Christine, along with the other thirty women survivors of the medical section stood at rigid attention as Sadok Sar and his aides filed into the elevated booth above the parade amphitheater near the center of the Great Base in Mare Moscoviense. She estimated that one-quarter of the population of the base was now assembled there, all under the watchful eyes of scores of Toman Daz guards in full armor and with weapons at the ready.

"You have been assembled here today to see firsthand the price of gross incompetence during this crisis!" began Sadok Sar's chief Aide, Number 13, in an amplified shrill voice, that echoed in the domed amphitheater. Near the elevated viewing booth stood a low pylon that had been recently constructed. It was topped with a hollow quartz crystal of enormous size, perhaps thirty feet in diameter, a walkway led to it. Along the walkway was a sad procession of Dr. Acra, the inventor of the unfortunate "Red Plague" that had caused one-third of the base to be vented to vacuum, several guards and Number 20, an Unash designated as the chief executioner for the Moon base. Acra was forced to walk through a booth and doused with water prior to being shoved roughly into the quartz crystal and the entrance sealed by a quartz slab. The executioner and guards then withdrew. A large drum beat filled the amphitheater as the hapless figure in the quartz crystal stood alone and began to wave his arms helplessly. Then a huge mirror outside the dome, 40 yards across, caught the rays of the Sun and focused them on the crystal and its occupant, the figure ignited into a brilliant flame inside the crystal, and in a few seconds was consumed. The smoke in the crystal then was then vented to the vacuum outside the amphitheater and disappeared. Tatiana noted with satisfaction that neither Kathy nor Christine betrayed any emotion at this terrible sight. *Good, some strength.*

The procession was then repeated, this time with Number 2, the former commander of space forces. Sadok Sar had decided that public execution in the solar crystal was a fitting reward for his loss of the Lagrange point space platform to the Errans. Then the smoke was vented to the hard vacuum outside the base. The crystal now stood empty, as if nothing had happened. The drum beat the dismissal, and everyone filed out.

Number 7 and his colleagues engaged in a lively debate, in the passage back to their quarters, over the reason for dousing the victims with water before their incineration in the crystal. The solar crystal was a new method of execution, whose technical details were puzzling to many. Opinion was divided between the engineering specialists, who felt the soaking with water was to lessen thermal shock on the crystal, and the lower ranking crewmen, who felt it was to delay ignition of the victim's flesh in order to prolong their suffering. Number 7 noted these comments with satisfaction, and viewed them as supportive of the new space commander, a grizzled veteran Unash called Number 21.

****

Richard Metternich looked relaxed and well as he relaxed after a workout in the Naval Hospital gym and a shower. He sat in his room in his athletic suit, looking attentively at James Bergman, the secretary of defense. His room had no bars on its windows.

"Dick I need you out of here and down at the Pentagon helping me, ASAP."

"Well I am flattered Jim, but I am not sure how much help I will be. I still slip into a sort of 'waking dream state' at odd intervals." said Metternich.

"Well, the doctors say you have made a miraculous recovery. They say you are now as sane as any man on the street."

"We both know that is a rather dubious endorsement, especially now." laughed Metternich. "The whole cosmos is insane now they tell me, so I don't really stand out like I used to."

694

"Yes! You need to be fully briefed," said Bergman. "The best place for that is down at the Pentagon. We have a limousine ready downstairs to take you to a hotel in Arlington, you'll get a full briefing at the Pentagon tomorrow morning."

"What is the basic situation?" asked Metternich, leaning forward. "They have kept me pretty well isolated here while I got better. But I gather the UFO cover-up failed and we are at war with the Greys." Bergman nodded in assent to this. Metternich leaned back, looked deep in thought.

"I regarded both developments as inevitable before they had me committed here," Metternich said, looking off into space. "That's probably why the Wizard had me committed," Metternich smiled as he said this. "The rest I could kind of figure out from the air raids and the Winter." he paused.

"But I am curious, how did the cover-up actually fail?" asked Metternich. "And if we are at war, how are we actually doing? I noticed the air raids at night have stopped, and it's a nice normal spring now, after an awful Winter."

"Well Dick we are doing pretty well basically," said Bergman soberly. "I was sure we would be crushed in few a weeks after the cover-up came crashing down, but instead we've done remarkably well. We're putting up one hell of a fight, as a matter of fact. I mean they tried terror raids at night and we shot down a lot of their ships, then they tried cutting off sunlight to the Earth, but the Navy stopped them in deep space, they also tried bacteriological warfare, but that apparently backfired on them. So they have basically thrown everything short of a full-scale invasion at us." Bergman smiled momentarily, then frowned. "It appears that the Greys were completely unprepared for a real war to break out here. But we are dealing with a situation of vast unknowns, sooner or later they are going recover their footing and send a major fleet here, we are trying to get ready for that."

"Who is Chairman of the Joint Chiefs?"

"Malcolm Burnham."

"Excellent, he is a damn good man."

"Yeah, they call him triple-A, because his standing order is "Attack, Attack, Attack."

"Good, that fits. We surprised them, then, Burnham keeps hitting them and never lets them regain their balance."

"How did the Cover-up fail?" asked Metternich.

"Oh well, it's complicated. But basically, this woman reporter, Cassandra Chen, took it down, her and that blonde, Pamela Monroe."

"They were the same ones who figured out the asteroid cover-up," said Metternich in wonder.

"Yeah, and what's even more unlikely, they are both still alive," said Bergman. "So they are not only smart but lucky."

"That's so strange," said Metternich in wonder, shaking his head. "You saw what the Magi did to me. I would have thought those two wouldn't stand a chance against the Wizard."

"Well, she was on the air the other night, looking great. It's been really good for morale. Excellent in fact."

"Astonishing..." said Metternich appearing deep in thought.

"Yeah, General Standish is CINC Space, and Charles Martel is the President, he's a former Navy fighter pilot."

"what is our relative shoot down rate?"

"At present, about three to one. We've brought down 243 of theirs, we've lost about 4,000 fighter pilots, doing it, but the trend is in our favor. They seem to be running out of ships, but we are building 100 fighters a day."

"Who owns low Earth Orbit?"

"We do, now," said Bergman smiling. Metternich nodded with satisfaction at this. "The rest will be in the full briefing down at the Pentagon, and I want you to report to work tomorrow morning. We have you checked in at the Arlington Hilton, a car will pick you up there at eight hundred tomorrow morning." Bergman put on his coat and prepared to leave.

"One last question. Where is the Wizard?" asked Metternich with concern.

"Oh, he sleeps with the fishes. The rest of the Magi are either dead, in Leavenworth awaiting trial or in hiding. We found the Wizard's body half eaten by dogs in a shit-pile."

"So he dies in a shit pile, and Cassandra Chen is on the news last night, looking good." That kind of tells you something," said Metternich looking deep in thought. He then rose. "OK, I'll see you tomorrow morning then, at the Pentagon," said Metternich shaking Bergman's hand. "If the cosmos has gone crazy, maybe a crazy man is just what you need now."

"Precisely..." said Bergman . *Desperate times require desperate measures...*

**** 

Cassandra was sitting in the backyard patio of her parent's house in the early evening, wearing a tee shirt and shorts. An enormous full moon had risen, and the sky was full of enormous turboprop airplanes and jet transports roaring overhead, leaving one after the other from El Toro Marine Base. The First Marine division was deploying.

She rose as the twilight had faded and went up to Pamela's room. Pamela was wearing her electric blue bathrobe and had her hair wound in a pink towel and was doing her nails.

Casandra sat down in a chair near her.

"Pammy?"

"Yes, Cassie."

697

"The Marines are going to the Moon."

"Yes," said Pamela carefully doing her nails in peach.

"So, we have to get Manny to send us to astronaut training, so we can go cover the war on the Moon," said Cassandra emphatically.

"Will they have clingy space suits?" asked Pamela holding up her nails and gazing at them with weariness.

"Of course," sighed Cassandra. "So, now we have to figure out how to pitch this to Manny."

"Yes," sighed Pamela. "I will figure out something while I am moon bathing. If you will pardon me, there is this magnificent Moon out. "Pamela looked with delight at the moonlight now pouring through the window. With that, she arose, smiled at Cassandra, took the towel off her hair and spread it on the floor in the Moonlight. She then shed her bathrobe revealing her beautiful body and lay down on her back in the patch of bright moonlight. She pulled out a set of mirrored sunglasses from a pocket on her robe and put them on. She wound her bathrobe into a roll and tucked it under her blonde head, now lit up in the brilliant moonlight. She then relaxed putting her arms up over her head. Her wedding ring sparkled brilliantly.

"Oooh, this is perfect Cassie," moaned Pamela. "Could you turn out the light over there Baby?"

****

## Chapter 15: Fujiyama

Madihira stood in the trench in the beautiful morning, facing the beautifully snow robed Mount Fujiyama beyond the forested hills in the distance. Many other journalists stood in the trench with her. She had her flash goggles pushed up back on her hair, which she had in a ponytail. She was wearing her tailored blue-green Indian Army fatigues. The sky was clear with flecks of jet contrails high in the sky. She waved happily and blew a kiss to her husband in the foreign military observers trench a hundred feet or so down the hill as he stood, resplendent in his officers uniform, among the multicolored row of uniforms of other foreign officers in the observer's trench. She tried to ignore the slight look of apprehension she saw on his smiling face, as he waved back. Beside her, Darrelle, her cameraman looked soberly out over the scene with binoculars. Rows of wheeled and tracked armored vehicles from the Japanese Self Defense Forces were arrayed several hundred yards ahead, waiting. The alien base was located in a high hill in the green forested foothills of Fujiyama.

"I sure hope these people know what they're doing," said Darrelle pensively. "They say this is standard procedure, the artillery will open up passages into the base, and troops will follow them in, like everywhere else. But the troops in the armored personnel carriers have to cross at least three miles out in the open to get to that hill."

"Where is the American unit?" asked Ma0aihira pulling up her binoculars near her face.

"Over there, the whole 29th Division, ten thousand men," said Darrelle, pointing. "I hear the officers from the Japanese 1st and 4th Divisions and the US 29th, had a real, roaring, drunk party last night," she said as she scanned the American infantry waiting beside their vehicles. "I heard drunk Americans shouting Banzai with the Japanese so loud everyone in Fujiyama prefecture could hear them. They said they wanted the aliens to hear them in that hill," continued Darrelle.

In the distance, suddenly, a flight of jet fighter-bombers flew in from the ocean over the brow of the hills from the East , they looked like a flock of dark specks. They all dropped napalm on the hill before streaking away.

The brilliant orange flames blossomed silently in the distance and mushroom clouds of black smoke arose. Madihira braced herself for the wall of sound she knew was racing towards them.

"Looks like the show has started," said Darrelle with the camera up and now filming. "Looks like they want to burn off all the foliage on the hills for the infantry assault." Artillery began to rain down on the hills now with brilliant white explosions of high explosive and phosphorus. Thunder arrived and Madihira looked up at a flock of startled birds rising into the beautiful blue sky, now full of white contrails.

"So far so good," shouted Darrell as the thunder rose in intensity. In an instant it became deafening. But Madiahira was transfixed by the startled birds rising into the contrail flecked sky. Suddenly a thought came to her, clear as crystal, *Time, it is a wheel.* She then turned to look at the burning foothills of Fujiyama. But all she saw was a blinding blue flash.

****

Pamela and Cassandra had just gotten off the plane at Reagan National Airport in Washington DC, when they were confronted with a crowd of stunned and horrified people staring at the television monitors in the terminal. They were getting off the plane excited and laughing but with slight puzzlement that no one at CNS was answering their phone calls. Women were crying, men were standing in transfixed horror at the images on the screen. After a moment of shock, Cassandra and Pamela stopped and looked up at the screen nearest them. Their hearts froze. It was the CNS news broadcast showing burning armored vehicles and burning human beings spilling out from them. The attack on the alien base at Fujiyama had been a disaster.

Suddenly the beautiful face of Madihira Kapoor appeared in a portrait on the screen, Darrelle's face also appeared. The caption below read: CNS Correspondents Killed. A parade of other correspondent's faces from other networks followed, also being reported as killed.

700

Cassandra tore her eyes away from the screen. A deep cold abyss opened in her soul. She turned and stared at Pamela who was looking at her now. Suddenly tears poured down both their faces, but then their looks of sorrow changed to sad strength and resolve.

"Let's go see Manny," said Cassandra with determination. "We can send for our luggage later," Pamela nodded gravely, wiping her eyes. Together they strode down the terminal with their mascara running, but with looks of steely resolve on their faces as they walked outside and hailed a cab to CNS headquarters.

****

"So in summary, Japanese losses are both the 1st and 4th Division of armored infantry basically wiped out, and the U.S. 29th ID lost approximately 80% dead or missing. Those wounded who could be recovered are dying of radiation exposure. Losses in armored vehicles are approximately 90%. Losses in aircraft, both Japanese and American are estimated as close to 150 fighter-bombers and bombers lost when they were sent to try to cover a ground force withdrawal. The aliens employed a massive proton beam of estimated energy 500 Billion electron volts and power estimated at 1 Terawatt during the pulses. Power was apparently shipped in from a remote base near the Mongolian Kazakhstan border via a tunnel or conduit stretching underground from there to Japan."

Bergman, his face ashen, nodded bitterly as the somber briefing at the Pentagon was concluded. The view graphs on the screen summarized the horrible losses of the attack.

"So we and Japanese have to pull back our perimeter outside of the range of the alien ray. That's fifteen kilometers." said the general, obviously shaken by the briefing he had just delivered, "Otherwise we are going to lose another 30,000 men."

General Ogarkov of the Russian Military Liaison Office will now brief us on their discovery of a hidden alien base in Kazakhstan that apparently supplied power for this attack.

General Ogarkov, in a full dress Russian Army uniform somberly took the podium and in heavily accented English began to speak as a map of Northeastern Asia appeared on the projection screen. A red cross was near a region of Kazakhstan called the Dzungaria Gate, and a wide blue line led from there to near Mt. Fuji in Japan.

"First, on behalf of the Russian High command and the Russian people, we wish to offer our condolences for the heavy loss of life in the unsuccessful attack on the alien base near Mt. Fuji. We understand the attack was repulsed by a single, very powerful directed energy beam from the alien base.  Power to create this beam was supplied partially by a base in Mongolia at the Dzungaria Gate which apparently shipped power as electromagnetic energy in a deep underground transmission line over 4,000 kilometers to the location in Japan. We are now airlifting drilling rigs from Siberia to drill down and set off mines along the transmission line to sever it.  We are also assembling a large force to attack the alien base at the Dzungarian Gate."

****

"No!" insisted Number 21. "We must use these reinforcements to stabilize or defenses of this base! The base on Erra is not defensible! Even if we can put our craft over the base, the Errans will flood the sky with their aircraft and we will be outnumbered forty to one! We will lose all the new ships!" Sadok Sar snarled in rage at this criticism of his plans.

"Are you all blind? We have just achieved a great victory on Erra!" yelled Sadok Sar.  "We can now re-establish psychological advantage, the yoke of fear!  Now is the time to put all our strength into preserving the base in Japan, if we hold it against the dung-eater  forces now, their will to resist will collapse!  Therefore you are ordered to attack their attempts to move against the base! That is an order!"

Number 7 stared straight ahead, fearing to do otherwise, as the Unash commanders nodded in assent with squinting eyes around the table. He nodded with them now, his head sinking low into a bow of assent. But he could not escape the thought that lurked deep within his mind, *I who have cheated death so many times, it is certain I will die now.*

"For the Genspore! Genspore!" shouted Sadok Sar, and the Unash and other commanders all joined in the cheer in unison. "The base in Japan must be held at all costs!"

****

"So I suddenly went into this dream state, and it was about Godzilla, and Tokyo, and Mysteroid. And I saw Godzilla trying to wade through a tornado of lightning," said Metternich. He was sitting in James Bergman's office. Bergman was looking at him nervously.

"So did you gain any insight from this dream?" asked Bergman.

"Yes, I realized that Japan has a higher concentration of electric power than any country on Earth, and we can divert it to attack the alien base."

"What can we turn it into?"

"Directed energy," said Metternich. "The only question is of what kind..."

Bergman starred at him, nodded.

"Richard I want you on a plane to Japan, I'm sending out Hans Bergenholm too. I want you to figure out what type of energy we can make to throw at that base !"

"Yes sir," said Metternich rising from his chair.

****

Cassandra and Pamela met and hugged several tearful women, including Darlene, as they walked resolutely down the hall to Manny's office at the CNS headquarters. Inside his office, Manny listened red-eyed behind his desk as Cassandra and Pamela stood in front of him, and Cassandra somberly explained that she and Pamela wanted to be sent to Japan to cover the military campaign being mounted there. Suddenly, his phone

703

rang. He answered it with apprehension. Then suddenly stood up behind his desk  to Cassandra and Pamela's amazement.  Manny wrote down a number on a notepad.

"Yes, Mr. President, we will do as you have requested…" said Manny staring ahead in shock. He then put down the phone in its cradle. Cassandra and Pamela starred at him.

"That was the President, from the White House, he has requested that you two be sent to cover the new military campaign. He said this is a major crisis and that the presence of you two will help troop morale." Manny sat down in his chair looking exhausted. He was staring down at his desk.

Cassandra got a sinking feeling as she read Manny's face.

"So, under the circumstances," Manny said slowly, "I am reluctantly agreeing with you two's request to be sent to the Far East to cover this military campaign.  The President  said I was to call a number he gave me at the Pentagon, and they would arrange your flights with fighter escort." He looked at them with a look of despair.

****

At the Space Center in Houston, Schwartzman was handed the phone and stood at attention,  as he heard the voice of General Burnham at the other end of the line.

"Schartz, I need you and your staff to ship out to Japan for this Fuji thing immediately. I am giving you a brevet promotion to Major General. Now I need you to move out there and break that alien base. You are  in command of the task force. If there is anything you need,  you'll get. This has absolute top priority now!"

"yes General," said Schwartzman, and put down the phone. He then turned to Arizona and Jason Parker.

"Gentleman lets saddle up. Where going to Japan," he said soberly. "They are sending us in." *Where angels fear to tread, they send us in…*

704

****

Cassandra was sitting with Pamela outside Manny's office. They were both smoking e-cigs. Their bags had arrived from the airport. They were thus already packed for their next journeys and ready to go. Cassandra was somberly staring at Manny's office door, as he was apparently negotiating their assignments. *At least we washed out clothes at Cassie's parent's place before we shipped out,* thought Pamela.

*What if I go insane on camera out there, what then?* Thought Cassandra as her bravado  faded, as they awaited details of their assignment to be worked out by Manny on the phone with the Pentagon.

"I keep imagining  Madihira walked out of that door," said Cassandra with a wavering voice. She had felt strong and fearless in Manny's office' now she felt increasingly weak and afraid.

"Cassie, stop!" said Pamela sharply.

"It has occurred to me,  that I have ceased to be a journalist and I am now a cheerleader for this war," said Cassandra quietly, after a pause.  "That's not the role I intended for myself."

"Jesus, Cassie! Do we have any other choice?" asked Pamela with exasperation. Her eyes were dark blue now as she inhaled vapor from her e-cig.

"I thought we did, yes,"  said Cassandra. "I thought I could be this classic objective journalist covering this war."

"Objectivity is a luxury," said Pamela sharply staring at the door also. "It's one of those things that goes overboard on a ship when it's in danger of sinking,  along with pianos and  last year's newspapers."

" But we are supposed to report the truth, and I see they want us out there now for propaganda,"said Cassandra.

"The truth, Cassie, is that we are staring defeat in the face!  If we can't destroy this base, then public morale will collapse and we will lose this war." Pamela turned and stared at Cassandra intently.  "So don't go wobbly on me now. You just got me talked into this damn assignment! Now we have to go out there, and look good."

"I am not going wobbly!" said Cassandra. "I am merely asking what our highest duty is?" She stared back at Pamela. "I mean, I was planning to ease back into doing the news..."

"My duty is to help win this war, and then report objectively on the victory parade afterwards," said Pamela intently. She was staring transfixed, at Manny's office door. "What is your duty?" she asked Cassandra, while still staring at the door.

Cassandra sat paralyzed for a moment after Pamela's question.

"I'm sorry, I never saw myself in this role we are in now."

"But we agreed when we started to bring down the cover-up, that it could lead to war! Now this is what we have, a war, complete with whole Army divisions getting barbecued, by vastly superior technology!" Pam was now staring at her intently.

"I know, but I realize now, that I always thought I would be dead by now," said Cassandra turning to face Pamela with a shaking voice. Pamela stared at her in shock, then shook her head.

"An excellent simplifying assumption Cassie, I must admit," said Pamela after a long pause. "You bring down the cover-up, but the aftermath is left for others to sort out. Is that right?" Her voice was becoming angry.

"No! I just don't know how to play this new role I am in...I am supposed to be a journalist or a cheerleader?" Cassandra said frantically. "How am I supposed to report objectively on a war I helped start?"

"It sounds like it's time for a new plan, Cassie," Pam said icily. She looked at Cassandra intently then looked ahead. "Well, girlfriend, I know what the hell I am doing. I helped start this war, and I am going to finish it." She took a long drag on her e-cigarette. Now I am going out there to see this nightmare through to the end, Cassie, with you or without you," said Pamela.

706

"No! I am going with you!" stammered Cassandra. "I just don't know how to act in this new role."

Suddenly, the door to Manny's office burst open and he walked out looking somber.

"OK you two," said Manny wearily. "You both need to go to Andrew's Air Force Base for transport. You, Pam, are going to Russia to cover the Russian task force into Kazakhstan. US military observers will be with you at all times. Cassie, you're going to Japan to cover the preparations there. Pamela will join you later there after the battle at Dzungaria. I'll send more detailed instructions later. But I want you two separated at all times, understand? You're going to cover different locations. Understand!" he said insistently. Cassandra and Pamela both rose and nodded somberly.

"And please, both of you be careful," said Manny, controlling his face.

They rode to airport silently, sitting close to each other.

At the Air Force flight line terminal, Pamela's flight was leaving quickly and they hugged each other outside the doors tightly before Pamela silently picked up her carry-on bags, then turned and joined the other military personnel running to board the C-17 jet transport. All amid the noise of turbines and the smell of burning jet fuel.

As she watched Pamela run gracefully up the ramp into the transport, Cassandra sat down shaking and watched the massive jet transport close its doors, then take off, followed by four F-51 Griffin fighters. She felt herself momentarily losing control and breaking into sobs, but forced herself to remain still and to have a calm face, as she watched the trail of smoke from the jet engines disappear into the deep blue sky. *No, I will see her again alive! I will see her again!* Cassandra forced herself to think.

On board the jet thundering through the sky, Pamela sat in a thinly padded metal seat between two officers in combat fatigues. The entire cargo bay of the transport was full of silent men, all with the same expression, a blank stare that seemed to focus at one thousand yards in the distance. Pamela buried her face in her hands and wept silently.

"God please help Cassie get her strength back…"

**\*\*\*\***

Cassandra watched carefully out the window as the C-130 Hercules came in low over the treetops to the landing strip with its four turboprops screaming as the pilot dropped the flaps and poured on the power for landing. She saw rows of artillery and trucks moving on a road near the airstrip with tanks and self- propelled guns and barrage rocket launchers marked with either the white star or rising sun. In the distance, she saw clouds of helicopters carrying towers made of shining girders, and farther in the distance, the peak of Mount Fujiyama. An American officer ran by up the aisle and shouted at her above the scream of the turbines as she felt the plane lurch sharply downward.

"GET YOUR HELMET ON DAMMIT! YOU'RE IN A COMBAT ZONE!" he yelled at her hoarsely. She tore her eyes away and put on her green camouflaged helmet of Kevlar. It had a metal EM shield on its outside, under the camouflaged cover. Her hands were shaking uncontrollably as she tried to buckle the chinstrap, but an American officer next to her batted her hands away and tightened it for her. Then the aircraft suddenly dove and Cassandra closed her eyes as she felt suddenly weightless. The transport slammed onto the runway and then the four mighty turboprops screamed as the props went into reverse pitch, slamming her forward against her safety harness. The plane screeched to a halt, and she heard the back cargo bay doors open and the unloading ramp drop with a crash onto the ground. The smell of burned jet fuel filled the plane.

"OFFLOAD! OFFLOAD!" someone was yelling in English as other harsh voices shouted orders in fierce Japanese, as she unbuckled her safety harness and rose and grabbed her camouflaged bag. She was wearing green camouflaged fatigues, only the white badge on her chest marked "press" distinguished her from the mass of camouflaged men with M-4 carbines now scrambling off the plane and down the ramp.

On the ground, she cringed as a Japanese officer lined up his men nearby and was screaming at them in fierce hoarse Japanese. The sight of them standing with fierce steeled faces with carbines at their sides filled her

708

with terror, a hereditary terror only a women of Chinese ancestry could feel.

"Ms. Chen?" said an American lieutenant  in a helmet and fatigues as he came up next to her. She turned shaking to face him. "Come with me," he said and grabbed her bag.  As the plane emptied,  hordes of ambulance Humvees rolled up and began offloading wounded prior to loading them on the plane. As the officer walked swiftly towards a waiting Humvee, she followed him. Litters carrying horribly wounded were carried by her in an endless stream,  men without arms, without legs, without faces; all seemed to be suffering from extensive burns. The nurses and soldiers carrying them had faces like frozen masks.  Mercifully she was in the Humvee, and it roared off the tarmac onto a road.  She covered her face with her hands trembling.

Suddenly, with her eyes closed,  she was seeing white tiles , endless corridors of white tiles and she was being taken to the Pain Section in Devils Mesa.

She tore her hands from her face forced her eyes wide, forced herself not to start screaming at the flashback.  She turned to the helmeted lieutenant,  who looked at her with concern.

"I'm sorry," she said, trying to steady her voice. *I must fight fear now, I must conquer fear. Just like these other people.* She thought. "I just got out of a hospital, but I'll be OK."  He nodded.

"Yeah, as you can see Ms. Chen,  we had a real rough day here," said the lieutenant. "Our  CO committed suicide afterward. But that's classified." The lieutenant turned and faced forward. "But we got a new commander now, who knows what he's doing." The officer seemed to say as much to himself as to Cassandra.

They were driving down a highway then stopped at a checkpoint at a cross roads. There was apparently some delay, and the lieutenant was conferring with grim Japanese soldiers manning the checkpoint. The Japanese soldiers were all smoking cigarettes calmly. She began to crave one. Cassandra noticed they were next to a  Bonsai Garden for tourists, now apparently abandoned. She stepped out of the Humvee. It was

709

actually a beautiful day, with the blue sky flecked with contrails. She wandered into the garden fastening her eyes on a small tree growing in it. She recoiled when she saw the tree trunk and branches were wrapped in heavy, black lacquered, steel wire. She suddenly saw herself back in Devil's Mesa strapped to a table with someone holding a black electrical wire in front of her face.

She cried out and ran from the stunted tree with tears streaming down her face through a grove of larger trees. Suddenly she was confronted with rows of wrecked and blackened armored vehicles. The odor of rotting and burned flesh filled her nostrils. At this, she sat down on a stone bench trembling and cried.

"I was supposed to be dead by now...I wasn't supposed to see all this," she wept. She covered her face with her hands, and sobbed, but all she saw then was white tiles, endless corridors of white tiles and masked troops in black. There was no escape. She felt her sanity slipping. *Help me! Help me!*

But suddenly she felt complete silence and uncovered her face and looked again at the horrid scene. A deep silence surrounded her.

"That was always the choice, wasn't it?" she gasped. "White tiles or blackened wreckage." Rage, white hot rage suddenly filled her. "It dies with a whimper, or dies fighting for life. " She wiped her face and stood. *We will live or die as a free people.*

"OK," she said regaining control of herself. "OK, I understand now. Thank you!" she added. She felt filled with strength. She heard the thunder of several sonic booms.

"Victory, I am alive so I can see victory, so I can help make victory!" she said aloud. Suddenly she felt alive, strong. "I WILL GET VICTORY!" she shouted at the sky. "MONKEY QUEEN WILL MAKE HAVOC IN HEAVEN! AND HEAVEN WILL BEND TO MY WILL!" She was waving her fist.

Suddenly she felt someone grab her arm and pull her back towards the entrance to the Bonsai garden. It was the lieutenant.

"Ms. Chen, what you just saw is classified!" he said gruffly. "Now stay near the Humvee back at the checkpoint, they have an air attack going on 20 kilometers from here so the entire war zone is locked down." He looked at her warily. She walked swiftly along beside him now. She stood tall and proud. *Monkey will make havoc in heaven, I swear to God,* she thought. A feeling of elation swept through her like she had not experienced since the downfall of the cover-up. *Victory, I will get victory.*

"Are you actually OK? I mean this is a combat zone. Just say the word and we can put you right back on a plane out of here," said the lieutenant. "We got enough psychological cases around here already."

"Yes, I am fine lieutenant, never better." she said as strongly as she could muster. "I was giving myself a pep talk." She forced a smile, as she spoke those words. Just then a formation of four F-51 Griffins, flew at tree top level over them headed towards the alien base near mount Fuji. The lieutenant ducked, but she forced herself to stand tall and not flinch. *Victory!* she thought. *That's all I care about now.*

**** 

The cargo bay doors opened with a crash and fierce sunlight flooded the inside of the Antonov 12 turboprop cargo plane. Pamela, dressed in American combat fatigues, together with a military attaché from the US embassy, rushed down the cargo ramp onto the runway in Rubtsovosk, south of Novosibirsk. There a Russian Army major waited for them beside a massively wheeled BTR armored personnel carrier. He wordlessly handed them both padded Russian tanker's helmets and motioned them into the open hatchway of the armored vehicle. In the cacophony of noise at the aerodrome, jet and turboprop military transports landed, disgorged cargo and took off again relentlessly. Formations of sleek Mig 29 and Sukhoi 35 jet fighters flew over with red stars on their wings, in a sky flecked with puffy white clouds. Soon the multi-wheeled armored carrier was rolling , joining a vast procession of armored vehicles and trucks on a highway leading from the airport. Soon, they were rolling across a pontoon bridge across a river. The ride was rough and Pamela was grateful for the padded tanker's helmet she had been given, as each lurch and bump in the road caused her head to bump

711

into the armored insides of the vehicle. She looked around warily at the rest of the crew in the vehicle. There was a Russian Army film crew, supposedly at her disposal. Major Henry Kravitz, the American military attaché looked grim as he faced her across the interior of the vehicle and spoke occasionally in Russian to the Russian military sharing the ride with them. The Major finally stood taller and looked at the Russian officer next to him. The Major tapped his neck with his fingers and suddenly the Russians broke into smiles and a bottle of vodka appeared and was passed around. Pamela took it and took a deep swig , feeling it burn her throat, and then passed it to the Russian soldier next to her, who laughed and took it from her smiling. The ride became rougher, she up looked out an open hatch on top of the vehicle and saw pine and birch trees above them. They were in the forest. Curious, she rose carefully and stuck her head out of the hatch. The smell of pine trees and diesel smoke filled her nostrils as she surveyed the column of armored vehicles and trucks driving through the forest on what appeared to be a narrow and rutted dirt road. Above, in the sky visible through the trees she saw the blue sky covered with contrails. The droning roar of the engine of the vehicle was loud and monotonous, and made all attempts at conversation useless, as they rolled south under the forest canopy towards the Dzungaria gate, where the enemy waited for them.

**** 

Cassandra leaped out of the Humvee as it rolled into an American military encampment. She was energized and curious. Manny had directed her go find the remaining members of the CNS news team and file a story. She had been told that the two remaining members were named Ian Finnegan, a cameraman and Michele O'Hara from a CNS affiliate in Oakland. *A pair of Irish lost in Japan,* she thought, *perfect.* The soldiers at the camp, an artillery base, all bore the same look, a brutalized wariness. She was directed to an Army tent marked CNS news. She opened the tent flap and stared inside. An obviously intoxicated Ian Finnegan, a large red-headed and bearded man in combat fatigues was sitting at a table covered with papers guzzling some Saki. A Japanese looking woman in fatigues was sleeping on a cot in the corner.

712

"You! Finnegan!" said Cassandra with annoyance. He stood up and turned face her with a startled look. *He is a hunk of manhood, I will admit,* she thought.

"We need to set up and file a story." she said. "Get your camera!" The tent was full of trash, mostly empty Saki bottles and MRE packages, overflowing from a 55-gallon diesel drum that had once been intended to a be a waste basket, but was now the center of a pile of debris.

"We don't have a camera, it got blown up last week with Maddy," Ian stammered. He seemed to be swaying dizzily as she looked around the disordered tent. "Who the hell are you?" he then asked, pulling out a cigarette and lighting it. Cassandra pulled off her helmet and unwound her long black hair.

"I am Cassandra Chen from CNS headquarters!" she said glaring at him after smoothing out her hair. "You may have heard of me! And I would be careful with open flame around here, it might ignite all the Saki fumes!" She looked around angrily. "Now, where is Michele O'Hara?" Ian motioned with his cigarette, towards the sleeping woman. Cassandra looked at her in amazement, she had expected a red-haired Irish wench.

"You on the cot! wake up!" said Cassandra loudly. The woman turned over and stared at her with red-rimmed eyes, that grew wide with amazement. The woman, who was pretty and had long dark brown hair, sat up groggily on the cot.

"I am sorry, I was taking a nap..." she said.

"I am Cassandra Chen," said Cassandra offering her hand. "We are supposed to file a story. Didn't anyone tell you I was coming here," she said impatiently. The woman meekly shook her hand.

"No, we haven't heard anything from anybody here since last week..." said Ian, sitting down woozily.

"Well, here I am!" said Cassandra emphatically. "Now we need a good spot to do a story with Mount Fuji in the background."

"We don't have our camera."

"Then use my phone camera, it can record ten minutes of video!"

Soon they were outside in the sunlight. With a line of 155-mm howitzers and snow-wreathed Mount Fuji in the background. The giant earth berm she had seen earlier, extended in front of the base and blocked any direct view of the base of the mountain. This was by design since it was reported that anyone trying to look at the alien base directly could be left permanently blind by UV rays emanating from it. Michele, the steadier of the two, held the I-phone with its camera, while Cassandra Chen gave a report.

"Hello, this is Cassandra Chen reporting from Fujiyama Prefecture in Japan where the US and Japanese Militaries are preparing for a renewed assault on the alien base hidden in one of the foothills of the mountain. Despite the terrible losses in last week's attack, morale is good here at this artillery base as reinforcements have arrived and a new commander has been put in charge. The weather here is beautiful, and this is helping preparations for a renewed assault to go forward rapidly." She noticed Michele smirk at these words as she said them.

In a minute they were finished, and Cassandra reviewed it and then, sent it to the local Army media officer who cleared it. She then uploaded it to an undersea cable terminal to be sent back to CNS.

"Do you really believe what you just reported?" asked Michele, whose birth name was Mioko.

"Yes, if I report imminent victory, it will happen!" said Cassandra putting her helmet back on and gazing at Michele intently. "I am on a mission from God. I was supposed to help bring down the UFO cover-up, and I did it. Now I am supposed to help us get victory in this war, and I will do it."

"But last week... They massacred our people, our weapons were like toys against them. We are news people, we are supposed to tell people the truth aren't we? Their technology is a hundred years ahead of us. The truth is we really don't have a chance against them." Michele stammered and began to cry. "Isn't it cruel to encourage people to have hope, when there isn't any?"

"Yes, they have technology 100 years ahead of us, but have to bring that technology 400 light years to use here," said Cassandra confidently, patting Michele on the shoulder. "As for hope, hope is a decision, and as for cruelty, well they are very cruel, so that's all we need to know." Cassandra turned and looked at Mount Fuji gleaming in the distance. "The cruelest thing to happen to us all is for us to surrender to them." Michele absorbed these words and then wandered back to the tent as Cassandra turned and watched her. *Do I really believe what I just said,* thought Cassandra, *yes I do!* Ian stood watching all of this. *Reporter yes, cheerleader maybe, but I am a reporter.*

"You shouldn't be hard on her. Her boyfriend got killed last week in the attack. He was a lieutenant in the infantry." said Ian. Cassandra sighed at this and looked at Ian.

"Ian let's get this place cleaned up and organized. And we need her to basically just follow the same script I just read from, OK? Otherwise, we will have to replace her. Now, I have to ship out tomorrow for Beijing for a few days. So you guys will have carry on without me till I get back." Ian nodded, looking bleary-eyed.

Later, Cassandra checked her email before she went to bed. Pam had sent her several links to Edward R. Murrow broadcasts from London during WWII. "Listen and learn, Idiot!" was the only message Pam had written with the links. *Idiot? The nerve of that woman!*

Cassandra listened to Murrow's reporting as the air raid sirens rose in the background in London, followed by the sound of bomb explosions. He conveyed an absolute allegiance to the truth as well as being adamantly opposed to the Nazis, and he did so effortlessly. The sound of the sirens made her tremble, reminding her of the endless nights in the hospital with the aliens flying over DC every night. But she fought her fear and listened to Murrow's sober and stoic accounts of the war. After a while, she felt strengthened.

"So that's how it is done, Pammy..." she said to herself in satisfaction.

**\*\*\*\***

715

"So I'm microwaving this day old coffee, and it hits me, boom!" said Metternich. He was sitting in an office in the headquarters of the Fuji task force across from an exhausted and impatient looking Hans Berganholm. "Microwaves! We can make 915 Megahertz microwaves at 98 percent efficiency. So we divert the Tokyo and Osaka power grids here and turn it into microwaves.

"But the range of the alien beam is fifteen kilometers, we can't focus microwave beams that far. It would take antennas a kilometer across!" protested Bergenholm.

"What is the diameter of our siege lines around the alien base?" asked Metternich.

"Twenty kilometers! We have to stay out of range."

"That's the diameter of our antenna then. We can phase lock the microwave generators with optical links. I have Toshiba working on it now." said Metternich. "I was trained as an Electrical Engineer before I became a policy wonk at the White House."

Bergenholm began stroking his beard and staring off into space. "AH HA!" he said suddenly and smiled.

****

A thunderous explosion rocked the BTR armored vehicle as the alien ships maneuvered over the forest above them in the red tracer-filled blue sky and the sound of automatic cannon fire was deafening. Soldiers were now firing shoulder-fired missiles at the sky. The Russians had put up a strong magnetic field around the group of vehicles Pamela was riding with from a central large vehicle. The field was deflecting the alien proton beams down to big lighting rods mounted on tracked armored vehicles so their energy flowed harmlessly to the ground. As she looked out a viewport, she saw one of the big cylindrical carbon resistors catch fire on the back of a tracked vehicle just in front of them after a ray strike. An older bald

Russian soldier leaped out of a hatch on the vehicle and began frantically swinging a big hammer at the burning cylinder and knocked it loose as the battle raged above their heads with brilliant streams of red tracers coming from every machine gun and anti-aircraft tank in the column. The bald soldier was joined by another soldier in a tankers helmet with a new resistor cylinder that they jammed into place and locked down. Suddenly the deafening roar of jet fighters filled the air and an air battle began over the forest. Pamela saw one brilliant flash and then a falling blue-white ball of fire, signifying a burning hull of an alien ship, followed by an earsplitting explosion.

****

Cassandra, dressed in an elegant black silk pantsuit, rode in the Foreign Ministry limousine through the streets of Beijing in mid-morning. The streets were crowded with cars buses and the ever-present bicycles. Everywhere were huge murals portraying a smiling Kang Sheng, former chief of the secret police, and now chairman of the Communist party. He was portrayed as plump and wearing a grey suit with a background of red. Equally ubiquitous were similar portraits of Chairman Mao. The images filled her with dread. China was in the midst of a political purge of Communist Party officials associated with the previous regime of Wen Ho Xing. The fear in the air was palpable. Near the Tiananmen Square, where the Ministries were located, the driver was forced to stop for a demonstration of young people carrying red banners and signs carrying Chinese characters she could not decipher. One read "denounced", but that was all she could make out. Her course in Chinese being many years in the past. The demonstration and its red banners passed, and they were soon at the Ministry of Foreign Affairs. Armed police were everywhere in front of the building as she followed a mild looking official into the huge building. Cassandra felt fear growing in her as they passed several armed guards at security posts in the halls and were waved through. She had been told she had to come to the Foreign Ministry that morning for "consultations with officials" and was expecting a lecture on what not to report from Xingjiang, where the Chinese army was deploying against the alien base located at the Dzhungarian Gate, a pass through the mountains on the old Silk Road in the region where Siberia met the steppes of Mongolia. The alien base was located only five kilometers from the shared

717

border between Kazakhstan and China, and hence its discovery had exacerbated tensions between China and Russia.

She was led to the ornate door of an office, which opened to reveal the Foreign Minister himself, Lao Tzu, a small man, sitting behind a huge desk. He looked at her and smiled warmly.

"Ms. Chen, it is good to see you again. I am honored that you could come and meet with me," he said, rising from his chair. He nodded to her official escort who turned and left with a smile. He then walked from behind his desk and approached her.

"Please come with me Ms. Chen," he said, and she followed him, slowly recovering from the shock of meeting with the head of the foreign ministry. He walked out into an open office area where several overstuffed chairs sat. There was a table also of fine lacquered wood with a pot of tea and cups. He motioned for her to sit down in a chair and poured hot tea into two fine china cups. She set her black purse on the floor and sat down in the chair he had indicated. The smell of the tea was wonderful. Then she noticed Lao Tzu's eyes dart from the left to right, and was suddenly afraid. *He is being watched, so am I. That's why he will not meet with me in his office!*

He sat down and raised a cup of tea, with a warm smile. She took the tea and drank. It was sweet and fragrant.

"Ms. Chen, I must take you to task for your reporting on the People's Republic of China. Your criticisms of this country are unfair and ill-informed." he suddenly said sharply. Startled, Cassandra looked up from her tea. Lao Tzu was no longer smiling.

"It is my job to report what I see, Minister," she replied firmly. "I thought we were going to talk about a war with aliens from outer space that threatens future human existence."

"You are a daughter of China! China is in great danger now!" he said ignoring her last statement. "Your duty is to report that which encourages the Chinese people and discourages their enemies." He looked at her

718

strangely, and his eyes darted from side to side. *I understand.* She thought. *He is putting on a show for whoever is watching him.*

"You must help us. We are your people," he said with his eyes lowered. With that, he handed her a set of papers.

"Here are your press credentials, passes and plane tickets," he said pointing to a set of papers on the table. "Be careful in the combat zone, it will be very dangerous. Your camera and crew will be provided by the People's Liberation Army, and all reports will be cleared  by my office. So make them uplifting to the people." He rose and clasped her hand,  she rose and bowed slightly in respect.

"Thank you, minister, for your counsel," she said as warmly as she could muster.

"I am glad you understand things better. To further enlighten you, I also have given you a ticket to the opera for tonight. I fear I cannot accompany you there, but do honor me by attending. The limousine will take you there from your hotel." he said now smiling. He then turned and left. *I am apparently considered too dangerous to talk to for very long...* she thought.

****

They were out of the forest now and rolling across the steppes of Mongolia , Pamela sought respite from the confines and unwashed body smells of the BTR by poking her head out of a top hatchway of the armored vehicle. The sky was deep blue and flanked with contrails , as far as she could see to either side,  waves of dark green armored vehicles and trucks were now emerging from the forest line and rolling southward. Many were towing artillery pieces. She paused and took some footage with the camera the Russians had provided. Suddenly a loud roar rose above the droning of the engines of the vehicles and in the distance, a huge missile rose, a dark speck rising on a pillar of fire,  rising  from a

719

mobile launcher. Another followed after it and then another and then a formation of Russian jet fighters roared over heading South. *These Russians look like they really mean it,* thought Pamela happily as she filmed.

Soon they had crossed , on a pontoon bridge, the river that marked the border and were plunging deeply into Kazakhstan.

****

Cassandra watched the dreary spectacle of the opera "Red Detachment of Women" with fascination. Finally, the end came and the hero was burned alive by his captors after he would not reveal the location of the Red detachment. Despite herself, she wept. *Yes, that is the choice we have,* she thought. *For most of the world's people, this is dirt simple. Only in the West do people try to see both sides of the question.*

****

Standing on the dark beach near the town of Fuji looking out into the broad expanse of Suruga Bay, now-General Schwartzman looked with satisfaction through his binoculars as the mighty battleships Wisconsin, Alabama, and Missouri as all wheeled  their gun turrets towards the Japanese coast  on the dim cloudy morning. Almost the entire US Seventh Fleet stood behind the battleships farther out to sea, and in the sky, thousands of jet fighters patrolled the skies. The aliens had tried to disrupt his attack preparations with several raids from space, but they had all been crushed. True, his forces had lost two fighters for every alien ship brought down, but it did not matter. Most of the pilots survived, and some were up flying again the next day. He had christened his operation to destroy the enemy base "Hammer of Thor." He had received a "blank check" from Supreme Allied Commander General Burnham and Secretary of Defense Bergman.  More  importantly, he was receiving  the mobilized energies and ingenuity of the entire Japanese nation, who, as General Morita, his Japanese second in command,  had said, 'we are re-engineering the entire nation of Japan into a weapon against the aliens.'

Schwartzman looked around him, now-General Jason Parker and now-Colonel  Arizona Jones stood beside  him in combat fatigues,  their faces now lit with the dull light of a cloudy dawn. Admiral Haynes, the US Chief of Naval Operations stood by also with his staff. General Morita of the Japanese Army, a tall muscular sumo wrestler of a man with a fierce mustache, and his staff in dark green fatigues stood also nearby on the beach. Schwartzman looked at his watch and watched the seconds race by. In ten seconds the battleships would open fire.

Schwartzman watched as the distant line of battleships erupted in brilliant light, lighting up even the clouds above them with reflected light as they began to fire, enormous clouds of yellow and orange flame blossoming around the muzzles of their 16-inch guns. In seconds, Schwartzman knew it would be raining down 1-ton shells full of diamond hard Teflon on to the alien base beyond the coastal range of hills. *Hammer Down* thought Schwartzman. The Japanese erupted in Banzai cheers at the sight. The hills blocked the alien's ray, which was strictly line of sight and was range-limited by the molecules of the atmosphere to fifteen kilometers at sea level in any case. The battleship guns had a range of twice that. Schwartzman turned and gave the thumbs-up sign to Admiral Haynes and General Morita, as the booming thunder of the distant Naval guns arrived. He turned and walked over to a large television screen in a tent to see the effect of the shells. The image was a fusion of visible light and infrared, showing the alien force-field in infrared in a dome over the hilltop near Mount Fuji in the distance. He was not disappointed by what he saw. The force field over the alien base, that had stopped ordinary artillery shells the week before, was now being pummeled with the battleship shells exploding deep inside it and shooting streamers of incandescent molten Teflon right into the hilltop that the alien base occupied.

"Looks like we are getting penetration of the shield, chief," said Parker. "They must know that the game is up now."

"How are we on power Arizona?" asked Schwartzman.

"We have the main power lines 75 percent complete from the Tokyo-Yokohama power grid, and 50 percent complete from the Osaka-Nagoya grid," said Arizona.

"Tell them to hurry up! The longer we take gives those maggots more time to prepare. I want that grid linked-up and synched-up by next week!"

"Yes, General!"

"Soon we will have more power than the aliens have, two terawatts! Then we'll see how their technology matches ours!" said Schwartzman as the air shook from the thunder of the huge guns far out in the sea, and light of the guns firing lit up the clouds from below and bathed the beach in a flickering firelight.

****

Pamela, standing outside in her now days-old combat fatigues and still wearing her Russian tankers helmet to hide her unwashed hair, stood on the Mongolian steppes as around her a massive Russian force was setting up artillery and barrage rocket batteries. It was a beautiful clear day. Fleets of jet fighters and bombers were flying overhead towards a range of mountains in the near distance. There was a large lake called Alakol. Intermittently, a fierily meteor-like spark would fall from the skies into the mountains, and the sky would light with flickering light visible even in the daylight. In the further distance, was a gap in the mountains which was the Dzhungarian Gate, connecting the Far East to the steppes of Central Asia. It had been the key pass through the mountains for the Silk Road of Ancient times. Now it was the site of a well concealed alien base.

"This is Pamela Monroe of CNS now reporting from the spear point of a Russian and Kazakh Army task force, as you can see behind us, this powerful Russian task force is now setting up artillery and rocket batteries to bombard the base which is roughly twenty kilometers in the distance and is only five kilometers from the border of Kazakhstan with China. We are told the Chinese have also brought up a large task force and will be bombarding the alien base from their side of the border."

****

Cassandra stood in her US Army combat fatigues and helmet in the bright sunlight beside the vigorous and youthful looking General Yueh Lai of the Chinese People's Liberation Army clad in desert camouflage. She was

722

looking north with special laser shielded binoculars across the border into Kazakhstan. Behind her, a salty lake called Lake Ebi lay dead. She was looking at Mongolian looking Kazakh cavalrymen with AK-74s who were riding small Mongolian ponies. They, in turn, were looking back at her also through binoculars. She noted that the Kazakhs, and even the ponies they rode, had anti-laser goggles covering their eyes.

The Russians she knew, were nearby, but concealed, manning high powered lasers. There had been numerous bloody clashes in the previous decades in the region between the Chinese and the Russians.

Behind them, the Chinese army was digging trenches and erecting protective earthen berms around row upon row of long-range heavy artillery. Soldiers in desert camouflage were rushing up to the General's aides giving reports in hoarse Mandarin Chinese and then saluting with a clenched fist held next to their heads.

"Cassie, you say you went to UCLA?" the general asked in perfect English. Cassie nodded as she continued to gaze through the binoculars.

"So did I for two years. I took Nuclear Engineering there, it was marvelous." General Yueh Lai said.

**\*\*\*\***

Manny Berkowitz watched with satisfaction as the faces of Cassandra and Pamela lit up the television screen as each gave their report from Dzhungaria. They both looked ravishing. Also queued up in the newscast was Michele O'Hara from Japan looking perky and animated as she reported on the massive buildup around the alien base near Fuji. The other networks appeared still stunned by the losses of the previous week and had not filed any stories from either site. *Market Share, we win this war by superior market share!* he thought.

**\*\*\*\***

"We will crush them with superior firepower! Their death rays have limited range in the atmosphere, and our artillery and rockets can reach farther," said General Gribkov's interpreter as Gribkov was making a hammering motion with his fist. Pamela simply listened, and nodded agreeably, noting, after the response to her first question, that General Gribkov did not like answering questions from reporters and preferred to make angry speeches. "Watch what happens in the next few days and you will see for yourselves!" the translator added after a long rant from Gribkov that even Pamela recognized was a sanitized version of the Russian tirade. "Now pardon me, I have to fight a battle!" the translator added, as Gribkov turned away, back to his aides.

"Well there you have it," said Pamela, looking radiant with her makeup perfect and her angelic face framed by her blonde locks. She had managed to have a bath after a torrential rainstorm had provided water, it had been heavenly, and it had allowed her to wash her hair for the first time in a week. "This is Pamela Monroe near the Dzhungarian Gate in Kazakhstan awaiting the Russian assault on the alien base located near here."

****

Cassandra was standing in a trench near General Yueh Lai, the clouds had passed and skies were perfectly clear. A feeling of tension in the Chinese camp was mounting as Casandra sensed that the time of the attack was near. She was scanning the deep blue skies, then she noticed silver glints. She watched in disbelief as two saucers darted out of the sky coming down straight for them. Without thinking, she instantly reached up and grabbed the General by his arm and yanked him down into the trench on top of her, her body cushioning his fall. She felt a shooting pain in her lower leg. In that same instant, the sky exploded with showers of yellow and green tracers and rockets as the surrounding army units opened fire on the saucers and the saucers fired also, triggering deafening explosions as the neatly stacked artillery ammunition next to the guns detonated. Clouds of dust filled the trench.

"Get me General Gu Li!" General Yueh Lai was yelling. "Where is the People's Liberation Army, Air Force! WHERE IS IT!" he yelled hoarsely. Cassandra heard this with her translator pod around her neck. As he struggled to get up off her. He managed to stand. They were both covered

724

with dust. Around them, outside the trench, flames, explosions and confused screaming was heard. Machine gun and automatic cannons still fired, but finally dwindled to nothing. The attack was apparently over.

"WHERE IS OUR AIR FORCE!" he yelled at her in English with an anguished tone as the noise ebbed. He got up and looked around, surveying the burning wreckage. He then turned to her and said slowly.

"You have saved my life, Cassandra. I am forever in your debt. Anything I can do for you that is in my power, I will do it." he said emotionally. He looked at her lovely form laying in the bottom of the trench and fell instantly in love with her.

"You can start by helping me up, I think I sprained my ankle," she said grimacing in pain.

"His strong hands pulled her up. Her ankle hurt badly, but any concern she had over the ankle vanished as she surveyed the results of the alien attack outside the trench. Hundreds of men were dead and blown to pieces or burned to a blackened crisp around them. Two of the general's aides, who had been standing next to him lay dead of shrapnel wounds from exploding artillery rounds. A wounded officer ran up to the General with his arm a bloody mass and asked if the general needed any medical help. When the general answered, that he was fine, the young officer fell over and died.

****

At the first light of dawn, the Russian rocket barrage opened up thunderously with thousands of long-range bombardment rockets flashing across the dark blue sky, as Pamela covered her ears while standing in a trench. After that, thousands of long-range artillery pieces opened fire as Pamela covered her ears tightly with palms of her hands and ducked down into the trench deeper. In the distance, the low mountain peak lit up with sparks of light and was finally glittering with a terrible scintillating brilliance.

725

Cassandra ducked low here trench as the artillery behind her fired with deafening noise that made the very air around her seem to shake like Jell-O. Even with ear protection, the noise was almost unbearable, shaking her insides. The bombardment continued for what seemed like an eternity, then with the glow of blue flares filling the trench the bombardment stopped. She rose on her crutches and looked with her binoculars. General Yueh was in the trench beside her with his staff.

"The Russians have begun their assault with their commandos in helicopters," said General Yueh with a certain awe as they watched.

"How can they? Our troops were slaughtered when they did that!" cried Cassandra.

"Well, they are doing it!" said the General in astonishment. As Cassandra watched the peak with her high power binoculars, it soon became apparent that besides the sight of blue tracers and flame throwers being used, no other sign of fighting was evident. After a half an hour, the peak was rocked by several brilliant explosions and then became quiet.

"Rodinya!,Rodinya! (Motherland)," the Russian troops were yelling in their trenches.

"What happened?" asked Pamela looking at the now peaceful looking mountain top. Only a fire seemed to be burning near the summit releasing a stream of black smoke.

"Well it looks like the Russian Spetznaz just helicopered in and took the place." said the American Military attaché in amazement. "Crazy bastards!" he muttered to himself. Several red flares appeared from the summit in the distance like sparks. The Russian troops began jumping out of their trenches and dancing.

"RODINYA, RODINYA!" they were yelling.

Cassandra was riding happily up to the terminal building in an open Humvee at the airport in the American sector near Fuji when Pamela emerged yelling excitedly. She ran up to the Humvee and hugged Cassandra excitedly. Ian Finnegan also appeared, and to Cassandra's amazement, appeared sober and with his beard well-trimmed. He grinned sheepishly as Cassandra hugged his neck from her seat. The airport was a tempest of activity with C130 Hercules turboprops, Blackhawk helicopters, and Osprey tilt-rotors landing and disgorging cargo and personnel, then taking off to allow more aircraft to land.

"Where is Michele?" asked Cassandra over the scream of the turbines as she was getting out of the Humvee painfully. Soldiers unloaded her bags . Ian grabbed her two bags as Pamela helped her into the terminal and they sat down at a table. Ian looked pained. Pamela adopted a blank look.

"Michele is on vacation right now," said Pamela levelly, the way she said it filled Cassandra with dread.

"What? Why?"

"Michele, she's originally from Sapporo up north on Hokkaido, a couple hundred miles north of here, and the aliens took her sister Hiroko and about forty other  of other women captive last night during a raid on Hokkaido," said Pamela grimly. "They took advantage of all the airpower being concentrated down here. The government just confirmed this a few hours ago. The aliens have sent a message to the Japanese government saying the women will be killed if the base is attacked.  So Michele fell apart when she was told this by her family. So... I gave her a vacation." said Pamela.

Cassandra looked somberly away from Pamela.

"That's so terrible," said Cassandra. Then she rose on her crutches. She paused.  "Well let's get started then. When is the attack supposed to start?"

"I would guess in the next day or so." said Pamela soberly." They seem to have set up a lot of big radar dishes around the perimeter and have been laying big power lines to them. They look like they are just about ready to

727

do something. Also, the alien base looks like it has been badly damaged by the naval and rocket bombardments. It looks fairly Lunar now. They have been hammering it for a week non-stop. So the alien power has been clearly degraded, so it looks good, for an attack soon.

****

"Jade and Blondie!, Jade and Blondie!" exclaimed several Japanese staffers talking excitedly in the hall outside the conference room. Schwartzman looked up from the map table he was studying with General Morita. Richard Metternich the special assistant to Secretary of Defense Bergman was also studying the map as was Hans Bergenholm their scientific advisor.

"What's all that noise about" asked Schwartzman with annoyance. He had only had four hours of sleep in the last 24 hours.

"It's your Jade and Blondie news team from CNS, they have arrived to cover the attack and are filing their reports. After the attack in the North last night, having them here is very good for morale," said General Morita. Schwartzman nodded thoughtfully. *Just on schedule.* He thought. *Uncanny timing as usual, either that, or there's a security leak.* The attack was planned for that night.

"Well let's give the girls a good show to report then," he said levelly, paused, "so, can we launch the attack tonight as planned? You have told me the power grids will be at maximum at ten o clock."

"Yes," said Bergenholm. "The Essex is also ready with the nuclear-driven laser and is in position in Suruga Bay and the charges in hill 523 are set. The power lines could use more testing, but even if we lose some we have some redundancy. We can continue the attack even if we lose ten lines, without power loss to the dishes. So we are pretty much as ready as we will ever be, except for the women"

"What women?" asked Schwartzman.

"I meant the women captives," said Bergenholm.

728

Schwartzman looked from Bergenholm to General Morita, who shook his head gravely.

"They are counted as dead already," said Morita grimly. "I have spoken with the Prime Minster, he says the attack must go forward as planned. That is the decision of the Cabinet. The Prime Minister said every day of delay will cost more lives in the end, and we have already lost too many here."

'What do you think then General Morita?"

"I say, go! Tonight!" said Morita sternly. Schwartzman turned to Admiral Clark, his Naval liaison.

"The 7th Fleet is ready General. I also say go! Tonight!"

"OK," said Schwartzman gruffly. It's on for tonight as we planned. 2200 hrs. is H-hour. God help us." He then turned and spoke to Parker and Arizona. "You guys get everything ready. I have to get some sleep before this thing pops tonight. Wake me at 20 hundred." He then wearily then went to his office and shut the door. Got down on his knees and prayed for success, then lay down on his cot and fell asleep.

**\*\*\*\***

In the alien fortress at Fujiyama, the alloy dome rang deafeningly as heavy battleship shells exploded against it and the force field above it.

"Number 7 stood with two of his deputies and watched as a medicaste Unash, Number 5, implored the commander Utok, a veteran warrior commander well known for his eccentricity, to return to the Moon. Utok sat in full armor listening to the medicaste above the din.

"But my Lord. We need your experience on the Moon, my Lord, and in any case, Number One has given you a direct order." With this last statement, Utok rose and pulled out a pistol, he then shot the medicaste officer dead. He then turned to Number 7.

729

"Take this message back to the Moon and deliver it to Number One! Tell him he should come here in person and tell me to abandon my people here. Tell him I find him utterly without honor!" he roared.

Suddenly there was a tremendous impact above them and the lights failed, then returned. In the halls below, they heard an Unash screaming.

"LET ME OUT ! LET ME OUT!" followed by a shot, and then silence.

"Now. Get out of here! While you still can!" yelled Utok at Number 7. Number 7 turned with his deputies and left the office. They were passed on the way out by a frantic looking medicaste officer in armor covered with dust, who ran into the office.

"My Lord the main field inductor for the force field has been damaged! Number 11 says it will fail completely in an hour if this bombardment continues. Also, the worker Oyans have broken out of their chambers on the lower levels and are running amok! We cannot get them back into their quarters."

Utok looked grimly down at the table before him and closed his eyes.

"Number 5, send the Toman Daz downstairs and have them liquidate the Oyans who will not return to their quarters. I fear we will have no more need of their labor after today, in any case." he opened his eyes and looked squarely at the officer. He then wrote an order on a piece of paper and signed it. "Also, take this order, and free the captive Erran women and send them down the one intact tunnel that leads to the sea and let them go free there. Take this order with you now and see that it is done personally. Tell the women that we do not hide behind hostages amongst true Unash warriors and that we Unash know how to die with honor. Tell them this! Then report back to me here when you have done this."

**\*\*\*\***

Cassandra was talking with Robert Schwartzman, and then he leaned over and kissed her.

Suddenly Cassandra awoke, it was Ian's voice.

"Cassie wake up! Something is happening!" she heard the roar of jet fighters above the building she was sleeping in. She sprang up from the cot she was sleeping on, cursed as she tried to put on her boot over her swollen ankle. Finally, she got it painfully laced up, grabbed her crutches and launched out of the door grabbing her helmet and goggles off a nail in the middle of the wall. It was a dark, cloudy night. Ian had the new camera and was setting it up. They would do a split screen of her and a view through a special camera on top of a pole that had a direct view of the alien base. In the darkness, she could make out an array of huge dish antennas was now in place around them. In between the crash of artillery, she heard the hum of electricity in vast amounts. Pamela, following Manny's orders, was on the far side of the perimeter.

"Pamela called me on the phone from the Japanese sector and said troops are deploying," said Ian.

****

Pamela was watching as hundreds of formerly camouflaged, huge metal mesh dish antennas were being uncovered and raised above the earthen berm in the Japanese sector, and the dishes pointed at the alien base. Maddox, her ever-present cameraman was there setting up the camera. He paused in the middle of his preparations, looked at her.

"Indeed, the shit is going down tonight," Maddox said with a faint smile.

Suddenly the artillery that had been pounding the hill for a week fell silent. It was a silence as terrifying as any scream in the night.

****

Schwartzman muttered a prayer and looked over the command post. The countdown was now in its last seconds. It was 20 hundred hours.

"We have power!" shouted a Japanese officer, Schwartzman looked north and saw the glow from the Tokyo bay suddenly fade. The entire City of Tokyo and Yokohama had blacked out, followed by Osaka and Nagoya to the South. Several million megawatts of power now flowed down power lines towards mount Fuji.

731

"Essex reports they are green on nuclear laser arming!"

Out in Suruga Bay, the aircraft carrier Essex, now modified into a directed energy weapons platform, turned a massive two story high domed turret on its flight deck towards mount Fuji and a huge visor lifted to reveal the fires of hell shining forth.

"We have microwaves!" shouted an officer. One million Industrial microwave Magnetrons flared to life at 98% efficiency pouring power in gigawatts into the antennas now ringing the perimeter. They were now synchronizing their waveforms to focus their power on the faraway hilltop. The hilltop began to glow a faint orange then blue as Saint Elmo's fire began to light the rocks around the summit.

"Synchronized microwave power at 90%, now 98% percent!"

"Fire the hill 523 charges!" shouted Schwartzman.

****

Cassandra stared at the hilltop and its eerie glow now filamenting into streamers reaching upward to make visible its force field. When a brilliant light lit up the sky like daylight. She pulled down her goggles to shield her eyes. Ten thousand tons of ammonium nitrate and fuel oil had vaporized hill 523 near the coast, now clearing a line of site between the Essex and its nuclear-powered 200-megawatt blue laser and the alien fortress. It took several seconds for the dust to clear the line of sight.

"Hill 523 is gone! Essex has clear line of sight to target!" shouted Parker

"LASER, LASER! NOW!" yelled Schwartzman, and the nuclear reactor housed in the massive turret went to high power, sucking a million tons of water a minute out of the bay to cool itself, and pouring the water back into the bay at boiling heat. From the laser leaped a blue ray of light so powerful that to even looking at it from the side within a mile of it was to risk blindness.

The laser beam came to a focused point in the middle of the mammoth microwave field. In a split- second, the air above the alien base broke down and ignited into a 5,000-degree plasma, brighter than the Sun. The

732

sky turned to day, illuminating the clouds with a harsh blue light, and the snowy slopes of mount Fuji shown like dawn.

The Plasma formed into a swirling torus and then stabilized. Then it began lowering over the hill summit, holding the alien base.

The plasma now tuned brilliant magenta as it rotated like a vortex and dropped onto the alien shield and chewed on it. The aliens in desperation tried to fire their death ray, but the magnetic field now in the plasma stopped it and added its power to the plasma vortex now tearing apart and short-circuiting the elaborately layered electric and magnetic field structure of the alien force shield. Now the power in the shield and death ray only added to the magenta inferno. The shield collapsed and the plasma bit deeply into the hilltop turning the plasma a blinding orange, until suddenly, the whole hilltop exploded brilliantly into an orange ball of fire a mile across rising to form a pillar of fire.

"The alien shield has collapsed, General and the plasma has penetrated the hilltop."

"Stop the directed energy attack, commence artillery bombardment," said Schwartzman. He looked to the north saw the glow of Tokyo slowly return to its former brilliance as the power was redirected. Around him for miles, the night was filled with jets of lights as a thousand long-range artillery pieces now poured shells into the hilltop. He watched with satisfaction as the artillery ripped what was left of the hilltop to pieces and a wave of cracking thunder rolled over him.

"HAMMER THEM! HAMMER THEM!" yelled Schwartzman.

*Victory* he thought. But in the distance, he saw the half moon rising between the clouds, as if in silent witness to what had occurred. The Moon was blood red from the smoke on the horizon. *You're next* thought Schwartzman, *take a good look.*

Arizona approached him smiling.

"General sir, we have a confirmed report that the captive women have been found released near the coastal town of Fuji." Schwartzman looked at Arizona in astonishment. "The women say that the aliens released them so that the aliens could die with honor."

"Well, I'll be damned," said Schwartzman in amazement. "Have that report confirmed again, and then release it to the press," he said as the rumble of the artillery continued.

A rising cheer was going up in the distance, thousands of troops, American and Japanese were yelling from their trenches "Banzai! Banzai!" as the alien base in the distance dissolved into fire and explosions. Its death fire brilliantly lighting the snows of Mount Fujiyama with a flickering golden light.

****

As they approached the lunar surface Douglas Forester spoke to his squadron.

"Fan out boys , the bombardment will begin any second , let's come in after it and hit Kepler crater again. Come in low and let's get solid hits!" Suddenly hundreds of tons of explosives and pre-sectioned steel prisms from warheads boosted from Earth orbit detonated with brilliant blue light then blossomed into red fireballs as "steel rain" from cortex warheads shredded the lunar surface around Kepler crater. Now the fighters dove in after the bombardment and watched the booster bodies, traveling at miles per second, impacting the lunar surface with white flashes. Now they were diving down on what was left of the alien structures in Kepler crater, and rockets streaked from the pods on the side of their space fighters to hit anything that looked artificial. Forester followed up with a string of twenty-millimeter tracer shells as the rockets impacted in waves of electric blue flashes. Clouds of lunar dust from the explosion rose, but he now pulled up back into space and fired his jets to accelerate back upwards. Soon the and squadron would be racing away from the Moon to the new space station at the L1 Lagrange point, poised above the nearside Lunar surface where they could rest, refit, and come back to hit the Moon yet again on the way back to the massive ALS station at L5.

734

"No ground fire this time sir," reported his wingman happily, we didn't lose anybody.  And it's getting harder to find targets; they seem to have quit trying to rebuild things above ground."

"Ditto sir.  It looks like they all got killed by the earth orbit bombardment or have pulled out," said another squadron member.

*We are getting close to being ready for the invasion,* thought Forester as they charged out into space.

****

The Space Frigate Dauntless was shaped like an arrowhead, the standard shape of most fighting spacecraft made by humans, with its plasma engines in the back and  presenting  glancing surfaces to laser weapons in most directions, was 500 feet long and fusion powered.  Its crew of 45 humans beings were now all in space suits and buckled into their seats. They were now far from Earth, having escaped its sphere of influence long ago. They now flew with several expended Saturn 7 upper stages far past the Moon. They had been following an inert and quiet conic section trajectory. But that was going to change very soon. They had their g-force reduction gear turned off to minimize their gravitic signature.

Captain Robert Forester, in his space suit and buckled into his seat on the bridge, was now watching the final countdown. The fusion power plant was now operating at full power, its power flowing into the inertial energy store that was spinning up with a rising whine and acting as power ballast.

"Main engine ignition in 10 seconds, on my mark, 3,2,1 Mark!" called out the  Navigation officer.

10, 9,  8, 7...

*Dear God, make our mission successful and bring me and my crew back to Earth...*

4,3,

*and may my wife and children be waiting for me, when I return...*

1, Zero, and main engine ignition.

Forester and everyone else was slammed back into their seats as the main engines ignited and gigawatts of synchrotron radiation power from the fusion power plant flowed into the target hydrogen plasmas in the main engines, which flashed into million degree heat and rammed out of their magnetic confinement and into space, generating tons of thrust. Soon the Dauntless, its massive arrow-shaped form, carrying nuclear-armed missiles, ten-megawatt laser cannon batteries, and proton plasma torpedo projectors, was racing into space far beyond Earth orbit. It was on a trajectory for deep space, and into Harm's Way.

****

"THIS IS AN UNJUST WAR! WE CANNOT WIN THIS WAR! ANY WAR THAT CANNOT BE WON IS UNJUST!" yelled Senator Tunney to the crowd at the peace rally.

"PEACE NOW! PEACE NOW!" the crowd was yelling in unison, many of the people crying.

"WE CANNOT ESCALATE THIS WAR! THERE MUST BE NO INVASION OF THE MOON! "yelled Senator Tunney.

****

In joyous aftermath of the victory at Mount Fuji, Cassandra was rolling down the runway to her plane in an open Humvee, resting her still painful ankle. She was leaving first, Pamela would follow in a few days. They were never allowed to fly on the same plane. As she neared her plane, she noticed another Humvee full of officers coming from the other direction on the flight line, it passed by them swiftly at a distance of only ten feet as she looked up. She suddenly felt torn and turned her head to look again at the tall man in the front seat. *Bob,* she thought. *It was him.*

A tear rolled down her cheek as she turned again to look desperately after his Humvee now lost in a cloud of dust.

****

## Chapter 16: D-Day, Sea of Storms

"The hyperdrive is losing efficiency, that is the meaning of the flashes of color outside the viewports," said Karlac in a worried tone.

"The hyperdrive is failing!" said Vikor. "The Samarans made their repairs too hastily!"

"Their repairs got us out of the Solerran system," said Karlac, looking now at the navigation computer screen. Amber was asleep in her bedroom. Vikor now slept on the floor. He had given up his quarters for her with seemingly uncharacteristic consideration. *Perhaps he has a heart after all?* wondered Karlac.

"Yes they did, indeed," said Vikor. "But to where, where are we now? I think this hyper-drive will fail very soon."

"We are near the Arrasian frontier, 10 light years from the Sotice system. I would rather not deal with them, their officials can be difficult."

"Are we near Temekula? I have friends there," asked Vikor.

"Yes, we are passing near it, it is only two light years, from here," said Karlac frowning. "But you know it is in the neutral zone. It is a lawless place and den of smugglers and thieves."

"Yes, like I said, I have friends there. But we won't have to deal with the Arrasians or be stranded in space. We can get repairs there, too. Do you have any gold on board?"

"I have a good universal credit account, it is good anywhere in the Eshalon."

"Yes, good, but Temekula isn't part of the Eshalon. That's why I asked if you have any gold. They don't like financial transactions that can be traced at Temekula." Karlac frowned at this.

"Yes, I have some gold. About a hundred sovereigns," said Karlac sourly. "I may be naïve, but I am not stupid."

"Good, that will make things run smoothly." Amber had awakened and was now standing by the table in the main cabin.

"Good morning, do you have any more of the red juice drink that comes in those cans?" she asked smiling.

Karlac and Vikor both turned to look at her. She looked radiant and was wearing her tight fitting lunar coveralls.

"I think we have some in the ceramic bottles, in the storage," said Vikor.

"Well, actually I wanted the kind in those cans, it has a slight metallic taste. I woke up thinking about it," said Amber.

Vikor and Karlac looked at each other and nodded.

"I will look," said Vikor.

"Yes, Amber," said Karlac smiling. "Good morning. Uh, we are going to stop someplace to get some more supplies. I did not stock this ship thinking I would have passengers. But, of course, I am delighted to have you on board. "

"What sort of place are we stopping at?" asked Amber, rubbing her stomach.

****

Colonel Robert Schwartzman emerged from his shower , and stepped into his hotel room in the Tokyo Hilton. He was feeling the excellent after-effects of his workout in the hotel gym an hour before. He was now just a Colonel again, his episode as being a brevet general officer was now over now that the battle at Fujiyama had ended. He was in Tokyo to receive a medal from the Japanese government in a private ceremony the next morning. *A little mopping up operation,* he laughed mentally.

He glanced out the windows and saw the vast lake of light that was Tokyo at night. *I helped save this, that is honor enough.* His thoughts then became more grim. *But does it make up for lost honor?* He glanced at his dress uniform, newly pressed and cleaned, lying on the bed. Instantly

738

noted that it was not where he had left it. With lightning reflexes he grabbed his Berretta 9mm from his bathrobe and primed it. His gaze fixated on a silhouette at the window he somehow had not noticed before, he cursed himself for inattentiveness as he held the gun with both hands pointed at it. He fought the impulse to shoot, then studied the figure more carefully. The silhouette wore his dress officer's cap and apparently his dress uniform jacket. He then saw that long brunette tresses fell down the back of the jacket as his eyes adjusted to the light in which the figure was surrounded, surrounded by the dazzling lights of Tokyo below.

"Colonel , Its very good to see you again." said a soothing feminine voice. The figure turned , it was a striking woman with high cheekbones and large blue eyes. She was wearing his officer's hat. She smiled. "you don't need to point your gun at me Colonel." She raised her slender arms and his dress uniform jacket slid off her shoulders revealing her standing naked in front of him. "I surrender." She said. He stared at her in astonishment. He lowered his pistol. Looked at her with exasperation.

"I remember you. You were in my hotel room in Morningstar, once."

"Excellent recall, Colonel, " she laughed. "as you will remember , I am a friendly alien from outer space, as you say here on this planet." she said lowered her arms and stepped towards him. His eyes swept her slender athletic frame. He put his gun down on a nearby bureau. *If she wanted to kill me, I would probably be dead already,* he thought in amazement.

"I suppose you're here to tell me the greys are our enemy again, or some other obvious piece of cosmic information," he said with a faint smile. She took off his hat and spun it like a Frisbee to a corner of the room with a grin.

"No , that's not why I am here Colonel Schwartzman," she starred deeply into his grey eyes, as if hypnotized, as she spoke, "You are hero of Fujiyama, and a deliverer of your people... " She then kissed him warmly, and pushed his bathrobe off his strong shoulders, so it fell to the floor.

"I only wish my people still had men such as you..." she gasped as she wrapped her arms around him and he embraced and kissed her deeply.

****

The Unash technician named Tadden, who worked with Dr. Ukla, guided Joseph to the spacecraft and assisted him in strapping himself into a seat.

"The ship is set to take off automatically. So sit here and do not touch anything, and it will fly automatically to a region of space called the Eshalon, where you will find friends. Nora, your friend will join you shortly for this journey, but we cannot bring you here to this ship together, they are even now rounding up all humans here to be shipped back to Erra."

"Why? Wouldn't it be good for me and her to go back to Erra."

"No, this order is from Sadok Sar, the commander on your Moon. He hates your people, so we decided to send you to the Eshalon worlds where we believe they will give you and Nora and Doctor Rosen sanctuary. So just wait here and don't touch anything. Nora will be with you soon."

The technician then shook Joseph's hand.

"A safe journey," said the technician and left the ship, shutting the hatch behind him.

A mile away in the space docking complex, Dr. Ukla, Nora, and Murray Rosen, his cylindrical life support system rolling on its treads while his bald head concentrated on guiding it. Dr. Ukla wore his usual white gown and Nora was wearing a blue coverall.

Suddenly, from around a corner came a group of armed Unash. The chief of them looked at Dr. Ukla grimly.

"Where are you taking this dung-eater?" said the chief of the guards pointing at Nora.

"I wish for her to see the operation of our dockyard," said Dr. Ukla.

"All Erran dung-eaters are ordered detained, for transport back to the Quzrada," said the chief Unash official. "She must come with us."

Nora kept her face controlled, she looked at Dr. Ukla, and Murray Rosen, whom the officials seemed to be ignoring.

"Goodbye Doctor," she said levelly. She walked over to the officials and they walked together in the opposite direction down the hall.

Dr. Ukla stood shaking, and closed his eyes, then began to walk. He and Murray Rosen went to the waiting spacecraft that would take them away to Vale, where Dr. Ukla had contacts and hoped to find friends. Murray Rosen began to cry, but Ukla told him quietly to stop. Together, they boarded a ship and departed for Vale.

On board his small ship, Joseph saw with despair that the ship was beginning to launch and wrestled with his straps to try and release them. Nora was not there.

Suddenly the ship took off on automatic, and he saw it rise above the atmosphere outside the forward viewport. He buried his face in his hands and wept like a child, as the craft dove deeply into the stars and away from the world of Nashan.

****

Cassandra and Pamela stood on the roof of the CNS building in Washington DC. It was past midnite and they were watching the sky to the south, it was a clear cold night. Japan was now a just a dream. Suddenly they both saw a string of bright white sparks of light in the sky.

"Here it goes," said Pamela, as the whole Southern sky now filled with white and yellowish sparks of light all headed to the East. The sparks then grew to clouds of bluish ghostly light that expanded and faded. "That's a salvo of the bombardment. Their preparing the nearside of the Moon for the invasion. That's thousands of tons of high explosive and fragmentation warheads, not to mention the impact of the booter upperstages."

"What are they hitting on the Moon now. " asked Cassandra, feeling a chill of awe and fear. *We are going there also...*

"Kepler Crater is one target I know of, the others are classified" said Pamela, staring at the horizon as a red crecent Moon began to rise.

**\*\*\*\***

Marshall Skana scowled in frustration. He was in the office of another high councilman named Soona.

"Why have all the Errans been taken away from Nashan? I had very much desired to speak to some of them!"

"Sadok Sar, the Commander of our mission at Erra requested it."

"Did he give a reason? The study of the Errans here is very useful to understand our coition operation at Erra, a mission I am very curious about now. I have heard recently that this mission may be encountering difficulties. Does this order by Sadok Sar mean that things are not going well at Erra in the Quzrada?" Councilman Soona was silent in response.

"Our mission in the Quzrada has encountered difficulties, yes," he said painfully. "And the Samar have sent a warlord to investigate. His report to the Samaran palace, I am told, will not be good. So the Samarans are displeased with us. Sadok Sar asked the warlord for more money, to cover the cost of the additional operations that are now necessary, but this request was rejected. The visiting warlord said that we would have to send a special ambassador to the Samaran Palace to request this additional money. This matter is most serious and cannot be discussed outside of the high council." Marshall Skana reacted in shock to this.

"Why was this not reported before the whole council?" demanded Skana in anger. "For many years we have gotten reports that the mission in the Quzrada has been going well! Always 'things are going well!' I have even said it is so going well at Erra that Sadok Sar would have been able to colonize not only Erra but five other worlds besides! I always worried that sending this individual was not good. I do not care if he is high-born! I looked into his history. He has failed at every other task given to him! I assumed he had been sent to the Quzrada so he could be forgotten. I

742

assumed that the real job of running things would be left to experts there! Now suddenly you tell me that things are in crisis in the Quzrada and that the Samar, who have paid us much gold, are displeased with us?" Marshall Skana stood and shook his fist at Soona. "I want to know if Erra is actually being colonized and how long it will take to complete this operation! If not, I want to know what has happened to all the supplies and personnel we have sent there!"

"Calm yourself most honorable Marshall, we cannot bring this before the full council at this time. It is a delicate matter and must be handled discreetly," said Soona. "We must instead request additional funds and time from the Samar, and secure this. Otherwise, the prime counselor will suffer grave embarrassment."

"What if the Samar refuse to grant us more money to solve this problem? What, in fact, is the problem at Erra?" asked Skana. Soona was silent for a moment. "Councilman Soona, I was chosen for this council because of my experience in war. In war, one must be realistic and objective! You must look at the facts! We are at war with the Unull. We cannot make peace with them, and they have taken several of our star systems. Only by maximum effort and efficient husbanding of resources can we push the Unull back and regain our systems! We cannot afford any problems in the Quzrada!"

"Rest assured, the Samar will grant our request. They have no choice," said Soona, closing his eyes. "I have agreed to go to Rigel, and insist to the Samar that more money be provided to us."

"My old friend, is that wise? Should not our ambassador at Rigel make this request?" responded Marshall Skana with concern.

"I serve the Genspore, Marshal Skana. One of the high council must go. The Samar will accede to our request because they have told us that they cannot allow any Archmetan power to arise in the Quzrada, and they cannot enter into the Quzrada with a fleet themselves. This would trigger a second war of the Quzrada, something they fear. So they have no choice."

"But, you have not answered my second question," said Marshal Skana, after a pause. "I ask again, my old friend, what are, exactly, the nature of the difficulties at Erra?" demanded Skana.

"War," said Soona painfully. "There is war at Erra, with the Errans. The Coition was to be accomplished peacefully, but now the Errans are fighting with us, and they are fighting very hard, this has greatly multiplied the difficulty of accomplishing coition, and its expense."

"There is war in Quzrada? At Erra?" asked Skana incredulously. "This is a disaster! We are already fighting a war with the Unull!"

"This cannot be discussed openly, even in the council. It is most secret. But it is not a disaster. Sadok Sar says the situation is under control. The Errans are vastly inferior to us in technology."

"This is the same Sadok Sar who has been telling us that everything has been going well! So this is truly a disaster! My Lord, Sadok Sar is not a trained commander of War!" gasped Skana. "What is our military posture at Erra? What is the order of battle? Can the Errans reach Una, where our base is?"

"No. The Errans will be crushed quickly with the forces we have available there. But this difficulty must remain a high secret until we can get more resources from the Samar. This means we cannot replace Sadok Sar until things are brought under control. He has many friends here, and it will cause too many questions to be asked if he is replaced. I take you into my confidence in this matter Marshall Skana. I assure you the situation at Erra is absolutely under control. Theoretically, the outcome of this war is already determined. So this is certainly not a disaster."

"No, War at Erra, it is not a disaster, it is a catastrophe," said Skana staring off into space. "I have seen war first-hand, my Lord. War in reality, it is not like war in theory. War is chaos."

"Yes, potentially," said Soona. "That is why I am going to Rigel to speak to the Samar. To argue for reason and order." he paused again. "But, Marshal Skana, my old friend, do not probe too deeply into this matter, there are things going on here involving the palace and the personage of the great Genspore.  Things much larger than a military skirmish at Erra, or even haggling over gold with the Samar, this thing is higher than the high council, and involves the future of the Genspore itself."

At this statement, Marshall Skana was filled with deep fear.

"What have we gotten ourselves into at Erra?"  he asked.

****

Robert Schartzman , Jason Parker and Arizona, stood on the roof of their barracks in Houston in their sweat soaked fatigues after a hard day's training.  They all watched through binoculars in both awe and satisfaction as the sky over them was filled with shooting stars, all headed to the East. After the sky cleared, a blood red Moon rose in the East.

"A couple more thousand tons of high explosives and shrapnel! A love note to shorty on the Moon! " laughed Parker. "Dear shorty, we be coming up for a visit soon! Don't worry if the place is a mess when we get there!"

"I just hope there's something left up there to kill when we get here," said Arizona,  still watching the Moon.

"You guys won't be talking like that when we get there," said Schwartzman levely, as he lowered his binoculars and stared at the Moon. "I can assure you."

****

Around the small reddish star called  Temekula,   orbited Temekula Station.  It  was a large, dark space station consisting of a large array of cylinders and spherical units seemingly stuck together at random that orbited close enough to the star for reasonable temperatures to be maintained and solar power to be generated,  but far way enough away for the frequent solar flares from the star to not be a problem.  No planet in the system occupied this cherished location, the planets of the system being either too hot or too cold,  so Temekula station was built, or rather had 'crystallized out of the vacuum'  and had grown by numerous haphazard additions.  Temekula was  ten light years from the Arrasian frontier.    The planets of the rest of the system were virtually lifeless, so the station was the system's main habitation.

The Arrasians were an Archmetan people governed by a theocracy with a puritanical bent and an appetite for high taxes. Thus, Temekula and other places nearby in the neutral zone were essential if the hypocrisies and inconveniences of the Arrasian culture were to be serviced properly. Given these conditions, Temekula was  located far enough away from the main bases of the Arrasian space forces to be safe from a surprise attack, and yet close enough to be convenient  for smugglers, pirates or simply cargo haulers trying to bypass Arrasian space and its absurd transit fees. Few members of the syndicate of families and gangs that cooperated in the running of Temekula station feared an attack by Arrasian forces now, however. Temekula Station had long since been recognized as being an essential safety valve by the Arrasian theocracy if they were to avoid real reform or revolution.  In fact, the ruling elites of Arrasia provided some of Temekula's best-paying clients.

The Song of Peace found a docking port near a repair yard, cluttered  with partially cannibalized wrecks, on the dark side of the station. The daylight side was mostly occupied by solar panels.

"Come with me, I have to renew some old friendships," said Vikor, putting on his coat and hat.

"I thought we were going to get our ship repaired,"  said Karlac in puzzlement.

"We are, but you just don't go to a repair yard here, you have to have connections," responded Vikor.

"Why do we have to come with you?  This place has a bad reputation.  I think Amber and I should just stay here," said Karlac looking out the viewport at the dark station.

"Yes," said Vikor  impatiently,  as he pulled out his laser pistol from its shoulder holster and checked its battery charge.  "However, I am the only one with a gun on this ship.  So you, and especially Amber here, have to come with me." He watched the words sink into Karlac.  Vikor noted that

746

Amber seemed to grasp his words perfectly and her face adopted a blank look. *Good, at least somebody on this ship understands reality,* he thought. "Oh yes, I'll need some of that gold," added Vikor.

Soon they had opened the hatch and paid a fee to the Vikhelm who manned it, and who seemed to know Vikor from before. They then walked down the broad hallway past the noisy saloons, 'love lounges', and the busy equipment and weapons markets of the station. Most of the people on the station were Arrasian, with dark blue skins and straight black hair, and they looked at them with amused curiosity. Amber walked between the two men, wearing her fine Samaran leather jacket, trying not to be afraid as they encountered a group of rough, space-suited greys, who glared at them and then walked by muttering.

"Wayyko," said Vikor with a blank look "neutral zone pirates, in the case of those Monchkini back there. They're deserters from the Unash fleet. You can tell by their suits with the emblems ripped off." Vikor paused. "The neutral zone collects people like that." They came to a large saloon lit with flashing, multicolored lights and an indecipherable sign, and followed Vikor inside.

Inside garish music was playing and an array of Archmetan and other species were standing at the bars and sitting at tables. They sat at an empty table by the wall. Vikor faced the room. Suddenly he rose and walked over to an older, handsome, Arrasian woman in a low-cut black dress. He kissed her passionately and then they both disappeared.

"Renewing old friendships indeed, "muttered Amber. Karlac tried to relax and look like he belonged in the place. However, he noticed that in a far corner of the bar, a body of an Arrasian was lying on the floor inert. As he watched a bystander started going through the pockets on the man's suit. Finally, what appeared to be a janitor appeared and dragged the body out a side door.

Suddenly, a powerfully built Arrasian in a spacesuit , followed by another and what looked like a Vikhelm approached the table where Karlac and Amber sat. The Arrasian in the spacesuit pulled up a chair and sat down at the table. He looked carefully at Amber, and then at Karlac.

747

"She is Erran?" he asked in a deep voice, pointing at her. His dark eyes were full of menace. "How much for her?" he asked after receiving no answer.

"How much for the girl?" he again asked Karlac in a deep voice. "She will fetch a good price on Sotice, I will pay you well."

"She is my associate, and she is not for sale," said Karlac firmly. "People are not for sale..." He sensed death casting its shadow over him. *May the Creator help us! Vikor come quickly! He thought desperately.* He began to plan to grab a chair and use it as a weapon.

"I have asked you politely, yet you refuse to bargain for her?" hissed the man. He pulled out a heavy laser pistol and laid it on the table pointing it at Karlac. "You should learn some manners."

Suddenly a deafening blast and blinding flash occurred and the figure in the spacesuit rose and fell backward screaming in a cloud of burning flesh. Amber then instantly raised a powerful Samaran laser pistol and fired it into the midsection of the Vikhelm who fell screaming backward to the floor. The remaining Arrasian dropped his half-drawn weapon as Amber rose and stepped around the table and hit him in the face with the red-hot barrel of her pistol and knocked him to the floor. She grabbed his gun and handed it backward to Karlac, who took it and laid it on the table in front of him. She then looked around the bar, blew a lock of her auburn hair out of her face, then stepped back and sat down. In all that time her blank expression had not changed. *Novocain face.*

"I grew up in Montana before they took me to the Moon. I know how to shoot," she said to Karlac levelly, still staring at the crowded bar. "This is a little going away gift from Zomal," she waved the laser pistol in the dim light. "I was going to tell you about it, Karlac, but I forgot," The living Arrasian slowly crawled across the floor, but someone nearby kicked him unconscious and people then rifled his pockets.

Vikor reappeared with the Arrasian woman on his arm. Her long black hair looked disordered. He looked in amazement at the two burned bodies on the floor and weapons both Amber and Karlac were holding as he approached.

748

"Nice place you brought us to, Vikor," said Amber levelly.

"Well, it's gone a little downhill since I was here last," Vikor said blankly. "This is my old friend Amaya. She can introduce us to the repair yard people we need."

"It is the war," she said sadly. "It has changed everything."

Vikor looked around nervously and leaned down over the table. "We should probably go," he whispered.

They were walking back to the dock area, when suddenly a grey alien in space suit without insignia stepped out in front of them. He was unarmed and waved his hand at them with his hand open.

"Earth-girl," he said in English. You and your friends are in great danger, my captain wants to help, and wishes to speak with you." Amber pulled out her gun in response, pointing it at the ceiling.

"I don't think so," she replied in English. Karlac froze and Vikor and Amaya looked around warily.

"I am Trona. You killed someone important back there in the bar, he was Ansol Taktarri, of the Taktarri Brothers clan. The whole Taktarri Brothers gang will be after you now."

"You killed one of the Taktarri brothers? Then you had better do as he asks," interjected Amaya suddenly. "If what he says is true, you are in great danger. The Taktarri are very powerful here! You should not have killed those men."

"She had no choice ," said Karlac quietly. "Trona, let us talk to your Captain and see what he says." The grey motioned for them to follow and marched ahead.

In between two shops, stood several Greys in spacesuits without insignia. All were armed, one was taller than the rest and wore a large pistol on his spacesuit belt.

"This is Captain Tookon," said Trona taking his place beside the captain.

"Can you understand me?" asked the Captain adjusting the translator amulet around his neck. His demeanor was not menacing but instead concerned.

"Yes," answered Karlac. "We did not intend to kill anyone here. We are merely trying to get our ship repaired and be on our way."

"You will never make it to Vale, Karlac of Delphin," said Tookon gruffly. "Everyone knows who you are and where you are headed. They also know your ship is slow and unarmed, and the Taktarri Brothers will be looking for you as soon as they return from the deep Quzrada. They will burn you out of space before you are halfway to Vale." He let his words sink in. "I instead offer an alternative to death," said Tookon looking at them intently. "Our ship is large, fast, and armed." The captain paused and raised his hand with three fingers extended." For much gold, we can load your ship into our cargo hold, and take you to Vale. But you must pay us three thousand drams of gold when we reach Vale. You can pay this amount at Vale?"

"Yes!" said Karlac.

"Do you have any gold with you?" asked Tookon leaning close.

"Yes," said Karlac and pulled out a gold coin and offered it to Tookon, who then took it, looked at it carefully, and then held it up to his crew, who gave grunts of ascent.

"Good , we must move quickly then..." said Tookon.

****

The Unash ship was spacious but spare, mostly bare metal with a few rugs and wall hangings, looking to Amber like they had been gathered at a hundred different garage sales. They had been invited up to the Captain's cabin for tea. Even his cabin was Spartan, with a large plastic table of bluish grey and small chairs sized for Unash, but still comfortable for a human, as long as they stretched out their legs.

Captain Tookon was friendly if serious, as he poured sweet fragrant tea into glass cups. Vikor, apparently restless since he had left Amaya behind at Temekula, said little but seemed to enjoy the tea.

"This is excellent tea," said Karlac to the Captain while Amber nodded and smiled. It did have a delightful taste, and she had been given it on the Moon.

"Yes Karlac of Delphin, it is from Nashan, my home world," said the Captain looking slightly sad. "It is rare in the Quzrada, especially now." The Captain paused, sipped his tea, then spoke again.

"Know this, Karlac of Delphin, I did not decide to help you and your associates get to Vale for gold. No, the gold merely pays for my crew."

"Why gold? It seems so old fashsioned, we even use it for money on Earth, " said Amber.

The Captian smiled.

"Yes, gold my dear. Everyone, advanced or primitive, takes gold as payment. It is bright and shiney and has only one stable isotope, so it cannot be traced. Gold from one star is like gold from any other. So it is the perfect currency for the Quzrada, where discrete transactions are the most important ones. Gold would have to be invented for the Quzrada if it did not exist."

The Captain continued. "But again, I did not agree to transport you and your ship for gold, it was because I had heard you were someone who could make peace and that you had come into the Quzrada to try to end the war at Erra."

"I have tried Captain Tookon," said Karlac. "But I confess, I did not understand how terrible the war at Erra was, or its causes."

"It is a catastrophe!" gasped Tookon nodding. "It has made me and my crew 'halk-Unash', renegades from our own people! The war draws my people into an interstellar war between the great powers in which we have neither the power nor wisdom to fight. I fear my people will be destroyed because of what will happen."

751

"How did this war begin? What brought your people into the Quzrada?" asked Karlac.

"Oh, it was the villainous Samar who did this thing! They said they would pay our people much gold and other precious metals if we colonized Erra, and the leaders of my people were blinded by greed to agree to this! They said 'Erra is a precious jewel, with much water, and we will have it and much gold also.' But things have not gone well, the whole operation was done poorly and was cursed with ill fortune! Marshall Tandu, a great man among our people, drank poison and made a death statement when he heard of the failures of our early expedition. He said that we should pull our forces out of the Quzrada because the Errans were excessively far from our bases, excessively advanced, and excessively warlike for this effort at colonization to succeed. It is called the argument of the 'Three Excesses.' Now the Unull and even the pirates of Bashan raid our supply convoys to Erra. Someone is paying the Bashani to attack us and are giving them heavy armaments. Who is doing this, we do not know. But I do know that the people of our space service are afraid to go into the Quzrada and now call it the 'Place of Death.' So great is the fear now, that our commanders made us all swear an oath before we left from our forward base in the Quzrada, called Rabmag. We had to swear that we would deliver our cargos to our base on Erra's moon, Una, or not return alive. They told us any crew who returned without certificates of delivery from Una, would be put to death. This is because only half the ships making the run from Rabmag to Erra make it there, and only one-half of those make it back to Rabmag."

"Why don't your people abandon this war?" asked Karlac. *If only it were that simple and logical.*

"I do not know, almost no-one on our home world even knows this war exists, much less that it is going so poorly. Our leaders tell the people nothing! So I arrived at Rabmag with my crew to transport cargo, and suddenly, they are arming my ship in the docking bay! 'Why,' I asked. And they said, ask no questions- only swear the oath and obey orders! So we go out in a convoy with many provisions and much rare metals to take to Una, with several warships accompanying our convoy, but still, we were

752

attacked half-way there!  By Unull I think, or maybe Bashani pirates.  The convoy was destroyed and only we escaped, as far as we know."

"Can you remember the ship types, of the group that attacked your convoy?" asked Karlac.

"Understand please, we did not  linger to look for any survivors or write an official report, I can tell you!  We simply ran from the place when we saw the destroyer near us explode.   So I and my crew, we met together, and voted to go renegade, since to try to go to Erra without escort  would be death, and to return to our base was death also." The Captain closed his eyes in a sign of grief for a moment.

"Now we try to make a living transporting cargos across the Quzrada.  Since we have no registry for our ship elsewhere,  we can operate only in this place where no ship carries a registry except  laser cannon. We made a living for a while doing this, but now the war grows worse in the Quzrada. Now,  in the Quzrada, we encounter warships, singly or in groups, often with masked identities. We do this more and more frequently.  We have seen what we are sure are warships of the Unash, and  the Unull  and now even Samar and the Annak.  If this pattern continues, the Vikhelm and Pleiadians will also enter, and there will be a second war of the Quzrada!" At these words, a chill fell over the room.

"I swear by the Creator of all stars, that I will not rest until I have negotiated peace in the Quzrada. I swear  it, Captain Tookon." said Karlac.

"Good, may the Creator of all Stars helps you."  said the Captain. He looked upon Amber quietly drinking her tea.

"Yes, and Amber of Erra, I wish you to know, that nothing would make me happier than for my people to depart from the Quzrada and leave your people in peace.  You are the first Erran I have ever met, and I am very pleased to have met you. I have absolutely no quarrel with you or your people.  I will also mention  that I saw you shoot the two slave dealers in the bar, and my man Trona saw this also and said to me afterward, 'the fools, they should have known  that Errans always carry guns and know

753

how to use them!' So now I understand why my people have not been able to take your planet from you!" He then laughed heartily.

"Well I only shot them because I thought they were going to shoot Karlac here, and he didn't have a gun," she said smiling.

"Well good, he can continue his peace mission then," said Tookon. He turned to Karlac, "Please be successful, end this war and bring peace again to the Quzrada, Karlac of Delphin. The Quzrada is the only country I have left now."

Later, they walked in the low-ceilinged passageways back to where their ship was stowed. The ship was humming along agreeably through hyperspace.

"I want you to know, Karlac, that protecting you was not the only reason I decided to fire at the man at the table when he pointed his gun at you," said Amber as they walked, keeping to the center of the domed passageway to avoid bumping their heads.

"Why did you do it then? I accept that it was necessary. I have learned that much on this journey." said Karlac sadly.

"I decided in that heartbeat of time that I would rather die than become a slave again," said Amber looking at him somberly. "So I pulled the trigger." Karlac noticed Vikor staring at him as she said this.

"I understand," said Karlac. "As I said, I have learned things I never imagined on this journey."

They returned to their ship, and Amber fell asleep in a chair by the table. Vikor, carefully placed a blanket over her, pointing out her firm grip on her laser pistol to Karlac as he did.

Karlac was sitting at the controls, looking at their progress towards Vale from the inertial navigation unit on the ship and the data being supplied by the Unash ship around them. They were making good speed on the agreed route that gave a wide berth to Arrasian space. Soon they would be in the relative safety of Vikhelmian space. Vikor came up to the controls and sat in the copilot seat.

"What is going to happen to her when you get her to Vale?" asked Vikor grimly. "She carries a child that the Samaran Ambassador thinks belongs to his household, and him also, probably."

"I don't know..." said Karlac staring out into the darkness of the cargo hold. "I came into this Quzrada thinking everyone in the cosmos was part of a family, and that reason and good will would triumph over everything else. Now I know the cosmos is the home of horror, misery, and cruelties I never imagined, and that hatred and death move the stars as surely as love and understanding. I am changed. I, who have forsworn violence and love of women in any form, have now held a weapon, and was ready to use it instantly to save a woman from a planet I barely heard of a year ago, and whom I now cannot quit thinking about."

"Oh, I miss the fair women of Erra," said Vikor. "Here is how I remember them, particularly that dark haired one who started this war." He pulled out the black rose from his pocket. It was held in a plastic bubble that preserved it still in bloom.

"So my friend, this journey has changed me also. I came to Erra caring for nothing except myself. I was a spy sent to a place no one cared about. They sent me there because I killed a man in a duel and wanted me in a forgotten place where no one could find me. Little did anyone know, it would turn into the center of the universe.

"The duel, was it a legal one in the arenas at Vale?" asked Karlac.

"No, this duel was in the bedchamber of a man who discovered me screwing his wife." said Vikor grimy. Karlac looked at him in horror. "Yes, I was young then and thinking with my cock." said Vikor. "We dueled with swords, I won and escaped. Unfortunately, I had killed a member of a powerful family in Vale, the Bloodaxe, so leaving Erra and returning to Vale, is not what I or my family had planned on my doing for a long time."

"What will you do, when we return to Vale?"

"Oh, I am not sure..." said Vikor staring out at the darkness beyond the cockpit.

"The objective for your unit will be strategic, Colonel . Your Rangers must take the Riphaeus Mountains' crest line, concentrating on these summits where we have identified alien observation posts. The Riphaeus Mountains are the high ground overlooking the main landing zone in Mare Cognitum, and must be taken and held at all costs. You will hold until relieved by the 1st Marines. As your unit will be one of the lead elements on the Lunar surface, you will have no provision for evacuation if things go south. Do you understand this assignment    Colonel? "Schwartzman stood at attention in General Joseph Collins office, who was Commander in Chief of the planned invasion of the Moon. A map of the mare Cognitum lay on the General's desk with the peaks of the Riphaeus Mountains marked in bright red circles.

"Yes General!" said Schwartzman.  "The 42nd Rangers  will get the job done, sir!" he said loudly.

"Then get your men ready Colonel, General Brennan will brief  your staff more extensively at your battalion CP. You are dismissed." said Collins rising and saluting . Schwartzman, who was standing resplendent in his green beret and dress uniform, returned the salute smartly, spun on his heel and left the office to the staff room outside. A line of other commanders was waiting to receive their orders.  In the distance, he heard distant thunder. It was a Saturn Seven launch from Brownsville going off on schedule and now echoing up the Gulf Coast. Another 300 tons now was headed for Low-Earth-Orbit.  The launches were now happening  three  times a day, every day. Combined with launches from Mississippi and Florida , Baikonur and Vostok, they were putting  3,000 tons of supplies in orbit a day. *Good,* he thought, *more ammo and MREs, for our assignment. Soon, that 3000 tons will be going to the Moon with us.*

Alicia Sepulveda  stood on the roof of the Pentagon with Abe Goldberg and CINC of space forces General Standish. They all gripped binoculars. It was night  and they were watching the clear sky to the south, it was a clear cold night. Suddenly they all  saw a string of bright white sparks of light in the sky. The sparks then grew to clouds of bluish ghostly light that expanded and faded.

"Soon we will be ready, we'll just keep hammering them, " said Standish grimly watching the display with binoculars. " then we are going up there ourselves and tear them another asshole. It's the one useful Cosmic skill humans excel at. "

"As you have said several times, Alicia, if the greys were truly intelligent they would have never come here..." said Goldberg as both Alica and him watching the expanding clouds of light with binoculars.

****

In the depths of the stone fortress by the sea on Tandol, Janek of Rigel, stood looking at the two naked men hung in chains from the ceiling of the underground chamber. They had both been beaten by Janek's retainers, who stood by them, and the bruised heads of the two naked men were now locked into steel clamps connected to the ceiling so that they could not move their heads. The room was lit by a fire burning on a stone hearth. The retainer nearest to the men was an immensely strong man named Talos.

"You two are lucky men," began Janek, his white hair and beard bright in the dim light of the fire, "for Hontal of Alnilam has survived your attempt to kill him. If he had died, you would have been guilty of killing an agent of the Emperor, and suffered the death of hot coals. But since he has recovered, and regained his knightly strength, I am inclined to be merciful to you both. This, despite the fact you were very difficult to track down and have put me to a great deal of trouble. I will therefore be especially merciful if you can answer my questions quickly." he smiled and listened to the pleadings of the two men.

"So, yes," continued Janek, "if you will both tell me who hired you to do this deed and the intentions of this plot, my mercy will know no bounds." Janek then reached towards the fire and pulled out a steel poker with a wooden handle, whose pointed end was white hot. He then held it in front of the face of the nearest man. The man whimpered piteously. "So who will be first to speak?" Janek then carefully pushed the white hot

757

iron into the man's right eye socket, with a sizzle.  The man was screaming in agony and the other man began to speak rapidly.

"We were hired by the House of Batelgeen! They were displeased with the report of Hontal from the Quzrada! So they paid us gold, and promised more gold when we did the killing!"

"Oh, that is much better!" laughed Janek. He stepped back towards the hearth, putting the hot poker back in the fire.

"And why did they do this?  Why? That is my question now.  To kill an agent of the Emperor, over a bad report?  This is a grave matter, and it must stem from a grave motivation, not just jealousy over a  displeasing report.  Hence, I know there is more to this story than merely a report." Janek looked at both of them carefully.  He smiled amiably.  The one men had a stream of blood coming from where his eye had been. "And you both, you were not a pair of marketplace idlers, hired to do a killing on the highway.  No, you are both trusted men of long employment  with the House of Batelgeen.  You are important men, hired to do an important job." Janek's smile suddenly vanished, his face adopted an angry snarl.

"So! What did you hear of the reason for the House of Batelgeen to meddle in the Quzrada?  Why does Batelgeen involve itself at Erra? Surely you must have heard of a reason?  I know both of you have both been invited to their banquets, and listened to their idle talk after much wine has been served.  So you have heard the reason! "

"My Lord we do not know! We were hired by them to kill Hontal of Alnilam," cried out the man who had lost an eye.

"Oh, I do not believe you," said Janek now smiling, pulling  the now white hot poker from the fire again and stepping toward the men.  Perhaps another eye must be sacrificed, or some other parts? Again, I ask, why is the House of Batelgeen so involved in doings at Erra? What have you heard?"

"The House of Batelgeen, it seeks to return to the throne!" shrieked the man who had lost and eye. "This is the rumor! I heard it at a banquet! It is the prophecy that a child of Erra will return the House of Batelgeen to the

758

throne! A child of two mothers! The house of Batelgeen seeks to bring this about at Erra! It is the Song of Erra!"

Janek stopped and turned suddenly, and stared in amazement at Talos his chief retainer, and motioned to him to come closer. Janek stepped closer to the fire and put the poker back in the fire. Talos came close to him beside the hearth.

"Talos, these men must not give any report of this interview to the House of Batelgeen." Janek motioned with his fingers across his throat, then waved his fingers like the waves of the sea.

"Yes my Lord," said Talos. Janek then left the chamber, climbed the steps to the battlements of the fortress, and stared out over the storm-tossed sea beyond.

\*\*\*\*

Manny Berkowitz was standing looking out the window of his office when Cassandra entered. She had come in late, after sleeping in that morning with jet lag. Bernie had lost weight and obviously toned up. Cassandra noted a plastic bag full of sliced carrots on his desk. He turned smiling to face Cassandra. *Oh no, this means trouble,* thought Cassandra.

"Cassie, thanks for seeing me so quickly, please shut the door and sit down. I hope you had a good trip to see your folks."

"Yes, Manny, have you thought about Pam and I going to astronaut training and getting space suits?" she asked sitting.

"Oh that, yes," he said sitting down.

"Well?" she asked insistently.

"Yeah, yeah, it seems like a good idea. We could turn it into a special. Bernie likes it."

"Well good then, we can do it soon then."

759

"Yes, let's start arranging it, and figure out a special around it. It will boost our ratings," said Manny with weary resignation.

"Our ratings are good, aren't they? I mean considering we are in a war to determine human survival, it's always good to have good ratings, right?" asked Cassandra sweetly.

"Yeah, I wanted to talk about something else." *Oh no,* thought Cassandra, *what now?*

"It's Pamela, she seems under the weather, recently," said Manny.

"She's told me she had a cold," said Cassandra defensively. "I hope that's allowed here."

"Yes and she seems to have gained some weight. You need to get her back in Zumba class." Cassandra frowned. She had just gotten back from seeing her parents for a week after the Far East trip. She had not seen Pamela except briefly since arriving the day before. *Perhaps Pam's face was a wee-bit rounder,* thought Cassandra. "I figured you could talk to her about it more diplomatically than me." *So it's my problem?* thought Cassandra , *I am supposed to fix this? Damn you Manny!*

"Sure, is there anything else?" asked Cassandra pleasantly. *I am gone for a week and everything falls apart.*

"No," said Manny offering her a carrot slice and smiling. Cassandra took a carrot slice thoughtfully, and turned and left. She would handle the 4 to 6 o'clock news, and Pam would cover until 8. Cassandra was already making plans. *How to engineer this?*

She walked down the hall to see Pamela. Pam was sitting in her small office staring out the window. Cassie came in and sat down. A row of cute stuffed animals stared cheerfully back at her.

Pamela turned to look at Cassandra, she had gained a little weight in the week since Cassandra had been gone. It was not much, but the camera magnified even small weight gains. *This is a crazy business. Back to Zumba class!* Thought Cassandra. But what struck Cassandra as she looked at Pam's face was a look of deep sadness. Pam started crying.

760

"What's wrong," asked Cassandra.

"My husband. It's been 6 months since Michael left on his secret mission. I haven't heard anything from him or the Navy. He is out in space someplace. They won't tell me where." The words cut Casandra like a knife. A feeling of emptiness and helplessness filled the room. "They tell me nothing, not even my contacts in the Navy high command staff, " Pamela said . "What does it mean, that much utter silence?" Cassandra could only shake her head sadly. She felt tears come to her own eyes.

"Let's have dinner after you get off at 8, baby, and have a few drinks," said Cassandra leaning forward and embracing Pamela warmly. They both wiped their eyes. Pamela nodded, they both smiled bravely. "I better get ready for the 4 o'clock," said Cassandra.

****

On the Space Frigate Dauntless, in the cramped control room, the Chief Medical officer Michael Donnelly stood by Captain Robert Forrester, who stood by the Captain's centrally positioned seat as the forward viewscreen zoomed into magnified view of their destination. It was the Jupiter Moon system. Jupiter, a mass of yellow and orange colors in bands, seemed to writhe and boil as it swam in a sea of utter blackness. Several multi-colored moons were visible. One was casting a black dot of a shadow on the planet. They were so far from home now, Earth might as well be in another universe.

"Navigation, what is our updated ETA for assuming Jupiter orbit." asked the Captain.

"48 hours, 11 minutes, Skipper," said Harris, the navigation officer.

"Mr. Dykstra, we are soon entering enemy occupied space, need to go to General Quarters in twelve hours." The Captain turned to Michael. Michael handed him the week's medical and morale report. The Captain quickly scanned it, then signed it. "Excellent Mr. Donnelly, please enter your report into the log.

The crew was very healthy, physically, and Captain Forester was an excellent commander, so morale was good. This meant Donnelly's chief job was to ensure that the ships food supply and atmosphere were as healthy as possible. The Skipper had told him that his main job was to 'keep the chow good and the air sweet.' This was no small task when the ship was recycling every piece of oxygen and organic matter. The system had been well tested back on Earth and in orbit, but that was close to a billion miles away now. The fact was, the waste system, and food and water systems were just different ends of the same loop. If anything went wrong, as the cook said 'it will be very bad for morale, if I quit eating what I am cooking.' So far everything had run unexpectedly well, but they hadn't seen any combat yet. Donnelly wondered how well hygiene in the system could be maintained if they suffered major battle damage.

The Space Frigate Dauntless now glided toward the Jupiter moon system like a spear point launched across the empty blackness. Donnelly turned and left the bridge ducking through the airtight hatch that connected it to the rest of the ship. He walked down the narrow, low-ceilinged hallway, whose walls and ceiling were thick with cables and junction boxes. He went past the Captain's quarters and officers mess, then the crewman's mess, then to his quarters/office next to sick bay. His nurse, one of the only three women among the crew of 45, looked up from looking at a sailor's eyes. She was a quite attractive brunette named Dorothy, and her looks ensured that no sailor would avoid sick bay if they got sick, or even suspected they were sick.

They were all a tiny bubble of human culture in an empty universe, now closing on Jupiter and its massive moon system. They were to there to find any alien bases in the Jupiter moon system, but more importantly, the suspected alien stargate believed operating there at the Sun- Jupiter Bergenholm point, where the tidal forces of Jupiter and the Sun created a region of "flat space." However, they were to approach the Bergenholm Point from Jupiter, not from the Sunward direction, and only after making sure the moon system held no bases. Still, Donnelly now rated their chances of ever seeing Earth again as only 50/50.

Donnelly went to his cramped office, sat down at his desk and looked fondly at a picture of Pamela posing in a tight blue sweater, smiling serenely. He kissed his hand and reached up and touched her picture. Because of complete radio silence on the mission he had not been able to send any messages home.

****

Cassandra had invited Pamela to her apartment as part of the "make Pamela more perky project" to spend the night and to watch the old German silent film, The Girl in the Moon. It had been made in Germany in 1929, just before the decent into the madness of the Third Reich and the catastrophe of World War Two. Pamela watched it mesmerized, while Cassandra drank wine and found herself staring out the window at the real Moon rising over the Potomac.

"Oh, there's Hitler," said Pamela pointing out one evil character. "You can tell by the way he combs his hair, even if he doesn't have a toothbrush mustache!"

The heroine appeared, a German blonde bombshell, "Oh, there I am Cassie! Thank you! This movie is very validating!" chortled Pamela. The characters all got in a big rocket and launched to the Moon with crowds of German citizens watching. They looked almost American, standing there in coats and hats. *So sad that the great disaster would engulf them later,* thought Cassandra. At that point in the movie, Cassandra found herself grabbing a pillow and holding it to herself, as Pamela made fun of the buxom heroine lying on a bed in the spacecraft struggling to breathe as the gravity forces built up.

"Ooh I feel this unbearable weight on my chest!" yelled out Pamela lying on her back on the couch. "Two of them actually!" she looked away from the movie and smiled at Cassandra mischievously.

"I've already lost two pounds, Cassie, thanks to you, which is good, but I will miss being a size 40 bra!" she added with a laugh.

Later, Cassandra was lying awake at 3:00 o'clock in the morning. She kept thinking about Bob Schwartzman. She regretted deeply now how they had parted. *I am sorry Bob, I didn't mean it* ....she thought. *I didn't mean it.*

763

She dreamed she was standing beside Robert Schwartzman, at a trial at The Hague. Robert Schwartzman was being condemned to death at the at the trial, for crimes against humanity from the UFO cover-up, and she was crying to him, *I love you, Bob, I love you...* as he was being led away. She awoke with tears in her eyes.

She looked up, Pamela was in her room. In the dim light, Cassandra could see that Pamela's hair was in disarray and she was naked. Tears were on her cheeks also.

"What wrong baby?" asked Cassandra, sitting up in her sheer violet night grown.

"Michael, I think he's dead," said Pamela sadly.

"Come to bed," said Cassandra. Pamela climbed in beside Cassandra. Pamela was soon asleep snuggled up next to her. Cassandra lay awake for a long period.

*I am caught between two loves, one that is forbidden, and another that is doomed,* she thought, as she slipped into sleep.

**** 

In the sick bay, Michael and his nurse Dorothy sat in their surgical scrubs by the airlock. Because they had to be able to treat wounded even if the ship lost pressurization, the sickbay had its own small airlock to pass wounded through. For wounded outside the airlock, they had little else except duct tape to try to keep the suits pressurized.

Michael knew they were now undergoing the most dangerous part of the Dauntless's space mission. They were braking to slow down and be captured into orbit around the moon Calisto in the Jovian system. To brake they had to increase their rest mass of the ship so that conservation of momentum would slow them down, then they had to do a plasma rocket burn to slip into orbit around Calisto. Michael knew both of these operations would create gravity and EM waves betraying their presence to whoever was watching in the Jovian system. He realized his life and

Dorothy's might be measured in hours. The whole ship was at battle stations, with everyone else in space suits and armor.

Sensing the mounting tension on the ship, Dorothy came over to him and kissed him deeply on the lips, and he put his arms around her. Out of the corner of his eye, he saw Pamela's portrait, and reached up and knocked it off the shelf as he and Dorothy embraced desperately.

****

Cassandra and Pamela were gyrating with a crowd of other women in the Zumba dancercise class. The look on both their faces was a peaceful weariness as the music pounded, and they moved sinuously to its beat, covered in perspiration. Both Cassandra and Pamela were now in top physical form.

****

Douglass Forrester, was once again diving for the Lunar surface, in this case, the Riphaeus mountains unloading rockets and tracer-explosive shells onto the apparently alien posts on the crests of the mountains before flying upwards back into deep space with the rest of his squadron. They were destroying the outposts every week, only to return, and see them rebuilt. Out of the corner of his eye, he could see a vast series of electric blue explosions over Kepler Crater showering it and the surrounding Lunar surface with hyper velocity steel fragments. This was followed by huge explosions and dust plumes as the Saturn 7 upper stages crashed into the Lunar surface and detonated.

****

In the vast concrete vacuum dome, Schwartzman led his men across simulated lunar dust at reduced gravity in armored space suits, firing their Kalashnikov Luna automatic assault rifles, equipped with bayonets, at pop-up targets of Greys. Above them, stars were painted on the steel roof. At first, combat moon-suit malfunctions had been common, but now, after three weeks "under the Moon Dome" the suits, the weapons, and his men were now operating like well-oiled machines.

****

Cassandra and Pamela stepped into the saucer in their new dark-blue form-fitting space suits, holding their helmets . They were both giddy with excitement  as John Grubenard motioned for them to sit and strap themselves in. They had both cut their hair to mid neck length so it would not interfere with their space helmets and they both put them on as did Grubenard.  They stared out of the clear Plexiglas dome above them, out at the green grass surrounding the helipad.  Above them was a deep blue sky.

"Dr. Grubenard, what are those vanes around the bottom of the craft?" asked Pamela as she finished strapping herself in.  " I don't remember them being there last time when I saw your ship."

"Please call me John, girls." he said, flipping switches and going down a checklist. "The vanes are new. Their called "Prometheans" or 'promo-vanes'. They increase lift versus power when we are near the ground. Some hot-shots  developed them recently in Nevada,"  he said distractedly.

Suddenly the turbines that powered the craft in the atmosphere started and began to whine at a higher and higher pitch, then there was a feeling of momentary weightlessness as the craft shot up into the sky at astonishing speed. Cassandra was watching the ground recede rapidly in a television screen, while Pamela was watching the sky above them turn a deeper and deeper blue while glancing at Grubenard's hands flying over the controls. The sky turned a deeper and deeper blue until it was a violet black and the stars appeared with the azure layer appearing only around them on the horizon.  But soon even the horizon fell away into a gentle curve of the Earth.  The turbines ebbed  and then fell silent. They were now running  the antigravity systems strictly on batteries.

"Oh my God, we're in space!" exclaimed Cassandra and grabbed Pamela's space-gloved hand with her own . Pamela, with the blue limb of the Earth arcing behind her head, merely smiled.

Now they were in low-Earth-orbit space but headed even higher. Soon among the stars near the bright limb of the Earth was a bright speck

766

growing larger. It was a donut-shaped space station, perhaps a hundred meters in diameter.

"That's an older one that had to rotate to have gravity." They closed on another bright object. "That is one of the new ones." He pointed to another space object in the distance. "This one was a triangular white structure with several spacecraft docked at it. "The new one uses electronic gravity so they can be built a lot lighter since they only have gravity on the inside of the modules." Cassandra could see a string of specks in the distance.

"What are those ?" asked Cassandra pointing at them.

"Lunar Boosters for the invasion; they must have thousands of them up here now." said Grubenard. "In fact, you didn't actually see that girls, it's classified."

They were now headed back into the atmosphere over Florida, the time in space being limited by their battery life. Soon they were back gliding in the atmosphere, enclosed in deep blueness. The turbines restarted, and soon they were partly gliding and partly "skimming", the term for floating on antigravity fields. Finally, they were descending towards the Kennedy Space center, and near the ground, the turbines whine turned into a roar as they descended onto the same Kennedy Space Center helipad that they had left from.

It had seemed like a dream, but it was in fact only a flight into space of an hour and a half. Cassandra felt giddy as she stepped out of the saucer and climbed down the thin aluminum ladder to the ground, pulling off her helmet and letting the sea breeze caress her hair. Pamela followed and then out came Grubenard, slim and fit in his silver space suit. As Pamela took off her space helmet and ran her fingers through her hair, Grubenard was quickly walking around the craft to inspect it. Cassandra caught Pamela looking at Grubenard with a transfixed dreamy gaze. *Oh no, Pammy* thought Cassandra.

\*\*\*\*

After four hours in electronic zero-g in the confined capsule, several rangers began to get space sick. Their helmets were wrestled off and vomit began floating around in the capsule in blobs.

"It's going to be a long two days, getting to the Moon," muttered Lt. Colonel Parker, sitting next to Schwartzman, who was reading Sun Tzu, the Art of War. Schwartzman merely smiled and closed his book as a glob of vomit floated by.

"Listen up you men! Nobody leaves this capsule until the vomiting stops!" he barked.

\*\*\*\*

In the Rose Garden of the White house, under a warm , clear blue sky, the band struck up Hail to the Chief and formations of Griffin jet fighters and newer, black triangle-shaped anti-gravity propelled Star-Eagle fighters flew over in a seemingly endless procession. There had already been a full military parade that morning , with Cassandra and Pamela riding in it, 'right behind the tanks' had noted Pamela happily. The hard-won victory at Fujiyama was being celebrated with wild abandon. As one official had told Cassandra 'In this war, morale is everything now…'

Cassandra and Pamela , Cassandra in a tan pantsuit and Pamela in a blue dress stood at attention as the President, looking happy and relaxed , approached them. An Air force fighter pilot , Captain Frank Gordon, credited with seven kills was also being awarded the congressional medal of honor that day, for, as it was said, 'heroic air and space actions , as well as heroic actions in the battle of the L5 Stable Lagrange Point. ' He had the flight name 'Titan,' before this, but now was called simply "Flash" in honor of his space exploits. He looked like any dashing fighter pilot with blonde crewcut hair.

Cassandra was the first in line to be given her medal, which the President put over her head on a dark blue sash. This done, he shook her hand and looked into her eyes.

"Cassandra , I want to thank you personally, for your bravery in ending the UFO Cover-up which has saved all of us. I also particularly want to thank

768

you for your brave words, on that day at the hospital when I was talking with you and they first told me about the discovery of the  greys cutting off the sunlight to Earth.  I knew you were suffering from deep trauma then,  because of what had happened to you , but  I remember exactly what you said, you said 'I am a little shaky now, but I am going to get well soon, and I am going to help you win this war'   I can tell you now, that if you hadn't spoken the brave words you said to me just then, I think I would have fallen into complete despair in the days after that when it looked like we might lose this war.  But your words sustained me, during those literally dark days.  You told me you were going to get well, and that we were going to win this war and I decided to believe you." He laughed helplessly.  " I mean,  you have been right about everything else.  Right?" She smiled and nodded awkwardly in response.

"I like being right , Mister President, that's for sure, " she laughed helplessly and nodded.  He then shook her hand warmly.

"So I just wanted to thank you for those words."  He added.

"Thankyou Mister President" said Cassandra  bowing her head slightly, before the President  moved  on to Pamela.  *I hardly believed those words myself, when I said them...* she thought in wonder.

"So how you today Pamela?" said the President.

"Just waiting for my next big news scoop, Mister President," said Pamela. The President smiled broadly at this, and put the Medal of Freedom around her neck.   "Your courage has been an inspiration to all of us Pamela," he said as he shook her hand.

"Thankyou Mister President, " said Pamela bowing her head slightly, before the President  moved  on to Captain Gordon.

Later that night,  at the White House Gala in their honor, Cassandra and Pamela both wearing stunning and daring pure-white strapless evening gowns entered the White House ballroom under brilliant lights. Their diamond necklaces sparked brilliantly as did their matching earrings. Their evening gowns looked like woven lightning under the lights and they smiled and waved to everyone from CNS and a distinguished group of Senators, Congressmen, Cabinet Officers, Generals, Admirals, and other high officials, as the White House orchestra played a musical fanfare to them. After dinner and some dancing, Cassandra found herself alone , holding a glass of wine, on a balcony in the warm night looking up the stars of above the lights of the city. *My child is up there somewhere...*

"I thought I'd find you someplace like this , " said Pamela from behind her, holding a glass of wine. Cassandra turned and smiled wearily at her.

"Well, we saved the world, what's next girlfriend?" asked Cassandra.

"Oh, just a few minor loose ends need to be dealt with , I suppose, my dear inspiration-to-humanity." laughed Pamela looked around the sky for the Moon and drinking some wine from her glass.

"The Moon is not due to rise for another half hour or so, I checked, " said Cassandra sipping some wine from her own glass. "I also just want to warn you Pamela, about our newly designated position as saviors of the human race, because, I have discovered tonight that the human race is actually a pretty rascally bunch."

"I'm shocked to hear this, Cassie ! On what salacious evidence have you arrived at this stunning conclusion, that saving this humanity may turn out to be a mixed blessing to the Cosmos?" laughed Pamela.

"I have been informed of this by no less than two Senators , who said they want me as their mistress. They mentioned this to me while we were dancing, " laughed Cassandra. " I told them I was very flattered."

"Well, I suppose people are offering us gifts of what they value the most! It is a sincere sign of gratitude, for sure!" giggled Pamela.

"To us, girlfriend, and to the human race, including its great rascals and everyone else..." said Cassandra lifting up her wineglass to the starry sky. Pamela clinked her half full glass with Cassandra's. They then watched in awe as the waning Moon, a blood red crescent, appeared and rose slowly above the horizon in the East.

****

Cassandra and Pamela skated furiously in their helmets, knee, and elbow pads, and red and gold uniforms dodged in and out of the wild melee of the Washington Press Woman's Roller Derby match. It was all being done for charity, but, as Pamela had noted, it was still a chance for old scores to be settled in the women's Washington Press Corps. They were naturally skating for the "CNS Power-Town CINNERS," and MSNBC was their fiercely competitive network rival, who was represented by the " "MSNBC Heart Breakers."

Pamela, whose skating name was "Little Miss Behavin," was sitting with Cassandra , whose skating name was "Sassy Cassie," was resting with a group of other CNS women skaters during half-time. The CNS CINNERS were ahead by 20 points and Pamela was trying increase team spirit.

"Why was the wife of the Alien Commander on the Moon happy?" she asked the team loudly with a broad smile.

"BECAUSE HE JUST GOT A BIG PROMOTION!" shouted the women, including Cassandra, then collapsing with helpless laughter.

"Why did they install urinals in the Alien headquarters on the Moon?"

"BECAUSE THE STAFF ALL GOT BIG PROMOTIONS TOO!" the women roared then jumped up and down with merriment.

"Finally, guys, why did the new chief alien nurse view all of this with alarm?" everyone looked at Pamela in puzzlement.

"Because she also got a promotion by mistake?" asked Cassandra with a snicker.

"No!" said Pamela with wide eyes. "It's because, where the nurse came from, no one ever got a promotion!" laughed Pamela. Everyone then laughed and charged out onto the derby floor shouting , "CNS SINNERS!

771

WERE THE BEST!" in unison. The team went on to win the game 124 to 105.

****

Marshall Skana stepped forward to examine the polished metal alloy box. The box was very cold, and moisture was frozen on it. They were in an entrance room near the high council chambers. The top of the box was bolted on. The Toman Daz guards who had delivered it from the spaceport, clad in polished armor of the palace, stood at attention around it, as a technician stepped forward and began removing the bolts. The Prime Counselor arrived with his bodyguards. He looked both happy and anxious.

"Councilman Soona has sent a signed message that the Samar have agreed to an additional payment," said the Prime Counselor to Marshall Skana with satisfaction while holding out the letter, "and this is the first shipment. Also, as he says the Samar have made this 'initial shipment' to prove their sincerity and their earnest desires concerning this matter." The Prime Counselor stepped forward eagerly, but Marshall Skana motioned him back in caution. "How much have they sent?" asked the Prime Counselor.

The lid was lifted up and Marshal Skana stepped forward and leaned over the edge of the box to look within. But he recoiled in horror and covered his eyes as he turned to the Prime Counselor. Inside of the metal box was Councilman Soona's frozen head, and a handful of Samaran gold coins in the frozen blood at the bottom of the box. There was also a note stuck on the surface of the frozen blood.

"My Lord, they have killed Lord Soona and sent his head back to us!" gasped Marshall Skana in horror. The prime Councilor shut his eyes in grief and shock at this. Marshal Skana turned and grimly took the note out of the box from beside his friend's lifeless head. He read the note, it was brief.

***"Perform the duty you agreed to do, for the price that was paid!"***

It was signed by Dakon, Commander of the Samaran Armed Forces.

772

"My Lord, we must declare a military emergency in the Quzrada!" said Marshall Skana. "And that fool Sadok Sar must be replaced!" he said, as he handed the bloody note to the Prime Counselor.

"I agree, we must send reinforcements to the Quzrada at once and declare it a zone of war!" said the Prime Councilor reading the note with shaking hands. "We must also send Sadok Sar a military assistant, to help him in this crisis!"

****

At the Pentagon, Metternich was sitting wearily in James Bergman's office, after returning from Japan. He had been involved in weeks of analysis of what had occurred in the battle. This had included digging up the ruins of the alien base along with its dead.

"Good job Richard!" you proved everybody wrong around here who said you were crazy. In fact, we're going to get you some sort of medal!"

"Yeah, I am pleased my Godzilla dream turned into something useful. But when it worked, I confess, I didn't feel that happy," said Metternich.

"Yeah, I understand. War is like that," said Bergman. He had pulled out a bottle of Jack Daniels and poured them both a shot glass full on his huge desk.

"War between two cultures as different as ours and Greys, it's like a collision of two views of reality. And different views of reality, it's like I understand that better than some," he said taking a glass. "So I found myself feeling some sympathy for the poor little bastards. They obviously never conceived of us putting up this much of a fight. Or if my read is correct, they were simply never authorized by their superiors to conceive of it."

"Yeah, but war often reveals such miscalculations, like Napoleon marching on Moscow. So much more so if you're from 400 light years away. So bottoms up Richard, and on to the next crisis!" said Bergman as they both drank their shots of whiskey.

****

Cassandra and Pamela, both clad in bikinis, soaked their aching bodies in a hot tube at a health spa, after the furious Roller Derby game.

"Oh, Pam, am so I glad this derby thing is over in two weeks," said Cassandra leaning back against the side of the hot tub. "Some bitch always manages to whack me right in the boobs."

"What activity is next to stay in shape for the astronaut testing, besides Zumba?" asked Pamela leaning back on the other side of the tub. "You know, we have got to be in good shape if we want to go to the Moon. I heard they are very strict."

"Twai Kwon Do, Pammy, and I found the perfect instructor for us. She's this tough Korean chick named Jenny Park. It's the best form of fighting karate they say, and she is really good."

"Good, I always wanted to learn karate," said Pamela. She chopped the air over the steaming water dreamily with her hand. "I would have thought you learned Kung Fu when you were a kid."

"No," said Cassandra. "I tried, but I only lasted a half hour In karate class. "Yes, Sensei! No Sensei!" said Cassandra in a comic voice. "I finally told him to go to hell! And then I marched out with my ponytail proudly bobbing in the air. It drove my parents crazy!" she said laughing. "But I am not as rebellious now, and I really want to learn karate because of where we're going."

"Sounds good Cassie. Now... the next item on the agenda: who do you want to go out with at CNS?"

Cassandra smiled.

"Actually, I was thinking of that Doug Miller person in the Sports Section. He has been especially friendly lately," said Cassandra.

"No! You can't go out with him! "said Pamela emphatically.

"Why not?"

"He has a low credit score!" said Pamela happily. "Remember, we have now become accidentally  rich in the middle of all of this!  And famous too! We have to be more careful!"

"How do you know his credit score? And I hope this isn't a personal question, Pammy," asked Cassandra skeptically.

"I have this new phone app!  All I need to do is type in someone's name and work location, and it gives me his credit score!" said Pamela happily.

"That's not only ridiculous Pammy, it's  probably  illegal."

"Why spoil  a clever idea with questions of legality?  Besides, you should go out with Bob Tierney in Financial News. He's hunky, and rumor has it that he has the hots for you!  Additionally, he has excellent credit!"

"He tried to sell me Lunar real estate last week! In the hall!" said Cassandra with a look of horror.  "I told him, 'first let's see how much blood it costs'."

"You didn't say that to him! That's sooo rude!" exclaimed Pamela.

"Well, I thought it, anyway," said Cassandra. "But I did say  that I was pleased that Wall Street was finally taking a Bullish position on this little war for human survival we are fighting."

"That's very rude too!  You know what I think?  I think you are chasing away perfectly hunky men because you still harbor romantic fantasies about your secret police Colonel, that Schwartzman guy."

"NO! That is absolutely false and untrue Pammy!  I am entertaining no such fantasies, romantic or otherwise!" said Cassandra indignantly.  "I think you should apologize for even suggesting such a ludicrous possibility!" she added splashing some water at Pamela. Who beamed.

"Oooh sorry," said Pamela, in mock regret. "But, methinks she doth protest too-much…" added Pamela with a serene smile.

"Au contraire, Pammy,  my protestations are entirely appropriate and proportional to the ridiculousness of your suggestion." retorted Cassandra holding her nose high. "I, on the other hand, methinks my married friend is becoming far too-much nosey about my affairs, business and otherwise. All, with the intention of vicarious and promotional voyeurism."

"Ha!" said Pamela smiling. "That is a totally lame answer," she leaned back and closed her eyes.

"Setting aside, temporarily, the subject of promotional voyeurism," said Cassandra. "I have heard the government is actually auctioning off Lunar real estate full of helium 3."

"Yes, I heard that too. It's either a sign the latest war bond drive has tanked or else it's a sign of irrational optimism down at the Pentagon," said Pamela sleepily and with her eyes still closed. "However, the price of helium 3 is now a billion dollars a gram. The Navy is buying it up everywhere it can," she moaned. "They are setting tanks of tritiated water in some countries to make helium 3 like it was wine. You see, once every twelve years, half the tritium turns to helium 3."

Cassandra suddenly raised her hand and looked at it in alarm.

"Pammy, we have to get out now ! Our skin is getting all pruney!" she said in horror.

**** 

Schwartzman , in his full spacesuit of silver, marched out under the dark dome of night stars in Houston Texas, his portable air conditioning unit purring away. His AK Luna carbine was at his side and he carried ten clips of ammunition for it. Behind him, equally armed, a line of fifty men marched also in lock step behind him. He disconnected his air conditioning unit and dropped it on a cart near the doorway. Many other men would be using it later that night. He was now marching up an aluminum ramp into a flying saucer-shaped, LOTS-4 transport, designed to carry 50 men into low-Earth-orbit, where their Saturn 7, Lunar transfer stage awaited them. In the distance, he could see bonfires burning in the Airborne units

776

barracks areas. The 82ⁿᵈ and 101ˢᵗ Division paratroopers were throwing all their money into bonfires, and dancing around them, signifying they weren't coming back to Earth until their mission was accomplished. The 101ˢᵗ had all shaved their heads in Mohawk haircuts. Schwartzman knew the 82ⁿᵈ and 101ˢᵗ were not transiting to Earth-orbit for several hours after he and his men had gone. His unit was part of the 82ⁿᵈ and part of the spearhead of the invasion.

Schwartzman marched into the saucer and took a seat in his designated spot near a small window, as commander of the 42ⁿᵈ Rangers Battalion, the first Army Battalion to land on the Moon. He connected his space suit to a new air conditioning hose and put on and buckled his safety harness. The inside of the saucer was bare metal, magnesium aluminum alloy, and his seat was just a metal ledge with a perforated metal plate for a seat and back. The other men were boarding now, seating was in two concentric rings with seats facing each other. Schwartzman glanced out the window and noted several other saucers being boarded. He turned and was facing Arizona and Jason Parker in their space suits. Their faces were without emotion. Soon everyone was seated and the hatchway was shut. Up above the domed ceiling, the pilot and co-pilot were doing final checkouts, and he could hear their boots on the floor as they took their seats. Soon the four turbo-alternators spun up with a rising whine and were finally singing together in a chorus. Then they were airborne in a sudden feeling of weightlessness.

Schwartzman glanced out the window as the ground fell away from them at astonishing speed. Since they were flying by gravity modification and were technically in "free fall", there was little sensation of motion. Soon the lights of Houston blazed below them, and he saw his and a formation of LOTS-4s rising above the dark Earth with its now pinpoints of light. They broke through a thin cloud layer, and the stars now blazed above them. He could see they were accelerating, and soon the Earth itself was a dark curve with faint green phosphorescent airglow beneath them. Then the main turbines eased back and finally cut-off. The turbo-alternators, by supplying both power and raw jet thrust from their exhausts, had done their job and run out of air. They were now flying strictly on fuel cells and a quiet APU or Auxiliary Power Unit, a small turbine power unit that ran on hydrazine monopropellant to supply extra power. Schwartzman could hear the APU throbbing. Out the window, he could see they were now flying parallel to the Earth and ascending into orbit. Since their gravity mass was now near zero, so was their inertial mass, so it took very little electric power to move them.  Dawn broke over them in space as they moved into the sunlight, and Earth below them was transformed into a beautiful blue and white curve. Gravity drives, at least those that he knew about, had nearly reached the Bergman Limit of an Earth radii, where gravity modification  reached a point of diminishing returns.  The real muscle for taking his men to the Moon would be a massive chemical booster, still the biggest means of releasing raw power available to humans.

Now they approached a large brilliant white object. Soon Schwartzman heard a metallic clang as the LOTS did an aggressive hard-dock. Men rose, floated to the hatchway and monitored its conditions. Then the hatchway opened, revealing a short tunnel into their landing capsule. It would be their home for the next two days while they transited to the Moon. Schwartzman glanced out the window as the men rose from their seats and began moving  through the hatchway using handholds.  The Saturn 7 upper stage, filled with hypergolic  fuels, Anhydrous Nitric Acid and Hydrazine, which could be stored in orbit for long periods and would ignite on contact in the rocket engines, stretched back from him. Now he rose, and moving by handholds in weightlessness, moved through the brightly lit hatch. Floating down a tunnel, he entered a cramped, cylindrical cabin full of men now buckling themselves into seats, their voices a chorus of laughter, cursing,  and off-color remarks. The men were all smiling fiercely.  Some saw him as he entered the capsule and saluted him.  He flew past them to the front of the cabin and took his designated seat in the very front of the cabin. He would be "point" on this expedition by choice. He buckled himself in.  They had simulated this part of the voyage several times, now it was for real.

A large digital clock near them showed 20 minutes and flying seconds until trans-Lunar burn.

"All right you Rangers! Buckle up and prepare for the burn!" he shouted. The fifty men in the capsule with him instantly fell silent and the only noise was the snapping and tightening of buckles.

Cassandra and Pamela, both carrying their Zumba workout bags, and weary after a furious workout, paused and looked at the dark, starlit sky. The whole sky seems suddenly full of comet-like streaks of white light. The number of them was vaster than they had ever seen before.

"There they go Cassie, it's the invasion, it's started," said Pamela somberly, as she watched transfixed.

"It's not just another pre-invasion bombardment?" asked Cassie staring at the moving lights.

"No," said Pamela shaking her head as she stared at the sky. "It's on, the invasion is on, I can feel it. I've had this feeling all day."

"God help us now," said Cassandra as she watched the whole sky now moving. She suddenly felt weightless, as if falling in into an abyss. *Bob is up there, I know it...*

****

In the capsule, Schwartzman stared out the small window. Rank has its privileges, thought Schwartzman. He had one of the few windows in the cramped landing capsule. *This ain't no pleasure cruise.* They had trained in a similar capsule on the ground, but the reality of it now sank into the pit of his stomach.

He saw the bombardment barrage boosters igniting up ahead as they crossed into darkness. Soon the sky ahead over the limb of the earth filled with white light as the boosters carrying 100 tons of explosive shrapnel cluster munitions each ignited and began their journey to the Moon. The great red number display was now counting down the last seconds and alarms were going off.

"BRACE FOR BURN! BRACE FOR THE BURN!" he bellowed.

In a few second they were in the final countdown. 5, 4, 3 , 2, 1, Zero.

The booster ignited, it felt like being kicked in the ass by a giant. This was no gentle gravity modification. This was raw chemical power, a thousand tons of thrust now pushing them to the Moon across the starry gulf. *Old school*, thought Schwartzman as he labored to breathe, and the thrust undulated. It was much rawer than the simulations, rougher. *Just like the men of Apollo experienced. If they could handle it, I sure as hell can!*

There was a brilliant light and an expanding ball of fire ahead of them and off to the right. He recognized that one of the boosters had exploded, probably killing an entire pod full of men. He simply looked away.

They were now on a raging pillar of fire, flying into the stars. For endless seconds the booster burned, Then the burn abruptly cut off, and he saw a cloud of droplets of vented unused fuel, surround the craft.

Everyone was silent. *No turning back now, we are absolutely committed.* He glanced back. The men all had the same look, a dull 1,000-yard stare. *I trained these guys well.*

Soon they emerged from the night side of the Earth, now traveling at 6 miles a second. They saw the Moonrise through the atmosphere. Then it was suddenly fully visible. It was not full, it was a waxing quarter moon, and they would be landing by Earthlight in the lunar night.

*No turning back. Victory or Death.*

\*\*\*\*

Cassandra and Pamela, both wearing dark blue space coveralls with American flag shoulder patches from their space training course, walked in awe down the underground corridor to the war room in the Pentagon, escorted by a Marine officer.

*What do you wear when invited to the war room at the Pentagon, certainly not our Zumba outfits,* thought Cassandra, recalling her discussion with Pamela. It was decided they should wear their space coveralls because they were comfortable and seemed appropriate. The war room was not as large as they expected and was dominated by a huge display showing Cis-Lunar Space, the Earth-Moon system. It was filled with golden sparks of light, the invasion fleet, concentrated near the Moon. Blue dots also moved near the Moon Space Forces, fighter bombers.

Cassandra gasped as she saw it, the number of golden sparks was in the thousands, hundreds of red lights were closer to the Lunar surface. The pre-landing bombardment barrage, that would hit the Lunar surface and tear it to pieces one last time, before the landing ships came in. She looked over at Pamela, who also stood awestruck.

"I guess you were right Pam, it was the beginning of the invasion we saw the other night," said Cassandra, "not just a bombardment."

"Of course, I was right, I am good at this job!" said Pamela staring at the display with a faint smile. But her smile faded as she stared transfixed. "Look at this. This is history Cassie," she gasped. Cassandra glanced around, and to her amazement saw Secretary of Defense James Bergman, Chairman of the Joint Chiefs, General Malcom Burnham , and the President of the United States all sitting together watching the big display with them. They all had a look that Cassandra recognized as somber desperation.

"This invasion has to succeed, it has to. If it fails...Please God let it succeed!" Cassandra muttered to herself, now watching the big display again, mesmerized. She could see the red lights now going out near the Moon, the bombardment barrage had arrived over the lunar surface.

****

They were now falling towards the Moon, and all sense of levity and bravado departed from the men. The forward viewscreen showed the wave of electric blue flashes covering the Oceanus Procellarum area of the Moon, as the bombardment wave arrived. Thousands of tons of explosives and pre-sectioned steel prisms tearing now at the Lunar surface, destroying anything alive or that sheltered life on the surface. Outside the small windows, they could see the lunar surface now rising up to embrace them. Only one sight heartened them, a squadron of heavily armed space fighters flew past them in a row, headed also for Procellarum.

After an alarm and countdown, they all secured their Moon suits, with smudge-gray lunar, camouflaged coveralls, with helmet's visors down and strapped themselves into their harnesses.

"5, 4, 3, 2 , 1,  Zero!" came a voice over the helmet radios.

Suddenly  the whole front hull of the spacecraft peeled back,  propelled by explosive  bolts  that    flew  away  revealing,  black,  star-studded  space around them and the grey- silver, Lunar surface in the front  of them rising now to meet them.  They could even see the Ripheasian Mountains below them,  a  silver  splash  across  a  cratered  grey  surface.  Then  the  entire spacecraft disassembled itself with each man now flying his own rocket pod.  No going back now, it was victory on the lunar surface  or death.

Schwartzman was now falling, strapped to his own pod as he watched his companions  all disperse into the distance.  He saw the Lunar horizon now rising around him as the Moon pulled  him into its embrace. He saw the bombardment still continuing below him with bright flashes. He took one last look at the Earth and thought of Cassandra.  Then ceased to think.


"Lord into thy will I commend my spirit," thought Schwartzman as he now fell into Procellarum,  seemingly alone .

The bombardment below him abruptly stopped except for the massive flares caused by the impact of the boosters.  Now he fell into the grey surface which filled his sight.

He  was  descending  at  many  kilometers  a  second  towards  the  Lunar surface and Ripheasian Mountains.  He began to make out peak 831, the objective  of  Bravo  Company.  He  was  falling  at  an  ever-increasing  rate through the airless void. He saw the peak, now memorized. He saw it triangulated  by  craters  Landsberg   C,   Udoxis  E,  and  F,  as  the  ground rushed up at him.

Suddenly a red light lit up inside his helmet with a countdown from 5 seconds.  He braced himself as the rocket booster under his feet fired, slowing his mad descent.  In ten seconds his speed into the ground slowed to a standstill and the booster then detached and his pod thruster took over. He was steering the thrusters to take him to Peak  831 of the Ripheasian Mountains. His heart began to pound as he knew the thrusters made him a target for any ground fire. But now he was nearing the upper slopes of the peak. He now leaned into the decent aiming to land on the very top of the peak. He now gripped his Luna Assault rifle, drew back it's bolt and pulled it from the straps on the front of his suit. Suddenly a stream of red tracers flew past him as he descended to the peak, right into a group of Lunar camouflaged greys in armored suits, who were coming out of a doorway on the peak slope. He trained his gun on them and fired, every fifth round a tracer. Tracers were now flying past him into the group of grey armored figures who now were falling and running about in confusion.

Abruptly his boots hit the Lunar soil and he leaped from the pod he had ridden down on and joined what was now a raging battle with the Greys. His own men were now landing all around him. Without thinking, they were running and firing up a slope to a bright hatchway in the side of the peak . A silent but brilliant explosion filled the hatchway and a small childlike figure flew out of it.  Now he was up to the hatchway and staring into it. It was a tunnel leading deep into the peak. The troops beside him were spraying tracers into its depths and throwing grenades down it, which exploded with sharp blue flashes.

"Colonel!" a voice crackled over the radio. His heart leaped at this. It meant radio silence was being broken because all his men were now on the Lunar surface. It was Arizona reporting: "This is Bravo Alpha Company reporting  we have taken peaks 921 and 910. Charlie Company is still engaged  at peak 730 and the connected ridgeline.  We are assembling here and will send a platoon into the tunnel to secure it."

"Jason, when you have reports from the company commanders,  I want them to send up flares signaling to the main landing forces that we have secured the Ripheasian crest line.  Schwartzman could see tracers and explosions further down the line of mountain peaks.  They seemed to have achieved complete surprise. It was baffling.

"Colonel Schwartzman, this is Major Bellamy of his Majesty's SAS, and we have secured peaks 521 , 456 and 458!"

Schwartzman looked over and saw what looked like silver specks descending like a snow storm to the west , it was the 101st and 82nd Airborne troops descending into their Oceanus Procellarum drop zone, near the Ripheasian Mountains his men had just seized. They were descending on the same sort of thrust pods his battalion had just used. Violet flares were now going up from the Ripheasian crest line, all objectives achieved. Several barrages of celebratory tracers also filled the sky.

"NO SHOOTING IN THE AIR, YOU MAY HIT THE MARINES! THIS IS COLONEL SCHWARTMAN!" He bellowed. "All units will now dig in and prepare for possible alien counterattack!" shouted Schwartzman into his radio. All company commanders will stand by for a radio conference."

He now looked and saw flares coming up to the west as the airborne troops assembled on the ground and began digging in. Their job was to block any alien ground force from Kepler Crater. He now looked to the East and saw descending specks of light now flare into brilliance near the surface. The 1st and 2nd Marine divisions were now making planet-fall. He saw one lander plummet straight and explode as it hit the surface, but the overwhelming majority were landing safely. Another lander then augured in and exploded. He saw no signs of alien resistance either to the East or West of the mountain peaks they now held.

"Oh my God, we are doing this thing! We are landing on the moon with only minimal resistance!"

****

In the war room, the tension seemed to ebb after what seemed like an eternity. Pamela noticed a more relaxed look on the face of the President as reports were being brought to him.

"What's happening ? " asked Cassandra, drinking some mineral water, as young handsome army officer walked by, after handing General Burnham a written report. He turned and smiled at her.

"So far so good," said the officer, a Captain. "The 101 and 82$^{nd}$ have landed with minimal casualties, the two Marine divisions have now landed also. The only fighting was on a range of mountains overlooking the main landing zone, but even there it was over quickly. The pre-landing bombardments seem to have made aliens evacuate the Lunar near side.

"You mean the landing has been largely unopposed?" Cassandra asked in amazement.

"Yes, at least so far. We are down in force, and the third wave is beginning to land with heavy equipment. They are setting up a base, and the mobile units are now moving out to Kepler Crater. First Infantry Division will be landing shortly."

\*\*\*\*

At Baikonur in Kazakhstan, night had fallen and General Baranov looked out at the dry plains now covered with lights. He watched the clock tick down the final seconds.

"Commence operation Firebird!" He shouted and General Gribkov , standing nearby, turned to his aides and began shouting orders. Soon, saucer-like transports full of elite troops were rising into the starry skies.

\*\*\*\*

"My God look at that," said Parker to Schwartzman. "The Jarheads have arrived to relieve us!" Several large armored Lunar tractors, six-wheeled vehicles with wide, flat, metal mesh tires, had come rolling up the gentle slope of the mountainside. The vehicles were called Lamptracs, or LAMPs, and were covered with Marines in armored space suits. They rolled up to Schwartzman's position and the Marines began dismounting. An officer in an armored Moon suit bounced up to Parker and Schwartzman and they exchanged salutes.

" Colonel Schwartzman , 42$^{nd}$ Ranger Battalion is relieved. We are the 103$^{rd}$ Marine Battalion. I am Colonel Girard. You are ordered to mount up, and we will transport your men to the zone held by the 82$^{nd}$ airborne on the far side of these mountains. "

"All right you Rangers, saddle up!" bellowed Schwartzman as he surveyed his men gathering around. They began climbing aboard the now empty LAMPS as the Marines took positions on the Ripheasian crest-line. Schwartzman looked with binoculars as he saw the scene being repeated on the mountain tops down the line. The Marines were unloading heavy armaments and supplies from the LAMPs. Soon they were rolling down the gentle Eastern slopes of the mountains, near to where the Navy CBs were building a Moon base. He was disappointed that they were going back down the mountainside the way the Marines had come up but was too exhausted to try and protest.

As they rolled past the moon base construction site to skirt around the South end of the mountains before heading North to the 82nd Division zone, they saw with satisfaction vast trenches being blasted into the lunar surface, and large tubes being rolled into them to form parts of a lunar base. The base would be named Apollo Base. The whole plain was now covered with workers, Lunar bulldozers, and cargo vehicles. Teams of men were also disassembling the Lunar Landers used by the Marines for use as Moon Base parts.

He saw a battalion of Marines standing in camouflaged Moon suits near their vehicles being addressed by their commander. Schwartzman tuned his radio to the local Marine channel.

"This is Colonel Hackett! Alright, you Marines, your mission is to advance to the far side of the Moon, locate those alien bases, and then you will secure those bases! Now Mount up! "

"UURAHH!" was the Marines response as then all bounced into their vehicles and began to roll, joining the mass of Marines that Schwartzman's battalion was now rolling with. Schwartzman turned his frequency back to this own unit's channel.

"We took our objective with only 48 men killed and twenty wounded," said Parker. "We must have killed 500 Greys. This day has begun pretty well. Colonel!" said Parker after conferring on the radio with the company commanders. "This campaign to take the alien lunar bases may go pretty much like the bases on Earth." Schwartzman had expected a large number of dead relative to wounded. To 'get hit' on the Moon usually meant the loss of spacesuit pressurization, even with armored self-sealing spacesuits, this could be instantly fatal. Still, Schwartzman nodded in satisfaction.

"Yes, it's good, Jason, but a day on the Moon lasts 28 earth days, so the rest of this day could still get interesting." *Next stop Kepler Crater.* He thought as he stared at the huge blue and white Earth, six times larger than a full moon, hanging beautifully over the Eastern horizon. A beautiful blue light illuminated everything like gentle daylight. This made Schwartzman feel happy and relieved for the first time in weeks. *Truly, not a bad start to our first few hours on the Moon,* he thought, as they rolled past an enormous rocket battery being set up by the Marines to defend the Apollo base. Then he looked out over the Moon and saw the Apollo Base being built.

*We are here to stay.*

**\*\*\*\***

"Good to see you, girls," said the President, with obvious relief, as he shook Cassandra's hand and then Pamela's. "You ought to try out the buffet dinner they have over there on the chow cart."

"Oh... thanks, Mister President, but we are in astronaut training now, and we have to really watch our weight!" said Cassandra cheerfully. Pamela nodded smiling.

"We did it! We have 60,000 men on the Moon and are getting dug in!" said Cassandra. "The aliens must have retreated back to the far side." The President nodded wearily, in response.

"That's what it looks right now, at least. But what these people have done so far makes little sense, I haven't had much luck predicting what they'll do." He grinned, Cassandra could see he had aged tremendously since the war had begun. "That's why I leave predicting alien actions to experts." He then walked on happily to talk to some people who looked like intelligence officials. Cassandra turned to Pamela, who looked deep in thought, and was now staring at the big display. It now showed blue arrows moving towards Kepler Crater, a formerly thriving alien base to

787

the West. The human position on the Moon now looked solid and dug in. Based on the arrows moving slowly on the Lunar surface on the display, it now appeared that the Marines and Paratroopers were rolling on armored vehicles towards Kepler.

"What do you think cosmic war, strategist? If I was the alien commander, I would have opposed this landing with everything I had," said Cassandra. "Why are they letting us get a foothold on the Moon?"

"Yes, but their main bases are on the far side, in the highlands of the far side," said Pamela. The near side of the Moon is covered with Maria, wide, flat, lava-covered plains, but the far side is all mountains and hills, excellent defensive terrain. They may have decided to hold a defensive line on the far side and wait for a big fleet to come rescue them. So they may be just trading real estate for time."

Pamela walked over to General Burnham, who was laughing jovially with some other officers. Cassandra followed her.

"Well, hello ladies," said General Burnham with a laugh. He was holding what looked like a glass of champagne.

"Looks like we're having a good day General," said Cassandra.

"Yes, just about as good a day as we could have hoped for so far." he said, glancing up at the display.

"How much longer do you think this war will last? Do you think they'll just give up and go home after this?" asked Pamela. General Burnham, looked deep in thought at this question.

"No," he said, shaking his head. His smile faded. "No, the lunar far side is like the Central Highlands of Vietnam, or like Italy in World War Two. It's good ground for defense. So this may be a long hard slog, to eliminate the far side bases." He sighed. "But today, right now, you are looking at one happy soldier," he said. He then excused himself and walked off to confer with some other generals.

Cassandra shot a knowing look at Pamela, who winked. *How does this girl figure out this stuff?* thought Cassandra.

788

"Well, the good news Cassie, is that this means we get to go to the Moon and report on a war there after all," said Pamela soberly.

****

Riding now in an Army LAMP, Schwartzman had taken off his helmet and was consulting a map as the vehicle lurched along, with its turbine engines running on NTO and hydrazine, whining reassuringly. Men were asleep with their helmets off, not advisable in a combat zone, but everyone was too exhausted to care. They were near the end of a long armored column crossing Oceanus Procellarum.

Kepler Crater had been reportedly found to house only the shattered ruins of an alien base, with many mummified alien bodies. This was being viewed by most of the forces, Airborne and Marine, with angry disappointment. The Marines had elected to set and detonate a bunch of deep demolition charges to break up any subsurface alien hold-out units, around the abandoned base. The airborne troops now mounted on vehicles, where ordered to move West.

"Well, at least our unit didn't bust our asses getting up there to find nuthin" said Arizona.

****

In Sinus Iridium, the Bay of Rainbows, General Baranov in his space suit got out of his lander and bounced in the weak lunar gravity to an area where several armored personnel carriers were parked. He pulled out a written speech and looked at the mass of Russian troops and vehicles massed across the Bay of Rainbows and into the adjoining Mare Frigoris. It was Lunar night, but the Earth, glowing brightly blue and white, provided ample light. *So we Russians have finally achieved the Moon.* He thought.

"Fellow Soldiers of Mother Russia!" he began, then he paused and suddenly threw away the speech." To hell with it! You know our mission here!" he laughed, and pulled out his pistol, loaded with red tracer ammunition for the occasion, and fired several celebratory shots, which were answered by a barrage of red and blue tracers going up into the

789

starry sky. He watched this with satisfaction, then walked to the nearest eight-wheeled armored personnel carrier and climbed in its open hatch. As he did, men rushed to the whole fleet of Russian vehicles. The elite Tula Airborne division and Taman Motorized Rifle Division began to roll. The Russian Army was now on the Moon, 30,000 strong, having landed without opposition, and was rolling East.

****

On the lunar far side, Tatiana stuck her head out into the hallway and watched with a slight smirk as the Unash ran about in panic in the aftermath of the space raid. *They look like ants on an anthill after you kick it,* she thought. She pulled her head back in the doorway, as she saw some Toman Daz warriors appearing down the hall. Kathy Davenport was standing by the door inside, looking frantic.

"What's happening!" asked Kathy.

"A space raid, I saw that some of the domes are burning a few kilometers from here. The Unash are so confused they haven't even shut off the oxygen to them. So they are burning like furnaces. One of the medicasts was screaming something about an invasion."

"The invasion has happened?" cried Kathy.

"I don't know. They look more panicked than usual, though," said Tatiana

"Do think the troops will come and rescue us?" asked Kathy.

Tatiana shook her head. The Taman Daz have orders to kill all of us if this place falls, so don't get hopeful. Hope is bad mental hygiene around here. Besides, if I know my own government, they will execute me as a traitor for working here for the Unash."

"The Americans won't do that! They will rescue us!" exclaimed Kathy.

"Don't say that! Don't talk about that ever again!" said Tatiana coldly. Kathy looked terrified at Tatiana. Tatiana now cracked the door and looked out again coldly. She saw a group of five Samaran warriors in armored spacesuits holding their helmets by their sides, marching down

790

the hall in lockstep as around them the Unash ran about, seemingly mindlessly. The look on the Samarans said everything. It was a look of stoic calm. She felt someone come up and stand close to her, startled, she pulled her head inside the door and shut it.

It was Christina looking at her in barely disguised fear. Tatiana pulled her close and embraced her.

"Don't worry child, it will be alright," she said, even though she did not believe it. *I believe in nothing now. I see the end of everything now.*

****

Zomal, the Samaran Lunar Commander ordered his men to stand outside the offices of Sadok Sar, the chief of the Unash on Moon.

"Where is Number 1, I must speak to him a once!" demanded Zomal. A docile looking medicast led him inside the offices. Number 1 sat on his throne, seemingly expressionless, his office had wide windows. A dome burned in the distance from the earlier raid.

"The Errans have landed troops and equipment on the other side of the Moon from us! I just thought you would like to know this! We must move forces there immediately and eject them."

"No, it is not necessary," said Number 1 slowly. "I have already analyzed the military situation, we need only hold the Errans and form defensive lines, and the fleet will come and destroy them. It will only take an hour to destroy them, once the fleet arrives."

"This is intolerable! You must move against them now! Give me a body of troops and I will do it!" yelled Zomal.

"Very well, you may have 1,000 of my Taman Daz troops, and you may use your own forces for whatever you like," said Sadok Sar impassively.

"I need more than this! I need at least ten thousand of your Toman Daz!" protested Zomal.

"They tell me the Samaran are great warriors, so you should need no more than what I have offered."

"Tell them to make ready at once then! We move to engage the Errans!" cried Zomal.

Zomal turned and marched out. He saw his second in command Tankos.

"Number 1 is a coward ! I go to fight the Errans, and I will return victorious of not at all so that the glory of the Samar may be preserved!" He then drew close.

"Brave Tankos, I go to victory or death, so the honor of the Samar may be maintained. You are to assume command and watch over the remaining garrison. I will take two men with me, but you are to protect the Erran women in the medical department, as they have long served us faithfully. They are of our house. This is also to preserve the honor of Samar." He paused.

"Also, Dr. Okoha of these dickless ones has showed me great disrespect, and since I am commander here, that means he has showed great disrespect to the Samaran Empire. So, I want you to personally requite this of him. " Zomal smiled. "Those are my final orders, should I not return."

Tankos lowered his eyes.

"Yes, my Lord."

****

■■■■■■■■■■■■■■■■■■■■■■■■■■■■■■■■■■■■■■■■■■■■■■■■

**Epilogue: Lacus Veris**

The Dauntless maneuvered, now in orbit around Ganymede, with mighty Jupiter lying beyond. The Dauntless had been in the Jovian system for several weeks now.

In the sick bay, after main duty hours, Michael and Dorothy lay together in bed asleep together. Pamela's picture had disappeared from the shelf above the desk and was stowed somewhere.

****

"Son of a Bitch!" yelled Parker of the radio as he scanned the lunar landscape to the North. Schwartzman immediately followed Parker's binoculars and pointed his own to the Northwest. They stood on high ground overlooking Lacus Veris in Mare Oriental on the Moon, with the 42nd Battalion and their vehicles arrayed behind them. They had been told to seize and hold the heights as the 101st and 82nd advanced to the South of them across the barren wastes of the central Mare Oriental. 82nd Division artillery was supposed to join them but was slowed by Moondust below the peak.

"The 101st lead elements are headed North! They have crossed the unit boundary into 1st Marine territory!" said Parker. A quick glance down at his map confirmed this to Schwartzman. The advance of the 1st Marines had been delayed by fighting at Kepler Crater with a grey holdout group. They had burst out of the ground during the demolition of what remained of the underground portion of the base. The flashes to the Northwest behind them told him the fighting was still going on. In front of them were steep cliffs and slopes leading down to plains of the Mare Oriental. Mare Oriental was a massive, double-ringed impact basin with a central uplift on the western end of the visible portion of the Moon's surface. The 101st and 82nd were advancing to the South of them.

"Inform General Blochman's headquarters that lead elements of his division are being observed headed Northwest into 1st Marines turf," said Schwartzman levelly to Arizona, who turned instantly to do the "Lunar Lope", a type of fast running, deemed the most efficient way to move rapidly on the Moon.

Suddenly, bright flashes of white and orange blossomed near the front of the 101st leading column's advance.

"Arizona! Tell 101st HQ we observe lead elements of 101st are now engaged in the Northwest Mare Oriental outer ring! Approximate Grid point Bravo X-ray Golf!" he yelled. Schwartzman zoomed in the binoculars, saw three 101st armored personnel carriers erupt into balls of orange fire on the plain of the Mare Oriental. "Tell Blochman they need air support!"

He did a quick mental estimate of the terrain ahead of them, concluded it was much too steep for the Lunar Armored Personnel carriers to advance down it to the plains, thousands of feet below, where the battle was now raging. He did a mental calculation of how long it would take them to get down to the Mare Oriental plain and into the battle.

"Let's get the boys dismounted and down this slope Jason! Let's get into this fight!" yelled Schwartzman. Parker saluted and began shouting orders. "Tell everyone to dump everything but ammo and oxygen! Let's move!" yelled Schwartzman as he did a mental estimate of how long it would take his men to get down the slopes and onto the plains, as the Northwest now lit up brilliantly with brilliant flashes and balls of fire. It looked like many hours. He took a last look at the Earth, hanging huge and beautiful in the black sky behind them. For a fraction of a second, he saw Cassandra's face floating beside it, then he turned and led his men down the steep slopes in front of him.

****

Cassandra and Pamela had been hopping like kangaroos in the lunar simulator dome at Houston in their Moon suits, under electronic 1/6th gravity and having a race, as the film crew taped them for their Lunar Training Special. This was great fun until Cassandra's space suit temperature regulator malfunctioned and the suit began to overheat. Because she had been racing Pamela across the 100-yard expanse of simulated lunar dust and both wanted desperately to win, Cassandra's suit temperature quickly spiked to 107 degrees Fahrenheit. She was suddenly drowning in sweat as she turned in dismay and tried to find the nearest airlock. She thought she saw one nearby but her suit visor then fogged up

794

so she could not see. Pamela quickly bounded over to her, grabbed her hand and led her to the airlock.

"Lunar Sim Control opened airlock door 12 immediately! We have a spacesuit malfunction!" yelled Pamela over the radio.

"This is Lunar Sim Control what is the nature of the malfunction?" came a man's voice on the radio.

Cassandra felt suddenly the nearness of death as she felt of wave of nausea pass over her. The seconds now seemed like lifetimes as she stood in front to the airlock, her body was now shaking. If she vomited inside her helmet it could be fatal. A thought came clear as crystal to her: *If I don't get out of the suit very soon I will die, either from high temperatures inside it or from the vacuum, when I tear my helmet off inside this chamber.*

"This is Lieutenant Monroe, US Navy! OPEN THE FUCKING  DOOR ON AIRLOCK 12! NOW!" Pamela yelled.

The airlock door opened to Cassandra's immense relief, revealing a light she could see even through her fogged over visor. She was now feeling dizzy as if she would faint. She felt Pamela pull her firmly into the airlock, then felt the shock of full earth gravity in the chamber. By sheer force of will,  she barely kept herself from vomiting into her sealed space helmet, knowing it might make her drown.  Pamela pushed her down on a seat in the airlock as the door shut and  Cassandra heard the welcome roar of oxygen rushing into the cramped airlock chamber. Soon it was at the same 1/5th atmosphere of pure oxygen as in their suits. She felt Pamela batting her hands away as she tried to wrench off her space helmet. Cassandra felt like she was in a suffocating steam room and could barely breathe, she fought panic. A tone sounded announcing full 1/5th atmosphere of oxygen, then Pamela somehow got Cassandra's helmet loose and pulled it off.  Cassandra, her face covered with sweat gasped the cool air in the airlock with relief as  Pamela deftly pulled off her own space helmet and stared at Cassandra with concern. They were both wearing smudged light-gray lunar camouflage coveralls over their spacesuits and were covered with grey simulated Moondust.

795

"Cassie, Cassie, are you OK?" demanded Pamela leaning close. Cassandra grabbed her gloved hand and held it in a death grip as she breathed in gasps and nodded.

"I think I'm going to throw up!" gasped Cassandra

"Please throw up in your helmet, if possible," came the man's voice over the intercom. Pamela grabbed Cassandra space helmet off the floor in annoyance and placed it in Cassandra's hands in front of her face. Drops of sweat were now falling into the helmet from her face. Pamela then sat down wearily on a metal bench facing Cassandra. Cassandra began fumbling with her spacesuit gloves while trying to balance the space helmet in one hand , Pamela leaned forward and quickly unsealed the gloves and pulled them off. Oh, what a relief to have one's hands in the open air! She felt her perspiration-soaked hands shedding moisture and cooling in the $1/5^{th}$ atmospheric oxygen. Pamela shed her gloves expertly. Pamela looked calm and collected and finally managed a faint smile at Cassandra.

"Don't let any pictures of me like this get out Pammy! I must look like a wreck!" said Cassandra in exasperation. "Just help me get out of this torture contraption they call a space suit!"

"Ms. Chen, this is Lunar Sim Control, we advise you stay in your space suit while in the airlock," came the voice over the intercom again. "The exertion of trying to get out of the suit will make you overheat again. We have the simulator physician standing by to look at you when you cycle back up to full atmospheric pressure."

"How long is that going to take to cycle?" asked Cassandra miserably.

"After a suit overheat, we recommend an hour and a half for cycling to full atmosphere."

"How about a half hour? Like normal?" retorted Cassandra.

"An hour and a half will be just fine!" said Pamela loudly. Motioning to Cassandra to be quiet.

"Cassie, be quiet and calm down, you'll cool off quicker," said Pamela emphatically. "Everything will be fine. Think how heroic and dramatic this will look on the Special." Cassandra looked down and nodded in resignation. The thought of thousands of men now on the moon in suits like she had just escaped from filled her with horror. There were no emergency airlocks on the Moon. A feeling of sad desperation overwhelmed her. *Bob*, she thought sadly. Cassandra saw men in armored space suits fighting with the Greys, everyone was dying. She could hardly bear it, then the vision disappeared.

Pamela turned on a flat screen TV, the only comfort in the small airlock. She deftly scanned channels, found a live feed channel from the Moon. It showed Apollo Base, cargo ships were landing and disgorging cargo, the 9th Infantry Division was now in the process of landing, and beside the landing zone , a column of armored vehicles was moving silently. In the black sky, the blue and white marbled Earth hung. There was no sound or commentary, only a steady movement of vehicles and occasional small figures in Moon suits. The alien scene was oddly hypnotic. Vehicles were now moving forward to dismantle the cargo landers and use the parts for building more of the base. Nothing was wasted at this stage of operations.

"We are beginning cycling to full atmosphere, make sure to pop your ears every minute or so," said the intercom. Cassandra was now feeling much better, the 1/5th atmosphere was drying out her hair and face and leaving them feeling cool. They had learned to apply baby lotion to their faces before going into space suits to prevent their skin from dying out. She felt the onrush of air as the re-pressure cycle advanced to take them back to full atmosphere at 80% nitrogen. She covered her mouth and yawned to pop her ears as Pamela did the same.

"Once there was a beautiful planet called the Heart. And the people there made joyous music. " began Pamela, staring at the lunar vista on the screen.

"Then came Grendle, that hideous fiend who had heard the music and became jealous. And he said, 'I will go to the Earth, called the Heart, silence this music and all this joyous sound, and make it the sound of weeping instead. So came Grendle to the Heart." Pamela paused.

"Once I was a young girl, trapped in Kansas, facing an evil interstellar empire. I lost my virginity by being raped on a spaceship at 15," said Pamela staring at the TV screen in amazement. "I was completely alone, I could tell no one what was happening to me. And when I tried to tell the government, they took me to a secret prison and raped me again and abused me to try and find out what I knew. To try and squeeze every drop of juice out of the raisin that I was then. Then the aliens took my unborn child..."

Cassandra felt overcome with sadness as she listened to Pamela.

"But somehow God heard my crying, and he helped me survive mentally and physically. Then He sent you to rescue me, and the whole world with me. "She turned and clasped Cassandra's hand. "Then you on your mission from God, to save the world, enlisted us in your Joan-of- Arc army and your fleet, and you brought down the secret government , whose major weapons were fear and terror. You forced that secret monster submarine, that dark undersea city, to the surface, and the forces you had marshaled there destroyed it utterly," said Pamela, her voice now a soothing whisper.

"You braved everything, Cassie, risked everything, endured everything, and in the end, you were victorious," continued Pamela.

"Well, let's not forget I was convinced I would die. That makes my so-called heroics thinly disguised madness, in a sense," said Cassandra.

"Oh ...admittedly, it was all an elaborate and highly creative scheme of suicide in your own mind Cassandra, I must admit, " said Pamela. "But it was also highly effective. Like a Kamikaze pilot sinking an aircraft carrier. But only someone who did not fear death, who actually was rushing to meet it, could have done what you have done." Pamela then turned to Cassandra and smiled serenely. She then turned back to the TV screen and stared at the Earth hanging above the endless movement of men and machines. "Then came Grendel to end all mirth. But now has come Beowulf, that mighty man of war, and he has seized Grendle, and will not release him..."

"Now what I faced alone in Kansas, the whole world faces with me," said Pamela staring at the screen. "When this war started, many people thought we would be crushed in a week by the Greys. Now look at us, a year and a half after the war began, and we have them retreating. In fact , this looks like a rout at this point. We are on the Moon and they don't seem to be able to do anything to stop us."

"Do you really think they have lost the war at this point? Do you think they will simply leave and go home?"

Pamela shook her head.

"No," said Pamela shaking here head somberly. "I know these people, remember? They will not give up now, I sense that they can't. They sense that their own survival is now at stake. But then the greys have suffered the results of an astronomical military miscalculation. Some people, the same people who thought we would be crushed in a week, have told me that this whole set of disasters the greys have suffered is merely some highly sophisticated strategy and that we humans are simply too stupid to understand. These are the same people who told me the Greys deliberately crashed their two spaceships at Roswell in order to give us fiber optics and Velcro. No, Cassie, what we are seeing on the Moon is not so much a successful invasion by the Allies, but rather the disastrous result of a failed invasion of Earth, caught in its preliminary stages, with exploiting forces exposed in forward positions. In a sense, the Greys have never been able to catch their breath since the night of the coup. But, no Cassie, this war isn't even close to being finished. This is only the end of the beginning. It will not even end on the Moon, it will end in space someplace when they send a fleet to rescue their Moon bases. That's what I think. So it will be the Navy that wins this war in the end, in some epic battle out in space. Great outcomes require great battles, that's Von Clausewitz. Sun Tzu, says the best way to win is without fighting, that was the grey's strategy all along, victory through terror. That is war on the cheap. But the way of this war is to be the way of Von Clausewitz, and that is a war that is down and dirty and bloody and costs everyone dearly."

**\*\*\*\***

Schwartzman waved his men to deploy behind the screen of a low ridge, as through the gap in the ridge, the battered remnants of two battalions of the 101st retreated. Their column consisting of a stream of armored personnel carriers filled and covered with wounded. In the distance to the West, brilliant flashes told of a battle taking place between the aliens and a rear guard of the 101st.

As Schwartzman's men deployed, using hand signals to keep radio silence, they dug an "L" ambush pattern across the track being made by the train of wounded retreating East. His hope was that the alien forces would simply follow the track and his battalion would ambush them. They had lugged, in addition to their small arms and machine guns, numerous 100-pound super claymore mines and the new 105 mm bazookas especially designed for the Moon.

Soon the Rangers had dug themselves foxholes and were lying in them waiting, as the flashes ebbed in the distance and the stream of APCs bearing wounded dried to a trickle. Arizona leaned close and pressed his helmet to Schwartzman's so he could hear by simple transmission of vibration between the metal.

"Boss, we picked up radio chatter from the 101st people: The 56th Battalion and 57th spotted some aliens and just went after them even though they were in the 1st Marine zone, but they got sucked into a trap to the West, so they were ordered by Blochman to withdraw directly to the East. 67th Battalion of the 101st is apparently making a last stand to cover the retreat of 56th and 57th. They say they can't move up the rest of the brigade. The 1st Marines are now moving West from the fight at Kepler Crater but won't be here for hours. "

"Where is the Air Force?" asked Schwartzman.

"Don't know Boss. Last I heard is they were all attacking the far side."

"Well, tell the men not to open fire until Parker and I fire red flares, we want to catch their force out in the open as much as possible.

"Yes, boss." Arizona rolled away across the moon dust to spread the word helmet to helmet down the line on the silver grey landscape under the black sky.

A single APC then came careening through the gap in the ridge, following the track. Then something bright hit it, and it blossomed into a ball of orange fire, throwing wreckage and bodies everywhere.

****

"So Cassie, your attack on the UFO cover-up was not madness in the classic sense, but merely a miscalculation," said Pamela, with a slight laugh. "I have been thinking about what you said a while back at CNS. I have concluded that you miscalculated, but God did not."

Cassandra nodded, noting she was now feeling happy.

"Yes, and because of it, I had no idea what to do after I survived. It was like landing this really big fish and then not knowing how to get it in the oven!"

"Yes! The fish was really big!" laughed Pamela stretching out her arms. "And that was just its mouth!"

"Oh, oh I just remembered," said Pamela. "There's this sea monster in the book of Job, in the Bible! Remember the guy I was reading about in the Bible back in the hospital? And all this terrible stuff happens to him. His family all dies and his camels run away! All of this just because the Devil tells God that Job only loves God because he is rich and has a big family and lots of camels!"

"So I remember asking you how it all turned out with Job," said Cassandra. "So a sea monster ate him in the end?" Cassandra laughed. Realizing she was now feeling giddy.

"No! No! Everything turned out all right in the end for Job. He got rich again and married some more wives and had more children. Then he asks God at the end of the book, 'why did all of this terrible stuff happen to me?'"

801

"Oh my God!" said Cassandra laughing. "The nitrogen! Pam, I think we're getting nitrogen raptures! Be careful! They're probably recording this all!" she laughed. "If anyone is listening, it's the nitrogen talking!" yelled Cassandra. Pamela beamed at this.

"So what did God say to Job?" said Cassandra becoming animated. Cassandra did an imitation of God with a deep voice, "Oh well, you see, Job, old buddy, the Devil and I had this bet going...and check out my cool sea monster..."

"No! No, God didn't say that!' exclaimed Pamela. "He answered Job out of A whirlwind of fire," Pamela moved her hands in whirling motion. "He said, where were you Job when I lit the fuse for the Big Bang? Huh? Where you when I made the stars of Orion and Pleiades? Where were you when I made my big sea monster?" Pamela stretched her arms out to indicate its huge size. "So he essentially, to paraphrase, told Job 'Job, you don't see the Big Picture'!"

"So he told Job not to try to figure it out? That Job couldn't understand it! That's it? That's the end of the story? That is so lame!" said Cassandra angrily.

"I liked it!" said Pamela smiling. "God, I never knew nitrogen could be so intoxicating," said Pamela shaking her head and laughing. "So, back to Job. In the end in the Bible, we're talking Job, doing really OK at the end and a God who is thinking big."

"Well I find that ending of the story to be only somewhat satisfying," said Cassandra. "If I had written it I would have had God tell Job all about the big plan and have Job be happy."

"Well Job was happy at the end and had even more camels than before, that much was accomplished , but as for arguing with God, he decided to just be quiet at the end and trust God "

"I like my ending much better..." said Cassandra, looking at the pressure gauge as they were nearing normal. Pamela was now watching the scene on the moon as another three cargo ships landed.

"Well, I may not understand the Big Picture completely but  One thing is for sure I know we are sure as hell not in Kansas anymore!" said Pamela

"Yes, screw Kansas!" laughed Cassandra as she glanced up and saw that they were at normal atmospheric pressure.

The door to the airlock opened, and Cassandra rose and rushed off to the dressing room past the puzzled looking doctor and took a long cold shower,  followed by Pamela, who as usual  gave a long explanation for Cassandra's behavior to the doctor.

**** 

The alien force arrived , apparently in hot pursuit of the retreating 101$^{st}$ battalions. They came pouring through the gap in a stream. To Schwartzman's amazement, it was all on foot with no armored vehicles or even spacecraft overhead. What arrived was a group of swiftly running humanoid figures, some of whom were the size of men, ranging down to half of human height. They were all carrying bulky weapons. When Schwartzman saw that the group of aliens had mostly cleared the gap he raised his flare gun and fired . The whole landscape exploded into fire and light as rockets, exploding claymore mines,  tracer bullets , clouds of lunar dust and ray beams transformed the landscape into a phantasmagorical light show. The aliens caught out in the open were mowed down. Like all successful ambushes, it was indistinguishable from a massacre. Finally, everything lay still. He gazed at the gap in the low ridge saw no evidence of more alien forces.  He drew his pistol and walked out into the debris-and-body strewn track in the lunar dust.

The bodies and fragments of bodies had swelled into frozen blobs of flesh, partly clothed with fragments of space suits, whose armor was apparently completely inadequate. This horrid form that bodies assumed in death on the Moon,  when their spacesuits were shredded,  had already earned the term "meatcicle" among the troops.  He glanced at the exploded wreck of the American armored personnel carrier full of bloated and burned human bodies. He saw that the fuel tanks , full of hydrazine and nitrogen tetroxide had exploded. *Note to headquarters, Lunar APCs need to be up-armored.* He then walked up and down the scattered field of bodies studying the field of alien dead.

*Looks like somebody threw this operation together without any preparation,* he thought but he found himself staring sadly at scores of dead greys, who looked in their space suits like dead children. He shook his head, turned to look at a human sized dead alien, near the lead. The spacesuit had a large blue star on it. *This one died a brave death,* he thought, *foolhardy, but brave.*

Schwartzman broke radio silence.

"Good job guys. Now you men all lay still and conserve your oxygen. NO TALKING. The Marines are moving up from the East, and they'll be here shortly. I'll fire a blue flare went they get close so they'll see us. " Schwartzman looked nervously down at his oxygen level, it was at ¼ . *Now if we can just get rescued before we run out of air, this operation will be a complete success. He went back and lay in his foxhole near Arizona. Schwartzman felt exhaustion overwhelm him. Arizona crawled up to him and pressed his helmet on Schwartzman's to speak without a radio.*

*"Arizona, how are the men, any letters home?" asked Schwartzman.*

"Two, Boss, they both took shrapnel through their face plates, it looks like. We also got three wounded." said Arizona. "but they're OK. Shrapnel with simple suit punctures. We got them duct taped. So they'll be OK." *Yeah, they'll be OK, provided we don't run out of oxygen before the Marines get here, thought Schwartzman wearily.*

*"Not bad, considering these same guys we just wasted, tore up the first brigade of the 101st, a new asshole," responded Schwartzman.*

"No, not bad at all Colonel," Arizona answered. *Death on the moon in combat, a good death,* thought Schwartzman.

"Boss, the Marines, how long will it take those jarheads to figure out there is nothing in front on them? I mean, will they hang back?" asked Arizona.

"Naw, my chief worry is they will run over us trying to get to the aliens. No, be quiet and lie still. Think of a picnic in the park back home. " *Yes, try to think of good thoughts.*

"What did it look like out there? I mean the enemy dead."

"It looked like the Children's Crusade, led by some Samar who wanted a brave death," said Schwartzman morosely. Arizona was silent for a long time after this.

"Well maybe this Lunar op will be done soon then, and we can go back to blue skies."

"Well, I am never going back to Earth, Arizona, not alive. I'll give myself two slugs to the head before I go back. All that is waiting for me back there is a cage, and you know it." Schwartzman said bitterly.

"Boss , you shouldn't think like that. You're tired. This French thing, it'll pass." said Arizona. " That whole thing is just political chicken-shit, and everybody knows it."

Schwartzman was too weary to respond. He instead felt for his pistol, patted it to reassure himself. *My one-way ticket.* Schwartzman rose and walked up slowly to a large boulder that stood about as high as his waist. He leaned heavily against it, cradling his flare gun. He forced himself to think of calm, positive thoughts. The Earth was just visible above a ridge to the East. *Cassie, I wonder how you are.*

Finally, after what seemed like an eternity, he saw movement to the East. He looked at it through his binoculars and saw it was a line of Marine armored personnel carriers. He raised his flare gun and fired a blue flare. It was answered by several blue flares from the approaching vehicles.

****

Baranov looked with satisfaction at the Russian Moon base, Gagarin, being constructed near the rim of crater Aristotle as his command van moved over the Sea of Frost on the northern Moon. He saw the Earth glowing beautifully above the horizon. Further East the Tula Guards Division was in the lead as they moved across the Lake of Dreams.

Suddenly, the horizon to the East was lit up by flashes.

****

Ragnar the Bold stepped through the door into the chambers of the Lord protector, who looked up from talking to some other councilors.

"My Lord, Jagar of Vale has reported that the Errans have launched a great invasion of the Moon of Erra, called Una. They seek to destroy the Unash bases there!"

The Lord Protector stood up from his chair.

"WHY CAN"T THEY JUST DIE!" the Lord Protector roared. "WHY PROLONG THIS! WHY FIGHT THE FATES?"

He glared at the words written in blood on the far wall of the chamber, 'avert not your eyes', poured himself a goblet of wine, and sat down again.

"Thank you  for your report most noble Ragnar...,"  he said somberly before lapsing into silence, and staring ahead into space.

****

On board the large star cruiser Thanon,  of the Unull fleet.  Semajse sat across from a Pleiadian military officer, named Samal,  with longish white hair and a ruggedly handsome, but grim, face as he took her report. They were both dressed in greyish blue space suits with metal neck rings for secure mounting of helmets, required clothing since they were still in the war zone of the Quzrada. They were in a conference room designed for the Unullians , who stood at only 4 feet tall, and hence the chairs they sat on and short legged desk that sat between them added discomfort to the already tense conversation between them.  Much had happened in the Pleiades in her absence.  The Sisterhood of Alcyone, who had ruled the Pleiades for two hundred years, making a society that was 'a model to all peoples' , had been "displaced. " The reason had been military incursions by the Samar,  as their war with the Tlax pressed closer to the stars of the Pleiades , and the sisterhood's apparent inability to deal with them.  The council of Maia now ruled,  a name unfamiliar to Semjase.

"Look, I was following orders from the government as it was. I was told to go to the Solerran system and find out as much as possible about the

806

Unash activities there. Those were precisely my orders, and I carried them out!" said Semjase sharply. " Read my reports!"

"Well, we want precise estimates of Unash ships, their types , and how many Samar ships visit and how often! We want to know how large the Unash facilities are, and their strength relative to the Errans. Instead, what you have told me lady Semjase is basically a travelogue diary of a tourist! This information is nearly worthless!"

"I tried to help people...I risked my life"

"You were sent their as a spy!" said Samal. "We need military information, not a sociological or humanitarian study! We are preparing for war with the Samar! They have taken Merop 4 and killed all the men and hauled off the colonies women and children as slaves! We are going to take it back!"

Semjase cringed mentally at these words. She fastened her gaze on the insignia on his chest. It was an ancient symbol of a blue dragon on a black background filled with stars. It had been the war flag of the Pleiadians during the war of the Quzrada. *War,* she thought. *The war I saw at Erra now reaches my own home stars.*

"As I have explained, " said Samal. " The sisterhood of Alcyone has been dissolved. They are no longer the government! The council of Maia now presides. You are hereby ordered to return to the Pleiades and report to fleet headquarters. Also , you are required to sign a loyalty oath to the council of Maia. " He produced a sheet with finely printed script on it and laid it in front of her on the table.

"Suppose I do not wish to sign any oath of loyalty to any council I have never heard of before?" she said, not looking at the loyalty oath, but instead starring at his green eyes.

"Then this would be a grave matter lady Semjase. I advise you to do this, given your association with the sisterhood, and the fact that you are of a great house, " said Samal, staring at her. " I would urge you to sign a loyalty oath before we rendezvous with the Pleiadian fleet elements when we reach the frontier. Otherwise you might be considered a disloyal person. " Samal rose from his chair and left the room, ducking down to clear the low doorway. Semjase grabbed the loyalty oath document and jammed it roughly into a pocket on her space suit, then left the room.

She wandered somberly down the hallway, filed with space suited Unull passing each other with clicking greetings. They were an unlikely looking species. They had ears but no eyes, using instead a complex electromagnetic field generated in their brains as both a synthetic aperture radar of their surroundings and as a main method of communication. They had basically no necks and a mouth full of sharp teeth on top of their heads , their conical shaped brains being buried in a thick skull in the back of their head. Despite the dramatic difference in sensory apparatus their social order and democratic government was strikingly similar to other cultures, as was their ability and appetite for war.

The Unull had been at war with the Unash for over a hundred years. It was a war that the Unash had started with the Unull by their aggressive expansion into Unullian space, and it was a war which the Unull now had sworn to finish. The alliance of the Unull and the Pleiadians seemed an unlikely one, since it involved species of such different physiologies and societal outlooks. But the alliance had served both peoples well. ' The Unull have learned from us and we have learned from the Unull ' remarked one of the sisterhood to Semjase, at her departure to the Quzrada.

*I must do a mind-bridge with Elsebeth, and find out what has happened....* She paused in the corridor and tried to initiate a mind-bridge but sensed nothing but utter sadness. She then ended her attempt.

Now Semjase wandered lost in the corridor, to the quarters of her and her crew, Samjeed and Tam, who sat in the hallway with their backs to the wall, looking glum and weary. Semjase sat down beside Samjeed, who avoided her eyes.

"You heard the Sisterhood has been deposed and the Council of Maia is now running the government?"

Samjeed nodded wearily without looking at her. Tam simply starred ahead.

"Have you both signed this loyalty oath to the Council of Maia? " she asked.

"Yes, "said Samjeed wearily. "I want to go home and see my wife and children, so did Tam, here. "

"Do either of you know who the Council of Maia is and what they stand for?"

"I know that they intend to take the Merope 4 system back from the Samar, and that's all I need to know right now. That, and they told me I could go home once I signed." Semjase looked at Samjeed in disbelief. He looked back at angrily , Tam also looked at her and nodded.

"Well I am not signing anything until I find out who is running the government and how they gained power! Then, I am headed back into the Quzrada."

"We are not going with you," said Samjeed sharply. Tam also nodded his ascent. "You got very lucky their last time, and also almost got us all killed. You go back their again and you'll die there. If you're lucky your death will be quick, if not, you're going to be first course in a Samaran banquet of revenge. I already told that Samal fellow , you're too emotional and reckless to be a good espionage agent. "

Semjase, stung by these words, rose silently from sitting and began walking down the hall again. She had walked several steps when a familiar soothing voice spoke within her mind. It was Tzan , an Unull commander who had been her liaison officer for a long time. She turned and looked at him standing behind her. The Unull were a strange species in appearance, but because of her long acquaintance with him she was happy to see him.

"I am sorry to hear of your distress , lady Semjase, with your new government and its officers. "

"What happened? How did this happen? "

"I know little of the details , but basically the Sisterhood, after the brave commander of your space forces, Jackan, chased away the Samar near Merope 7, rather than giving him some sort of commendation, they instead charged him with insubordination and had him arrested. The Samar heard of this , and interpreted this as a sign of weakness by the Sisterhood, and so they returned in force and took the entire Merope 4 system. They killed all the men, and sold the women and children into slavery, as is their habit. The third and fourth planets of the system are now being settled by Samaran colonists. So a group of former fleet officers seized the government palace at Pleone, and declared the Council of Alcyone to be dissolved for reasons of great incompetence and cowardice. The members of former the sisterhood are all under house arrest, which we Unul think is a rather mild punishment. We, in fact, we have commended your new government for its leniency. "

"You mean your government acquiesced to this ?"

"We had little choice." Tzan responded. We still are much helped by your government in our war effort, and the new government has said it will increase its levels of aid to us. Plus, unlike the Sisterhood of Alcyone , the officials of your new government do not serve us the kraydit, when they deliver us shipments of arms and equipment."

"What is the kraydit?" asked Semjase in exasperation.

"The kyadit is a mixture of bitter herbs and medicine we give to our children with their main meal of the day to make them healthy and remind them that life is sometimes bitter. It also means a "tiresome lecture", for the Sisterhood always insisted on giving us tiresome lectures about peace and understanding when they delivered their shipments of armaments to us. Tzan projected a humorous image into her mind, of several Unaull senior officers , sitting beside cargo boxes of lethal equipment, while listening patiently, like a bunch of bored Erran housecats, to a lecture from Abigail, one of the prominent members of the Sisterhood, about the virtues of peace and understanding in the Cosmos. Semjase smiled despite herself. "So we get armaments in increased amounts , but without lectures, from your new government. So we Unull are happy. Also, we have never forgotten that your people saved us from being eaten alive by the Unash, so we remain grateful. "

"But now we are going to have a war," lamented Semjase, "what has happened to my people's creed 'an example to all peoples'. "

"Well , as someone who has known war all my life, I consider that the Pleiadians are now making themselves a most excellent example for any people in the cosmos , who are themselves confronted with mindless aggression. The first rule of being an 'example to all peoples in the cosmos' is to survive, this gets the attention of all peoples, so that they may learn from your example, " said Tzan with a sense of merriment. He then became more somber. "As you know the Unash killed a billion of my people, not all of them quickly. Many they killed slowly as they dissected us alive to satiate their curiosity about our unusual physiology. Semjase cringed mentally at the images in Tzan's mind projected. "Well are the Unash called the 'authors of atrocity' by the other peoples who know them. That is why our word for the Unash is 'Kyya' which means 'demon.' If not for you people's help we would have been eaten alive by them and destroyed. Know always that we are eternally grateful to your people for this. However, our experience of life and death in cosmos is much different than your people's, and so is our outlook. I note you have seen several battles and much death, brave Semjase. Consider this as knowledge that you possess that others of your people do not. You must go home and educate them. Your knowledge will comfort them in their sorrow over the passing of former things. "

"I don't want to go home now, Tzan. Especially if people like Samal are running things. " thought Semjase sadly.

"But you must, noble and brave Semjase. Samal is a good man, he is just not from the Pleiades you knew. Circumstances have changed your culture. There is much sorrow over this, but your people must let go of sorrow and take up the sword joyfully now. The way of life is to defy death now. We Unull understand this, and your people must also.

" However, your people need you to report first hand on what is happening at Erra. Despite our great gratitude to your people, we have always regarded you Pleidians as somewhat delusional. Your stars have enjoyed peace for a long time, but your Sisterhood had forgotten that your stars enjoyed peace because your people were mighty in war in the past. They defeated both the Samaran and Vikhelm and everyone else. But your people have forgotten that peace must be earned. You, however, have seen the horror and terror of the war the Unash are waging against the Errans, and have helped its victims. Your account must be heard in the councils of Pleone, as the accounts of those who escaped the rapine and slaughter at Merope 4 are heard. You will help to save your people by these reports and ease their sorrow."

Semjase thought deeply on this. She understood that Tzan was had also been reading her memories of the Quzrada and Erra, she did not attempt to block this. She sensed mounting sadness in his mind as he read her memories.

"I must also tell you of a remarkable thing," said Tzan, suddenly as if to change the subject, "that we have learned, noble Semjase. It concerns an older planet that we recaptured from the Unash several years ago. It was devastated, of course, but we found the Unash had made a remarkable archeological excavation in one area. In the excavation we found a temple with complex inscriptions that we had not known about. In the inscriptions, which were in ancient old galactic, dating from seven-to-ten millions of years ago, we found that the prophecy of the 'great Ruler coming forth from Erra' was present, with star maps indicating the center of Quzrada, so their was no mistaking the location of Solerra. So this prophecy of the "ruler of all stars being a son of Erra" predates the Song of Erra by millions of years. And not only was the prophecy present but the inscription records that a powerful race , in order to prevent the prophecy being fulfilled , came to the Solerra system and destroyed the culture that was then living there on the fourth planet of Solerra, called now the Red Planet. The race apparently ignored Erra, seeing no intelligent beings there. "

"So the Solerra system has seen great tragedy before, because of the same prophecy, which is far older than we had guessed. We Unull think this prophecy is why the Unash are still trying to conquer Erra even though their attempt is doomed to failure. We know the Errans have resolved to detonate thousands of nuclear weapons on Erra to destroy it if

812

they lose the war. So the Unash cannot conquer it, and the Unash losses are now terrible, yet they will not abandon this effort. This is not logical if the Unash merely wanted to possess Erra inact. The Errans have invaded Una , the Moon of Erra, with force and power, and threaten the Unash bases there. It would be logical for the Unash to simply retreat and admit failure, but they will not. So this makes sense to us Unull, if the Unash believe that possessing Erra, even as a smoking cinder, somehow gives their species primacy. As it is, we fear that the Unash may send a major fleet ino the Quzrada to destroy Erra and rescue their bases, and we fear also the Samar will also send a fleet as well to make sure this is done properly by the Unash. The Samar , we know are pressing the Unash to send a fleet even now to do this."

"We cannot allow that to happen, not two planetary massacres in the same star system , over the same prophecy! The Cosmos will not allow it." said Semjase vehemently.

"That is why you must return home to your people, and give them your report, most noble and brave Semjase."

She was of a great house and duty was her first thought, always.

****

In her cool shower, Cassandra relaxed as her body temperature became normal and she felt herself again. She had no idea how long she had been there. She imagined herself on the peak of some beautiful mountain in a cool breeze, looking up at a clear blue sky. *I did die, actually, at Morningstar. Then, I was dead inside, but still walking around. Now I am alive again, somehow, like Lazarus.*

*Pamela's child is somewhere on the Moon perhaps, and my child ...* Cassandra suddenly felt lost in the stars without number , lost in Orion near the Pleiades. But she suddenly saw her child, a beautiful daughter smiling with an impish grin and laughing, dressed in golden silken clothes, and Cassandra felt suddenly happy. The child embraced her, its tiny arms clinging to her neck.

"Mama," the child said to her. Then she was gone, and Cassandra was standing in the cool shower alone.

"Your love... it saved me baby Hamster..." she gasped. She opened her eyes. Looked at the tiles of the shower. *My child is out there... in the stars,* she thought, *someday I'll understand...*

\*\*\*\*

"My Lord," said Marshall Skana, after entering the office of the high Councilor. "The Errans have invaded Una with large forces. The moon is tidally locked and they have landed on the side of Una facing Erra. They clearly intend to take our great base of the far-side of Una using ground assault." The high Councilor stared at him transfixed from his chair. "We have just received this message, and the Samar will also know of it!"

"The impudent fools! We must send reinforcements!" said the High Councilor.

"We must send a mighty fleet, my Lord," said Marshall Skana gravely. "This affair must be finished! And finished quickly!" But doubt tore at Skana as he said this. *Erra is the heart of the Quzrada, and it is so very far away. How can we possibly wage a war effectively there?*

\*\*\*\*

Colonel Robert Schwartzman lay on a pile of grey lunar gravel that was sealed with spray-on plastic, in the Marine Corps' frontline pressurized shelter, with his space helmet and space gloves off, relaxing while the rest of his battalion slept or played cards. He was smoking an e-cig, a habit he had picked up only recently. Out the nearby portal, he could see the Earth floating like a blue-white apparition above the silver horizon, in the black sky, as below it an endless stream of trucks and Lunar APCs covered with space-suited Marines rolled past. This was followed by a column of light tanks. He reflected on the fact that he felt hopelessly trapped by the UFO cover-up only two years ago. Parker and Arizona came over bearing hot coffee and sat down beside him looking happy and relieved. Schwartzman recognized the smell of gin in the coffee as he drank. *These Marines do know how to supply their people, after all,* he thought.

"You young men don't realize how far we've come on this road, " he said drinking some more coffee. "I can remember just a few years ago, marching into a news station in Lexington Kentucky one night, on assignment, with the rest of the  Carney in tow, all of us in trench coats and hats, real life G-Men, and telling this pretty news anchor that she was going to have to spike a breaking local news story  about a man biting a dog. The police are looking for him, but we already have him." Schwartzman laughed. "Boy was she upset! She says 'this is literally a man bites dog story!' She then demands to know 'why do we have to spike it? '" Schwartzman grinned and puffed on his e-cig. "Women are always asking me 'why'," he added.

"So Chief, what did you tell her?" asked Parker grinning.

"I told her she couldn't run the 'man bites dog' story  BECAUSE THE MAN WAS FROM OUTER SPACE!"  answered Schwartzman with a grin. Whereupon they all collapsed in laughter.

***To be continued in Book III of the Morningstar-UFO Trilogy***

Alphabetical List of principal characters by stellar origin

Kenneth Forester – Father of Robert , Douglass, and Joseph Forrester, owner of a tree farm in Medford Oregon.

Abraham Goldberg Ph.D. - Chief of Defense Science Board.

Charles Martel- Former Navy fighter pilot , and Senator, now President of the United States.

Richard Metternich- former top aide to James Bergman, "chemically lobotomized" by leaders of the UFO cover-up.

Pamela Monroe ( real name Elena Monochenko) – blonde news anchor at CNS and chief ally of Cassandra Chen in bringing down the UFO cover-up, former UFO abductee, and subject of highly classified government programs.

Captain George "Samurai" Nakajima USAF – ace fighter pilot.

Dr. George Petrosian- a senior psychiatrist at Arlington Hospital specializing in post-traumatic stress cases, badly wounded on the night of the collapse of the UFO cover-up. Prior physician of Pamela Monroe now helping Cassandra Chen.

Florence Rivers- Chief nurse in the 'X-ray exposed' section of Arlington Hospital.

Col. Robert Schwartzman USA- leader of the "carney men" special forces unit assigned to support the UFO cover-up , lover of Cassandra Chen, led a successful mutiny against the UFO cover-up leadership and led a rescue mission to save her at Devil's Mesa at Morningstar Colorado, where she was held prisoner after the collapse of the UFO cover-up. Now commander of 42nd Ranger battalion.

Alicia Sepulveda-Steel Ph.D. - Deputy chief of Defense Science Board, the hero of Sepulveda Asteroid Intercept.

Colonel Patrick Steel USMC – astronaut and former marine fight pilot, husband of Alicia Sepulveda.

817

Senator Dennis Toomey of Massachusetts- leader of peace movement hoping to end the war with the Unash or 'grey' aliens.

Major Lamar Jamison – USA, member of 82nd airborne, assistant to James Bergman.

President Vladimir Yurivich Petrov –President of Russia and staunch ally of the United States during the alien war.

General Contstantine Maximilovich Boronov- renowned Russian commander

General Victor Gribkov – general of Russian Army subordinate to Bornonov

Major Yuri Ivanovich Kokorin- Russian Special Forces "spetnatz" commander

General Vitaly Gregorovich Samarsky- Russian Army intelligence officer

General Babiyev – Interior Ministry forces commander, sworn enemy of Pamela Monroe

Samar- Archmetian aliens

Hontal of Alnilam- an honored knight of the realm, warlord, special emissary of the Samaran Empire to the Solerran ( Solar) System.

Bekar of Batelgean (Betelgeuse) - Warlord of the important Batelgean house (or clan) of the Samar, formerly the Royal House of the Samaran Empire.

Dakon of Rigel – Chief of Armed Forces for the Samaran Empire

Krayus of Rigel, Lord ambassador of the Samar to Vale of the Vikhelm

Koton of Batelgean- former commander of the Samaran Lunar garrison , who dies in battle on Earth.

Nor of Bellatrix – Duchess of the house of Bellatrix , a warrior princess, and ally of Bekar of Battelgean.

Janek of Saiph – Chief Deputy to Dakon of Rigel and highly honored veteran warrior.

Gamal of Alnilam – loyal bodyguard and retainer of Hontal of Alnilam , a much-decorated warrior.

Tankos of Alnik – deputy of Zomal of Bellatrix in the Samaran lunar garrison

Zomal of Alnik -  Acting commander of the Samar Lunar garrison sometimes referred to as Zomal of Beltran since he bears allegiance to Bellatrix

Quinton of Rigel-  a veteran Captian of the Samaran Starfleet, sent on many voyages for the Palace. He conveys Hontal to Erra and back.

Vikhelm – Archmetian aliens

Quantal of Valekone, The Lord protector, chief leader of the Vikhelm , head of the Eshalon alliance against the Xix.

Swarus of Vanon,  Marshall of the Vikhelm – chief commander of Vikhelm armed forces and deputy of Quantal of Valkone.

Jagar of Vale -master of the Vikhelm star fleets.

Ragnar the Bold, a former leader of war of great renown in times past.

Norden the wise- a respected member of the council of Quantal of Valone

Satya the Poetess- a reputed witch, and prophetess among the Vikhelm

Vikor of Vale- a Vikhelm spy stranded by the outbreak of war on Earth ( Erra)

Karlac of Delphin -  a high regarded resolver of disputes and quarrels within the Eschalon , a member of the Order of Delpin , a monastic order dedicated to enlightenment and peace.

Dolas of Delphin- head of the order of Delphin.

## Pleiadians- Archmetan

Semjase of Pleone -  Pleiadian intelligence agent sent to Earth

Sanjeev - pilot for Semjase

Tam ( short for Tamil – Engineer on Semjase's mission

## The Unash and subject species

Sadok Sar "Number 1" supreme commander of the Unash in the Solerra ( Solar) system

Number 7 an Idelkite Hybrid who is in command of Idelkite space forces supporting the Unash.

Dr. Acra- the developer of the "Red Death" a bioengineered version of Rocky mountain Spotted Fever.

Dr. Ukla -  an Unash Scientist doing research on humanity who has become a friend to human beings and fervently wants peace between the Unash and humanity.

Dr.  Okoha- a notorious Unash experimenter on human beings at Crater Daedalus.

Unit Oyka- a sadistic Unash guard of lowest caste

Dr. Vasa – a researcher on Nashan who is sympathetic to the human plight.

Marshall Skana- – A renowned former military commander of the Unash who is high caste. He is a member of the ruling council of the Unash on Nashan

Councilman Soona- a highcaste Unash who sits on the most high council

The Prime Councilman- head of the Most high Council of the Unash , the supreme ruling coucil of the Unash Empire

Captian Tookon – a deserter from the Unash fleet, now a renegade freighter captain in the Quzrada.

Glossary of Terms and Acronyms

Archmetan- an extraterrestrial human, one of many races scattered throughout the galaxy by some powerful agency. Genetically compatible with humans. Humans are considered Archmetan and have mixed hertiage, being related to several Archmetan peoples, cheifly Samar, Pleiadian, and Vikhelm.

Archmetia- the swath of Archmetan peoples across the galaxy.

ADN- Ammonium Di-Nitromine a powerful oxidizer for rocket fuels and some explosives formula

Aluminol- Ammonium nitrate fuel oil and powdered aluminum mixture , with more power than Amfo, used for large-scale demolitions.

APC -armored personnel carrier, a wheeled or tracked, lightly armored, vehicle , designed for transporting personnel in combat.

Amfo- Ammonium nitrate and fuel oil. A cheap explosive used for large explosive charges.

C-4- noun - US military plastic explosive- a mixture of RDX and plasticizer

C-4- verb- to blow up something

Cortex- Coordinated Explosive - a high explosive shaped charge based on a phased array of detonators embedded in high explosive. Used to create directed jets of shrapnel in missile warheads and shells.

821

D-He3 fusion- Fusion power from Deuterium and Helium-3 fusion reactions in a magnetically polarized plasma. Preferred by the military because of light weight, lack of radioactivity, and direct EM output.

DT fusion - Fusion power from Deuterium and Tritium fusion reactions. Used mostly for neutron production to drive fission for fixed site power. Requires handling of radioactivity and thermal production of power.

Deuterium- "D" A non-radioactive isotope of hydrogen found in water, also known as 'heavy hydrogen'. It is burned in magnetically polarized plasmas with Helium -3 three to create compact fusion energy with direct conversion to electricity and no radioactivity.

"Diamond Blue- a high-efficiency blue-green laser based on mono-crystalline diamond doped with atomic oxygen.

Diamond Teflon- a form of Teflon plastic that has been highly cross-branched by intense gamma radiation and so has near-diamond hardness, developed by the Russians. It can penetrate heavy EM force fields without being affected.

Electronic Gravity - gravity fields created by GEM technology for human use.

EM-electromagnetism

EMP- EM pulse often designed to disrupt alien spacecraft gravity drives or flight control systems

Erra- old galactic name for Earth , from root "erron"- 'beautiful one'

F-51 Griffin fighter – an evolved form of the F-15 fighter with canards , with optical fluidic-hydraulic flight, controls it is highly resistant to EM jamming and has GEM gravity reduction for the pilot to allow rapid maneuvers. Designed for rapid manufacture and operation from unimproved airstrips, it is the main atmospheric fighter of the USAF and Navy.

F-71 Scorpion - An upgraded fighter version of the SR-71 capable of Mach 5 using optofluidic hydraulic flight controls to be resistant to EM jamming.

F-81 Super Hellcat- a trans-atmospheric fighter

F-91 Hyper Viper- also called "Hyper" a deep space fighter variant of the F-81.

Fly's Eye – a dome-shaped microwave phased array antenna designed to launch powerful EMP pulses at alien craft to disrupt or destroy their flight systems.

GEM – Gravity-Electro-Magnetism, a unified field theory used to modify gravity fields for flight or artificial gravity.

Gravitics- Gravity modification used for flight , also called "antigravity" or GEM propulsion

Gravity reduction- GEM systems used to reduce g-forces on pilots and allow rapid maneuvers in fighter aircraft.

Grey- Unash alien or a servile species

Helium 3 –"He-3" A rare, non-radioactive, isotope of helium used along with deuterium to create compact fusion power with no radiation and direct EM power production.  Reserved almost exclusively for use in military spacecraft power plants.  Can be manufactured on Earth in fission reactors but is also present in vast amounts on the Lunar surface.

HMX- Cyclo-Methylene Tetra-nitrosamine 'Her majestie's explosive'- a very powerful high explosive developed by the British, used in warheads and shells.

Magnetometer- a sensor that detects variations in magnetic field created by the powerful magnetic fields used in gravitic drives of alien spacecraft.

Magneto- Proximity fuse- "Magneto" a warhead fuse for missiles and shells sensitive to the magnetic fields generated by alien gravity drives.

MIB -"Man in Black" humanoid aliens , called Verspucians, mercenaries employed on Earth by the Unash.

MIG 500- a transatmospheric and deep space fighter developed by the Russians

Quzrada -  Litterally "crossing place" or "cross roads"  region. The neutral zone  with the Solar System at its center, known to humans as the 'local bubble'

SOCOM – Special Forces Command – A US military command that directs special forces operations and missions.  US Military Rangers, SEALS, Airforce Commandos, and other special operations forces fall under its command.

Seraf drive - Synchrotron Radiation Fusion Drive – A method of coupling fusion energy from a D-He3

Solerra- old galactic name for Sol,  literally, 'star ( single ) of Erra'

Solerran- Solar system or human being

Tallin- Titanium-Aluminum-Nickle Nitride.a bronze colored superalloy used in many human military systems because of its high strength and light weight.

X-ray- extraterrestrial – from military alphabet "x"

USA – US Army

USAF- US Air Force

USMC- US Marine Corps

USN – US Navy

Star Map: viewed from above the Galactic Disk

Galactic Core ↑

# The Eschalon

VIKHELM
*
* Alpha Sagittae    Antares

ARRAS

UNASH                    *
* SS Cygni              Alpha Crux
        The Quzrada    ANNAK
        Sol *

UNULL

Polaris            *    Betelgeuse
*
        The            SAMAR
        Pleiades

200 light years
⊢————————⊣

↓                    Rigel *

Galactic Rim

Made in the USA
Middletown, DE
25 September 2017